THE DESIGN OF FICTION

THE DESIGN OF FICTION

Mark   *Josephine*   *Hester*
HARRIS   HARRIS   HARRIS

THOMAS Y. CROWELL COMPANY
New York   *Established 1834*

Copyright © 1976 by Mark Harris

All Rights Reserved

Except for use in a review, the reproduction or utilization of this work
in any form or by any electronic, mechanical, or other means,
now known or hereafter invented, including photocopying and recording,
and in any information storage and retrieval system is forbidden
without the written permission of the publisher.

Library of Congress Cataloging in Publication Data
Main entry under title:

The Design of fiction.

   1. Short stories. I. Harris, Mark. 1922-
II. Harris, Josephine. III. Harris, Hester.
PZ1.D423   [PN6014]   808.8'31   75-26521
ISBN 0-690-00851-1

THOMAS Y. CROWELL COMPANY
666 Fifth Avenue
New York, New York 10019

Typography by Chris Simon

Manufactured in the United States of America

For permission to use copyrighted materials, grateful acknowledgment
is made to the copyright holders listed on the pages following
the last page of text, which are hereby made a part of this copyright page.

TO MY BROTHERS

*with love from this third,
Hester Jill*

AND FOR MURIEL SIMPSON

Contents

The Stories ix
The Authors xi
Who the Editors Are xiii
Preface xv

INTRODUCTION

The Writer's View 3
The Reader's View 5

PART ONE: THE WRITER'S VIEW

I. REALISM 9

The Use of Force   *William Carlos Williams* 9
The Procurator of Judaea   *Anatole France* 16

II. HIGH STYLE VERSUS JUST PLAIN GOOD:
THE RIGHT WORDS AND THEIR ORDER 27

The Sire de Malétroit's Door   *Robert Louis Stevenson* 30
The Short Happy Life of Francis Macomber
   Ernest Hemingway 46
The Curious Case of Benjamin Button   *F. Scott Fitzgerald* 72
But For This . . .   *Lajos Zilahy* 93

III. HUMOR 97

A Hunger Artist   *Franz Kafka* 98
Dying   *Richard Stern* 106
The Gonzaga Manuscripts   *Saul Bellow* 118
The Iron Fist of Oligarchy   *Mark Harris* 140

CONTENTS

IV. THE READER	157
The Ambitious Guest *Nathaniel Hawthorne*	158
The Real Right Thing *Henry James*	165
Life-Story *John Barth*	177

PART TWO: THE READER'S VIEW

V. MYTH AND SYMBOL	191
Persephone *Meridel Le Sueur*	192
Red Leaves *William Faulkner*	201

VI. ALLEGORY	221
Hook *Walter Van Tilburg Clark*	222
A Mother's Tale *James Agee*	238
Death of a Favorite *J. F. Powers*	255

VII. DREAM AS CRISIS	275
In Dreams Begin Responsibilities *Delmore Schwartz*	276
An Occurrence at Owl Creek Bridge *Ambrose Bierce*	283
The Secret Room *Alain Robbe-Grillet*	292
The Seven Riders *Dino Buzzati*	297

VIII. ARCHETYPES AND STEREOTYPES: THE ARTIFICIAL NIGGER AND THE IMAGINARY JEW	301
A Simple Heart *Gustave Flaubert*	303
The Imaginary Jew *John Berryman*	332
The Artificial Nigger *Flannery O'Connor*	340
Counterparts *James Joyce*	357

IX. IRONY—EPIPHANY	367
Bliss *Katherine Mansfield*	368
Fifty Pounds *A. E. Coppard*	378
Barbados *Paule Marshall*	391

X. THE SHAPE OF FICTION	405
The Wife of Martin Guerre *Janet Lewis*	405

HANDBOOK FOR TEACHERS AND STUDENTS	469

The Stories

The Ambitious Guest   *Nathaniel Hawthorne*   158
The Artificial Nigger   *Flannery O'Connor*   340
Barbados   *Paule Marshall*   391
Bliss   *Katherine Mansfield*   368
But For This . . .   *Lajos Zilahy*   93
Counterparts   *James Joyce*   357
The Curious Case of Benjamin Button   *F. Scott Fitzgerald*   72
Death of a Favorite   *J. F. Powers*   255
Dying   *Richard Stern*   106
Fifty Pounds   *A. E. Coppard*   378
The Gonzaga Manuscripts   *Saul Bellow*   118
Hook   *Walter Van Tilburg Clark*   222
A Hunger Artist   *Franz Kafka*   98
The Imaginary Jew   *John Berryman*   332
In Dreams Begin Responsibilities   *Delmore Schwartz*   276
The Iron Fist of Oligarchy   *Mark Harris*   140
Life-Story   *John Barth*   177
A Mother's Tale   *James Agee*   238
An Occurrence at Owl Creek Bridge   *Ambrose Bierce*   283
Persephone   *Meridel Le Sueur*   192
The Procurator of Judaea   *Anatole France*   16
The Real Right Thing   *Henry James*   165
Red Leaves   *William Faulkner*   201
The Secret Room   *Alain Robbe-Grillet*   292
The Seven Riders   *Dino Buzzati*   297
The Short Happy Life of Francis Macomber   *Ernest Hemingway*   46
A Simple Heart   *Gustave Flaubert*   303
The Sire de Malétroit's Door   *Robert Louis Stevenson*   30
The Use of Force   *William Carlos Williams*   9
The Wife of Martin Guerre   *Janet Lewis*   405

The Authors

James Agee (1909–1955) American
John Barth (1930–) American
Saul Bellow (1915–) American
John Berryman (1914–1972) American
Ambrose [Gwinnett] Bierce (1842–1914?) American
Dino Buzzati (1870–1953) Italian
Walter Van Tilburg Clark (1909–1971) American
A[lfred] E[dgar] Coppard (1878–1957) English
William Faulkner (1897–1962) American
F[rancis] Scott Fitzgerald (1896–1940) American
Gustave Flaubert (1821–1880) French
Anatole France (1844–1924) French
Mark Harris (1922–) American
Nathaniel Hawthorne (1804–1864) American
Ernest Hemingway (1898–1961) American

Henry James (1843–1916) American
James Joyce (1882–1941) Irish
Franz Kafka (1833–1924) Austrian
Meridel Le Sueur (1900–) American
Janet Lewis (1899–) American
Katherine Mansfield (1888–1923) English
Paule Marshall (1929–) American
Flannery O'Connor (1925–1964) American
J[ames] F[arl] Powers (1917–) American
Alain Robbe-Grillet (1922–) French
Delmore Schwartz (1913–1966) American
Richard Stern (1928–) American
Robert Louis Balfour Stevenson (1850–1894) Scottish
William Carlos Williams (1883–1963) American
Lajos Zilahy (1891–1974) Hungarian

Who the Editors Are

Mark Harris published his first novel in 1946. He has been a journalist. From 1948 to 1951 he was a student of the creative-writing program directed by Alan Swallow at the University of Denver. He received his doctoral degree in American Studies at the University of Minnesota. For twenty years he has been teacher and writer. Among his novels are *The Southpaw, The Goy, Killing Everybody,* and *Wake Up, Stupid.* His screenplay, *Bang the Drum Slowly,* was adapted from his novel of the same name. He is presently professor of English at the University of Pittsburgh.

Josephine Harris received her doctoral degree in psycholinguistics at Purdue University; her master's degree was in literature. She has taught at San Francisco State University and elsewhere, most recently at the California Institute of the Arts, as Dean of Complementary Education.

Hester Harris is a student in the Department of Physics and Astronomy at San Francisco State University. She formed an early affection for literature, perhaps as a result of her parents' commitment. In the preparation of this anthology her collaboration with her parents was full and complete: often the editors cannot be certain from page to page whose text is whose.

Preface

Begin! Enjoy! The editors enjoyed reading stories long before they thought about making an anthology. One of the great tasks in the teaching of literature is to help teachers and students to relax. The pursuit of literature ought not to be a chore, a duty, a punishment, an assignment to drudgery, but a pleasure whose reward may be the most personal illumination: for each of us, in Frost's language, "a momentary stay against confusion."

Some stories survive, standing the test of time and change. Most of the stories in this book have been chosen from among those which appear to have defied aging, which remain moving, affecting, graceful in style, and surprising in outcome to us even after many readings, even after we have long known "how it comes out," and even beyond long interruptions when, returning to a particular story, we find that it speaks to us again.

Other stories in this volume have not yet lived that long. Perhaps they will. Long-lived or short, these are stories which emancipated the editors, who have been at one time or another students, teachers, writers, and always readers.

Making spirit into book requires a different kind of organization. The editors have shaken down a thousand reading experiences to thirty stories, then arranged the stories by category. Each of the central categories is accompanied by editorial comment. Sometimes commentary follows a story; sometimes not. In this respect, as with respect to the book as a whole, we have wanted to live flexibly, speaking *as needed* rather than merely to fulfill the conditions of a format. For that reason, not all our commentaries are equal. Some are longer than others; some are in the text, some are in the Handbook. This has made sense to us in a way a mere equalizing formula has not made sense, and we hope it will be seen as useful.

Likewise, some stories are more difficult then others, and some are rather difficult indeed. Literature broadens experience, as all true education does. Work which is not at first or easily comprehensible often

PREFACE

becomes beautifully clear when considered in friendly spirit by a teacher drawing from personal experience and from the experence of criticism; to students, drawing from teachers, that which was obscure early in the semester may soon appear lucid and meaningful.

Every story in this volume is rational. None is a trick. Serious and meaningful, they await our penetration. Thought and discussion will illuminate them; patience, brief perplexity or even dark frustration often go with the literary territory. Then the work produces light. Give Emily Dickinson the last word on the subject of literary apprehension. She knew the problem.

> Tell all the truth but tell it slant,
> Success in circuit lies,
> Too bright for our infirm delight
> The truth's superb surprise;
>
> As lightning to the children eased
> With explanation kind,
> The truth must dazzle gradually
> Or every man be blind.

For us, the mood of the volume matters a great deal. We want to stress fluidity—we don't want to pretend that a given story or our related commentary belongs to an inescapable category. We cross lines. We integrate. We think of categories as shuttles, taking us from one place to another. We do not enjoy expertism. We do not admire mystification. Our whole value may be to remind the teacher and student that the goal of reading is not a scholarly professionalism but the natural act of learning things about the world each of us has joined.

One of the objectives of the teaching of English ought to be (if it isn't) the advancement of that speciality which is merely humane. In preparing this volume the editors had in mind not only the student of English but students of other things as well, with whom we wish to speak in good English as much about the pleasure of reading as the technicalities of scholarship.

Making a book, we also made a Handbook, and put it at the end. We felt that some thoughts and procedures were more appropriate to the book than to the Handbook, and *vice versa*, but we urge upon every teacher his or her own approach. Openness is best. Teachers will make many discoveries in these stories which the editors have not made, and students will make more. Begin, enjoy, and share, the fewer secrets the better.

THE DESIGN
OF FICTION

INTRODUCTION

The Writer's View

The men and women who wrote these stories did not write them for a college anthology. Indeed, we can scarcely know why anyone writes a story. The author may not know, or, knowing, may even conceal the reasons. Perhaps he had in mind the fame which print might bring. Perhaps he was thinking of money. Perhaps he hoped to change mankind's idea of itself; or of him; or her. Or he might have thought to send off secret messages to his wife, his associates, his enemies. Perhaps it was all of these together. It comes to this: We cannot exhume the author's intention.

The place where we are reading these stories is different from the place where the author wrote them. Crucial circumstances vary. In the context of the schoolhouse (red brick or multiversity) we may make the mistake of imagining that a story was written for this setting—to test our aptitude for symbol searching, for theme detection, for the identification of sources and likenesses, or for the discovery of historical parallels. But these are tasks we undertake after *the fact. The story was written* before *the fact.*

In the moment of writing, the author was no scholar or student. He wrote primarily out of feeling, out of emotion, out of some impulse or desire to speak, to say, out of some humor, some rage, some display, some revenge, some idea or hope he wished to express for the relief of his own feelings. An author writes with passion as well as with mind.

The author may not have been aware of the symbols we now detect—i.e., the further meaning a word may have. We may see dimensions in a story which would surprise the author, and yet if he were seated among us in the classroom he might confess—"Yes, yes, I sort of meant that, I guess, now that you mention it I can see where you see it your way."

It seems rather indirect, though, to cast one's feelings in the form of a story; mere make-believe. Why not come out directly and say what's on one's mind? Why not write an essay, a letter to the editor? One might paint a picture or snap a photograph to illustrate his complaint. Alas, the writer writes. He can do no other. If he is a writer of fiction he writes

INTRODUCTION

fiction: that is the form his feelings take. It is natural to him. He cannot help himself.

We love the sound of a good story, its rhythms, its excellent phrases, the very words themselves. Maybe we can never know precisely what the story is "about." It just is. It sounds. This, too, the writer may have felt: it sounded right.

He may be less certain of its meaning than its sound. For instance, in discussing the last sentence of his story, "The Portable Phonograph," Walter Van Tilburg Clark speaks of having "plucked the proper closing note," not in a "considered" way, but by luck. His sentence was: "On the inside of the bed, next the wall, he could feel with his hand the comfortable lead pipe."

> It seemed to me that sentence plucked the proper closing note, one that might linger for a time with a tenuous but moving reminder of the whole intention. If so, it was so, happily, by means of the very last phrase, and particularly by means of the one word "comfortable." Nothing in the phrase was considered, not "comfortable" any more than the rest, but even as it came, that "comfortable" tickled me, not so much because of its immediate implication, in which the paradox was clear enough, as for some remote, redoubling connotation which I could not, at the moment, catch hold of. Then, a few seconds after I had poked home the final period, it came to me. I had done a bit of lucky thieving from Bill of Avon. . . . Remember how Juliet, walking in the tomb, and not yet aware that Romeo is dead, murmurs drowsily to the gentle Friar Lawrence, "Oh, comfortable Friar—"?*

Lucky it was. The writer depends upon luck to carry him along; upon rhythm; upon the people of his story to make their own ways out of their own necessities. A mere idea with which the writer began may have had to give way to the reality of the characters of his story, in the same way that the actors in a play may produce a play the playwright never intended.

The language of fiction is its own language, and we may be advancing upon deceptive ground when we try to translate a story from its own language into other terms. Beware the phrase, "In other words. . . ." Few writers of fiction are formal sociologists, although readers interested in sociology may find a story rewarding. The author of "The Use of Force," who is a physician, uses his medical experience to support the authenticity of his story, not to offer a medical program.

In creating the fiction itself the writer is beyond sociology, beyond medicine, beyond (not above) any branch of study. It was the feeling of

---

* "The Ghost of an Apprehension," in *The Pacific Spectator*, Summer 1949.

INTRODUCTION

a story which inspired the author, and we receive the author's feeling first. We hope to avoid becoming entrapped by the data or substance of a story, by philosophy or metaphysics, or by the wrong questions generally. Asking freely, we discover in time which questions are fruitful. Sometimes the authors are telling us things to ask, as Henry James may be doing in this volume in "The Real Right Thing."

The Reader's View

If the passion and the emotion are the artist's distillation of experience, we may sensibly begin, as readers, by trying to feel, not analyze.

Then we move with our feelings toward intellect. We are creatures of intellect (that is why we are in the schoolhouse). We know enough about the fabulous human mind to realize how much deductive and inductive procedure our thinking pursues. We conclude that art must also be shaped in these ways.

The writer writes. Very well, we read. If the creation of a short story is an act of intense narrative compression, the reading of the same is an act of intense narrative abstraction. Our first task is to see the story whole, piercing its data and its substance, seizing its feeling. We must transcend time, place, occupation, or other local factors and considerations unifying the story in order to receive the story fully: to see any structure whole we stand back before becoming involved with detail at the expense of the overall view.

First, we ought to pursue the print for a total effect. Then we can read for a gathering-in of the parts that make the whole, the building units that form the structure. We can talk in terms of plot, characters, style, and setting, but the end—and the beginning—is not in explication but in emotion.

Is the impact of emotion in a short story a momentary thing, a permanence of feeling, a changeling? Is this impact a criterion for telling good from bad? Or bad from worse? Or excellent from indifferent? We have read a story and we have felt it. Our author humanly wrote it, and we humanly read it. The feeling passed from writer to reader. In some ways our lives are different now.

So, we begin with feeling. We finish reading a story, it serves us, it excites us, it turns us on, it changes our lives—for the moment. We run from the room to show this marvelous story to a friend. We make him read it on the spot, saying "Here's the best story ever written," and he reads it and says, "What's so hot about it?"

INTRODUCTION

Perhaps we should have said, "This is the best story ever written for me, at this hour of my life." Tomorrow will bring another hour, another story, and next month, next year, still another.

Not the story, of course, but the reader has changed. Not a syllable of the story has been altered, but a psychological transaction has occurred; the reader's life has changed.

Judgment is relative, and we must live with the fact of relativity without descending into chaos. Let us avoid rigid categories and ranks. We need never decide which are the ten best stories of all the ages, nor even the hundred best, nor which stories are better than others, nor which stories we ought to read as "good for us."

The excitement of discovery must never be diminished, deplored, or discouraged. We must never be ashamed of our literary affections. We must never fear our own judgments upon the grounds that it may not be "right" to hold such a view of a story—may not be intellectually "respectable," may not be "in." Consensus is not the goal of literature.

Just as agreement about excellence eludes us, so does agreement about the "meaning" of a story. Each of us may like a story, be moved by it, equally proclaim it a good story, an excellent story, and yet each of us may admire it for different reasons. We may not agree upon its "meaning" or even its outcome, and we ought to be eager not to betray the totality of the story by resorting to simple paraphrase—"this story says that honesty is the best policy." No, the best policy may be to learn to live with doubt. On the other hand, we must rein in, too, from "going all the way" once the way is discovered, into seeing metaphor, allegory, symbolism, and myth in everything.

We must learn to see a story whole.

PART ONE
THE WRITER'S VIEW

I | Realism

I have been reading and writing and studying fiction for a quarter of a century, but I cannot give you a good definition of "realism." To tell you the truth, I'm not sure you should want one.

I cannot recall ever meeting a writer who spoke of a work of his own in terms of its being "realistic," or who could be certain whether it was or it wasn't. Once a work of fiction is done, the writer doesn't appear to be interested in many of its aspects which seem to interest teachers, students, and other readers. Many writers, for example, once they are at a distance from a story, seem uncertain about its "meaning," and in the most exasperating way they agree to the possibilities of interpretations somewhat remote even from those with which they thought they had begun.

I have been teaching English in colleges for twenty years, but I never begin a class discussion of a story without a certain nervousness. As a means of getting past my nervousness, and past all this doubt and uncertainty regarding definitions, motives, meanings, and intentions, I frequently begin a semester's first day with a very short story I read for the first time on a high stool behind the cash register at Tro Harper's Book Store in San Francisco in 1954. I was working at that book store because, although I was a professor, I hadn't any money. My wife made me Poor Boy sandwiches and I took them to work with me and read books behind the cash register. When I read "The Use of Force" it almost knocked me off the stool.

THE USE OF FORCE

William Carlos Williams

They were new patients to me, all I had was the name, Olson. Please come down as soon as you can, my daughter is very sick.

When I arrived I was met by the mother, a big startled-looking woman, very clean and apologetic who merely said, Is this the doctor? and let me

REALISM

in. In the back, she added. You must excuse us, doctor, we have her in the kitchen where it is warm. It is very damp here sometimes.

The child was fully dressed and sitting on her father's lap near the kitchen table. He tried to get up, but I motioned for him not to bother, took off my overcoat and started to look things over. I could see that they were all very nervous, eyeing me up and down distrustfully. As often, in such cases, they weren't telling me more than they had to, it was up to me to tell them; that's why they were spending three dollars on me.

The child was fairly eating me up with her cold, steady eyes, and no expression to her face whatever. She did not move and seemed, inwardly, quiet; an unusually attractive little thing, and as strong as a heifer in appearance. But her face was flushed, she was breathing rapidly, and I realized that she had a high fever. She had magnificent blond hair, in profusion. One of those picture children often reproduced in advertising leaflets and the photogravure sections of the Sunday papers.

She's had a fever for three days, began the father and we don't know what it comes from. My wife has given her things, you know, like people do, but it don't do no good. And there's been a lot of sickness around. So we tho't you'd better look her over and tell us what is the matter.

As doctors often do I took a trial shot at it as a point of departure. Has she had a sore throat?

Both parents answered me together, No . . . No, she says her throat don't hurt her.

Does your throat hurt you? added the mother to the child. But the little girl's expression didn't change nor did she move her eyes from my face.

Have you looked?

I tried to, said the mother, but I couldn't see.

As it happens we had been having a number of cases of diphtheria in the school to which this child went during that month and we were all, quite apparently, thinking of that, though no one had as yet spoken of the thing.

Well, I said, suppose we take a look at the throat first. I smiled in my best professional manner and asking for the child's first name I said, come on, Mathilda, open your mouth and let's take a look at your throat.

Nothing doing.

Aw, come on, I coaxed, just open your mouth wide and let me take a look. Look, I said opening both hands wide, I haven't anything in my hands. Just open up and let me see.

Such a nice man, put in the mother. Look how kind he is to you. Come on, do what he tells you to. He won't hurt you.

At that I ground my teeth in disgust. If only they wouldn't use the word "hurt" I might be able to get somewhere. But I did not allow myself

THE USE OF FORCE

to be hurried or disturbed but speaking quietly and slowly I approached the child again.

As I moved my chair a little nearer suddenly with one cat-like movement both her hands clawed instinctively for my eyes and she almost reached them too. In fact she knocked my glasses flying and they fell, though unbroken, several feet away from me on the kitchen floor.

Both the mother and father almost turned themselves inside out in embarrassment and apology. You bad girl, said the mother, taking her and shaking her by one arm. Look what you've done. The nice man . . .

For heaven's sake, I broke in. Don't call me a nice man to her. I'm here to look at her throat on the chance that she might have diphtheria and possibly die of it. But that's nothing to her. Look here, I said to the child, we're going to look at your throat. You're old enough to understand what I'm saying. Will you open it now by yourself or shall we have to open it for you?

Not a move. Even her expression hadn't changed. Her breaths however were coming faster and faster. Then the battle began. I had to do it. I had to have a throat culture for her own protection. But first I told the parents that it was entirely up to them. I explained the danger but said that I would not insist on a throat examination so long as they would take the responsibility.

If you don't do what the doctor says you'll have to go to the hospital, the mother admonished her severely.

Oh yeah? I had to smile to myself. After all, I had already fallen in love with the savage brat, the parents were contemptible to me. In the ensuing struggle they grew more and more abject, crushed, exhausted while she surely rose to magnificent heights of insane fury of effort bred of her terror of me.

The father tried his best, and he was a big man but the fact that she was his daughter, his shame at her behavior and his dread of hurting her made him release her just at the critical moment several times when I had almost achieved success, till I wanted to kill him. But his dread also that she might have diphtheria made him tell me to go on, go on though he himself was almost fainting, while the mother moved back and forth behind us raising and lowering her hands in an agony of apprehension.

Put her in front of you on your lap, I ordered, and hold both her wrists.

But as soon as he did the child let out a scream. Don't, you're hurting me. Let go of my hands. Let them go I tell you. Then she shrieked terrifyingly, hysterically. Stop it! Stop it! You're killing me!

Do you think she can stand it, doctor! said the mother.

You get out, said the husband to his wife. Do you want her to die of diphtheria?

REALISM

Come on now, hold her, I said.

Then I grasped the child's head with my left hand and tried to get the wooden tongue depressor between her teeth. She fought, with clenched teeth, desperately! But now I also had grown furious—at a child. I tried to hold myself down but I couldn't. I know how to expose a throat for inspection. And I did my best. When finally I got the wooden spatula behind the last teeth and just the point of it into the mouth cavity, she opened up for an instant but before I could see anything she came down again and gripping the wooden blade between her molars she reduced it to splinters before I could get it out again.

Aren't you ashamed, the mother yelled at her. Aren't you ashamed to act like that in front of the doctor?

Get me a smooth-handled spoon of some sort, I told the mother. We're going through with this. The child's mouth was already bleeding. Her tongue was cut and she was screaming in wild hysterical shrieks. Perhaps I should have desisted and come back in an hour or more. No doubt it would have been better. But I have seen at least two children lying dead in bed of neglect in such cases, and feeling that I must get a diagnosis, now or never I went at it again. But the worst of it was that I too had got beyond reason. I could have torn the child apart in my own fury and enjoyed it. It was a pleasure to attack her. My face was burning with it.

The damned little brat must be protected against her own idiocy, one says to one's self at such times. Others must be protected against her. It is social necessity. And all these things are true. But a blind fury, a feeling of adult shame, bred of a longing for muscular release are the operatives. One goes on to the end.

In a final unreasoning assault I overpowered the child's neck and jaws. I forced the heavy silver spoon back of her teeth and down her throat till she gagged. And there it was—both tonsils covered with membrane. She had fought valiantly to keep me from knowing her secret. She had been hiding that sore throat for three days at least and lying to her parents in order to escape just such an outcome as this.

Now truly she *was* furious. She had been on the defensive before but now she attacked. Tried to get off her father's lap and fly at me while tears of defeat blinded her eyes.

Where was the power of this story that it should knock me off the stool? I think the point of the power may have been the word "pleasure" in the fourth paragraph from the end—"I could have torn the child apart in my own fury and enjoyed it. It was a pleasure to attack her. My face was burning with it."

I had not been reading the story analytically. I was simply between

THE USE OF FORCE

customers. I had been open *to the story. I did not expect to be examined on it, and I did not expect to examine anyone else. Open, defenseless, I was a broad target for paradoxes which reminded me of myself at certain moments—beyond reason, the pleasure of attack, the burning face, soon followed by the rationalization of it all! "The damned little brat must be protected against her own idiocy, one says to one's self at such times. Others must be protected against her. It is a social necessity."*

In that moment I acknowledged myself. Living in the world, as I do (you too?), I slowly came to see that story as a comment on many people and things beyond myself. Of course it is a comment upon force itself (it is useful to consider titles); upon warfare; upon the justification of the use of force by person against person, man against woman; upon secret springs of rapine men may feel within themselves, even if the man be a most respectable physician charging three dollars a visit. I did not know all that on a first reading, but I felt *much, unable to name what I had felt.*

This is a superb story to begin any class with, and so we begin this book with it, too. It is shorter than almost any other story in the book, and yet it has everything—a rhythm so compelling it defies the need for quotation marks, dramatic shape, form, suspense, action, plot, characterization, confrontation, a beginning, a middle, an end, and a profound message in a setting so simple we run the danger of its sailing past.

I have read the story aloud to students at least a hundred times. I can almost recite it. Its rhythms often return to me when something in daily life makes me think, "Oh yes, social necessity." First we feel *a story. Then we remember it.*

Because Dr. Williams looked into himself he saw us, and he helps us to see into ourselves. I do not think that was his motive. I think he meant only to describe a familiar, recurring sensation he had experienced on his medical rounds, this divided emotion of pleasure and fury, duty and shame. I have a suspicion unsupported by any evidence that "The Use of Force" is either a fragment once intended as part of a longer work, or that it is a prose paraphrase of a poem Dr. Williams planned. But I cannot know. I never spoke to Dr. Williams. And could he even remember exactly how it had been formed, or why? The creation of a work of fiction may be something like the mother's sensation of childbirth: labor done, child produced, the memory fades.

We may speculate upon motives, meanings, intentions, and definitions, for such speculation is interesting and tempting. But we need not expect to arrive at firm conclusions, for when a story departs its author it becomes many things to many people.

Teachers, students, how many all told are in your class?

That's how many stories any story is.

REALISM

Teachers, students, don't be nervous. Be open. Let a story knock you off your stool, if it will.

All right, if you insist, here's a timid thought toward a definition of "realism."

Realism: *the characters in a work of fiction are exactly what they are, seen as if in a plain straightforward photograph; looked at direct, without distortion; nevertheless symbolic, as all things are symbolic; "Symbols are what fly off everything" [Robert Frost].*

Certain fiction which we call "realistic" may be so precisely because the author is close to his (or her) subject. He may have in his pocket at the actual moment of writing a straightforward photograph of his central character, hero, or adversary—Dr. Williams perhaps had a photograph of himself or of Mathilda ("One of those picture children often reproduced in advertising leaflets and the photogravure sections of the Sunday papers").

Most of the fiction in this volume is realistic, coming at its realism in various ways from various directions. But some of the work included— "The Curious Case of Benjamin Button," or "A Hunger Artist"—is clearly not realistic, although it is certainly true that even fiction which is not in itself "realistic" may in critical ways affect our reactions to the very real lives we lead. We say of events of our lives that they are "Alice-in-Wonderlandish," or that they are "Kafkaesque." For Kafka, "real" life was indescribable in realistic terms: he required an unreal setting (a "hunger artist" in a "small barred cage") for an adequate description of life as he felt it.

Writers wish to express real conditions of life. They are often angry about the lives they see around them, or about injustices they see or personally experience. They are offended by conditions, even as they are awed, they laugh, they sink into melancholy, and they are often overcome by nostalgia. They invite events to enter their awareness, and they make the most of uninvited intrusions. "Therefore," wrote Henry James, "if I should certainly say to a novice, 'Write from experience and from experience only,' I should feel that this was rather a tantalizing monition if I were not careful immediately to add, 'Try to be one of the people on whom nothing is lost!' "

The realism of "The Procurator of Judea" appears to arise less from an intensely personal concern (the alarming introspections of a physician) than from certain reflections upon history.

THE USE OF FORCE

History, however, is also now. We live now. Anatole France lived then. But our then was his now; he cared for his own times mainly, he hoped to modify or improve them, and he was awed, as men of reflection often are, by that phenomenon of history often reduced to clichés: ". . . there's nothing new under the sun . . . history repeats itself."

Anatole France lived from 1844 to 1924. Learned in classical literature, he was also deeply involved in the political crises of his country—after whom he had renamed himself—at the beginning of the twentieth century.

He remained reflective, knowing enough history to avoid becoming drowned in the present. Is Anatole France's account of a meeting of two men in the time of Christ upon a street in Rome precisely realistic? Or is it based, instead, upon the author's projection of the life of his own country in 1900? Very likely it is the latter. And we in turn stand upon a street in Rome created by Anatole France in his own time in another country. The realism *fails, but the point is gained, and we see, as the author intends us to see, how very like our own time were Roman years, and how very like the time of Anatole France—how, in short, history is continuous, how history goes about in a circle, and how human passions endure beyond superficial change.*

Anatole France may also be instructing us to beware our hypocrisy, pointing out to us, if we will but hear, how we whose civilization adores Christ, especially during high holiday seasons, might be indifferent to Him were He our contemporary. If we recall Anatole France's humane role in the Dreyfus case, we may imagine that he is warning us against casualness regarding individual fate: Dreyfus, a French Jew, accused of betraying his country, sentenced to detention for life on Devil's Island, was exonerated after twelve years of a controversy during which Anatole France and others of his countrymen risked lives and reputations to focus interest upon an unpopular cause.

Is "The Procurator of Judea" a Treatise *upon Nature of exactly the sort Lamia reads when we meet him? Nothing more is made of the* Treatise, *but in retrospect the detail is suggestive (nothing illuminates a story like a second reading), for the story as a whole may be addressing itself to Nature: ours, France's, Rome's.*

Two men meet. They have not seen one another for twenty years. The name Lamia *means nothing to us. But* Pontius Pilate! *The final moment of the story—Pilate's small remark—is a moment so real, so realistic, that it elevates the story to success; and it illuminates, by the way, 2000 years of history. Yes. Read on.*

15

REALISM

THE PROCURATOR OF JUDAEA

Anatole France

Aelius Lamia, born in Italy of illustrious parents, had not yet discarded the *toga praetexta* when he set out for the schools of Athens to study philosophy. Subsequently he took up his residence at Rome, and in his house on the Esquiline, amid a circle of youthful wastrels, abandoned himself to licentious courses. But being accused of engaging in criminal relations with Lepida, the wife of Sulpicious Quirinus, a man of consular rank, and being found guilty, he was exiled by Tiberius Caesar. At that time he was just entering his twenty-fourth year. During the eighteen years that his exile lasted he traversed Syria, Palestine, Cappadocia, and Armenia, and made prolonged visits to Antioch, Caesarea, and Jerusalem. When, after the death of Tiberius, Caius was raised to the purple, Lamia obtained permission to return to Rome. He even regained a portion of his possessions. Adversity had taught him wisdom.

He avoided all intercourse with the wives and daughters of Roman citizens, made no efforts towards obtaining office, held aloof from public honours, and lived a secluded life in his house on the Esquiline. Occupying himself with the task of recording all the remarkable things he had seen during his distant travels, he turned, as he said, the vicissitudes of his years of expiation into a diversion for his hours of rest. In the midst of these calm employments, alternating with assiduous study of the works of Epicurus, he recognized with a mixture of surprise and vexation that age was stealing upon him. In his sixty-second year, being afflicted with an illness which proved in no slight degree troublesome, he decided to have recourse to the waters at Baiae. The coast at that point, once frequented by the halcyon, was at this date the resort of the wealthy Roman, greedy of pleasure. For a week Lamia lived alone, without a friend in the brilliant crowd. Then one day, after dinner, an inclination to which he yielded urged him to ascend the incline, which, covered with vines that resembled bacchantes, looked out upon the waves.

Having reached the summit he seated himself by the side of a path beneath a terebinth, and let his glances wander over the lovely landscape. To his left, livid and bare, the Phlegraean plain stretched out towards the ruins of Cumae. On his right, Cape Misenum plunged its abrupt spur beneath the Tyrrhenian sea. Beneath his feet luxurious Baiae, following the graceful outline of the coast, displayed its gardens, its villas thronged with statues, its porticos, its marble terraces along the shores of the blue ocean where the dolphins sported. Before him, on the other side of the bay, on the Campanian coast, gilded by the already sinking sun, gleamed

THE PROCURATOR OF JUDAEA

the temples which far away rose above the laurels of Posilippo, whilst on the extreme horizon Vesuvius looked forth smiling.

Lamia drew from a fold of his toga a scroll containing the *Treatise upon Nature*, extended himself upon the ground, and began to read. But the warning cries of a slave necessitated his rising to allow of the passage of a litter which was being carried along the narrow pathway through the vineyards. The litter being uncurtained, permitted Lamia to see stretched upon the cushions as it was borne nearer to him the figure of an elderly man of immense bulk, who, supporting his head on his hand, gazed out with a gloomy and disdainful expression. His nose, which was aquiline, and his chin, which was prominent, seemed desirous of meeting across his lips, and his jaws were powerful.

From the first moment Lamia was convinced that the face was familiar to him. He hesitated a moment before the name came to him. Then suddenly hastening towards the litter with a display of surprise and delight—

"Pontius Pilate!" he cried. "The gods be praised who have permitted me to see you once again!"

The old man gave a signal to the slaves to stop, and cast a keen glance upon the stranger who had addressed him.

"Pontius, my dear host," resumed the latter, "have twenty years so far whitened my hair and hollowed my cheeks that you no longer recognize your friend Aelius Lamia?"

At this name Pontius Pilate dismounted from the litter as actively as the weight of his years and the heaviness of his gait permitted him, and embraced Aelius Lamia again and again.

"Gods! what a treat it is to me to see you once more! But, alas, you call up memories of those long-vanished days when I was Procurator of Judaea in the province of Syria. Why, it must be thirty years ago that I first met you. It was at Caesarea, whither you came to drag out your weary term of exile. I was fortunate enough to alleviate it a little, and out of friendship, Lamia, you followed me to that depressing place Jerusalem, where the Jews filled me with bitterness and disgust. You remained for more than ten years my guest and my companion, and in converse about Rome and things Roman we both of us managed to find consolation—you for your misfortunes, and I for my burdens of State."

Lamia embraced him afresh.

"You forget two things, Pontius; you are overlooking the facts that you used your influence on my behalf with Herod Antipas, and that your purse was freely open to me."

"Let us not talk of that," replied Pontius, "since after your return to Rome you sent me by one of your freedmen a sum of money which repaid me with usury."

REALISM

"Pontius, I could never consider myself out of your debt by the mere payment of money. But tell me, have the gods fulfilled your desires? Are you in the enjoyment of all the happiness you deserve? Tell me about your family, your fortunes, your health."

"I have withdrawn to Sicily, where I possess estates, and where I cultivate wheat for the market. My oldest daughter, my best-beloved Pontia, who has been left a widow, lives with me, and directs my household. The gods be praised, I have preserved my mental vigour; my memory is not in the least degree enfeebled. But old age always brings in its train a long procession of griefs and infirmities. I am cruelly tormented with gout. And at this very moment you find me on my way to the Phlegraean plain in search of a remedy for my sufferings. From that burning soil, whence at night flames burst forth, proceed acrid exhalations of sulphur, which, so they say, ease the pains and restore suppleness to the joints. At least, the physicians assure me that it is so."

"May you find it so in your case, Pontius! But, despite the gout and its burning torments, you scarcely look as old as myself, although in reality you must be my senior by ten years. Unmistakably you have retained a greater degree of vigour than I ever possessed, and I am overjoyed to find you looking so hale. Why, dear friend, did you retire from the public service before the customary age? Why, on resigning your governorship in Judaea, did you withdraw to a voluntary exile on your Sicilian estates? Give me an account of your doings from the moment that I ceased to be a witness of them. You were preparing to suppress a Samaritan rising when I set out for Cappadocia, where I hoped to draw some profit from the breeding of horses and mules. I have not seen you since then. How did that expedition succeed? Pray tell me. Everything interests me that concerns you in any way."

Pontius Pilate sadly shook his head.

"My natural disposition," he said, "as well as a sense of duty, impelled me to fulfil my public responsibilities, not merely with diligence, but even with ardour. But I was pursued by unrelenting hatred. Intrigues and calumnies cut short my career in its prime, and the fruit it should have looked to bear has withered away. You ask me about the Samaritan insurrection. Let us sit down on this hillock. I shall be able to give you an answer in few words. Those occurrences are as vividly present to me as if they had happened yesterday.

"A man of the people, of persuasive speech—there are many such to be met with in Syria—induced the Samaritans to gather together in arms on Mount Gerizim (which in that country is looked upon as a holy place) under the promise that he would disclose to their sight the sacred vessels which in the ancient days of Evander and our father, Aeneas, had been

THE PROCURATOR OF JUDAEA

hidden away by an eponymous hero, or rather a tribal deity, named Moses. Upon this assurance the Samaritans rose in rebellion; but having been warned in time to forestall them, I dispatched detachments of infantry to occupy the mountain, and stationed cavalry to keep the approaches to it under observation.

"These measures of prudence were urgent. The rebels were already laying siege to the town of Tyrathaba, situated at the foot of Mount Gerizim. I easily dispersed them, and stifled the as yet scarcely organized revolt. Then, in order to give a forcible example with as few victims as possible, I handed over to execution the leaders of the rebellion. But you are aware, Lamia, in what strait dependence I was kept by the proconsul Vitellius, who governed Syria not in, but against the interests of Rome, and looked upon the provinces of the empire as territories which could be farmed out to tetrarchs. The head-men among the Samaritans, in their resentment against me, came and fell at his feet lamenting. To listen to them, nothing had been further from their thoughts than to disobey Caesar. It was I who provoked the rising, and it was purely in order to withstand my violence that they had gathered together round Tyrathaba. Vitellius listened to their complaints, and handing over the affairs of Judaea to his friend Marcellus, commanded me to go and justify my proceedings before the Emperor himself. With a heart overflowing with grief and resentment I took ship. Just as I approached the shores of Italy, Tiberius, worn out with age and the cares of empire, died suddenly on the selfsame Cape Misenum, whose peak we see from this very spot magnified in the mists of evening. I demanded justice of Caius, his successor, whose perception was naturally acute, and who was acquainted with Syrian affairs. But marvel with me, Lamia, at the maliciousness of fortune, resolved on my discomfiture. Caius then had in his suite at Rome the Jew Agrippa, his companion, the friend of his childhood, whom he cherished as his own eyes. Now Agrippa favoured Vitellius, inasmuch as Vitellius was the enemy of Antipas, whom Agrippa pursued with his hatred. The Emperor adopted the prejudices of his beloved Asiatic, and refused even to listen to me. There was nothing for me to do but bow beneath the stroke of unmerited misfortune. With tears for my meat and gall for my portion, I withdrew to my estates in Sicily, where I should have died of grief if my sweet Pontia had not come to console her father. I have cultivated wheat, and succeeded in producing the fullest ears in the whole province. But now my life is ended; the future will judge between Vitellius and me."

"Pontius," replied Lamia, "I am persuaded that you acted towards the Samaritans according to the rectitude of your character, and solely in the interests of Rome. But were you not perchance on that occasion a trifle

REALISM

too much influenced by that impetuous courage which has always swayed you? You will remember that in Judaea it often happened that I who, younger than you, should naturally have been more impetuous than you, was obliged to urge you to clemency and suavity."

"Suavity towards the Jews!" cried Pontius Pilate. "Although you have lived amongst them, it seems clear that you ill understand those enemies of the human race. Haughty and at the same time base, combining an invincible obstinacy with a despicably mean spirit, they weary alike your love and your hatred. My character, Lamia, was formed upon the maxims of the divine Augustus. When I was appointed Procurator of Judaea, the world was already penetrated with the majestic ideal of the *pax romana*. No longer, as in the days of our internecine strife, were we witnesses to the sack of a province for the aggrandisement of a proconsul. I knew where my duty lay. I was careful that my actions should be governed by prudence and moderation. The gods are my witnesses that I was resolved upon mildness, and upon mildness only. Yet what did my benevolent intentions avail me? You were at my side, Lamia, when, at the outset of my career as ruler, the first rebellion came to a head. Is there any need for me to recall the details to you? The garrison had been transferred from Casarea to take up its winter quarters at Jerusalem. Upon the ensigns of the legionaries appeared the presentment of Caesar. The inhabitants of Jerusalem, who did not recognize the indwelling divinity of the Emperor, were scandalized at this, as though, when obedience is compulsory, it were not less abject to obey a god than a man. The priests of their nation appeared before my tribunal imploring me with supercilious humility to have the ensigns removed from within the holy city. Out of reverence for the divine nature of Caesar and the majesty of the empire, I refused to comply. Then the rabble made common cause with the priests, and all around the pretorium portentous cries of supplication arose. I ordered the soldiers to stack their spears in front of the tower of Antonia, and to proceed, armed only with sticks like lictors, to disperse the insolent crowd. But, heedless of blows, the Jews continued their entreaties, and the more obstinate amongst them threw themselves on the ground and, exposing their throats to the rods, deliberately courted death. You were a witness of my humiliation on that occasion, Lamia. By the order of Vitellius I was forced to send the insignia back to Caesarea. That disgrace I had certainly not merited. Before the immortal gods I swear that never once during my term of office did I flout justice and the laws. But I am grown old. My enemies and detractors are dead. I shall die unavenged. Who will now retrieve my character?"

He moaned and lapsed into silence. Lamia replied—

"That man is prudent who neither hopes nor fears anything from the uncertain events of the future. Does it matter in the least what estimate men may form of us hereafter? We ourselves are after all our own witnesses, and our own judges. You must rely, Pontius Pilate, on the testimony you yourself bear to your own rectitude. Be content with your own personal respect and that of your friends. For the rest, we know that mildness by itself will not suffice for the work of government. There is but little room in the actions of public men for that indulgence of human frailty which the philosophers recommend."

"We'll say no more at present," said Pontius. "The sulphureous fumes which rise from the Phlegraean plain are more powerful when the ground which exhales them is still warm beneath the sun's rays. I must hasten on. Adieu! But now that I have rediscovered a friend, I should wish to take advantage of my good fortune. Do me the favour, Aelius Lamia, to give me your company at supper at my house to-morrow. My house stands on the seashore, at the extreme end of the town in the direction of Misenum. You will easily recognize it by the porch which bears a painting representing Orpheus surrounded by tigers and lions, whom he is charming with the strains from his lyre.

"Till to-morrow, Lamia," he repeated, as he climbed once more into his litter. "To-morrow we will talk about Judaea."

The following day at the supper hour Lamia presented himself at the house of Pontius Pilate. Two couches only were in readiness for occupants. Creditably but simply equipped, the table held a silver service in which were set out beccaficos in honey, thrushes, oysters from the Lucrine lake, and lampreys from Sicily. As they proceeded with their repast, Pontius and Lamia interchanged inquiries with one another about their ailments, the symptoms of which they described at considerable length, mutually emulous of communicating the various remedies which had been recommended to them. Then, congratulating themselves on being thrown together once more at Baiae, they vied with one another in praise of the beauty of that enchanting coast and the mildness of the climate they enjoyed. Lamia was enthusiastic about the charms of the courtesans who frequented the seashore laden with golden ornaments and trailing draperies of barbaric broidery. But the aged Procurator deplored the ostentation with which by means of trumpery jewels and filmy garments foreigners and even enemies of the empire beguiled the Romans of their gold. After a time they turned to the subject of the great engineering feats that had been accomplished in the country; the prodigious bridge constructed by Caius between Puteoli and Baiae, and the canals which Augustus excavated to convey the waters of the ocean to Lake Avernus and the Lucrine lake.

REALISM

"I also," said Pontius, with a sigh, "I also wished to set afoot public works of great utility. When, for my sins, I was appointed Governor of Judaea, I conceived the idea of furnishing Jerusalem with an abundant supply of pure water by means of an aqueduct. The elevation of the levels, the proportionate capacity of the various parts, the gradient for the brazen reservoirs to which the distribution pipes were to be fixed—I had gone into every detail, and decided everything for myself with the assistance of mechanical experts. I had drawn up regulations for the superintendents so as to prevent individuals from making unauthorized depredations. The architects and the workmen had their instructions. I gave orders for the commencement of operations. But far from viewing with satisfaction the construction of that conduit, which was intended to carry to their town upon its massive arches not only water but health, the inhabitants of Jerusalem gave vent to lamentable outcries. They gathered tumultuously together, exclaiming against the sacrilege and impiousness, and, hurling themselves upon the workmen, scattered the foundation stones. Can you picture to yourself, Lamia, a filthier set of barbarians? Nevertheless, Vitellius decided in their favour, and I received orders to put a stop to the work."

"It is a knotty point," said Lamia, "how far one is justified in devising things for the commonweal against the will of the populace."

Pontius Pilate continued as though he had not heard this interruption.

"Refuse an aqueduct! What madness! But whatever is of Roman origin is distasteful to the Jews. In their eyes we are an unclean race, and our very presence appears a profanation to them. You will remember that they would never venture to enter the pretorium for fear of defiling themselves, and that I was consequently obliged to discharge my magisterial functions in an open-air tribunal on that marble pavement your feet so often trod.

"They fear us and they despise us. Yet is not Rome the mother and warden of all those peoples who nestle smiling upon her venerable bosom? With her eagles in the van, peace and liberty have been carried to the very confines of the universe. Those whom we have subdued we look on as our friends, and we leave those conquered races, nay, we secure to them the permanence of their customs and their laws. Did Syria, aforetime rent asunder by its rabble of petty kings, ever even begin to taste of peace and prosperity until it submitted to the armies of Pompey? And when Rome might have reaped a golden harvest as the price of her goodwill, did she lay hands on the hoards that swell the treasuries of barbaric temples? Did she despoil the shrine of Cybele at Pessinus, or the Morimene and Cicilian sanctuaries of Jupiter, or the temple of the Jewish god at Jerusalem? Antioch, Palmyra, and Apamea, secure despite their wealth,

THE PROCURATOR OF JUDAEA

and no longer in dread of the wandering Arab of the desert, have erected temples to the genius of Rome and the divine Caesar. The Jews alone hate and withstand us. They withhold their tribute till it is wrested from them, and obstinately rebel against military service."

"The Jews," replied Lamia, "are profoundly attached to their ancient customs. They suspected you, unreasonably I admit, of a desire to abolish their laws and change their usages. Do not resent it, Pontius, if I say that you did not always act in such a way as to disperse their unfortunate illusion. It gratified you, despite your habitual self-restraint, to play upon their fears, and more than once have I seen you betray in their presence the contempt with which their beliefs and religious ceremonies inspired you. You irritated them particularly by giving instructions for the sacerdotal garments and ornaments of their high priest to be kept in ward by your legionaries in the Antonine tower. One must admit that though they have never risen like us to an appreciation of things divine, the Jews celebrate rites which their very antiquity renders venerable."

Pontius Pilate shrugged his shoulders.

"They have very little exact knowledge of the nature of the gods," he said. "They worship Jupiter, yet they abstain from naming him or erecting a statue of him. They do not even adore him under the semblance of a rude stone, as certain of the Asiatic peoples are wont to do. They know nothing of Apollo, of Neptune, of Mars, nor of Pluto, nor of any goddess. At the same time, I am convinced that in days gone by they worshipped Venus. For even to this day their women bring doves to the altar as victims; and you know as well as I that the dealers who trade beneath the arcades of their temple supply those birds in couples for sacrifice. I have ever been told that on one occasion some madmen proceeded to overturn the stalls bearing these offerings, and their owners with them. The priests raised an outcry about it, and looked on it as a case of sacrilege. I am of opinion that their custom of sacrificing turtle-doves was instituted in honour of Venus. Why are you laughing, Lamia?"

"I was laughing," said Lamia, "at an amusing idea which, I hardly know how, just occurred to me. I was thinking that perchance some day the Jupiter of the Jews might come to Rome and vent his fury upon you. Why should he not? Asia and Africa have already enriched us with a considerable number of gods. We have seen temples in honour of Isis and the dog-faced Anubis erected in Rome. In the public squares, and even on the race-courses, you may run across the Bona Dea of the Syrians mounted on an ass. And did you never hear how, in the reign of Tiberius, a young patrician passed himself off as the horned Jupiter of the Egyptians, Jupiter Ammon, and in this disguise procured the favours of an illustrious lady who was too virtuous to deny anything to a God? Beware, Pontius, lest the

REALISM

invisible Jupiter of the Jews disembark some day on the quay at Ostia!"

At the idea of a god coming out of Judaea, a fleeting smile played over the severe countenance of the Procurator. Then he replied gravely—

"How would the Jews manage to impose their sacred law on outside peoples when they are in a perpetual state of tumult amongst themselves as to the interpretation of that law? You have seen them yourselves, Lamia, in the public squares, split up into twenty rival parties, with staves in their hands, abusing each other and clutching one another by the beard. You have seen them on the steps of the temple, tearing their filthy garments as a symbol of lamentation, with some wretched creature in a frenzy of prophetic exaltation in their midst. They have never realized that it is possible to discuss peacefully and with an even mind those matters concerning the divine which yet are hidden from the profane and wrapped in uncertainty. For the nature of the immortal gods remains hidden from us, and we cannot arrive at a knowledge of it. Though I am of opinion, none the less, that it is a prudent thing to believe in the providence of the gods. But the Jews are devoid of philosophy, and cannot tolerate any diversity of opinions. On the contrary, they judge worthy of the extreme penalty all those who on divine subjects profess opinions opposed to their law. And as, since the genius of Rome has towered over them, capital sentences pronounced by their own tribunals can only be carried out with the sanction of the proconsul or the procurator, they harry the Roman magistrate at any hour to procure his signature to their baleful decrees, they besiege the pretorium with their cries of 'Death!' A hundred times, at least, have I known them, mustered, rich and poor together, all united under their priests, make a furious onslaught on my ivory chair, seizing me by the skirts of my robe, by the thongs of my sandals, and all to demand of me—nay, to exact from me—the death sentence on some unfortunate whose guilt I failed to perceive, and as to whom I could only pronounce that he was as mad as his accusers. A hundred times, do I say! Not a hundred, but every day and all day. Yet it was my duty to execute their law as if it were ours, since I was appointed by Rome not for the destruction, but for the upholding of their customs, and over them I had the power of the rod and the axe. At the outset of my term of office I endeavoured to persuade them to hear reason; I attempted to snatch their miserable victims from death. But this show of mildness only irritated them the more; they demanded their prey, fighting around me like a horde of vultures with wing and beak. Their priests reported to Caesar that I was violating their law, and their appeals, supported by Vitellius, drew down upon me a severe reprimand. How many times did I long, as the Greeks used to say, to dispatch accusers and accused in one convoy to the crows!

THE PROCURATOR OF JUDAEA

"Do not imagine, Lamia, that I nourish the rancour of the discomfited, the wrath of the superannuated, against a people which in my person has prevailed against both Rome and tranquility. But I foresee the extremity to which sooner or later they will reduce us. Since we cannot govern them, we shall be driven to destroy them. Never doubt it. Always in a state of insubordination, brewing rebellion in their inflammatory minds, they will one day burst forth upon us with a fury beside which the wrath of the Numidians and the mutterings of the Parthians are mere child's play. They are secretly nourishing preposterous hopes, and madly premeditating our ruin. How can it be otherwise, when, on the strength of an oracle, they are living in expectation of the coming of a prince of their own blood whose kingdom shall extend over the whole earth? There are no half measures with such a people. They must be exterminated. Jerusalem must be laid waste to the very foundation. Perchance, old as I am, it may be granted me to behold the day when her walls shall fall and the flames shall envelop her houses, when her inhabitants shall pass under the edge of the sword, when salt shall be strown on the place where once the temple stood. And in that day I shall at length be justified."

Lamia exerted himself to lead the conversation back to a less acrimonious note.

"Pontius," he said, "it is not difficult for me to understand both your long-standing resentment and your sinister forebodings. Truly, what you have experienced of the character of the Jews is nothing to their advantage. But I lived in Jerusalem as an interested onlooker, and mingled freely with the people, and I succeeded in detecting certain obscure virtues in these rude folk which were altogether hidden from you. I have met Jews who were all mildness, whose simple manners and faithfulness of heart recalled to me what our poets have related concerning the Spartan lawgiver. And you yourself, Pontius, have seen perish beneath the cudgels of your legionaries simple-minded men who have died for a cause they believed to be just without revealing their names. Such men do not deserve our contempt. I am saying this because it is desirable in all things to preserve moderation and an even mind. But I own that I never experienced any lively sympathy for the Jews. The Jewesses, on the contrary, I found extremely pleasing. I was young then, and the Syrian women stirred all my senses to response. Their ruddy lips, their liquid eyes that shone in the shade, their sleepy gaze pierced me to the very marrow. Painted and stained, smelling of nard and myrrh, steeped in odours, their physical attractions are both rare and delightful."

Pontius listened impatiently to these praises.

"I was not the kind of man to fall into the snares of the Jewish women," he said; "and since you have opened the subject yourself, Lamia,

25

REALISM

I was never able to approve of your laxity. If I did not express with sufficient emphasis formerly how culpable I held you for having intrigued at Rome with the wife of a man of consular rank, it was because you were then enduring heavy penance for your misdoings. Marriage from the patrician point of view is a sacred tie; it is one of the institutions which are the support of Rome. As to foreign women and slaves, such relations as one may enter into with them would be of little account were it not that they habituate the body to a humiliating effeminacy. Let me tell you that you have been too liberal in your offerings to the Venus of the Market-place; and what, above all, I blame in you is that you have not married in compliance with the law and given children to the Republic, as every good citizen is bound to do."

But the man who had suffered exile under Tiberius was no longer listening to the venerable magistrate. Having tossed off his cup of Falernian, he was smiling at some image visible to his eye alone.

After a moment's silence he resumed in a very deep voice, which rose in pitch by little and little—

"With what languorous grace they dance, those Syrian women! I knew a Jewess at Jerusalem who used to dance in a poky little room, on a threadbare carpet, by the light of one smoky little lamp, waving her arms as she clanged her cymbals. Her loins arched, her head thrown back, and, as it were, dragged down by the weight of her heavy red hair, her eyes swimming with voluptuousness, eager, languishing, compliant, she would have made Cleopatra herself grow pale with envy. I was in love with her barbaric dances, her voice—a little raucous and yet so sweet—her atmosphere of incense, the semi-somnolescent state in which she seemed to live. I followed her everywhere. I mixed with the vile rabble of soldiers, conjurers, and extortioners with which she was surrounded. One day, however, she disappeared, and I saw her no more. Long did I seek her in disreputable alleys and taverns. It was more difficult to learn to do without her than to lose the taste for Greek wine. Some months after I lost sight of her, I learned by chance that she had attached herself to a small company of men and women who were followers of a young Galilean thaumaturgist. His name was Jesus; he came from Nazareth, and he was crucified for some crime, I don't quite know what. Pontius, do you remember anything about the man?"

Pontius Pilate contracted his brows, and his hand rose to his forehead in the attitude of one who probes the deeps of memory. Then after a silence of some seconds—

"Jesus?" he murmured, "Jesus—of Nazareth? I cannot call him to mind."

II | High Style Versus Just Plain Good: The Right Words and Their Order

There is no such person as an objective reader, no such thing as objective literary judgment. Fiction grows out of a particular concern in human time and in human space; mathematically expressed, it is a function of these—the end result of a combination of factors: an equation.

The reader and the writer vacillate. A book that makes no sense to the child ("there aren't any pictures") may, years later, be meaningful to the adult. That which was deeply moving to someone young may, years later, seem to be only a distant part of growing up. A "ladies' novel," racy at the turn of the century, is prudish now. Edith Wharton seems tame. Oscar Wilde says in his preface to The Picture of Dorian Gray, *"There is no such thing as a moral or an immoral book. Books are well written, or badly written. That is all."*

Style is the unique arrangement of words into sentences, the division of sentences by punctuation, and the process of delicate decision which organizes these sentences into paragraphs. Each writer has his own way of utilizing the mechanics available to him. This is his *style. Style, like fingerprints, may take one of a number of general forms, but no writing style is ever exactly like another. The rhythm of writing, the intuitive comma that appears or doesn't, the feeling that a sentence must end* here, *is a rhythm either inborn or so early conditioned that it is almost innate.*

The variables of time, place, person, choice, taste, and personal experience affect style. Usually an author must struggle to construct what he writes, to create the best sentence to say his say, but the original sense of flow is that unique characteristic, style.

Style is impulse. Style is phenomenal. How different is a sentence written by Ernest Hemingway from a sentence of Robert Louis Stevenson! Hemingway's writing is staccato, curt, direct, his sentences abrupt: his training had been much in newspapers. Stevenson is gentler with a softer delivery. Hemingway uses a period where Stevenson might prefer a comma. Hemingway's language is deceptively simple. He is not a wordy man. The narrative of "The Short Happy Life of Francis Macomber" is

HIGH STYLE VERSUS JUST PLAIN GOOD

straightforward and uncomplicated. It bears no excess of adjectives, no cushioning of blows with words.

Yet the emotions Hemingway challenges, in this story and in his other writings, are highly complex. They are not less than the themes of Henry James—but think how James would have written such a story, the long study he would have made of it, attenuating the relationships, and surely setting the whole indoors.

Hemingway delivers it right up front, no extraneous material, no thoughtful speculative asides. He understates. In his succinctness lies much of his power as a stylist.

Some writing is joy to read almost for the style alone, as in a poem, which may "feel" before it "means." In some stories the sentences glide so smoothly they invite the eye to follow effortlessly; their precision is so fine that ease of reading increases pleasure. Such a story is "The Sire de Malétroit's Door," whose sentences are long, light, clear, and lilting.

Then, too, some fiction is not so refined, its style not so right. The world possesses much more literature than great literature. Thus we know a style which is serviceable storytelling, somehow not great but just plain good. Such fiction, although its style is less perfectly wrought than "The Short Happy Life of Francis Macomber" or "The Sire de Malétroit's Door," holds other kinds of significance.

If "The Curious Case of Benjamin Button" fails of the supremacy of style of "Macomber" or "The Sire" it nevertheless merits praise, retains the interest of many readers, and is admired by some readers above "better" stories. Its author is F. Scott Fitzgerald, whose style elsewhere is remarkable. The Great Gatsby and Tender Is the Night are outstanding American fiction. But "The Curious Case of Benjamin Button" is just plain good.

Perhaps we should try to view "Benjamin Button" as an isolated act of creative energy, separate from its author, separate from whatever else he has written, and separate from the circumstances of his life. That procedure would be ideal, but we cannot help knowing certain facts of Fitzgerald's life and work. Thus, if we come to "Benjamin Button" with the thought that its style is the style of "a lesser Fitzgerald" we deprive ourselves of the real pleasures of the story. Let us view its "writtenness" aside from its historical importance.

The setting for this story is Fitzgeraldian enough. Wealthy, southern, socially prominent families figure often in Fitzgerald's work. For the rest, however, if we did not know its author we might not guess him.

HIGH STYLE VERSUS JUST PLAIN GOOD

The story was published in 1922 by Charles Scribner's Sons two years after that house published Fitzgerald's first novel, This Side of Paradise. *That novel is the only long work by Fitzgerald which does not deal with the failure of a marriage, and which offers its main character reason for hope. It is a young man's self-discovery, composed by Fitzgerald when he was twenty-two or twenty-three years old. Certainly it is "well-written," though his style was not yet perfected. It won fame for him in America and in Europe.*

It would seem that Fitzgerald wrote "The Curious Case of Benjamin Button" either before he wrote his first novel, or at some time while he was at work on it. Its delayed publication may suggest that he was a better publisher's risk now that he was known as the author of This Side of Paradise. *Obviously the story is early work, atypical Fitzgerald.*

It is a fantasy, a kind of modern fairy tale—to grow younger, to move through time backward, eventually attaining childhood. These thoughts have occurred universally, and they belong to what Carl Jung calls the collective unconscious. Ponce de León searched Florida for a fountain of youth, James Barrie wrote Peter and Wendy, *and an old Japanese fairy tale tells of a woman who drank too deeply of a magic stream, regressed to infancy, and was discovered in the reeds by her husband, who took her home to raise her.*

To that tradition "The Curious Case of Benjamin Button" belongs. When we know, however, that Fitzgerald wrote it, we may speculate also that it represents his fantasy of immortality. The writer, of all people, leaving himself to the world on paper, exists long after his body's departure. In theme, if not in style, this story is much like Hawthorne's "The Ambitious Guest," found elsewhere in this volume.

Clearly, "But For This . . ." is less than high style. It is a memorable story for the force of its idea, its notion, its haunting nature, not for excellence of other kinds. One of the editors read this story at a very young age and could never dismiss it from mind. Its recent impact can never equal its first impact—but impact exists, its force exists, and the story truly survives its own stylistic deficiencies. It did, at least, for someone, and will again for someone else.

The discovery which motivated the writing of "But For This . . ." may now strike its mark again in readers coming to the story for the first time. The story was published many years ago, and it has passed through time and space without loss.

Other readers, however, may remain unmoved. Judgment is subjective: the equations of fiction vary from story to story, style to style, person to person, writer to reader.

HIGH STYLE VERSUS JUST PLAIN GOOD

THE SIRE DE MALETROIT'S DOOR

Robert Louis Stevenson

Denis de Beaulieu was not yet two-and-twenty, but he counted himself a grown man, and a very accomplished cavalier into the bargain. Lads were early formed in that rough, warfaring epoch; and when one has been in a pitched battle and a dozen raids, has killed one's man in an honourable fashion, and knows a thing or two of strategy and mankind, a certain swagger in the gait is surely to be pardoned. He had put up his horse with due care, and supped with due deliberation; and then, in a very agreeable frame of mind, went out to pay a visit in the grey of the evening. It was not a very wise proceeding on the young man's part. He would have done better to remain beside the fire or go decently to bed. For the town was full of the troops of Burgundy and England under a mixed command; and though Denis was there on safe-conduct, his safe-conduct was like to serve him little on a chance encounter.

It was September, 1429; the weather had fallen sharp; a flighty piping wind, laden with showers, beat about the township; and the dead leaves ran riot along the streets. Here and there a window was already lighted up; and the noise of men-at-arms making merry over supper within, came forth in fits and was swallowed up and carried away by the wind. The night fell swiftly; the flag of England, fluttering on the spire-top, grew ever fainter and fainter against the flying clouds—a black speck like a swallow in the tumultuous, leaden chaos of the sky. As the night fell the wind rose and began to hoot under archways and roar amid the tree-tops in the valley below the town.

Denis de Beaulieu walked fast and was soon knocking at his friend's door; but though he promised himself to stay only a little while and make an early return, his welcome was so pleasant, and he found so much to delay him, that it was already long past midnight before he said good-bye upon the threshold. The wind had fallen again in the meanwhile; the night was as black as the grave; not a star, nor a glimmer of moonshine, slipped through the canopy of cloud. Denis was ill-acquainted with the intricate lanes of Château Landon; even by daylight he had found some trouble in picking his way; and in this absolute darkness he soon lost it altogether. He was certain of one thing only—to keep mounting the hill; for his friend's house lay at the lower end, or tail, of Château Landon, while the inn was up at the head under the great church spire. With this clue to go upon he stumbled and groped forward, now breathing more freely in open places where there was a good slice of sky overhead, now feeling along the wall in stifling closes. It is an eerie and mysterious position to be thus submerged in opaque blackness in an almost unknown town. The silence is terrifying in its possibilities. The touch of cold window bars to the exploring hand startles the man like the touch of a toad; the inequalities of the pavement shake his heart into his mouth; a piece of denser darkness threatens an ambuscade or a chasm in the pathway; and where the air is brighter, the houses put on strange and bewildering appearances, as if to lead him farther from his way. For Denis, who had to regain his inn without attracting notice, there was real danger as well as mere discomfort in the walk; and he went warily and boldly at once, and at every corner paused to make an observation.

He had been for some time threading a lane so narrow that he could touch a wall with either hand, when it began to open out and go sharply downward. Plainly this lay no longer in the direction of his inn; but the hope of a little more light tempted him forward to reconnoitre. The lane ended in a terrace with a bartisan wall, which gave an outlook between high houses, as out of an embrasure, into the valley lying dark and formless several hundred feet below. Denis looked down, and could discern a few tree-tops waving and a single speck of brightness where the river ran across a weir. The weather was clearing up, and the sky had lightened, so as to show the outline of the heavier clouds and the dark margin of the hills. By the uncertain glimmer, the house on his left hand should be a place of some pretensions; it was surmounted by several pinnacles and turret-tops; the round stern of a chapel, with a fringe of flying buttresses, projected boldly from the main block; and the door was sheltered under a deep porch carved with figures and overhung by two long gargoyles. The windows of the chapel gleamed through their intricate tracery with a light as of many tapers, and threw out the buttresses and the peaked roof in a more intense blackness against the sky. It was plainly the hotel of some great family of the neighbourhood; and as it reminded Denis of a town house of his own at Bourges, he stood for some time gazing up at it and mentally gauging the skill of the architects and the consideration of the two families.

There seemed to be no issue to the terrace but the lane by which he had reached it; he could only retrace his steps, but he had gained some notion of his whereabouts, and hoped by this means to hit the main thoroughfare and speedily regain the inn. He was reckoning without that chapter of accidents which was to make this night memorable above all others in his career; for he had not gone back above a hundred yards before he saw a light coming to meet him, and heard loud voices speaking together in the echoing of the lane. It was a party of men-at-arms going the night round with torches. Denis assured himself that they had all been making free with the wine-bowl, and were in no mood to be particular about safe-conducts or the niceties of chivalrous war. It was as like as not that they would kill him like a dog and leave him where he fell. The situation was inspiriting but nervous. Their own torches would conceal him from sight, he reflected; and he hoped that they would drown the noise of his footsteps with their own empty voices. If he were but fleet and silent, he might evade their notice altogether.

Unfortunately, as he turned to beat a retreat, his foot rolled upon a pebble; he fell against the wall with an ejaculation, and his sword rang loudly on the stones. Two or three voices demanded who went there—some in French, some in English; but Denis made no reply, and ran the faster down the lane. Once upon the terrace, he paused to look back. They still kept calling after him, and just then began to double the pace in pursuit, with a considerable clank of armour, and great tossing of the torchlight to and fro in the narrow jaws of the passage.

Denis cast a look around and darted into the porch. There he might escape observation, or—if that were too much to expect—was in a capital posture whether for parley or defence. So thinking, he drew his sword and tried to set his back against the door. To his surprise, it yielded behind his weight; and though he turned in a moment, continued to swing back on oiled and noiseless hinges, until it stood wide open on a black exterior. When things fall out opportunely for the person concerned, he is not apt to be critical about the how or why, his own immediate personal convenience seeming a sufficient reason for the strangest oddities and revolutions in our sublunary things; and so Denis, without a moment's hesitation, stepped within and partly closed the door behind him to conceal his place of refuge. Nothing was further from his thoughts than to close it altogether; but for some inexplicable reason—perhaps by a spring or a weight—the ponderous mass of oak whipped itself out of his fingers and clanked to, with a formidable rumble and a noise like the falling of an automatic bar.

The round, at that very moment, debouched upon the terrace and proceeded to summon him with shouts and curses. He heard them ferreting in the dark corners; the stock of a lance even rattled along the outer surface of the door behind which he stood; but these gentlemen were in too high a humour to be long delayed, and soon made off down a corkscrew pathway which had escaped Denis's observation, and passed out of sight and hearing along the battlements of the town.

Denis breathed again. He gave them a few minutes' grace for fear of accidents, and then groped about for some means of opening the door and slipping forth again. The inner surface was quite smooth, not a handle, not a moulding, not a projection of any sort. He got his finger-nails round the edges and pulled, but the mass was immovable. He shook it, it was as firm as a rock. Denis de Beaulieu frowned and gave vent to a little noiseless whistle. What ailed the door? he wondered. Why was it open? How came it to shut so easily and so effectually after him? There was something obscure and underhand about all this, that was little to the young man's fancy. It looked like a snare; and yet who would suppose a snare in such a quiet by-street and in a house of so prosperous and even noble an exterior? And yet—snare or no snare, intentionally or unintentionally—here he was, prettily trapped; and for the life of him he could see no way out of it again. The darkness began to weigh upon him. He gave ear; all was silent without, but within and close by he seemed to catch a faint sighing, a faint sobbing rustle, a little stealthy creak—as though many persons were at his side, holding themselves quite still, and governing even their respiration with the extreme of slyness. The idea went to his vitals with a shock, and he faced about suddenly as if to defend his life. Then, for the first time, he became aware of a light about the level of his eyes and at some distance in the interior of the house—a vertical thread of light, widening towards the bottom, such as might escape between two wings of arras over a doorway. To see anything was a relief to Denis; it was like a piece of solid ground to a man labouring in a morass; his mind seized upon it with avidity; and he stood staring at it and trying to piece together some logical conception of his surroundings. Plainly there was a flight of steps ascending from his own level to that of this illuminated doorway; and indeed he thought he could make out another thread of light, as fine as a needle and as faint as phosphorescence, which might very well be reflected along the polished wood of a handrail. Since he had begun to suspect that he was not alone, his heart had continued to beat with smothering violence, and an intolerable desire for action of any sort had possessed itself of his spirit. He was in deadly peril, he believed. What could be more natural than to mount the staircase, lift the curtain, and confront his difficulty at once? At least he would be dealing with something tangible; at least he would be no longer in the dark. He stepped slowly forward with outstretched hands, until his foot struck the bottom step; then he rapidly scaled the stairs, stood for a moment to compose his expression, lifted the arras and went in.

He found himself in a large apartment of polished stone. There were three doors; one on each of three sides; all similarly curtained with tapestry. The fourth side was occupied by two large windows and a great stone chimney-piece, carved with the arms of the Malétroits. Denis recognised the bearings, and was gratified to find himself in such good hands. The room was strongly illuminated; but it contained little furniture except a chair or two, the hearth was innocent of fire, and the pavement was but sparsely strewn with rushes clearly many days old.

On a high chair beside the chimney, and directly facing Denis as he entered, sat a little old gentleman in a fur tippet. He sat with his legs crossed and his hands folded, and a cup of spiced wine stood by his elbow on a bracket on the wall. His countenance had a strongly masculine cast; not properly human, but such as we see in the bull, the goat, or the domestic boar; something equivocal and wheedling, something greedy, brutal, and dangerous. The upper lip was inordinately full, as though swollen by a blow or a toothache; and the smile, the peaked eyebrows, and the small, strong eyes were quaintly and almost comically evil in expression. Beautiful white hair hung straight all around his head, like a saint's, and fell in a single curl upon the tippet. His beard and moustache were the pink of venerable sweetness. Age, probably in consequence of inordinate precautions, had left no mark upon his hands; and the Malétroit hand was famous. It would be difficult to imagine anything at once so fleshy and so delicate in design; the taper, sensual fingers were like those of one of Leonardo's women; the fork of the thumb made a dimpled protuberance when closed; the nails were perfectly shaped, and of a dead, surprising whiteness. It rendered his aspect tenfold more redoubtable, that a man with hands like these should keep them devoutly folded in his lap like a virgin martyr—that a man with so intense and startling an expression of face should sit patiently on his seat and contemplate people with an unwinking stare, like a god, or a god's statue. His quiescence seemed ironical and treacherous, it fitted so poorly with his looks.

Such was Alain, Sire de Malétroit.

Denis and he looked silently at each other for a second or two.

"Pray step in," said the Sire de Malétroit. "I have been expecting you all the evening."

He had not risen, but he accompanied his words with a smile and a slight but courteous inclination of the head. Partly from the smile, partly from the strange musical murmur with which the Sire prefaced his observation, Denis felt a strong shudder of disgust go through his marrow. And what with disgust and honest confusion of mind, he could scarcely get words together in reply.

"I fear," he said, "that this is a double accident. I am not the person you suppose me. It seems you were looking for a visit; but for my part, nothing was further from my thoughts—nothing could be more contrary to my wishes—than this intrusion."

"Well, well," replied the old gentleman indulgently, "here you are, which is the main point. Seat yourself, my friend, and put yourself entirely at your ease. We shall arrange our little affairs presently."

THE SIRE DE MALÉTROIT'S DOOR

Denis perceived that the matter was still complicated with some misconception, and he hastened to continue his explanations.

"Your door..." he began.

"About my door?" asked the other, raising his peaked eyebrows. "A little piece of ingenuity." And he shrugged his shoulders. "A hospitable fancy! By your own account, you were not desirous of making my acquaintance. We old people look for such reluctance now and then; and when it touches our honour, we cast about until we find some way of overcoming it. You arrive uninvited, but believe me, very welcome."

"You persist in error, sir," said Denis. "There can be no question between you and me. I am a stranger in this countryside. My name is Denis, damoiseau de Beaulieu. If you see me in your house, it is only——"

"My young friend," interrupted the other, "you will permit me to have my own ideas on that subject. They probably differ from yours at the present moment," he added with a leer, "but time will show which of us is in the right."

Denis was convinced he had to do with a lunatic. He seated himself with a shrug, content to wait the upshot; and a pause ensued, during which he thought he could distinguish a hurried gabbling as of prayer from behind the arras immediately opposite him. Sometimes there seemed to be but one person engaged, sometimes two; and the vehemence of the voice, low as it was, seemed to indicate either great hast or an agony of spirit. It occurred to him that this piece of tapestry covered the entrance to the chapel he had noticed from without.

The old gentleman meanwhile surveyed Denis from head to foot with a smile, and from time to time emitted little noises like a bird or a mouse, which seemed to indicate a high degree of satisfaction. This state of matters became rapidly insupportable; and Denis, to put an end to it, remarked politely that the wind had gone down.

The old gentleman fell into a fit of silent laughter, so prolonged and violent that he became quite red in the face. Denis got upon his feet at once, and put on his hat with a flourish.

"Sir," he said, "if you are in your wits, you have affronted me grossly. If you are out of them, I flatter myself I can find better employment for my brains than to talk with lunatics. My conscience is clear; you have made a fool of me from the first moment; you have refused to hear my explanations; and now there is no power under God will make me stay here any longer; and if I cannot make my way out in a more decent fashion, I will hack your door in pieces with my sword."

The Sire de Malétroit raised his right hand and wagged it at Denis with the fore and little fingers extended.

"My dear nephew," he said, "sit down."

"Nephew!" retorted Denis, "you lie in your throat;" and he snapped his fingers in his face.

"Sit down, you rogue!" cried the old gentleman, in a sudden harsh voice, like the barking of a dog. "Do you fancy," he went on, "that when I had made my little contrivance for the door I had stopped short with that? If you prefer to be bound hand and foot till your bones ache, rise and try to go away. If you choose to remain a free young buck, agreeably conversing with an old gentleman—why, sit where you are in peace, and God be with you."

"Do you mean I am a prisoner?" demanded Denis.

"I state the facts," replied the other. "I would rather leave the conclusion to yourself."

Denis sat down again. Externally he managed to keep pretty calm; but within, he was now boiling with anger, now chilled with apprehension. He no longer felt convinced that he was dealing with a madman. And if the old gentleman was sane, what, in God's name, had he to look for? What absurd or tragical adventure had befallen him? What countenance was he to assume?

While he was thus unpleasantly reflecting, the arras that overhung the chapel door was raised, and a tall priest in his robes came forth and, giving a long, keen stare at Denis, said something in an undertone to Sire de Malétroit.

"She is in a better frame of spirit?" asked the latter.

"She is more resigned, messire," replied the priest.

"Now the Lord help her, she is hard to please!" sneered the old gentleman. "A likely stripling—not ill-born—and of her own choosing, too? Why, what more would the jade have?"

"The situation is not usual for a young damsel!" said the other, "and somewhat trying to her blushes."

"She should have thought of that before she began the dance. It was none of my choosing, God knows that: but since she is in it, by our Lady, she shall carry it to the end." And then addressing Denis, "Monsieur de Beaulieu," he asked, "may I present you to my niece? She had been waiting your arrival, I may say, with even greater impatience than myself."

Denis had resigned himself with a good grace—all he desired was to know the worst of it as speedily as possible; so he rose at once, and bowed in acquiescence. The Sire de Malétroit followed his example and limped, with the assistance of the chaplain's arm, towards the chapel door. The priest pulled aside the arras, and all three entered. The building had considerable architectural pretensions. A light groining sprang from six stout columns, and hung down in two rich pendants from the centre of

THE SIRE DE MALETROIT'S DOOR

the vault. The place terminated behind the altar in a round end, embossed and honeycombed with a superfluity of ornament in relief, and pierced by many little windows shaped like stars, trefoils, or wheels. These windows were imperfectly glazed, so that the night air circulated freely in the chapel. The tapers, of which there must have been half a hundred burning on the altar, were unmercifully blown about; and the light went through many different phases of brilliancy and semi-eclipse. On the steps in front of the altar knelt a young girl richly attired as a bride. A chill settled over Denis as he observed her costume; he fought with desperate energy against the conclusion that was thrust upon his mind; it could not—it should not —be as he feared.

"Blanche," said the Sire, in his most flute-like tones, "I have brought a friend to see you, my little girl; turn round and give him your pretty hand. It is good to be devout; but it is necessary to be polite, my niece."

The girl rose to her feet and turned towards the new comers. She moved all of a piece; and shame and exhaustion were expressed in every line of her fresh young body; and she held her head down and kept her eyes upon the pavement, as she came slowly forward. In the course of her advance, her eyes fell upon Denis de Beaulieu's feet—feet of which he was justly vain, be it remarked, and wore in the most elegant accoutrement even while travelling. She paused—started, as if his yellow boots had conveyed some shocking meaning—and glanced suddenly up into the wearer's countenance. Their eyes met; shame gave place to horror and terror in her looks; the blood left her lips; with a piercing scream she covered her face with her hands and sank upon the chapel floor.

"That is not the man!" she cried. "My uncle, that is not the man!"

The Sire de Malétroit chirped agreeably. "Of course not," he said; "I expected as much. It was so unfortunate you could not remember his name."

"Indeed," she cried, "indeed, I have never seen this person till this moment—have never so much as set eyes upon him—I never wish to see him again. Sir," she said, turning to Denis, "if you are a gentleman, you will bear me out. Have I ever seen you—have you ever seen me—before this accursed hour?"

"To speak for myself, I have never had that pleasure," answered the young man. "This is the first time, messire, that I have met with your engaging niece."

The old gentleman shrugged his shoulders.

"I am distressed to hear it," he said. "But it is never too late to begin. I had little more acquaintance with my own late lady ere I married her; which proves," he added with a grimace, "that these impromptu marriages may often produce an excellent understanding in the long run. As the bridegroom is to have a voice in the matter, I will give him two hours to make up for lost time before we proceed with the ceremony." And he turned towards the door, followed by the clergyman.

The girl was on her feet in a moment. "My uncle, you cannot be in earnest," she said. "I declare before God I will stab myself rather than be forced on that young man. The heart rises at it; God forbid such marriages; you dishonour your white hair. Oh, my uncle, pity me! There is not a woman in all the world but would prefer death to such a nuptial. Is it possible," she added, faltering, "is it possible that you do not believe me—that you still think this"—and she pointed at Denis with a tremor of anger and contempt—"that you still think *this* to be the man?"

"Frankly," said the old gentleman, pausing on the threshold, "I do. But let me explain to you once for all, Blance de Malétroit, my way of thinking about this affair. When you took it into your head to dishonour my family and the name that I have borne, in peace and war, for more than threescore years, you forfeited, not only the right to question my designs, but that of looking me in the face. If your father had been alive, he would have spat on you and turned you out of doors. His was the hand of iron. You may bless your God you have only to deal with the hand of velvet, mademoiselle. It was my duty to get you married without delay. Out of pure goodwill, I have tried to find your own gallant for you. And I believe I have succeeded. But before God and all the holy angels, Blanche de Malétroit, if I have not, I care not one jackstraw. So let me recommend you to be polite to our young friend; for upon my word, your next groom may be less appetising."

And with that he went out, with the chaplain at his heels; and the arras fell behind the pair.

The girl turned upon Denis with flashing eyes.

"And what, sire," she demanded, "may be the meaning of all this?"

"God knows," returned Denis gloomily. "I am a prisoner in this house, which seems full of mad people. More I know not; and nothing do I understand."

"And pray how came you here?" she asked.

He told her as briefly as he could. "For the rest," he added, "perhaps you will follow my example, and tell me the answer to all these riddles, and what, in God's name, is like to be the end of it."

She stood silent for a little, and he could see her lips tremble and her tearless eyes burn with a feverish lustre. Then she pressed her forehead in both hands.

"Alas, how my head aches!" she said wearily—"to say nothing of my poor heart! But it is due to you to know my story, unmaidenly as it must seem. I am called Blanche de Malétroit; I have been without father or mother for—oh! for as long as I can recollect, and indeed I have been most unhappy all my life. Three months ago a young captain began to stand near me every day in church. I could see that I pleased him; I am much to blame, but I was so glad that anyone should love me; and when he passed me a letter, I took it home with me and read it with great pleasure. Since that time he has written many. He was so anxious to speak with me, poor fellow! and kept asking me to leave the door open some evening that we might have two words upon the stair. For he knew how much my uncle trusted me." She gave something like a sob at that, and it was a moment before she could go on. "My uncle is a hard man, but he is very shrewd," she said at last. "He has performed many feats in war, and was a great person at court, and much trusted by Queen Isabeau in old days. How he came to suspect me I cannot tell; but it is hard to keep anything from his knowledge; and this morning, as we came from mass, he took my hand in his, forced it open, and read my little billet, walking by my side all the while. When he had finished, he gave it back to me with great politeness. It contained another request to have the door left open; and this has been the ruin of us all. My uncle kept me strictly in my room until evening, and then ordered me to dress myself as you see me—a hard mockery for a young girl, do you not think so? I suppose, when he could not prevail with me to tell him the young captain's name, he must have laid a trap for him: in which, alas! you have fallen in the anger of God. I looked for much confusion; for how could I tell whether he was willing to take me for his wife on these sharp terms? He might have been trifling with me from the first; or I might have made myself too cheap in his eyes. But truly I had not looked for such a shameful punishment as this! I could not think that God would let a girl be so disgraced before a young man. And now I have told you all; and I can scarcely hope that you will not despise me."

Denis made her a respectful inclination.

"Madam," he said, "you have honoured me by your confidence. It remains for me to prove that I am not unworthy of the honour. Is Messire de Malétroit at hand?"

"I believe he is writing in the salle without," she answered.

"May I lead you thither, madam?" asked Denis, offering his hand with his most courtly bearing.

She accepted it; and the pair passed out of the chapel, Blanche in a very drooping and shamefast condition, but Denis strutting and ruffling in the consciousness of a mission, and the boyish certainty of accomplishing it with honour.

The Sire de Malétroit rose to meet them with an ironical obeisance.

"Sir," said Denis with the grandest possible air, "I believe I am to have some say in the matter of this marriage; and let me tell you at once, I will be no party to forcing the inclination of this young lady. Had it been freely offered to me, I should have been proud to accept her hand, for I perceive she is as good as she is beautiful; but as things are, I have now the honour, messire, of refusing."

Blanche looked at him with gratitude in her eyes; but the old gentleman only smiled and smiled, until his smile grew positively sickening to Denis.

"I am afraid," he said, "Monsieur de Beaulieu, that you do not perfectly understand the choice I have to offer you. Follow me, I beseech you, to this window." And he led the way to one of the large windows which stood open on the night. "You observe," he went on, "there is an iron ring in the upper masonry, and reeved through that, a very efficacious rope. Now, mark my words; if you should find your disinclination to my niece's person insurmountable, I shall have you hanged out of this window before sunrise. I shall only proceed to such an extremity with the greatest regret, you may believe me. For it is not at all your death that I desire, but my niece's establishment in life. At the same time, it must come to that if you prove obstinate. Your family, Monsieur de Beaulieu, is very well in its way; but if you sprang from Charlemagne, you should not refuse the hand of a Malétroit with impunity—not if she had been as common as the Paris road—not if she were as hideous as the gargoyle over my door. Neither my niece nor you, nor my own private feelings, move me at all in this matter. The honour of my house has been compromised; I believe you to be the guilty person; at least you are now in the secret; and you can hardly wonder if I request you to wipe out the stain. If you will not, your blood be on your own head! It will be no great satisfaction to me to have your interesting relics kicking their heels in the breeze below my windows; but half a loaf is better than no bread, and if I cannot cure the dishonour, I shall at least stop the scandal."

There was a pause.

"I believe there are other ways of settling such imbroglios among gentlemen," said Denis. "You wear a sword, and I hear you have used it with distinction."

The Sire de Malétroit made a signal to the chaplain, who crossed the room with long silent strides and raised the arras over the third of the three doors. It was only a moment before he let it fall again; but Denis had time to see a dusky passage full of armed men.

"When I was a little younger, I should have been delighted to honour you, Monsieur de Beaulieu," said Sire Alain; "but I am now too old. Faithful retainers are the sinews of age, and I must employ the strength I have. This is one of the hardest things to swallow as a man grows up

THE SIRE DE MALÉTROIT'S DOOR

in years; but with a little patience, even this becomes habitual. You and the lady seem to prefer the salle for what remains of your two hours; and as I have no desire to cross your preference, I shall resign it to your use with all the pleasure in the world. No haste!" he added, holding up his hand, as he saw a dangerous look come into Denis de Beaulieu's face. "If your mind revolts against hanging, it will be time enough two hours hence to throw yourself out of the window or upon the pikes of my retainers. Two hours of life are always two hours. A great many things may turn up in even as little a while as that. And, besides, if I understand her appearance, my niece has still something to say to you. You will not disfigure your last hours by a want of politeness to a lady?"

Denis looked at Blanche, and she made him an imploring gesture.

It is likely that the old gentleman was hugely pleased at this symptom of an understanding; for he smiled on both, and added sweetly: "If you will give me your word of honour, Monsieur de Beaulieu, to wait my return at the end of two hours before attempting anything desperate, I shall withdraw my retainers, and let you speak in greater privacy with mademoiselle."

Denis again glanced at the girl, who seemed to beseech him to agree.

"I give you my word of honour," he said.

Messire de Malétroit bowed, and proceeded to limp about the apartment, clearing his throat the while with that odd musical chirp which had already grown so irritating in the ears of Denis de Beaulieu. He first possessed himself of some papers which lay upon the table; then he went to the mouth of the passage and appeared to give an order to the men behind the arras; and lastly he hobbled out through the door by which Denis had come in, turning upon the threshold to address a last smiling bow to the young couple, and followed by the chaplain with a hand-lamp.

No sooner were they alone than Blanche advanced towards Denis with her hands extended. Her face was flushed and excited, and her eyes shone with tears.

"You shall not die!" she cried, "you shall marry me after all."

"You seem to think, madam," replied Denis, "that I stand much in fear of death."

"Oh, no, no," she said, "I see you are no poltroon. It is for my own sake—I could not bear to have you slain for such a scruple."

"I am afraid," returned Denis, "that you underrate the difficulty, madam. What you may be too generous to refuse, I may be too proud to accept. In a moment of noble feeling towards me, you forgot what you perhaps owe to others."

He had the decency to keep his eyes upon the floor as he said this, and after he had finished, so as not to spy upon her confusion. She stood silent

HIGH STYLE VERSUS JUST PLAIN GOOD

for a moment, then walked suddenly away, and falling on her uncle's chair, fairly burst out sobbing. Denis was in the acme of embarrassment. He looked round, as if to seek for inspiration, and seeing a stool, plumped down upon it for something to do. There he sat, playing with the guard of his rapier, and wishing himself dead a thousand times over, and buried in the nastiest kitchen-heap in France. His eyes wandered round the apartment, but found nothing to arrest them. There were such wide spaces between the furniture, the light fell so badly and cheerlessly over all, the dark outside air looked in so coldly through the windows, that he thought he had never seen a church so vast, nor a tomb so melancholy. The regular sobs of Blanche de Malétroit measured out the time like the ticking of a clock. He read the device upon the shield over and over again, until his eyes became obscured; he stared into shadowy corners until he imagined they were swarming with horrible animals; and every now and again he awoke with a start, to remember that his last two hours were running, and death was on the march.

Oftener and oftener, as the time went on, did his glance settle on the girl herself. Her face was bowed forward and covered with her hands, and she was shaken at intervals by the convulsive hiccup of grief. Even thus she was not an unpleasant object to dwell upon, so plump and yet so fine, with a warm brown skin, and the most beautiful hair, Denis thought, in the whole world of womankind. Her hands were like her uncle's; but they were more in place at the end of her young arms and looked infinitely soft and caressing. He remembered how her blue eyes had shone upon him, full of anger, pity, and innocence. And the more he dwelt on her perfections, the uglier death looked, and the more deeply was he smitten with penitence at her continued tears. Now he felt that no man could have the courage to leave a world which contained so beautiful a creature; and now he would have given forty minutes of his last hour to have unsaid his cruel speech.

Suddenly a hoarse and ragged peal of cockrow rose to their ears from the dark valley below the windows. And this shattering noise in the silence of all around was like a light in a dark place, and shook them both out of their reflections.

"Alas, can I do nothing to help you?" she said, looking up.

"Madam," replied Denis, with a fine irrelevancy, "if I have said anything to wound you, believe me, it was for your own sake and not for mine."

She thanked him with a tearful look.

"I feel your position cruelly," he went on. "The world has been bitter hard on you. Your uncle is a disgrace to mankind. Believe me, madam, there is no young gentleman in all France but would be glad of my opportunity to die in doing you a momentary service."

"I know already that you can be very brave and generous," she answered. "What I *want* to know is whether I can serve you—now or afterwards," she added, with a quaver.

"Most certainly," he answered with a smile. "Let me sit beside you as if I were a friend, instead of a foolish intruder; try to forget how awkwardly we are placed to one another; make my last moments go pleasantly; and you will do me the chief service possible."

"You are very gallant," she added, with a yet deeper sadness . . "very gallant . . . and it somehow pains me. But draw nearer, if you please; and if you find anything to say to me, you will at least make certain of a very friendly listener. Ah! Monsieur de Beaulieu," she broke forth—"ah! Monsieur de Beaulieu, how can I look you in the face?" And she fell to weeping again with a renewed effusion.

"Madam," said Denis, taking her hand in both of his, "reflect on the little time I have before me, and the great bitterness into which I am cast by the sight of your distress. Spare me, in my last moment, the spectacle of what I cannot cure even with the sacrifice of my life."

"I am very selfish," answered Blanche. "I will be braver, Monsieur de Beaulieu, for your sake. But think if I can do you no kindness in the future —if you have no friends to whom I could carry your adieux. Charge me as heavily as you can; every burden will lighten, by so little, the invaluable gratitude I owe you. Put it in my power to do something more for you than weep."

"My mother is married again, and has a young family to care for. My brother Guichard will inherit my fiefs; and if I am not in error, that will content him amply for my death. Life is a little vapour that passeth away, as we are told by those in holy orders. When a man is in a fair way and sees all life open in front of him, he seems to himself to make a very important figure in the world. His horse whinnies to him; the trumpets blow and the girls look out of windows as he rides into town before his company; he receives many assurances of trust and regard—sometimes by express in a letter—sometimes face to face, with persons of great consequence falling on his neck. It is not wonderful if his head is turned for a time. But once he is dead, were he as brave as Hercules or as wise as Solomon, he is soon forgotten. It is not ten years since my father fell, with many other knights around him, in a very fierce encounter, and I do not think that any one of them, nor so much as the name of the fight, is now remembered. No, no, madam, the nearer you come to it, you see that death is a dark and dusty corner, where a man gets into his tomb and has

HIGH STYLE VERSUS JUST PLAIN GOOD

the door shut after him till the judgment day. I have few friends just now, and once I am dead I shall have none."

"Ah, Monsieur de Beaulieu!" she exclaimed, "you forget Blanche de Malétroit."

"You have a sweet nature, madam, and you are pleased to estimate a little service far beyond its worth."

"It is not that," she answered. "You mistake me if you think I am so easily touched by my own concerns. I say so, because you are the noblest man I have ever met; because I recognise in you a spirit that would have made even a common person famous in the land."

"And yet here I die in a mouse-trap—with no more noise about it than my own squeaking," answered he.

A look of pain crossed her face, and she was silent for a while. Then a light came into her eyes, and with a smile she spoke again.

"I cannot have my champion think meanly of himself. Anyone who gives his life for another will be met in Paradise by all the heralds and angels of the Lord God. And you have no such cause to hang your head. For . . . Pray, do you think me beautiful?" she asked, with a deep flush.

"Indeed, madam, I do," he said.

"I am glad of that," she answered heartily. "Do you think there are many men in France who have been asked in marriage by a beautiful maiden—with her own lips—and who have refused her to her face? I know you men would half despise such a triumph; but believe me, we women know more of what is precious in love. There is nothing that should set a person higher in his own esteem; and we women would prize nothing more dearly."

"You are very good," he said; "but you cannot make me forget that I was asked in pity and not for love."

"I am not so sure of that," she replied, holding down her head. "Hear me to an end, Monsieur de Beaulieu. I know how you must despise me; I feel you are right to do so; I am too poor a creature to occupy one thought of your mind, although, alas! you must die for me this morning. But when I asked you to marry me, indeed, and indeed, it was because I respected and admired you, and loved you with my whole soul, from the very moment that you took my part against my uncle. If you had seen yourself, and how noble you looked, you would pity rather than despise me. And now," she went on, hurriedly checking him with her hand, "although I have laid aside all reserve and told you so much, remember that I know your sentiments towards me already. I would not, believe me, being nobly born, weary you with importunities into consent. I too have a pride of my own: and I declare before the holy Mother of God, if you should now go back from your word already given, I would no more marry you than I would marry my uncle's groom."

Denis smiled a little bitterly.

"It is a small love," he said, "that shies at a little pride."

She made no answer, although she probably had her own thoughts.

"Come hither to the window," he said, with a sigh. "Here is the dawn."

And indeed the dawn was already beginning. The hollow of the sky was full of essential daylight, colourless and clean; and the valley underneath was flooded with a grey reflection. A few thin vapours clung in the coves of the forest or lay along the winding course of the river. The scene disengaged a surprising effect of stillness, which was hardly interrupted when the cocks began once more to crow among the steadings. Perhaps the same fellow who had made so horrid a clangour in the darkness not half an hour before, now sent up the merriest cheer to greet the coming day. A little wind went bustling and eddying among the tree-tops underneath the windows. And still the daylight kept flooding insensibly out of the east, which was soon to grow incandescent and cast up that red-hot cannonball, the rising sun.

Denis looked out over all this with a bit of a shiver. He had taken her hand, and retained it in his almost unconsciously.

"Has the day begun already?" she said; and then, illogically enough: "the night has been so long! Alas! what shall we say to my uncle when he returns?"

"What you will," said Denis, and he pressed her fingers in his.

She was silent.

"Blanche," he said, with a swift, uncertain, passionate utterance, "you have seen whether I fear death. You must know well enough that I would as gladly leap out of that window into the empty air as lay a finger on you without your free and full consent. But if you care for me at all do not let me lose my life in a misapprehension; for I love you better than the whole world! and though I will die for you blithely, it would be like all the joys of Paradise to live on and spend my life in your service."

As he stopped speaking, a bell began to ring loudly in the interior of the house; and a clatter of armour in the corridor showed that the retainers were returning to their post, and the two hours were at an end.

"After all that you have heard?" she whispered, leaning towards him with her lips and eyes.

"I have heard nothing," he replied.

"The captain's name was Florimond de Champdivers," she said in his ear.

"I did not hear it," he answered, taking her supple body in his arms and covering her wet face with kisses.

A melodious chirping was audible behind, followed by a beautiful chuckle, and the voice of Messire de Malétroit wished his nephew a good morning.

THE SHORT HAPPY LIFE OF FRANCIS MACOMBER

Ernest Hemingway

It was now lunch time and they were all sitting under the double green fly of the dining tent pretending that nothing had happened.

"Will you have lime juice or lemon squash?" Macomber asked.

"I'll have a gimlet," Robert Wilson told him.

"I'll have a gimlet too. I need something," Macomber's wife said.

"I suppose it's the thing to do," Macomber agreed. "Tell him to make three gimlets."

The mess boy had started them already, lifting the bottles out of the canvas cooling bags that sweated wet in the wind that blew through the trees that shaded the tents.

"What had I ought to give them?" Macomber asked.

"A quid would be plenty," Wilson told him. "You don't want to spoil them."

"Will the headman distribute it?"

"Absolutely."

Francis Macomber had, half an hour before, been carried to his tent from the edge of the camp in triumph on the arms and shoulders of the cook, the personal boys, the skinner and the porters. The gun-bearers had taken no part in the demonstration. When the native boys put him down at the door of his tent, he had taken all their hands, received their congratulations, and then gone into the tent and sat on the bed until his wife came in. She did not speak to him when she came in and he left the ten at once to wash his face and hands in the portable wash basin outside and go over to the dining tent to sit in a comfortable canvas chair in the breeze and the shade.

"You've got your lion," Robert Wilson said to him, "and a damned fine one too."

Mrs. Macomber looked at Wilson quickly. She was an extremely handsome and well-kept woman of the beauty and social position which had, five years before, commanded five thousand dollars as the price of endors-

SHORT HAPPY LIFE OF FRANCIS MACOMBER

ing, with photographs, a beauty product which she had never used. She had been married to Francis Macomber for eleven years.

"He is a good lion, isn't he?" Macomber said. His wife looked at him now. She looked at both these men as though she had never seen them before.

One, Wilson, the white hunter, she knew she had never truly seen before. He was about middle height with sandy hair, a stubby mustache, a very red face and extremely cold blue eyes with faint white wrinkles at the corners that grooved merrily when he smiled. He smiled at her now and she looked away from his face at the way his shoulders sloped in the loose tunic he wore with the four big cartridges held in loops where the left breast pocket should have been, at his big brown hands, his old slacks, his very dirty boots and back to his red face again. She noticed where the baked red of his face stopped in a white line that marked the circle left by his Stetson hat that hung now from one of the pegs of the tent pole.

"Well, here's to the lion," Robert Wilson said. He smiled at her again and, not smiling, she looked curiously at her husband.

Francis Macomber was very tall, very well built if you did not mind that length of bone, dark, his hair cropped like an oarsman, rather thin-lipped, and was considered handsome. He was dressed in the same sort of safari clothes that Wilson wore except that his were new, he was thirty-five years old, kept himself very fit, was good at court games, had a number of big-game fishing records, and had just shown himself, very publicly, to be a coward.

"Here's to the lion," he said. "I can't ever thank you for what you did."

Margaret, his wife, looked away from him and back to Wilson.

"Let's not talk about the lion," she said.

Wilson looked over at her without smiling and now she smiled at him.

"It's been a very strange day," she said. "Hadn't you ought to put your hat on even under the canvas at noon? You told me that, you know."

"Might put it on," said Wilson.

"You know you have a very red face, Mr. Wilson," she told him and smiled again.

"Drink," said Wilson.

"I don't think so," she said. "Francis drinks a great deal, but his face is never red."

"It's red today," Macomber tried a joke.

"No," said Margaret. "It's mine that's red today. But Mr. Wilson is always red."

"Must be racial," said Wilson. "I say, you wouldn't like to drop my beauty as a topic, would you?"

"I've just started on it."

"Let's chuck it," said Wilson.

"Conversation is going to be so difficult," Margaret said.

"Don't be silly, Margot," her husband said.

"No difficulty," Wilson said. "Got a damn fine lion."

Margot looked at them both and they both saw that she was going to cry. Wilson had seen it coming for a long time and he dreaded it. Macomber was past dreading it.

"I wish it hadn't happened. Oh, I wish it hadn't happened," she said and started for her tent. She made no noise of crying but they could see that her shoulders were shaking under the rose-colored, sun-proofed shirt she wore.

"Women upset," Wilson said to the tall man. "Amounts to nothing. Strain on the nerves and one thing'n another."

"No," said Macomber. "I suppose that I rate that for the rest of my life now."

"Nonsense. Let's have a spot of the giant killer," said Wilson. "Forget the whole thing. Nothing to it anyway."

"We might try," said Macomber. "I won't forget what you did for me though."

"Nothing," said Wilson. "All nonsense."

So they sat there in the shade where the camp was pitched under some wide-topped acacia trees with a boulder-strewn cliff behind them, and a stretch of grass that ran to the bank of a boulder-filled stream in front with forest beyond it, and drank their just-cool lime drinks and avoided one another's eyes while the boys set the table for lunch. Wilson could tell that the boys all knew about it now and when he saw Macomber's personal boy looking curiously at his master, while he was putting dishes on the table he snapped at him in Swahili. The boy turned away with his face blank.

"What were you telling him?" Macomber asked.

"Nothing. Told him to look alive or I'd see he got about fifteen of the best."

"What's that? Lashes?"

"It's quite illegal," Wilson said. "You're supposed to fine them."

"Do you still have them whipped?"

"Oh, yes. They could raise a row if they chose to complain. But they don't. They prefer it to the fines."

"How strange!" said Macomber.

"Not strange, really," Wilson said. "Which would you rather do? Take a good birching or lose your pay?"

The he felt embarrassed at asking it and before Macomber could answer he went on, "We all take a beating every day, you know, one way or another."

This was no better. "Good God," he thought "I am a diplomat, aren't I?"

"Yes, we take a beating," said Macomber, still not looking at him. "I'm awfully sorry about that lion business. It doesn't have to go any further, does it? I mean no one will hear about it, will they?"

"You mean will I tell it at the Mathaiga Club?" Wilson looked at him now coldly. He had not expected this. So he's a bloody four-letter man as well as a bloody coward, he thought. I rather liked him too until today. But how is one to know about an American?

"No," said Wilson. "I'm a professional hunter. We never talk about our clients. You can be quite easy on that. It's supposed to be bad form to ask us not to talk though."

He had decided now that to break would be much easier. He would eat, then, by himself and could read a book with his meals. They would eat by themselves. He would see them through the safari on a very formal basis—what was it the French called it? Distinguished consideration—and it would be a damn sight easier than having to go through this emotional trash. He'd insult him and make a good clean break. Then he could read a book with his meals and he'd still be drinking their whiskey. That was the phrase for it when a safari went bad. You ran into another white hunter and you asked "How is everything going?" and he answered. "Oh, I'm still drinking their whiskey," and you knew everything had gone to pot.

"I'm sorry," Macomber said and looked at him with his American face that would stay adolescent until it became middle-aged, and Wilson noted his crew-cropped hair, fine eyes only faintly shifty, good nose, thin lips and handsome jaw. "I'm sorry I didn't realize that. There are lots of things I don't know."

So what could he do, Wilson thought. He was all ready to break it off quickly and neatly and here the beggar was apologizing after he had just insulted him. He made one more attempt. "Don't worry about me talking," he said. "I have a living to make. You know in Africa no woman ever misses her lion and no white man ever bolts."

"I bolted like a rabbit," Macomber said.

Now what in hell were you going to do about a man who talked like that, Wilson wondered.

Wilson looked at Macomber with his flat, blue, machine-gunner's eyes and the other smiled back at him. He had a pleasant smile if you did not notice how his eyes showed when he was hurt.

"Maybe I can fix it up on buffalo," he said. "We're after them next, aren't we?"

"In the morning if you like," Wilson told him. Perhaps he had been wrong. This was certainly the way to take it. You most certainly could not tell a damned thing about an American. He was all for Macomber again. If you could forget this morning. But, of course, you couldn't. The morning had been about as bad as they come.

"Here comes the Memsahib," he said. She was walking over from her tent looking refreshed and cheerful and quite lovely. She had a very perfect oval face, so perfect that you expected her to be stupid. But she wasn't stupid, Wilson thought, no, not stupid.

"How is the beautiful red-faced Mr. Wilson? Are you feeling better, Francis, my pearl?"

"Oh, much," said Macomber.

"I've dropped the whole thing," she said, sitting down at the table. "What importance is there to whether Francis is any good at killing lions? That's not his trade. That's Mr. Wilson's trade. Mr. Wilson is really very impressive killing anything. You do kill anything, don't you?"

"Oh, anything," said Wilson. "Simply anything." They are, he thought, the hardest in the world; the hardest, the cruelest, the most predatory and the most attractive and their men have softened or gone to pieces nervously as they have hardened. Or is it that they pick men they can handle? They can't know that much at the age they marry, he thought. He was grateful that he had gone through his education on American women before now because this was a very attractive one.

"We're going after buff in the morning," he told her.

"I'm coming," she said.

"No, you're not."

"Oh, yes, I am. Mayn't I, Francis?"

"Why not stay in camp?"

"Not for anything," she said. "I wouldn't miss something like today for anything."

When she left, Wilson was thinking, when she went off to cry, she seemed a hell of a fine woman. She seemed to understand, to realize, to be hurt for him and for herself and to know how things really stood. She is away for twenty minutes and now she is back. simply enamelled in that American female cruelty. They are the damnedest women. Really the damnedest.

"We'll put on another show for you tomorrow," Francis Macomber said.

"You're not coming," Wilson said.

"You've very mistaken," she told him. "And I want *so* to see you perform again. You were lovely this morning. That is if blowing things' heads off is lovely."

"Here's the lunch," said Wilson. "You're very merry, aren't you?"

"Why not? I didn't come out here to be dull."

"Well, it hasn't been dull," Wilson said. He could see the boulders in the river and the high bank beyond with the trees and he remembered the morning.

"Oh, no," she said. "It's been charming. And tomorrow. You don't know how I look forward to tomorrow."

"That's eland he's offering you," Wilson said.

"They're the big cowy things that jump like hares, aren't they?"

"I suppose that describes them," Wilson said.

"It's very good meat," Macomber said.

"Did you shoot it, Francis?" she asked.

"Yes."

"They're not dangerous, are they?"

"Only if they fall on you," Wilson told her.

"I'm so glad."

"Why not let up on the bitchery just a little, Margot," Macomber said, cutting the eland steak and putting some mashed potato, gravy and carrot on the down-turned fork that tined through the piece of meat.

"I suppose I could," she said, "since you put it so prettily."

"Tonight we'll have champagne for the lion," Wilson said. "It's a bit too hot at noon."

"Oh, the lion," Margot said. "I'd forgotten the lion!"

So, Robert Wilson thought to himself, she *is* giving him a ride, isn't she? Or do you suppose that's her idea of putting up a good show? How should a woman act when she discovers her husband is a bloody coward? She's damn cruel but they're all cruel. They govern, of course, and to govern one has to be cruel sometimes. Still, I've seen enough of their damn terrorism.

"Have some more eland," he said to her politely.

That afternoon, late, Wilson and Macomber went out in the motor car with the native driver and the two gun-bearers. Mrs. Macomber stayed in the camp. It was too hot to go out, she said, and she was going with them in the early morning. As they drove off Wilson saw her standing under the big tree, looking pretty rather than beautiful in her faintly rosy khaki, her dark hair drawn back off her forehead and gathered in a knot low on her neck, her face as fresh, he thought, as though she were in England. She waved to them as the car went off through the swale of high grass and curved around through the trees into the small hills of orchard bush.

HIGH STYLE VERSUS JUST PLAIN GOOD

In the orchard bush they found a herd of impala, and leaving the car they stalked one old ram with long, wide-spread horns and Macomber killed it with a very creditable shot that knocked the buck down at a good two hundred yards and sent the herd off bounding wildly and leaping over one another's backs in long, leg-drawn-up leaps as unbelievable and as floating as those one makes sometimes in dreams.

"That was a good shot," Wilson said. "They're a small target."

"Is it a worth-while head?" Macomber asked.

"It's excellent," Wilson told him. "You shoot like that and you'll have no trouble."

"Do you think we'll find buffalo tomorrow?"

"There's a good chance of it. They feed out early in the morning and with luck we may catch them in the open."

"I'd like to clear away that lion business," Macomber said. "It's not very pleasant to have your wife see you do something like that."

I should think it would be even more unpleasant to do it, Wilson thought, wife or no wife, or to talk about it having done it. But he said, "I wouldn't think about that any more. Any one could be upset by his first lion. That's all over."

But that night after dinner and a whiskey and soda by the fire before going to bed, as Francis Macomber lay on his cot with the mosquito bar over him and listened to the night noises it was not all over. It was there, exactly as it happened with some parts of it indelibly emphasized and he was miserably ashamed at it. But more than shame he felt cold, hollow fear in him. The fear was still like a cold slimy hollow in all the emptiness where once his confidence had been and it made him feel sick. It was still there with him now.

It had started the night before when he had wakened and heard the lion roaring somewhere up along the river. It was a deep sound and at the end there were sort of coughing grunts that made him seem just outside the tent, and when Francis Macomber woke in the night to hear it he was afraid. He could hear his wife breathing quietly, asleep. There was no one to tell he was afraid, nor to be afraid with him, and, lying alone, he did not know the Somali proverb that says a brave man is always frightened three times by a lion; when he first sees his track, when he first hears him roar and when he first confronts him. Then while they were eating breakfast by lantern light out in the dining tent, before the sun was up, the lion roared again and Francis thought he was just at the edge of camp.

"Sounds like an old-timer," Robert Wilson said, looking up from his kippers and coffee. "Listen to him cough."

"Is he very close?"

"A mile or so up the stream."

"Will we see him?"

"We'll have a look."

"Does his roaring carry that far? It sounds as though he were right in camp."

"Carries a hell of a long way," said Robert Wilson. "It's strange the way it carries. Hope he's a shootable cat. The boys said there was a very big one about here."

"If I get a shot, where should I hit him," Macomber asked, "to stop him?"

"In the shoulders," Wilson said. "In the neck if you can make it. Shoot for bone. Break him down."

"I hope I can place it properly," Macomber said.

"You shoot very well," Wilson told him. "'Take your time. Make sure of him. The first one in is the one that counts."

"What range will it be?"

"Can't tell. Lion has something to say about that. Won't shoot unless it's close enough so you can make sure."

"At under a hundred yards?" Macomber asked.

Wilson looked at him quickly.

"Hundred's about right. Might have to take him a bit under. Shouldn't chance a shot at much over that. A hundred's a decent range. You can hit him wherever you want at that. Here comes the Memsahib."

"Good morning," she said. "Are we going after that lion?"

"As soon as you deal with your breakfast," Wilson said. "How are you feeling?"

"Marvellous," she said. "I'm very excited."

"I'll just go and see that everything is ready," Wilson went off. As he left the lion roared again.

"Noisy beggar," Wilson said. "We'll put a stop to that."

"What's the matter, Francis?" his wife asked him.

"Nothing," Macomber said.

"Yes there is," she said. "What are you upset about?"

"Nothing," he said.

"Tell me," she looked at him. "Don't you feel well?"

"It's that damned roaring," he said. "It's been going on all night, you know."

"Why didn't you wake me," she said. "I'd love to have heard it."

"I've got to kill the damned thing," Macomber said, miserably.

"Well, that's what you're out here for, isn't it?"

"Yes. But I'm nervous. Hearing the thing roar gets on my nerves."

"Well then, as Wilson said, kill him and stop his roaring."

"Yes, darling," said Francis Macomber. "It sounds easy, doesn't it?"

"You're not afraid, are you?"

"Of course not. But I'm nervous from hearing him roar all night."

"You'll kill him marvellously," she said. "I know you will. I'm awfully anxious to see it."

"Finish your breakfast and we'll be starting."

"It's not light yet," she said. "This is a ridiculous hour."

Just then the lion roared in a deep-chested moaning, suddenly guttural, ascending vibration that seemed to shake the air and ended in a sigh and a heavy, deep-chested grunt.

"He sounds almost here," Macomber's wife said.

"My God," said Macomber. "I hate that damned noise."

"It's very impressive."

"Impressive. It's frightful."

Robert Wilson came up then carrying his short, ugly, shockingly big-bored .505 Gibbs and grinning.

"Come on," he said. "Your gun-bearer has your Springfield and the big gun. Everything's in the car. Have you solids?"

"Yes."

"I'm ready," Mrs. Macomber said.

"Must make him stop that racket," Wilson said. "You get in front. The Memsahib can sit back here with me."

They climbed into the motor car and, in the gray first daylight, moved off up the river through the trees. Macomber opened the breech of his rifle and saw he had metal-cased bullets, shut the bolt and put the rifle on safety. He saw his hand was trembling. He felt in his pocket for more cartridges and moved his fingers over the cartridges in the loops of his tunic front. He turned back to where Wilson sat in the rear seat of the doorless, box-bodied motor car beside his wife, them both grinning with excitement, and Wilson leaned forward and whispered.

"See the birds dropping. Means the old boy has left his kill."

On the far bank of the stream Macomber could see, above the trees, vultures circling and plummeting down.

"Chances are he'll come to drink along here," Wilson whispered. "Before he goes to lay up. Keep an eye out."

They were driving slowly along the high bank of the stream which here cut deeply to its boulder-filled bed, and they wound in and out through big trees as they drove. Macomber was watching the opposite bank when he felt Wilson take hold of his arm. The car stopped.

"There he is," he heard the whisper. "Ahead and to the right. Get out and take him. He's a marvellous lion."

Macomber saw the lion now. He was standing almost broadside, his great head up and turned toward them. The early morning breeze that blew toward them was just stirring his dark mane, and the lion looked huge, silhouetted on the rise of bank in the gray morning light, his shoulders heavy, his barrel of a body bulking smoothly.

"How far is he?" asked Macomber, raising his rifle.

"About seventy-five. Get out and take him."

"Why not shoot from where I am?"

"You don't shoot them from cars," he heard Wilson saying in his ear. "Get out. He's not going to stay there all day."

Macomber stepped out of the curved opening at the side of the front seat, onto the step and down onto the ground. The lion still stood looking majestically and coolly toward this object that his eyes only showed in silhouette, bulking like some super-rhino. There was no man smell carried toward him and he watched the object, moving his great head a little from side to side. Then watching the object, not afraid, but hesitating before going down the bank to drink with such a thing opposite him, he saw a man figure detach itself from it and he turned his heavy head and swung away toward the cover of the trees as he heard a cracking crash and felt the slam of a .30-06 220-grain solid bullet that bit his flank and ripped in sudden hot scalding nausea through his stomach. He trotted, heavy, big-footed, swinging wounded full-bellied, through the trees toward the tall grass and cover, and the crash came again to go past him ripping the air apart. Then it crashed again and he felt the blow as it hit his lower ribs and ripped on through, blood sudden hot and frothy in his mouth, and he galloped toward the high grass where he could crouch and not be seen and make them bring the crashing thing close enough so he could make a rush and get the man that held it.

Macomber had not thought how the lion felt as he got out of the car. He only knew his hands were shaking and as he walked away from the car it was almost impossible for him to make his legs move. They were stiff in the thighs, but he could feel the muscles fluttering. He raised the rifle, sighted on the junction of the lion's head and shoulders and pulled the trigger. Nothing happened though he pulled until he thought his finger would break. Then he knew he had the safety on and as he lowered the rifle to move the safety over he moved another frozen pace forward, and the lion seeing his silhouette now clear of the silhouette of the car, turned and started off at a trot, and as Macomber fired, he heard a whunk that meant that the bullet was home; but the lion kept on going. Macomber shot again and every one saw the bullet throw a spout of dirt beyond the trotting lion. He shot again, remembering to lower his aim, and they all heard the bullet hit, and the lion went into a gallop and was in the tall grass before he had the bolt pushed forward.

HIGH STYLE VERSUS JUST PLAIN GOOD

Macomber stood there feeling sick at his stomach, his hands that held the Springfield still cocked, shaking, and his wife and Robert Wilson were standing by him. Beside him too were the two gun-bearers chattering in Wakamba.

"I hit him," Macomber said. "I hit him twice."

"You gut-shot him and you hit him somewhere forward." Wilson said without enthusiasm. The gun-bearers looked very grave. They were silent now.

"You may have killed him," Wilson went on. "We'll have to wait a while before we go in to find out."

"What do you mean?"

"Let him get sick before we follow him up."

"Oh," said Macomber.

"He's a hell of a fine lion," Wilson said cheerfully. "He's gotten into a bad place though."

"Why is it bad?"

"Can't see him until you're on him."

"Oh," said Macomber.

"Come on," said Wilson. "The Memsahib can stay here in the car. We'll go to have a look at the blood spoor."

"Stay here, Margot," Macomber said to his wife. His mouth was very dry and it was hard for him to talk.

"Why?" she asked.

"Wilson says to."

"We're going to have a look," Wilson said. "You stay here. You can see even better from here."

"All right."

Wilson spoke in Swahili to the driver. He nodded and said, "Yes, Bwana."

Then they went down the steep bank and across the stream, climbing over and around the boulders and up the other bank, pulling up by some projecting roots, and along it until they found where the lion had been trotting when Macomber first shot. There was dark blood on the short grass that the gun-bearers pointed out with grass stems, and that ran away behind the river bank trees.

"What do we do?" asked Macomber.

"Not much choice," said Wilson. "We can't bring the car over. Bank's too steep. We'll let him stiffen up a bit and then you and I'll go in and have a look for him."

"Can't we set the grass on fire?" Macomber asked.

"Too green."

"Can't we send beaters?"

Wilson looked at him appraisingly. "Of course we can," he said. "But it's just a touch murderous. You see we know the lion's wounded. You can drive an unwounded lion—he'll move on ahead of a noise—but a wounded lion's going to charge. You can't see him until you're right on him. He'll make himself perfectly flat in cover you wouldn't think would hide a hare. You can't very well send boys in there to that sort of a show. Somebody bound to get mauled."

"What about the gun-bearers?"

"Oh, they'll go with us It's their *shauri*. You see, they signed on for it. They don't look too happy though, do they?"

"I don't want to go in there," said Macomber. It was out before he knew he'd said it.

"Neither do I," said Wilson very cheerily. "Really no choice though." Then, as an afterthought, he glanced at Macomber and saw suddenly how he was trembling and the pitiful look on his face.

"You don't have to go in, of course," he said. "That's what I'm hired for, you know. That's why I'm so expensive."

"You mean you'd go in by yourself? Why not leave him there?"

Robert Wilson, whose entire occupation had been with the lion and the problem he presented, and who had not been thinking about Macomber except to note that he was rather windy, suddenly felt as though he had opened the wrong door in a hotel and seen something shameful.

"What do you mean?"

"Why not just leave him?"

"You mean pretend to ourselves he hasn't been hit?"

"No. Just drop it."

"It isn't done."

"Why not?"

"For one thing, he's certain to be suffering. For another, some one else might run onto him."

"I see."

"But you don't have to have anything to do with it."

"I'd like to," Macomber said. "I'm just scared, you know."

"I'll go ahead when we go in," Wilson said, "with Kongoni tracking. You keep behind me and a little to one side. Chances are we'll hear him growl. If we see him we'll both shoot. Don't worry about anything. I'll keep you backed up. As a matter of fact, you know, perhaps you'd better not go. It might be much better. Why don't you go over and join the Memsahib while I just get it over with?"

"No, I want to go."

"All right," said Wilson. "But don't go in if you don't want to. This is my *shauri* now, you know."

"I want to go," said Macomber.

They sat under a tree and smoked.

"Want to go back and speak to the Memsahib while we're waiting?" Wilson asked.

"No."

"I'll just step back and tell her to be patient."

"Good," said Macomber. He sat there, sweating under his arms, his mouth dry, his stomach hollow feeling, wanting to find courage to tell Wilson to go and finish off the lion without him. He could not know that Wilson was furious because he had not noticed the state he was in earlier and sent him back to his wife. While he sat there Wilson came up. "I have your big gun," he said. "Take it. We've given him time, I think. Come on."

Macomber took the big gun and Wilson said:

"Keep behind me and about five yards to the right and do exactly as I tell you." Then he spoke in Swahili to the two gun-bearers who looked the picture of gloom.

"Let's go," he said.

"Could I have a drink of water?" Macomber asked. Wilson spoke to the older gun-bearer, who wore a canteen on his belt, and the man unbuckled it, unscrewed the top and handed it to Macomber, who took it noticing how heavy it seemed and how hairy and shoddy the felt covering was in his hand. He raised it to drink and looked ahead at the high grass with the flat-topped trees behind it. A breeze was blowing toward them and the grass rippled gently in the wind. He looked at the gun-bearer and he could see the gun-bearer was suffering too with fear.

Thirty-five yards into the grass the big lion lay flattened out along the ground. His ears were back and his only movement was a slight twitching up and down of his long, black-tufted tail. He had turned at bay as soon as he had reached this cover and he was sick with the wound through his full belly, and weakening with the wound through his lungs that brought a thin foamy red to his mouth each time he breathed. His flanks were wet and hot and flies were on the little openings the solid bullets had made in his tawny hide, and his big yellow eyes, narrowed with hate, looked straight ahead, only blinking when the pain came as he breathed, and his claws dug in the soft baked earth. All of him, pain, sickness, hatred and all of his remaining strength, was tightening into an absolute concentration for a rush. He could hear the men talking and he waited, gathering all of himself into this preparation for a charge as soon as the men would come into the grass. As he heard their voices his tail stiffened to twitch up and down, and, as they came into the edge of the grass, he made a coughing grunt and charged.

Kongoni, the old gun-bearer, in the lead watching the blood spoor, Wilson watching the grass for any movement, his big gun ready, the second gun-bearer looking ahead and listening, Macomber close to Wilson, his rifle cocked, they had just moved into the grass when Macomber heard the blood-choked coughing grunt, and saw the swishing rush in the grass. The next thing he knew he was running; running wildly, in panic in the open, running toward the stream.

He heard the *ca-ra-wong!* of Wilson's big rifle, and again in a second crashing *carawong!* and turning saw the lion, horrible-looking now, with half his head seeming to be gone, crawling toward Wilson in the edge of the tall grass while the red-faced man worked the bolt on the short ugly rifle and aimed carefully as another blasting *carawong!* came from the muzzle, and the crawling, heavy, yellow bulk of the lion stiffened and the huge, mutilated head slid forward and Macomber, standing by himself in the clearing where he had run, holding a loaded rifle, while two black men and a white man looked back at him in contempt, knew the lion was dead. He came toward Wilson, his tallness all seeming a naked reproach, and Wilson looked at him and said:

"Want to take pictures?"

"No," he said.

That was all any one had said until they reached the motor car. Then Wilson had said:

"Hell of a fine lion. Boys will skin him out. We might as well stay here in the shade."

Macomber's wife had not looked at him nor he at her and he had sat by her in the back seat with Wilson sitting in the front seat. Once he had reached over and taken his wife's hand without looking at her and she had removed her hand from his. Looking across the stream to where the gun-bearers were skinning out the lion he could see that she had been able to see the whole thing. While they sat there his wife had reached forward and put her hand on Wilson's shoulder. He turned and she had leaned forward over the low seat and kissed him on the mouth.

"Oh, I say," said Wilson, going redder than his natural baked color.

"Mr. Robert Wilson," she said. "The beautiful red-faced Mr. Robert Wilson."

Then she sat down beside Macomber again and looked away across the stream to where the lion lay, with uplifted, white-muscled, tendon-marked naked forearms, and white bloating belly, as the black men fleshed away the skin. Finally the gun-bearers brought the skin over, wet and heavy, and climbed in behind with it, rolling it up before they got in, and the motor car started. No one had said anything more until they were back in camp.

HIGH STYLE VERSUS JUST PLAIN GOOD

That was the story of the lion. Macomber did not know how the lion had felt before he started his rush, nor during it when the unbelievable smash of the .505 with a muzzle velocity of two tons had hit him in the mouth, nor what kept him coming after that, when the second ripping crash had smashed his hind quarters and he had come crawling on toward the crashing, blasting thing that had destroyed him. Wilson knew something about it and only expressed it by saying, "Damned fine lion," but Macomber did not know how Wilson felt about things either. He did not know how his wife felt except that she was through with him.

His wife had been through with him before but it never lasted. He was very wealthy, and would be much wealthier, and he knew she would not leave him ever now. That was one of the few things that he really knew. He knew about that, about motor cycles—that was earliest—about motor cars, about duck-shooting, about fishing, trout, salmon and big-sea, about sex in books, many books, too many books, about all court games, about dogs, not much about horses, about hanging on to his money, about most of the other things his world dealt in, and about his wife not leaving him. His wife had been a great beauty and she was still a great beauty in Africa, but she was not a great enough beauty any more at home to be able to leave him and better herself and she knew it. She had missed the chance to leave him and he knew it. If he had been better with women she would probably have started to worry about him getting another new, beautiful wife; but she knew too much about him to worry about him either. Also, he had always had a great tolerance which seemed the nicest thing about him if it were not the most sinister.

All in all they were known as a comparatively happily married couple, one of those whose disruption is often rumored but never occurs, and as the society columnist put it, they were adding more than a spice of *adventure* to their much envied and ever-enduring *Romance* by a *Safari* in what was known as *Darkest Africa* until the Martin Johnsons lighted it on so many silver screens where they were pursuing *Old Simba* the lion, the buffalo, *Tembo* the elephant and as well collecting specimens for the Museum of Natural History. This same columnist had reported them *on the verge* at least three times in the past and they had been. But they always made it up. They had a sound basis of union. Margot was too beautiful for Macomber to divorce her and Macomber had too much money for Margot to leave him.

It was now about three o'clock in the morning and Francis Macomber, who had been asleep a little while after he had stopped thinking about the lion, wakened and then slept again, woke suddenly, frightened in a dream of the bloody-headed lion standing over him, and listening while his heart pounded, he realized that his wife was not in the other cot in the tent. He lay awake with that knowledge for two hours.

At the end of that time his wife came into the tent, lifted her mosquito bar and crawled cozily into bed.

"Where have you been?" Macomber asked in the darkness.

"Hello," she said. "Are you awake?"

"Where have you been?"

"I just went out to get a breath of air."

"You did, like hell."

"What do you want me to say, darling?"

"Where have you been?"

"Out to get a breath of air."

"That's a new name for it. You *are* a bitch."

"Well, you're a coward."

"All right," he said. "What of it?"

"Nothing as far as I'm concerned. But please let's not talk, darling, because I'm very sleepy."

"You think that I'll take anything."

"I know you will, sweet."

"Well, I won't."

"Please, darling, let's not talk. I'm so very sleepy."

"There wasn't going to be any of that. You promised there wouldn't be."

"Well, there is now," she said sweetly.

"You said if we made this trip that there would be none of that. You promised."

"Yes, darling. That's the way I meant it to be. But the trip was spoiled yesterday. We don't have to talk about it, do we?"

"You don't wait long when you have an advantage, do you?"

"Please let's not talk. I'm so sleepy, darling."

"I'm going to talk."

"Don't mind me then, because I'm going to sleep." And she did.

At breakfast they were all three at the table before daylight and Francis Macomber found that, of all the many men that he had hated, he hated Robert Wilson the most.

"Sleep well?" Wilson asked in his throaty voice, filling a pipe.

"Did you?"

"Topping," the white hunter told him.

You bastard, thought Macomber, you insolent bastard.

So she woke him when she came in, Wilson thought, looking at them both with his flat, cold eyes. Well, why doesn't he keep his wife where she belongs? What does he think I am, a bloody plaster saint? Let him keep her where she belongs. It's his own fault.

"Do you think we'll find buffalo?" Margot asked, pushing away a dish of apricots.

"Chance of it," Wilson said and smiled at her. "Why don't you stay in camp?"

"Not for anything," she told him.

"Why not order her to stay in camp?" Wilson said to Macomber.

"You order her," said Macomber coldly.

"Let's not have any ordering, nor," turning to Macomber, "any silliness, Francis," Margot said quite pleasantly.

"Are you ready to start?" Macomber asked.

"Any time," Wilson told him. "Do you want the Memsahib to go?"

"Does it make any difference whether I do or not?"

The hell with it, thought Robert Wilson. The utter complete hell with it. So this is what it's going to be like. Well, this is what it's going to be like, then.

"Makes no difference," he said.

"You're sure you wouldn't like to stay in camp with her yourself and let me go out and hunt the buffalo?" Macomber asked.

"Can't do that," said Wilson. "Wouldn't talk rot if I were you."

"I'm not talking rot. I'm disgusted."

"Bad word, disgusted."

"Francis, will you please try to speak sensibly?" his wife said.

"I speak too damned sensibly," Macomber said. "Did you ever eat such filthy food?"

"Something wrong with the food?" asked Wilson quietly.

"No more than with everything else."

"I'd pull yourself together, laddybuck," Wilson said very quietly. "There's a boy waits at table that understands a little English."

"The hell with him."

Wilson stood up and puffing on his pipe strolled away, speaking a few words in Swahili to one of the gun-bearers who was standing waiting for him. Macomber and his wife sat on at the table. He was staring at his coffee cup.

"If you make a scene I'll leave you, darling," Margot said quietly.

"No, you won't."

"You can try it and see."

"You won't leave me."

"No," she said. "I won't leave you and you'll behave yourself."

"Behave myself? That's a way to talk. Behave myself."

"Yes. Behave yourself."

"Why don't *you* try behaving?"

"I've tried it so long. So very long."

"I hate that red-faced swine," Macomber said. "I loathe the sight of him."

"He's really *very* nice."

"Oh, *shut up*," Macomber almost shouted. Just then the car came up and stopped in front of the dining tent and the driver and the two gun-bearers got out. Wilson walked over and looked at the husband and wife sitting there at the table.

"Going shooting?" he asked.

"Yes," said Macomber, standing up. "Yes."

"Better bring a woolly. It will be cool in the car," Wilson said.

"I'll get my leather jacket," Margot said.

"The boy has it," Wilson told her. He climbed into the front with the driver and Francis Macomber and his wife sat, not speaking, in the back seat.

Hope the silly beggar doesn't take a notion to blow the back of my head off, Wilson thought to himself. Women *are* a nuisance on safari.

The car was grinding down to cross the river at a pebbly ford in the gray daylight and then climbed, angling up the steep bank, where Wilson had ordered a way shovelled out the day before so they could reach the parklike wooded rolling country on the far side.

It was a good morning, Wilson thought. There was a heavy dew and as the wheels went through the grass and low bushes he could smell the odor of the crushed fronds. It was an odor like verbena and he liked this early morning smell of the dew, the crushed bracken and the look of the tree trunks showing black through the untracked, parklike country. He had put the two in the back seat out of his mind now and was thinking about buffalo. The buffalo that he was after stayed in the daytime in a thick swamp where it was impossible to get a shot, but in the night they fed out into an open stretch of country and if he could come between them and their swamp with the car, Macomber would have a good chance at them in the open. He did not want to hunt buff with Macomber in thick cover. He did not want to hunt buff or anything else with Macomber at all, but he was a professional hunter and he had hunted with some rare ones in his time. If they got buff today there would only be rhino to come and the poor man would have gone through his dangerous game and things might pick up. He'd have nothing more to do with the woman and Macomber would get over that too. He must have gone through plenty of that before by the looks of things. Poor beggar. He must have a way of getting over it. Well, it was the poor sod's own bloody fault.

He, Robert Wilson, carried a double size cot on safari to accommodate any windfalls he might receive. He had hunted for a certain clientele, the international, fast, sporting set, where the women did not feel they were getting their money's worth unless they had shared that cot with the white hunter. He despised them when he was away from them although he liked some of them well enough at the time, but he made his living by them; and their standards were his standards as long as they were hiring him.

They were his standards in all except the shooting. He had his own standards about the killing and they could live up to them or get some one else to hunt them. He knew, too, that they all respected him for this. This Macomber was an odd one though. Damned if he wasn't. Now the wife. Well, the wife. Yes, the wife. Hm, the wife. Well he'd dropped all that. He looked around at them. Macomber sat grim and furious. Margot smiled at him. She looked younger today, more innocent and fresher and not so professionally beautiful. What's in her heart God knows, Wilson thought. She hadn't talked much last night. At that it was a pleasure to see her.

The motor car climbed up a slight rise and went on through the trees and then out into a grassy prairie-like opening and kept in the shelter of the trees along the edge, the driver going slowly and Wilson looking carefully out across the prairie and all along its far side. He stopped the car and studied the opening with his field glasses. Then he motioned to to driver to go on and the car moved slowly along, the driver avoiding wart-hog holes and driving around the mud castles ants had built. Then, looking across the opening, Wilson suddenly turned and said,

"By God, there they are!"

And looking where he pointed, while the car jumped forward and Wilson spoke in rapid Swahili to the driver, Macomber saw three huge, black animals looking almost cylindrical in their long heaviness, like big black tank cars, moving at a gallop across the far edge of the open prairie. They moved at a stiff-necked, stiff bodied gallop and he could see the upswept wide black horns on their heads as they galloped heads out; the heads not moving.

"They're three old bulls,' Wilson said. "We'll cut them off before they get to the swamp."

The car was going a wild forty-five miles an hour across the open and as Macomber watched, the buffalo got bigger and bigger until he could see the gray, hairless, scabby look of one huge bull and how his neck was a part of his shoulders and the shiny black of his horns as he galloped a little behind the others that were strung out in that steady plunging gait; and then, the car swaying as though it had just jumped a road, they drew up close and he could see the plunging hugeness of the bull, and the dust in his sparsely haired hide, the wide boss of horn and his outstretched, wide-nostrilled muzzle, and he was raising his rifle when Wilson shouted, "Not from the car, you fool!" and he had no fear, only hatred of Wilson, while the brakes clamped on and the car skidded, plowing sideways to an almost stop and Wilson was out on one side and he on the other, stumbling as his feet hit the still speeding-by of the earth, and then he was shooting at the bull as he moved away, hearing the bullets whunk into him, emptying his rifle at him as he moved steadily away, finally remembering to get his shots forward into the shoulder, and, as he fumbled to re-load, he saw the bull was down. Down on his knees, his big head tossing, and seeing the other two still galloping he shot at the leader and hit him. He shot again and missed and he heard the *carawonging* roar as Wilson shot and saw the leading bull slide forward onto his nose.

"Get that other," Wilson said. "Now you're shooting!"

But the other bull was moving steadily at the same gallop and he missed, throwing a spout of dirt, and Wilson missed and the dust rose in a cloud and Wilson shouted, "Come on. He's too far!" and grabbed his arm and they were in the car again, Macomber and Wilson hanging on the sides and rocketing swayingly over the uneven ground, drawing up on the steady, plunging, heavy-necked, straight-moving gallop of the bull.

They were behind him and Macomber was filling his rifle, dropping shells onto the ground, jamming it, clearing the jam, then they were almost up with the bull when Wilson yelled "Stop," and the car skidded so that it almost swung over and Macomber fell forward onto his feet, slammed his bolt forward and fired as far forward as he could aim into the galloping, rounded black back, aimed and shot again, then again, then again, and the bullets, all of them hitting, had no effect on the buffalo that he could see. Then Wilson shot, the roar deafening him, and he could see the bull stagger. Macomber shot again, aiming carefully, and down he came, onto his knees.

"All right," Wilson said. "Nice work. That's the three."

Macomber felt a drunken elation.

"How many times did you shoot?" he asked.

"Just three," Wilson said. "You killed the first bull. The biggest one. I helped you finish the other two. Afraid they might have got into cover. You had them killed. I was just mopping up a little. You shot damn well."

"Let's go to the car," said Macomber. "I want a drink."

"Got to finish off that buff first," Wilson told him. The buffalo was on his knees and he jerked his head furiously and bellowed in pig-eyed, roaring rage as they came toward him.

"Watch he doesn't get up," Wilson said. Then, "Get a little broadside and take him in the neck just behind the ear."

Macomber aimed carefully at the center of the huge, jerking rage-driven neck and shot. At the shot the head dropped forward.

"That does it," said Wilson. "Got the spine. They're a hell of a looking thing, aren't they?"

"Let's get the drink," said Macomber. In his life he had never felt so good.

In the car Macomber's wife sat very white faced. "You were marvellous, darling," she said to Macomber. "What a ride."

"Was it rough?" Wilson asked.

"It was frightful. I've never been more frightened in my life."

"Let's all have a drink," Macomber said.

"By all means," said Wilson. "Give it to the Memsahib." She drank the neat whiskey from the flask and shuddered a little when she swallowed. She handed the flask to Macomber who handed it to Wilson.

"It was frightfully exciting," she said. "It's given me a dreadful headache. I didn't know you were allowed to shoot them from cars though."

"No one shot from cars," said Wilson coldly.

"I mean chase them from cars."

"Wouldn't ordinarily," Wilson said. "Seemed sporting enough to me though while we were doing it. Taking more chance driving that way across the plain full of holes and one thing and another than hunting on foot. Buffalo could have charged us each time we shot if he liked. Gave him every chance. Wouldn't mention it to any one though. It's illegal if that's what you mean."

"It seemed very unfair to me," Margot said, "chasing those big helpless things in a motor car."

"Did it?" said Wilson.

"What would happen if they heard about it in Nairobi?"

"I'd lose my licence for one thing. Other unpleasantnesses," Wilson said, taking a drink from the flask. "I'd be out of business."

"Really?"

"Yes, really."

"Well," said Macomber, and he smiled for the first time all day. "Now she has something on you."

"You have such a pretty way of putting things, Francis," Margot Macomber said. Wilson looked at them both. If a four-letter man marries a five-letter woman, he was thinking, what number of letters would their children be? What he said was, "We lost a gun-bearer. Did you notice it?"

"My God, no," Macomber said.

"Here he comes," Wilson said. "He's all right. He must have fallen off when we left the first bull."

Approaching them was the middle-aged gun-bearer, limping along in his knitted cap, khaki tunic, shorts and rubber sandals, gloomy-faced and disgusted looking. As he came up he called out to Wilson in Swahili and they all saw the change in the white hunter's face.

"What does he say?" asked Margot.

"He says the first bull got up and went into the bush," Wilson said with no expression in his voice.

"Oh," said Macomber blankly.

"Then it's going to be just like the lion," said Margot, full of anticipation.

"It's not going to be a damned bit like the lion," Wilson told her. "Did you want another drink, Macomber?"

"Thanks, yes," Macomber said. He expected the feeling he had had about the lion to come back but it did not. For the first time in his life he really felt wholly without fear. Instead of fear he had a feeling of definite elation.

"We'll go and have a look at the second bull," Wilson said. "I'll tell the driver to put the car in the shade."

"What are you going to do? asked Margaret Macomber.

"Take a look at the buff," Wilson said.

"I'll come."

"Come along."

The three of them walked over to where the second buffalo bulked blackly in the open, head forward on the grass, the massive horns swung wide.

"He's a very good head," Wilson said. "That's close to a fifty-inch spread."

Macomber was looking at him with delight.

"He's hateful looking," said Margot. "Can't we go into the shade?"

"Of course," Wilson said. "Look," he said to Macomber, and pointed. "See that patch of bush?"

"Yes."

"That's where the first bull went in. The gun-bearer said when he fell off the bull was down. He was watching us helling along and the other two buff galloping. When he looked up there was the bull up and looking at him. Gun-bearer ran like hell and the bull went off slowly into that bush."

"Can we go in after him now?" asked Macomber eagerly.

Wilson looked at him appraisingly. Damned if this isn't a strange one, he thought. Yesterday he's scared sick and today he's a ruddy fire eater.

"No, we'll give him a while."

"Let's please go into the shade," Margot said. Her face was white and she looked ill.

They made their way to the car where it stood under a single, widespreading tree and all climbed in.

"Chances are he's dead in there," Wilson remarked. "After a little we'll have a look."

Macomber felt a wild unreasonable happiness that he had never known before.

"By God, that was a chase," he said. "I've never felt any such feeling. Wasn't it marvellous, Margot?"

"I hated it."

"Why?"

"I hated it," she said bitterly. "I loathed it."

"You know I don't think I'd ever be afraid of anything again," Macomber said to Wilson. "Something happened in me after we first saw the buff and started after him. Like a dam bursting. It was pure excitement."

"Cleans out your liver," said Wilson. "Damn funny things happen to people."

Macomber's face was shining. "You know something did happen to me," he said. "I feel absolutely different"

His wife said nothing and eyed him strangely. She was sitting far back in the seat and Macomber was sitting forward talking to Wilson who turned sideways talking over the back of the front seat.

"You know, I'd like to try another lion," Macomber said. "I'm really not afraid of them now. After all what can they do to you?"

"That's it," said Wilson. "Worst one can do is kill you. How does it go? Shakespeare. Damned good. See if I can remember. Oh, damned good. Used to quote it to myself at one time. Let's see. 'By my troth, I care not; a man can die but once; we owe God a death and let it go which way it will he that dies this year is quit for the next.' Damned fine, eh?"

He was very embarrassed, having brought out this thing he had lived by, but he had seen men come of age before and it always moved him. It was not a matter of their twenty-first birthday.

It had taken a strange chance of hunting, a sudden precipitation into action without opportunity for worrying beforehand, to bring this about with Macomber, but regardless of how it had happened it had most certainly happened. Look at the beggar now, Wilson thought. It's that some of them stay little boys so long, Wilson thought. Sometimes all their lives. Their figures stay boyish when they're fifty. The great American boy-men. Damned strange people. But he liked this Macomber now.

Damned strange fellow. Probably meant the end of cuckoldry too. Well, that would be a damn good thing. Damned good thing. Beggar had probably been afraid all his life. Don't know what started it. But over now. Hadn't had time to be afraid with the buff. That and being angry too. Motor car too. Motor cars made it familiar. Be a damn fire eater now. He'd seen it in the war work the same way. More of a change than any loss of virginity. Fear gone like an operation. Something else grew in its place. Main thing a man had. Made him into a man. Women knew it too. No bloody fear.

From the far corner of the seat Margaret Macomber looked at the two of them. There was no change in Wilson. She saw Wilson as she had seen him the day before when she had first realized what his great talent was. But she saw the change in Francis Macomber now.

"Do you have that feeling of happiness about what's going to happen?" Macomber asked, still exploring his new wealth.

"You're not supposed to mention it," Wilson said, looking in the other's face. "Much more fashionable to say you're scared. Mind you, you'll be scared too, plenty of times."

"But you *have* a feeling of happiness about action to come?"

"Yes," said Wilson. "There's that. Doesn't do to talk too much about all this. Talk the whole thing away. No pleasure in anything if you mouth it up too much."

"You're both talking rot," said Margot. "Just because you've chased some helpless animals in a motor car you talk like heroes."

"Sorry," said Wilson. "I have been gassing too much." She's worried about it already, he thought.

"If you don't know what we're talking about why not keep out of it?" Macomber asked his wife.

"You've gotten awfully brave, awfully suddenly," his wife said contemptuously, but her contempt was not secure. She was very afraid of something.

Macomber laughed, a very natural hearty laugh. "You know I have," he said. "I really have."

"Isn't it sort of late?" Margot said bitterly. Because she had done the best she could for many years back and the way they were together now was no one person's fault.

"Not for me," said Macomber.

Margot said nothing but sat back in the corner of the seat.

"Do you think we've given him time enough?" Macomber asked Wilson cheerfully.

"We might have a look," Wilson said. "Have you any solids left?"

"The gun-bearer has some."

Wilson called in Swahili and the older gun-bearer, who was skinning out one of the heads, straightened up, pulled a box of solids out of his pocket and brought them over to Macomber, who filled his magazine and put the remaining shells in his pocket.

"You might as well shoot the Springfield,' Wilson said. "You're used to it. We'll leave the Mannlicher in the car with the Memsahib. Your gun-bearer can carry your heavy gun. I've this damned cannon. Now let me tell you about them." He had saved this until the last because he did not want to worry Macomber. "When a buff comes he comes with his head high and thrust straight out. The boss of the horns covers any sort of a brain shot. The only shot is straight into the nose. The only other shot is into his chest or, if you're to one side, into the neck or the shoulders. After they've been hit once they take a hell of a lot of killing. Don't try anything fancy. Take the easiest shot there is. They've finished skinning out that head now. Should we get started?"

He called to the gun-bearers, who came up wiping their hands, and the older one got into the back.

"I'll only take Kongoni," Wilson said. "The other can watch to keep the birds away."

As the car moved slowly across the open space toward the island of brushy trees that ran in a tongue of foliage along a dry water course that cut the open swale, Macomber felt his heart pounding and his mouth was dry again, but it was excitement, not fear.

"Here's where he went in," Wilson said. Then to the gun-bearer in Swahili, "Take the blood spoor."

The car was parallel to the patch of bush. Macomber, Wilson and the gun-bearer got down. Macomber, looking back, saw his wife, with the rifle by her side, looking at him. He waved to her and she did not wave back.

The brush was very thick ahead and the ground was dry. The middle-aged gun-bearer was sweating heavily and Wilson had his hat down over his eyes and his red neck showed just ahead of Macomber. Suddenly the gun-bearer said something in Swahili to Wilson and ran forward.

"He's dead in there," Wilson said. "Good work," and he turned to grip Macomber's hand and as they shook hands, grinning at each other, the gun-bearer shouted wildly and they saw him coming out of the bush sideways, fast as a crab, and the bull coming, nose out, mouth tight closed, blood dripping, massive head straight out, coming in a charge, his little pig eyes bloodshot as he looked at them. Wilson, who was ahead was kneeling shooting, and Macomber, as he fired, unhearing his shot in the roaring of Wilson's gun, saw fragments like slate burst from the huge boss of the horns, and the head jerked, he shot again at the wide nostrils and saw the horns jolt again and fragments fly, and he did not see Wilson now and, aiming carefully, shot again with the buffalo's huge bulk almost on him and his rifle almost level with the on-coming head, nose out, and he could see the little wicked eyes and the head started to lower and he felt a sudden white-hot, blinding flash explode inside his head and that was all he ever felt.

Wilson had ducked to one side to get in a shoulder shot. Macomber had stood solid and shot for the nose, shooting a touch high each time and hitting the heavy horns, splintering and chipping them like hitting a slate roof, and Mrs. Macomber, in the car, had shot at the buffalo with the 6.5 Mannlicher as it seemed about to gore Macomber and had hit her husband about two inches up and a little to one side of the base of his skull.

Francis Macomber lay now, face down, not two yards from where the buffalo lay on his side and his wife knelt over him with Wilson beside her.

"I wouldn't turn him over," Wilson said.

The woman was crying hysterically.

"I'd get back in the car," Wilson said. "Where's the rifle?"

She shook her head, her face contorted. The gun-bearer picked up the rifle.

"Leave it as it is," said Wilson. Then, "Go get Abdulla so that he may witness the manner of the accident."

He knelt down, took a handkerchief from his pocket, and spread it over Francis Macomber's crew-cropped head where it lay. The blood sank into the dry, loose earth.

Wilson stood up and saw the buffalo on his side, his legs out, his thinly-haired belly crawling with ticks. "Hell of a good bull," his brain registered automatically. "A good fifty inches, or better. Better." He called to the driver and told him to spread a blanket over the body and stay by it. Then he walked over to the motor car where the woman sat crying in the corner.

"That was a pretty thing to do," he said in a toneless voice. "He *would* have left you too."

"Stop it," she said.

"Of course it's an accident," he said. "I know that."

"Stop it," she said.

"Don't worry," he said. "There will be a certain amount of unpleasantness but I will have some photographs taken that will be very useful at the inquest. There's the testimony of the gun-bearers and the driver too. You're perfectly all right."

"Stop it," she said.

"There's a hell of a lot to be done," he said. "And I'll have to send a truck off to the lake to wireless for a plane to take the three of us into Nairobi. Why didn't you poison him? That's what they do in England."

"Stop it. Stop it. Stop it," the woman cried.

Wilson looked at her with his flat blue eyes.

"I'm through now," he said. "I was a little angry. I'd begun to like your husband."

"Oh, please stop it," she said. "Please, please stop it."

"That's better," Wilson said. "Please is much better. Now I'll stop."

THE CURIOUS CASE OF BENJAMIN BUTTON

F. Scott Fitzgerald

As long ago as 1860 it was the proper thing to be born at home. At present, so I am told, the high gods of medicine have decreed that the first cries of the young shall be uttered upon the anesthetic air of a hospital, preferably a fashionable one. So young Mr. and Mrs. Roger Button were fifty years ahead of style when they decided, one day in the summer of 1860, that their first baby should be born in a hospital. Whether this anachronism had any bearing upon the astonishing history I am about to set down will never be known.

I shall tell you what occurred, and let you judge for yourself.

The Roger Buttons held an enviable position, both social and financial, in ante-bellum Baltimore. They were related to the This Family and the That Family, which, as every Southerner knew, entitled them to membership in that enormous peerage which largely populated the Confederacy. This was their first experience with the charming old custom of having babies—Mr. Button was naturally nervous. He hoped it would be a boy so that he could be sent to Yale College in Connecticut, at which institution Mr. Button had been known for four years by the somewhat obvious nickname of "Cuff."

On the September morning consecrated to the enormous event he arose nervously at six o'clock, dressed himself, adjusted an impeccable stock, and hurried forth through the streets of Baltimore to the hospital, to determine whether the darkness of the night had borne in new life upon its bosom.

When he was approximately a hundred yards from the Maryland Private Hospital for Ladies and Gentlemen he saw Doctor Keene, the family physician, descending the front steps, rubbing his hands together with a washing movement—as all doctors are required to do by the unwritten ethics of their profession.

Mr. Roger Button, the president of Roger Button & Co., Wholesale Hardware, began to run toward Doctor Keene with much less dignity than was expected from a Southern gentleman of that picturesque period. "Doctor Keene!" he called. "Oh, Doctor Keene!"

The doctor heard him, faced around, and stood waiting, a curious expression settling on his harsh, medicinal face as Mr. Button drew near.

"What happened?" demanded Mr. Button, as he came up in a gasping rush. "What was it? How is she? A boy? Who it is? What——"

"Talk sense!" said Doctor Keene sharply. He appeared somewhat irritated.

"Is the child born?" begged Mr. Button.

Doctor Keene frowned. "Why, yes, I suppose so—after a fashion." Again he threw a curious glance at Mr. Button.

"Is my wife all right?"

"Yes."

"Is it a boy or a girl?"

"Here now!" cried Doctor Keene in a perfect passion of irritation, "I'll ask you to go and see for yourself. Outrageous!" He snapped the last word out in almost one syllable, then he turned away muttering: "Do you imagine a case like this will help my professional reputation? One more would ruin me—ruin anybody."

"What's the matter?" demanded Mr. Button, appalled. "Triplets?"

"No, not triplets!" answered the doctor cuttingly. "What's more, you can go and see for yourself. And get another doctor. I brought you into the world, young man, and I've been physician to your family for forty years, but I'm through with you! I don't want to see you or any of your relatives again! Good-by!"

Then he turned sharply, and without another word climbed into his phaeton, which was waiting at the curbstone, and drove severely away.

Mr. Button stood there upon the sidewalk, stupefied and trembling from head to foot. What horrible mishap had occurred? He had suddenly lost all desire to go into the Maryland Private Hospital for Ladies and Gentlemen—it was with the greatest difficulty that, a moment later, he forced himself to mount the steps and enter the front door.

A nurse was sitting behind a desk in the opaque gloom of the hall. Swallowing his shame, Mr. Button approached her.

"Good morning," she remarked, looking at him pleasantly.

"Good morning. I—I am Mr. Button."

HIGH STYLE VERSUS JUST PLAIN GOOD

At this a look of utter terror spread itself over the girl's face. She rose to her feet and seemed about to fly from the hall, restraining herself only with the most apparent difficulty.

"I want to see my child," said Mr. Button.

The nurse gave a little scream. "Oh—of course!" she cried hysterically. "Upstairs. Right upstairs. Go—*up!*"

She pointed the direction, and Mr. Button, bathed in a cool perspiration, turned falteringly, and began to mount to the second floor. In the upper hall he addressed another nurse who approached him, basin in hand. "I'm Mr. Button," he managed to articulate. "I want to see my——"

Clank! The basin clattered to the floor and rolled in the direction of the stairs. Clank! Clank! It began a methodical descent as if sharing in the general terror which this gentleman provoked.

"I want to see my child!" Mr. Button almost shrieked. He was on the verge of collapse.

Clank! The basin had reached the first floor. The nurse regained control of herself, and threw Mr. Button a look of hearty contempt.

"All *right*, Mr. Button," she agreed in a hushed voice. "Very *well!* But if you *knew* what state it's put us all in this morning! It's perfectly outrageous! The hospital will never have the ghost of a reputation after——"

"Hurry!" he cried hoarsely, "I can't stand this!"

"Come this way, then, Mr. Button."

He dragged himself after her. At the end of a long hall they reached a room from which proceeded a variety of howls—indeed, a room which, in later parlance, would have been known as the "crying-room." They entered. Ranged around the walls were half a dozen white-enameled rolling cribs, each with a tag tied at the head.

"Well," gasped Mr. Button, "which is mine?"

"There!" said the nurse.

Mr. Button's eyes followed her pointing finger, and this is what he saw. Wrapped in a voluminous white blanket, and partially crammed into one of the cribs, there sat an old man apparently about seventy years of age. His sparse hair was almost white, and from his chin dripped a long smoke-colored beard, which waved absurdly back and forth, fanned by the breeze coming in at the window. He looked up at Mr. Button with dim, faded eyes in which lurked a puzzled question.

"Am I mad?" thundered Mr. Button, his terror resolving into rage. "Is this some ghastly hospital joke?"

"It doesn't seem like a joke to us," replied the nurse severely. "And I don't know whether you're mad or not—but this is most certainly your child."

The cool perspiration redoubled on Mr. Button's forehead. He closed his eyes, and then, opening them, looked again. There was no mistake—he was gazing at a man of threescore and ten—a baby of threescore and ten, a baby whose feet hung over the sides of the crib in which it was reposing.

The old man looked placidly from one to the other for a moment, and then suddenly spoke in a cracked and ancient voice. "Are you my father?" he demanded.

Mr. Button and the nurse started violently.

"Because if you are," went on the old man querulously, "I wish you'd get me out of this place—or, at least, get them to put a comfortable rocker in here."

"Where in God's name did you come from? Who are you?" burst out Mr. Button frantically.

"I can't tell you *exactly* who I am," replied the querulous whine, "because I've only been born a few hours—but my last name is certainly Button."

"You lie! You're an impostor!"

The old man turned wearily to the nurse. "Nice way to welcome a newborn child," he complained in a weak voice. "Tell him he's wrong, why don't you?"

"You're wrong, Mr. Button," said the nurse severely. "This is your child, and you'll have to make the best of it. We're going to ask you to take him home with you as soon as possible—some time today."

"Home?" repeated Mr. Button incredulously.

"Yes, we can't have him here. We really can't, you know."

"I'm glad of it," whined the old man. "This is a fine place to keep a youngster of quiet tastes. With all this yelling and howling, I haven't been able to get a wink of sleep. I asked for something to eat"—here his voice rose to a shrill note of protest—"and they brought me a bottle of milk!"

Mr. Button sank down upon a chair near his son and concealed his face in his hands. "My heavens!" he murmured, in an ecstasy of horror. "What will people say? What must I do?"

"You'll have to take him home," insisted the nurse—"immediately!"

A grotesque picture formed itself with dreadful clarity before the eyes of the tortured man—a picture of himself walking through the crowded streets of the city with this appalling apparition stalking by his side. "I can't. I can't," he moaned.

People would stop to speak to him, and what was he going to say? He would have to introduce this—this septuagenarian: "This is my son, born early this morning." And then the old man would gather his blanket

HIGH STYLE VERSUS JUST PLAIN GOOD

around him and they would plod on, past the bustling stores, the slave market—for a dark instant Mr. Button wished passionately that his son was black—past the luxurious houses of the residential district, past the home for the aged....

"Come! Pull yourself together," commanded the nurse.

"See here," the old man announced suddenly, "if you think I'm going to walk home in this blanket, you're entirely mistaken."

"Babies always have blankets."

With a malicious crackle the old man held up a small white swaddling garment. "Look!" he quavered. "*This* is what they had ready for me."

"Babies always wear those," said the nurse primly.

"Well," said the old man, "this baby's not going to wear anything in about two minutes. This blanket itches. They might at least have given me a sheet."

"Keep it on! Keep it on!" said Mr. Button hurriedly. He turned to the nurse. "What'll I do?"

"Go downtown and buy your son some clothes."

Mr. Button's son's voice followed him down into the hall: "And a cane, father. I want to have a cane."

Mr. Button banged the outer door savagely....

2

"Good morning," Mr. Button said, nervously, to the clerk in the Chesapeake Dry Goods Company. "I want to buy some clothes for my child."

"How old is your child, sir?"

"About six hours," answered Mr. Button, without due consideration.

"Babies' supply department in the rear."

"Why, I don't think—I'm not sure that's what I want. It's—he's an unusually large-size child. Exceptionally—ah—large."

"They have the largest child's sizes."

"Where's the boys' department?" inquired Mr. Button, shifting his ground desperately. He felt that the clerk must surely scent his shameful secret.

"Right here."

"Well——" He hesitated. The notion of dressing his son in men's clothes was repugnant to him. If, say, he could only find a very large boy's suit, he might cut off that long and awful beard, dye the white hair brown, and thus manage to conceal the worst, and to retain something of his own self-respect—not to mention his position in Baltimore society.

But a frantic inspection of the boys' department revealed no suits to fit the newborn Button. He blamed the store, of course—in such cases it is the thing to blame the store.

"How old did you say that boy of yours was?" demanded the clerk curiously.

"He's—sixteen."

"Oh, I beg your pardon, I thought you said *six hours*. You'll find the youths' department in the next aisle."

Mr. Button turned miserably away. Then he stopped, brightened, and pointed his finger toward a dressed dummy in the window display. "There!" he exclaimed. "I'll take that suit, out there on the dummy."

The clerk stared. "Why," he protested, "that's not a child's suit. At least it *is*, but it's for fancy dress. You could wear it yourself!"

"Wrap it up," insisted his customer nervously. "That's what I want."

The astonished clerk obeyed.

Back at the hospital Mr. Button entered the nursery and almost threw the package at his son. "Here's your clothes," he snapped out.

The old man untied the package and viewed the contents with a quizzical eye.

"They look sort of funny to me," he complained. "I don't want to be made a monkey of——"

"You've made a monkey of me!" retorted Mr. Button fiercely. "Never you mind how funny you look. Put them on—or I'll—or I'll *spank* you." He swallowed uneasily at the penultimate word, feeling nevertheless that it was the proper thing to say.

"All right, father"—this with a grotesque simulation of filial respect—"you've lived longer; you know best. Just as you say."

As before, the sound of the word "father" caused Mr. Button to start violently.

"And hurry."

"I'm hurrying, father."

When his son was dressed Mr. Button regarded him with depression. The costume consisted of dotted socks, pink pants, and a belted blouse with a wide white collar. Over the latter waved the long whitish beard, drooping almost to the waist. The effect was not good.

"Wait!"

Mr. Button seized a hospital shears and with three quick snaps amputated a large section of the beard. But even with this improvement the ensemble fell far short of perfection. The remaining brush of scraggy hair, the watery eyes, the ancient teeth, seemed oddly out of tone with the gayety of the costume. Mr. Button, however, was obdurate—he held out his hand. "Come along!" he said sternly.

His son took the hand trustingly. "What are you going to call me, dad?" he quavered as they walked from the nursery—"just 'baby' for a while? till you think of a better name?"

HIGH STYLE VERSUS JUST PLAIN GOOD

Mr. Button grunted. "I don't know," he answered harshly. "I think we'll call you Methuselah."

3

Even after the new addition to the Button family had had his hair cut short and then dyed to a sparse unnatural black, had had his face shaved so close that it glistened, and had been attired in small-boy clothes made to order by a flabbergasted tailor, it was impossible for Mr. Button to ignore the fact that his son was a poor excuse for a first family baby. Despite his aged stoop, Benjamin Button—for it was by this name they called him instead of by the appropriate but invidious Methuselah—was five feet eight inches tall. His clothes did not conceal this, nor did the clipping and dyeing of his eyebrows disguise the fact that the eyes underneath were faded and watery and tired. In fact, the baby nurse who had been engaged in advance left the house after one look, in a state of considerable indignation.

But Mr. Button persisted in his unwavering purpose. Benjamin was a baby, and a baby he should remain. At first he declared that if Benjamin didn't like warm milk he could go without food altogether, but he was finally prevailed upon to allow his son bread and butter, and even oatmeal by way of a compromise. One day he brought home a rattle and, giving it to Benjamin, insisted in no uncertain terms that he should "play with it," whereupon the old man took it with a weary expression and could be heard jingling it obediently at intervals throughout the day.

There can be no doubt, though, that the rattle bored him, and that he found other and more soothing amusements when he was left alone. For instance, Mr. Button discovered one day that during the preceding week he had smoked more cigars than ever before—a phenomenon which was explained a few days later when, entering the nursery unexpectedly, he found the room full of faint blue haze and Benjamin, with a guilty expression on his face, trying to conceal the butt of a dark Havana. This, of course, called for a severe spanking, but Mr. Button found that he could not bring himself to administer it. He merely warned his son that he would "stunt his growth."

Nevertheless he persisted in his attitude. He brought home lead soldiers, he brought toy trains, he brought large pleasant animals made of cotton, and, to perfect the illusion which he was creating—for himself at least—he passionately demanded of the clerk in the toy store whether "the paint would come off the pink duck if the baby put it in his mouth." But, despite all his father's efforts, Benjamin refused to be interested. He would steal down the back stairs and return to the nursery with a volume of the "Encyclopaedia Britannica," over which he would pore through an

THE CURIOUS CASE OF BENJAMIN BUTTON

afternoon, while his cotton cows and his Noah's ark were left neglected on the floor. Against such a stubbornness Mr. Button's efforts were of little avail.

The sensation created in Baltimore was, at first, prodigious. What the mishap would have cost the Buttons and their kinsfolk socially cannot be determined, for the outbreak of the Civil War drew the city's attention to other things. A few people who were unfailingly polite racked their brains for compliments to give to the parents—and finally hit upon the ingenious device of declaring that the baby resembled his grandfather, a fact which, due to the standard state of decay common to all men of seventy, could not be denied. Mr. and Mrs. Roger Button were not pleased, and Benjamin's grandfather was furiously insulted.

Benjamin, once he left the hospital, took life as he found it. Several small boys were brought to see him, and he spent a stiff-jointed afternoon trying to work up an interest in tops and marbles—he even managed, quite accidentally, to break a kitchen window with a stone from a slingshot, a feat which secretly delighted his father.

Thereafter Benjamin contrived to break something every day, but he did these things only because they were expected of him, and because he was by nature obliging.

When his grandfather's initial antagonism wore off, Benjamin and that gentleman took enormous pleasure in one another's company. They would sit for hours, these two so far apart in age and experience, and, like old cronies, discuss with tireless monotony the slow events of the day. Benjamin felt more at ease in his grandfather's presence than in his parents'—they seemed always somewhat in awe of him and, despite the dictatorial authority they exercised over him, frequently addressed him as "Mr."

He was as puzzled as anyone else at the apparently advanced age of his mind and body at birth. He read up on it in the medical journal, but found that no such case had been previously recorded. At his father's urging he made an honest attempt to play with other boys, and frequently he joined in the milder games—football shook him up too much, and he feared that in case of a fracture his ancient bones would refuse to knit.

When he was five he was sent to kindergarten, where he was initiated into the art of pasting green paper on orange paper, of weaving colored maps and manufacturing eternal cardboard necklaces. He was inclined to drowse off to sleep in the middle of these tasks, a habit which both irritated and frightened his young teacher. To his relief she complained to his parents, and he was removed from the school. The Roger Buttons told their friends that they felt he was too young.

By the time he was twelve years old his parents had grown used to him. Indeed, so strong is the force of custom that they no longer felt that he was different from any other child—except when some curious anomaly reminded them of the fact. But one day a few weeks after his twelfth birthday, while looking in the mirror, Benjamin made, or thought he made, an astonishing discovery. Did his eyes deceive him, or had his hair turned in the dozen years of his life from white to iron-gray under its concealing dye? Was the network of wrinkles on his face becoming less pronounced? Was his skin healthier and firmer, with even a touch of ruddy winter color? He could not tell. He knew that he no longer stooped and that his physical condition had improved since the early days of his life.

"Can it be——?" he thought to himself, or rather, scarcely dared to think.

He went to his father. "I am grown," he announced determinedly. "I want to put on long trousers."

His father hesitated. "Well," he said finally, "I don't know. Fourteen is the age for putting on long trousers—and you are only twelve."

"But you'll have to admit," protested Benjamin, "that I'm big for my age."

His father looked at him with illusory speculation. "Oh, I'm not so sure of that," he said. "I was as big as you, when I was twelve."

This was not true—it was all part of Roger Button's silent agreement with himself to believe in his son's normality.

Finally a compromise was reached. Benjamin was to continue to dye his hair. He was to make a better attempt to play with boys of his own age. He was not to wear his spectacles or carry a cane in the street. In return for these concessions he was allowed his first suit of long trousers. . . .

4

Of the life of Benjamin Button between his twelfth and twenty-first year I intend to say little. Suffice to record that they were years of normal ungrowth. When Benjamin was eighteen he was erect as a man of fifty; he had more hair and it was of a dark gray; his step was firm, his voice had lost its cracked quaver and descended to a healthy baritone. So his father sent him up to Connecticut to take examinations for entrance to Yale College. Benjamin passed his examination and became a member of the freshman class.

On the third day following his matriculation he received a notification from Mr. Hart, the college registrar, to call at his office and arrange his schedule. Benjamin, glancing in the mirror, decided that his hair needed a new application of its brown dye, but an anxious inspection of his bureau drawer disclosed that the dye bottle was not there. Then he remembered —he had emptied it the day before and thrown it away.

He was in a dilemma. He was due at the registrar's in five minutes. There seemed to be no help for it—he must go as he was. He did.

"Good morning," said the registrar politely. "You've come to inquire about your son."

"Why, as a matter of fact, my name's Button——" began Benjamin, but Mr. Hart cut him off.

"I'm very glad to meet you, Mr. Button. I'm expecting your son here any minute."

"That's me!" burst out Benjamin. "I'm a freshman."

"What!"

"I'm a freshman."

"Surely you're joking."

"Not at all."

The registrar frowned and glanced at a card before him. "Why, I have Mr. Benjamin Button's age down here as eighteen."

"That's my age," asserted Benjamin, flushing slightly.

The registrar eyed him wearily. "Now surely, Mr. Button, you don't expect me to believe that."

Benjamin smiled wearily. "I am eighteen," he repeated.

The registrar pointed sternly to the door. "Get out," he said. "Get out of college and get out of town. You are a dangerous lunatic."

"I am eighteen."

Mr. Hart opened the door. "The idea!" he shouted. "A man of your age trying to enter here as a freshman. Eighteen years old, are you? Well, I'll give you eighteen minutes to get out of town."

Benjamin walked with dignity from the room, and half a dozen undergraduates, who were waiting in the hall, followed him curiously with their eyes. When he had gone a little way he turned around, faced the infuriated registrar, who was still standing in the doorway, and repeated in a firm voice: "I am eighteen years old."

To a chorus of titters which went up from the group of undergraduates, Benjamin walked away.

But he was not fated to escape so easily. On his melancholy walk to the railroad station he found that he was being followed by a group, then by a swarm, and finally by a dense mass of undergraduates. The word had gone around that a lunatic had passed the entrance examinations for Yale and attempted to palm himself off as a youth of eighteen. A fever of excitement permeated the college. Men ran hatless out of classes, the football team abandoned its practice and joined the mob, professors' wives, with bonnets awry and bustles out of position, ran shouting after the procession, from which proceeded a continual succession of remarks aimed at the tender sensibilities of Benjamin Button.

"He must be the Wandering Jew!"

"He ought to go to prep school at his age!"

"Look at the infant prodigy!"

"He thought this was the old men's home."

"Go up to Harvard!"

Benjamin increased his gait, and soon he was running. He would show them! He *would* go to Harvard, and then they would regret these ill-considered taunts!

Safely on board the train for Baltimore, he put his head from the window. "You'll regret this!" he shouted.

"Ha-ha!" the undergraduates laughed. "Ha-ha-ha!" It was the biggest mistake that Yale College had ever made....

5

In 1880 Benjamin Button was twenty years old, and he signalized his birthday by going to work for his father in Roger Button & Co., Wholesale Hardware. It was in that same year that he began "going out socially" —that is, his father insisted on taking him to several fashionable dances. Roger Button was now fifty, and he and his son were more and more companionable—in fact, since Benjamin had ceased to dye his hair (which was still grayish) they appeared the same age, and could have passed for brothers.

One night in August they got into the phaeton attired in their full-dress suits and drove out to a dance at the Shevlins' country house, situated just outside of Baltimore. It was a gorgeous evening. A full moon drenched the road to the lustreless color of platinum, and late-blooming harvest flowers breathed into the motionless air aromas that were like low, half-heard laughter. The open country, carpeted for rods around with bright wheat, was translucent as in the day. It was almost impossible not to be affected by the sheer beauty of the sky—almost.

"There's a great future in the dry-goods business," Roger Button was saying. He was not a spiritual man—his esthetic sense was rudimentary.

"Old fellows like me can't learn new tricks," he observed profoundly. "It's you youngsters with energy and vitality that have the great future before you."

Far up the road the lights of the Shevlins' country house drifted into view, and presently there was a sighing sound that crept persistently toward them—it might have been the fine plaint of violins or the rustle of the silver wheat under the moon.

They pulled up behind a handsome brougham whose passengers were disembarking at the door. A lady got out, then an elderly gentleman, then another young lady, beautiful as sin. Benjamin started; an almost chemical change seemed to dissolve and recompose the very elements of his body. A rigor passed over him, blood rose into his cheeks, his forehead, and there was a steady thumping in his ears. It was first love.

The girl was slender and frail, with hair that was ashen under the moon and honey-colored under the sputtering gas lamps of the porch. Over her shoulders was thrown a Spanish mantilla of softest yellow, butterflied in black; her feet were glittering buttons at the hem of her bustled dress.

Roger Button leaned over to his son. "That," he said, "is young Hildegarde Moncrief, the daughter of General Moncrief."

Benjamin nodded coldly. "Pretty little thing," he said indifferently. But when the negro boy had led the buggy away, he added: "Dad, you might introduce me to her."

They approached a group of which Miss Moncrief was the centre. Reared in the old tradition, she curtsied low before Benjamin. Yes, he might have a dance. He thanked her and walked away—staggered away.

The interval until the time for his turn should arrive dragged itself out interminably. He stood close to the wall, silent, inscrutable, watching with murderous eyes the young bloods of Baltimore as they eddied around Hildegarde Moncrief, passionate admiration in their faces. How obnoxious they seemed to Benjamin; how intolerably rosy! Their curling brown whiskers aroused in him a feeling equivalent to indigestion.

But when his own time came, and he drifted with her out upon the changing floor to the music of the latest waltz from Paris, his jealousies and anxieties melted from him like a mantle of snow. Blind with enchantment, he felt that life was just beginning.

"You and your brother got here just as we did, didn't you?" asked Hildegarde, looking up at him with eyes that were like bright blue enamel.

Benjamin hesitated. If she took him for his father's brother, would it be best to enlighten her? He remembered his experience at Yale, so he decided against it. It would be rude to contradict a lady; it would be criminal to mar this exquisite occasion with the grotesque story of his origin. Later, perhaps. So he nodded, smiled, listened, was happy.

"I like men of your age," Hildegarde told him. "Young boys are so idiotic. They tell me how much champagne they drink at college, and how much money they lose playing cards. Men of your age know how to appreciate women."

Benjamin felt himself on the verge of a proposal—with an effort he choked back the impulse.

"You're just the romantic age," she continued—"fifty. Twenty-five is too worldly-wise; thirty is apt to be pale from overwork; forty is the age of long stories that take a whole cigar to tell; sixty is—oh, sixty is too near seventy; but fifty is the mellow age. I love fifty."

HIGH STYLE VERSUS JUST PLAIN GOOD

Fifty seemed to Benjamin a glorious age. He longed passionately to be fifty.

"I've always said," went on Hildegarde, "that I'd rather marry a man of fifty and be taken care of than marry a man of thirty and take care of *him*."

For Benjamin the rest of the evening was bathed in a honey-colored mist. Hildegarde gave him two more dances, and they discovered that they were marvellously in accord on all the questions of the day. She was to go driving with him on the following Sunday, and then they would discuss all these questions further.

Going home in the phaeton just before the crack of dawn, when the first bees were humming and the fading moon glimmered in the cool dew, Benjamin knew vaguely that his father was discussing wholesale hardware.

". . . And what do you think should merit our biggest attention after hammers and nails?" the elder Button was saying.

"Love," replied Benjamin absent-mindedly.

"Lugs?" exclaimed Roger Button. "Why, I've just covered the question of lugs."

Benjamin regarded him with dazed eyes just as the eastern sky was suddenly cracked with light, and an oriole yawned piercingly in the quickening trees. . . .

6

When, six months later, the engagement of Miss Hildegarde Moncrief to Mr. Benjamin Button was made known (I say "made known," for General Moncrief declared he would rather fall upon his sword than announce it), the excitement in Baltimore society reached a feverish pitch. The almost forgotten story of Benjamin's birth was remembered and sent out upon the winds of scandal in picaresque and incredible forms. It was said that Benjamin was really the father of Roger Button, that he was his brother who had been in prison for forty years, that he was John Wilkes Booth in disguise—and, finally, that he had two small conical horns sprouting from his head.

The Sunday supplements of the New York papers played up the case with fascinating sketches which showed the head of Benjamin Button attached to a fish, to a snake, and, finally, to a body of solid brass. He became known, journalistically, as the Mystery Man of Maryland. But the true story, as is usually the case, had a very small circulation.

However, everyone agreed with General Moncrief that it was "criminal" for a lovely girl who could have married any beau in Baltimore to throw herself into the arms of a man who was assuredly fifty. In vain Mr. Roger Button published his son's birth certificate in large type in the

Baltimore *Blaze*. No one believed it. You had only to look at Benjamin and see.

On the part of the two people most concerned there was no wavering. So many of the stories about her fiancé were false that Hildegarde refused stubbornly to believe even the true one. In vain General Moncrief pointed out to her the high mortality among men of fifty—or, at least, among men who looked fifty; in vain he told her of the instability of the wholesale hardware business. Hildegarde had chosen to marry for mellowness—and marry she did. . . .

7

In one particular, at least, the friends of Hildegarde Moncrief were mistaken. The wholesale hardware business prospered amazingly. In the fifteen years between Benjamin Button's marriage in 1880 and his father's retirement in 1895, the family fortune was doubled—and this was due largely to the younger member of the firm.

Needless to say, Baltimore eventually received the couple to its bosom. Even old General Moncrief became reconciled to his son-in-law when Benjamin gave him the money to bring out his "History of the Civil War" in twenty volumes, which had been refused by nine prominent publishers.

In Benjamin himself fifteen years had wrought many changes. It seemed to him that the blood flowed with new vigor through his veins. It began to be a pleasure to rise in the morning, to walk with an active step along the busy, sunny street, to work untiringly with his shipments of hammers and his cargoes of nails. It was in 1890 that he executed his famous business coup: he brought up the suggestion that *all nails used in nailing up the boxes in which nails are shipped are the property of the shippee*, a proposal which became a statute, was approved by Chief Justice Fossile, and saved Roger Button and Company, Wholesale Hardware, more than *six hundred nails every year*.

In addition, Benjamin discovered that he was becoming more and more attracted by the gay side of life. It was typical of growing enthusiasm for pleasure that he was the first man in the city of Baltimore to own and run an automobile. Meeting him on the street, his contemporaries would stare enviously at the picture he made of health and vitality.

"He seems to grow younger every year," they would remark. And if old Roger Button, now sixty-five years old, had failed at first to give a proper welcome to his son he atoned at last by bestowing on him what amounted to adulation.

And here we come to an unpleasant subject which it will be well to pass over as quickly as possible. There was only one thing that worried Benjamin Button: his wife had ceased to attract him.

At that time Hildegarde was a woman of thirty-five, with a son, Roscoe, fourteen years old. In the early days of their marriage Benjamin had worshiped her. But, as the years passed, her honey-colored hair became an unexciting brown, the blue enamel of her eyes assumed the aspect of cheap crockery—moreover, and most of all, she had become too settled in her ways, too placid, too content, too anemic in her excitements, and too sober in her taste. As a bride it had been she who had "dragged" Benjamin to dances and dinners—now conditions were reversed. She went out socially with him, but without enthusiasm, devoured already by that eternal inertia which comes to live with each of us one day and stays with us to the end.

Benjamin's discontent waxed stronger. At the outbreak of the Spanish-American War in 1898 his home had for him so little charm that he decided to join the army. With his business influence he obtained a commission as captain, and proved so adaptable to the work that he was made a major, and finally a lieutenant-colonel just in time to participate in the celebrated charge up San Juan Hill. He was slightly wounded, and received a medal.

Benjamin had become so attached to the activity and excitement of army life that he regretted to give it up, but his business required attention, so he resigned his commission and came home. He was met at the station by a brass band and escorted to his house.

8

Hildegarde, waving a large silk flag, greeted him on the porch, and even as he kissed her he felt with a sinking of the heart that these three years had taken their toll. She was a woman of forty now, with a faint skirmish line of gray hairs in her head. The sight depressed him.

Up in his room he saw his reflection in the familiar mirror—he went closer and examined his own face with anxiety, comparing it after a moment with a photograph of himself in uniform taken just before the war.

"Good Lord!" he said aloud. The process was continuing. There was no doubt of it—he looked now like a man of thirty. Instead of being delighted, he was uneasy—he was growing younger. He had hitherto hoped that once he reached a bodily age equivalent to his age in years, the grotesque phenomenon which had marked his birth would cease to function. He shuddered. His destiny seemed to him awful, incredible.

When he came downstairs Hildegarde was waiting for him. She appeared annoyed, and he wondered if she had at last discovered that there was something amiss. It was with an effort to relieve the tension between them that he broached the matter at dinner in what he considered a delicate way.

"Well," he remarked lightly, "everybody says I look younger than ever."

Hildegarde regarded him with scorn. She sniffed. "Do you think it's anything to boast about?"

"I'm not boasting," he asserted uncomfortably.

She sniffed again. "The idea," she said, and after a moment: "I should think you'd have enough pride to stop it."

"How can I?" he demanded.

"I'm not going to argue with you," she retorted. "But there's a right way of doing things and a wrong way. If you've made up your mind to be different from everybody else, I don't suppose I can stop you, but I really don't think it's very considerate."

"But, Hildegarde, I can't help it."

"You can too. You're simply stubborn. You think you don't want to be like anyone else. You always have been that way, and you always will be. But just think how it would be if everyone else looked at things as you do —what would the world be like?"

As this was an inane and unanswerable argument Benjamin made no reply, and from that time on a chasm began to widen between them. He wondered what possible fascination she had ever exercised over him.

To add to the breach, he found, as the new century gathered headway, that his thirst for gayety grew stronger. Never a party of any kind in the city of Baltimore but he was there, dancing with the prettiest of the young married women, chatting with the most popular of the débutantes, and finding their company charming, while his wife, a dowager of evil omen, sat among the chaperons, now in haughty disapproval, and now following him with solemn, puzzled, and reproachful eyes.

"Look!" people would remark. "What a pity! A young fellow that age tied to a woman of forty-five. He must be twenty years younger than his wife." They had forgotten—as people inevitably forget—that back in 1880 their mammas and papas had also remarked about this same ill-matched pair.

Benjamin's growing unhappiness at home was compensated for by his many new interests. He took up golf and made a great success of it. He went in for dancing: in 1906 he was an expert at "The Boston," and in 1908 he was considered proficient at the "Maxixe," while in 1909 his "Castle Walk" was the envy of every young man in town.

His social activities, of course, interfered to some extent with his business, but then he had worked hard at wholesale hardware for twenty-five years and felt that he could soon hand it on to his son, Roscoe, who had recently graduated from Harvard.

He and his son were, in fact, often mistaken for each other. This pleased Benjamin—he soon forgot the insidious fear which had come over him on his return from the Spanish-American War, and grew to take a naïve pleasure in his appearance. There was only one fly in the delicious ointment—he hated to appear in public with his wife. Hildegarde was almost fifty, and the sight of her made him feel absurd. . . .

9

One September day in 1910—a few years after Roger Button & Co., Wholesale Hardware, had been handed over to young Roscoe Button—a man, apparently about twenty years old, entered himself as a freshman at Harvard University in Cambridge. He did not make the mistake of announcing that he would never see fifty again nor did he mention the fact that his son had been graduated from the same institution ten years before.

He was admitted, and almost immediately attained a prominent position in the class, partly because he seemed a little older than the other freshmen, whose average age was about eighteen.

But his success was largely due to the fact that in the football game with Yale he played so brilliantly, with so much dash and with such a cold, remorseless anger that he scored seven touchdowns and fourteen field goals for Harvard, and caused one entire eleven of Yale men to be carried singly from the field, unconscious. He was the most celebrated man in college.

Strange to say, in his third or junior year he was scarcely able to "make" the team. The coaches said that he had lost weight, and it seemed to the more observant among them that he was not quite as tall as before. He made no touchdowns—indeed, he was retained on the team chiefly in hope that his enormous reputation would bring terror and his disorganization to the Yale team.

In his senior year he did not make the team at all. He had grown so slight and frail that one day he was taken by some sophomores for a freshman, an incident which humiliated him terribly. He became known as something of a prodigy—a senior who was surely no more than sixteen —and he was often shocked at the worldliness of some of his classmates. His studies seemed harder to him—he felt that they were too advanced. He had heard his classmates speak of St. Midas', the famous preparatory school, at which so many of them had prepared for college, and he determined after his graduation to enter himself at St. Midas', where the sheltered life among boys his own size would be more congenial to him.

THE CURIOUS CASE OF BENJAMIN BUTTON

Upon his graduation in 1914 he went home to Baltimore with his Harvard diploma in his pocket. Hildegarde was now residing in Italy, so Benjamin went to live with his son, Roscoe. But though he was welcomed in a general way, there was obviously no heartiness in Roscoe's feeling toward him—there was even perceptible a tendency on his son's part to think that Benjamin, as he moped about the house in adolescent mooniness, was somewhat in the way. Roscoe was married now and prominent in Baltimore life, and he wanted no scandal to creep out in connection with his family.

Benjamin, no longer persona grata with the débutantes and younger college set, found himself left much alone, except for the companionship of three or four fifteen-year-old boys in neighborhood. His idea of going to St. Midas' school recurred to him.

"Say," he said to Roscoe one day, "I've told you over and over that I want to go to prep school."

"Well, go, then," replied Roscoe shortly. The matter was distasteful to him, and he wished to avoid a discussion.

"I can't go alone," said Benjamin helplessly. "You'll have to enter me and take me up there."

"I haven't got time," declared Roscoe abruptly. His eyes narrowed and he looked uneasily at his father. "As a matter of fact," he added, "you'd better not go on with this business much longer. You better pull up short. You better—you better"—he paused and his face crimsoned as he sought for words—"you better turn right around and start back the other way. This has gone too far to be a joke. It isn't funny any longer. You—you behave yourself!"

Benjamin looked at him, on the verge of tears.

"And another thing," continued Roscoe, "when visitors are in the house I want you to call me 'Uncle'—not 'Roscoe,' but 'Uncle,' do you understand? It looks absurd for a boy of fifteen to call me by my first name. Perhaps you'd better call me 'Uncle' *all* the time, so you'll get used to it."

With a harsh look at his father, Roscoe turned away....

10

At the termination of this interview, Benjamin wandered dismally upstairs and stared at himself in the mirror. He had not shaved for three months, but he could find nothing on his face but a faint white down with which it seemed unnecessary to meddle. When he had first come home from Harvard, Roscoe had approached him with the proposition that he should wear eyeglasses and imitation whiskers glued to his cheeks, and it had seemed for a moment that the farce of his early years was to be repeated. But whiskers had itched and made him ashamed. He wept and Roscoe had reluctantly relented.

Benjamin opened a book of boys' stories, "The Boy Scouts in Bimini Bay," and began to read. But he found himself thinking persistently about the war. America had jointed the Allied cause during the preceding month, and Benjamin wanted to enlist, but, alas, sixteen was the minimum age, and he did not look that old. His true age, which was fifty-seven, would have disqualified him, anyway.

There was a knock at his door, and the butler appeared with a letter bearing a large official legend in the corner and addressed to Mr. Benjamin Button. Benjamin tore it open eagerly, and read the enclosure with delight. It informed him that many reserve officers who had served in the Spanish-American War were being called back into service with a higher rank, and it enclosed his commission as brigadier-general in the United States Army with orders to report immediately.

Benjamin jumped to his feet fairly quivering with enthusiasm. This was what he had wanted. He seized his cap and ten minutes later he had entered a large tailoring establishment on Charles Street, and asked in his uncertain treble to be measured for a uniform.

"Want to play soldier, sonny?" demanded a clerk, casually.

Benjamin flushed. "Say! Never mind what I want!" he retorted angrily. "My name's Button and I live on Mt. Vernon Place, so you know I'm good for it."

"Well," admitted the clerk, hesitatingly, "if you're not, I guess your daddy is, all right."

Benjamin was measured, and a week later his uniform was completed. He had difficulty in obtaining the proper general's insignia because the dealer kept insisting to Benjamin that a nice Y. W. C. A. badge would look just as well and be much more fun to play with.

Saying nothing to Roscoe, he left the house one night and proceeded by train to Camp Mosby, in South Carolina, where he was to command an infantry brigade. On a sultry April day he approached the entrance to the camp, paid off the taxicab which had brought him from the station, and turned to the sentry on guard:

"Get someone to handle my luggage!" he said briskly.

The sentry eyed him reproachfully. "Say," he remarked, "where you goin' with the general's duds, sonny?"

Benjamin, veteran of the Spanish-American War, whirled upon him with fire in his eye, but with, alas, a changing treble voice.

"Come to attention!" he tried to thunder; he paused for breath—then suddenly he saw the sentry snap his heels together and bring his rifle to the present. Benjamin concealed a smile of gratification, but when he glanced around, his smile faded. It was not he who had inspired obedience, but an imposing artillery colonel who was approaching on horseback.

THE CURIOUS CASE OF BENJAMIN BUTTON

"Colonel!" called Benjamin shrilly.

The colonel came up, drew rein, and looked coolly down at him with a twinkle in his eyes. "Whose little boy are you?" he demanded kindly.

"I'll soon darn well show you whose little boy I am!" retorted Benjamin in a ferocious voice. "Get down off that horse!"

The colonel roared with laughter.

"You want him, eh, general?"

"Here!" cried Benjamin desperately. "Read this." And he thrust his commission toward the colonel.

The colonel read it, his eyes popping from their sockets.

"Where'd you get this?" he demanded, slipping the document into his own pocket.

"I got it from the Government, as you'll soon find out!"

"You come along with me," said the colonel with a peculiar look. "We'll go up to headquarters and talk this over. Come along."

The colonel turned and began walking his horse in the direction of headquarters. There was nothing for Benjamin to do but follow with as much dignity as possible—meanwhile promising himself a stern revenge.

But this revenge did not materialize. Two days later, however, his son Roscoe materialized from Baltimore, hot and cross from a hasty trip, and escorted the weeping general, *sans* uniform, back to his home.

11

In 1920 Roscoe Button's first child was born. During the attendant festivities, however, no one thought it "the thing" to mention that the little grubby boy, apparently about ten years of age, who played around the house with lead soldiers and a miniature circus was the new baby's own grandfather.

No one disliked the little boy whose fresh, cheerful face was crossed with just a hint of sadness, but to Roscoe Button his presence was a source of torment. In the idiom of his generation, Roscoe did not consider the matter "efficient." It seemed to him that his father, in refusing to look sixty, had not behaved like a "red-blooded he-man"—this was Roscoe's favorite expression—but in a curious and perverse manner. Indeed, to think about the matter for as much as a half hour drove him to the edge of insanity. Roscoe believed that "live wires" should keep young, but carrying it out on such a scale was—was—was inefficient. And there Roscoe rested.

Five years later Roscoe's little boy had grown old enough to play childish games with little Benjamin under the supervision of the same nurse. Roscoe took them both to kindergarten on the same day and Benjamin found that playing with little strips of colored paper, making mats and chains and curious and beautiful designs, was the most fascinating game in the world. Once he was bad and had to stand in the corner—then he cried—but for the most part there were gay hours in the cheerful room, with the sunlight coming in the windows and Miss Bailey's kind hand resting for a moment now and then in his tousled hair.

Roscoe's son moved up into the first grade after a year, but Benjamin stayed on in the kindergarten. He was very happy. Sometimes when other tots talked about what they would do when they grew up a shadow would cross his little face as if in a dim, childish way he realized that those were things in which he was never going to share.

The days flowed on in monotonous content. He went back a third year to the kindergarten, but he was too little now to understand what the bright shining strips of paper were for. He cried because the other boys were bigger than he and he was afraid of them. The teacher talked to him, but though he tried to understand he could not understand at all.

He was taken from the kindergarten. His nurse, Nana, in her starched gingham dress, became the center of his tiny world. On bright days they walked in the park; Nana would point at a great gray monster and say "elephant," and Benjamin would say it after her, and when he was being undressed for bed that night he would say it over and over aloud to her: "Elyphant, elyphant, elyphant." Sometimes Nana let him jump on the bed, which was fun, because if you sat down exactly right it would bounce you up on your feet again, and if you said "Ah" for a long time while you jumped you got a very pleasing broken vocal effect.

He loved to take a big cane from the hatrack and go around hitting chairs and tables with it and saying: "Fight, fight, fight." When there were people there the old ladies would cluck at him, which interested him, and the young ladies would try to kiss him, which he submitted to with mild boredom. And when the long day was done at five o'clock he would go upstairs with Nana and be fed oatmeal and nice soft mushy foods with a spoon.

There were no troublesome memories in his childish sleep; no token came to him of his brave days at college, of the glittering years when he flustered the hearts of many girls. There were only the white, safe walls of his crib and Nana and a man who came to see him sometimes, and a great big orange ball that Nana pointed at just before his twilight bed hour and called "sun." When the sun went his eyes were sleepy—there were no dreams, no dreams to haunt him.

The past—the wild charge at the head of his men up San Juan Hill; the first years of his marriage when he worked late into the summer dusk down in the busy city for young Hildegarde whom he loved; the days before that when he sat smoking far into the night in the gloomy old

Button house on Monroe Street with his grandfather—all these had faded like substantial dreams from his mind as though they had never been.

He did not remember. He did not remember clearly whether the milk was warm or cool at his last feeding or how the days passed—there was only his crib and Nana's familiar presence. And then he remembered nothing. When he was hungry he cried—that was all. Through the noons and nights he breathed and over him there were soft mumbling and murmurings that he scarcely heard, and faintly differentiated smells, and light and darkness.

Then it was all dark, and his white crib and the dim faces that moved above him, and the warm sweet aroma of the milk, faded out altogether from his mind.

BUT FOR THIS . . .

LaJos Zilahy

He didn't stop to wash the turpentine from his hands, but merely dried them on the rag that was hanging on a nail behind the door.

Then he untied the green carpenter's apron from his waist and shook the shavings from his trousers.

He put on his hat and, before going out the door, turned to the old carpenter who was standing with his back to him, stirring the glue. His voice was weary as he said:

"Goodnight."

A strange mysterious feeling had shivered in him since morning.

There had been a bad taste in his mouth.

For a moment his hand would stop moving the plane, and his eyes would close, tired.

He went home and listlessly ate his supper.

He lived at an old woman's, the widow of Ferenz Borka, in a dark little room which had once been a wood shed.

That night—on the fourth day of October, 1874—at a quarter past one in the morning, the journeyman carpenter, John Kovacs, died.

He was a soft-spoken, sallow-faced man, with sagging shoulders and a rusty mustache.

He died at the age of thirty-five.

Two days later, they buried him.

He left no wife, nor child behind, no one but a cook living in Budapest in the service of a bank president, by the name of Torday.

She was John Kovacs' cousin.

HIGH STYLE VERSUS JUST PLAIN GOOD

Five years later, the old carpenter in whose shop he had worked, died, and nine years later death took the old woman in whose shed he had lived.

Fourteen years later, Torday's cook, John Kovacs' cousin, died.

Twenty-one years later—in the month of March in 1895—in a pub at the end of Kerepesiut, cabbies sat around a red clothed table drinking wine.

It was late in the night, it must have been three o'clock. They sprawled with their elbows on the table, shaking with raucous laughter.

Clouds of thick smoke from vile cigars curled around them. They recalled the days of their military service.

One of them, a big, ruddy-faced, double-chinned coachman whom they called Fritz, was saying:

"Once my friend, the corporal, made a recruit stick his head into the stove . . ."

And at this point he was seized by a violent fit of laughter as he banged the table with palm of his hand.

"Jeez!" he roared.

The veins swelled on his neck and temples and for many minutes he choked, twitched and shook with convulsive laughter.

When he finally calmed down he continued, interrupting himself with repeated guffaws.

"He made him stick his head into the stove and in there he made him shout one hundred times 'Herr Zugsfierer, ich melde gehorsammst' . . . poor chump, there he was on all fours and we paddled his behind till the skin almost split on our fingers."

Again he stopped to get over another laughing spell.

Then he turned to one of the men. "Do you remember, Franzi?" Franzi nodded.

The big fellow put his hand to his forehead.

"Now . . . what was the fellow's name . . ."

Franzi thought for a moment and then said: "Ah . . . a . . . Kovacs . . . John Kovacs."

That was the last time ever a human voice spoke the name of John Kovacs.

On November the tenth, in 1899, a woman suffering from heart disease was carried from an O Buda tobacco factory to St. John's Hospital. She must have been about forty-five years old.

They put her on the first floor in ward number 3.

She lay there on the bed, quiet and terrified; she knew she was going to die.

It was dark in the ward, the rest of the patients were already asleep: only a wick sputtered in a small blue oil lamp.

BUT FOR THIS . . .

Her eyes staring wide into the dim light, the woman reflected upon her life.

She remembered a summer night in the country, and a gentle-eyed young man, with whom—their fingers linked—she was roaming over the heavy scented fields and through whom that night she became a woman.

That young man was John Kovacs and his face, his voice, the glance of his eyes had now returned for the last time.

But this time his name was not spoken, only in the mind of this dying woman did he silently appear for a few moments. The following year a fire destroyed the Calvinist rectory and its dusty records that contained the particulars of the birth and death of John Kovacs.

In January, 1901, the winter was hard.

Toward evening in the dark a man dressed in rags climbed furtively over the ditch that fenced in the village cemetery.

He stole two wooden crosses to build a fire.

One of the crosses had marked the grave of John Kovacs.

Again two decades passed.

In 1923, in Kecskemet, a young lawyer sat at his desk making an inventory of his father's estate.

He opened every drawer and looked carefully through every scrap of paper.

On one was written: "Received 4 Florins, 60 kraciers. The price of two chairs polished respectfully Kovacs John."

The lawyer glanced over the paper, crumpled it in his hand and threw it into the wastepaper basket.

The following day the maid took out the basket and emptied its contents in the far end of the courtyard.

Three days later it rained.

The crumpled paper soaked through and only this much remained on it: ". . . Kova . . . J. . . ."

The rain had washed away the rest; the letter "J" was barely legible.

These last letters were the last lines, the last speck of matter that remained of John Kovacs.

A few weeks later the sky rumbled and the rain poured down as though emptied from buckets.

On that afternoon the rain washed away the remaining letters.

The letter "v" resisted longest, because there where the line curves in the "v" John Kovacs had pressed on his pen.

Then the rain washed that away too.

And in that instant—forty-nine years after his death—the life of the journeyman carpenter ceased to exist and forever disappeared from this earth. . . . But for this . . .

III | Humor

"I am not laughing, what you see are tears," an old man says in the final speech of Faulkner's remarkable novel, A Fable. Where fiction is richest, laughing and crying mingle. Life merges with death. All things contain their opposites. Good guys are partly bad guys and bad guys are partly good guys.

The greatest humor is that which is most meaningful and most real (most "realistic") because it is most truly connected to its own polarity, which is sadness, tragedy. Great comedy thrives on juxtaposition, depending for its success upon the reader's sharing with the author laughter in the shadow of whatever doom. To laugh with Kafka's "A Hunger Artist," or with Richard Stern's "Dying," requires us to learn to laugh in spite of pain; it requires us, too, to see through our texts in ways we may never have done before, for in the past we have been solemn about death.

Proposition: truly funny stories are very often about death.

Truly funny stories often appear also to be about the authors' chagrin regarding their own occupations. It may be true that writers would decline to exchange their occupations for any other. "We lead the freest and zestfullest life of anybody in the entire world," William Gibson has written, "and complain because we are not also rich as magnates, famous as movie stars, powerful as presidents." But it appears to be the nature of writers to feel abused, put upon, mistreated, exploited, swindled, deprived of dignity. Their self-pity is an occupational hazard, and for good reason: writers require indignation.

The writer knows that it is not he who is abused, but everyone else. He generalizes himself. His first stimulation to write may have arisen from his sense of having been abused, but now that writing has become the habit of his life he must maintain his stimulation—his inspiration—even though the very act of writing has carried him by catharsis beyond that early pain.

Of course he retains resemblances to himself. Kafka, the writer, disguises himself as "a hunger artist" to express his sense of the callousness of relationships. Stern, professor of English, becomes for a moment

HUMOR

"Instructor in Plant Physiology" to express his rage in comic terms against death reduced to sentimentality. Bellow, in "'The Gonzaga Manuscripts," appears to liberate laughter by a contemplation of the earnest, innocent young Clarence, who might even be, one guesses, Saul Bellow himself at a time past when he was green.

Indignation inspires resistance. "I would prefer not to," is the theme of a story of Herman Melville, while Kafka's "hunger artist" says, "I can't help it . . . I couldn't find the food I liked. If I had found it, believe me, I should have made no fuss and stuffed myself like you or anyone else."

But when the writer dwells too long in self-pity he knows that his case is somewhat weak, and he laughs: in the end the writer may be luckiest after all, freest and zestfullest because it is only he who articulates his condition, only he whose complaint is heard. He has the last word.

Commonly, the writer feels himself insulted by circumstances. Franz Kafka was afflicted in a number of ways. His health was poor. He was incompetent or timid at love, depressed by anti-Semitism, and abused by his father. Feeling himself to be a writer, Kafka was enslaved all his life to boring workaday labor, mainly for insurance agencies in Prague. Apparently he took no pleasure even in the distant prospect of posthumous fame, ordering that his unpublished manuscripts be destroyed unread at his death. His executor circumvented his will in an act for which the world has had reason to be grateful.

A HUNGER ARTIST

Franz Kafka*

During these last decades the interest in professional fasting has markedly diminished. It used to pay very well to stage such great performances under one's own management, but today that is quite impossible. We live in a different world now. At one time the whole town took a lively interest in the hunger artist; from day to day of his fast the excitement mounted; everybody wanted to see him at least once a day; there were people who bought season tickets for the last few days and sat from morning till night in front of his small barred cage: even in the nighttime there were visiting hours, when the whole effect was heightened by torch flares; on fine days the cage was set out in the open air, and then it was

* Translated by Willa and Edwin Muir.

the children's special treat to see the hunger artist; for their elders he was often just a joke that happened to be in fashion, but the children stood open-mouthed, holding each other's hands for greater security, marveling at him as he sat there pallid in black tights, with his ribs sticking out so prominently, not even on a seat but down among straw on the ground, sometimes giving a courteous nod, answering questions with a constrained smile, or perhaps stretching an arm through the bars so that one might feel how thin it was, and then again withdrawing deep into himself, paying no attention to anyone or anything, not even to the all-important striking of the clock that was the only piece of furniture in his cage, but merely staring into vacancy with half-shut eyes, now and then taking a sip from a tiny glass of water to moisten his lips.

Besides casual onlookers there were also relays of permanent watchers selected by the public, usually butchers, strangely enough, and it was their task to watch the hunger artist day and night, three of them at a time, in case he should have some secret recourse to nourishment. This was nothing but a formality, instituted to reassure the masses, for the initiates knew well enough that during his fast the artist would never in any circumstances, not even under forcible compulsion, swallow the smallest morsel of food; the honor of his profession forbade it. Not every watcher, of course, was capable of understanding this, there were often groups of night watchers who were very lax in carrying out their duties and deliberately huddled together in a retired corner to play cards with great absorption, obviously intending to give the hunger artist the chance of a little refreshment, which they supposed he could draw from some private hoard. Nothing annoyed the artist more than such watchers; they made him miserable; they made his fast seem unendurable; sometimes he mastered his feebleness sufficiently to sing during their watch for as long as he could keep going, to show them how unjust their suspicions were. But that was of little use; they only wondered at his cleverness in being able to fill his mouth even while singing. Much more to his taste were the watchers who sat close up to the bars, who were not content with the dim night lighting of the hall but focused him in the full glare of the electric pocket torch given them by the impresario. The harsh light did not trouble him at all, in any case he could never sleep properly, and he could always drowse a little, whatever the light, at any hour, even when the hall was thronged with noisy onlookers. He was quite happy at the prospect of spending a sleepless night with such watchers: he was ready to exchange jokes with them, to tell them stories out of his nomadic life, anything at all to keep them awake and demonstrate to them again that he had no eatables in his cage and that he was fasting as not one of them could fast. But his happiest moment was when the morning came and an enormous breakfast was brought them, at his expense, on which they flung themselves with the keen appetite of healthy men after a weary night of wakefulness. Of course there were people who argued that this breakfast was an unfair attempt to bribe the watchers, but that was going rather too far, and when they were invited to take on a night's vigil without a breakfast, merely for the sake of the cause, they made themselves scarce, although they stuck stubbornly to their suspicions.

Such suspicions, anyhow, were a necessary accompaniment to the profession of fasting. No one could possibly watch the hunger artist continuously, day and night, and so no one could produce first-hand evidence that the fast had really been rigorous and continuous: only the artist himself could know that, he was therefore bound to be the sole completely satisfied spectator of his own fast. Yet for other reasons he was never satisfied: it was not perhaps mere fasting that had brought him to such skeleton thinness that many people had regretfully to keep away from his exhibitions, because the sight of him was too much for them, perhaps it was dissatisfaction with himself that had worn him down. For he alone knew, what no other initiate knew, how easy it was to fast. It was the easiest thing in the world. He made no secret of this, yet people did not believe him, at the best they set him down as modest; most of them, however, thought he was out for publicity or else was some kind of cheat who found it easy to fast because he had discovered a way of making it easy, and then had the impudence to admit the fact, more or less. He had to put up with all that, and in the course of time had got used to it, but his inner dissatisfaction always rankled, and never yet, after any term of fasting—this must be granted to his credit—had he left the cage of his own free will. The longest period of fasting was fixed by his impresario at forty days, beyond that term he was not allowed to go, not even in great cities, and there was good reason for it, too. Experience had proved that for about forty days the interest of the public could be stimulated by a steadily increasing pressure of advertisement, but after that the town began to lose interest, sympathetic support began notably to fall off: there were of course local variations as between one town and another or one country and another, but as a general rule forty days marked the limit. So on the fortieth day the flower-bedecked cage was opened, enthusiastic spectators filled the hall, a military band played, two doctors entered the cage to measure the results of the fast which were announced through a megaphone, and finally two young ladies appeared, blissful at having been selected for the honor, to help the hunger artist down the few steps leading to a small table on which was spread a carefully chosen invalid repast. And at this very moment the artist always turned stubborn. True, he would entrust his bony arms to the outstretched helping hands of the ladies bending over him, but stand up he would not. Why stop fasting at this particular moment, after forty days of it? He had held out for a long time, an illimitably long time; why stop now, when he was in his best fasting form, or rather, not quite in his best fasting form? Why should he be cheated of the fame he would get for fasting longer, for being not only the record hunger artist of all time, which presumably he was already, but for beating his own record by a performance beyond human imagination, since he felt that there were no limits to his capacity for fasting? His public pretended to admire him so much, why should it have so little patience with him; if he could endure fasting longer, why shouldn't the public endure it? Besides, he was tired, he was comfortable sitting in the straw, and now he was supposed to lift himself to his full height and go down to a meal the very thought of which gave him a nausea that only the presence of the ladies kept him from betraying, and even that with an effort. And he looked up into the eyes of the ladies who were apparently so friendly and in reality so cruel, and shook his head, which felt too heavy on its strengthless neck. But then there happened yet again what always happened. The impresario came forward, without a word—for the band made speech impossible—lifted his arms in the air above the artist, as if inviting Heaven to look down upon its creature here in the straw, this suffering martyr, which indeed he was, although in quite another sense; grasped him round the emaciated waist, with exaggerated caution, so that the frail condition he was in might be appreciated; and committed him to the care of the blenching ladies, not without secretly giving him a shaking so that his legs and body tottered and swayed. The artist now submitted completely; his head lolled on his breast as if it had landed there by chance; his body was hollowed out; his legs in a spasm of self-preservation clung close to each other at the knees, yet scraped on the ground as if it were not really solid ground, as if they were only trying to find solid ground; and the whole weight of his body, a featherweight after all, relapsed onto one of the ladies, who, looking round for help and panting a little—this post of honor was not at all what she had expected it to be—first stretched her neck as far as she could to keep her face at least free from contact with the artist, then finding this impossible, and her more fortunate companion not coming to her aid but merely holding extended on her own trembling hand the little bunch of knucklebones that was the artist's, to the great delight of the spectators burst into tears and had to be replaced by an attendant who had long been stationed in readiness. Then came the food, a little of which the impresario managed to get between the artist's lips, while he sat in a kind of half-fainting trance, to the accompaniment of cheerful patter designed to distract the public's attention from the artist's condi-

HUMOR

tion; after that a toast was drunk to the public, supposedly prompted by a whisper from the artist in the impresario's ear; the band confirmed it with a mighty flourish, the spectators melted away, and no one had any cause to be dissatisfied with the proceedings, no one except the hunger artist himself, he only, as always.

So he lived for many years, with small regular intervals of recuperation, in visible glory, honored by the world, yet in spite of that troubled in spirit, and all the more troubled because no one would take his trouble seriously. What comfort could he possibly need? What more could he possibly wish for? And if some good-natured person, feeling sorry for him, tried to console him by pointing out that his melancholy was probably caused by fasting, it could happen, especially when he had been fasting for some time, that he reacted with an outburst of fury and to the general alarm began to shake the bars of his cage like a wild animal. Yet the impresario had a way of punishing these outbreaks which he rather enjoyed putting into operation. He would apologize publicly for the artist's behavior, which was only to be excused, he admitted, because of the irritability caused by fasting; a condition hardly to be understood by well-fed people; then by natural transition he went on to mention the artist's equally incomprehensible boast that he could fast for much longer than he was doing; he praised the high ambition, the good will, the great self-denial undoubtedly implicit in such a statement; and then quite simply countered it by bringing out photographs, which were also on sale to the public, showing the artist on the fortieth day of a fast lying in bed almost dead from exhaustion. This perversion of the truth, familiar to the artist though it was, always unnerved him afresh and proved too much for him. What was a consequence of the premature ending of his fast was here presented as the cause of it! To fight against this lack of understanding, against a whole world of non-understanding, was impossible. Time and again in good faith he stood by the bars listening to the impresario, but as soon as the photographs appeared he always let go and sank with a groan back on to his straw, and the reassured public could once more come close and gaze at him.

A few years later when the witnesses of such scenes called them to mind, they often failed to understand themselves at all. For meanwhile the aforementioned change in public interest had set in: it seemed to happen almost overnight; there may have been profound causes for it, but who was going to bother about that; at any rate the pampered hunger artist suddenly found himself deserted one fine day by the amusement seekers, who went streaming past him to other more favored attractions. For the last time the impresario hurried him over half Europe to discover whether the old interest might still survive here and there; all in vain;

everywhere, as if by secret agreement, a positive revulsion from professional fasting was in evidence. Of course it could not really have sprung up so suddenly as all that, and many premonitory symptoms which had not been sufficiently remarked or suppressed during the rush and glitter of success now came retrospectively to mind, but it was now too late to take any countermeasures. Fasting would surely come into fashion again at some future date, yet that was no comfort for those living in the present. What, then, was the hunger artist to do? He had been applauded by thousands in his time and could hardly come down to showing himself in a street booth at village fairs, and as for adopting another profession, he was not only too old but too fanatically devoted to fasting. So he took leave of the impresario, his partner in an unparalleled career, and hired himself to a large circus; in order to spare his own feelings he avoided reading the conditions of his contract.

A large circus with its enormous traffic in replacing and recruiting men, animals and apparatus can always find a use for people at any time, even for a hunger artist, provided of course that he does not ask too much, and in this particular case anyhow it was not only the artist who was taken on but his famous and long-known name as well, indeed considering the peculiar nature of his performance, which was not impaired by advancing age, it could not be objected that here was an artist past his prime, no longer at the height of his professional skill, seeking a refugee in some quiet corner of a circus, on the contrary, the hunger artist averred that he could fast as well as ever, which was entirely credible, he even alleged that if he were allowed to fast as he liked, and this was at once promised him without more ado, he could astound the world by establishing a record never yet achieved, a statement which certainly provoked a smile among the other professionals, since it left out of account the change in public opinion, which the hunger artist in his zeal conveniently forgot.

He had not, however, actually lost his sense of the real situation and took it as a matter of course that he and his cage should be stationed, not in the middle of the ring as a main attraction, but outside, near the animal cages, on a site that was after all easily accessible. Large and gaily painted placards made a frame for the cage and announced what was to be seen inside it. When the public came thronging out in the intervals to see the animals, they could hardly avoid passing the hunger artist's cage and stopping there for a moment, perhaps they might even have stayed longer had not those pressing behind them in the narrow gangway, who did not understand why they should be held up on their way towards the excitements of the menagerie, made it impossible for anyone to stand gazing quietly for any length of time. And that was the reason why the

HUMOR

hunger artist, who had of course been looking forward to these visiting hours as the main achievement of his life, began instead to shrink from them. At first he could hardly wait for the intervals; it was exhilarating to watch the crowds come streaming his way, until only too soon—not even the most obstinate self-deception, clung to almost consciously, could hold out against the fact—the conviction was borne in upon him that these people, most of them, to judge from their actions, again and again, without exception, were all on their way to the menagerie. And the first sight of them from the distance remained the best. For when they reached his cage he was at once deafened by the storm of shouting and abuse that arose from the two contending factions, which renewed themselves continuously, of those who wanted to stop and stare at him—he soon began to dislike them more than the others—not out of real interest but only out of obstinate self-assertiveness, and those who wanted to go straight on to the animals. When the first great rush was past, the stragglers came along, and these, whom nothing could have prevented from stopping to look at him as long as they had breath, raced past with long strides, hardly even glancing at him, in their haste to get to the menagerie in time. And all too rarely did it happen that he had a stroke of luck, when some father of a family fetched up before him with his children, pointed a finger at the hunger artist and explained at length what the phenomenon meant, telling stories of earlier years when he himself had watched similar but much more thrilling performances, and the children, still rather uncomprehending, since neither inside nor outside school had they been sufficiently prepared for this lesson—what did they care about fasting?— yet showed by the brightness of their intent eyes that new and better times might be coming. Perhaps, said the hunger artist to himself many a time, things would be a little better if his cage were set not quite so near the menagerie. That made it too easy for people to make their choice, to say nothing of what he suffered from the stench of the menagerie, the animals' restlessness by night, the carrying past of raw lumps of flesh for the beasts of prey, the roaring at feeding times, which depressed him continually. But he did not dare to lodge a complaint with the management; after all, he had the animals to thank for the troops of people who passed his cage, among whom there might always be one here and there to take an interest in him, and who could tell where they might seclude him if he called attention to his existence and thereby to the fact that, strictly speaking, he was only an impediment on the way to the menagerie.

A small impediment, to be sure, one that grew steadily less. People grew familiar with the strange idea that they could be expected, in times like these, to take an interest in a hunger artist, and with this familiarity the verdict went out against him. He might fast as much as he could, and he did so; but nothing could save him now, people passed him by. Just try to explain to anyone the art of fasting! Anyone who has no feeling for it cannot be made to understand it. The fine placards grew dirty and illegible, they were torn down; the little notice board telling the number of fast days achieved, which at first was changed carefully every day, had long stayed at the same figure, for after the first few weeks even this small task seemed pointless to the staff; and so the artist simply fasted on and on, as he had once dreamed of doing, and it was no trouble to him, just as he had always foretold, but no one counted the days, no one, not even the artist himself, knew what records he was already breaking, and his heart grew heavy. And when once in a time some leisurely passer-by stopped, made merry over the old figure on the board and spoke of swindling, that was in its way the stupidest lie ever invented by indifference and inborn malice, since it was not the hunger artist who was cheating, he was working honestly, but the world was cheating him of his reward.

Many more days went by, however, and that too came to an end. An overseer's eye fell on the cage one day and he asked the attendants why this perfectly good stage should be left standing there unused with dirty straw inside it; nobody knew, until one man, helped out by the notice board, remembered about the hunger artist. They poked into the straw with sticks and found him in it. "Are you still fasting?" asked the overseer, "when on earth do you mean to stop?" "Forgive me, everybody," whispered the hunger artist; only the overseer, who had his ear to the bars, understood him. "Of course," said the overseer, and tapped his forehead with a finger to let the attendants know what state the man was in, "we forgive you." "I always wanted you to admire my fasting," said the hunger artist. "We do admire it," said the overseer, affably. "But you shouldn't admire it," said the hunger artist. "Well then we don't admire it," said the overseer, "but why shouldn't we admire it?" "Because I have to fast, I can't help it," said the hunger artist. "What a fellow you are," said the overseer, "and why can't you help it?" "Because," said the hunger artist, lifting his head a little and speaking, with his lips pursed, as if for a kiss, right into the overseer's ear, so that no syllable might be lost, "because I couldn't find the food I liked. If I had found it, believe me, I should have made no fuss and stuffed myself like you or anyone else." These were his last words, but in his dimming eyes remained the firm though no longer proud persuasion that he was still continuing to fast.

"Well, clear this out now!" said the overseer, and they buried the hunger artist, straw and all. Into the cage they put a young panther. Even

HUMOR

the most insensitive felt it refreshing to see this wild creature leaping around the cage that had so long been dreary. The panther was all right. The food he liked was brought him without hesitation by the attendants; he seemed not even to miss his freedom; his noble body, furnished almost to the bursting point with all that it needed, seemed to carry freedom around with it too: somewhere in his jaw it seemed to lurk; and the joy of life streamed with such ardent passion from his throat that for the onlookers it was not easy to stand the shock of it. But they braced themselves, crowded round the cage, and did not want ever to move away.

DYING

Richard Stern

Dreben's first call came while Bly was in the laboratory. Mrs. Shearer's pale coniform budded with announcement: "He says it's urgent."

"Can't come." Watching the smear of kineton coax soluble nitrogens from the right leaf bulge, a mobilization of nutrient which left the ravaged context sere, yellow, senescent. "What kinda urgent?"

"Wouldn't say. An odd one." Her bud, seamed, cracked, needful of a good smear itself, trichloro-hydroxyphenyl, petrolatums, lipids: a chapstick; or lip-stick to mask its aging.

"Get the number." Eyes on the ravenous patch of leaf. Molisch, Curtis, and Clark had shown that mobilizing forces were strongest in flowers and fruits, less strong in growing points, still less strong in lateral buds, weakest in roots. Bly was checking on partial senescence, revving up one section of a tobacco leaf at the expense of another.

Two hours later, he drew the yellow Message Slip from his box: Name: F. Dorfman Dreben; Number: Bl 6-4664; Message: Please return call; Message Taken By: LES.

He knew no Dorfman Dreben, needed nothing from Bl 6-4664. The yellow slip floated toward the waste basket.

The second call came that night while he read President Kennedy's favorite book—he was going through the *Life* magazine list one by one—*John Quincy Adams and the State of the Union*, by Samuel F. Bemis.

"Professor Bly?"

"*Der spricht.*"

"Professor Bly?"

"I am Bly."

"F. Dorfman Dreben, F. Dorfman Dreben Enterprises, I called you at 2:40 this afternoon."

DYING

"My boss wouldn't let me go to the phone, Mr. Dreben. What can I do you for?" Bly held the receiver a foot away, six pock marks in the auditing cup, six at the center of the speaker's circular rash. A great machine. From the solitary six, as much of F. Dorfman Dreben as could be electrically transmitted from voice box A to Ear Drum Y appealed. "It was your poem in *Harper's* right, Professor?"

The forty-fourth poem he'd written since high school, the eleventh since his appointment as Instructor in Plant Physiology, Division of the Biological Sciences, The University of Chicago, the seventh reproduced for public satisfaction (cf. Raleigh *News* and *Observer*, December 1954, "Blackie! Thy very name meant life!"; the Wake Forest *Lit,* "Sonnet on Your Easter Bonnet," Fall, 1956, and four others in the same publication) and the only one which had brought him money ($35.00) and fame (notice in the Chicago *Maroon,* a call from the U. of Chicago Public Relations Officer resulting in six lines in the Chicago *Sun-Times,* four comments from students, bemused, pleased, uneasy, mocking, even stupefyingly, joyous, responses from colleagues, one letter from a lady in Milledgeville, Georgia, declaring the poem "the most beautiful I have read in years" requesting a manuscript copy for the Milledgeville Pantosocratic Society, and today, one, then a second, call from F. Dorfman Dreben, F. Dorfman Dreben Enterprises). "All mine."

"A great poem," said the six pock marks. Seven lines unrhymed, iambic tetrameter with frequent substitutions, title, "In Defense of Decrepitude," epigraph, "A characteristic consequence of senescence is the occurrence of death," theme, "O death, thy sting is life." "Which explains, besides congratulations, my call, Professor."

"You're too kind." 2 cubed plus 4 squared equals my age, the square root of 576, a dayful of years.

"Not kind, Professor. Needy. I need your help."

You? And I, and my tobacco leaves, and Plant Physiology, students, the University, *Harper's,* girls—mostly unknown—children—unconceived.

"Though perhaps it will be of help to you too, Professor. Your helping me."

And the greatest of these. "Explain, Mr. Dreben."

"Easily. Here is our situation. My mother, may her soul, lies on her death bed. A week, a month, who knows, a day, will no longer be with us."

"I'm very sorry." His right eye, nose bone, and right cheek leaked—not sorrow—upon a curl of purple violets (*V. cucullata*) filling a six-by-eight print, glassed-over, above the phone, a retreat of flesh towards hollow, though not sorrowful, limpidity. He was mostly eye. Bly the Eye. Eye had mobilized the nutrient that might have fleshed his flesh.

HUMOR

made him at twenty-four husband, father, house-holder, mortgage-payer. Assistant Professor of Plant Physiology ("Get a loada Bly. Claims he looks like a violet").

"Thank you sincerely, Professor. I can tell you're a man of feeling. It showed in the poem, and that's why I call. Because more than a man of feeling, you're a master of words." No. Master of Science. Doctor of Philosophy, but no M.W., except honorary, University of Dorfman-Dreben. "We are in need. Sister and I. What we want to do is to put on mother's stone, already purchased, a short verse, original in nature, only for her. For such a verse, we are inaugurating a contest, prize two hundred dollars. I am officially inviting you to enter the contest with a verse suitable for permanent inscription." The *cucullata* smeared its fuzzy purple into his small jaw, bruised his neck. He was being mobilized for the assault on stone. Bly the Eye reporting. M.W., O.N. (Original in Nature). "A month ago, I wrote this Robert Frost. Saw him on the Inaugural Day. One month and haven't had a line from him. Not even a 'no'. Once they get into politics they're through."

"Through?"

"Poets. Two weeks ago, I wrote Sandburg. Same result. Negative. They're not interested in a business man's dollar. I tried writing one on my own. Failure. My sister tried. Also. Then my sister saw your poem in *Harper's.* 'Right in Chicago,' she said. 'A sign.'"

"I was in politics," said Bly. Treasurer of the Arista, Binyon High School. John Quincy Adams, defeated by Jackson, turned to poetry. *Duncan Macmorrogh* or *The Conquest of Ireland.* Epic in four cantos.

"If my mother could have read it, she would say, 'This is the poet for my stone.'"

Bly's mother, "Mother Bly," as his sister's husband, Lember, the John Bircher, called her, had carried the sonnet "Blackie" around in her wallet until its shreds had married those of the Brussels streetcar stub, souvenir of the European week which was the product of her mother's death and legacy. He had sent his mother neither a copy of *Harper*'s nor notice of his poem's presence there; evil communication corrupteth good parents. The viper generation that sent no sign. But he could use two hundred dollars, no doubt of it. The summer at the Oceanographic Institute at Wood's Hole was stale for him. He wanted his own week in Europe. He wanted to marry—girl unknown—though he had his nourished eye on a couple in Plant Physiology 263. A new suit. A car.

"Just a short poem, Professor. Maybe four lines. Rhymed."

"Rhymed'll cost you two-fifty."

The pock marks paused. "Who knows? I'll expect to hear from you

DYING

then? F. Dorfman Dreben, 342 Wacker Drive; Bl 6-4664. Any time, day or night. Messages will be taken. I'm very grateful."

Bly sat down under the violets, took up the telephone pad and wrote non-stop:

> Claramae Dreben droops like a leaf.
> Her chest is still heaving, her boy's full of grief.

He pushed the eraser laterally on his forehead, once, twice.

> When she is nothing but dried skin and bone
> Two hundred smackers will carve grief in stone.

Two errors, "Claramae," odds against, one in two thousand, and "Two hundred smackers," which would not buy Bly's rhymed lines. No, a third error: the whole thing.

Bly threw the quatrain under the couch and picked up *John Quincy Adams* who was thinking of going into Congress despite his son's assertion that it would be beneath an ex-president's dignity. An hour later, in bed, he thought first of the kineton smear and the alpha aminoisobutyne acid he would apply to it tomorrow, then of Miss Gammon, a wiry little number in Pl. Phys. 263.

He didn't think of Dorfman Dreben until the third call, five days later. He was home eating the Tai Gum How he had sent up from Sixty-Third Street twice a week. "I called you last night, Professor. Failed to get you."

"Forgive me."

"F. Dorfman Dreben. Mother is sinking."

"I was out, Mr. D." The weekly meeting of the instructors in zoology and botany, papers read, discussion, a good meeting.

Bly sat down under the *cucullata*, the Tai Gum How crawling with porcine force up his stomach cavity. "Mr. Dreben. I must have led you astray. I'm no poet. I've written very few poems. Even if I were a poet, I couldn't take the time to work on a poem now. After all, I didn't even know your mother. Not even her name."

The pock marks were silent. Then, softly, "Clarissa, Professor. A beautiful name."

Bly got up. Almost one in two thousand. A sign. "Yes."

"You are a poet, Professor. No doubt of it. We are not looking for epics. A simple verse, original in nature. Any minute will be her last. I could feel so comforted telling her her resting place will be honored."

At lunch, a joke about the Irishman on his deathbed, sniffing ham

HUMOR

cooking in the kitchen, managing to call to his wife for a piece, being refused. "You know better than that, Flaherty. It's for the wake."

"A simple verse at fifty, maybe sixty-one dollars a line. That's not a bad rate in any business."

Cottonwood brushed against the wire screen, the fluff comas breaking off, falling. Behind a violet shield of cotton cloud, the day's sun bowed good night. "Maybe I can try, Mr. Dreben. But listen, if you don't get a note from me this week, you'll know I couldn't do it. I'm not much on elegies. Not exactly a specialty of the house." Tai Gum How/Hot off the sow/One man's meat/Another man's Frau. Dermot O'Flaherty, Epic in Four Graves.

"You'll try then, Professor?"

"I'll try, Mr. D. If I send it on, please remit the two-fifty by certified cheque. Also, my name is not to be signed to or be associated with the verse. The Division might not approve. And finally, we must never communicate again."

"Wel——"

"Not *au revoir* but good-bye, Mr. D. You either will or will not hear from me within a hundred-and-sixty-eight hours." The pock marks chattered as the receiver plunged.

That evening, Bly sat back in his easy chair and thought about dying. In some ways, he was an expert. There was dying *en masse*, annually, dying deciduously, dying from the top—tulips, spring wheat, Dean Swift —dying from the bottom—he, Bly, nearly died there from the need to live there five or six times a week. Molisch in *Der Lebensauer der Pflanzen* showed that the century plant (*Agave americana,* L.) is a centenarian only when it can't become reproductive for a hundred years. "The most conspicuous factor associated with plant senescence is reproduction." The nutrient was mobilized into the fruit, and the rest suffered. Clarissa Dreben had conceived and spawned F. Dorfman, and who knows if it didn't kill her? Filial sentiments of a matricide. He, Bly, would at times have sold ten of his dayful of years for a few hours with even Mrs. Shearer's dying buds. People dying, Drebens dying. What to say? "Nuts." (Indehiscent, polycarpellary, one-seeded fruits, woodily pericarped. "Fine examination there, Bly.")

He picked up *The State of the Union,* then put it down, ran around the corner to the Trebilcocks and suggested that there was still enough light for a quick badminton game. He and Oscar tied the net cords to the apple trees, laid out the boundary stones, and whacked the birdie till the dark wouldn't let them guess where it was. He told them his assignment, and, telling it, laughed at its absurdity. The next day, he told it at the physiologists' table, elaborating it with echoes of the

Flaherty story. That was it. May passed, and thoughts of the dying Clarissa died with it. Teaching, the study of senescence, the preparation of a paper to be given at the June meetings of the American Association of Plant Physiologists, and then Phyllis Gammon, drove the drebitis from his system.

He had traversed the difficult teacher-student chasm between "Miss Gammon" and "Phyllis." There'd been coffee, then Tai Gum How, then intimate conversation, then amorous relations with the wiry young physiologist from Cumberland, Maryland, who herself remarked about, and thus arrested, the humorous notice of hot gammons and Cumberland Gaps. A girl after if not Bly's heart, at least his mobilizing centers. Even the thought of sacramental union entered his orderly mind without disordering it. Not that there had to be a crash program. Phyllis was no raving beauty, no sex-pot. Her discernible virtues were not those prized in the Bedsheet Derby. She was his, more or less for the asking, a splendid alteration in his life.

He was playing badminton with her at the Trebilcocks when Dreben showed up. A June Sunday that squeezed heat from the stones and thickened the air with summer sounds. They played in shorts, Bly shirtless, asweat. The apple trees were misty with green, their branches wild with the coming weight of the rosy balls busy now sucking nutrient from the sap. The yard ran with children, four Trebilcocks, five Grouts, assorted derivations from China, Ireland, the Baltic, Africa, a running sea of life, rising in the trees, covering the flower borders, drifting through the Jungle Gym and miniature geodesic dome in the yard. Bly and Phyllis —a little wiry for shorts but a great pull on him—whacked the feathered cork over the net while Trebilcock and his wife poured a gallon of Savoia Red back and forth toward their glasses. Bly and Phyllis swigged away between points, so that by the time the dark, bald, bespectacled man in the hound's-tooth winter overcoat strode through the yards, through the quieting children, he was drunk enough almost to disbelieve his presence. "Professor Bly?" Bly saw the black eyes scoot up and down behind the spectacles, and the thinking, "This? A professor? A poet? A sweaty squirt slapping a piece of cork at a sweaty girl, boozing on a run-down lawn. What gives?"

"Yes, I'm Bly. What can I do for you?" though he knew it was Dreben.

Hand out of the hound's-tooth sleeve, shaken by Bly. "F. Dorfman Dreben, Professor. You remember. A month back. Excuse my bothering you here Sunday. Your landlady directed——"

"Over here, Mr. Dreben," and Bly led the man by the hound's-tooth elbow to a corner where a rickety bench leaned on an elm. "You want

HUMOR

to talk with me about the poetry, even though I told you that silence meant inability to bring back the bacon." His bare chest, both narrow and puffy, a snake of hair winding sweatily down towards his shorts, did not enforce the harsh chill of voice, blue eyes, nostrils, shivering with hauteur.

Dreben's rear sank to the bench, the dark, bald skull lowered to the hound-toothed sternum. In the Renoir blaze of yard, he was a funereal smear. Sobered, easier, Bly said, "I'm sorry, Mr. Dreben. If I could have done the job, I'd have done it. Has, is——?"

"Two weeks ago. Smiling." Spoken to his bright Oxfords. "She rests under two thousand dollars worth of granite. Bare. Waiting the expression of our love." The head was up, spectacles catching the gold thrusts of light.

"What can I do, Mr. Dreben? I don't have time. I'm a full-time physiologist." He spread his hands, or rather one hand and one badminton raquet. Then, blushed for the latter, and for the guzzled Savoia, for the lawn, for Phyllis, for—as a matter of fact—life. "Except for sheer physical relaxation, every now and then. I don't have the thinking energy for poetry, and poetry takes energy and time. Took me eight works—I mean weeks—to write the one you read."

The head, a darkly golden Arp egg, appealed. "Please," it said. "We know you're the one for us. Two hundred and fifty dollars, a prize in a contest, permanent commemoration on granite."

He'd almost forgotten the gold. On the grass, wiry legs folded against each other, strong knees raised toward an assuredly pointed dickey, straw-head apple-rosy with its own and the sun's heat, his hot gammon. Two hundred and fifty would give them a hot little week or two up on the Michigan Dunes. "In the mail by Tuesday, Mr. Dreben. Something will be in the mail. You send the cheque by return mail."

Dreben was up, hound-toothed arms churning, off. Not a word. Was silence a contractual ceremony? At the net, he ducked, head deploying for a half-second stare at the three staring guzzlers, then sideswiping half a dozen racing children, he disappeared.

Five hours later, in Michener's Book Store, Bly skimmed a volume on burials and funeral customs. He learned: that in common law, one is responsible for persons dying under one's roof; that corpses were considered sinfully infectious by Persians who placed them in Dakmas, "towers of silence," where birds defleshed them; that West African Negroes wear white at funerals; that the Roman funeral dresses—black—were called *lugubria*; that Patagonians interred horses, Vikings ships, Hindus and Wends widows, and the Egyptians books with their dead. Books, thought Bly. This was about where he came in with Dreben.

DYING

Though for the Egyptians, the books were for the dead's guidance, whereas his poem was for display, the display of expensive devotion which could summon something "original in nature," a freshly created object to bury with a freshly-uncreated subject.

Bly walked home in the hot streets, past the humming student taverns, the boarded store fronts, the waste lands of the Land Clearance Commission, the crazy blue whirl-lights of the police cars, the cottonwood elms sighing in the heat. Life, such as it was, mobilized in the growing points. In Michener's he'd been down where the forces were weakest, in the roots of death, where only an odd Dreben, dark in his hound's-tooth winter coat, mobilized for them.

Out of the gashed window of what had been, three weeks ago, a TASTEE FREEZE BAR, the idea for his mortuary poem came to him.

"Systems in internal equilibrium approach states of perfect order as the temperature lowers toward absolute zero." The third law of thermodynamics which Oscar Trebilcock was using as base for research into frozen protozoa; out of the defunct ice-creamery it slipped and made for the granite above Clarissa Dreben. "Yes," said Bly, Master of Science, to Bly, Master of Words. "Death is perfect order, life disorder." Dodging a lump of dog dung in the cracked pavement, Bly, the Word-Master, thought.

> Clarissa Dreben, know at last,
> Your disorder's been and past.

He stepped off a lawn signed "No dogs. Grass chemically treated," and finished:

> Showing others why they die,
> Under granite, perfect lie.

A great breath in his small chest and a proud look at the prinked-out sky. He'd done it. He ran up the block, up his stairs, called Phyllis and recited it to her. Her response did not dampen him; she was no flatterer. He typed it out on Department of Plant Physiology stationery, just stopped himself from putting an air-mail stamp on the envelope, and ran downstairs and two blocks to the Fifty-Third Street mailbox, pick-up at 6:45 A.M.

He must have lain awake till pick-up time, drenched in thoughts of gods and death as perfect systems, the former discarded by his mind's razor, Occam's, the latter retained, warmly, the spur to research, poetry, the ordering of disorder. His President's hero, Quincy Adams, filled volumes dodging the subject. That's what one did. One wasn't dragged by the beast, one saddled it and rode elsewhere. He was grateful to

HUMOR

Clarissa and F. Dorfman, and went to sleep thinking well of them, the sun firing itself through the soot smears on his window.

The next week he gave his Senescence paper at the Plant Physiology Meetings in the Palmer House. A minor triumph which brought him two job offers which he brought to his department chairman for squeezing out a raise and promotion. He saw no one but physiologists and Phyllis, the latter at supper, though one supper extended to breakfast.

At the end of June, the Trebilcocks left for their yearly month in Wisconsin, and Bly remembered the Michigan cabin that he'd planned to rent with his Dreben money. It had not been sent, nor had there been any word at all from F. Dorfman. "Call the man," said Phyllis from the bed, where she lay, covered, with his sweat and her own. He didn't have to look up the number, Bl 6-4664. He dialed and reached a message service, left his name, number and any hope of getting through to Dreben.

Half an hour later, though, the phone rang.

"Hello, Mr. Dreben. I called to find out why I haven't heard from you."

"Yes. I was going to call. We've been considering the entries until just this afternoon, Professor. We've reached our decision. I was going to call. As I said. I'm afraid that the decision has gone against your fine poem."

Bly held the phone off for two or three seconds, the six pock marks whirling in the heat. "What are you doing, Leon?" Phyllis in white socks, the bare remainder curved toward him like an interrogation mark.

He said, "You'd invited other—there were other poets writing verses for you?"

"Two others, Professor. Baldwin Kerner, editor of the Township School year-book, a fine young poet, and then a dear friend of my sister's, Mrs. Reiser."

"Which won?"

"I have only one."

"Who won the contest?"

"Baldwin. His poem was not quite so forcibly expressed as yours, but it was beautiful and true to nature and mother. Of course, he knew her."

"Is there a second prize?"

Pause. "Yes. You won honorable mention."

Bly lay the phone on the tiny rubber towers, reached behind him to touch Phyllis, who reached around to touch him. No plant in evolutionary history had ever contrived such mingling. Then the animal spirits mobilized in the reproductive centers, and he and Phyllis faced each other.

DYING

Part of the laughter of "A Hunger Artist" undoubtedly arises from the exactitude of detail of the author's fantasy. With what precision he tells us of all the daily routine and ritual of an occupation no man ever practiced! With what satisfaction he might have smiled at the success of his first sentence, the earnest sound of history with which it proceeds! "During these last decades the interest in professional fasting has markedly diminished."

Almost immediately he adds, "We live in a different world now," but that is Kafka's way of saying Not at all, Not at all, for the professional faster—the hunger artist—who never lived, then or now, lives now, and his name is Franz Kafka, who changes identity from time to time. He awoke one morning, in "The Metamorphosis," to find himself "transformed in his bed into a gigantic insect . . . lying on his hard, as it were armor-plated, back. . . ." Abused, mistreated, put upon, Kafka has also imagined the world as a penal colony. Do we all feel so? To the extent that we do, Kafka speaks for us as well as for himself, and bids us laugh together at our common entrapment, for in Kafka the contemplation of our helpless mortality inevitably produces laughter, though he gloomily sees us as bugs upon our backs.

The "hunger artist" bears many resemblances to a writer. He performs for an "impresario" who may be editor, publisher, or patron, and for skeptical spectators—readers—who believe that he really eats on the sly, or that his true hunger is only for publicity. In fact, however, the hunger artist may be "the sole completely satisfied spectator of his own fast," that very Kafka who ordered the destruction of his manuscripts.

The public, the reader, "apparently so friendly and in reality so cruel," is represented at one point as a young lady "selected for the honor" like a Miss America, who makes every effort "to keep her face at least free from contact with the artist." In "Dying," Dreben avoids contact with the poet, too. He wants the poem (he thinks) but not the untouchable poet sweating at badminton. As for the impresario, not even the truest performance is sufficient: the artist must look *like the public expectation of him. Therefore the impresario "secretly" gives the artist a "shaking so that his legs and body tottered and swayed" in a crowd-pleasing manner. For the impresario, merely to be passively wasted by hunger is never enough.*

How difficult the artist is, the impresario might say. He is "honored by the world, yet in spite of that troubled in spirit." Why must he be so difficult? Between public and impresario, on one hand, and the artist on the other, the gulf appears infinite. Nothing can be done "against a whole world of non-understanding." Kafka could only laugh.

HUMOR

The laughter of "Dying" emerges from a conflict similar to the conflict encountered in "A Hunger Artist." Public and impresario are merged in a single figure, a Chicago businessman named Dorfman Dreben, obtuse, cynical, revealing his own barrenness by his inability to believe that the poet, Bly, cannot simply dash off a deeply felt utterance for a fee. "After all," Bly pleads, "I didn't even know your mother. Not even her name." How can he write feelingly? Shall he fake an emotion for two hundred dollars? "Just a short poem, Professor. Maybe four lines. Rhymed." "Rhymed'll cost you two-fifty," the poet replies, but irony is lost upon the businessman who can never believe in the poet's resistance, for he half believes the poet has *a pay rate—so much for rhymed, so much for unrhymed—even as he believes that sentimentality and a monument adequately embrace a real emotion.*

The poet succumbs to temptation. It is an old story. He should have known from the start that accommodation is never possible, but one goes on, hoping always for a miracle, a windfall, that "hot little week or two up on the Michigan Dunes." God knows Bly could have dashed off rhymes easily enough. His head was full of rhymes. But he couldn't do it. The writer within him wouldn't permit it. "I would prefer not to." And then he did *do it, after all. . . .*

❧❧❧

We must not be humorless regarding humor. Great humorists, like the best practical jokers, keep a straight face when they care to. A teacher tells of his difficulty in teaching Bellow's story, "A Sermon by Doctor Pep," to a class whose interests lay elsewhere than in literature. They were sociologists, anthropologists, various kinds of social scientists, philosophers, and psychologists, they were serious, they were earnest—so serious and so earnest they thought that everyone else, including the crazed man of the Bellow story, was as serious and earnest as they.

The problem may also arise with Bellow's "The Gonzaga Manuscripts." Students may so deeply identify with the earnestness of Clarence Feiler that they will lose the humor of him. ("Jokes about me are not funny," somebody once said.) Will students, in short, miss the point of "The Gonzaga Manuscripts"? Will teachers miss the point? Maybe the editors have missed the point. Bellow's tone and mood are uniquely his own. Is the author laughing, or are those tears we see?

"You take it big," says Miss Ungar to Clarence. She favors his taking things big, she admires his serious tourism, although she herself is inclined to be a bit blasé, jaded.

One of the things Clarence takes big is Gonzaga's poetry. Like the hunger artist, like Professor Bly, like Sy Appleman in "The Iron Fist of Oligarchy," Clarence is serious about his art to the point of self-sacrifice. Something of the authors themselves is contained in each of these stories of "humor." Perhaps the stories did not begin as humor. But if they began in self-pity the mood was one none of the authors could sustain.

We admire the young Clarence. His quest is fine. He is above pettiness, above meanness. Man, he believes, can rise above expectations—"Money doesn't have to do that to you," he exclaims. And yet, whatever Clarence touches turns us toward laughter. He is "good," he is "religious," but he is also the awkward victim of his own earnestness: he will offer a wife not love but "leadership"; his beard is less a beard than "a project, to give his life shape"; and the poetry he adores, even allowing for loss in its imagined translation, is ludicrously this:

> These few bits of calcium my teeth are,
> And these few ohms my brain is,
> May make you think I am nothing but puny.
> Let me tell you, sir,
> I am like any creature—
> A creature.

But perhaps you feel that this poetry is good. You are moved. Then that's the problem when we read Bellow, deciding where the tone actually lies.

Bellow does not tell us what he feels about Clarence. He shows us Clarence reflected against other people; he shows us how Clarence behaves, and the poetry Clarence admires. Clarence is mirrored by situation, like the young man courting in "In Dreams Begin Responsibilities," elsewhere in this volume: "It is evident that the respect in which my father is held in this house is tempered by a good deal of mirth. He is impressive, but also very awkward."

Almost everyone else in "The Gonzaga Manuscripts" is enclosed in his or her own obsessions, just as is Clarence. "If you came here with the intention of having fun, you won't have it in Madrid," a lady says to Clarence. "I've been here twenty years and never had any." She cannot distinguish between her own experience and life generally, nor between Clarence and America generally. She blames him for the atomic bomb, which causes the bad weather in Spain. "The weather has never been normal since the atom thing started...."

Lacking experience, Clarence mistakes other people's motives. He categorizes people. "He had thought that the kind of woman who became engaged to an airline pilot might look down on him." Later he thinks, "Perhaps she was not really in love with her fiancé. Clarence now had the *impression that the black-marketing was not her idea but the pilot's. It embarrassed her, but she was too loyal to admit it to him."*

He is even a victim of the very weather he has been accused of creating. On his way to a dinner party of importance to his search for the Gonzaga manuscripts he is caught in the rain. He enters his host's house *"clumsily in his sodden wool suit. It has a shameful smell, like a wet dog."*

Bellow, in this story, offers no clear hints or signs identifying his work as humor. He offers us the scene, which we must then experience for ourselves. He plays no canned laughter on a sound track to guide us. When, in fact, Clarence met *"a family of laughers"* they weren't at all funny. *"They laughed when they spoke and when you answered."* Like other moments during his ill-fated journey, this moment frustrates Clarence.

Clarence will not recover the Gonzaga manuscripts. Perhaps those manuscripts no longer even exist

But his quest is sincere and touching, and if he does not gain the manuscripts he gains experience of life. Looking back upon himself some day, he too may be amused. Innocence exposed, where nobody is hurt, is part of the stuff of humor.

THE GONZAGA MANUSCRIPTS

Saul Bellow

Buttoned to the throat in a long, soft overcoat, dark green, Clarence Feiler got off the Hendaye Express in the Madrid station. It was late afternoon and it was raining, and the station with its throng and its dim orange lights seemed sunken under darkness and noise. The gaunt horse-like Spanish locomotives screamed off their steam and the hurrying passengers struggled in the narrow gates. Porters and touts approached Clarence, obviously a foreigner by his small blond beard, blue eyes, almost brimless hat, long coat and crepe-soled shoes. But he carried his own bag and had no need of them. This was not his first visit to Madrid. An old limousine took him to the Pension La Granja, where he had a room reserved. This limousine probably had run on the boulevards of Madrid before Clarence was born but it was mechanically still beautiful. In the spacious darkness of the back seat the windows were like the glass of an old cabinet, and he listened happily to the voice of the wonderful old motor. Where could you get another ride like this, on such an evening, through such a place? Clarence loved Spanish cities, even the poorest and barrenest, and the capitals stirred his heart as no other places did. He had first come as an undergraduate, a mere kid, studying Spanish literature at the University of Minnesota; and then he had come again and seen the ruins of the Civil War. This time he came not as a tourist but on a quest. He had heard from a Spanish Republican refugee in California, where he now lived, that there were more than a hundred poems by Manuel Gonzaga somewhere in Madrid. Not a single Spanish publishing house could print them because they were so critical of the Army and the state. It was hard to believe that poems by one of the greatest of modern Spanish geniuses could be suppressed, but the refugee gave Clarence reliable proof that it was so. He showed him letters to one of Gonzaga's nephews from a man named Gúzman del Nido, Gonzaga's friend and literary executor, with whom he had served in North Africa, admitting that he had once had the poems but had given them up to a certain Countess del Camino since most of them were love poems addressed to her. The countess had died during the war, her home had been looted, and he didn't know what had become of the poems.

"Perhaps he doesn't care either," said the refugee. "He's one of these people who think everything has come to an end anyway, and they might as well live comfortably. Gúzman del Nido lives very comfortably. He's rich. He is a member of the Cortes."

"Money doesn't have to do that to you," said Clarence, who had a little money himself. He was not exactly a rich man, but he didn't have to work for a living. "He must have a bad character not to care about his friend's work. And such work! You know, I was just killing time in graduate school till I came across Gonzaga. The year I spent doing my thesis on *Los Huesos Secos* was the first good year I had had since I was a boy. There hasn't been anything like it since. I'm not much on modern poetry in English. Some of it is very fine, of course, but it doesn't express much wish to live. To live as a creature, that is. As if it were not good enough. But the first time I opened Gonzaga I read:

> These few bits of calcium my teeth are,
> May make you think I am nothing but puny.
> And these few ohms my brain is,
> Let me tell you, sir,
> I am like any creature—
> A creature.

I felt right away and in spite of this ironical turn that I was in touch with a poet who could show me how to go on, and what attitude to take toward life. The great, passionate poems carried me away, like 'The Poem of Night,' which I still know by heart from beginning to end and which often seems like the only thing I really have got—" Clarence was sometimes given to exaggerating. "Or take the poem called 'Confession,' the one that goes:

> I used to welcome all
> And now I fear all.
> If it rained it was comforting
> And if it shone, comforting,
> But now my very weight is dreadful . . .

When I read that, Gonzaga made me understand how we lose everything by trying to become everything. This was the most valuable lesson of my life, I think. Gosh! There should be someone trying to find those posthumous poems. They ought not to be given up. They must be marvelous."

He felt, suddenly, as if he had been thrown into a race, terribly excited, full of effort, feverish—and profoundly grateful. For Clarence had not found his occupation and had nothing to do. He did not think it right to marry until he had found something and could offer a wife leadership. His beard was grown not to hide weaknesses but as a project, to give his life shape. He was becoming an eccentric; it was all he could do with his good impulses. As yet he did not realize that these impulses were religious. He was too timid to say he believed in God, and he couldn't think that it would matter to anyone what he believed. Since he was weak, it would be said, he must have some such belief. However, he was really enthusiastic about Gonzaga, and to recover this inspired Spaniard's poems was something that mattered. And "Does it really matter?" was always the test question. It filled Clarence with secret pleasure to know that he was not indifferent, at bottom pretending. It *did* matter, and what mattered might save him. He was in Madrid not to perform an act of cultural piety but to do a decent and necessary thing, namely, bring the testimony of a great man before the world. Which certainly could use it.

As soon as he arrived at the Pension La Granja and the lamps were lit in his room, a comfortable large room with balconies facing the trees of the Retiro, Madrid's biggest park, Clarence called for the porter and sent off two letters. One was addressed to Gúzman del Nido, Gonzaga's comrade-in-arms of the Moroccan War and literary executor, and the other to a Miss Faith Ungar on García de Paredes Street. This Miss Ungar was an art student, or rather student of art history; her fiancé was an airline pilot who brought in cheaper pesetas from Tangiers. Clarence disliked black-marketing, but the legal rate of exchange was ridiculous; he was prepared to pay a lot of money for those manuscripts and at eighteen to one he might spend a small fortune.

His landlady came to welcome him to the pension—a pale, big woman with a sort of turban of hair wound spirally to a point. She came also to collect his passport and other travel papers for police inspection and to give him a briefing on her guests. A retired general was the oldest. She had also some people from British Shell and the widow of a Minister and six members of a Brazilian trade delegation, so the dining room was full. "And are you a tourist?" she said, glancing at the *triptico*, the elaborate police document all travelers have to carry in Spain.

"In a way," said Clarence, guardedly. He didn't like to be thought of as a tourist, and yet secrecy was necessary. Gonzaga's poems, though unpublished, would probably come under the head of national treasures.

"Or have you come to study something?"

"Yes, that's it."

"There's a great deal here to interest people from a country as new as yours."

"There certainly is," he said, his rosy beard-lengthened face turned to her, seeming perfectly sincere. The color of his mouth was especially vivid in the lamplight. It was not yet full evening and the rain was stopping. Beyond the trees of the Retiro the sky was making itself clear of clouds, and a last yellow daylight pierced the water-gray. Trolley sparks scratched green within the locust trees.

A bell rang, an old handbell, announcing dinner. A maid passed, ringing it proudly, her shoulders thrown back.

The guests were eating soup in the dining room, an interior room, not very airy, with dark red, cloth-covered walls. The Brazilians were having a lively conversation. The old general, feeble-headed, eyes nearly extinct, was bothering the soup with his spoon but not eating. Doña Elvia seated Clarence with a hefty British lady; he knew he must expect to have trouble with her. She was in a bad way. Her face was heavily made up; she thought she was a person of charm, and she did have a certain charm, but her eyes were burning. Tresses of dark-reddish hair fought strongly for position on her head.

"If you came here with the intention of having fun, you won't have it in Madrid. I've been here twenty years and never had any," she said. "By now I'm so tired out I don't even look for any. I don't read any books, I don't go to the cinema, and I can just barely stand to read *Coyote* and look at the funnies. I can't understand why so many Americans want to come here. They're all over the place. One of your bishops was arrested at Santander for bathing without the top of his costume."

"Really?"

"They're very strict in Spain about dress. I suppose if they had known he was a bishop they would have let him alone. However, in the water. . . ."

HUMOR

"It's strange," said Clarence. "Well, anyway, he's not one of *my* bishops. I have no bishops."

"You do have Congressmen, though. Two of those had their pants stolen while taking a nap on the Barcelona Express. The thieves reached into the compartment from the roof. It happened in broad daylight. They carried about two thousand dollars each. Don't they have pocketbooks? Why do they carry so much money in their pockets?"

Clarence frowned. "Yes, I read about that," he said. "I can't tell you why they carry so much money in their trouser pockets. Maybe that's the custom down South. It's none of my business, though."

"I'm afraid I'm annoying you," she said. She was not afraid at all; a bold look of enjoyment had entered her eyes. She was trying to bait him. Why? he wondered; he found no ready answer.

"You're not annoying me."

"If I am," she said, "it's not absolutely my fault. You know Stendhal once wrote there was a secret principle of unhappiness in the English."

"Is that so?" he said. He looked at her with deep interest. What a busted-up face; fully of unhappy vigor and directionless intelligence. Yes, she was astonishing. He felt sorry for her and yet lucky to have met her, in spite of everything.

"He may have been right. You see, I used to read widely once. I was a cultivated person. But the reason for it was sex, and that went."

"Oh, come, I wouldn't say—"

"I shouldn't be talking like this. It's partly the weather. It's been raining so hard. It isn't supposed to rain like this in the summer. I've never seen so much damned rain. You people may be to blame for that."

"*Who* people? Which people?"

"It could be because of the atom bomb," she said. "The weather has never been normal since the atom thing started. Nobody can tell what this radioactive stuff is doing. Perhaps it's the beginning of the end."

"You make me feel very strange," said Clarence. "But why are the American bombs the dangerous ones? There are others."

"Because one always reads of the Americans exploding them. They do it under water. Holes are torn in the ocean bottom. The cold water rushes in and cools the core of the earth. Then the surface shrinks. No one can tell what will happen. It's affected the weather already."

Clarence's color grew very high and he looked dazed. He paid no attention to his broiled meat and french-fried potatoes. "I don't keep up much with science," he said. "I remember I did read somewhere that industry gives off six billion tons of carbon dioxide every year and so the earth is growing warmer because the carbon dioxide in the air is opaque to heat radiation. All that means that the glaciers won't be coming back."

"Yes, but what about Carbon Fourteen? You Americans are filling the air with Carbon Fourteen, which is very dangerous."

"I don't know about it. I am not all Americans. You are not all the English. You didn't lick the Armada, I didn't open the West. You are not Winston Churchill, I am not the Pentagon."

"I believe you are some sort of fanatic," she announced.

"And I believe you're a nasty old bag!" he said, enraged. He left the table and went to his room.

Half an hour later she knocked at his door. "I'm terribly sorry," she said. "I suppose I did go too far. But it's all right, we're friends now, aren't we? It does you so much good to be angry. It really is good." She did, now, look very friendly and happy.

"It's all right. I'm sorry too," he said.

After all, how would feuding with this Englishwoman help him with his quest? And then there were wrong ways and right ways of going about it. Gonzaga's poems should be recovered in the spirit of Gonzaga himself. Otherwise, what was the use?

Considering it all next morning, he saw that this Miss Walsh, the Englishwoman, had done him a service by baiting him. Unwittingly, she offered a test of his motive. He could not come to Spain and act badly, blindly. So he was deepened in his thought and in his purpose, and felt an increased debt to Gonzaga and to those poems.

He was in a hurry next morning to get to a bookstore and see what Gonzaga items there were in print. Impatiently he turned himself out of the comfortable bed, pulled on his underpants, dealt nervously with his cuff-buttons, washed at his little sink with the glass shelves and pointed faucets, and combed his hair and whiskers with his palms. Odors of soil and flowers came from the Retiro across the freshly watered street. The morning was clear, still and blue. He took one bite of the brick bits of toast the maid brought, sipped from the immense cup of bitter café-au-lait, and then rushed out to find a bookstore.

At Bucholz's he found only a single volume he had not seen before, a collection of letters from Gonzaga to his father. The frontispiece showed Gonzaga in his lieutenant's uniform—a small man, by Clarence's standard —sitting up straight at the keyboard of an old-fashioned piano, his large eyes opened directly into the camera. Underneath he had noted, "Whenever I am lucky enough to come upon a piano in one of these Moroccan towns, I can, after playing for ten or fifteen minutes, discover how I really feel. Otherwise I am ignorant." Clarence's face colored with satisfaction as he stooped and looked. What a man this Gonzaga was—what a personality! On the very first page was an early version of a poem he had always admired, the one that began:

HUMOR

>   Let me hear a sound
>   Truly not my own;
>   The voice of another,
>   Truly other. . . .

The book engrossed him entirely until eleven o'clock. With a sort of hungry emotion, he sat at a café table and read it from cover to cover. It was beautiful. He thanked God for sending him the Republican refugee who had given him the idea of coming to Spain.

Reluctantly he left the café and took a cab to García de Paredes Street, where Miss Ungar lived. He hated to do it, but he needed the pesetas, and it was unavoidable.

Again he was lucky. She was not at all the kind of person you would have expected a black-marketing art student to be; she was young and unusually attractive with a long, intelligent white face. Her hair was drawn tightly back over her elongated head and tied off in an arched, sparkling tail. Her eyes were extremely clear. Clarence was greatly taken with her. Even the fact that her teeth, because of the contrast with her very fair skin, were not too bright, impressed him. It proved to him that she was genuine. On a ribbon round her neck she wore a large silver medal.

"Is that a religious thing you're wearing?"

"No. Do you want to look at it?" She bent forward so that it swung free. He picked up the warm piece of silver and read: *Helene Waite Award for Historical Studies.*

"You won it?"

"Yes."

"Then why are you in this kind of business?"

"And what did you come here for?" she said.

"I need pesetas."

"And we need dollars. My fiancé and I want to buy a house."

"I see."

"Besides, it's a way of meeting a lot of people. You'd be surprised how few interesting people an American woman in Madrid can meet. I can't spend all my time in the Prado or at the Library. The embassy people are about as interesting as a plate of cold cuts. My fiancé only gets here twice a month. Are you on a holiday?"

"Sort of."

She didn't believe him. She knew he had come with a definite purpose. He could not say why, but this pleased him.

"How do you like the Granja?"

"It's all right. An Englishwoman there lammed into me last night, first about the atom bomb and then saying that I must be a fanatic. She thought I was peculiar."

"Everybody has to make it as he can," she said.

"That's exactly the way I feel about it."

He had thought that the kind of woman who became engaged to an airline pilot might look down on him. She didn't, not in the least. Soon he was wondering how that sort of man could interest her.

"If you have no other plans, why don't you come to lunch with me," he said, "and save me from that Miss Walsh?"

They went out to eat. Though the day had grown hot, she stopped in the courtyard to put on a pair of net gloves; women without gloves were considered common in Madrid. For his part Clarence thought the momentary grasp of her fingers as she worked them into the gloves was wonderful; what a lot of life she had! Her white face gave off a pleasant heat. As they walked, she told him she couldn't give him many pesetas just yet; she'd pay whatever rate was quoted in the *Tribune* on the day the money arrived. That day, Clarence reflected, would also be the day on which her pilot arrived; he had no business to be disturbed by that, and yet it did disturb him.

Near the Naval Ministry they were stopped by a procession. Priests with banners led it, and after them came a statue of the Virgin carried by four men. A group of barefooted widows followed in their mourning with black mantillas. Old women passed, carrying tapers. Most of these appeared to be old maids, and the flames made a clear additional light near each face. A band played Beethoven's Funeral March. Above the walls of the ministry trees shot their leaves; there was the same odor of flowers and soil that Clarence had smelled that morning, of graves, of summer pines. Across the square, on the car tracks, a welding arc hummed and scalded. The dazzling mouths of the horns were carried past and the fires in the daylight moved away, but it was the bare white feet of the widows treading on the dusty asphalt paving that Clarence watched, and when they were gone he said to Miss Ungar, "Wasn't that splendid? I'm glad I'm here."

His brows had risen; his face was so lively that Miss Ungar laughed and said, "You take it big. I like the way you take it. You ought to be sure to visit Toledo. Have you ever been there?"

"No."

"I go often. I'm doing a study. Come with me next time I go. I can show you lots of things there."

"There's nothing I'd like better. When do you go next?"

"Tomorrow."

He was disappointed. "Oh, I'm sorry, I can't make it tomorrow," he said. "I arrived yesterday and I'm going to be very busy for a while. Just give me a rain-check, will you? I'll hold you to this. But there is something special I came to do—you guessed it, I suppose—and I can't take the time to go anywhere now. I'm all keyed up."

"Is this mission of yours a secret?"

"In a way. There's an illegal side to it, probably. But I don't think you'd tell on me, and I'm so full of it I'm willing to talk. Have you ever heard of a poet named Gonzaga?"

"Gonzaga? I must have. But I don't think I ever read his poems."

"You should read them. He was very great, one of the most original of modern Spanish poets, and in the class of Juan Ramón Jiménez, Lorca, and Machado. I studied him at school and he means a lot to me. To understand what he did, you have to think first of modern literature as a sort of grand council considering what mankind should do next, how they should fill their mortal time, what they should feel, what they should see, where they should get their courage, how they should love, how they should be pure or great, and all the rest. This advice of literature has never done much good. But you see God doesn't rule over men as he used to, and for a long time people haven't been able to feel that life was firmly attached at both ends so that they could stand confidently in the middle and trust the place where they were. That kind of faith is missing, and for many years poets have tried to supply a substitute. Like 'the unacknowledged legislators' or 'the best is yet to be,' or Walt Whitman saying that whoever touched him could be sure he was touching a man. Some have stood up for beauty, and some have stood up for perfect proportion, and the very best have soon gotten tired of art for its own sake. Some took it as their duty to behave like brave performers who try to hold down panic during a theater fire. Very great ones have quit, like Tolstoi, who became a reformer, or like Rimbaud, who went to Abyssinia, and at the end of his life was begging of a priest, '*Montrez-moi. Montrez* . . . Show me something.' Frightening, the lives some of these geniuses led. Maybe they assumed too much responsibility. They knew that if by their poems and novels *they* were fixing values, there must be something wrong with the values. One man can't furnish them. Oh, he may try, if his inspiration is for values, but not if his inspiration is for words. If you throw the full responsibility for meaning and for the establishing of good and evil on poets, they are doomed to go down. However, the poets reflected what was happening to everyone. There are people who feel that they are responsible for *everything*. Gonzaga is free from this, and that's why I love him. Here. See what he says in some of these letters. I found this marvelous collection this morning."

His long hands shaking, he pressed flat the little book on the table of the restaurant. Miss Ungar's quiet face expressed more than intellectual interest. "Listen. He writes to his father: 'Many feel they must say it all, whereas all has been said, unsaid, resaid so many times that we are bound to feel futile unless we understand that we are merely adding our voices. Adding them when moved by the spirit. Then and then only.' Or this: 'A poem may outlive its subject—say, my poem about the girl who sang songs on the train—but the poet has no right to expect this. The poem has no greater privilege than the girl.' You see what kind of man he was?"

"Impressive—really!" she said. "I see that."

"I've come to Spain to find some of his unpublished poems. I have some money, and I've never really been able to find the thing that I wanted to do. I'm not original myself, except in some minor way. Anyhow, that's why I'm here. Lots of people call themselves leaders, healers, priests, and spokesmen for God, prophets or witnesses, but Gonzaga was a human being who spoke only as a human being; there was nothing spurious about him. He tried never to misrepresent; he wanted to see. To move you he didn't have to do anything, he merely had to be. We've made the most natural things the hardest of all. Unfortunately for us all, he was killed while still young. But he left some poems to a certain Countess del Camino, and I'm here to locate them."

"It's a grand thing. I wish you luck. I hope people will help you."

"Why shouldn't they?"

"I don't know, but don't you expect to run into trouble?"

"Do you think I ought to expect to?"

"If you want my honest opinion, yes."

"I may get the poems—why, just like that," he said. "You never can tell."

"Started, by God!" he said when he received an answer from Gúzman del Nido. The member of the Cortes invited him to dinner. All that day he was in a state, and the weather was peculiarly thick, first glaring sunshine, then explosive rains. "See what I told you," said Miss Walsh. But when Clarence went out late in the afternoon, the sky was clear and pale again and the Palm Sunday leaves braided in the ironwork of balconies were withering in the sunlight. He walked to the Puerta del Sol with its crowd of pleasure-seekers, beggars, curb-haunters, wealthy women, soldiers, cops, lottery-ticket and fountain-pen peddlers, and priests, humble door-openers, chair-menders, and musicians. At seven-thirty he boarded a streetcar, following directions; it seemed to take him to every other point of the city first. Finally, with the wisp of trolley paper still in his hand, he got off and mounted a bare stone alley at the top of which was the del Nido villa. Suddenly there was another cloudburst—*una tormenta* was what the Madrileños called it. No doorway offered cover and he was drenched. At the gate he had to wait a long while for the porter to answer his ring, perhaps five minutes in the hard rain. This would probably give comfort to the Englishwoman with her atomic theories. His nervous long eyes seemed to catch some of the slaty blue of the pouring rain-cloud; his blond beard darkened, and he pulled in his shoulders. The tall gate opened. The porter held out an umbrella in his brown fist. Clarence walked past him to the door of the house. The rain stopped when he was halfway up the path.

So he was at a disadvantage when Gúzman del Nido came forward to meet him. He walked clumsily in his sodden wool suit. It had a shameful smell, like wet dog.

"How do you do, Señor Feiler. What a shame about the rain. It has ruined your suit but it gives your face a fine color."

They shook hands, and it came over Clarence with a thrill as he looked at the high-bridged nose and dark, fine-textured skin of del Nido that he was in touch with Gonzaga himself—this round-shouldered man in his linen suit, bowing his sloping head, smiling with sharp teeth, with his hairless hand and big-boned wrist and his awkward fanny, he had been Gonzaga's friend and belonged within the legend. Clarence at once sensed that he would make him look foolish if he could, through the irony of his very complete manners. He also realized that del Nido was the sort of person who cut everyone down to size, Gonzaga included; precisely the sort of man to whom Gonzaga had written: *"Go away! You have no holy ones."*

"The letter I sent you—" Clarence managed to begin. They were hurrying toward the dining room; other guests were waiting.

"We can discuss it later."

"I understand you gave certain poems to the Countess del Camino," he said.

But del Nido was speaking with another guest. The candles were lit and the company sat down.

Clarence had no appetite.

He was sitting between an Italian Monsignore and an Egyptian lady who had lived in New York and spoke a very slangy English. There was a German gentleman, too, who headed some insurance company; he sat between Señora del Nido and her daughter. From his end of the table, del Nido with his narrow sleek head and his forward-curved teeth shining with valuable crowns, dominated the conversation. About his eyes the skin was twisted in curious laugh-wrinkles. Impressed, appalled, too, Clarence asked himself again and again how Gonzaga could have trusted such a person. A maker of witticisms, as Pascal had said, a bad character.

When these words of Pascal came into his head, Clarence turned to the Monsignore as a man to whom this might make sense. But the Monsignore was interested mostly in stamp-collecting. Clarence was not, so the Monsignore had nothing further to say to him. He was a gloomy, fleshy man whose hair grew strongly and low over the single deep wrinkle of his forehead.

Gúzman del Nido kept on talking. He talked about modern painting, about mystery stories, about old Russia, about the movies, about Nietzsche. Dreamy-looking, the daughter seemed not to listen; his wife expanded some of his remarks. The daughter stared with close-set eyes into the candle flames. The Egyptian lady was amused by the strong smell of Clarence's rain-shrinking clothes. She made a remark about wet wool. He was grateful for the absence of electric lights.

"An American was arrested in Córdoba," said Gúzman del Nido. "He stole the hat of a *Guardia Civil* for a souvenir."

"Isn't that unusual!"

"He'll find the jail smaller than the jails at home. I hope you won't mind if I tell a story about Americans and the size of things in Spain."

"Why should I mind?" said Clarence.

"Splendid. Well, there was an American whose Spanish host could not impress him. Everything was larger in America. The skyscrapers were bigger than the palaces. The cars were bigger. The cats were bigger. At last his host placed a lobster between his sheets and when the horrified American saw it his host said, 'This is one of our bedbugs. I don't think you can beat that.'"

For some reason this fetched Clarence more than it did the others. He uttered a bark of laughter that made the candlelights bend and flutter.

"Perhaps you'll tell us an American story," said del Nido.

Clarence thought. "Well, here's one," he said. "Two dogs meet in the street. Old friends. One says, 'Hello.' The other answers, 'Cock-a-doodle-do!' 'What does that mean? What's this cock-a-doodle-do stuff?' 'Oh,' says he, 'I've been studying foreign languages.'"

Dead silence. No one laughed. The Egyptian lady said, "I'm afraid you laid an egg." Clarence was angry.

"Is this story told in English or in American?" del Nido asked.

That started a discussion. Was American really a sort of English? Was it a language? No one seemed sure, and Clarence at last said, "I don't know whether or not it is a language, but there is *something* spoken. I've seen people cry in it and so forth, just as elsewhere."

"We deserved that," said del Nido. "It's true, we're not fair to Americans. In reality the only true Europeans left are Americans."

"How so?"

HUMOR

"The Europeans themselves do not have the peace of mind to appreciate what's best. Life is too hard for us, society too unstable."

Clarence realized that he was being shafted; del Nido was satirizing his quest; he undoubtedly meant that Clarence could not comprehend Gonzaga's poems. An ugly hatred for del Nido grew and knotted in his breast. He wanted to hit him, to strangle him, to trample him, to pick him up and hurl him at the wall. Luckily del Nido was called to the phone, and Clarence stared out his rage at the empty place, the napkin, the silver, the crest of the chair. Only Señorita del Nido seemed aware that he was offended.

Once more Clarence told himself that there was a wrong way to go about obtaining the poems, a way contrary to their spirit. That did much to calm him. He managed to get down a few spoonfuls of ice cream and mastered himself.

"Why are you so interested in Gonzaga?" said del Nido to him later in the garden, under the date palms with their remote leaves.

"I studied Spanish literature in college and became a Gonzagian."

"Wasn't that rather strange, though? You must forgive me, but I see my poor old friend Gonzaga, who was Spanish of the Spanish, in that terrible uniform we used to wear, and our hands and faces bruised and baked and chapped by the desert sun, and I ask myself why he should have had an effect . . ."

"I don't know why. I'd like to understand it myself; but the fact that he did is what you start with."

"I have made an interesting observation about poets and their lives. Some are better in real life than in their work. You read bitter poems and then you find the poet is personally very happy and good-tempered. Some are worse in their personality than you would guess from their work. They are luckier, in a way, because they have a chance to correct their faults and improve themselves. Best of all are the ones who are exactly the same inside and out, in the spoken word and the written. To be what you seem to be is the objective of true culture. Gonzaga was of the second type."

"Was he?" It occurred to Clarence that del Nido was trying to make himself more interesting to him than Gonzaga could be, to push Gonzaga out.

"I think I can tell you one reason why Gonzaga appeals to me," said Clarence. "He got away from solving *his* own problem. I often feel this way about it: a poem is great because it is absolutely necessary. Before it came silence. After it comes more silence. It begins when it must and ends when it must, and therefore it's not personal. It's 'the sound truly not my own.'" Now he was proving to del Nido that he *could* comprehend; at the same time he knew that he was throwing away his effort.

THE GONZAGA MANUSCRIPTS

Gúzman del Nido was fundamentally indifferent. Indifferent, indifferent, indifferent! He fundamentally did not care. What can you do with people who don't fundamentally care! "But you know why I came to you. I want to know what became of Gonzaga's last poems. What were they like?"

"They were superb love poems. But I don't know where they are now. They were dedicated to the Countess del Camino and I was supposed to hand them on to her. Which I did."

"There aren't any copies?" said Clarence, trembling as del Nido spoke of the poems.

"No. They were for the countess."

"Of course. But they were also for everyone else."

"There's plenty of poetry already, for everyone. Homer, Dante, Calderón, Shakespeare. Have you noticed how much difference it makes?"

"It should make a difference. Besides, Calderón wasn't your friend. But Gonzaga was. Where's the countess now? The poor woman is dead, isn't she? And what happened to those poems? Where do you think the poems can be?"

"I don't know. She had a secretary named Polvo, a fine old man. A few years ago he died, too. The old man's nephews live in Alcalá de Henares. Where Cervantes was born, you know. They're in the civil service, and they're very decent people, I hear."

"You never even asked them what happened to your friend's poems?" cried Clarence, astonished. "Didn't you want to find them?"

"I thought eventually I'd try to trace them. I'm sure the countess would have taken good care of her poems."

This was where the discussion stopped, and Clarence was just as glad that it couldn't continue; he sensed that Gúzman del Nido would have liked to give him the dirt on Gonzaga—revelations involving women, drunkenness and dope-taking, bribery, gonorrhea, or even murder. Gonzaga had escaped into the army; that was notorious. But Clarence didn't want to hear del Nido's reminiscences.

It's natural to suppose, because a man is great, that the people around him must have known how to respond to greatness, but when those people turn out to be no better than Gúzman del Nido you wonder what response greatness really needs.

This was what Clarence was saying to Miss Ungar several days later.

"He's glad he doesn't have the poems," said Miss Ungar. "If he had them he'd feel obliged to do something about them, and he's afraid of that because of his official position."

"That's right. Exactly," said Clarence. "But he did me one favor anyway. He put me on to the countess's secretary's nephews. I've written them and they've invited me to Alcalá de Henares. They didn't mention the poems but maybe they were just being discreet. I'd better start being more discreet myself. There's something unpleasant going on, lately."

"What is it?"

"I think the police have an eye on me."

"Oh, come!"

"I do. I'm serious. My room was searched yesterday. I know it was. My landlady didn't answer one way or another when I asked her. She didn't even bother."

"It's too peculiar for anything," Miss Ungar said, laughing in amazement. "But why should they search? What for?"

"I suppose I just inspire suspicion. And then I made a mistake with my landlady the day after my visit to del Nido. She's a very patriotic character. She has a retired general in the pension, too. Well, she was talking to me the other morning and among other things she told me how healthy she was, strong as a rock—*una roca*—a sort of Gibraltar. And like a dumbbell I said, without even thinking, '*Gibraltar Español!*' That was an awful boner."

"Why?"

"During the war, you see, when the British were taking such a pounding there was a great agitation for the return of Gibraltar to Spain. The slogan was *Gibraltar Español!* Of course they don't like to be reminded that they were dying for the British to get it good and hot from Germany. Well, she probably thinks I'm a political secret somebody. And she was just plain offended."

"But what difference does it really make, as long as you don't do anything illegal?"

"When you're watched closely you're bound sooner or later to do *something*," he said.

He went out to Alcalá on a Sunday afternoon and met the two nephews of Don Francisco Polvo and their wives and daughters.

They proved to be a family of laughers. They laughed when they spoke and when you answered. You saw nothing in the town but sleepy walls, and parched trees and stones. The brothers were squat, sandy-haired, broad-bellied men.

"We're having tea in the garden," said Don Luis Polvo. He was called "the Englishman" by the others because he had lived in London for several months twenty years ago; they addressed him as "My Lord," and he obliged them by acting like an *Inglés*. He even owned a scotch terrier named *Duglas*. The family cried to him, "Now's your chance to speak English, Luis. Speak to him!"

"Jolly country, eh?" Luis said. That was about all he could manage.

"Very."

"More, more!"

"Charing Cross."

"Go on, Luis, say more."

"Piccadilly. And that's all I can remember."

The tea was served. Clarence drank and sweltered. Lizards raced in the knotty grapevines and by the well. . . . The wives were embroidering. The laughing daughters were conversing in French, obviously about Clarence. Nobody appeared to believe what he said. Lanky and pained he sat in what looked to be a suit made of burlap, with his tea. Instead of a saucer, he felt as though he were holding on to the rim of Saturn.

After tea they showed him through the house. It was huge, old, bare, thick-walled and chill, and it was filled with the portraits and the clothing of ancestors—weapons, breastplates, helmets, daggers, guns. In one room where the picture of a general in the Napoleonic Wars was hung, a fun-making mood seized the brothers. They tried on plumed hats, then sabers, and finally full uniforms. Wearing spurs, medals, musty gloves, they went running back to the terrace where the women sat. Don Luis dragged a sword, his seat hung down and the cocked hat sagged broken, opening in the middle on his sandy baldness. With a Napoleonic musket, full of self-mockery, he performed the manual-at-arms to uproarious laughter. Clarence laughed, too, his cheeks creased; he couldn't explain however why his heart was growing heavier by the minute.

Don Luis aimed the musket and shouted, *"La bomba atómica! Poum!"*

The hit he scored with this was enormous. The women shrieked, swiveling their fans, and his brother fell on his behind in the sanded path, weeping with laughter. The terrier *Duglas* leaped into Don Luis's face, fiercely excited.

Don Luis threw a stick and cried, "Fetch, fetch, *Duglas! La bomba atómica! La bomba atómica!"*

The blood stormed Clarence's head so furiously he heard the strange noise of it. This was another assault on him. Oh! he thought frantically, the things he had to bear! The punishment he had to take trying to salvage those poems!

As if in the distance, the voice of Don Luis cried, "Hiroshima! Nagasaki! Bikini! Good show!" He flung the stick and the dog bounded on taut legs, little *Duglas,* from the diminished figure of his master and back—the tiny white and brown animal, while laughter incessantly pierced the dry air of the garden.

It was not a decent joke, even though Don Luis in that split hat and the withered coat was mocking the dead military grandeur of his own country. That didn't even the score. The hideous stun of the bomb and

HUMOR

its unbearable, death-brilliant mushroom cloud filled Clarence's brain. This was not right.

He managed to stop Don Luis. He approached him, laid a hand on the musket, and asked to speak with him privately. It made the others laugh. The ladies started to murmur about him. An older woman said, "*Es gracioso*"; the girls seemed to disagree. He heard one of them answer, "*Non, il n'est pas gentil.*" Proudly polite, Clarence faced it out. "Damn their damn tea!" he said to himself. His shirt was sticking to his back.

"We did not inherit my uncle's papers," said Don Luis. "Enough, *Duglas!*" He threw the stick down the well. "My brother and I inherited this old house and other land but if there were papers they probably went to my cousin Pedro Alvarez-Polvo who lives in Segovia. He's a very interesting fellow. He works for the *Banco Español* but is a cultivated person. The countess had no family. She was fond of my uncle. My uncle was extremely fond of Alvarez-Polvo. They shared the same interests."

"Did your uncle ever speak of Gonzaga?"

"I don't recall. The countess had a large number of artistic admirers. This Gonzaga interests you very much, doesn't he?"

"Yes. Why shouldn't I be interested in him? You may some day be interested in an American poet."

"*I?* No!" Don Luis laughed, but he was startled.

What people! Damn these dirty laughers! Clarence waited until Don Luis's shocked and latterly somewhat guilty laughter ended, and his broad yap, with spacious teeth, closed—his lips shook with resistance to closing, and finally remained closed.

"Do you think your cousin Alvarez-Polvo would know . . ."

"He would know a lot," said Don Luis, composed. "My uncle confided in him. *He* can tell you something definite, you can count on him. I'll give you a letter of introduction to him."

"If it's not too much trouble."

"No, no, the pleasure is mine." Don Luis was all courtesy.

After returning to Madrid on the bus through the baking plain of Castile, Clarence phoned Miss Ungar. He wanted her sympathy and comfort. But she didn't invite him to come over. She said, "I can give you the pesetas tomorrow." That was her tactful way of informing him that the pilot had landed, and he thought she sounded regretful. Perhaps she was not really in love with her fiancé. Clarence now had the impression that the black-marketing was not her idea but the pilot's. It embarrassed her, but she was too loyal to admit it to him.

"I'll come by later in the week. There's no hurry," he said. "I'm busy anyway."

It would hurt him to do it, but he'd cash a check at the American Express tomorrow at the preposterous legal rate of exchange.

Disappointed, Clarence hung up. *He* should have a woman like that. It passed dimly over his mind that a live woman would make a better quest than a dead poet. But the poet was already *there*; the woman not. He sent a letter to Alvarez-Polvo, washed all over, and lay reading Gonzaga by a buzzing light under the canopy of his bed.

He arrived in Segovia early one Sunday morning. It was filled with sunlight, the clouds were silk-white in the mountain air. Their shadows wandered over the slopes of the bare sierra like creatures that crept and warmed themselves on the soil and rock. All over the old valley were convents, hermitages, churches, towers, the graves of San Juan and other mystical saints. At the highest point of Segovia was the Alcázar of Isabella the Catholic. And passing over the town with its many knobby granite curves that divided the sky was the aqueduct, this noble Roman remnant, as bushy as old men's ears. Clarence stood at the window of his hotel and looked at this conjured rise of stones that bridged the streets. It got him, all of it—the ancient mountain slopes worn as if by the struggles of Jacob with the angel, the spires, the dry glistening of the atmosphere, the hermit places in green hideaways, the sheep bells' clunk, the cistern water dropping, while beams came as straight as harpwires from the sun. All of this, like a mild weight, seemed to press on him; it opened him up. He felt his breath creep within him like a tiny pet animal.

He went down through the courtyard. There the cistern of fat stone held green water, full of bottom-radiations from the golden brass of the faucets. Framed above it in an archway were ladies' hair styles of twenty years ago—a brilliantine advertisement. Ten or so beautiful señoritas with bangs, singles, and windswept bobs smiled like various priestesses of love. Therefore Clarence had the idea that this cistern was the Fountain of Youth. And also that it was something Arcadian. He said, " 'Ye glorious nymphs!' " and burst out laughing. He felt happy—magnificent! The sun poured over his head and embraced his back hotly.

Smiling, he rambled up and down the streets. He went to the Alcázar. Soldiers in German helmets were on guard. He went to the cathedral. It was ancient but the stones looked brand-new. After lunch he sat at the café in front of the aqueduct waiting for Alvarez-Polvo. On the wide sloping sidewalk there were hundreds of folding chairs, empty, the paint blazed off them and the wood emerging as gray as silverfish. The long low windows were open, so that inside and outside mingled their air, the yellow and the sombre, the bar brown and the sky clear blue. A gypsy woman came out and gave Clarence the eye. She was an entertainer, but whether a real gypsy or not was conjectural. In the phrase he had heard, some of these girls were *Gitanas de miedo*, or strictly from hunger. But he sat and studied the aqueduct, trying to imagine what sort of machinery they could have used to raise the stones.

A black hearse with mourners who trod after it slowly, and with all the plumes, and carvings of angels and death-grimacers, went through the main arch to the cemetery. After ten minutes it came galloping back with furious lashing of the horses, the silk-hatted coachman standing, yacking at them. Only a little later the same hearse returned with another procession of mourners who supported one another, weeping aloud, grief pushing on their backs. Through the arch again. And once more the hearse came flying back. With a sudden tightness of the guts Clarence thought, Why all these burials at once? Was this a plague? He looked at the frothy edge of his glass with horror.

But Alvarez-Polvo set his mind at rest. He said, "The hearse was broken all week. It has just been repaired."

He was a strange-looking man. His face seemed to have been worked by three or four diseases and then abandoned. His nose swelled out and shrunk his eyes. He had a huge mouth, like his cousin Don Luis. He wore a beret, and a yellow silk sash was wound around his belly. Clarence often had noticed that short men with big bellies sometimes held their arms ready for defense as they walked, but at heart expected defeat. Alvarez-Polvo, too, had that posture. However, his brown, mottled, creased, sunlit face with kinky hair escaping from the beret seemed to declare that he had a soul like a drum. If you struck, you wouldn't injure him. You'd hear a sound.

"You know what I've come for?" said Clarence.

"Yes, I do know. But let's not start talking business right away. You've never been in Segovia before, I assume, and you must let me be hospitable. I'm a proud Segoviano—proud of this ancient, beautiful city, and it would give me pleasure to show you the principal places."

At the words "talking business" Clarence's heart rose a notch. Was it only a matter of settling the price? Then he had the poems! Something in Clarence flapped with eager joy, like a flag in the wind.

"By all means. For a while. It is beautiful. Never in my life have I seen anything so gorgeous as Segovia."

Alvarez-Polvo took his arm.

"With me you will not only see, you will understand. I have made a study of it. I'm a lover of such things. I seldom have an opportunity to express it. Wherever I take my wife, she is interested only in *novelas morbosas*. At Versailles she sat and read Ellery Queen. In Paris, the same.

In Rome, the same. If she lives to the end of time, she will never run out of *novelas morbosas."*

From this remark, without notice, he took a deep plunge into the subject of women, and he carried Clarence with him. Women, women women! All the types of Spanish beauty. The Granadinas, the Malagueñas, the Castellanas, the Cataluñas. And then the Germans, the Greeks, the French, the Swedes! He tightened his hold on Clarence and pulled him close as he boasted and complained and catalogued and confessed. He was ruined! They had taken his money, his health, his time, his years, his life, women had—innocent, mindless, beautiful, ravaging, insidious, malevolent, chestnut, blond, red, black. . . . Clarence felt hemmed in by women's faces, and by women's bodies.

"I suppose you'd call this a Romanesque church, wouldn't you?" Clarence said, stopping.

"Of course it is," said Alvarez-Polvo. "Just notice how the Renaissance building next to it was designed to harmonize with it."

Clarence was looking at the pillars and their blunted faces of humorous, devil-beast humanities, the stone birds, demon lollers, apostles. Two men carried by a spring and mattress in a pushcart. They looked like the kings of Shinar and Elam defeated by Abraham.

"Come, have a glass of wine," said Alvarez-Polvo. "I'm not allowed to drink since my operation, but you must have something."

When could they begin to talk about the poems? Clarence was impatient. Gonzaga's poems would mean little if anything to a man like this, but in spite of his endless gallant bunk and his swagger and his complaints about having broken his springs in the service of love and beauty, he was probably a very cunning old fuff. He wanted to stall Clarence and find out what the poems were worth to him. And so Clarence gazed, or blinked, straight ahead, and kept a tight grip on his feelings.

In the *bodega* were huge barrels, copper fittings, innumerable bottles duplicated in the purple mirror, platters of *mariscos,* crawfish bugging their eyes on stalks, their feelers cooked into various last shapes. From the middle of the floor rose a narrow spiral staircase. It mounted—who-knew-where? Clarence tried to see but couldn't. A little torn-frocked beggar child came selling lottery tickets. The old chaser petted her; she wheedled; she took his small hand and laid her cheek to it. Still talking, he felt her hair. He stroked his fill and sent her away with a coin.

Clarence drank down the sweet, yellow Malaga.

"Now," said Alvarez-Polvo, "I will show you a church few visitors ever see."

They descended to the lower part of town, down littered stairways of stone, by cavelike homes and a lot where runty boys were passing a football with their heads, and dribbling and hooking it with their boots.

"Here," Alvarez-Polvo said. "This wall is of the tenth century and this one of the seventeenth."

The air inside the church was dark, thick as ointment. Hollows of dark red and dark blue and heavy yellow slowly took shape, and Clarence began to see the altar, the columns.

Alvarez-Polvo was silent. The two men were standing before a harshly crowned Christ. The figure was gored deeply in the side, rust-blooded. The head-cover of thorns was too wide and heavy to be borne. As he confronted it, Clarence felt that it threatened to scratch the life out of him, to scratch him to the heart.

"The matter that interests us both . . ." Alvarez-Polvo then said.

"Yes, yes, let's go somewhere and have a talk about it. You got the poems among your uncle's papers. Do you have them here in Segovia?"

"Poems?" said Alvarez-Polvo, turning the dark and ruined face from the aisle. "That's a strange word to use for them."

"Do you mean they're not in that form? What are they, then? What are they written in?"

"Why, the usual legal language. According to law."

"I don't understand."

"Neither do I. But I can show you what I'm talking about. Here. I have one with me. I brought it along." He drew a document from his pocket.

Clarence held it, trembling. It was heavy, glossy and heavy. He felt an embossed surface. Yes, there was a seal on it. What had the countess done with the poems? This paper was emblazoned with a gilt star. He sought light and read, within an elaborate border of wavy green, *Compañia de Minas, S.A.*

"Is this— It can't be. You've given me the wrong thing." His heart was racing. "Look in your pocket again."

"The wrong thing?"

"It looks like shares of stock."

"Then it isn't the wrong thing. It's what it's supposed to be, mining stock. Isn't that what you're interested in?"

"Of course not! Certainly not! What kind of mine?"

"It's a pitchblende mine in Morocco, that's what it is."

"What in the name of anything do I want with pitchblende!" Clarence shouted.

"What any sensible man would want. To sell it. Pitchblende has uranium in it. Uranium is used in atom bombs."

Oh, dear God!

"*Claro. Para la bomba atómica.*"

"What have I to do with atom bombs? What do I care about atom bombs! To hell with atom bombs!" Clarence cried out, furious.

"I understand you were a financier."

"Me? Do I look like one?"

"Yes, of course you do. More English than American, I thought. But a financier. Aren't you?"

"I am not. I came about the poems of Gonzaga, the poems owned by the Countess del Camino. Love poems dedicated to her by the poet Manuel Gonzaga."

"Manuel? The soldier? The little fellow? The one that was her lover in nineteen-twenty-eight? He was killed in Morocco."

"Yes, yes! What did your uncle do with the poems?"

"Oh, that's what you were talking about. Why, my uncle did nothing with them. The countess did, herself. She had them buried with her. She took them to the grave."

"Buried! With her, you say! And no copies?"

"I doubt it. My uncle had instructions from her, and he was very loyal. He lived by loyalty. My uncle—"

"Oh, damn! Oh, damn it! And didn't he leave you anything in that collection of papers that has to do with Gonzaga? No journals, no letters that mention Gonzaga? Nothing?"

"He left me these shares in the mine. They're valuable. Not yet, but they will be if I can get capital. But you can't raise money in Spain. Spanish capital is cowardly, ignorant of science. It is still in the Counter-Reformation. Let me show you the location of this mine." He opened a map and began to explain the geography of the Atlas Mountains.

Clarence walked out on him—ran, rather than walked. He had to get out of Segovia. Quickly. Immediately. Panting, enraged, choking, he clambered from the lower town.

As soon as he entered his room at the hotel he knew that his valise had been searched. Storming, he slammed it shut and dragged it down the stairs, past the cistern, and into the lobby.

He called in a shout to the manager, "Why must the police come and turn my things upside down?"

White-faced and stern, the manager said, "You must be mistaken, señor."

"I am not mistaken. Why must the police bother foreign visitors?"

A man rose angrily from a chair in the lobby. He wore an old suit with a mourning band on the arm.

"These Englismen!" he said with fury. "They don't know what hospitality is. They come here and enjoy themselves, and criticize our country, and complain about police. What hypocrisy! There are more police in England. The whole world knows you have a huge jail in Liverpool, filled with Masons. Five thousand Masons are *encarcelados* in Liverpool alone."

Clarence couldn't reply. He stared. Then he paid his bill and left. All the way to Madrid he sat numb and motionless in his second-class seat.

As the train left the mountains, the heavens seemed to split; a rain began to fall, heavy and sudden, boiling on the wide plain.

He knew what to expect from that redheaded Miss Walsh at dinner.

THE IRON FIST OF OLIGARCHY

Mark Harris

You will never again hear of anything so tragic as the career of Sy Appleman. However, let me begin with Mrs. Governour. One must begin somewhere.

Mrs. Governour was a tall, thin, insane widow of fifty-five living in Richie, Illinois, with a Toy Manchester Terrier bitch named Champion Princess Gloriosa, whose bloodlines were beyond reproach. She was fourteen years old (the human equivalent of ninety-eight), and so it was natural that one morning she died, dragging her little rug into the livingroom, curling herself up, and expiring. "Gloriosa!" screamed Mrs. Governour. "What are you doing here, you naughty child? Bad, bad girl, get back where you belong," beating the dog with a supple maple twig.

Of course the dog refused to stir. The veterinarian was summoned, one Logan McLean, a brother, as it happened, of Walter McLean, owner of Radio Station KRIC in Richie, for whom Sy Appleman worked for two years. "There's not too much sense beating her," said the veterinarian, "the animal's dead. I'll tell you what I'll do, I'll just dispose of the remains."

Mrs. Governour had other plans, however, for the repose of her dog. "You can't possibly think," she said, "that I'm just going to throw Gloriosa down a hole in the ground." Therefore, with the veterinarian's assistance, she groomed the dead dog, dressed it in a plaid vest, tied blue ribbons to its collar, and drove with this burden a hundred miles to St. Louis. When Logan McLean presented her with a bill for five dollars she refused to pay it, accusing him of having murdered her dog. Eleven months later he brought suit against her in Richie Municipal Court, introducing witnesses to prove that he could have had no possible motive for murder, and after a trial of a day and a half he was awarded his fee and legal costs. It was a struggle.

In St. Louis she witnessed the interment of her dog in a vault sold to her by Laughter In The Glen, Inc., which promised her that fresh lilies of the valley would be placed regularly before the dog's resting-place, and assured her that the vault was immune to flood, fire, or other natural disaster. Service was read by an officer of Laughter In The Glen, choosing as his text *Genesis* VIII, 17, "Bring forth with thee every living thing that is with thee, of all flesh, both of fowl, and of cattle. . . ." Then he presented her with a bill for $600, which she immediately paid.

Now, Sy Appleman, whose true name was not Seymour, as you might suspect, but Samuel, or Sam, was at that time the all-round man, or boy, at Radio Station KRIC in Richie. He had been born in New York City, where he had received a degree in Dramatic Art, son of Harry Appleman, a Radio producer of note in the heyday of Radio, later transferring his talents to Television, where he is highly thought of throughout the industry as a man of dynamic magnetism. The job in Richie was Sy's first. He had accepted it more or less to please his father, who had gone to some effort to make the connection.

Radio, in Harry Appleman's opinion, was then on the threshold of becoming an Art form, forced into an agonizing reappraisal of itself in view of the threat of Televison, and therefore really only in its infancy, screaming for young men of talent and ingenuity to revolutionize the industry, exactly the medium for Sy's fine voice, his expressiveness, his clean-cut nature, and his co-operative spirit. In short, a challenge.

Of course Richie was terribly hot, and Sy never took the heat well, gasping and suffocating at seventy-five degrees or over, but he loved every minute of the job up to a point. Everything that a voice could do in small Radio was his to do, his finger was on the pulse of the town. He was always courteous, always anxious to promote good public relations, meanwhile forming a sound sense of community life, and learning Radio from every conceivable point of view. What enthusiasm he had!

And what a small salary! He was paid $32.50 a week, raised to $35 in his second year, which he budgeted very carefully in order not to depend upon his father. If his father sent him a check he sent it back. He rented a small room in the home of people named Klein, owners of a jewelry store in Richie. They had a daughter, Teddy, an intelligent girl who wore no make-up and read magazines containing articles entitled "The Iron Fist of Oligarchy." At first, Sy's tastes at this young stage of life directed him toward girls less intelligent but more glamorous than Teddy, with the result that he formed friendships with several, although never concurrently, skating on the lake in the winter, or walking arm in arm about the town late at night, Sy, as they walked, pointing out the important houses of the town and describing their residents' political or commercial affiliations. He was on speaking terms with every important person of the place since, in addition to reading local news on KRIC, he gathered it. He also read national and international news torn from the teletype, enunciating well, and allocating to each item proper feeling and respect, never reading with cynicism what ought to have been read with gravity, and clearly differentiating in tone between commercial announcements, on the one hand, and items of importance to mankind. He was a true humanitarian, God bless him, we need more of his type. He made every effort to pronounce the names of foreign persons and places in a manner even a native would have approved, and to distinguish between fact and hearsay, charge and conviction, or wish and actuality.

In the summer, his preferred destination was the slaughterhouse, which was refrigerated, although I cannot doubt, as he has told me, that most of the girls of Richie disliked it, since it smelled bad and was splattered with blood. He often went there with Teddy Klein, who did not object, and who even found in a slaughterhouse rich material for serious conversation. In the slaughterhouse they talked about man's relationship to animals, of the ethics of killing them, and of the wonders and dangers of man's technological control of his environment, thoughts which you and I had when we were younger.

Well, why should I keep you in suspense? Just before he eventually left Richie they were married, and in time had four children, the first a boy, named Richie, simply Richie, not Richard, as you might suspect. Perhaps he has a middle name, poor little darling, but if so I was never informed of it. Thus you can see that he retained a favorable memory of Richie, Illinois, where his pulse had been on everything, and where his work had been full of variety, as it cannot help but be for an all-round man in small Radio. She was not beautiful, but they were devoted. Afterward, when his pockets spilled over with nothing but money, and he could have picked and chosen among varieties, or his father at the drop of a hint could have boosted a girl to national prominence in a single night, he took no liberties. His agent in Hollywood, Peggy Flanagan, not only thought the world of him but was eleven or twelve times as beautiful as the former Teddy Klein, but Sy never so much as pecked her forehead. The three other children were born on the Coast, where Sy and his growing family lived in a splendid home between Hollywood and Topanga, thoroughly air-conditioned, and blessed with a swimming pool shaped like a star, for the house had been built by the late Star Weber, hero of more than two hundred Westerns, a tragic story, but not this one. Suffice it to say he returned home one night, announced to his widow that he had been first on the draw at the pass two hundred times too often, drained the pool, leaped onto the divingboard, and jack-knifed headfirst in.

Additionally, in Richie, Illinois, Sy was soon conducting his own morning show, which unquestionably revolutionized Radio, at least in Richie. It was a work of Art, carefully planned, although not without its moments of sheer inspiration, as I shall relate. It was a *balanced* show. In music, for example, he reduced the quantity of pop and increased the quantity of classical, most of the latter from his own store of records. One portion of his program he called Human Take All, absolutely unrehearsed, unrecorded, untaped, and unnetworked, during which he interviewed a scholar or artist if by chance such a person appeared in the vicinity of Richie. If no scholar or artist were available, he invited to the studio someone entirely undistinguished, as, for example, a slaughterhouse worker, an electrical repairman, a policeman, a barber, a grocery clerk, a schoolteacher, inquiring into the details of their jobs, what hours they kept, what their principal problems were, what their secret ambitions were, whether they were bored, and so forth. I have heard recordings of these shows, and you may believe me they were every inch original. Moreover, there were no complaints.

One day, after delivering a commercial announcement on behalf of the Ralston Purina Company of St. Louis, advocating the use of Purina Dog Chow For Eager Eaters, and Purina Kibbled Meal For High Energy Requirements, Sy thought, in a moment of sheer inspiration, to embellish his statements with a few barks such as a happy and appreciative dog might make after a meal of such variety. Mr. Walter McLean, owner of KRIC, looked up from his desk and smiled at Sy, for he was always proud of the young man's resourcefulness, and a few moments later the telephone rang.

Sy allowed it to ring several times. Little did he know that this was the ring of Fate. Had he known he would have snapped up the telephone in a twinkling, for he was much like all of us, anxious to know his Fate, good or bad, sitting and waiting for *the* telephone call. One receives many, until sometimes life is nothing but a ringing, and one considers unlisting his number. On the other hand, one keeps his number listed, never daring to disconnect himself from Fate. It was Mrs. Governour, demanding to know whose Toy Manchester Terrier she had just heard.

"It wasn't actually a Toy Manchester Terrier," Sy said politely.

"You're being impertinent, young man," she said, "because I guess I ought to know her when I hear her."

"It wasn't a her," Sy said, "it was a him."

"You're not being truthful," she said.

HUMOR

"Just a minute," said Sy, "I'll look." He laughed. (Laughing at Fate, what an irony!) He whispered to Mr. McLean the substance of Mrs. Governour's remarks. "By golly," said Sy back into the phone, "you're right, ma'am, and many thanks for calling."

"I want to see her," said Mrs. Governour.

"But you really can't," said Sy. "Frankly, ma'am, it was only a sound, to be truthful."

"Has she been altered?" Mrs. Governour inquired.

"Hang up and tell her to go to hell," said Mr. McLean, but this was not a thing Sy Appleman could do. If anything, he was a humanitarian, and therefore, in response to Mrs. Governour's request, he called the dog to the telephone, saying, "Here, doggie, speak to the nice lady," which the dog did, barking several times into the phone until Mrs. Governour at last permitted Sy to leave the line. When he met Teddy Klein for lunch that day she said "Woof." (First laughing at Fate, and now saying "Woof" to Fate, irony piled on irony!)

Had Mrs. Governour been satisfied with one single telephone conversation, things might have been different, but she saw no inconvenience to anyone in calling every day to speak to the dog, so that what first was humorous soon became an annoyance, almost in the nature of a pain in the ass, even to a humanitarian like Sy Appleman. Once she came to the studio in the hope of seeing the dog. Sy told her it had died in the night, but this was a possibility she was unable to grasp. Therefore he said the dog had gone away on a two-week vacation. She described to him the murder of the dog by Mr. Logan McLean, and the funeral in St. Louis, presented him with a copy of the script of the sermon, and she went home again, but in two weeks her calls were resumed, and Sy was able to tell her, with perfect truth, that *he* was leaving, not for two weeks but forever.

"And tell her you're taking your dog with you," said Mr. McLean.

"And taking my dog with me," said Sy. "But, ma'am, I have a plan if you have a phonograph. Mr. McLean says if you'll pay for the materials I can make you a little recording of the dog barking, and you can play it on your phonograph night and day."

"Will it be expensive?" asked Mrs. Governour.

"About a dollar," said Sy.

It was agreed. Sy made the record, beginning with a few moments of yipping and howling in his own voice, followed by a statement, "Here, doggie, here's your food," and the dog barked "Thank you," and later "Good morning" and "'Good night" and "Where's my leash?" and whatnot until Sy had cut a record of decent size, which he labeled MANCHESTER TOY TERRIER (*with Sy Appleman*).

THE IRON FIST OF OLIGARCHY

That record will someday be a collector's item. More than that. It is not alone the record of a man imitating a dog, but a tragic poem illustrating the stage of civilization in the calendar year 1950. No doubt things have changed in the decade since, but in 1950, in Richie, Illinois, a young man of some talent received from his unseen audience only one request—to speak not in his own voice but in the voice of a dog. This is demeaning to a man. Sy Appleman had many intelligent things to say in his own voice, ideas he had formed on life from alert living, ideas on Dramatic Art from his studies at college, ideas on love from loving Teddy Klein, ideas on international news, ideas on budgeting for the simple life, ideas on heat, ideas on enunciation and pronunciation, even ideas on dogs. Soon after he reached New York the record was sent on to him by Mr. Walter McLean, since Mrs. Governour refused to pay the dollar charge.

It goes without saying, the experiences of Sy and Teddy Appleman in New York were nothing short of perfect bliss. Here were a healthy and energetic young man and his beautiful, or intelligent bride, free of all the restraints of childhood, and not yet apprehensive of the encroachments of age, surrounded by amiable friends old and new, and by cultural benefits of every sort, living on love, as the saying goes. From a financial point of view they could not be envied, but New York is a Paradise of open-air amusements, and the boulevards and parks are free.

Their apartment was not spacious. To be perfectly straightforward with you, it consisted of only a single room in a house owned by the University, although the rent was less reasonable than you might expect from a non-profit institution. When I first visited them they had no furniture except a crib for Richie, soon to be born, although they had also received, from a friend in the rug business, a rug. Sy's father, seeing their condition, sent them a bed and chairs, and they slept on the bed, I suppose, but piled the chairs in the corner until one night, after a furious argument with his father, Sy agreed to unpile them and distribute them about the room, although I never saw him actually sit on one. There is no questioning the fact that Harry Appleman in argument is a forbidding man. When angered, or even overcome by mere friendly enthusiasm, he pounds the fist of one hand into the other with such violence that it is reminiscent of whipcrack or gunfire. He is not a tall man, but he stands exceptionally erect on all occasions, and his hair is fully gray, and extremely striking. The room also contained a guitar, records, and a photograph which we heard on the first night I made their acquaintance.

But rather than tell you all the details of their life in New York, let me give you a glimpse of Sy and Teddy such as I had one warm night as I walked down their street. They were sitting at the open window of

HUMOR

their dark room, facing the street, he bare-chested and she bare-shouldered, he with his arm about her, sitting so peacefully, so completely fulfilled, so utterly content to be alone with themselves, so pleased with this moment and with the world and with all that was in it, that they would not have noticed me as I passed if I had fired a cannon into their faces. Chairs and rugs they did not need.

I was at this time writing a little family show which Harry Appleman was producing, but which was bound to fail. We perked it up for awhile with a kindly Uncle, suggested by Harry Appleman and subsequently played with such success for many years by Melvin Aloy. Following introductions, Harry encouraged Sy to play us the records of his days in Radio in Richie. Reluctantly he did so, sitting on a stack of books and closing his eyes and groaning, and saying after each record, "Well, that's plenty," but his father said, "No, go on, go on," and Sy put on another record. A father is a father. His father thought the records all very well, smiling and nodding or occasionally offering criticisms of a minor nature, such as "You were talking too much there, not allowing your guest to explore himself."

And finally! History! Because when Sy played the record of the Toy Manchester Terrier talking to Mrs. Governour his father became inspired, pounding his fist several times—a regular bombardment—leaping to his feet and losing all control, dancing a jig on the floor, laughing and holding his ribs, absolutely convulsed, and he said to me, "The dog is the missing ingredient over and above the kindly Uncle, minimize the family and accentuate the dog. Sy will read the dog. Do you realize that this is a country that can't get enough of dogs? Hail and farewell, my moment of truth is heralded by the voice of a Toy Manchester Terrier."

"It wasn't a Toy Manchester Terrier," Sy said. "It was just a dog barking, no particular dog."

"Sy, give me your answer and think it over later," said his father. "Let me tell you something, Television is in its infancy, on the threshold of becoming an Art, dying and bleeding while waiting for young men of talent and ingenuity to revolutionize the industry."

"No," said Sy.

"For you," said his father, "Television will be easier than falling off a log."

"I don't want to do something easy," Sy said. "'I want to do something hard."

"A tremendous challenge," his father said.

"To bark like a dog?" Sy asked. "Thousands of actors can satisfactorily bark like a dog. Why not get an actual dog?"

I will not bore you with the reasons why actual dogs have never been heard on "Kanine Kapers." For a short period of time in 1956, when Sy was sulking in his tent, or mansion, we attempted to work with dogs, but the chief problems are three: dogs are dirty and smelly; dogs do not always bark on cue, however well-trained, since they cannot read scripts; and the employment of a dog also requires the employment of a trainer, who is frequently more of a nuisance than the animal itself.

"As a favor to your father," cried Harry Appleman, grasping Sy by the shoulders and kissing him on both cheeks. "Now you are about to become a father yourself, change your little darling's diapers night and day, feed him his mush, bathe him, wash him, tie his shoes, wipe his nose and what-not else, shower him with gifts and protect him from the bruises of life until he can stand upright and manly on his own two sturdy feet, direct his intellectual development, nurture his genius and talent and ingenuity, pray that he will be wealthy—and rush at night a thousand times to the side of his cradle for fear he has stopped his breathing." Here Harry rushed to the cradle, laid his forehead on the crossbar, his arms dangling at his sides, and wept.

"Don't be so goddamn emotional," Sy said, standing by his father with an arm around his shoulder, but he was moved and so were we all.

Of course, you would never expect Sy Appleman to offer anything less than his absolute best. Bark like a dog?—just any old dog? Not Sy. If he were to bark at all he would bark accurately, because for him the point of life was not to fall off a log but to do whatever he was called upon to do with energy and enthusiasm, confronting not only the simpler demands of a given task but its most rigid complexities, believe me. The research he accomplished! He went to dozens of kennels in New York, Westchester, Jersey, and I believe southern Connecticut, soon learning to bark the bark of breeds most people will never hear of. Have you ever heard, let us say, of an Affenpinscher? A Bouvier des Flandres? A Keeshonden? Welsh Corgis? Lhasa Apsos? Now you are speaking of rarities in the kingdom of dogs, and Sy Appleman knew them by their bark.

We shot three pilot films of the "Kanine Kapers" series in four days in a studio in Manhattan, everybody working for carfare from what looked at best like a risky script. Melvin Aloy played Uncle, Caldwell Burris played Father, and Rhoda Sibilia Mother, all remaining with us throughout the years. Unfortunately, from season to season we must recast the children as they outgrow their roles, although we always attempt to retain them as long as we humanly can. And then when we break the new child in, you may be sure we sweat hammer and nails while effecting the transition. You see, it is a business ridden with superstition, the reason being that nobody has anything definite to go on, so

HUMOR

that we must depend exclusively upon omens and portents. When something works, nobody knows why. Succeed or fail, there's no accounting for it. For these three pilot films Sy was paid $110, retroactive contingent on selling a sponsor.

After the pilot series he retired, as he thought, from his career in Television. Never mind this getting on in life. This was an attitude he maintained even after the show was sold. He stood firm, literally unmoved. "It's sold, it's sold," his father shouted, but Sy replied calmly, "Things are sold every day, so don't be so emotional. Beef is sold every day in Richie, Illinois, rice in China, coffee in Brazil, candy in Woolworth's, Coca-Cola in bottles. In short, leave me alone, I have only a certain limited capacity for rejoicing."

"Only thirteen weeks," his father said. "I plead with you, in memory of your mother. I'll pay you $220 a week. Consider your babe in arms. To sophisticated minds like yours and Teddy's the natural beauties and cultural benefits of the City of New York may be nourishment enough, but these things cannot pacify a baby. On top of everything," he added, "your father's problems have now increased beyond all possible control."

This was true. With a sponsor, our budget was relatively tremendous, the agency hovered over our every move, we were forced to infinite care with every detail, and all the members of the company were continually prostrated with nervous anxiety. Add to this the fact that we were shooting the new series at the same time we were trying to transfer the operation to Hollywood, and you will understand that Sy allowed himself finally to be persuaded to assist, carrying out his own end of things to perfection in spite of a severe collapse brought on by the heat. He bought a Frigikoola air-conditioner for his apartment, or room, although it burst through the limits of his budget, costing $299.99—let's say $300—plus installation charges. He quickly reimbursed himself with an appearance on the Ed Sullivan show, then in its infancy, where he imitated a True Boxer Type reading "'From Here to Eternity" to a Dandie Dinmont, and a Rhodesian Ridgeback explaining Canasta to a somewhat backward Alaskan Malamute. This was so successful that he received numerous invitations to appear on Radio and Television, and another to appear before a convention of veterinarians in Dallas. The letter from the veterinarians he neatly tore in half and threw away, but later retrieved and carried with him for weeks. Whenever he took the letter from his pocket he became blue, downcast by the thought of going all the way to Dallas to bark like a dog, and yet he could not surrender it, although I encouraged him either to answer it or throw it way. But how could he throw it away? The fee was $1,000 plus expenses, a sum he could not honestly deprive his family of, especially with another baby on the way.

THE IRON FIST OF OLIGARCHY

He also kept his money in his pocket, I think in the hope he would lose it. Possibly the continual barking was getting him down. Think how often you have beeen praised for something you have done so many times that now you are beginning to lose interest in it—some anecdote, for example, which you are asked to repeat over and over again until you wish you had never told it the first time. Think how often we say of our job, "Yes, I know it sounds thrilling, but after awhile it becomes a bore, and I feel the need for a change." Let me even mention love and marriage, pointing out to you how often we change our husbands and wives, buy a new car, grow a mustache and shave it off, cook a new dish, drive home by a different route, anything for a change. "Variety is the spice of life." Good God, even a dog needs a change off from Purina Dog Chow to Purina Kibbled Meal as the days go by. The man was made for better things.

The public saw their first "Kanine Kapers" in September. Within thirteen weeks it was a national institution. In private conversation the industry expected it to decline shortly like everything else, but officially the agencies were taking no chances, so that we were soon underwritten eighteen months into the future. Harry Appleman himself had no idea how he had achieved what he had achieved. Nor did he care to know. He wished only to continue, and the way to do so is to repeat the performance over and over again, respecting the omens and portents, employing the same names and the same faces and the same voices and the same plot and the same music without variation or improvement or experiment or innovation, even down to the same cameras on the same lot at the same hour of morning on the same days of the week, throwing parties to reduce the boredom, raising wages to introduce the idea of progress, and promising that someday it will end, halfway hoping it will but halfway hoping it won't until someday, at long last, to everyone's relief and despair, it finally does.

The moment we saw we were in for a good thing we rushed back East, finding Sy studying for his courses on the floor, and rocking the cradle with his foot. We pleaded with him to return with us to the Coast, he had never seen the Golden West, but he complained that he had seen the show on Television, and it was infantile and foolish and a certain sign that the moment was coming which would witness the decline and fall of America, and so forth, further complaining that the show lacked *teamwork*, he never met the actors, the actors never met the writer, the writer had no control over the music, and he wished he were back in Richie, Illinois.

However, this is standard procedure throughout the industry, except in the rare event of a producer who feels it may be beneficial to all con-

HUMOR

cerned to have a general idea of the total show, in which case a round-table is held beforehand, sometimes for an hour. To make a long story short, tears were followed by compromise, his father agreeing to inject a team spirit into the production by holding regular round-tables, in return for which Sy would come out for thirty-nine weeks at $440 a week, and I flew back with Harry. As I recall, Sy and Teddy and Richie stopped off in Richie, Illinois, where the Kleins were greeted with the first sight of their new grandson, and Sy staged a huge emotional scene, kissing the earth at the Town Square, then down to Dallas for the veterinarians, then a week's engagement in Reno, and then to the Coast, where they arrived in good health and spirits, and took up their new life.

It goes without saying, their experiences on the Coast were nothing short of perfect bliss up to a point. Their house was more unique than any I have ever seen, but at the same time by no means inexpensive. The truth is, in that environment there are only mansions or shacks, the middle class having withered away. There is no such thing as medium, although the house was somewhat cheaper than another of the same quality because of its history. In a community ridden by superstition nobody wants to live in the shadow of suicide, which is looked upon as a form of failure. For years nobody would buy the house from the widow, no matter how she disguised its past. In addition to pool and air-conditioning throughout, it was entirely mechanized, built along the lines of the Indian cliff-houses at Acoma, New Mexico, where Star Weber had shot many of his Westerns. In structure it consisted of one immense principal room with ladders leading upward into numerous small bedrooms, bath, kitchen, and what-not.

All things prospered, there were four children and they grew, sunburned from toe to crown, and Teddy increased in beauty, although she was widely criticized for refusing to wear make-up, and Sy's income doubled from time to time until it had grown beyond all reason. He forgot whose face was on the dollar bill, his voice was insured by his father for $1,000,000, he seemed serene.

Of course, especially when the weather was hot, he was a man of temperament, frequently threatening to leave us and return to Richie, Illinois, where he could always obtain a job for $35 a week in Radio, and supplement his income by helping out Teddy's father in the jewelry business. Often he bought tickets to Richie, carried them in his pocket awhile, then tore them up. He complained that his bark was now perfected beyond the wildest dream of man and dog, that there was nowhere left to go but down, and at such times he spoke of suicide, inquiring among his intimates if any had heard of a new and original way, never before tried, such as jumping out of a dirigible, burying himself in sand, or hanging himself from a Television aerial.

In 1956, as I have related, he left us for a short period of time, remaining in his home *incommunicado*, where he undertook to write a friendly letter to every person he had ever met in his life, under whatever circumstance and regardless of how briefly, as a means of returning to that point in his existence where he had taken the wrong turn, but little was accomplished. The fact was that he had passed the point of return. He could not return to Richie or to Radio or to school, not now. Too many people depended upon him, from his father to his smallest child, poor little darling.

Two years ago he broke off all direct relations with his father, refusing to speak with him, so that communication between them was conducted by his agent, Peggy Flanagan. When his moods were at their worst they sat for long hours in his pool, each on the tip of a star, Sy, Peggy, Harry, conferring until the mood had passed and his spirits were recovered, so that he appeared for work on the following day full of good cheer again, with a smile and a quip and a bark for everyone. Originally he engaged her to find other work for him in Television, which she promised to do, and perhaps tried, although why she should have tried I cannot imagine, since he was now earning $1,760 a week. Bark, yes, this she could have found for him all over town, besieged he was, make no mistake, because he was an omen and a portent of success. After all, the industry is the industry, you do what you do. A man turns a screw, as he does in Detroit. "I can play the piano or guitar," he said, "I can sing a little, even whistle, or hum, read from the classics, interpret philosophy, saw wood, wire electricity, I am a man of numerous parts, I have a face, I can speak," but the industry is vast, versatility is not required. Send out a call for two men who can hum, and a thousand will knock at your door. "Television is only in its infancy," he said, "soon it will be an Art, it is bleeding and dying for young men of talent and ingenuity to revolutionize the industry," but this is not so. He did not see things clearly in his mind.

One morning, about three o'clock, Teddy discovered him draining the pool, and I went when she called, throwing my clothes on over my pajamas, and thinking, "Fortunately such a beautiful pool takes a long time to drain." It was early June. Let me guarantee you I drove at breakneck speed, resolved that if I were not too late I would make every effort in the future to know him better, and understand him, and comfort him in his melancholy moods. He needed a vacation. We all needed a vacation. I had written eight thousand pages of "Kanine Kapers."

A mile away I could see the lights of his house, and the revolving red

HUMOR

light of an ambulance, or police car. As I approached I perceived that there were several such vehicles, as well as emergency fire equipment, dozens of automobiles from all the neighborhood and scores of people gathered on the lawn beneath the floodlights, so that I almost had the feeling, with my pajamas beneath my clothes, that I was attending one of those come-as-you-were-when-invited parties, of which we have such a number these days. Then I heard the singing.

Everyone was singing "I'll Never Smile Again," Sy leading them with his hands, in his bathing suit, on the divingboard, and all the light pouring down. For an actor, it was Paradise. Among those present was Dr. Joe Jack, a physician and friend of the family, who, when he saw me approach, said "Sing, sing, for all you're worth," and I joined in song. There was a foot of water in the pool below him, or perhaps eighteen inches, as one of the firemen later estimated. With wrenches the firemen had turned the water on again, but the inflow was only, so to speak, a drop in the bucket. They had also endeavored to run a safety net beneath the board, but the width of the pool prevented their doing so. Floating in the pool was a rope with which a neighbor, Oliver Wells, a Western player, had attempted to lasso him, but this, too, had somehow failed. When he saw me he barked in my honor, saying, "Here is the man who has written my speeches," howling and baying and setting up a howling and a baying in reply from all the dogs of the neighborhood, magnificent power and range of the sort I never knew he had, since we had never required it.

The firemen now struck upon the plan of nudging him with a long pole, in the hope that he would fall into the pool and suffer only scrapes and bruises. Joe Jack opposed this. The best course, he said, was to stall for the light of day, which might cast a different aspect upon things, and meanwhile sing according to Sy's directions for all we were worth. He also suggested that the children be brought, which they were, blinking and rubbing their eyes under the lights, falling asleep and waking, falling asleep again, but at last waking and standing together beside the pool and singing a song with their father which they had sung together on many evenings. It was from a Pooh book, Sy singing the words, the children singing the "tiddely pom," while Dr. Jack instructed the oldest, Richie, to call to his father, "Daddy, we love you, we will miss you, remember that you always told us to make sure the water is in the pool."

SY.	The more it snows
CHILDREN.	Tiddely pom
SY.	The more it goes
CHILDREN.	Tiddely pom
SY.	The more it goes

THE IRON FIST OF OLIGARCHY

CHILDREN.   Tiddely pom
SY.   On snowing.

The boy's words had no effect upon his father. "Thank you for your sentiments," Sy said, "and I wish you a merry Christmas. Remember how versatile your father was, I can sing, lead the choir, bark, and dive." He prepared to dive, but Dr. Jack called, "No, just one more song, your versatile voice is entrancing us all," ordering the firemen to try the use of the long pole, as they had planned, which they in turn decided against, bringing instead a long hose which they intended to play upon him and cause him to fall instead of dive. He consented to lead us one final time, issuing instructions, and we sang it in the following way:

SY.   And nobody knows
CHORUS OF VOICES.   Tiddely pom
SY.   How cold my toes
CHORUS OF VOICES.   Tiddely pom
SY.   How cold my toes
CHORUS OF VOICES.   Tiddely pom
SY.   Are growing.

"Let me bring you a coat," I shouted.

This he paused to consider, when his father arrived, and the cold spell passed, and he began to grow warm, wiping the sweat from his face, gasping, suffocating, strangulating, and calling out, "Turn on the air-conditioner," which Dr. Jack and I promised to do, bending with wrenches at the base of the board where it was attached to the ladder, informing him that we were turning on the air-conditioner, in the hope that we could loosen the board and tip him into the pool, where he might suffer only scrapes and bruises.

"Sy," his father shouted, pounding his fist into his palm, "come down off there before you make a fool of yourself," and Sy replied, "Don't be emotional," but even so, hearing the voice of his father he came, and the crew from the ambulance seized him. Tell me if it is not as tragic as I promised. His mind is gone. Sorely we miss him. For the time being we are finding it possible to transcribe his barking from the old films, and beginning in September we will gain time with thirteen weeks of Critic's Choices (re-runs), meanwhile training a new voice. We are not without confidence, but you may believe me that we are sweating hammer and nails while effecting the transition.

"One must begin somewhere," says the narrator (not the author) of "The Iron Fist of Oligarchy." "All you have to do is write one true sentence," Hemingway wrote. "Write the truest sentence that you know. So finally I would write one true sentence, and then go on from there." A poem, wrote Frost, "begins in delight, it inclines to the impulse, it assumes direction with the first line laid down, it runs a course of lucky events, and ends in a clarification of life...."

I began somewhere with a true sentence, a first line, on June 23, 1959. In May we had acquired a dog, a transaction which had brought me once more into contact with people I recalled from earlier dog transactions—they talked about dogs as if dogs were people. Thus the "tall, thin, insane widow" who buries her dog in Laughter In The Glen, Inc. Perhaps she asked Professor Bly to write a poem for the vault.

I had once worked as a reporter for a newspaper in Port Chester, N.Y., an experience easily transferred to a radio station in Richie, Ill., where I have never been. But I have lived in the Middle West, suffocating in the summer humidity with Sy Appleman.

I spent the eventing of May 8, 1959, with a friend named Dick Drinnon, who mentioned an article or book, The Iron Fist of Oligarchy. The title clung to the inside of my head, as things do, like the memory of certain friends seen one night "sitting at the open window of their dark room, facing the street, he bare-chested and she bare-shouldered, he with his arm about her ... so pleased with this moment and with the world and with all that was in it, that they would not have noticed me as I passed if I had fired a cannon into their faces." Or that old song, "I'll Never Smile Again." Or the lines of Pooh.

I'd never seen a swimming pool shaped like a star, but I'd heard about one from my friend Robert Russell, who walked many miles with me on the streets of San Francisco, telling me tales of life in Hollywood.

Who is Melvin Aloy in "The Iron Fist of Oligarchy"? My Diary for April 24, 1959, tells me that "On the 'Sergeant Bilko' show on TV tonight I saw Allen Melvin, whom I knew back at Evander Childs High in 1938–9."

Details, memories, hints, suggestions, fragments. They drop into place once a main idea gets started. Images line up for me, like actors lining up for a job. They have heard that a piece of fiction is on the make.

The main idea was this: actors, performers, writers are usually unable to escape some speciality the world has attached to them. They perform without growth, without latitude, barking like a dog, crossing their eyes, imitating the president, imitating Donald Duck, although in the beginning they had hoped to transcend their first triumphs. Sy Appleman's first triumph was his clever barking. He escaped at least into an ambulance.

My own first triumph was fiction in the colloquial idiom of an imagined baseball player, and during this period of three months, when "The Iron

THE IRON FIST OF OLIGARCHY

Fist of Oligarchy" was conceived and written, I had been particularly oppressed by requests to do over and over and over again the tales I had already "done" enough.

Looking back upon my story more than a decade later I see what I missed then. It wasn't right to blame everything on Sy's father, or on society. I see now (as people told me even then) that a good deal of the blame must fall upon Sy himself. He invited his fate. I don't think he really *kept his money in his pocket in the hope of losing it.* I think I was idealizing him, as a way of idealizing myself: people would think it was I who was careless of money.

Sy was something of an exhibitionist. If he was really *in rebellion against his commercial success he could have walked out of it by walking out of it.* Sometimes an actor or a writer will perform even against his best critical judgment—better to perform than not to perform. I saw too shallowly into Sy. I should have asked, "If he really intended to commit suicide why did he invite the whole neighborhood and set a stage with 'all the light pouring down'?" For an actor, it was Paradise.

Or did I understand all this then? I cannot say.

M.H.

IV | The Reader

Dear reader, assist the poor writer, for he is only human, like you. We do sometimes tend to forget his mere humanness. Inside the schoolhouse, with his portrait on the wall, his books upon the shelves—even the very building named for him—we often commit the error of reverence. We think that the writer is infallible, that he knew all along the answers to the questions critics ask, that he knew what he was doing every moment of the way, or that he knew the true meaning of his fiction even before he began.

But the portrait of Nathaniel Hawthorne on the wall was made when he was nearing age sixty. His story, "The Ambitious Guest," on the other hand, was written at age thirty, when he was a doubtful young man worrying about what might become of him, if anything, and whether he stood a chance of living long enough to complete at least enough writing to make a first impression. This we read into his fiction, for "the ambitious guest" is surely Hawthorne himself, placed by himself into the record at age thirty, all his fears upon parade.

The writer does worry at every age about his fame, about his fortune, and about the interpretations students and teachers and critics will make of his fiction. Yet he also hopes that nobody will too blithely equate his fiction with his life—how do we know the ambitious guest is Hawthorne?

Because these matters are on the writer's mind he writes of them, having learned with experience to seek the material of fiction among his own obsessions. The writer must face his own vanity, his own fears, exploiting his own preoccupations. Finally, however, "the artist was what he did— *he was nothing else." So Henry James insists in our story, as he insisted often throughout his fiction. He resisted inquiry into his life. When the biographer undertakes to "do" the writer, as Withermore undertakes to "do" Ashton Doyne in "The Real Right Thing," the very ghost of the writer is aroused.*

That may be how it ought *to be. The demands we make upon the writer may be unjust, although they appear to be inevitable, for readers at all times seem to want to know about a writer's private life. For better or for worse, we thereby force the writer to deal with the reader as well as with himself. He tells us of his problems in getting started (as John Barth does in "Life-Story"), and how he wishes us to read him, the distance he wishes us to keep, and what he wishes us to do with his bones when he's dead. Without us he cannot go on. Yet we cause him vast difficulty, he wishes we did not exist, he wishes no criticism existed—and yet, how can he achieve fame if we do not exist? How can he say the things he wishes to say if he has no audience to say them to? Whitman spoke for all writers: "To have great poets there must be great audiences, too."*

THE AMBITIOUS GUEST

Nathaniel Hawthorne

One September night a family had gathered round their hearth, and piled it high with the driftwood of mountain streams, the dry cones of the pine, and the splintered ruins of great trees that had come crashing down the precipice. Up the chimney roared the fire, and brightened the room with its broad blaze. The faces of the father and mother had a sober gladness; the children laughed; the eldest daughter was the image of Happiness at seventeen; and the aged grandmother, who sat knitting in the warmest place, was the image of Happiness grown old. They had found the "herb, heart's-ease," in the bleakest spot of all New England. This family were situated in the Notch of the White Hills, where the wind was sharp throughout the year, and pitilessly cold in the winter—giving their cottage all its fresh inclemency before it descended on the valley of the Saco. They dwelt in a cold spot and a dangerous one; for a mountain towered above their heads, so steep, that the stones would often rumble down its sides and startle them at midnight.

The daughter had just uttered some simple jest that filled them all with mirth, when the wind came through the Notch and seemed to pause before their cottage—rattling the door, with a sound of wailing and lamentation, before it passed into the valley. For a moment it saddened them, though there was nothing unusual in the tones. But the family were glad again when they perceived that the latch was lifted by some traveler, whose footsteps had been unheard amid the dreary blast which heralded his approach, and wailed as he was entering, and went moaning away from the door.

Though they dwelt in such a solitude, these people held daily converse with the world. The romantic pass of the Notch is a great artery, through

THE AMBITIOUS GUEST

which the lifeblood of internal commerce is continually throbbing between Maine, on one side, and the Green Mountains and the shores of the St. Lawrence, on the other. The stagecoach always drew up before the door of the cottage. The wayfarer, with no companion but his staff, paused here to exchange a word, that the sense of loneliness might not utterly overcome him ere he could pass through the cleft of the mountain, or reach the first house in the valley. And here the teamster, on his way to Portland market, would put up for the night; and, if a bachelor, might sit an hour beyond the usual bedtime, and steal a kiss from the mountain maid at parting. It was one of those primitive taverns where the traveler pays only for food and lodging, but meets with a homely kindness beyond all price. When the footsteps were heard, therefore, between the outer door and the inner one, the whole family rose up, grandmother, children, and all, as if about to welcome some one who belonged to them, and whose fate was linked with theirs.

The door was opened by a young man. His face at first wore the melancholy expression, almost despondency, of one who travels a wild and bleak road, at nightfall and alone, but soon brightened up when he saw the kindly warmth of his reception. He felt his heart spring forward to meet them all, from the old woman, who wiped a chair with her apron, to the little child that held out its arms to him. One glance and smile placed the stranger on a footing of innocent familiarity with the eldest daughter.

"Ah, this fire is the right thing!" cried he; "especially when there is such a pleasant circle round it. I am quite benumbed; for the Notch is just like the pipe of a great pair of bellows; it has blown a terrible blast in my face all the way from Bartlett."

"Then you are going towards Vermont?" said the master of the house, as he helped to take a light knapsack off the young man's shoulders.

"Yes; to Burlington, and far enough beyond," replied he. "I meant to have been at Ethan Crawford's tonight; but a pedestrian lingers along such a road as this. It is no matter, for, when I saw this good fire, and all your cheerful faces, I felt as if you had kindled it on purpose for me, and were waiting my arrival. So I shall sit down among you, and make myself at home."

The frank-hearted stranger had just drawn his chair to the fire when something like a heavy footstep was heard without, rushing down the steep side of the mountain, as with long and rapid strides, and taking such a leap in passing the cottage as to strike the opposite precipice. The family held their breath, because they knew the sound, and their guest held his by instinct.

"The old mountain has thrown a stone at us, for fear we should forget him," said the landlord, recovering himself. "He sometimes nods his head and threatens to come down; but we are old neighbors, and agree together pretty well upon the whole. Besides we have a sure place of refuge hard by if he should be coming in good earnest."

Let us now suppose the stranger to have finished his supper of bear's meat; and, by his natural felicity of manner, to have placed himself on a footing of kindness with the whole family, so that they talked as freely together as if he belonged to their mountain brood. He was of a proud, yet gentle spirit—haughty and reserved among the rich and great; but ever ready to stoop his head to the lowly cottage door, and be like a brother or a son at the poor man's fireside. In the household of the Notch he found warmth and simplicity of feeling, the pervading intelligence of New England, and a poetry of native growth, which they had gathered when they little thought of it from the mountain peaks and chasms, and at the very threshold of their romantic and dangerous abode. He had traveled far and alone; his whole life, indeed, had been a solitary path; for, with the lofty caution of his nature, he had kept himself apart from those who might otherwise have been his companions. The family, too, though so kind and hospitable, had that consciousness of unity among themselves, and separation from the world at large, which, in every domestic circle, should still keep a holy place where no stranger may intrude. But this evening a prophetic sympathy impelled the refined and educated youth to pour out his heart before the simple mountaineers, and constrained them to answer him with the same free confidence. And thus it should have been. Is not the kindred of a common fate a closer tie than that of birth?

The secret of the young man's character was a high and abstracted ambition. He could have borne to live an undistinguished life, but not to be forgotten in the grave. Yearning desire had been transformed to hope; and hope, long cherished, had become like certainty that, obscurely as he journeyed now, a glory was to beam on all his pathway—though not, perhaps, while he was treading it. But when posterity should gaze back into the gloom of what was now the present, they would trace the brightness of his footsteps, brightening as meaner glories faded, and confess that a gifted one had passed from his cradle to his tomb with none to recognize him.

"As yet," cried the stranger—his cheek glowing and his eye flashing with enthusiasm—"as yet, I have done nothing. Were I to vanish from the earth tomorrow, none would know so much of me as you: that a nameless youth came up at nightfall from the valley of the Saco, and opened his heart to you in the evening, and passed through the Notch by sunrise, and was seen no more. Not a soul would ask, 'Who was he?

Whither did the wanderer go?' But I cannot die till I have achieved my destiny. Then, let Death come! I shall have built my monument!"

There was a continual flow of natural emotion, gushing forth amid abstracted reverie, which enabled the family to understand this young man's sentiments, though so foreign from their own. With quick sensibility of the ludicrous, he blushed at the ardor into which he had been betrayed.

"You laugh at me," said he, taking the eldest daughter's hand, and laughing himself. "You think my ambition as nonsensical as if I were to freeze myself to death on the top of Mount Washington, only that people might spy at me from the country round about. And, truly, that would be a noble pedestal for a man's statue!"

"It is better to sit here by this fire!" answered the girl, blushing, "and be comfortable and contented, though nobody thinks about us."

"I suppose," said her father, after a fit of musing, "there is something natural in what the young man says; and if my mind had been turned that way, I might have felt just the same. It is strange, wife, how his talk has set my head running on things that are pretty certain never to come to pass."

"Perhaps they may," observed the wife. "Is the man thinking what he will do when he is a widower?"

"No, no!" cried he, repelling the idea with reproachful kindness. "When I think of your death, Esther, I think of mine, too. But I was wishing we had a good farm in Bartlett, or Bethlehem, or Littleton, or some other township round the White Mountains; but not where they could tumble on our heads. I should want to stand well with my neighbors and be called Squire, and sent to General Court for a term or two; for a plain, honest man may do as much good there as a lawyer. And when I should be grown quite an old man, and you an old woman, so as not to be long apart, I might die happy enough in my bed, and leave you all crying around me. A slate gravestone would suit me as well as a marble one—with just my name and age, and a verse of a hymn, and something to let people know that I lived an honest man and died a Christian."

"There now!" exclaimed the stranger; "it is our nature to desire a monument, be it slate or marble, or a pillar of granite, or a glorious memory in the universal heart of man."

"We're in a strange way, tonight," said the wife, with tears in her eyes. "They say it's a sign of something, when folks' minds go a wandering so. Hark to the children!"

They listened accordingly. The younger children had been put to bed in another room, but with an open door between, so that they could be heard talking busily among themselves. One and all seemed to have caught the infection from the fireside circle, and were outvying each other in wild wishes, and childish projects of what they would do when they came to be men and women. At length a little boy, instead of addressing his brothers and sisters, called out to his mother.

"I'll tell you what I wish, mother," cried he. "I want you and father and grandma'm, and all of us, and the stranger too, to start right away, and go and take a drink out of the basin of the Flume!"

Nobody could help laughing at the child's notion of leaving a warm bed, and dragging them from a cheerful fire, to visit the basin of the Flume—a brook which tumbles over the precipice, deep within the Notch. The boy had hardly spoken when a wagon rattled along the road, and stopped a moment before the door. It appeared to contain two or three men, who were cheering their hearts with the rough chorus of a song, which resounded, in broken notes, between the cliffs, while the singers hesitated whether to continue their journey or put up here for the night.

"Father," said the girl, "they are calling you by name."

But the good man doubted whether they had really called him, and was unwilling to show himself too solicitous of gain by inviting people to patronize his house. He therefore did not hurry to the door; and the lash being soon applied, the travelers plunged into the Notch, still singing and laughing, though their music and mirth came back drearily from the heart of the mountain.

"There, mother!" cried the boy, again. "They'd have given us a ride to the Flume."

Again they laughed at the child's pertinacious fancy for a night ramble. But it happened that a light cloud passed over the daughter's spirit; she looked gravely into the fire, and drew a breath that was almost a sigh. It forced its way, in spite of a little struggle to repress it. Then starting and blushing, she looked quickly round the circle, as if they had caught a glimpse into her bosom. The stranger asked what she had been thinking of.

"Nothing," answered she, with a downcast smile. "Only I felt lonesome just then."

"Oh, I have always had a gift of feeling what is in other people's hearts," said he, half seriously. "Shall I tell the secrets of yours? For I know what to think when a young girl shivers by a warm hearth, and complains of lonesomeness at her mother's side. Shall I put these feelings into words?"

"They would not be a girl's feelings any longer if they could be put into words," replied the mountain nymph, laughing, but avoiding his eye.

THE AMBITIOUS GUEST

All this was said apart. Perhaps a germ of love was springing in their hearts, so pure that it might blossom in Paradise, since it could not be matured on earth; for women worship such gentle dignity as his; and the proud, contemplative, yet kindly soul is oftenest captivated by simplicity like hers. But while they spoke softly, and he was watching the happy sadness, the lightsome shadows, the shy yearnings of a maiden's nature, the wind through the Notch took a deeper and drearier sound. It seemed, as the fanciful stranger said, like the choral strain of the spirits of the blast, who in old Indian times had their dwellings among these mountains, and made their heights and recesses a sacred region. There was a wail along the road, as if a funeral were passing. To chase away the gloom, the family threw pine branches on their fire, till the dry leaves crackled and the flame arose, discovering once again a scene of peace and humble happiness. The light hovered about them fondly, and caressed them all. There were the little faces of the children, peeping from their bed apart, and here the father's frame of strength, the mother's subdued and careful mien, the high-browed youth, the budding girl, and the good old grandam, still knitting in the warmest place. The aged woman looked up from her task, and, with fingers ever busy, was the next to speak.

"Old folks have their notions," said she, "as well as young ones. You've been wishing and planning, and letting your heads run on one thing and another, till you've set my mind a wandering too. Now what should an old woman wish for, when she can go but a step or two before she comes to her grave? Children, it will haunt me night and day till I tell you."

"What is it, mother?" cried the husband and wife at once.

Then the old woman, with an air of mystery which drew the circle closer round the fire, informed them that she had provided her grave-clothes some years before—a nice linen shroud, a cap with a muslin ruff, and everything of a finer sort than she had worn since her wedding day. But this evening an old superstition had strangely recurred to her. It used to be said, in her younger days, that if anything were amiss with a corpse, if only the ruff were not smooth, or the cap did not set right, the corpse in the coffin and beneath the clods would strive to put up its cold hands and arrange it. The bare thought made her nervous.

"Don't talk so, grandmother!" said the girl, shuddering.

"Now"—continued the old woman, with singular earnestness, yet smiling strangely at her own folly—"I want one of you, my children—when your mother is dressed and in the coffin—I want one of you to hold a looking-glass over my face. Who knows but I may take a glimpse at myself, and see whether all's right?"

THE READER

"Old and young, we dream of graves and monuments," murmured the stranger youth. "I wonder how mariners feel when the ship is sinking, and they, unknown and undistinguished, are to be buried together in the ocean—that wide and nameless sepulchre?"

For a moment, the old woman's ghastly conception so engrossed the minds of her hearers that a sound abroad in the night, rising like the roar of a blast, had grown broad, deep, and terrible, before the fated group were conscious of it. The house and all within it trembled; the foundations of the earth seemed to be shaken, as if this awful sound were the peal of the last trump. Young and old exchanged one wild glance, and remained an instant, pale, affrighted, without utterance, or power to move. Then the same shriek burst simultaneously from all the lips.

"The Slide! The Slide!"

The simplest words must intimate, but not portray, the unutterable horror of the catastrophe. The victims rushed from their cottage, and sought refuge in what they deemed a safer spot—where, in contemplation of such an emergency, a sort of barrier had been reared. Alas! they had quitted their security, and fled right into the pathway of destruction. Down came the whole side of the mountain, in a cataract of ruin. Just before it reached the house, the stream broke into two branches—shivered not a window there, but overwhelmed the whole vicinity, blocked up the road, and annihilated everything in its dreadful course. Long ere the thunder of the great Slide had ceased to roar among the mountains, the mortal agony had been endured, and the victims were at peace. Their bodies were never found.

The next morning, the light smoke was seen stealing from the cottage chimney up the mountain side. Within, the fire was yet smouldering on the hearth, and the chairs in a circle round it, as if the inhabitants had but gone forth to view the devastation of the Slide, and would shortly return, to thank Heaven for their miraculous escape. All had left separate tokens, by which those who had known the family were made to shed a tear for each. Who has not heard their name? The story has been told far and wide, and will forever be a legend of these mountains. Poets have sung their fate.

There were circumstances which led some to suppose that a stranger had been received into the cottage on this awful night, and had shared the catastrophe of all its inmates. Others denied that there were sufficient grounds for such a conjecture. Woe for the high-souled youth, with his dream of Earthly Immortality! His name and person utterly unknown; his history, his way of life, his plans, a mystery never to be solved, his death and his existence equally a doubt! Whose was the agony of that death moment?

THE REAL RIGHT THING

Henry James

I

When, after the death of Ashton Doyne—but three months after—George Withermore was approached, as the phrase is, on the subject of a "volume," the communication came straight from his publishers, who had been, and indeed much more, Doyne's own; but he was not surprised to learn, on the occurrence of the interview they next suggested, that a certain pressure as to the early issue of a Life had been brought to bear upon them by their late client's widow. Doyne's relations with his wife had been, to Withermore's knowledge, a very special chapter—which would present itself, by the way, as a delicate one for the biographer; but a sense of what she had lost, and even of what she had lacked, had betrayed itself, on the poor woman's part, from the first days of her bereavement, sufficiently to prepare an observer at all initiated for some attitude of reparation, some espousal even exaggerated of the interests of a distinguished name. George Withermore was, as he felt, initiated; yet what he had not expected was to hear that she had mentioned him as the person in whose hands she would most promptly place the materials for a book.

These materials—diaries, letters, memoranda, notes, documents of many sorts—were her property, and wholly in her control, no conditions at all attaching to any portion of her heritage; so that she was free at present to do as she liked—free, in particular, to do nothing. What Doyne would have arranged had he had time to arrange could be but supposition and guess. Death had taken him too soon and too suddenly, and there was all the pity that the only wishes he was known to have expressed were wishes that put it positively out of account. He had broken short off—that was the way of it; and the end was ragged and needed trimming. Withermore was conscious, abundantly, how close he had stood to him, but he was not less aware of his comparative obscurity. He was young, a journalist, a critic, a hand-to-mouth character, with little, as yet, as was vulgarly said, to show. His writings were few and small, his relations scant and vague. Doyne, on the other hand, had lived long enough—above all had had talent enough—to become great, and among his many friends gilded also with greatness were several to whom his wife would have struck those who knew her as much more likely to appeal.

The preference she had, at all events, uttered—and uttered in a roundabout, considerate way that left him a measure of freedom—made our

THE READER

young man feel that he must at least see her and that there would be in any case a good deal to talk about. He immediately wrote to her, she as promptly named an hour, and they had it out. But he came away with his particular idea immensely strengthened. She was a strange woman, and he had never thought her an agreeable one; only there was something that touched him now in her bustling, blundering impatience. She wanted the book to make up, and the individual whom, of her husband's set, she probably believed she might most manipulate was in every way to help it to make up. She had not taken Doyne seriously enough in life, but the biography should be a solid reply to every imputation on herself. She had scantly known how such books were constructed, but she had been looking and had learned something. It alarmed Withermore a little from the first to see that she would wish to go in for quantity. She talked of "volumes"—but he had his notion of that.

"My thought went straight to *you*, as his own would have done," she had said almost as soon as she rose before him there in her large array of mourning—with her big black eyes, her black wig, her big black fan and gloves, her general gaunt, ugly, tragic, but striking and, as might have been thought from a certain point of view, "elegant" presence. "You're the one he liked most; oh, *much*!"—and it had been quite enough to turn Withermore's head. It little mattered that he could afterward wonder if she had known Doyne enough, when it came to that, to be sure. He would have said for himself indeed that her testimony on such a point would scarcely have counted. Still, there was no smoke without fire; she knew at least what she meant, and he was not a person she could have an interest in flattering. They went up together, without delay, to the great man's vacant study, which was at the back of the house and looked over the large green garden—a beautiful and inspiring scene, to poor Withermore's view—common to the expensive row.

"You can perfectly work here, you know," said Mrs. Doyne: "you shall have the place quite to yourself—I'll give it all up to you; so that in the evenings, in particular, don't you see? for quiet and privacy, it will be perfection."

Perfection indeed, the young man felt as he looked about—having explained that, as his actual occupation was an evening paper and his earlier hours, for a long time yet, regularly taken up, he would have to come always at night. The place was full of their lost friend; everything in it had belonged to him; everything they touched had been part of his life. It was for the moment too much for Withermore—too great an honour and even too great a care; memories still recent came back to him, and, while his heart beat faster and his eyes filled with tears, the pressure of his loyalty seemed almost more than he could carry. At the sight of his

THE REAL RIGHT THING

tears Mrs Doyne's own rose to her lids, and the two, for a minute, only looked at each other He half expected her to break out: "Oh, help me to feel as I know you know I want to feel!" And after a little one of them said, with the other's deep assent—it didn't matter which: "It's here that we're *with* him." But it was definitely the young man who put it, before they left the room, that it was there he was with *them.*

The young man began to come as soon as he could arrange it, and then it was, on the spot, in the charmed stillness, between the lamp and the fire and with the curtains drawn, that a certain intenser consciousness crept over him. He turned in out of the black London November; he passed through the large, hushed house and up the red-carpeted staircase where he only found in his path the whisk of a soundless, trained maid, or the reach, out of a doorway, of Mrs. Doyne's queenly weeds and approving tragic face; and then, by a mere touch of the well-made door that gave so sharp and pleasant a click, shut himself in for three or four warm hours with the spirit—as he had always distinctly declared it—of his master. He was not a little frightened when, even the first night, it came over him that he had really been most affected, in the whole matter, by the prospect, the privilege and the luxury, of this sensation. He had not, he could now reflect, definitely considered the question of the book—as to which there was here, even already, much to consider: he had simply let his affection and admiration—to say nothing of his gratified pride—meet, to the full, the temptation Mrs Doyne had offered them.

How did he know, without more thought, he might begin to ask himself, that the book was, on the whole, to be desired? What warrant had he ever received from Ashton Doyne himself for so direct and, as it were, so familiar an approach? Great was the art of biography, but there were subjects and subjects. He confusedly recalled, so far as that went, old words dropped by Doyne over contemporary compilations, suggestions of how he himself discriminated as to other heroes and other panoramas. He even remembered how his friend, at moments, would have seemed to show himself as holding that the "literary" career might—save in the case of a Johnson and a Scott, with a Boswell and a Lockhart to help—best content itself to be represented. The artist was what he *did*—he was nothing else. Yet how, on the other hand, was not *he*, George Withermore, poor devil, to have jumped at the chance of spending his winter in an intimacy so rich? It had been simply dazzling—that was the fact. It hadn't been the "terms," from the publishers—though these were, as they said at the office, all right; it had been Doyne himself, his company and contact and presence—it had been just what it was turning out, the possibility of an intercourse closer than that of life. Strange that death, of the two things, should have the fewer mysteries and secrets! The first night our young man was alone in the room it seemed to him that his master and he were really for the first time together.

II

Mrs Doyne had for the most part let him expressively alone, but she had on two or three occasions looked in to see if his needs had been met, and he had the opportunity of thanking her on the spot for the judgment and zeal with which she had smoothed his way. She had to some extent herself been looking things over and had been able already to muster several groups of letters; all the keys of drawers and cabinets she had, moreover, from the first placed in his hands, with helpful information as to the apparent whereabouts of different matters. She had put him, in a word, in the fullest possible possession, and whether or no her husband had trusted her, she at least, it was clear, trusted her husband's friend. There grew upon Withermore, nevertheless, the impression that, in spite of all these offices, she was not yet at peace, and that a certain unappeasable anxiety continued even to keep step with her confidence. Though she was full of consideration, she was at the same time perceptibly *there*: he felt her, through a supersubtle sixth sense that the whole connection had already brought into play, hover, in the still hours, at the top of landings and on the other side of doors, gathered from the soundless brush of her skirts the hint of her watchings and waitings. One evening when, at his friend's table, he had lost himself in the depths of correspondence, he was made to start and turn by the suggestion that some one was behind him. Mrs Doyne had come in without his hearing the door, and she gave a strained smile as he sprang to his feet. "I hope," she said, "I haven't frightened you."

"Just a little—I was so absorbed. It was as if, for the instant," the young man explained, "it had been himself."

The oddity of her face increased in her wonder. "Ashton?"

"He does seem so near," said Withermore.

"To you too?"

This naturally struck him. "He does then to you?"

She hesitated, not moving from the spot where she had first stood, but looking round the room as if to penetrate its duskier angles. She had a way of raising to the level of her nose the big black fan which she apparently never laid aside and with which she thus covered the lower half of her face, her rather hard eyes, above it, becoming the more ambiguous. "Sometimes."

"Here," Withermore went on, "it's as if he might at any moment come in. That's why I jumped now. The time is so short since he really used to —it only *was* yesterday. I sit in his chair, I turn his books, I use his pens,

THE REAL RIGHT THING

I stir his fire, exactly as if, learning he would presently be back from a walk, I had come up here contentedly to wait. It's delightful—but it's strange."

Mrs Doyne, still with her fan up, listened with interest. "Does it worry you?"

"No—I like it."

She hesitated again. "Do you ever feel as if he were—a—quite—a—personally in the room?"

"Well, as I said just now," her companion laughed, "on hearing you behind me I seemed to take it so. What do we want, after all," he asked, "but that he shall be with us?"

"Yes, as you said he would be—that first time." She stared in full assent. "He *is* with us."

She was rather portentous, but Withermore took it smiling. "Then we must keep him. We must do only what he would like."

"Oh, only that, of course—only. But if he *is* here——?" And her sombre eyes seemed to throw it out, in vague distress, over her fan.

"It shows that he's pleased and wants only to help? Yes, surely; it must show that."

She gave a light gasp and looked again round the room. "Well," she said as she took leave of him, "remember that I too want only to help." On which, when she had gone, he felt sufficiently—that she had come in simply to see he was all right.

He was all right more and more, it struck him after this, for as he began to get into his work he moved, as it appeared to him, but the closer to the idea of Doyne's personal presence. When once this fancy had begun to hang about him he welcomed it, persuaded it, encouraged it, quite cherished it, looking forward all day to feeling it renew itself in the evening, and waiting for the evening very much as one of a pair of lovers might wait for the hour of their appointment. The smallest accidents humoured and confirmed it, and by the end of three or four weeks he had come quite to regard it as the consecration of his enterprise. Wasn't it what settled the question of what Doyne would have thought of what they were doing? What they were doing was what he wanted done, and they could go on, from step to step, without scruple or doubt. Withermore rejoiced indeed at moments to feel this certitude: there were times of dipping deep into some of Doyne's secrets when it was particularly pleasant to be able to hold that Doyne desired him, as it were, to know them. He was learning many things that he had not suspected, drawing many curtains, forcing many doors, reading many riddles, going, in general, as they said, behind almost everything. It was at an occasional sharp turn of some of the duskier of these wanderings "behind" that he really, of a sudden, most felt himself, in the intimate, sensible way, face to face with his friend; so that he could scarcely have told, for the instant, if their meeting occurred in the narrow passage and tight squeeze of the past, or at the hour and in the place that actually held him. Was it '67, or was it but the other side of the table?

Happily, at any rate, even in the vulgarest light publicity could ever shed, there would be the great fact of the way Doyne was "coming out." He was coming out too beautifully—better yet than such a partisan as Withermore could have supposed. Yet, all the while, as well, how would this partisan have represented to any one else the special state of his own consciousness? It wasn't a thing to talk about—it was only a thing to feel. There were moments, for instance, when, as he bent over his papers, the light breath of his dead host was as distinctly in his hair as his own elbows were on the table before him. There were moments when, had he been able to look up, the other side of the table would have shown him this companion as vividly as the shaded lamplight showed him his page. That he couldn't at such a juncture look up was his own affair, for the situation was ruled—that was but natural—by deep delicacies and fine timidities, the dread of too sudden or too rude an advance. What was intensely in the air was that if Doyne *was* there it was not nearly so much for himself as for the young priest of his altar. He hovered and lingered, he came and went, he might almost have been, among the books and the papers, a hushed, discreet librarian, doing the particular things, rendering the quiet aid, liked by men of letters.

Withermore himself, meanwhile, came and went, changed his place, wandered on guests either definite or vague; and more than once, when, taking a book down from a shelf and finding in it marks of Doyne's pencil, he got drawn on and lost, he had heard documents on the table behind him gently shifted and stirred, had literally, on his return, found some letter he had mislaid pushed again into view, some wilderness cleared by the opening of an old journal at the very date he wanted. How should he have gone so, on occasion, to the special box or drawer, out of fifty receptacles, that would help him, had not his mystic assistant happened, in fine prevision, to tilt its lid, or to pull it half open, in just the manner that would catch his eye?—in spite, after all, of the fact of lapses and intervals in which, *could* one have really looked, one would have seen somebody standing before the fire a trifle detached and over-erect—somebody fixing one the least bit harder than in life.

III

That this auspicious relation had in fact existed, had continued, for two or three weeks, was sufficiently proved by the dawn of the distress with which our young man found himself aware that he had, for some reason, from a certain evening, begun to miss it. The sign of that was an abrupt, surprised sense—on the occasion of his mislaying a marvellous unpublished page which, hunt where he would, remained stupidly, irrecoverably lost—that his protected state was, after all, exposed to some confusion and even to some depression. If, for the joy of the business, Doyne and he had, from the start, been together, the situation had, within a few days of his first new suspicion of it, suffered the odd change of their ceasing to be so. That was what was the matter, he said to himself, from the moment an impression of mere mass and quantity struck him as taking, in his happy outlook at his material, the place of his pleasant assumption of a clear course and a lively pace. For five nights he struggled; then, never at his table, wandering about the room, taking up his references only to lay them down, looking out of the window, poking the fire, thinking strange thoughts and listening for signs and sounds not as he suspected or imagined, but as he vainly desired and invoked them, he made up his mind that he was, for the time at least, forsaken.

The extraordinary thing thus became that it made him not only sad not to feel Doyne's presence, but in a high degree uneasy. It was stranger, somehow, that he shouldn't be there than it had ever been that he *was*—so strange indeed at last that Withermore's nerves found themselves quite inconsequently affected. They had taken kindly enough to what was of an order impossible to explain, perversely reserving their sharpest state for the return to the normal, the supersession of the false. They were remarkably beyond control when, finally, one night, after resisting an hour or two, he simply edged out of the room. It had only now, for the first time, become impossible to him to remain there. Without design, but panting a little and positively as a man scared, he passed along his usual corridor and reached the top of the staircase. From this point he saw Mrs Doyne looking up at him from the bottom quite as if she had known he would come; and the most singular thing of all was that, though he had been conscious of no notion to resort to her, had only been prompted to relieve himself by escape, the sight of her position made him recognize it as just, quickly feel it as a part of some monstrous oppression that was closing over both of them. It was wonderful how, in the mere modern London hall, between the Tottenham Court Road rugs and the electric light, it came up to him from the tall black lady, and went again from him down to her, that he knew what she meant by looking as if he would know. He descended straight, she turned into her own little lower room, and there, the next thing, with the door shut, they were, still in silence and with queer faces, confronted over confessions that had taken sudden life from these two or three movements. Withermore gasped as it came to him why he had lost his friend. "He has been with *you*?"

With this it was all out—out so far that neither had to explain and that, when "What do you suppose is the matter?" quickly passed between them, one appeared to have said it as much as the other. Withermore looked about at the small bright room in which, night after night, she had been living her life as he had been living his own upstairs. It was pretty, cosy, rosy; but she had by turns felt in it what he had felt and heard in it what he had heard. Her effect there—fantastic black, plumed and extravagant, upon deep pink—was that of some "decadent" coloured print, some poster of the newest school. "You understood he had left me?" he asked.

She markedly wished to make it clear. "This evening—yes. I've made things out."

"You knew—before—that he was with me?"

She hesitated again. "I felt he wasn't with *me*. But on the stairs——"

"Yes?"

"Well—he passed, more than once. He was in the house. And at your door——"

"Well?" he went on as she once more faltered.

"If I stopped I could sometimes tell. And from your face," she added, "to-night, at any rate, I knew your state."

"And that was why you came out?"

"I thought you'd come to me."

He put out to her, on this, his hand, and they thus, for a minute, in silence, held each other clasped. There was no peculiar presence for either, now—nothing more peculiar than that of each for the other. But the place had suddenly become as if consecrated, and Withermore turned over it again his anxiety. "What *is* then the matter?"

"I only want to do the real right thing," she replied after a moment.

"And are we not doing it?"

"I wonder. Are *you* not?"

He wondered too. "To the best of my belief. But we must think."

"We must think," she echoed. And they did think—thought, with intensity, the rest of that evening together, and thought, independently—Withermore at least could answer for himself—during many days that followed. He intermitted for a little his visits and his work, trying, in meditation, to catch himself in the act of some mistake that might have accounted for their disturbance. Had he taken, on some important point —or looked as if he might take—some wrong line or wrong view? had he somewhere benightedly falsified or inadequately insisted? He went back at last with the idea of having guessed two or three questions he might have been on the way to muddle; after which he had, above stairs, another

THE REAL RIGHT THING

period of agitation, presently followed by another interview, below, with Mrs Doyne, who was still troubled and flushed.

"He's there?"

"He's there."

"I knew it!" she returned in an odd gloom of triumph. Then as to make it clear: "He has not been again with *me*."

"Nor with me again to help," said Withermore.

She considered. "Not to help?"

"I can't make it out—I'm at sea. Do what I will, I feel I'm wrong."

She covered him a moment with her pompous pain. "How do you feel it?"

"Why, by things that happen. The strangest things. I can't describe them—and you wouldn't believe them."

"Oh yes, I would!" Mrs Doyne murmured.

"Well, he intervenes." Withermore tried to explain. "However I turn, I find him."

She earnestly followed. " 'Find' him?"

"I meet him. He seems to rise there before me."

Mrs Doyne, staring, waited a little. "Do you mean you see him?"

"I fell as if at any moment I may. I'm baffled. I'm checked." Then he added: "I'm afraid."

"Of *him*?" asked Mrs Doyne.

He thought. "Well—of what I'm doing."

"Then what, that's so awful, *are* you doing?"

"What you proposed to me. Going into his life."

She showed, in her gravity, now, a new alarm. "And don't you *like* that?"

"Doesn't *he*? That's the question. We lay him bare. We serve him up. What is it called? We give him to the world."

Poor Mrs Doyne, as if on a menace to her hard atonement, glared at this for an instant in deeper gloom. "And why shouldn't we?"

"Because we don't know. There are natures, there are lives, that shrink. He mayn't wish it," said Withermore. "We never asked him."

"How *could* we?"

He was silent a while. "Well, we ask him now. That's after all, what our start has, so far, represented. We've put it to him."

"Then—if he has been with us—we've had his answer."

Withermore spoke now as if he knew what to believe. "He hasn't been 'with' us—he has been against us."

"Then why did you think——"

"What I *did* think, at first—that what he wishes to make us feel is his sympathy? Because, in my original simplicity, I was mistaken. I was—I

173

don't know what to call it—so excited and charmed that I didn't understand. But I understand at last. He only wanted to communicate. He strains forward out of his darkness; he reaches toward us out of his mystery; he makes us dim signs out of his horror."

" 'Horror'?" Mrs Doyne gasped with her fan up to her mouth.

"At what we're doing." He could by this time piece it all together. "I see now that at first——"

"Well, what?"

"One had simply to feel he was there, and therefore not indifferent. And the beauty of that misled me. But he's there as a protest."

"Against *my* Life?" Mrs Doyne wailed.

"Against *any* Life. He's there to *save* his Life. He's there to be let alone."

"So you give up?" she almost shrieked.

He could only meet her. "He's there as a warning."

For a moment, on this, they looked at each other deep. "You *are* afraid!" she at last brought out.

It affected him, but he insisted. "He's there as a curse!"

With that they parted, but only for two or three days; her last word to him continuing to sound so in his ears that, between his need really to satisfy her and another need presently to be noted, he felt that he might not yet take up his stake. He finally went back at his usual hour and found her in her usual place. "Yes, I *am* afraid," he announced as if he had turned that well over and knew now all it meant. "But I gather that you're not."

She faltered, reserving her word. "What is it you fear?"

"Well, that if I go on I *shall* see him."

"And then——?"

"Oh, then," said George Withermore, "I *should* give up!"

She weighed it with her lofty but earnest air. "I think, you know, we must have a clear sign."

"You wish me to try again?"

She hesitated. "You see what it means—for me—to give up."

"Ah, but *you* needn't," Withermore said.

She seemed to wonder, but in a moment she went on.

"It would mean that he won't take from me——" But she dropped for despair.

"Well, what?"

"Anything," said poor Mrs Doyne.

He faced her a moment more. "I've thought myself of the clear sign. I'll try again."

174

THE REAL RIGHT THING

As he was leaving her, however, she remembered. "I'm only afraid that to-night there's nothing ready—no lamp and no fire."

"Never mind," he said from the foot of the stairs; "I'll find things."

To which she answered that the door of the room would probably, at any rate, be open; and retired again as if to wait for him. She had not long to wait; though, with her own door wide and her attention fixed, she may not have taken the time quite as it appeared to her visitor. She heard him, after an interval, on the stair, and he presently stood at her entrance, where, if he had not been precipitate, but rather, as to step and sound, backward and vague, he showed at least as livid and blank.

"I give up."

"Then you've seen him?"

"On the threshold—guarding it."

"Guarding it?" She glowed over her fan. "Distinct?"

"Immense. But dim. Dark. Dreadful," said poor George Withermore.

She continued to wonder. "You didn't go in?"

The young man turned away. "He forbids!"

"You say *I* needn't," she went on after a moment. "Well then, need I?"

"See him?" George Withermore asked.

She waited an instant. "Give up."

"You must decide." For himself he could at last but drop upon the sofa with his bent face in his hands. He was not quite to know afterwards how long he had sat so; it was enough that what he did next know was that he was alone among her favourite objects. Just as he gained his feet, however, with this sense and that of the door standing open to the hall, he found himself afresh confronted, in the light, the warmth, the rosy space, with her big black perfumed presence. He saw at a glance, as she offered him a huger, bleaker stare over the mask of her fan, that she had been above; and so it was that, for the last time, they faced together their strange question. "You've seen him?" Withermore asked.

He was to infer later on from the extraordinary way she closed her eyes and, as if to steady herself, held them tight and long, in silence, that beside the unutterable vision of Ashton Doyne's wife his own might rank as an escape. He knew before she spoke that all was over. "I give up."

George Withermore's allusion to Boswell is suggestive. Henry James had no way of knowing the things we have learned since, following the piecemeal discoveries of portions of the massive journal maintained by

Boswell and, so successfully concealed that they preserved their privacy from the year of his death, 1795, until their discovery in scattered out-of-the-way corners in this century. Readers of Boswell's Life of Johnson had long supposed that Boswell was an obsequious humble follower of the powerful Johnson—a kind of clerk or scribe.

But Boswell's own life, we know now, was rich, full, diverse, passionate, turning from youthful comedy to bloodless tragedy even while Boswell appeared only to be sitting at the great man's feet, asking convenient questions. No man kept himself better out of his own book than Boswell kept himself out of the Life. He was artist, gathering and organizing his materials, and writing them up with a style equal to the style of his subject, but keeping himself, as far as we could see, always aloof. He was what he did. The wretched fellow of the journal hardly matters. It is as if he is someone else.

❧❧❧

John Barth, in "Life-Story," presents the writer at the most dreary of all possible hours, in the most familiar place, at the one purely unavoidable task—"in his study attempting to draft the opening pages of a new short story." The time is nine o'clock on a Monday morning—the time for all good men to be at work. Our author has difficulty getting started today. Most authors do. So does everybody have trouble getting started writing, whether freshmen at their themes or scholars at their monographs.

Soon it is ten o'clock. The writer appears to have spent a full hour between the middle of one paragraph and the end of the next. He is on the point of abandoning the whole thing.

Why so slow? What's stopping him? "Another story about a writer writing a story!" he complains, ". . . and why should a reader be interested?" He need not look far to see hurried readers impatient of his contemplation of his own processes. His wife and daughters prefer "entertainment . . . arresting circumstance, bold character, trenchant action," nothing so deep as he feels compelled to provide. Besides, he is restless himself, he leaves his desk, he lights his pipe, he spies one Gloria sunbathing. Is Gloria his mistress? We do know that his mistress entered his study, at least in his imagination. But on the other hand he has told us that he has no mistress. Of course he may be saying that, or writing that, out of his awareness that his wife will read his writings if only to find out secrets. Is he therefore speaking sideways to her? Or is he telling us the truth? Regardless, some sort of story is taking shape here, and we are relieved on behalf of the writer.

Experience has demonstrated to the writer (whoever he is) of "Life-Story" that "his fiction inevitably made public his private life." This is a variation upon James's idea in "The Real Right Thing"—the writer was what he did; leave his life alone lest you arouse his ghost.

Perhaps this was one of the basic impulses for fiction, to reveal the writer, or to allow him to reveal himself, even while he finds protection in the ambiguity of storytelling. Somewhere in human history exists that first genius who discovered that he could tell his own story by pretending to be telling someone else's; by pretending to be "making this all up," or by pretending it was all a dream, a myth.

It was a clever way of dealing with the reader, of entertaining the reader while putting off his or her biographical curiosity. At the same time, of course, it served the reader, too, for the reader now could read about himself *with the same pretense to disengagement.*

How irritating human beings are! They're so human. They're so subjective. They want to see things the writer hadn't intended them to see. They see things he hadn't meant. Conversely, they fail to see his meaning —or what he thought he meant; or what he remembered meaning.

LIFE-STORY

John Barth

I

Without discarding what he'd already written he began his story afresh in a somewhat different manner. Whereas his earlier version had opened in a straightforward documentary fashion and then degenerated or at least modulated intentionally into irrealism and dissonance he decided this time to tell his tale from start to finish in a conservative, "realistic," unself-conscious way. He being by vocation an author of novels and stories it was perhaps inevitable that one afternoon the possibility would occur to the writer of these lines that his own life might be a fiction, in which he was the leading or an accessory character. He happened at the time[1] to be in his study attempting to draft the opening pages of a new short story; its general idea had preoccupied him for some months along with other general ideas, but certain elements of the conceit, without which he could scarcely proceed, remained unclear. More specifically: narrative plots may be imagined as consisting of a "ground-situation" (Scheherazade desires not to die) focused and dramatized by a "vehicle-situation" (Scheherazade

---

[1] 9:00 A.M., Monday, June 20, 1966.

beguiles the King with endless stories), the several incidents of which have their final value in terms of their bearing upon the "ground-situation." In our author's case it was the "vehicle" that had vouchsafed itself, first as a germinal proposition in his commonplace book—D comes to suspect that the world is a novel, himself a fictional personage—subsequently as an articulated conceit explored over several pages of the workbook in which he elaborated more systematically his casual inspirations: since D is writing a fictional account of this conviction he has indisputably a fictional existence in his account, replicating what he suspects to be his own situation. Moreover E, hero of D's account, is said to be writing a similar account, and so the replication is in both ontological directions, et cetera. But the "ground-situation"—some state of affairs on D's part which would give dramatic resonance to his attempts to prove himself factual, assuming he made such attempts—obstinately withheld itself from his imagination. As is commonly the case the question reduced to one of stakes: what were to be the consequences of D's—and finally E's—disproving or verifying his suspicion, and why should a reader be interested?

What a dreary way to begin a story he said to himself upon reviewing his long introduction. Not only is there no "ground-situation," but the prose style is heavy and somewhat old-fashioned, like an English translation of Thomas Mann, and the so-called "vehicle" itself is at least questionable: self-conscious, vertiginously arch, fashionably solipsistic, unoriginal—in fact a convention of twentieth-century literature. Another story about a writer writing a story! Another regressus in infinitum! Who doesn't prefer art that at least overtly imitates something other than its own processes? That doesn't continually proclaim "Don't forget I'm an artifice!"? That takes for granted its mimetic nature instead of asserting it in order (not so slyly after all) to deny it, or vice-versa? Though his critics sympathetic and otherwise described his own work as avant-garde, in his heart of hearts he disliked literature of an experimental, self-despising, or overtly metaphysical character, like Samuel Beckett's, Marian Cutler's, Jorge Borges's. The logical fantasies of Lewis Carroll pleased him less than straight-forward tales of adventure, subtly sentimental romances, even densely circumstantial realism like Tolstoy's. His favorite contemporary authors were John Updike, Georges Simenon, Nicole Riboud. He had no use for the theater of absurdity, for "black humor," for allegory in any form, for apocalyptic preachments meretriciously tricked out in dramatic garb.

Neither had his wife and adolescent daughters, who for that matter preferred life to literature and read fiction when at all for entertainment. Their kind of story (his too, finally) would begin if not once upon a time

LIFE-STORY

at least with arresting circumstance, bold character, trenchant action. C flung away the whining manuscript and pushed impatiently through the french doors leading to the terrace from his oak-wainscoted study. Pausing at the stone balustrade to light his briar he remarked through a lavender cascade of wisteria that lithe-limbed Gloria, Gloria of timorous eye and militant breast, had once again chosen his boat-wharf as her basking-place.

By Jove he exclaimed to himself. It's particularly disquieting to suspect not only that one is a fictional character but that the fiction one's in—the fiction one is—is quite the sort one least prefers. His wife entered the study with coffee and an apple-pastry, set them at his elbow on his work table, returned to the living room. Ed' pelut' kondo nedode; nyoing nyang. One manifestation of schizophrenia as everyone knows is the movement from reality toward fantasy, a progress which not infrequently takes the form of distorted and fragmented representation, abstract formalism, an increasing preoccupation, even obsession, with pattern and design for their own sakes—especially patterns of a baroque, enormously detailed character—to the (virtual) exclusion of representative "content." There are other manifestations. Ironically, in the case of graphic and plastic artists for example the work produced in the advanced stages of their affliction may be more powerful and interesting than the realistic productions of their earlier "sanity." Whether the artists themselves are gratified by this possibility is not reported.

B called upon a literary acquaintance, B——, summering with Mrs. B and children on the Eastern Shore of Maryland. "You say you lack a ground-situation. Has it occurred to you that circumstance may be your ground-situation? What occurs to me is that if it is it isn't. And conversely. The case being thus, what's really wanting after all is a well-articulated vehicle, a foreground or upstage situation to dramatize the narrator's or author's grundladge. His what. To write merely C comes to suspect that the world is a novel, himself a fictional personage is but to introduce the vehicle; the next step must be to initiate its uphill motion by establishing and complicating some conflict. I would advise in addition the eschewal of overt and self-conscious discussion of the narrative process. The via negativa and its positive counterpart are it is to be remembered poles after all of the same cell. Returning to his study.

If I'm going to be a fictional character G declared to himself I want to be in a rousing good yarn as they say, not some piece of avant-garde preciousness. I want passion and bravura action in my plot, heroes I can admire, heroines I can love, memorable speeches, colorful accessory characters, poetical language. It doesn't matter to me how naively linear the anecdote is; never mind modernity! How reactionary J appears to be.

THE READER

How will such nonsense sound thirty-six years from now?[2] As if. If he can only get K through his story I reflected grimly; if he can only retain his self-possession to the end of this sentence; not go mad; not destroy himself and/or others. Then what I wondered grimly. Another sentence fast, another story. Scheherazade my only love! All those nights you kept your secret from the King my rival, that after your defloration he was unnecessary, you'd have killed yourself in any case when your invention failed.

Why could he not begin his story afresh X wondered, for example with the words why could he not begin his story afresh et cetera? Y's wife came into the study as he was about to throw out the baby with the bathwater. "Not for an instant to throw out the baby while every instant discarding the bathwater is perhaps a chief task of civilized people at this hour of the world."[3] I used to tell B——that without success. What makes you so sure it's not a film he's in or a theater-piece?

Because U responded while he certainly felt rather often that he was merely acting his own role or roles he had no idea who the actor was, whereas even the most Stanislavsky methodist would presumably if questioned closely recollect his offstage identity even onstage in mid-act. Moreover a great part of T's "drama," most of his life in fact, was non-visual, consisting entirely in introspection, which the visual dramatic media couldn't manage easily. He had for example mentioned to no one his growing conviction that he was a fictional character, and since he was not given to audible soliloquizing a "spectator" would take him for a cheerful, conventional fellow, little suspecting that et cetera. It was of course imaginable that much goes on in the mind of King Oedipus in addition to his spoken sentiments; any number of interior dramas might be being played out in the actors' or characters' minds, dramas of which the audience is as unaware as are V's wife and friends of his growing conviction that he's a fictional character—but everything suggested that the medium of his life was prose fiction—moreover a fiction narrated from either the first-person or the third-person-omniscient point of view.

Why is it L wondered with mild disgust that both K and M for example choose to write such stuff when life is so sweet and painful and full of such a variety of people, places, situations, and activities other than self-conscious and after all rather blank introspection? Why is it N wondered et cetera that both M and O et cetera when the world is in such parlous explosive case? Why et cetera et cetera et cetera when the world, which was in the beginning, is now evidently nearing the end of its road? Am I

[2] 10:00 A.M., Monday, June 20, 1966.
[3] 11:00 A.M., Monday, June 20, 1966.

LIFE-STORY

being strung out in this ad libitum fashion I wondered merely to keep my author from the pistol? What sort of story is it whose drama lies always in the next frame out? If Sinbad sinks it's Scheherazade who drowns; whose neck one wonders is on her line?

II

Discarding what he'd already written as he could wish to discard the mumbling pages of his life he began his story afresh, resolved this time to eschew overt and self-conscious discussion of his narrative process and to recount instead in the straight-forwardest manner possible the several complications of his character's conviction that he was a character in a work of fiction, arranging them into dramatically ascending stages if he could for his readers' sake and leading them (the stages) to an exciting climax and denouement if he could.

He rather suspected that the medium and genre in which he worked—the only ones for which he felt any vocation—were moribund if not already dead. The idea pleased him. One of the successfullest men he knew was a blacksmith of the old school who et cetera. He meditated upon the grandest sailing-vessel ever built, the *France II*, constructed in Bordeaux in 1911 not only when but because the age of sail had passed. Other phenomena that consoled and inspired him were the great flying-boat *Hercules*, the zeppelin *Hindenburg*, the *Tsar Pushka* cannon, the then-record Dow-Jones industrial average of 381.17 attained on September 3, 1929.

He rather suspected that the society in which he persisted—the only one with which he felt any degree of identification—was moribund if not et cetera. He knew beyond any doubt that the body which he inhabited—the only one et cetera—was et cetera. The idea et cetera. He had for thirty-six years lacking a few hours been one of our dustmote's three billion tenants give or take five hundred million, and happening to be as well a white male citizen of the United States of America he had thirty-six years plus a few hours more to cope with one way or another unless the actuarial tables were mistaken, not bloody likely, or his term was unexpectedly reduced.

Had he written for his readers' sake? The phrase implied a thitherto-unappreciated metaphysical dimension. Suspense. If his life was a fictional narrative it consisted of three terms—teller, tale, told—each dependent on the other two but not in the same ways. His author could as well tell some other character's tale or some other tale of the same character as the one being told as he himself could in his own character as author; his "reader" could as easily read some other story, would be well advised to; but his own "life" depended absolutely on a particular author's original

THE READER

persistence, thereafter upon some reader's. From this consideration any number of things followed, some less tiresome than others. No use appealing to his author, of whom he'd come to dislike even to think. The idea of his playing with his characters' and his own self-consciousness! He himself tended in that direction and despised the tendency. The idea of his or her smiling smugly to himself as the "words" flowed from his "pen" in which his protagonist's unhappy inner life was exposed! Ah he had mistaken the nature of his narrative; he had thought it very long, longer than Proust's, longer than any German's, longer than *The Thousand Nights and a Night* in ten quarto volumes. Moreover he'd thought it the most prolix and pedestrian *tranche-de-vie* realism, unredeemed by even the limited virtues of colorful squalor, solid specification, an engaging variety of scenes and characters—in a word a bore, of the sort he himself not only would not write but would not read either. Now he understood that his author might as probably resemble himself and the protagonist of his own story-in-progress. Like himself, like his character aforementioned, his author not impossibly deplored the obsolescence of humanism, the passing of *savoir-vivre*, et cetera; admired the outmoded values of fidelity, courage, tact, restraint, amiability, self-discipline, et cetera; preferred fictions in which were to be found stirring actions, characters to love as well as ditto to despise, speeches and deeds to affect us strongly, et cetera. He too might wish to make some final effort to put by his fictional character and achieve factuality or at least to figure in if not be hero of a more attractive fiction, but be caught like the writer of these lines in some more or less desperate tour de force. For him to attempt to come to an understanding with such an author were as futile as for one of his own creations to et cetera.

But the reader! Even if his author were his only reader as was he himself of his work-in-progress as of the sentence-in-progress and his protagonist of his, et cetera, his character as reader was not the same as his character as author, a fact which might be turned to account. What suspense.

As he prepared to explore this possibility one of his mistresses whereof he had none entered his brown study unannounced. "The passion of love," she announced, "which I regard as no less essential to a satisfying life than those values itemized above and which I infer from my presence here that you too esteem highly, does not in fact play in your life a role of sufficient importance to sustain my presence here. It plays in fact little role at all outside your imaginative and/or ary life. I tell you this not in a criticizing spirit, for I judge you to be as capable of the sentiment aforementioned as any other imagin[ative], deep-feeling man in good physical health more or less precisely in the middle of the road of our life. What hampers, even cripples you in this regard is your final preference, which I refrain from analyzing, for the sedater, more responsible pleasures of monogamous fidelity and the serener affections of domesticity, notwithstanding the fact that your enjoyment of these is correspondingly inhibited though not altogether spoiled by an essentially romantical, unstable, irresponsible, death-wishing fancy. V. S. Pritchett, English critic and author, will put the matter succinctly in a soon-to-be-written essay on Flaubert, whose work he'll say depicts the course of ardent longings and violent desires that rise from the horrible, the sensual, and the sadistic. They turn into the virginal and mystical, only to become numb by satiety. At this point pathological boredom leads to a final desire for death and nothingness—the Romantic syndrome. If, not to be unfair, we qualify somewhat the terms horrible and sadistic and understand satiety to include a large measure of vicariousness, this description undeniably applies to one aspect of yourself and your work; and while your ditto has other, even contrary aspects, the net fact is that you have elected familial responsibilities and rewards—indeed, straight-laced middle-classness in general—over the higher expenses of spirit and wastes of shame attendant upon a less regular, more glamorous style of life. So to elect is surely admirable for the layman, even essential if the social fabric, without which there can be no culture, is to be preserved. For the artist, however, and in particular the writer, whose traditional material has been the passions of men and women, the choice is fatal. You having made it I bid you goodnight probably forever."

Even as she left he reached for the sleeping pills cached conveniently in his writing desk and was restrained from their administration only by his being in the process of completing a sentence, which he cravenly strung out at some sacrifice of rhetorical effect upon realizing that he was et cetera. Moreover he added hastily he had not described the intruder for his readers' vicarious satiety: a lovely woman she was, whom he did not after all describe for his readers' et cetera inasmuch as her appearance and character were inconstant. Her interruption of his work inspired a few sentences about the extent to which his fiction inevitably made public his private life, though the trespasses in this particular were as nothing beside those of most of his profession. That is to say, while he did not draw his characters and situations directly from life nor permit his author-protagonist to do so, any moderately attentive reader of his oeuvre, his what, could infer for example that its author feared for example schizophrenia, impotence creative and sexual, suicide—in short living and dying. His fictions were preoccupied with these fears among their other, more serious preoccupations. Hot dog. As of the sentence-in-progress he was not in fact unmanageably schizophrenic, impotent in either respect, or dead by his own hand, but there was always the next sentence to worry about. But there was always the next sentence to worry about. In sum he concluded hastily such limited self-exposure did not constitute a misdemeanor, representing or mis as it did so small an aspect of his total self, negligible a portion of his total life—even which totalities were they made public would be found remarkable only for their being so unremarkable. Well shall he continue.

Bearing in mind that he had not developed what he'd mentioned earlier about turning to advantage his situation vis-à-vis his "reader" (in fact he deliberately now postponed his return to that subject, sensing that it might well constitute the climax of his story) he elaborated one or two ancillary questions, perfectly aware that he was trying, even exhausting, whatever patience might remain to whatever readers might remain to whoever elaborated yet another ancillary question. Was the novel of his life for example a *roman à clef*? Of that genre he was as contemptuous as of the others aforementioned; but while in the introductory adverbial clause it seemed obvious to him that he didn't "stand for" anyone else, any more than he was an actor playing the role of himself, by the time he reached the main clause he had to admit that the question was unanswerable, since the "real" man to whom he'd correspond in a *roman à clef* would not be also in the *roman à clef* and the characters in such works were not themselves aware of their irritating correspondences.

Similarly unanswerable were such questions as when "his" story (so he regarded it for convenience and consolement though for all he knew he might be not the central character; it might be his wife's story, one of his daughter's, his imaginary mistress's, the man-who-once-cleaned-his-chimney's) began. Not impossibly at his birth or even generations earlier: a *Bildungsroman*, an *Erziehungsroman*, a *roman fleuve*. ! More likely at the moment he became convinced of his fictional nature: that's where he'd have begun it, as he'd begun the piece currently under his pen. If so it followed that the years of his childhood and younger manhood weren't "real," he'd suspected as much, in the first-order sense, but a mere "background" consisting of a few well-placed expository insinuations, perhaps misleading, or inferences, perhaps unwarranted, from strategic hints in his present reflections. God so to speak spare his readers from heavyfooted forced expositions of the sort that begin in the countryside near—in May of the year—it occurred to the novelist—that his own life might be a—, in which he was the leading or an accessory character. He happened at the time to be in the oak-wainscoted study of the old family summer residence; through a lavender cascade of hysteria he observed that his wife had once again chosen to be the subject of this clause, itself the direct object of his observation. A lovely woman she was, whom he did not

LIFE-STORY

describe in keeping with his policy against drawing characters from life as who should draw a condemnee to the gallows. Begging his pardon. Flinging his tiresome tale away he pushed impatiently through the French windows leading from his study to a sheer drop from the then-record high into a nearly fatal depression.

He clung onto his narrative depressed by the disproportion of its ratiocination to its dramatization, reflection to action. One had heard *Hamlet* criticized as a collection of soliloquies for which the implausible plot was a mere excuse; witnessed Italian operas whose dramatic portions were no more than interstitial relief and arbitrary continuity between the arias. If it was true that he didn't take his "real" life seriously enough even when it had him by the throat, the fact didn't lead him to consider whether the fact was a cause or a consequence of his tale's tedium or both.

Concluding these reflections he concluded these reflections: that there was at this advanced page still apparently no ground-situation suggested that his story was dramatically meaningless. If one regarded the absence and his vain endeavors to supply the defect, as itself a sort of ground-situation, did his life-story thereby take on a kind of meaning? A "dramatic" sort he supposed, though of so sophistical a character as more likely to annoy than to engage.

III

The reader! You, dogged, uninsultable, print-oriented bastard, it's you I'm addressing, who else, from inside this monstrous fiction. You've read me this far, then? Even this far? For what discreditable motive? How is it you don't go to a movie, watch TV, stare at a wall, play tennis with a friend, make amorous advances to the person who comes to your mind when I speak of amorous advances? Can nothing surfeit, saturate you, turn you off? Where's your shame?

Having let go this barrage of rhetorical or at least unanswered questions and observing himself nevertheless in midst of yet another sentence he concluded and caused the "hero" of his story to conclude that one or more of three things must be true: 1) his author was his sole and indefatigable reader; 2) he was in a sense his own author, telling his story to himself, in which case in which case; and/or 3) his reader was not only tireless and shameless but sadistic, masochistic if he was himself.

For why do you suppose—you! you!—he's gone on so, so relentlessly refusing to entertain you as he might have at a less desperate than this hour of the world[4] with felicitous language, exciting situation, unforgettable character and image? Why has he as it were ruthlessly set about not

[4] 11:00 P.M., Monday, June 20, 1966.

THE READER

to turn you away? Because your own author bless and damn you his life is in your hands! He writes and reads himself; don't you think he knows who gives his creatures their lives and deaths? Do they exist except as he or others read their words? Age except we turn their pages? And can he die until you have no more of him? Time was obviously when his author could have turned the trick; his pen had once to left-to-right it through these words as does your kindless eye and might have ceased at any one. This. This. And did not as you see but went on like an Oriental torture-master to the end.

But you needn't! He exclaimed to you. In vain. Had he petitioned you instead to read slowly in the happy parts, what happy parts, swiftly in the painful no doubt you'd have done the contrary or cut him off entirely. But as he longs to die and can't without your help you force him on, force him on. Will you deny you've read this sentence? This? To get away with murder doesn't appeal to you, is that it? As if your hands weren't inky with other dyings! As if he'd know you'd killed him! Come on. He dares you.

In vain. You haven't: the burden of his knowledge. That he continues means that he continues, a fortiori you too. Suicide's impossible: he can't kill himself without your help. Those petitions aforementioned, even his silly plea for death—don't you think he understands their sophistry, having authored their like for the wretches he's authored? Read him fast or slow, intermittently, continuously, repeatedly, backward, not at all, he won't know it; he only guesses someone's reading or composing sentences such as this one; the net effect is that there's a net effect, of continuity and an apparently consistent flow of time, though his pages do seem to pass more swiftly as they near his end.

To what conclusion will he come? He'd been about to append to his own tale inasmuch as the old analogy between Author and God, novel and world, can no longer be employed unless deliberately as a false analogy, certain things follow: 1) fiction must acknowledge its fictitiousness and metaphoric invalidity or 2) choose to ignore the question or deny its relevance or 3) establish some other, acceptable relation between itself, its author, its reader. Just as he finished doing so however his real wife and imaginary mistresses entered his study; "It's a little past midnight" she announced with a smile; "do you know what that means?"

Though she'd come into his story unannounced at a critical moment he did not describe her, for even as he recollected that he'd seen his first light just thirty-six years before the night incumbent he saw his last: that he could not after all be a character in a work of fiction inasmuch as such a fiction would be of an entirely different character from what he thought of as fiction. Fiction consisted of such monuments of the imagination as

LIFE-STORY

Cutler's *Morganfield*, Riboud's *Tales Within Tales*, his own creations; fact of such as for example read those fictions. More, he could demonstrate by syllogism that the story of his life was a work of fact: though assaults upon the boundary between life and art, reality and dream, were undeniably a staple of his own and his century's literature as they'd been of Shakespeare's and Cervantes's, yet it was a fact that in the corpus of fiction as far as he knew no fictional character had become convinced as had he that he was a character in a work of fiction. This being the case and he having in fact become thus convinced it followed that his conviction was false. "Happy birthday," said his wife et cetera, kissing him et cetera to obstruct his view of the end of the sentence he was nearing the end of, playfully refusing to be nay-said so that in fact he did at last as did his fictional character end his ending story endless by interruption cap his pen.

The wife of Ashton Doyne, committing the remains of her husband to the young biographer, "had not taken Doyne seriously enough in life." The wife of the writer in "Life-Story" may not take her husband seriously enough.

Writers may feel neglected. Therefore, in one way or another, they often choose to write of neglected people, themselves in extremis, *of humble, obscure people who may be reflections of themselves: the "ambitious guest," Felicité in "A Simple Heart," the slaughtered beasts of James Agee, the obliterated carpenter of "But For This . . .", the mortal hawk Hook, the "hunger artist," the violated child of "Counterparts."*

If the writer is not himself outstandingly victimized he has nevertheless the imagination of what it must be like to be so. He is sensitive to the way the world works, if not for himself then for others. The writer makes symbols of things, especially of himself.

PART TWO
THE READER'S VIEW: SOURCES OF IMAGERY

V | Myth and Symbol

A sage once remarked that fiction is the lie we tell ourselves to identify our humanity. A philosopher-psychologist, Carl Jung, refined the idea when he referred to the "collective unconscious" of the human race. He meant that we share the sense of imagination and ritual about our humanity that results in patters of form, of worship, of social behavior universally recognizable. One of these patterns, in which all the foregoing come together, is tale-telling.

We are all tale-tellers from our earliest times, although some of us become better at it than others do as time goes by. But our experience at telling and whatever it is we share of the collective unconscious make us communicants in the ritual of story. As readers, therefore, we are already a distance toward understanding the tale-tellers of this book. We have something in common. It is helpful to understand that writers are discussing our commonality in their work, each writer in a special way with a special feeling. They write out of the simplicity of their humanity and the complexity of their culture and their psychology. In the same way, we read.

Two of the very useful tools writers draw upon they share with us as readers—myth and symbol. Both are rich sources of imagery, "mental pictures," which like the sage's lie, help identify our humanity.

Now then, let us try Northrop Frye's helpful distinctions about such mythical patterns as dawn-birth-spring; evening-death-winter; the opposing or antithetical powers of darkness, revival, or resurrection.* In Frye's view, the human cycle of waking and dreaming corresponds to the natural cycle of light and darkness, and the seeking of the one when the other is upon us. In literature, Frye believes, the central myth is the Quest, the search. Using his insight, we speculate that fiction can reflect at a concrete level the human search for light or dark, present in myth at the abstract level as the hero-god Quest. With the help of Meridel Le Sueur's title, "Persephone," our speculation thus reflects the parallel between the

* Northrop Frye, *Anatomy of Criticism* (Princeton, N.J.: Princeton University Press, 1957).

MYTH AND SYMBOL

events of her narrative and the details of the myth of Demeter and Persephone.

One interpretation of human events is that the outcome of life is predetermined, foretold in advance by certain forces. Such an interpretation is called "fate," and fate takes many forms. In Greek and Roman mythology, for instance, it was believed that three goddesses, Atropos, Clotho, and Lachesis, controlled each destiny. Eventually, Western economics produced the philosophy of "determinism"—not fate now, but "scientific" doctrine expounding the belief that certain class systems and working conditions delimit possibility. Emile Zola, a French writer, was influenced by the doctrine of economic determinism. But Thomas Hardy, an Englishman, wrote of a universe whose utter indifference to a puny force called "man" produced another kind of determinism, fate not by design but by accident.

Elsewhere in this book, the legendlike quality of Hawthorne's "The Ambitious Guest" suggests that "accident" is the product of a larger control. We are reminded of an ancient Dutch proverb full of malevolence, "Man plans, and God laughs."

Call it what you will, a larger control or force, accident, magic, or history. Writers can take a moment and make us aware that we are seeing this moment from a vantage point in solved time and space, a long way out, watching our own past unfold. "The Procurator of Judaea" in another section of the book presents us with such a moment; it deals with the Christ, a grave and portentous symbol. Forthcoming here we have another historical moment, that presented by William Faulkner. It deals in great part with American Indians, that special world symbol of the "noble savage."

Myth and symbol are intricate parts of history and psychology, the usable past which the literary sensibility translates into the "shock of recognition," the insights we most humanly share. "For England and St. George," Shakespeare has his kingly hero, Henry V, shout to his soldiers. It is rallying cry against fate. But for the millions of children who have loved the fairy tale, St. George slew the dragon not for England but for the preservation of dreams.

PERSEPHONE

Meridel Le Sueur

We boarded the train at a Kansas town. Its black houses sat low amidst the fields which were hardening and darkening now the summer was over. The corn had been shocked, the seed lay in the granaries, the earth had closed, and now the sun hung naked in the sky. All was over—the festival, the flowering, the harvesting. Dark days had come and I was taking the daughter of Freda away to discover, if I could, the malady which made her suffer.

As the train moved from the station I watched Freda standing on the platform, her round face shadowed by the train as it passed between her and the low sun. The daughter leaned against the window for the last sight of her mother; as we left the town she sat with her small head bent as if half broken from her body.

We sped through the dying country, fleeing through the low land. Upon the fields as they lay upturned and dark, clear to the sound swinging sky-line, there fell the eerie wan light of the dying season. The train as it traveled through this dim sea of light became uncanny and frail, touched, too, with the bright delicacy of decay. But upon the daughter of Freda the last light dwelt intimately as she lay half sleeping, like the fields, fatally within the cycle of the dying earth.

Fatigued after the preparations for the journey, she rested in utter weariness. Her black garments hung, about to exhaust her, while out from them like sudden flowers sprang her hands and face. Over her great eyes the lids were lowered and gave to her whole being a magical abstraction, as if she looked eternally within, or down through the earth. Only her mouth had tasted of violent fruit; it drooped in her face and turned red when she coughed, which she did frequently, dipping her head like a blind bird.

As I watched her an old pain brewed within me: a faint nostalgia which had come upon me all my life when looking upon her, or when in the presence of her mother, as if upon seeing these two women a kind of budding came about on all the secret unflowered tendrils of my being, to blossom and break in the spaces of a strange world, far from my eyes and hands.

Just when the round and naked sun hung on the horizon, three bulls, standing in the dim, nether light, turned and loped towards our train.

"The black bull," I said, "looked like your husband's."

She lifted the white lids from her eyes, but did not speak. When I repeated what I said, she turned away without answering and sat with her hands in her lap, her eyes lowered, in an attitude so fatal and hopeless that I knew it was of no use to take her on this train, through these fields, past these rivers and houses to our destination. Nothing lay in these things that could mitigate her illness. The malady was too deep.

As we sped through the fields, the fantastic conquering of distance threw a magic over us so that terrible and vast things became possible.

With the dying of the sun the train traveled through a colossal cave, between the closed earth and the closed sky and I half forgot our departure and our destination.

I have always expected some metamorphosis to take place in Freda and her daughter—a moment when the distant look would, by miracle, go from their eyes and they would reveal their nativity in some awful gesture. Nothing had ever happened beyond the natural ritual of our common farm life. But there came upon me now the old mystic credulity as I watched Freda's daughter sitting motionless, her white lids rounding over her eyes, her face glowing in the gloom.

Lying there, she contained like a white seed the mystery of her origin. The marks of living were slight upon her, for from the first she seemed to carry most strongly the mark of a perpetual death. Paradoxically I thought that because death was her intimate, I could never come nearer her mystery than to her birth on the prairies, in the spring as the first white violets bloomed.

For the women of the Kansas town, shading their eyes, had seen Freda coming from the prairies, walking and carrying the child.

"Whose baby is that?" the woman asked her when she had come to them.

And she answered, "Mine." And uncovered for them to see, bending down to them.

"When was it born?" these women to whom birth was a great dread, asked.

She answered smiling. "In the night." And she went into a store and bought some goods with little flowers marked on it in which she wrapped the baby.

That year the days were bright and the earth bountiful. For each ear of corn heretofore, there were now two. The sun ripened all that had been sown. The soil was so hot we could not suffer our bare feet upon it. Freda's lands were the most fertile of all.

Her husband, Frantz, the strongest man in the country, was a plowman. We saw him in the fields, dark and stocky, driving his big flanked horses, astride the black furrows that turned behind him. When he came to our fields we were frightened by his narrow eyes buried in the flesh, and by his hands matted with hair.

Together, Frantz and Freda plowed the fields; there was a feeling abroad that never had Freda sown a seed that had not come to fruition. It was true that for her everything blossomed.

In the spring we met her in the fields or in the thickets, where the first flowers were springing alone. In the full, golden light she came towards us, full-bosomed, with baskets of wild berries hanging on her bright arms. When we ran to her, she gave us gifts, berries, nuts, and wild fruits unknown to us.

At harvest time she worked in the fields with the men. When we brought her water she straightened from the earth to loom above us, curving against the sky; a strong odor would come from her, like the odor of the earth when it is just turned; her yellow hair would glisten round her face and we thought it grew from her head exactly as the wheat grew from the earth. Once when she leaned over me, I grew faint with the fertile odor and at the same time drops of perspiration fell from her temples on my face.

When her mare was seen hitched outside the houses of the town, we knew that a great, natural, and dreadful thing was taking place within. The house became, after that, marked, possessing a strange significance of birth. We children, while the mare waited, sat on the curb watching for Freda, who, when she came, passed in a kind of confusion of her great body, the golden hair, and the strong, sweet odor. We would watch the hips of the horse, with Freda upon her, disappearing down the road, past the houses of the town, out into the open plains.

The child of Freda, delicate and pale from the first, was not much known or seen about. She came to town on the first spring days, with her mother, riding in the wagon, atop the early vegetables. She carried with her always, falling from her hands, the first white violets. It did not astonish us that she was thus privy to the first stirrings of the season, since we glimpsed her through all the year in the prairies, by the streams, or hidden in the nooks of the fragrant hills. In the fall, returning from berry hunting, she brushed past us in the chill dusk. In the winter, as we went to the frozen creek, we glimpsed her peering from the naked bush. In the spring we saw her come by her mother, with the first violets. She never spoke to us, but covered her enormous eyes with her lids, standing quite still, before us but irrevocably hidden.

On Saturdays as Freda went about the town she hid behind her skirts, her eyes lowered in her slim, pale face. Some women would stop in the streets and say she was idiotic because of her little head. To me, however, she had a strange grace, with her swelling body, her little head and pale face, her eyes like minerals, and her hair light like her mother's but fine and thin as if it had grown outside the light of the sun.

When Freda and her husband were plowing the fields, the girl, who grew very tall, would run in the wake of the plow, singing. Franz hated her, as everyone knew, and he hated her singing. When Freda with her horses went plunging through the black waves to the horizon, he would leave his plow and strike at the girl. She would veer away as if only the wind had struck her, still singing.

When I could run away from the town I used to lie in the damp thicket which bordered their field and watch them: the dark man straddling the furrows, following the rumps of his horses, holding the plow to the heavy soil; Freda with her skirts on the earth, the horses turning their great eyes to look back at her, the fields lying about her with their living secrets—I watched with satisfaction these two heavy figures, turning the vast earth, moving upon her stillnesses, and the slim girl, like an antelope, running in the fields beside them, singing high and shrill.

She coughed beside me, dipping her little head like a bird. Now no song was in her.

Outside rapidly past us moved the thickets, the fields, the villages. A woman stood in a doorway, half invisible in the dusk, hoisting a baby on her hip—a man came down the road with his team, the white breath of the horses flying from them in the dusk.

The visible world was sinking into another sea, into a faint dusk. The daughter of Freda lay like a fallen and despoiled angel, traveling through darkness, lost to the realm of her nativity, with neither memory nor anticipation. Still I watched her trying to spin around her the stuff of reality. Did there exist for her the seed of our common life or had she eaten only the fruit of perpetual strangeness and death? All that had happened to her, all the incidents of her life, I brought to bear upon her, but I had easier made a mark upon the wind. These things had made no mark upon her. The only mark was her mark upon life, upon all of us who saw her as a frail lost child in the fields of her mother, as a woman ravished by strangeness.

The young farm boys, still delicate with the wind and the fire which is the mark of light and air before the fields harden them, were the only ones who came close to Freda's daughter. They often told us in the evenings that they had met her in the thickets or coming across the fields, and had talked with her. But then they would say no more.

The older youths found it impossible to snare the footsteps of the delicate girl. Strange to say, on the other hand, the firm and serious farm youth were convinced of her wantonness, while old ladies rocking on their porches hinted dark things of her.

But one night a man came to town, from the West, driving his cattle, packed and bellowing, through the deserted streets.

The next morning people said to each other, "Did you hear the cattle going by in the night?" We children thought it had been only a dream until, early in the morning, we saw on the lawn the deep prints of cloven hoofs. When I went for the morning milk, just outside the town, I saw the cattle where they stood sleeping, knee-deep in the grass and mist. As I was passing a man sat up, from where he too had been sleeping, and looked at me from the grasses. His beard stood out like bracken. From his low forehead the black hair sprang. When I saw him about to rise, I ran into the town shouting to my brothers that the cattle they had heard and thought were only the sound in a dream, had really gone down our streets, and had stopped on the outskirts of the town.

It came to be known that the man I had seen in the grasses went by the name of March. Saturday he came into the town riding a splendid horse. He went about the streets talking in a loud voice to the country people. He was to be seen too, at the horse barns, or at public auctions. Saturday nights he herded what cattle he had purchased, sometimes only a fine bull, to the pasture he had bought next to Freda's land. He became famous through the countryside for his pedigreed bulls. The farmers came in season to lead them to their own pastures for breeding.

It happened in a very subtle way that the countryside came to think of Freda and her daughter and the man March, all three together, as somehow of the same blood. All the vital acts of farm life came to move around one or the other of them. Freda and her husband seemed intimate with the fields, and the half mystical rites of planting and reaping. It was said in wonder that Freda even brought in the lambs as they were dropped in the fields in the spring as if she knew their time. She appeared to the women at the oven and her appearance augured good bread. It was out their road the farmers went for the breeding of their cows. The very lay of the land with its rich dark color was strange, so was the magic they had with the earth and with natural things. Freda's daughter held a more strange mystery. She seemed half evil at times. But after she saved the life of a boy, when his body had turned black, they sought her out for palliatives.

So that it came about that the country people, as they dreamed over their work in the spring and autumn, were half unconsciously touched by the mystery of their tasks—a mystery between their own action and the secret of what they acted upon, by virtue of which alliance everything they did prospered and yielded in the field, the vine, the flesh. Probably because they were, in a manner of speaking, without a God, when in their dream, in a kind of blind ecstasy over the earth, within the heat, they attributed dimly to the figure of Freda, and with her the other two, an alliance and an intimacy with the virtue and the mystery, along with something sinister, of the natural things of which their lives were made.

After the corn had been husked and the dreary Kansas cold had set in, I was wandering in the thicket which ran along the stream in a little curve of the fields below Freda's. The pale sun, casting no shadow, shone on the naked sod and the land, low and flat, swelled a little to the sky. This side of Freda's the bulls stood in the wind, quite still.

I had just left the path and gone further into the thickets for berries, when, out of the dying woods, with only a slight sound like a bird's, ran the daughter of Freda. March came after her. I could hear his feet strike the bare ground, and saw as he ran past me, his black beard and hair struck by the wind as he ran into the open. She had climbed the barbed wire fence and was running in the bull pasture, through the crisp grasses toward her mother's. But three bulls turned at the farthest fence and eyed her. When she turned back, frightened, March was running to her. Then she stood binding her skirts around her, her small head, like a dying birds, thrown back. As she seemed about to cry out, he came upon her and bore her with him into the grasses. A young bull struck the ground with his forefeet and loped toward the sun. I ran back into the thicket.

The next days I was filled with terror because of what I had seen. I dared not go upon the road to the fields, or even out under the sky. The third day I came home and there in the dusk was Freda, leaning in our door.

"She is gone," I heard her say.

My mother spoke from the dark kitchen. "And is he gone too, with all the cattle?"

"Yes," said Freda and stood suffering in the dusk. After a while she walked away down the dim road.

Frantz came in the night, knocking and pounding at our door to know where she had gone.

That winter she grew very old. The farmers, through the frosty moonlight, saw her wandering the barren plains. Children screamed when she approached the town. She seemed like an old woman whose time of fertility has gone. In the nights she came knocking at the doors of the village to ask for her daughter.

That year the spring never came. The flowers died beneath the ground and the fields burned in the sun.

Through the hot days of spring we saw her far off, unreal in the simmering heat. We found her by the old well in our orchard, sitting, sorrowing on the stones, her hair wild and white. We were young girls from school with bright ribbons in our hair. We had come to cool our faces over the black opening of the well and to cry down its sides to hear the sweet, far echo answer us. But when we saw her there we drew together, whispering and peering at her. She rose and came toward us, no longer bright and bold, but still terrible, looming above us. She went among us as we hid our faces in our aprons, stroking our hair and arms, calling each of us by the same name. It was a name I had never heard before and I could never, after that, remember it. She peered at each of us so close that we trembled when her breath came upon us. When she turned her sad eyes to the well again we ran from her in every direction, through the orchard, and for the rest of the afternoon watched her from behind the trees as she sat on the stones of the well, sorrowing.

One evening late in summer, as the land lay still beneath the drought, my brother came from the fields, and standing before us with the heat of the day on his face, he said, "I saw Freda's daughter walking toward her mother's."

That night the country people thought it strange that the first rains fell, plunging ceaselessly into the earth.

The train stopped at a siding amidst the prairies in a sudden silence. The woman, aroused, sat up with her eyes wide open.

"How far are we?" she asked in a light voice.

I answered her very low, "From where?"

Before she could answer a fit of coughing shook her and the train started again.

The lights were lit. She was timid about going into the diner, but at last, with vague gestures, lifting her pale hands she put over her head an old velvet hat and rose and went down the aisle, forlorn and pale, with a kind of assaulted and pathetic dignity.

I came behind her, looking at the tall body as it moved with its peculiar grace. It was like this she had come back to Freda's, with this delicate, hopeless grace, as if she had touched strange fruits and eaten pale and deathless seeds.

After the summer, March had come back, driving his bulls through the street to the old pasture. He had knocked at Freda's door and Freda had given her daughter back to him. She had gone to live in his low hut. When we passed we saw her come out of the door to throw the dishwater over the bare ground. Her thick black skirts, given her now by the women of the town, would be pulling and dragging about her, her little head would swirl up from them, free as a serpent's. After she had thrown the water she would stand still, tall and hopeless, in that terrible abstraction, looking toward us with her blind, deep eyes.

In the diner she seated herself with timid, quick movements, then sat with her eyes lowered. Some arrangement of the heavy skirt annoyed her; she fingered it delicately beneath the table. She coughed, turning her head and frowning. In an effort to suppress the cough the tears started, and did not fall, but hung there magnifying her great eyes. Suddenly, unable to bear the light, she closed them. Again the lids covered her eyes, by some bewitchment her face became beautiful and eternal. I felt again the imminent metamorphosis as if she were about to change before my eyes and as always in haste as if to prevent a phenomenon which I both hoped for and dreaded, I spoke.

"Did you see the fine bulls that ran toward our train?"

She lifted her eyes and looked at me, but did not answer.

"I believe the black one was the one your husband sold the upstate farmer." She was looking at me. "Did you see the bulls just before dark?"

"No," she said and the answer startled me.

Whether it was the natural desolateness of traveling between places, likely to give to the form of what reality we know a vast and fabulous temper, or the sorrow of the dying year, I do not know, but back in the car, I became desolate and afraid.

For the remaining hours I sat opposite, watching her sleeping. I brooded over her, half expectant as if about to startle from the mist that covered her, the winged bird which was the secret of her being. I watched her with pain as she moved me with her ancient mystery, as of something half remembered.

It seemed to me again that a metamorphosis was about to take place here on this train, going through Kansas, that the bounds of all that I had known would be shattered before me. Lying before me, she lost what semblance of reality she ever had and seemed to glow and live in other elements than I knew.

What strange realms had thrust her forth to be born of her mother in the night, to put upon her the burden of endless movement through fields, upon the earth, through many days under the burder of shadowless nights, marked with the mark of strangeness to be usurped by an unfamiliar man, to walk through unfamiliar places, and to carry unfamiliar burdens.

Watching her glow before me with her terrible veiled identity, a strangeness of everything came upon me and a terror. I felt suddenly that after this journey, in which after all nothing had happened, I should never be the same; that by looking upon her I was partaking of some poisonous drug, like the poison of early spring flowers and the poison of late berries.

I dared not move in my terror, afraid she might stir, but she sat still, preoccupied, with her eyes hidden, dreaming of what she had never forgotten. Cautiously I came near to her mystery. She among us all had known that living was a kind of dying. When in these realms, she had refused to partake of our fruits and so become enamored, but had closed herself in the dream which is real and from which we die when we are born.

Soon now we would come upon the city glittering on the plain, above the bluffs of the river. A terror of all that lived came upon me; a terror of Freda's daughter who lay as if dead, glowing already in the mineral worlds of her strange lord. Because of the terror I said to myself, this woman is only the wife of a Kansas stockman—but who is the stockman? We saw him driving his bulls through the night, but who is he? Who is her mother? We saw her in the ripe fields, and turning the soil to fertility —but who is she?

All in that town came to me, all I had known passed before me, and I said, who are they? And I did not know.

RED LEAVES

William Faulkner

I

The two Indians crossed the plantation toward the slave quarters. Neat with whitewash, of baked soft brick, the two rows of houses in which lived the slaves belonging to the clan, faced one another across the mild shade of the lane marked and scored with naked feet and with a few homemade toys mute in the dust. There was no sign of life.

"I know what we will find," the first Indian said.

"What we will not find," the second said. Although it was noon, the lane was vacant, the doors of the cabins empty and quiet; no cooking smoke rose from any of the chinked and plastered chimneys.

"Yes. It happened like this when the father of him who is now the Man died."

"You mean, of him who was the Man."

"Yao."

The first Indian's name was Three Basket. He was perhaps sixty. They were both squat men, a little solid, burgherlike; paunchy, with big heads, big, broad, dust-colored faces of a certain blurred serenity like carved heads on a ruined wall in Siam or Sumatra, looming out of a mist. The sun had done it, the violent sun, the violent shade. Their hair looked like sedge grass on burnt-over land. Clamped through one ear Three Basket wore an enameled snuffbox.

"I have said all the time that this is not the good way. In the old days there were no quarters, no Negroes. A man's time was his own then. He had time. Now he must spend most of it finding work for them who prefer sweating to do."

"They are like horses and dogs."

"They are like nothing in this sensible world. Nothing contents them save sweat. They are worse than the white people."

"It is not as though the Man himself had to find work for them to do."

"You said it. I do not like slavery. It is not the good way. In the old days, there was the good way. But not now."

"You do not remember the old way either."

"I have listened to them who do. And I have tried this way. Man was not made to sweat."

"That's so. See what it has done to their flesh."

"Yes. Black. It has a bitter taste, too."

"You have eaten of it?"

"Once. I was young then, and more hardy in the appetite than now. Now it is different with me."

"Yes, They are too valuable to eat now."

"There is a bitter taste to the flesh which I do not like."

"They are too valuable to eat, anyway, when the white men will give horses for them."

They entered the lane. The mute, meager toys—the fetish-shaped objects made of wood and rags and feathers—lay in the dust about the patinaed doorsteps, among bones and broken gourd dishes. But there was no sound from any cabin, no face in any door; had not been since yesterday, when Issetibbeha died. But they already knew what they would find.

It was in the central cabin, a house a little larger than the others, where at certain phases of the moon the Negroes would gather to begin their ceremonies before removing after nightfall to the creek bottom, where they kept the drums. In this room they kept the minor accessories, the cryptic ornaments, the ceremonial records which consisted of sticks daubed with red clay in symbols. It had a hearth in the center of the floor, beneath a hole in the roof, with a few cold wood ashes and a suspended iron pot. The window shutters were closed; when the two Indians entered, after the abashless sunlight they could distinguish nothing with the eyes save a movement, shadow, out of which eyeballs rolled, so that the place appeared to be full of Negroes. The two Indians stood in the door.

"Yao," Basket said. "I said this is not the good way."

"I don't think I want to be here," the second said.

"That is black man's fear which you smell. It does not smell as ours does."

"I don't think I want to be here."

"Your fear has an odor too."

"Maybe it is Issetibbeha which we smell."

"Yao. He knows. He knows what we will find here. He knew when he died what we should find here today." Out of the rank twilight of the room the eyes, the smell, of Negroes rolled about them. "I am Three Basket, whom you know," Basket said into the room. "We are come from the Man. He whom we seek is gone?" The Negroes said nothing. The smell of them, of their bodies, seemed to ebb and flux in the still hot air. They seemed to be musing as one upon something remote, inscrutable. They were like a single octopus. They were like the roots of a huge tree uncovered, the earth broken momentarily upon the writhen, thick, fetid tangle of its lightless and outraged life. "Come," Basket said. "You know our errand. Is he whom we seek gone?"

"They are thinking something," the second said. "I do not want to be here."

"They are knowing something," Basket said.

"They are hiding him, you think?"

"No. He is gone. He has been gone since last night. It happened like this before, when the grandfather of him who is now the Man died. It took us three days to catch him. For three days Doom lay above the ground, saying, 'I see my horse and my dog. But I do not see my slave. What have you done with him that you will not permit me to lie quiet?'"

"They do not like to die."

"Yao. They cling. It makes trouble for us, always. A people without honor and without decorum. Always a trouble."

"I do not like it here."

"Nor do I. But then, they are savages; they cannot be expected to regard usage. That is why I say that this way is a bad way."

"Yao. They cling. They would even rather work in the sun than to enter the earth with a chief. But he is gone."

The Negroes had said nothing, made no sound. The white eyeballs rolled, wild, subdued; the smell was rank, violent. "Yes, they fear," the second said. "What shall we do now?"

"Let us go and talk with the Man."

"Will Moketubbe listen?"

"What can he do? He will not like to. But he is the Man now."

"Yao. He is the Man. He can wear the shoes with the red heels all the time now." They turned and went out. There was no door in the door frame. There were no doors in any of the cabins.

"He did that anyway," Basket said.

"Behind Issetibbeha's back. But now they are his shoes, since he is the Man."

"Yao. Issetibbeha did not like it. I have heard. I know that he said to Moketubbe: 'When you are the Man, the shoes will be yours. But until then, they are my shoes.' But now Moketubbe is the Man; he can wear them."

"Yao," the second said. "He is the Man now. He used to wear the shoes behind Issetibbeha's back, and it was not known if Issetibbeha knew this or not. And then Issetibbeha became dead, who was not old, and the shoes are Moketubbe's, since he is the Man now. What do you think of that?"

"I don't think about it," Basket said. "Do you?"

"No," the second said.

"Good," Basket said. "You are wise."

II

The house sat on a knoll, surrounded by oak trees. The front of it was one story in height, composed of the deck house of a steamboat which had gone ashore and which Doom, Issetibbeha's father, had dismantled with his slaves and hauled on cypress rollers twelve miles home overland. It took them five months. His house consisted at the time of one brick wall. He set the steamboat broadside on to the wall, where now the chipped and flaked gilding of the rococo cornices arched in faint splendor above the gilt lettering of the stateroom names above the jalousied doors.

Doom had been born merely a subchief, a Mingo, one of three children on the mother's side of the family. He made a journey—he was a young man then and New Orleans was a European city—from north Mississippi to New Orleans by keel boat, where he met the Chevalier Sœur Blonde de Vitry, a man whose social position, on its face, was as equivocal as Doom's own. In New Orleans, among the gamblers and cutthroats of the river front, Doom, under the tutelage of his patron, passed as the chief, the Man, the hereditary owner of that land which belonged to the male side of the family; it was the Chevalier de Vitry who spoke of him as *l'Homme* or *de l'Homme,* and hence Doom.

They were seen everywhere together—the Indian, the squat man with a bold, inscrutable, underbred face, and the Parisian, the expatriate, the friend, it was said, of Carondelet and the intimate of General Wilkinson. Then they disappeared, the two of them, vanishing from their old equivocal haunts and leaving behind them the legend of the sums which Doom was believed to have won, and some tale about a young woman, daughter of a fairly well-to-do West Indian family, the son and brother of whom sought Doom with a pistol about his old haunts for some time after his disappearance.

Six months later the young woman herself disappeared, boarding the Saint Louis packet, which put in one night at a wood landing on the north

RED LEAVES

Mississippi side, where the woman, accompanied by a Negro maid, got off. Four Indians met her with a horse and wagon, and they traveled for three days, slowly, since she was already big with child, to the plantation, where she found that Doom was now chief. He never told her how he accomplished it, save that his uncle and his cousin had died suddenly. Before that time the house had consisted of a brick wall built by shiftless slaves, against which was propped a thatched lean-to divided into rooms and littered with bones and refuse, set in the center of ten thousand acres of matchless parklike forest where deer grazed like domestic cattle. Doom and the woman were married there a short time before Issetibbeha was born, by a combination itinerant minister and slave trader who arrived on a mule, to the saddle of which was lashed a cotton umbrella and a three-gallon demijohn of whiskey. After that, Doom began to acquire more slaves and to cultivate some of his land, as the white people did. But he never had enough for them to do. In utter idleness the majority of them led lives transplanted whole out of Africa jungles, save on the occasions when, entertaining guests, Doom coursed them with dogs.

When Doom died, Issetibbeha, his son, was nineteen. He became proprietor of the land and of the quintupled herd of blacks for which he had no use at all. Though the title of Man rested with him, there was a hierarchy of cousins and uncles who ruled the clan and who finally gathered in squatting conclave over the Negro question, squatting profoundly beneath the golden names above the doors of the steamboat.

"We cannot eat them," one said.

"Why not?"

"There are too many of them."

"That's true," a third said. "Once we started, we should have to eat them all. And that much flesh diet is not good for man."

"Perhaps they will be like deer flesh. That cannot hurt you."

"We might kill a few of them and not eat them," Issetibbeha said.

They looked at him for a while. "What for?" one said.

"That is true," a second said. "We cannot do that. They are too valuable; remember all the bother they have caused us, finding things for them to do. We must do as the white men do."

"How is that?" Issetibbeha said.

"Raise more Negroes by clearing more land to make corn to feed them, then sell them. We will clear the land and plant it with food and raise Negroes and sell them to the white men for money."

"But what will we do with this money?" a third said.

They thought for a while.

"We will see," the first said. They squatted, profound, grave.

"It means work," the third said.

"Let the Negroes do it," the first said.

"Yao. Let them. To sweat is bad. It is damp. It opens the pores."

"And then the night air enters."

So they cleared the land with the Negroes and planted it in grain. Up to that time the slaves had lived in a huge pen with a lean-to roof over one corner, like a pen for pigs. But now they began to build quarters, cabins, putting the young Negroes in the cabins to mate; five years later Issetibbeha sold forty head to a Memphis trader, and he took the money and went abroad upon it, his maternal uncle from New Orleans conducting the trip. At that time the Chevalier Sœur Blonde de Vitry was an old man in Paris, in a toupee and a corset and a careful, toothless old face fixed in a grimace quizzical and profoundly tragic. He borrowed three hundred dollars from Issetibbeha and in return he introduced him into certain circles; a year later Issetibbeha returned home with a gilt bed, a pair of girandoles by whose light it was said that Pompadour arranged her hair while Louis smirked at his mirrored face across her powdered shoulder, and a pair of slippers with red heels. They were too small for him, since he had not worn shoes at all until he reached New Orleans on his way abroad.

He brought the slippers home in tissue paper and kept them in the remaining pocket of a pair of saddlebags filled with cedar shavings, save when he took them out on occasion for his son, Moketubbe, to play with. At three years of age Moketubbe had a broad, flat, Mongolian face that appeared to exist in a complete and unfathomable lethargy, until confronted by the slippers.

Moketubbe's mother was a comely girl whom Issetibbeha had seen one day working in her shift in a melon patch. He stopped and watched her for a while—the broad, solid thighs, the sound back, the serene face. He was on his way to the creek to fish that day, but he didn't go any farther; perhaps while he stood there watching the unaware girl he may have remembered his own mother, the city woman, the fugitive with her fans and laces and her Negro blood, and all the tawdry shabbiness of that sorry affair. Within the year Moketubbe was born; even at three he could not get his feet into the slippers. Watching him in the still, hot afternoon as he struggled with the slippers with a certain monstrous repudiation of fact, Issetibbeha laughed quietly to himself. He laughed at Moketubbe's antics with the shoes for several years, because Moketubbe did not give up trying to put them on until he was sixteen. Then he quit. Or Issetibbeha thought he had. But he had merely quit trying in Issetibbeha's presence. Issetibbeha's newest wife told him that Moketubbe had stolen and hidden the shoes. Issetibbeha quit laughing then, and he sent the woman away, so that he was alone. "Yao," he said, "I too like being alive, it seems." He sent for Moketubbe. "I give them to you," he said.

Moketubbe was twenty-five then, unmarried. Issetibbeha was not tall, but he was taller by six inches than his son and almost a hundred pounds lighter. Moketubbe was already diseased with flesh, with a pale, broad, inert face and dropsical hands and feet. "They are yours now," Issetibbeha said, watching him. Moketubbe had looked at him once when he entered, a glance brief, discreet, veiled.

"Thanks," he said.

Issetibbeha looked at him. He could never tell if Moketubbe saw anything, looked at anything. "Why will it not be the same if I give the slippers to you?"

"Thanks," Moketubbe said. Issetibbeha was using snuff at the time; a white man had shown him how to put the powder into his lip and scour it against his teeth with a twig of gum or of alphea.

"Well," he said, "a man cannot live forever." He looked at his son, then his gaze went blank in turn, unseeing, and he mused for an instant You could not tell what he was thinking, save that he said half aloud: "Yao. But Doom's uncle had no shoes with red heels." He looked at his son again, fat, inert. "Beneath all that, a man might think of doing anything and it not be known until too late." He sat in a splint chair hammocked with deer thongs. "He cannot even get them on; he and I are both frustrated by the same gross meat which he wears. He cannot even get them on. But is that my fault?"

He lived for five years longer, then he died. He was sick one night, and though the doctor came in a skunkskin vest and burned sticks, Issetibbeha died before noon.

That was yesterday; the grave was dug, and for twelve hours now the people had been coming in wagons and carriages and on horseback and afoot, to eat the baked dog and the succotash and the yams cooked in ashes and to attend the funeral.

III

"It will be three days," Basket said, as he and the other Indian returned to the house. "It will be three days and the food will not be enough; I have seen it before."

The second Indian's name was Louis Berry. "He will smell too, in this weather."

"Yao. They are nothing but a trouble and a care."

"Maybe it will not take three days."

"They run far. Yao. We will smell this Man before he enters the earth. You watch and see if I am not right."

They approached the house.

"He can wear the shoes now," Berry said. "He can wear them now in man's sight."

"He cannot wear them for a while yet," Basket said. Berry looked at him. "He will lead the hunt."

"Moketubbe?" Berry said. "Do you think he will? A man to whom even talking is travail?"

"What else can he do? It is his own father who will soon begin to smell."

"That is true," Berry said. "There is even yet a price he must pay for the shoes. Yao. He has truly bought them. What do you think?"

"What do you think?"

"What do you think?"

"I think nothing."

"Nor do I. Issetibbeha will not need the shoes now. Let Moketubbe have them; Issetibbeha will not care."

"Yao. Man must die."

"Yao. Let him; there is still the Man."

The bark roof of the porch was supported by peeled cypress poles, high above the texas of the steamboat, shading an unfloored banquette where on the trodden earth mules and horses were tethered in bad weather. On the forward end of the steamboat's deck sat an old man and two women. One of the woman was dressing a fowl, the other was shelling corn. The old man was talking. He was barefoot, in a long linen frock coat and a beaver hat.

"This world is going to the dogs," he said. "It is being ruined by white men. We got along fine for years and years, before the white men foisted their Negroes upon us. In the old days the old men sat in the shade and ate stewed deer's flesh and corn and smoked tobacco and talked of honor and grave affairs; now what do we do? Even the old wear themselves into the grave taking care of them that like sweating." When Basket and Berry crossed the deck he ceased and looked up at them. His eyes were querulous, bleared; his face was myriad with tiny wrinkles. "He is fled also," he said.

"Yes," Berry said, "he is gone."

"I knew it. I told them so. It will take three weeks, like when Doom died. You watch and see."

"It was three days, not three weeks," Berry said.

"Were you there?"

"No," Berry said. "But I have heard."

"Well, I was there," the old man said. "For three whole weeks, through the swamps and the briers—" They went on and left him talking.

What had been the saloon of the steamboat was now a shell, rotting slowly; the polished mahogany, the carving glinting momentarily and fading through the mold in figures cabalistic and profound; the gutted windows were like cataracted eyes. It contained a few sacks of seed or grain, and the fore part of the running gear of a barouche, to the axle of which two C-springs rusted in graceful curves, supporting nothing. In one corner a fox cub ran steadily and soundlessly up and down a willow cage; three scrawny gamecocks moved in the dust, and the place was pocked and marked with their dried droppings.

They passed through the brick wall and entered a big room of chinked logs. It contained the hinder part of the barouche, and the dismantled body lying on its side, the window slatted over with willow withes, through which protruded the heads, the still, beady, outraged eyes and frayed combs of still more game chickens. It was floored with packed clay; in one corner leaned a crude plow and two hand-hewn boat paddles. From the ceiling, suspended by four deer thongs, hung the gilt bed which Issetibbeha had fetched from Paris. It had neither mattress nor springs, the frame criss-crossed now by a neat hammocking of thongs.

Issetibbeha had tried to have his newest wife, the young one, sleep in the bed. He was congenitally short of breath himself, and he passed the nights half reclining in his splint chair. He would see her to bed and, later, wakeful, sleeping as he did but three or four hours a night, he would sit in the darkness and simulate slumber and listen to her sneak infinitesimally from the gilt and ribboned bed, to lie on a quilt pallet on the floor until just before daylight. Then she would enter the bed quietly again and in turn simulate slumber, while in the darkness beside her Issetibbeha quietly laughed and laughed.

The girandoles were lashed by thongs to two sticks propped in a corner where a ten-gallon whiskey keg lay also. There was a clay hearth; facing it, in the splint chair, Moketubbe sat. He was maybe an inch better than five feet tall, and he weighed two hundred and fifty pounds. He wore a broadcloth coat and no shirt, his round, smooth copper balloon of belly swelling above the bottom piece of a suit of linen underwear. On his feet were the slippers with the red heels. Behind his chair stood a stripling with a punkah-like fan made of fringed paper. Moketubbe sat motionless, with his broad, yellow face with its closed eyes and flat nostrils, his flipperlike arms extended. On his face was an expression profound, tragic, and inert. He did not open his eyes when Basket and Berry came in.

"He has worn them since daylight?" Basket said.

"Since daylight," the stripling said. The fan did not cease. "You can see."

"Yao," Basket said. "We can see." Moketubbe did not move. He

MYTH AND SYMBOL

looked like an effigy, like a Malay god in frock coat, drawers, naked chest, the trivial scarlet-heeled shoes.

"I wouldn't disturb him, if I were you," the stripling said.

"Not if I were you," Basket said. He and Berry squatted. The stripling moved the fan steadily. "O Man," Basket said, "listen." Moketubbe did not move. "He is gone," Basket said.

"I told you so," the stripling said. "I knew he would flee. I told you."

"Yao," Basket said. "You are not the first to tell us afterward what we should have known before. Why is it that some of you wise men took no steps yesterday to prevent this?"

"He does not wish to die," Berry said.

"Why should he not wish it?" Basket said.

"Because he must die some day is no reason," the stripling said. "That would not convince me either, old man."

"Hold your tongue," Berry said.

"For twenty years," Basket said, "while others of his race sweat in the fields, he served the Man in the shade. Why should he not wish to die, since he did not wish to sweat?"

"And it will be quick," Berry said. "It will not take long."

"Catch him and tell him that," the stripling said.

"Hush," Berry said. They squatted, watching Moketubbe's face. He might have been dead himself. It was as though he were cased so in flesh that even breathing took place too deep within him to show.

"Listen, O Man," Basket said. "Issetibbeha is dead. He waits. His dog and his horse we have. But his slave has fled. The one who held the pot for him, who ate of his food, from his dish, is fled. Issetibbeha waits."

"Yao," Berry said.

"This is not the first time," Basket said. "This happened when Doom, thy grandfather, lay waiting at the door of the earth. He lay waiting three days, saying, 'Where is my Negro?' And Issetibbeha, thy father, answered, 'I will find him. Rest; I will bring him to you so that you may begin the journey.'"

"Yao," Berry said.

Moketubbe had not moved, had not opened his eyes.

"For three days Issetibbeha hunted in the bottom," Basket said. "He did not even return home for food, until the Negro was with him; then he said to Doom, his father, 'Here is thy dog, thy horse, thy Negro; rest.' Issetibbeha, who is dead since yesterday, said it. And now Issetibbeha's Negro is fled. His horse and his dog wait with him, but his Negro is fled."

"Yao," Berry said.

Moketubbe had not moved. His eyes were closed; upon his supine monstrous shape there was a colossal inertia, something profoundly im-

RED LEAVES

mobile, beyond and impervious to flesh. They watched his face, squatting.

"When thy father was newly the Man, this happened," Basket said. "And it was Issetibbeha who brought back the slave to where his father waited to enter the earth." Moketubbe's face had not moved, his eyes had not moved. After a while Basket said, "Remove the shoes."

The stripling removed the shoes. Moketubbe began to pant, his bare chest moving deep, as though he were rising from beyond his unfathomed flesh back into life, like up from the water, the sea. But his eyes had not opened yet.

Berry said, "He will lead the hunt."

"Yao," Basket said. "He is the Man. He will lead the hunt."

IV

All that day the Negro, Issetibbeha's body servant, hidden in the barn, watched Issetibbeha's dying. He was forty, a Guinea man. He had a flat nose, a close, small head; the inside corners of his eyes showed red a little, and his prominent gums were a pale bluish red above his square, broad teeth. He had been taken at fourteen by a trader off Kamerun, before his teeth had been filed. He had been Issetibbeha's body servant for twenty-three years.

On the day before, the day on which Issetibbeha lay sick, he returned to the quarters at dusk. In that unhurried hour the smoke of the cooking fires blew slowly across the street from door to door, carrying into the opposite one the smell of the identical meat and bread. The women tended them; the men were gathered at the head of the lane, watching him as he came down the slope from the house, putting his naked feet down carefully in a strange dusk. To the waiting men his eyeballs were a little luminous.

"Issetibbeha is not dead yet," the headman said.

"Not dead," the body servant said. "Who not dead?"

In the dusk they had faces like his, the different ages, the thoughts sealed inscrutable behind faces like the death masks of apes. The smell of the fires, the cooking, blew sharp and slow across the strange dusk, as from another world, above the lane and the pickaninnies naked in the dust.

"If he lives past sundown, he will live until daybreak," one said.

"Who says?"

"Talk says."

"Yao. Talk says. We know but one thing." They looked at the body servant as he stood among them, his eyeballs a little luminous. He was breathing slow and deep. His chest was bare; he was sweating a little. "He knows. He knows it."

"Let us let the drums talk."

"Yao. Let the drums tell it."

The drums began after dark. They kept them hidden in the creek bottom. They were made of hollowed cypress knees, and the Negroes kept them hidden; why, none knew. They were buried in the mud on the bank of a slough; a lad of fourteen guarded them. He was undersized, and a mute; he squatted in the mud there all day, clouded over with mosquitoes, naked save for the mud with which he coated himself against the mosquitoes, and about his neck a fiber bag containing a pig's rib to which black shreds of flesh still adhered, and two scaly barks on a wire. He slobbered onto his clutched knees, drooling; now and then Indians came noiselessly out of the bushes behind him and stood there and contemplated him for a while and went away, and he never knew it.

From the loft of the stable where he lay hidden until dark and after, the Negro could hear the drums. They were three miles away, but he could hear them as though they were in the barn itself below him, thudding and thudding. It was as though he could see the fire too, and the black limbs turning into and out of the flames in copper gleams. Only there would be no fire. There would be no more light there than where he lay in the dusty loft, with the whispering arpeggios of rat feet along the warm and immemorial ax-squared rafters. The only fire there would be the smudge against mosquitoes where the women were nursing children crouched, their heavy, sluggish breasts nippled full and smooth into the mouths of men children; contemplative, oblivious of the drumming, since a fire would signify life.

There was a fire in the steamboat, where Issetibbeha lay dying among his wives, beneath the lashed girandoles and the suspended bed. He could see the smoke, and just before sunset he saw the doctor come out, in a waistcoat made of skunk skins, and set fire to two clay-daubed sticks at the bows of the boat deck. "So he is not dead yet," the Negro said into the whispering gloom of the loft, answering himself; he could hear the two voices, himself and himself:

"Who not dead?"

"You are dead."

"Yao, I am dead," he said quietly. He wished to be where the drums were. He imagined himself springing out of the bushes, leaping among the drums on his bare, lean, greasy, invisible limbs. But he could not do that, because man leaped past life into where death was; he dashed into death and did not die because when death took a man, it took him just this side of the end of living. It was when death overran him from behind, still in life. The thin whisper of rat feet died in fainting gusts along the rafters. Once he had eaten rat. He was a boy then, but just come to America.

RED LEAVES

They had lived ninety days in a three-foot-high 'tween deck in tropic latitudes, hearing from topside the drunken New England captain intoning aloud from a book which he did not recognize for ten years afterward to be the Bible. Squatting in the stable so, he had watched the rat, civilized, by association with man reft of its inherent cunning of limb and eye; he had caught it without difficulty, with scarce a movement of his hand, and he ate it slowly, wondering how any of the rats had escaped so long. At that time he was still wearing the single white garment which the trader, a deacon in the Unitarian church, had given him, and he spoke then only his native tongue.

He was naked now, save for a pair of dungaree pants bought by Indians from white men, and an amulet slung on a thong about his hips. The amulet consisted of one half of a mother-of-pearl lorgnon which Issetibbeha had brought back from Paris, and the skull of a cottonmouth moccasin. He had killed the snake himself and eaten it, save the poison head. He lay in the loft, watching the house, the steamboat, listening to the drums, thinking of himself among the drums.

He lay there all night. The next morning he saw the doctor come out, in his skunk vest, and get on his mule and ride away, and he became quite still and watched the final dust from beneath the mule's delicate feet die away, and then he found that he was still breathing and it seemed strange to him that he still breathed air, still needed air. Then he lay and watched quietly, waiting to move, his eyeballs a little luminous, but with a quiet light, and his breathing light and regular, and saw Louis Berry come out and look at the sky. It was good light then, and already five Indians squatted in their Sunday clothes along the steamboat deck; by noon there were twenty-five there. That afternoon they dug the trench in which the meat would be baked, and the yams; by that time there were almost a hundred guests—decorous, quiet, patient in their stiff European finery— and he watched Berry lead Issetibbeha's mare from the stable and tie her to a tree, and then he watched Berry emerge from the house with the old hound which lay beside Issetibbeha's chair. He tied the hound to the tree too, and it sat there, looking gravely about at the faces. Then it began to howl. It was still howling at sundown, when the Negro climbed down the back wall of the barn and entered the spring branch, where it was already dusk. He began to run then. He could hear the hound howling behind him, and near the spring, already running, he passed another Negro. The two men, the one motionless and the other running, looked for an instant at each other as though across an actual boundary between two different worlds. He ran on into full darkness, mouth closed, fists doubled, his broad nostrils bellowing steadily.

He ran on in the darkness. He knew the country well, because he had hunted it often with Issetibbeha, following on his mule the course of the fox or the cat beside Issetibbeha's mare; he knew it as well as did the men who would pursue him. He saw them for the first time shortly before sunset of the second day. He had run thirty miles then, up the creek bottom, before doubling back; lying in a pawpaw thicket he saw the pursuit for the first time. There were two of them, in shirts and straw hats, carrying their neatly rolled trousers under their arms, and they had no weapons. They were middle-aged, paunchy, and they could not have moved very fast anyway; it would be twelve hours before they could return to where he lay watching them. "So I will have until midnight to rest," he said. He was near enough to the plantation to smell the cooking fires, and he thought how he ought to be hungry, since he had not eaten in thirty hours. "But it is more important to rest," he told himself. He continued to tell himself that, lying in the pawpaw thicket, because the effort of resting, the need and the haste to rest, made his heart thud the same as the running had done. It was as though he had forgot how to rest, as though the six hours were not long enough to do it in, to remember again how to do it.

As soon as dark came he moved again. He had thought to keep going steadily and quietly through the night, since there was nowhere for him to go, but as soon as he moved he began to run at top speed, breasting his panting chest, his broad-flaring nostrils through the choked and whipping darkness. He ran for an hour, lost by then, without direction, when suddenly he stopped, and after a time his thudding heart unraveled from the sound of the drums. By the sound they were not two miles away; he followed the sound until he could smell the smudge fire and taste the acrid smoke. When he stood among them the drums did not cease; only the headman came to him where he stood in the drifting smudge, panting, his nostrils flaring and pulsing, the hushed glare of his ceaseless eyeballs in his mud-daubed face as though they were worked from lungs.

"We have expected thee," the headman said. "Go, now."

"Go?"

"Eat, and go. The dead may not consort with the living; thou knowest that."

"Yao. I know that." They did not look at one another. The drums had not ceased.

"Wilt thou eat?" the headman said.

"I am not hungry. I caught a rabbit this afternoon, and ate while I lay hidden."

"Take, some cooked meat with thee, then."

He accepted the cooked meat, wrapped in leaves, and entered the creek bottom again; after a while the sound of the drums ceased. He walked steadily until daybreak. "I have twelve hours," he said. "Maybe more, since the trail was followed by night." He squatted and ate the meat and wiped his hands on his thighs. Then he rose and removed the dungaree pants and squatted again beside a slough and coated himself with mud—face, arms, body and legs—and squatted again, clasping his knees, his head bowed. When it was light enough to see, he moved back into the swamp and squatted again and went to sleep so. He did not dream at all. It was well that he moved, for, waking suddenly in broad daylight and the high sun, he saw the two Indians. They still carried their neatly rolled trousers; they stood opposite the place where he lay hidden, paunchy, thick, soft-looking, a little ludicrous in their straw hats and shirt tails.

"This is wearying work," one said.

"'I'd rather be at home in the shade myself," the other said. "But there is the Man waiting at the door to the earth."

"Yao." They looked quietly about; stooping, one of them removed from his shirt tail a clot of cockleburs. "Damn that Negro," he said.

"Yao. When have they ever been anything but a trial and a care to us?"

In the early afternoon, from the top of a tree, the Negro looked down into the plantation. He could see Issetibbeha's body in a hammock betweeen the two trees where the horse and the dog were tethered, and the concourse about the steamboat was filled with wagons and horses and mules, with carts and saddlehorses, while in bright clumps the women and the smaller children and the old men squatted about the long trench where the smoke from the barbecuing meat blew slow and thick. The men and the big boys would all be down there in the creek bottom behind him, on the trail, their Sunday clothes rolled carefully up and wedged into tree crotches. There was a clump of men near the door to the house, to the saloon of the steamboat, though, and he watched them, and after a while he saw them bring Moketubbe out in a litter made of buckskin and persimmon poles; high hidden in his leafed nook the Negro, the quarry, looked quietly down upon his irrevocable doom with an expression as profound as Moketubbe's own. "Yao," he said quietly. "He will go then. That man whose body has been dead for fifteen years, he will go also."

In the middle of the afternoon he came face to face with an Indian. They were both on a footlog across a slough—the Negro gaunt, lean, hard, tireless and desperate; the Indian thick, soft-looking, the apparent embodiment of the ultimate and the supreme reluctance and inertia. The Indian made no move, no sound; he stood on the log and watched the Negro plunge into the slough and swim ashore and crash away into the undergrowth.

Just before sunset he lay behind a down log. Up the log in slow pro-

MYTH AND SYMBOL

cession moved a line of ants. He caught them and ate them slowly, with a kind of detachment, like that of a dinner guest eating salted nuts from a dish. They too had a salt taste, engendering a salivary reaction out of all proportion. He ate them slowly, watching the unbroken line move up the log and into oblivious doom with a steady and terrific undeviation. He had eaten nothing else all day; in his caked mud mask his eyes rolled in reddened rims. At sunset, creeping along the creek bank toward where he had spotted a frog, a cottonmouth moccasin slashed him suddenly across the forearm with a thick, sluggish blow. It struck clumsily, leaving two long slashes across his arm like two razor slashes, and half sprawled with its own momentum and rage, it appeared for the moment utterly helpless with its own awkwardness and choleric anger. "Olé, Grandfather," the Negro said. He touched its head and watched it slash him again across his arm, and again, with thick, raking awkward blows. "It's that I do not wish to die," he said. Then he said it again—"It's that I do not wish to die—in a quiet tone, of slow and low amaze, as though it were something that, until the words had said themselves, he found that he had not known, or had not known the depth and extent of his desire.

V

Moketubbe took the slippers with him. He could not wear them very long while in motion, not even in the litter where he was slung reclining, so they rested upon a square of fawnskin upon his lap—the cracked, frail slippers a little shapeless now, with their scaled patent-leather surface and buckless tongues and scarlet heels, lying upon the supine, obese shape just barely alive, carried through swamp and brier by swinging relays of men who bore steadily all day long the crime and its object, on the business of the slain. To Moketubbe it must have been as though, himself immortal, he were being carried rapidly through hell by doomed spirits which, alive, had contemplated his disaster, and, dead, were oblivious partners to his damnation.

After resting for a while, the litter propped in the center of the squatting circle and Moketubbe motionless in it, with closed eyes and his face at once peaceful for the instant and filled with inescapable foreknowledge, he could wear the slippers for a while. The stripling put them on him, forcing his big, tender, dropsical feet into them; whereupon into his face came again that expression, tragic, passive, and profoundly attentive, which dyspeptics wear. Then they went on. He made no move, no sound, inert in the rhythmic litter out of some reserve of inertia, or maybe of some kingly virtue such as courage or fortitude. After a time they set the litter down and looked at him, at the yellow face like that of an idol, beaded over with sweat. Then Three Basket or Louis Berry would say: "Take them off. Honor has been served." They would remove the shoes. Moketubbe's face would not alter, but only then would his breathing become perceptible, going in and out of his pale lips with a faint ah-ah-ah sound, and they would squat again while the couriers and the runners came up.

"Not yet?"

"Not yet. He is going east. By sunset he will reach Mouth of Tippah. Then he will turn back. We may take him tomorrow."

"Let us hope so. It will not be too soon."

"Yao. It has been three days now."

"When Doom died, it took only three days."

"But that was an old man. This one is young."

"Yao. A good race. If he is taken tomorrow, I will win a horse."

"May you win it."

"Yao. This work is not pleasant."

That was the day on which the food gave out at the plantation. The guests returned home and came back the next day with more food, enough for a week longer. On that day Issetibbeha began to smell; they could smell him for a long way up and down the bottom when it got hot toward noon and the wind blew. But they didn't capture the Negro on that day, nor the next. It was about dusk on the sixth day when the couriers came up to the litter; they had found blood. "He has injured himself."

"Not bad, I hope," Basket said. "We cannot send with Issetibbeha one who will be of no service to him."

"Nor whom Issetibbeha himself will have to nurse and care for," Berry said.

"We do not know," the courier said. "He has hidden himself. He has crept back into the swamp. We have left pickets."

They trotted with the litter now. The place where the Negro had crept into the swamp was an hour away. In the hurry and excitement they had forgotten that Moketubbe still wore the slippers; when they reached the place Moketubbe had fainted. They removed the slippers and brought him to.

With dark, they former a circle about the swamp. They squatted, clouded over with gnats and mosquitoes: the evening star burned low and close down the west, and the constellations began to wheel overhead. "We will give him time," they said. "Tomorrow is just another name for today."

"Yao. Let him have time." Then they ceased, and gazed as one into the darkness where the swamp lay. After a while the noise ceased, and soon the courier came out of the darkness.

"He tried to break out."

"But you turned him back?"

"He turned back. We feared for a moment, the three of us. We could smell him creeping in the darkness, and we could smell something else, which we did not know. That was why we feared, until he told us. He said to slay him there, since it would be dark and he would not have to see the face when it came. But it was not that which we smelled; he told us what it was. A snake had struck him. That was two days ago. The arm swelled, and it smelled bad. But it was not that which we smelled then, because the swelling had gone down and his arm was no larger than that of a child. He showed us. We felt the arm, all of us did; it was no larger than that of a child. He said to give him a hatchet so he could chop the arm off. But tomorrow is today also."

"Yao. Tomorrow is today."

"We feared for a while. Then he went back into the swamp."

"That is good."

"Yao. We feared. Shall I tell the Man?"

"I will see," Basket said. He went away. The courier squatted, telling again about the Negro. Basket returned. "The man says that is good. Return to your post."

The courier crept away. They squatted about the litter; now and then they slept. Some time after midnight the Negro waked them. He began to shout and talk to himself, his voice coming sharp and sudden out of the darkness, then he fell silent. Dawn came; a white crane flapped slowly across the jonquil sky. Basket was awake. "Let us go now," he said. "It is today."

Two Indians entered the swamp, their movements noisy. Before they reached the Negro they stopped, because he began to sing. They could see him, naked and mud-caked, sitting on a log, singing. They squatted silently a short distance away, until he finished. He was chanting something in his own language, his face lifted to the rising sun. His voice was clear, full, with a quality wild and sad. "Let him have time," the Indians said, squatting, patient, waiting. He ceased and they approached. He looked back and up at them through the cracked mud mask. His eyes were bloodshot, his lips cracked upon his square short teeth. The mask of mud appeared to be loose on his face, as if he might have lost flesh since he put it there; he held his left arm close to his breast. From the elbow down it was caked and shapeless with black mud. They could smell him, a rank smell. He watched them quietly until one touched him on the arm. "Come," the Indian said. "You ran well. Do not be ashamed."

VI

As they neared the plantation in the tainted bright morning, the Negro's eyes began to roll a little, like those of a horse. The smoke from the cooking pit blew low along the earth and upon the squatting and waiting guests about the yard and upon the steamboat deck, in their bright, stiff harsh finery; the women, the children, the old men. They had sent couriers along the bottom, and another on ahead, and Issetibbeha's body had already been removed to where the grave waited, along with the horse and the dog, though they could still smell him in death about the house where he had lived in life. The guests were beginning to move toward the grave when the bearers of Moketubbe's litter mounted the slope.

The Negro was the tallest there, his high, close, mud-caked head looming above them all. He was breathing hard, as though the desperate effort of the six suspended and desperate days had capitulated upon him at once; although they walked slowly, his naked scarred chest rose and fell above the close-clutched left arm. He looked this way and that continuously, as if he were not seeing, as though sight never quite caught up with the looking. His mouth was open a little upon his big white teeth; he began to pant. The already moving guests halted, pausing, looking back, some with pieces of meat in their hands, as the Negro looked about at their faces with his wild, restrained, unceasing eyes.

"Will you eat first?" Basket said. He had to say it twice.

"Yes," the Negro said. "That's it. I want to eat."

The throng had begun to press back toward the center; the word passed to the outermost: "He will eat first."

They reached the steamboat. "Sit down," Basket said. The Negro sat on the edge of the deck. He was still panting, his chest rising and falling, his head ceaseless with its white eyeballs, turning from side to side. It was as if the inability to see came from within, from hopelessness, not from absence of vision. They brought food and watched quietly as he tried to eat it. He put the food into his mouth and chewed it, but chewing, the half-masticated matter began to emerge from the corners of his mouth and to drool down his chin, onto his chest, and after a while he stopped chewing and sat there, naked, covered with dried mud, the plate on his knees, and his mouth filled with a mass of chewed food, open his eyes wide and unceasing, panting and panting. They watched him, patient, implacable, waiting.

"Come," Basket said at last.

"It's water I want," the Negro said. "I want water."

The well was a little way down the slope toward the quarters. The

MYTH AND SYMBOL

slope lay dappled with the shadows of noon, of that peaceful hour when, Issetibbeha napping in his chair and waiting for the noon meal and the long afternoon to sleep in, the Negro, the body servant, would be free. He would sit in the kitchen door then, talking with the women that prepared the food. Beyond the kitchen the lane between the quarters would be quiet, peaceful, with the women talking to one another across the lane and the smoke of the dinner fires blowing upon the pickaninnies like ebony toys in the dust.

"Come," Basket said.

The Negro walked among them, taller than any. The guests were moving on toward where Issetibbeha and the horse and the dog waited. The Negro walked with his high ceaseless head, his panting chest. "Come," Basket said. "You wanted water."

"Yes," the Negro said. "Yes." He looked back at the house, then down to the quarters, where today no fire burned, no face showed in any door, no pickaninny in the dust, panting. "It struck me here, raking me across this arm; once, twice, three times. I said, 'Olé, Grandfather.'"

"Come now," Basket said. The Negro was still going through the motion of walking, his knee action high, his head high, as though he were on a treadmill. His eyeballs had a wild, restrained glare, like those of a horse. "You wanted water," Basket said. "Here it is."

There was a gourd in the well. They dipped it full and gave it to the Negro, and they watched him try to drink. His eyes had not ceased rolling as he tilted the gourd slowly against his caked face. They could watch his throat working and the bright water cascading from either side of the gourd, down his chin and breast. Then the water stopped. "Come," Basket said.

"Wait," the Negro said. He dipped the gourd again and tilted it against his face, beneath his ceaseless eyes. Again they watched his throat working and the unswallowed water sheathing broken and myriad down his chin, channeling his caked chest. They waited, patient, grave, decorous, implacable; clansman and guest and kin. Then the water ceased, though still the empty gourd tilted higher and higher, and still his black throat aped the vain motion of his frustrated swallowing. A piece of water-loosened mud carried away from his chest and broke at his muddy feet, and in the empty gourd they could hear his breath: ah-ah-ah.

"Come," Basket said, taking the gourd from the Negro and hanging it back in the well.

VI | Allegory

Allegory reaches far back into literary history. It has served as a convenient and necessary tool: a disguise. Good *allegory may be all the more pointed because it* is *allegory; a symbol may be a more concise expression than the thing it symbolizes; representation may be more obvious than presentation.*

Allegory is a way of saying by not saying. Hence it is the fiction *that must say. If it is good fiction, its allegorical intent will succeed. First it must be a story—the good writer knows that story is paramount.*

All fiction is to some extent allegory, implication and symbol, but some fiction exists which is clearly allegorical. Such is the menagerie of "Hook," "A Mother's Tale," and "Death of a Favorite," for the animal kingdom offers the greatest source of allegorical inspiration.

This triangle of beastly experience is rooted in human tradition. The tales would be meaningless unless each creature—bovine, feline, and fowl—held a special significance for human sensation. Each creature imparts a different texture, represents a distinct level of consciousness and a separate place in man's ecology. Each writer has chosen the animal which best suits the needs of his own fable. Think of the qualities of the three—the cow, the cat, the bird—how unique each is, how different each is from any other living creature.

Characteristics which are physically evident in a species may often be the source of its symbolic meanings in fables and in fairy tales, or in any metaphorical use we make of its members in our writing or in our speech. Conversely, the personification to which we subject animals is visible in their bodies. A bird is not a cat is not a cow.

Our literary recognition of the qualities that make a creature what it is belongs to the human verbal tradition. It is partly inborn and partly learned. We are parties to a universal understanding. The very appearance of the animal in fiction implies that recognition and draws on its role in oral and written legend. Without it, the allegory would fail.

As we move through this fiction we perceive an allegorical continuum, although each story has its own evolution. The writer did not write with classification in mind, but to release himself creatively. He wrote out of

ALLEGORY

that part of himself that is Hook, that is alone, and that screams for the equilibrium of self-expression. Writing well is a most personal act. We have before us the personal acts completed, final drafts, printed, published, now to be read. And one of the beauties of an act so private or personal is its power to encompass ideas or feelings shared by the reader. Reader and writer are assisted in their sharing by the common language allegory.

HOOK

Walter Van Tilburg Clark

Hook, the hawks' child, was hatched in a dry spring among the oaks beside the seasonal river, and was struck from the nest early. In the drouth his single-willed parents had to extend their hunting ground by more than twice, for the ground creatures upon which they fed died and dried by the hundreds. The range became too great for them to wish to return and feed Hook, and when they had lost interest in each other they drove Hook down into the sand and brush and went back to solitary courses over the bleaching hills.

Unable to fly yet, Hook crept over the ground, challenging all large movements with recoiled head, erected, rudimetary wings, and the small rasp of his clattering beak. It was during this time of abysmal ignorance and continual fear that his eyes took on the first quality of a hawk, that of being wide, alert and challenging. He dwelt, because of his helplessness, among the rattling brush which grew between the oaks and the river. Even in his thickets and near the water, the white sun was the dominant presence. Except in the dawn, when the land wind stirred, or in the late afternoon, when the sea wind became strong enough to penetrate the half-mile inland to this turn in the river, the sun was the major force, and everything was dry and motionless under it. The brush, small plants and trees alike husbanded the little moisture at their hearts; the moving creatures waited for dark, when sometimes the sea fog came over and made a fine, soundless rain which relieved them.

The two spacious sounds of his life environed Hook at this time. One was the great rustle of the slopes of yellowed wild wheat, with over it the chattering rustle of the leaves of the California oaks, already as harsh and individually tremulous as in autumn. The other was the distant whisper of the foaming edge of the Pacific, punctuated by the hollow shoring of the waves. But these Hook did not yet hear, for he was attuned by fear and hunger to the small, spasmodic rustlings of live things. Dry, shrunken, and nearly starved, and with his plumage delayed, he snatched at beetles, dragging in the sand to catch them. When swifter and stronger birds and animals did not reach them first, which was seldom, he ate the small, silver fish left in the mud by the failing river. He watched, with nearly chattering beak, the quick, thin lizards pause, very alert, and raise and lower themselves, but could not catch them because he had to raise his wings to move rapidly, which startled them.

Only one sight and sound not of his world of microscopic necessity was forced upon Hook. That was the flight of the big gulls from the beaches, which sometimes, in quealing play, came spinning back over the foothills and the river bed. For some inherited reason, the big, ship-bodied birds did not frighten Hook, but angered him. Small and chewed-looking, with his wide, already yellowing eyes glaring up at them, he would stand in an open place on the sand in the sun and spread his shaping wings and clatter his bill like shaken dice. Hook was furious about the swift, easy passage of gulls.

His first opportunity to leave off living like a ground owl came accidentally. He was standing in the late afternoon in the red light under the thicket, his eyes half-filmed with drowse and the stupefaction of starvation, when suddenly something beside him moved, and he struck, and killed a field mouse driven out of the wheat by thirst. It was a poor mouse, shriveled and lice ridden, but in striking, Hook had tasted blood, which raised nest memories and restored his nature. With started neck plumage and shining eyes, he tore and fed. When the mouse was devoured, Hook had entered hoarse adolescence. He began to seek with a conscious appetite, and to move more readily out of shelter. Impelled by the blood appetite, so glorious after his long preservation upon the flaky and bitter stuff of bugs, he ventured even into the wheat in the open sun beyond the oaks, and discovered the small trails and holes among the roots. With his belly often partially filled with flesh, he grew rapidly in strength and will. His eyes were taking on their final change, their yellow growing deeper and more opaque, their stare more constant, their challenge less desperate. Once during this transformation, he surprised a ground squirrel, and although he was ripped and wing-bitten and could not hold his prey, he was not dismayed by the conflict, but exalted. Even while the wing was still drooping and the pinions not grown back, he was excited by other ground squirrels and pursued them futilely, and was angered by their dusty escapes. He realized that his world was a great arena for killing, and felt the magnificence of it.

The two major events of Hook's young life occurred in the same day. A little after dawn he made the customary essay and succeeded in flight. A little before sunset, he made his first sustained flight of over two hundred yards, and at its termination struck and slew a great buck squirrel whose thrashing and terrified gnawing and squealing gave him a wild delight. When he had gorged on the strong meat, Hook stood upright, and in his eyes was the stare of the hawk, never flagging in intensity but never swelling beyond containment. After that the stare had only to grow more deeply challenging and more sternly controlled as his range and deadliness increased. There was no change in kind. Hook had mastered the first of the three hungers which are fused into the single, flaming will of a hawk, and he had experienced the second.

The third and consummating hunger did not awaken in Hook until the following spring, when the exultation of space had grown slow and steady in him, so that he swept freely with the wind over the miles of coastal foothills, circling, and ever in sight of the sea, and used without struggle the warm currents lifting from the slopes, and no longer desired to scream at the range of his vision, but intently sailed above his shadow swiftly climbing to meet him on the hillsides, sinking away and rippling across the brush-grown canyons.

That spring the rains were long, and Hook sat for hours, hunched and angry under their pelting, glaring into the fogs of the river valley, and killed only small, drenched things flooded up from their tunnels. But when the rains had dissipated, and there were sun and sea wind again, the game ran plentiful, the hills were thick and shining green, and the new river flooded about the boulders where battered turtles climbed up to shrink and sleep. Hook then was scorched by the third hunger. Ranging farther, often forgetting to kill and eat, he sailed for days with growing rage, and woke at night clattering on his dead tree limb, and struck and struck and struck at the porous wood of the trunk, tearing it away. After days, in the draft of a coastal canyon miles below his own hills, he came upon the acrid taint he did not know but had expected, and sailing down it, felt his neck plumes rise and his wings quiver so that he swerved unsteadily. He saw the unmated female perched upon the tall and jagged stump of a tree that had been shorn by storm, and he stooped, as if upon game. But she was older than he, and wary of the gripe of his importunity, and banked off screaming, and he screamed also at the intolerable delay.

At the head of the canyon, the screaming pursuit was crossed by another male with a great wing-spread, and the light golden in the fringe of his plumage. But his more skillful opening played him false against the ferocity of the twice-balked Hook. His rising maneuver for position was cut short by Hook's wild, upward swoop, and at the blow he raked desperately and tumbled off to the side. Dropping, Hook struck him again, struggled to clutch, but only raked and could not hold, and, diving, struck once more in passage, and then beat up, yelling triumph, and saw the crippled antagonist side-slip away, half-tumble once, as the ripped wing failed to balance, then steady and glide obliquely into the cover of brush on the canyon side. Beating hard and stationary in the wind above the bush that covered his competitor, Hook waited an instant, but when the bush was still, screamed again, and let himself go off with the current, reseeking, infuriated by the burn of his own wounds, the thin choke-thread of the acrid taint.

On a hilltop projection of stone two miles inland, he struck her down, gripping her rustling body with his talons, beating her wings down with his wings, belting her head when she whimpered or thrashed, and at last clutching her neck with his hook and, when her coy struggles had given way to stillness, succeeded.

In the early summer, Hook drove the three young ones from their nest, and went back to lone circling above his own range. He was complete.

II

Throughout that summer and the cool, growthless weather of the winter, when the gales blew in the river canyon and the ocean piled upon the shore, Hook was master of the sky and the hills of his range. His flight became a lovely and certain thing, so that he played with the treacherous currents of the air with a delicate ease surpassing that of the gulls. He could sail for hours, searching the blanched grasses below him with telescopic eyes, gaining height against the wind, descending in mile-long, gently declining swoops when he curved and rode back, and never beating either wing. At the swift passage of his shadow within their vision, gophers, ground squirrels and rabbits froze, or plunged gibbering into their tunnels beneath matted turf. Now, when he struck, he killed easily in one hard-knuckled blow. Occasionally, in sport, he soared up over the river and drove the heavy and weaponless gulls downstream again, until they would no longer venture inland.

There was nothing which Hook feared now, and his spirit was wholly belligerent, swift and sharp, like his gaze. Only the mixed smells and incomprehensible activities of the people at the Japanese farmer's home, inland of the coastwise highway and south of the bridge across Hook's river, troubled him. The smells were strong, unsatisfactory and never clear, and the people, though they behaved foolishly, constantly running in and out of their built-up holes, were large, and appeared capable, with fearless eyes looking up at him, so that he instinctively swerved aside from them. He cruised over their yard, their gardens, and their bean fields, but he would not alight close to their buildings.

But this one area of doubt did not interfere with his life. He ignored it, save to look upon it curiously as he crossed, his afternoon shadow sliding

ALLEGORY

in an instant over the chicken-and-crate-cluttered yard, up the side of the unpainted barn, and then out again smoothly, just faintly, liquidly rippling over the furrows and then over the stubble of the grazing slopes. When the season was dry, and the dead earth blew on the fields, he extended his range to satisfy his great hunger, and again narrowed it when the fields were once more alive with the minute movements he could not only see but anticipate.

Four times that year he was challenged by other hawks blowing up from behind the coastal hills to scud down his slopes, but two of these he slew in mid-air, and saw hurtle down to thump on the ground and lie still while he circled, and a third, whose wing he tore, he followed closely to earth and beat to death in the grass, making the crimson jet out from its breast and neck into the pale wheat. The fourth was a strong flier and experienced fighter, and theirs was a long, running battle, with brief, rising flurries of striking and screaming, from which down and plumage soared off.

Here, for the first time, Hook felt doubts, and at moments wanted to drop away from the scoring, burning talons and the twisted hammer strokes of the strong beak, drop away shrieking, and take cover and be still. In the end, when Hook, having outmaneuvered his enemy and come above him, wholly in control, and going with the wind, tilted and plunged for the death rap, the other, in desperation, threw over on his back and struck up. Talons locked, beaks raking, they dived earthward. The earth grew and spread under them amazingly, and they were not fifty feet above it when Hook, feeling himself turning toward the underside, tore free and beat up again on heavy, wrenched wings. The other, stroking swiftly, and so close to down that he lost wing plumes to a bush, righted himself and planed up, but flew on lumberingly between the hills and did not return. Hook screamed the triumph, and made a brief pretense of pursuit, but was glad to return, slow and victorious, to his dead tree.

In all these encounters Hook was injured, but experienced only the fighter's pride and exultation from the sting of wounds received in successful combat. And in each of them he learned new skill. Each time the wounds healed quickly, and left him a more dangerous bird.

In the next spring, when the rains and the night chants of the little frogs were past, the third hunger returned upon Hook with a new violence. In his quest, he came into the taint of a young hen. Others too were drawn by the unnerving perfume, but only one of them, the same with which Hook had fought his great battle, was a worthy competitor. This hunter drove off two, while two others, game but neophytes, were glad enough that Hook's impatience would not permit him to follow and kill. Then the battle between the two champions fled inland, and was a tactical marvel, but Hook lodged the neck-breaking blow, and struck again as they dropped past the treetops. The blood had already begun to pool on the gray, fallen foliage as Hook flapped up between branches, too spent to cry his victory. Yet his hunger would not let him rest until, late in the second day, he drove the female to ground, among the laurels of a strange river canyon.

When the two fledglings of this second brood had been driven from the nest, and Hook had returned to his own range, he was not only complete, but supreme. He slept without concealment on his bare limb, and did not open his eyes when, in the night, the heavy-billed cranes coughed in the shadows below him.

III

The turning point of Hook's career came that autumn, when the brush in the canyons rustled dryly and the hills, mowed close by the cattle, smoked under the wind as if burning. One midafternoon, when the black clouds were torn on the rim of the sea and the surf flowered white and high on the rocks, raining in over the low cliffs, Hook rode the wind diagonally across the river mouth. His great eyes, focused for small things stirring in the dust and leaves, overlooked so large and slow a movement as that of the Japanese farmer rising from the brush and lifting the two black eyes of his shotgun. Too late Hook saw and, startled, swerved, but wrongly. The surf muffled the reports, and nearly without sound, Hook felt the minute whips of the first shot, and the astounding, breath-taking blow of the second.

Beating his good wing, tasting the blood that quickly swelled into his beak, he tumbled off with the wind and struck into the thickets on the far side of the river mouth. The branches tore him. Wild with rage, he thrust up and clattered his beak, challenging, but when he had fallen over twice, he knew that the trailing wing would not carry, and then heard the boots of the hunter among the stones in the river bed and, seeing him loom at the edge of the bushes, crept back among the thickest brush and was still. When he saw the boots stand before him, he reared back, lifting his good wing and cocking his head for the serpent-like blow, his beak open but soundless, his great eyes hard and very shining. The boots passed on. The Japanese farmer, who believed that he had lost chickens, and who had cunningly observed Hook's flight for many afternoons, until he could plot it, did not greatly want a dead hawk.

When Hook could hear nothing but the surf and the wind in the thicket, he let the sickness and shock overcome him. The fine film of the inner lid dropped over his big eyes. His heart beat frantically, so that it made the plumage of his shot-aching breast throb. His own blood

ALLEGORY

throttled his breathing. But these things were nothing compared to the lightning of pain in his left shoulder, where the shot had bunched, shattering the airy bones so the pinions trailed on the ground and could not be lifted. Yet, when a sparrow lit in the bush over him, Hook's eyes flew open again, hard and challenging, his good wing was lifted and his beak strained open. The startled sparrow darted piping out over the river.

Throughout that night, while the long clouds blew across the stars and the wind shook the bushes about him, and throughout the next day, while the clouds still blew and massed until there was no gleam of sunlight on the sand bar, Hook remained stationary, enduring his sickness. In the second evening, the rains began. First there was a long, running patter of drops upon the beach and over the dry trees and bushes. At dusk there came a heavier squall, which did not die entirely, but slacked off to a continual, spaced splashing of big drops, and then returned with the front of the storm. In long, misty curtains, gust by gust, the rain swept over the sea, beating down its heaving, and coursed up the beach. The little jets of dust ceased to rise about the drops in the fields, and the mud began to gleam. Among the boulders of the river bed, darkling pools grew slowly.

Still Hook stood behind his tree from the wind, only gentle drops reaching him, falling from the upper branches and then again from the brush. His eyes remained closed, and he could still taste his own blood in his mouth, though it had ceased to come up freshly. Out beyond him, he heard the storm changing. As rain conquered the sea, the heave of the surf became a hushed sound, often lost in the crying of the wind. Then gradually, as the night turned toward morning, the wind also was broken by the rain. The crying became fainter, the rain settled toward steadiness, and the creep of the waves could be heard again, quiet and regular upon the beach.

At dawn there was no wind and no sun, but everywhere the roaring of the vertical, relentless rain. Hook then crept among the rapid drippings of the bushes, dragging his torn sail, seeking better shelter. He stopped often and stood with the shutters of film drawn over his eyes. At mid-morning he found a little cave under a ledge at the base of the sea cliff. Here, lost without branches and leaves about him, he settled to await improvement.

When, at midday of the third day, the rain stopped altogether, and the sky opened before a small, fresh wind, letting light through to glitter upon a tremulous sea, Hook was so weak that his good wing trailed also to prop him upright, and his open eyes were lusterless. But his wounds were hardened, and he felt the return of hunger. Beyond his shelter, he heard the gulls flying in great numbers and crying their joy at the cleared air. He could even hear, from the fringe of the river, the ecstatic and unstinted bubblings and chirpings of the small birds. The grassland, he felt, would be full of the stirring anew of the close-bound life, the undrowned insects clicking as they dried out, the snakes slithering down, heads half erect, into the grasses where the mice, gophers and ground squirrels ran and stopped and chewed and licked themselves smoother and drier.

With the aid of this hunger, and on the crutches of his wings, Hook came down to stand in the sun beside his cave, whence he could watch the beach. Before him, in ellipses on tilting planes, the gulls flew. The surf was rearing again, and beginning to shelve and hiss on the sand. Through the white foam-writing it left, the long-billed pipers twinkled in bevies, escaping each wave, then racing down after it to plunge their fine drills into the minute double holes where the sand crabs bubbled. In the third row of breakers two seals lifted sleek, streaming heads and barked, and over them, trailing his spider legs, a great crane flew south. Among the stones at the foot of the cliff, small red and green crabs made a little, continuous rattling and knocking. The cliff swallows glittered and twanged on aerial forays.

The afternoon began auspiciously for Hook also. One of the two gulls which came squabbling above him dropped a freshly caught fish to the sand. Quickly Hook was upon it. Gripping it, he raised his good wing and cocked his head with open beak at the many gulls which had circled and come down at once toward the fall of the fish. The gulls sheered off, cursing raucously. Left alone on the sand, Hook devoured the fish and, after resting in the sun, withdrew again to his shelter.

IV

In the succeeding days, between rains, he foraged on the beach. He learned to kill and crack the small green crabs. Along the edge of the river mouth, he found the drowned bodies of mice and squirrels and even sparrows. Twice he managed to drive feeding gulls from their catch, charging upon them with buffeting wing and clattering beak. He grew stronger slowly, but the shot sail continued to drag. Often, at the choking thought of soaring and striking and the good, hot-blood kill, he strove to take off, but only the one wing came up, winnowing with a hiss, and drove him over onto his side in the sand. After these futile trials, he would rage and clatter. But gradually he learned to believe that he could not fly, that his life must now be that of the discharged nestling again. Denied the joy of space, without which the joy of loneliness was lost, the joy of battle and killing, the blood lust, became his whole concentration. It was his hope, as he charged feeding gulls, that they would turn and offer battle, but they never did. The sandpipers, at his approach, fled peeping, or, like

ALLEGORY

a quiver of arrows shot together, streamed out over the surf in a long curve. Once, pent beyond bearing, he disgraced himself by shrieking challenge at the business-like heron which flew south every evening at the same time. The heron did not even turn his head, but flapped and glided on.

Hook's shame and anger became such that he stood awake at night. Hunger kept him awake also, for these little leavings of the gulls could not sustain his great body in its renewed violence. He became aware that the gulls slept at night in flocks on the sand, each with one leg tucked under him. He discovered also that the curlews and the pipers, often mingling, likewise slept, on the higher remnant of the bar. A sensation of evil delight filled him in the consideration of protracted striking among them.

There was only half of a sick moon in a sky of running but far-separated clouds on the night when he managed to stalk into the center of the sleeping gulls. This was light enough, but so great was his vengeful pleasure that there broke from him a shrill scream of challenge as he first struck. Without the power of flight behind it, the blow was not murderous, and this newly discovered impotence made Hook crazy, so that he screamed again and again as he struck and tore at the felled gull. He slew the one, but was twice knocked over by its heavy flounderings, and all the others rose above him, weaving and screaming, protesting in the thin moonlight. Wakened by their clamor, the wading birds also took wing, startled and plaintive. When the beach was quiet again, the flocks had settled elsewhere, beyond his pitiful range, and he was left alone beside the single kill. It was a disappointing victory. He fed with lowering spirit.

Thereafter, he stalked silently. At sunset he would watch where the gulls settled along the miles of beach, and after dark he would come like a sharp shadow among them, and drive with his hook on all sides of him, till the beating of a poorly struck victim sent the flock up. Then he would turn vindictively upon the fallen and finish them. In his best night, he killed five from one flock. But he ate only a little from one, for the vigor resulting from occasional repletion strengthened only his ire, which became so great at such a time that food revolted him. It was not the joyous, swift, controlled hunting anger of a sane hawk, but something quite different, which made him dizzy if it continued too long, and left him unsatisfied with any kill.

Then one day, when he had very nearly struck a gull while driving it from a gasping yellowfin, the gull's wing rapped against him as it broke for its running start, and, the trailing wing failing to support him, he was knocked over. He flurried awkwardly in the sand to regain his feet, but his mastery of the beach was ended. Seeing him, in clear sunlight, struggling after the chance blow, the gulls returned about him in a flashing cloud, circling and pecking on the wing. Hook's plumage showed quick little jets of irregularity here and there. He reared back, clattering and erecting the good wing, spreading the great, rusty tail for balance. His eyes shone with a little of the old pleasure. But it died, for he could reach none of them. He was forced to turn and dance awkwardly on the sand, trying to clash bills with each tormentor. They banked up quealing and returned, weaving about him in concentric and overlapping circles. His scream was lost in their clamor, and he appeared merely to be hopping clumsily with his mouth open. Again he fell sideways. Before he could right himself, he was bowled over, and a second time, and lay on his side, twisting his neck to reach them and clappering in blind fury, and was struck three times by three successive gulls, shrieking their flock triumph.

Finally he managed to roll to his breast, and to crouch with his good wing spread wide and the other stretched nearly as far, so that he extended like a gigantic moth, only his snake head, with its now silent scimitar, erect. One great eye blazed under its level brow, but where the other had been was a shallow hole from which thin blood trickled to his russet gap.

In this crouch, by short stages, stopping repeatedly to turn and drive the gulls up, Hook dragged into the river canyon and under the stiff cover of the bitter-leafed laurel. There the gulls left him, soaring up with great clatter of their valor. Till nearly sunset Hook, broken spirited and enduring his hardening eye socket, heard them celebrating over the waves.

When his will was somewhat replenished, and his empty eye socket had stopped the twitching and vague aching which had forced him often to roll ignominiously to rub it in the dust, Hook ventured from the protective lacings of his thicket. He knew fear again, and the challenge of his remaining eye was once more strident, as in adolescence. He dared not return to the beaches, and with a new, weak hunger, the home hunger, enticing him, made his way by short hunting journeys back to the wild wheat slopes and the crisp oaks. There was in Hook an unwonted sensation now, that of the ever-neighboring possibility of death. This sensation was beginning, after his period as a mad bird on the beach, to solidify him into his last stage of life. When, during his slow homeward passage, the gulls wafted inland over him, watching the earth with curious, miserish eyes, he did not cower, but neither did he challenge, either by opened beak or by raised shoulder. He merely watched carefully, learning his first lessons in observing the world with one eye.

At first the familiar surroundings of the bend in the river and the tree with the dead limb to which he could not ascend, aggravated his humiliation, but in time, forced to live cunningly and half-starved, he lost much

ALLEGORY

of his savage pride. At the first flight of a strange hawk over his realm, he was wild at his helplessness, and kept twisting his head like an owl, or spinning in the grass like a small and feathered dervish, to keep the hateful beauty of the wind-rider in sight. But in the succeeding weeks, as one after another coasted his beat, his resentment declined, and when one of the raiders, a haughty yearling, sighted his up-staring eye, and plunged and struck him dreadfully, and failed to kill him only because he dragged under a thicket in time, the second of his great hungers was gone. He had no longer the true lust to kill, no joy of battle, but only the poor desire to fill his belly.

Then truly he lived in the wheat and the brush like a ground owl, ridden with ground lice, dusty or muddy, ever half-starved, forced to sit for hours by small holes for petty and unsatisfying kills. Only once during the final months before his end did he make a kill where the breath of danger recalled his valor, and then the danger was such as a hawk with wings and eyes would scorn. Waiting beside a gopher hole, surrounded by the high, yellow grass, he saw the head emerge, and struck, and was amazed that there writhed in his clutch the neck and dusty coffin-skull of a rattlesnake. Holding his grip, Hook saw the great, thick body slither up after, the tip an erect, strident blur, and writhe on the dirt of the gopher's mound. The weight of the snake pushed Hook about, and once threw him down, and the rising and falling whine of the rattles made the moment terrible, but the vaulted mouth, gaping from the closeness of Hook's gripe, so that the pale, envenomed sabers stood out free, could not reach him. When Hook replaced the grip of his beak with the grip of his talons, and was free to strike again and again at the base of the head, the struggle was over. Hook tore and fed on the fine, watery flesh, and left the tattered armor and the long, jointed bone for the marching ants.

When the heavy rains returned, he ate well during the period of the first escapes from flooded burrows, and then well enough, in a vulture's way, on the drowned creatures. But as the rains lingered, and the burrows hung full of water, and there were no insects in the grass and no small birds sleeeping in the thickets, he was constantly hungry, and finally unbearably hungry. His sodden and ground-broken plumage stood out raggedly about him, so that he looked fat, even bloated, but underneath it his skin clung to his bones. Save for his great talons and clappers, and the rain in his down, he would have been like a handful of air. He often stood for a long time under some bush or ledge, heedless of the drip, his one eye filmed over, his mind neither asleep or awake, but between. The gurgle and swirl of the brimming river, and the sound of chunks of the bank cut away to splash and dissolve in the already muddy flood, became familiar to him, and yet a torment, as if that great, ceaselessly working power of water ridiculed his frailty, within which only the faintest spark of valor still glimmered. The last two nights before the rain ended, he huddled under the floor of the bridge on the coastal highway, and heard the palpitant thunder of motors swell and roar over him. The trucks shook the bridge so that Hook, even in his famished lassitude, would sometimes open his one great eye wide and startled.

V

After the rains, when things became full again, bursting with growth and sound, the trees swelling, the thickets full of song and chatter, the fields, turning green in the sun, alive with rustling passages, and the moonlit nights strained with the song of the peepers all up and down the river and in the pools in the fields, Hook had to bear the return of the one hunger left him. At times this made him so wild that he forgot himself and screamed challenge from the open ground. The fretfulness of it spoiled his hunting, which was now entirely a matter of patience. Once he was in despair, and lashed himself through the grass and thickets, trying to rise when that virgin scent drifted for a few moments above the current of his own river. Then, breathless, his beak agape, he saw the strong suitor ride swiftly down on the wind over him, and heard afar the screaming fuss of the harsh wooing in the alders. For that moment even the battle heart beat in him again. The rim of his good eye was scarlet, and a little bead of new blood stood in the socket of the other. With beak and talon, he ripped at a fallen log, and made loam and leaves fly from about it.

But the season of love passed over to the nesting season, and Hook's love hunger, unused, shriveled in him with the others, and there remained in him only one stern quality befitting a hawk, and that the negative one, the remnant, the will to endure. He resumed his patient, plotted hunting, now along a field of the Japanese farmer, but ever within reach of the river thickets.

Growing tough and dry again as the summer advanced, inured to the family of the farmer, whom he saw daily, stooping and scraping with sticks in the ugly, open rows of their fields, where no lovely grass rustled and no life stirred save the shameless gulls, which walked at the heels of the workers, gobbling the worms and grubs as they turned up, Hook became nearly content with his shard of life. The only longing or resentment to pierce him was that which he suffered occasionally when forced to hide at the edge of the mile-long bean field from the wafted cruising

ALLEGORY

and the restive, down-bent gaze of one of his own kind. For the rest, he was without flame, a snappish, dust-colored creature, fading into the grasses he trailed through, and suited to his petty ways.

At the end of that summer, for the second time in his four years, Hook underwent a drouth. The equinoctial period passed without a rain. The laurel and the rabbit-brush dropped dry leaves. The foliage of the oaks shriveled and curled. Even the night fogs in the river canyon failed. The farmer's red cattle on the hillside lowed constantly, and could not feed on the dusty stubble. Grass fires broke out along the highway, and ate fast in the wind, filling the hollows with the smell of smoke, and died in the dirt of the shorn hills. The river made no sound. Scum grew on its vestigial pools, and turtles died and stank among the rocks. The dust rode before the wind, and ascended and flowered to nothing between the hills and every sunset was red with the dust in the air. The people in the farmer's house quarreled, and even struck one another. Birds were silent, and only the hawks flew much. The animals lay breathing hard for very long spells, and ran and crept jerkily. Their flanks were fallen in, and their eyes were red.

At first Hook gorged at the fringe of the grass fires on the multitudes of tiny things that came running and squeaking. But thereafter there were the blackened strips on the hills, and little more in the thin, crackling grass. He found mice and rats, gophers and ground-squirrels, and even rabbits, dead in the stubble and under the thickets, but so dry and fleshless that only a faint smell rose from them, even on the sunny days. He starved on them. By early December he had wearily stalked the length of the eastern foothills, hunting at night to escape the voracity of his own kind, resting often upon his wings. The queer trail of his short steps and great horned toes zigzagged in the dust and was erased by the wind at dawn. He was nearly dead, and could make no sound through the horn funnels of his clappers.

Then one night the dry wind brought him, with the familiar, lifeless dust, another familiar scent, troublesome, mingled and unclear. In his vision-dominated brain he remembered the swift circle of his flight a year past, crossing in one segment, his shadow beneath him, a yard cluttered with crates and chickens, a gray barn and then again the plowed land and the stubble. Traveling faster than he had for days, impatient of his shrunken sweep, Hook came down to the farm. In the dark wisps of cloud blown among the stars over him, but no moon, he stood outside the wire of the chicken run. The scent of fat and blooded birds reached him from the shelter, and also within the enclosure was water. At the breath of the water, Hook's gorge contracted, and his tongue quivered and clove in its groove of horn. But there was the wire. He stalked its perimeter and found no opening. He beat it with his good wing, and felt it cut but not give. He wrenched at it with his beak in many places, but could not tear it. Finally, in a fury which drove the thin blood through him, he leaped repeatedly against it, beating and clawing. He was thrown back from the last leap as from the first, but in it he had risen so high as to clutch with his beak at the top wire. While he lay on his breast on the ground, the significance of this came upon him.

Again he leapt, clawed up the wire, and, as he would have fallen, made even the dead wing bear a little. He grasped the top and tumbled within. There again he rested flat, searching the dark with quick-turning head. There was no sound or motion but the throb of his own body. First he drank at the chill metal trough hung for the chickens. The water was cold, and loosened his tongue and his tight throat, but it also made him drunk and dizzy, so that he had to rest again, his claws spread wide to brace him. Then he walked stiffly, to stalk down the scent. He trailed it up the runway. Then there was the stuffy, body-warm air, acrid with droppings, full of soft rustlings as his talons clicked on the board floor. The thick, white shapes showed faintly in the darkness. Hook struck quickly, driving a hen to the floor with one blow, its neck broken and stretched out stringily. He leaped the still pulsing body, and tore it. The rich, streaming blood was overpowering to his dried senses, his starved, leathery body. After a few swallows, the flesh choked him. In his rage, he struck down another hen. The urge to kill took him again, as in those nights on the beach. He could let nothing go. Balked of feeding, he was compelled to slaughter. Clattering, he struck again and again. The henhouse was suddenly filled with the squawking and helpless rushing and buffeting of the terrified, brainless fowls.

Hook reveled in mastery. Here was game big enough to offer weight against a strike, and yet unable to soar away from his blows. Turning in the midst of the turmoil, cannily, his fury caught at the perfect pitch, he struck unceasingly. When the hens finally discovered the outlet, and streamed into the yard, to run around the fence, beating and squawking, Hook followed them, scraping down the incline, clumsy and joyous. In the yard, the cock, a bird as large as he, and much heavier, found him out and gave valiant battle. In the dark, and both earthbound, there was little skill, but blow upon blow, and only chance parry. The still squawking hens pressed into one corner of the yard. While the duel went on, a dog, excited by the sustained scuffling, began to bark. He continued to bark, running back and forth along the fence on one side. A light flashed on in an uncurtained window of the farmhouse, and streamed whitely over the crates littering the ground.

Enthralled by his old battle joy, Hook knew only the burly cock before

ALLEGORY

him. Now, in the farthest reach of the window light, they could see each other dimly. The Japanese farmer, with his gun and lantern, was already at the gate when the finish came. The great cock leapt to jab with his spurs and, toppling forward with extended neck as he fell, was struck and extinguished. Blood had loosened Hook's throat. Shrilly he cried his triumph. It was a thin and exhausted cry, but within him as good as when he shrilled in mid-air over the plummeting descent of a fine foe in his best spring.

The light from the lantern partially blinded Hook. He first turned and ran directly from it, into the corner where the hens were huddled. They fled apart before his charge. He essayed the fence, and on the second try, in his desperation, was out. But in the open dust, the dog was on him, circling, dashing in, snapping. The farmer, who at first had not fired because of the chickens, now did not fire because of the dog, and, when he saw that the hawk was unable to fly, relinquished the sport to the dog, holding the lantern up in order to see better. The light showed his own flat, broad, dark face as sunken also, the cheekbones very prominent, and showed the torn-off sleeves of his shirt and the holes in the knees of his overalls. His wife, in a stained wrapper, and barefooted, heavy black hair hanging around a young, passionless face, joined him hesitantly, but watched, fascinated and a little horrified. His son joined them too, encouraging the dog, but quickly grew silent. Courageous and cruel death, however it may afterward sicken the one who has watched it, is impossible to look away from.

In the circle of the light, Hook turned to keep the dog in front of him. His one eye gleamed with malevolence. The dog was an Airedale, and large. Each time he pounced, Hook stood ground, raising his good wing, the pinions newly torn by the fence, opening his beak soundlessly, and, at the closest approach, hissed furiously, and at once struck. Hit and ripped twice by the whetted horn, the dog recoiled more quickly from several subsequent jumps and, infuriated by his own cowardice, began to bark wildly. Hook maneuvered to watch him, keeping his head turned to avoid losing the foe on the blind side. When the dog paused, safely away, Hook watched him quietly, wing partially lowered, beak closed, but at the first move again lifted the wing and gaped. The dog whined, and the man spoke to him encouragingly. The awful sound of his voice made Hook for an instant twist his head to stare up at the immense figures behind the light. The dog again sallied, barking, and Hook's head spun back. His wing was bitten this time, and with a furious side-blow, he caught the dog's nose. The dog dropped him with a yelp, and then, smarting, came on more warily, as Hook propped himself up from the ground again between his wings. Hook's artificial strength was waning, but his heart still stood to the battle, sustained by a fear of such dimension as he had never known before, but only anticipated when the arrogant young hawk had driven him to cover. The dog, unable to find any point at which the merciless, unwinking eye was not watching him, the parted beak waiting, paused and whimpered again.

"Oh, kill the poor thing," the woman begged.

The man, though, encouraged the dog again, saying, "Sick him; sick him."

The dog rushed bodily. Unable to avoid him, Hook was bowled down, snapping and raking. He left long slashes, as from the blade of a knife, on the dog's flank, but before he could right himself and assume guard again, was caught by the good wing and dragged, clattering, and seeking to make a good stroke from his back. The man following them to keep the light on them, and the boy went with him, wetting his lips with his tongue and keeping his fists closed tightly. The woman remained behind, but could not help watching the diminished conclusion.

In the little, palely shining arena, the dog repeated his successful maneuver three times, growling but not barking, and when Hook thrashed up from the third blow, both wings were trailing, and dark, shining streams crept on his black-fretted breast from the shoulders. The great eye flashed more furiously than it ever had in victorious battle, and the beak still gaped, but there was no more clatter. He faltered when turning to keep front; the broken wings played him false even as props. He could not rise to use his talons.

The man had tired of holding the lantern up, and put it down to rub his arm. In the low, horizontal light, the dog charged again, this time throwing the weight of his forepaws against Hook's shoulder, so that Hook was crushed as he struck. With his talons up, Hook raked at the dog's belly, but the dog conceived the finish, and furiously worried the feathered bulk. Hook's neck went limp, and between his gaping clappers came only a faint chittering, as from some small kill of his own in the grasses.

In this last conflict, however, there had been some minutes of the supreme fire of the hawk whose three hungers are perfectly fused in the one will; enough to burn off a year of shame.

Between the great sails the light body lay caved and perfectly still. The dog, smarting from his cuts, came to the master and was praised. The woman, joining them slowly, looked at the great wingspread, her husband raising the lantern that she might see it better.

"Oh, the brave bird," she said.

ALLEGORY

A MOTHER'S TALE

James Agee

The calf ran up the hill as fast as he could and stopped sharp. "Mama!" he cried, all out of breath. "What *is* it! What are they *doing*! Where are they *going*!"

Other spring calves came galloping too.

They all were looking up at her and awaiting her explanation, but she looked out over their excited eyes. As she watched the mysterious and majestic thing they had never seen before, her own eyes became even more than ordinarily still, and during the considerable moment before she answered, she scarcely heard their urgent questioning.

Far out along the autumn plain, beneath the sloping light, an immense drove of cattle moved eastward. They went at a walk, not very fast, but faster than they could imaginably enjoy. Those in front were compelled by those behind; those at the rear, with few exceptions, did their best to keep up; those who were locked within the herd could no more help moving than the particles inside a falling rock. Men on horses rode ahead, and alongside, and behind, or spurred their horses intensely back and forth, keeping the pace steady, and the herd in shape; and from man to man a dog sped back and forth incessantly as a shuttle, barking, incessantly, in a hysterical voice. Now and then one of the men shouted fiercely, and this like the shrieking of the dog was tinily audible above a low and awesome sound which seemed to come not from the multitude of hooves but from the center of the world, and above the sporadic bawlings and bellowings of the herd.

From the hillside this tumult was so distant that it only made more delicate the prodigious silence in which the earth and sky were held; and, from the hill, the sight was as modest as its sound. The herd was virtually hidden in the dust it raised, and could be known, in general, only by the horns which pricked this flat sunlit dust like briars. In one place a twist of the air revealed the trembling fabric of many backs; but it was only along the near edge of the mass that individual animals were discernible, small in a driven frieze, walking fast, stumbling and recovering, tossing their armed heads, or opening their skulls heavenward in one of those cries which reached the hillside long after the jaws were shut.

From where she watched, the mother could not be sure whether there were any she recognized. She knew that among them there must be a son of hers; she had not seen him since some previous spring, and she would not be seeing him again. Then the cries of the young ones impinged on her bemusement: "Where are they gong?"

She looked into their ignorant eyes.

"Away," she cried.

"Where?" they cried. "Where? Where?" her own son cried again.

She wondered what to say.

"On a long journey."

"But where *to*?" they shouted. "Yes, where *to*?" her son exclaimed, and she could see that he was losing his patience with her, as he always did when he felt she was evasive.

"I'm not sure," she said.

Their silence was so cold that she was unable to avoid their eyes for long.

"Well, not *really* sure. Because, you see," she said in her most reasonable tone, "I've never seen it with my own eyes, and that's the only way to *be* sure; *isn't* it."

They just kept looking at her. She could see no way out.

"But I've *heard* about it," she said with shallow cheerfulness, "from those who *have* seen it, and I don't suppose there's any good reason to doubt them."

She looked away over them again, and for all their interest in what she was about to tell them, her eyes so changed that they turned and looked, too.

The herd, which had been moving broadside to them, was being turned away, so slowly that like the turning of stars it could not quite be seen from one moment to the next; yet soon it was moving directly away from them, and even during the little while she spoke and they all watched after it, it steadily and very noticeably diminished, and the sounds of it as well.

"It happens always about this time of year," she said quietly while they watched. "Nearly all the men and horses leave, and go into the North and the West."

"Out on the range," her son said, and by his voice she knew what enchantment the idea already held for him.

"Yes," she said, "out on the range." And trying, impossibly, to imagine the range, they were touched by the breath of grandeur.

"And then before long," she continued, "everyone has been found, and brought into one place; and then . . . what you see, happens. All of them.

"Sometimes when the wind is right," she said more quietly, "you can hear them coming long before you can see them. It isn't even like a sound, at first. It's more as if something were moving far under the ground. It makes you uneasy. You wonder, why, what in the world can *that* be! Then you remember what it is and then you can really hear it. And then finally, there they all are."

ALLEGORY

She could see this did not interest them at all.

"But where are they *going*?" one asked, a little impatiently.

"I'm coming to that," she said; and she let them wait. Then she spoke slowly but casually.

"They are on their way to a railroad."

There, she thought; that's for that look you all gave me when I said I wasn't sure. She waited for them to ask; they waited for her to explain.

"A railroad," she told them, "is great hard bars of metal lying side by side, or so they tell me, and they go on and on over the ground as far as the eye can see. And great wagons run on the metal bars on wheels, like wagon wheels but smaller, and these wheels are made of solid metal too. The wagons are much bigger than any wagon you've ever seen, as big as, big as sheds, they say, and they are pulled along on the iron bars by a terrible huge dark machine, with a loud scream."

"Big as *sheds*?" one of the calves said skeptically.

"Big *enough*, anyway," the mother said. "I told you I've never seen it myself. But those wagons are so big that several of us can get inside at once. And that's exactly what happens."

Suddenly she became very quiet, for she felt that somehow, she could not imagine just how, she had said altogether too much.

"Well, *what* happens," her son wanted to know. "What do you mean, *happens*."

She always tried hard to be a reasonably modern mother. It was probably better, she felt, to go on, than to leave them all full of imaginings and mystification. Besides, there was really nothing at all awful about what happened . . . if only one could know *why*.

"Well," she said, "it's nothing much really. They just—why, when they all finally *get* there, why there are all the great cars waiting in a long line, and the big dark machine is up ahead . . . smoke comes out of it, they say . . . and . . . well, then, they just put us into the wagons, just as many as will fit in each wagon, and when everybody is in, why . . . she hesitated, for again, though she couldn't be sure why, she was uneasy.

"Why then," her son said, "the train takes them away."

Hearing that word, she felt a flinching of the heart. Where had he picked it up, she wondered, and she gave him a shy and curious glance. Oh dear, she thought. I should never have even *begun* to explain. "Yes," she said, "when everybody is safely in, they slide the doors shut."

They were all silent for a little while. Then one of them asked thoughtfully, "Are they taking them somewhere they don't want to go?"

"Oh, I don't think so," the mother said. "I imagine it's very nice."

"*I* want to go," she heard her son say with ardor. "I want to go right

A MOTHER'S TALE

now," he cried. "Can I, Mama? *Can* I? *Please?*" And looking into his eyes, she was overwhelmed by sadness.

"Silly thing," she said, "there'll be time enough for that when you're grown up. But what I very much hope," she went on, "is that instead of being chosen to go out on the range and to make the long journey, you will grow up to be very strong and bright so they will decide that you may stay here at home with Mother. And you, too," she added, speaking to the other little males; but she could not honestly wish this for any but her own, least of all for the eldest, strongest and most proud, for she knew how few are chosen.

She could see that what she said was not received with enthusiasm.

"But I want to go," her son said.

"Why?" she asked. "I don't think any of you realize that it's a great *honor* to be chosen to stay. A great privilege. Why, it's just the most ordinary ones are taken out onto the range. But only the very pick are chosen to stay here at home. If you want to go out on the range," she said in hurried and happy inspiration, "all you have to do is be ordinary and careless and silly. If you want to have even a chance to be chosen to stay, you have to try to be stronger and bigger and braver and brighter than anyone else, and that takes *hard work. Every day.* Do you see?" And she looked happily and hopefully from one to another. "Besides," she added, aware that they were not won over, "I'm told it's a very rough life out there, and the men are unkind.

"Don't you see," she said again; and she pretended to speak to all of them, but it was only to her son.

But he only looked at her. "Why do you want me to stay home?" he asked flatly; in their silence she knew the others were asking the same question.

"Because it's safe here," she said before she knew better; and realized she had put it in the most unfortunate way possible. "Not safe, not just that," she fumbled. "I mean . . . because here we *know* what happens, and what's going to happen, and there's never any doubt about it, never any reason to wonder, to worry. Don't you see? It's just *Home*," and she put a smile on the word, "where we all know each other and are happy and well."

They were so merely quiet, looking back at her, that she felt they were neither won over nor alienated. Then she knew of her son that he, anyhow, was most certainly not persuaded, for he asked the question she most dreaded: "Where do they go on the train?" And hearing him, she knew that she would stop at nothing to bring that curiosity and eagerness, and that tendency toward skepticism, within safe bounds.

ALLEGORY

"Nobody knows," she said, and she added, in just the tone she knew would most sharply engage them, "Not for sure, anyway."

"What do you mean, *not for sure,*" her son cried. And the oldest, biggest calf repeated the question, his voice cracking.

The mother deliberately kept silence as she gazed out over the plain, and while she was silent they all heard the last they would ever hear of all those who were going away: one last great cry, as faint almost as a breath; the infinitesimal jabbing vituperation of the dog; the solemn muttering of the earth.

"Well," she said, after even this sound was entirely lost, "there was one who came back." Their instant, trustful eyes were too much for her. She added, "Or so they say."

They gathered a little more closely around her, for now she spoke very quietly.

"It was my great-grandmother who told me," she said. "She was told it by *her* great-grandmother, who claimed she saw it with her own eyes, though of course I can't vouch for that. Because of course I wasn't even dreamed of then; and Great-grandmother was so very, very old, you see, that you couldn't always be sure she knew quite *what* she was saying."

Now that she began to remember it more clearly, she was sorry she had committed herself to telling it.

"Yes," she said, "the story is, there was one, *just* one, who ever came back, and he told what happened on the train, and where the train went and what happened after. He told it all in a rush, they say, the last things first and every which way, but as it was finally sorted out and gotten into order by those who heard it and those they told it to, this is more or less what happened:

"He said that after the men had gotten just as many of us as they could into the car he was in, so that their sides pressed tightly together and nobody could lie down, they slid the door shut with a startling rattle and a bang, and then there was a sudden jerk, so strong they might have fallen except that they were packed so closely together, and the car began to move. But after it had moved only a little way, it stopped as suddenly as it had started, so that they all nearly fell down again. You see, they were just moving up the next car that was joined on behind, to put more of us into it. He could see it all between the boards of the car, because the boards were built a little apart from each other, to let in air."

Car, her son said again to himself. Now he would never forget the word.

"He said that then, for the first time in his life, he became very badly frightened, he didn't know why. But he was sure, at that moment, that there was something dreadfully to be afraid of. The others felt this same

242

great fear. They called out loudly to those who were being put into the car behind, and the others called back, but it was no use; those who were getting aboard were between narrow white fences and then were walking up a narrow slope and the men kept jabbing them as they do when they are in an unkind humor, and there was no way to go but on into the car. There was no way to get out of the car, either: he tried, with all his might, and he was the one nearest the door.

"After the next car behind was full, and the door was shut, the train jerked forward again, and stopped again, and they put more of us into still another car, and so on, and on, until all the starting and stopping no longer frightened anybody; it was just something uncomfortable that was never going to stop, and they began instead to realize how hungry and thirsty they were. But there was no food and no water, so they just had to put up with this; and about the time they became resigned to going without their suppers (for now it was almost dark), they heard a sudden and terrible scream which frightened them even more deeply than anything had frightened them before, and the train began to move again, and they braced their legs once more for the jolt when it would stop, but this time, instead of stopping, it began to go fast, and then even faster, so fast that the ground nearby slid past like a flooded creek and the whole country, he claimed, began to move too, turning slowly around a far mountain as if it were all one great wheel. And then there was a strange kind of disturbance inside the car, he said, or even inside his very bones. He felt as if everything in him was *falling,* as if he had been filled full of a heavy liquid that all wanted to flow one way, and all the others were leaning as he was leaning, away from this queer heaviness that was trying to pull them over, and then just as suddenly this leaning heaviness was gone and they nearly fell again before they could stop leaning against it. He could never understand what this was, but it too happened so many times that they all got used to it, just as they got used to seeing the country turn like a slow wheel, and just as they got used to the long cruel screams of the engine, and the steady iron noise beneath them which made the cold darkness so fearsome, and the hunger and the thirst and the continual standing up, and the moving on and on and on as if they would never stop."

"*Didn't* they ever stop?" one asked.

"Once in a great while," she replied. "Each time they did," she said, "he thought, Oh, now *at* last! *At last* we can get out and stretch our tired legs and lie down! *At last* we'll be given food and water! But they never let them out. And they never gave them food or water. They never even cleaned up under them. They had to stand in their manure and in the water they made."

ALLEGORY

"Why did the train stop?" her son asked; and with somber gratification she saw that he was taking all this very much to heart.

"He could never understand why," she said. "Sometimes men would walk up and down alongside the cars, and the more nervous and the more trustful of us would call out; but they were only looking around, they never seemed to do anything. Sometimes he could see many houses and bigger buildings together where people lived. Sometimes it was far out in the country and after they had stood still for a long time they would hear a little noise which quickly became louder, and then became suddenly a noise so loud it stopped their breathing, and during this noise something black would go by, very close, and so fast it couldn't be seen. And then it was gone as suddenly as it had appeared, and the noise became small, and then in the silence their train would start up again.

"Once, he tells us, something very strange happened. They were standing still, and cars of a very different kind began to move slowly past. These cars were not red, but black, with many glass windows like those in a house; and he says they were as full of human beings as the car he was in was full of our kind. And one of these people looked into his eyes and smiled, as if he liked him, or as if he knew only too well how hard the journey was.

"So by his account it happens to them, too," she said, with a certain pleased vindictiveness. "Only they were sitting down at their ease, not standing. And the one who smiled was eating."

She was still, trying to think of something; she couldn't quite grasp the thought.

"But didn't they *ever* let them out?" her son asked.

The oldest calf jeered. "Of *course* they did. He came back, didn't he? How would he ever come back if he didn't get out?"

"They didn't let them out," she said, "for a long, long time."

"How long?"

"So long, and he was so tired, he could never be sure. But he said that it turned from night to day and from day to night and back again several times over, with the train moving nearly all of this time, and that when it finally stopped, early one morning, they were all so tired and so discouraged that they hardly even noticed any longer, let alone felt any hope that anything would change for them, ever again; and then all of a sudden men came up and put up a wide walk and unbarred the door and slid it open, and it was the most wonderful and happy moment of his life when he saw the door open, and walked into the open air with all his joints trembling, and drank the water and ate the delicious food they had ready for him; it was worth the whole terrible journey."

Now that these scenes came clear before her, there was a faraway shining in her eyes, and her voice, too, had something in it of the faraway.

"When they had eaten and drunk all they could hold they lifted up their heads and looked around, and everything they saw made them happy. Even the trains made them cheerful now, for now they were no longer afraid of them. And though these trains were forever breaking to pieces and joining again with other broken pieces, with shufflings and clashings and rude cries, they hardly paid them attention any more, they were so pleased to be in their new home, and so surprised and delighted to find they were among thousands upon thousands of strangers of their own kind, all lifting up their voices in peacefulness and thanksgiving, and they were so wonderstruck by all they could see, it was so beautiful and so grand.

"For he has told us that now they lived among fences as white as bone, so many, and so spiderishly complicated, and shining so pure, that there's no use trying even to hint at the beauty and the splendor of it to anyone who knows only the pitiful little outfittings of a ranch. Beyond these mazy fences, through the dark and bright smoke which continually turned along the sunlight, dark buildings stood shoulder to shoulder in a wall as huge and proud as mountains. All through the air, all the time, there was an iron humming like the humming of the iron bar after it has been struck to tell the men it is time to eat, and in all the air, all the time, there was that same strange kind of iron strength which makes the silence before lightning so different from all other silence.

"Once for a little while the wind shifted and blew over them straight from the great buildings, and it brought a strange and very powerful smell which confused and disturbed them. He could never quite describe this smell, but he has told us it was unlike anything he had ever known before. It smelled like old fire, he said, and old blood and fear and darkness and sorrow and most terrible and brutal force and something else, something in it that made him want to run away. This sudden uneasiness and this wish to run away swept through every one of them, he tells us, so that they were all moved at once as restlessly as so many leaves in a wind, and there was great worry in their voices. But soon the leaders among them concluded that it was simply the way men must smell when there are a great many of them living together. Those dark buildings must be crowded very full of men, they decided, probably as many thousands of them, indoors, as there were of us, outdoors; so it was no wonder their smell was so strong and, to our kind, so unpleasant. Besides, it was so clear now in every other way that men were not as we had always supposed, but were doing everything they knew how to make us comfortable and happy, that we ought to just put up with their smell, which after all they couldn't help, any more than we could help our own. Very likely

ALLEGORY

men didn't like the way we smelled, any more than we liked theirs. They passed along these ideas to the others, and soon everyone felt more calm, and then the wind changed again, and the fierce smell no longer came to them, and the smell of their own kind was back again, very strong of course, in such a crowd, but ever so homey and comforting, and everyone felt easy again.

"They were fed and watered so generously, and treated so well, and the majesty and the loveliness of this place where they had all come to rest was so far beyond anything they had ever known or dreamed of, that many of the simple and ignorant, whose memories were short, began to wonder whether that whole difficult journey, or even their whole lives up to now, had ever really been. Hadn't it all been just shadows, they murmured, just a bad dream?

"Even the sharp ones, who knew very well it had all really happened, began to figure that everything up to now had been made so full of pain only so that all they had come to now might seem all the sweeter and the more glorious. Some of the oldest and deepest were even of a mind that all the puzzle and tribulation of the journey had been sent us as a kind of harsh trying or proving of our worthiness; and that it was entirely fitting and proper that we could earn our way through to such rewards as these, only through suffering, and through being patient under pain which was beyond our understanding; and that now at the last, to those who had borne all things well, all things were made known: for the mystery of suffering stood revealed in joy. And now as they looked back over all that was past, all their sorrows and bewilderments seemed so little and so fleeting that, from the simplest among them even to the most wise, they could feel only the kind of amused pity we feel toward the very young when, with the first thing that hurts them or they are forbidden, they are sure there is nothing kind or fair in all creation, and carry on accordingly, raving and grieving as if their hearts would break."

She glanced among them with an indulgent smile, hoping the little lesson would sink home. They seemed interested but somewhat dazed. I'm talking way over their heads, she realized. But by now she herself was too deeply absorbed in her story to modify it much. *Let* it be, she thought, a little impatient; it's over *my* head, for that matter.

"They had hardly before this even wondered that they were alive," she went on, "and now all of a sudden they felt they understood *why* they were. This made them very happy, but they were still only beginning to enjoy this new wisdom when quite a new and different kind of restiveness ran among them. Before they quite knew it they were all moving once again, and now they realized that they were being moved, once more, by men, toward still some other place and purpose they could not know. But

A MOTHER'S TALE

during these last hours they had been so well that now they felt no uneasiness, but all moved forward calm and sure toward better things still to come; he has told us that he no longer felt as if he were being driven, even as it became clear that they were going toward the shade of those great buildings; but guided.

"He was guided between fences which stood ever more and more narrowly near each other, among companions who were pressed ever more and more closely against one another; and now as he felt their warmth against him it was not uncomfortable, and his pleasure in it was not through any need to be close among others through anxiousness, but was a new kind of strong and gentle delight, at being so very close, so deeply of his own kind, that it seemed as if the very breath and heartbeat of each one were being exchanged through all that multitude, and each was another, and others were each, and each was a multitude, and the multitude was one. And quieted and made mild within this melting, they now entered the cold shadow cast by the buildings, and now with every step the smell of the buildings grew stronger, and in the darkening air the glittering of the fences was ever more queer.

"And now as they were pressed ever more intimately together he could see ahead of him a narrow gate, and he was strongly pressed upon from either side and from behind, and went in eagerly, and now he was between two fences so narrowly set that he brushed either fence with either flank, and walked alone, seeing just one other ahead of him, and knowing of just one other behind him, and for a moment the strange thought came to him, that the one ahead was his father, and that the one behind was the son he had never begotten.

"And now the light was so changed that he knew he must have come inside one of the gloomy and enormous buildings, and the smell was so much stronger that it seemed almost to burn his nostrils, and the swell and the somber new light blended together and became some other thing again, beyond his describing to us except to say that the whole air beat with it like one immense heart and it was as if the beating of this heart were pure violence infinitely manifolded upon violence: so that the uneasy feeling stirred in him again that it would be wise to turn around and run out of this place just as fast and as far as ever he could go. This he heard, as if he were telling it to himself at the top of his voice, but it came from somewhere so deep and so dark inside him that he could only hear the shouting of it as less than a whisper, as just a hot and chilling breath, and he scarcely heeded it, there was so much else to attend to.

"For as he walked along in this sudden and complete loneliness, he tells us, this wonderful knowledge of being one with all his race meant less and less to him, and in its place came something still more wonderful: he knew what it was to be himself alone, a creature separate and

ALLEGORY

different from any other, who had never been before, and would never be again. He could feel this in his whole weight as he walked, and in each foot as he put it down and gave his weight to it and moved above it, and in every muscle as he moved, and it was a pride which lifted him up and made him feel large, and a pleasure which pierced him through. And as he began with such wondering delight to be aware of his own exact singleness in this world, he also began to understand (or so he thought) just why these fences were set so very narrow, and just why he was walking all by himself. It stole over him, he tells us, like the feeling of a slow cool wind, that he was being guided toward some still more wonderful reward or revealing, up ahead, which he could not of course imagine, but he was sure it was being held in store for him alone.

"Just then the one ahead of him fell down with a great sigh, and was so quickly taken out of the way that he did not even have to shift the order of his hooves as he walked on. The sudden fall and the sound of that sigh dismayed him, though, and something within him told him that it would be wise to look up: and there he saw Him.

"A little bridge ran crosswise above the fences. He stood on this bridge with His feet as wide apart as He could set them. He wore spattered trousers but from the belt up He was naked and as wet as rain. Both arms were raised high above His head and in both hands He held an enormous Hammer. With a grunt which was hardly like the voice of a human being, and with all His strength, He brought this Hammer down into the forehead of our friend: who, in a blinding blazing, heard from his own mouth the beginning of a gasping sigh; then there was only darkness."

Oh, this is *enough!* it's *enough!* she cried out within herself, seeing their terrible young eyes. How *could* she have been so foolish as to tell so much!

"What happened then?" she heard, in the voice of the oldest calf, and she was horrified. This shining in their eyes: was it only excitement? no pity? no fear?

"What happened?" two others asked.

Very well, she said to herself. I've gone so far; now I'll go the rest of the way. She decided not to soften it, either. She'd teach them a lesson they wouldn't forget in a hurry.

"Very well," she was surprised to hear herself say aloud.

"How long he lay in this darkness he couldn't know, but when he began to come out of it, all he knew was the most unspeakably dreadful pain. He was upside down and very slowly swinging and turning, for he was hanging by the tendons of his heels from great frightful hooks, and he has told us that the feeling was as if his hide were being torn from him inch by inch, in one piece. And then as he became more clearly aware he found that this was exactly what was happening. Knives would sliver and slice along both flanks, between the hide and the living flesh; then there was a moment of most precious relief; then red hands seized his hide and there was a jerking of the hide and a tearing of tissue which it was almost as terrible to hear as to feel, turning his whole body and the poor head at the bottom of it; and then the knives again.

"It was so far beyond anything he had ever known unnatural and amazing that he hung there through several more such slicings and jerkings and tearings before he was fully able to take it all in: then, with a scream, and a supreme straining of all his strength, he tore himself from the hooks and collapsed sprawling to the floor and, scrambling right to his feet, charged the men with the knives. For just a moment they were so astonished and so terrified they could not move. Then they moved faster than he had ever known men could—and so did all the other men who chanced to be in his way. He ran down a glowing floor of blood and down endless corridors which were hung with the bleeding carcasses of our kind and with bleeding fragments of carcasses, among blood-clothed men who carried bleeding weapons, and out of that vast room into the open, and over and through one fence after another, shoving aside many an astounded stranger and shouting out warnings as he ran, and away up the railroad toward the West.

"How he ever managed to get away, and how he ever found his way home, we can only try to guess. It's told that he scarcely knew, himself, by the time he came to this part of his story. He was impatient with those who interrupted him to ask about that, he had so much more important things to tell them, and by then he was so exhausted and so far gone that he could say nothing very clear about the little he did know. But we can realize that he must have had really tremendous strength, otherwise he couldn't have outlived the Hammer; and that strength such as his— which we simply don't see these days, it's of the olden time—is capable of things our own strongest and bravest would sicken to dream of. But there was something even stronger than his strength. There was his righteous fury, which nothing could stand up against, which brought him out of that fearful place. And there was his high and burning and heroic purpose, to keep him safe along the way, and to guide him home, and to keep the breath of life in him until he could warn us. He did manage to tell us that he just followed the railroad, but how he chose one among the many which branched out from that place, he couldn't say. He told us, too, that from time to time he recognized shapes of mountains and other landmarks, from his journey by train, all reappearing backward and with a changed look and hard to see, too (for he was shrewd enough to travel mostly at night), but still recognizable. But that isn't enough

ALLEGORY

to account for it. For he has told us, too, that he simply *knew* the way; that he didn't hesitate one moment in choosing the right line of railroad, or even think of it as choosing; and that the landmarks didn't really guide him, but just made him the more sure of what he was already sure of; and that whenever he *did* encounter human beings—and during the later stages of his journey, when he began to doubt he would live to tell us, he traveled day and night—they never so much as moved to make him trouble, but stopped dead in their tracks, and their jaws fell open.

"And surely we can't wonder that their jaws fell open. I'm sure yours would, if you had seen him as he arrived, and I'm very glad I wasn't there to see it, either, even though it is said to be the greatest and most momentous day of all the days that ever were or shall be. For we have the testimony of eyewitnesses, how he looked, and it is only too vivid, even to hear of. He came up out of the East as much staggering as galloping (for by now he was so worn out by pain and exertion and loss of blood that he could hardly stay upright), and his heels were so piteously torn by the hooks that his hooves doubled under more often than not, and in his broken forehead the mark of the Hammer was like the socket for a third eye.

"He came to the meadow where the great trees made shade over the water. 'Bring them all together!' he cried out, as soon as he could find breath. 'All!' Then he drank; and then he began to speak to those who were already there: for as soon as he saw himself in the water it was as clear to him as it was to those who watched him that there was no time left to send for the others. His hide was all gone from his head and his neck and his forelegs and his chest and most of one side and a part of the other side. It was flung backward from his naked muscles by the wind of his running and now it lay around him in the dust like a ragged garment. They say there is no imagining how terrible and in some way how grand the eyeball is when the skin has been taken entirely from around it: his eyes, which were bare in this way, also burned with pain, and with the final energies of his life, and with his desperate concern to warn us while he could; and he rolled his eyes wildly while he talked, or looked piercingly from one to another of the listeners, interrupting himself to cry out, '*Believe* me! Oh, *believe* me!' For it had evidently never occurred to him that he might not be believed, and must make this last great effort, in addition to all he had gone through for us, to *make* himself believed; so that he groaned with sorrow and with rage and railed at them without tact or mercy for their slowness to believe. He had scarcely what you could call a voice left, but with this relic of a voice he shouted and bellowed and bullied us and insulted us, in the agony of his concern. While

A MOTHER'S TALE

he talked he bled from the mouth, and the mingled blood and saliva hung from his chin like the beard of a goat.

"Some say that with his naked face, and his savage eyes, and that beard and the hide lying off his bare shoulders like shabby clothing, he looked almost human. But others feel this is an irreverence even to think; and others, that it is a poor compliment to pay the one who told us, at such cost to himself, the true ultimate purpose of Man. Some did not believe he had ever come from our ranch in the first place, and of course he was so different from us in appearance and even in his voice, and so changed from what he might ever have looked or sounded like before, that nobody could recognize him for sure, though some were sure they did. Others suspected that he had been sent among us with his story for some mischievous and cruel purpose, and the fact that they could not imagine what this purpose might be, made them, naturally, all the more suspicious. Some believed he was actually a man, trying—and none too successfully, they said—to disguise himself as one of us; and again the fact that they could not imagine why a man would do this, made them all the more uneasy. There were quite a few who doubted that anyone who could get into such bad condition as he was in, was fit even to give reliable information, let alone advice, to those in good health. And some whispered, even while he spoke, that he had turned lunatic; and many came to believe this. It wasn't only that his story was so fantastic; there was good reason to wonder, many felt, whether anybody in his right mind would go to such trouble for others. But even those who did not believe him listened intently, out of curiosity to hear so wild a tale, and out of the respect it is only proper to show any creature who is in the last agony.

"What he told, was what I have just told you. But his purpose was away beyond just the telling. When they asked questions, no matter how curious or suspicious or idle or foolish, he learned, toward the last, to answer them with all the patience he could and in all the detail he could remember. He even invited them to examine his wounded heels and the pulsing wound in his head as closely as they pleased. He even begged them to, for he knew that before everything else, he must be believed. For unless we could believe him, wherever could we find any reason, or enough courage to do the hard and dreadful things he told us we must do!

"It was only these things, he cared about. Only for these, he came back."

Now clearly remembering what these things were, she felt her whole being quail. She looked at the young ones quickly and as quickly looked away.

ALLEGORY

"While he talked," she went on, "and our ancestors listened, men came quietly among us; one of them shot him. Whether he was shot in kindness or to silence him is an endlessly disputed question which will probably never be settled. Whether, even, he died of the shot, or through his own great pain and weariness (for his eyes, they say, were glazing for some time before the men came), we will never be sure. Some suppose even that he may have died of his sorrow and his concern for us. Others feel that he had quite enough to die of, without that. All these things are tangled and lost in the disputes of those who love to theorize and to argue. There is no arguing about his dying words, though; they were very clearly remembered:

" *'Tell them! Believe!'* "

After a while her son asked. "What did he tell them to do?"

She avoided his eyes. "There's a great deal of disagreement about that, too," she said after a moment. "You see, he was so very tired."

They were silent.

"So tired," she said, "some think that toward the end, he really *must* have been out of his mind."

"Why?" asked her son.

"Because he was so tired out and so badly hurt."

They looked at her mistrustfully.

"And because of what he told us to do."

"What did he tell us to do?" her son asked again.

Her throat felt dry. "Just . . . things you can hardly bear even to think of. That's all."

They waited. "Well, *what?*" her son asked in a cold, accusing voice.

" *'Each one is himself,'* " she said shyly. " *'Not of the herd. Himself alone.'* That's one."

"What else?"

" *'Obey nobody. Depend on none.'* "

"What else?"

She found that she was moved. " *'Break down the fences,'* " she said less shyly. " ' *Tell everybody, everywhere.'* "

"Where?"

"Everywhere. You see, he thought there must be ever so many more of us than we had ever known."

They were silent, "What else?" her son asked.

" *'For if even a few do not hear me, or disbelieve me, we are all betrayed.'* "

"Betrayed?"

"He meant, doing as men want us to. Not for ourselves, or the good of each other."

A MOTHER'S TALE

They were puzzled.

"Because, you see, he felt there was no other way." Again her voice altered: *" 'All who are put on the range are put onto trains. All who are put onto trains meet the Man With The Hammer. All who stay home are kept there to breed others to go onto the range, and so betray themselves and their kind and their children forever.*

" 'We are brought into this life only to be victims; and there is no other way for us unless we save ourselves.'

"Do you understand?"

Still they were puzzled, she saw; and no wonder, poor things. But now the ancient lines rang in her memory, terrible and brave. They made her somehow proud. She began actually to want to say them.

" 'Never be taken,' " she said. *" 'Never be driven. Let those who can, kill Man. Let those who cannot, avoid him.' "*

She looked around at them.

"What else?" her son asked, and in his voice there was a rising valor.

She looked straight into his eyes. *" 'Kill the yearlings,' "* she said very gently. *" 'Kill the calves.' "*

She saw the valor leave his eyes.

"Kill *us*?"

She nodded, *" 'So long as Man holds dominion over us,' "* she said. And in dread and amazement she heard herself add, *" 'Bear no young.' "*

With this they all looked at her at once in such a way that she loved her child, and all these others, as never before; and there dilated within her such a sorrowful and marveling grandeur that for a moment she was nothing except her own inward whisper, "Why, *I* am one alone. And of the herd, too. Both at once. All one."

Her son's voice brought her back: "Did they do what he told them to?"

The oldest one scoffed, "Would we be here, if they had?"

"They say some did," the mother replied. "Some tried. Not all."

"What did the men do to them?" another asked.

"I don't know," she said. "It was such a very long time ago."

"Do you believe it?" asked the oldest calf.

"There are some who believe it," she said.

"Do *you*?"

"I'm told that far back in the wildest corners of the range there are some of us, mostly very, very old ones, who have never been taken. It's said that they meet, every so often, to talk and just to think together about the heroism and the terror of two sublime Beings. The One Who Came Back, and The Man With The Hammer. Even here at home, some of the old ones, and some of us who are just old-fashioned, believe it, or parts of it anyway. I know there are some who say that a hollow at the center of the forehead—a sort of shadow of the Hammer's blow—is a sign of very special ability. And I remember how Great-grandmother used to sing an old, pious song, let's see now, yes, 'Be not like dumb-driven cattle, be a hero in the strife.' But there aren't many. Not any more."

"Do *you* believe it?" the oldest calf insisted; and now she was touched to realize that every one of them, from the oldest to the youngest, needed very badly to be sure about that.

"Of course not, silly," she said; and all at once she was overcome by a most curious shyness, for it occurred to her that in the course of time, this young thing might be bred to her. "It's just an old, old legend." With a tender little laugh she added, lightly, "We use it to frighten children with."

By now the light was long on the plain and the herd was only a fume of gold near the horizon. Behind it, dung steamed, and dust sank gently to the shattered ground. She looked far away for a moment, wondering. Something—it was like a forgotten word on the tip of the tongue. She felt the sudden chill of the late afternoon and she wondered what she had been wondering about. "Come, children," she said briskly, "it's high time for supper." And she turned away; they followed.

The trouble was, her son was thinking, you could never trust her. If she said a thing was so, she was probably just trying to get her way with you. If she said a thing wasn't so, it probably was so. But you never could be sure. Not without seeing for yourself. I'm going to go, he told himself; I don't care *what* she wants. And if it isn't so, why then I'll live on the range and make the great journey and find out what *is* so. And if what she told was true, why then I'll know ahead of time and the one I will charge is The Man With The Hammer. I'll put Him and His Hammer out of the way forever, and that will make me an even better hero than The One Who Came Back.

So, when his mother glanced at him in concern, not quite daring to ask her question, he gave her his most docile smile, and snuggled his head against her, and she was comforted.

The littlest and youngest of them was doing double skips in his efforts to keep up with her. Now that he wouldn't be interrupting her, and none of the big ones would hear and make fun of him, he shyly whispered his question, so warmly moistly ticklish that she felt as if he were licking her ear.

"What is it, darling?" she asked, bending down.

"What's a train?"

DEATH OF A FAVORITE

J. F. Powers

I had spent most of the afternoon mousing—a matter of sport with me and certainly not of diet—in the sunburnt fields that begin at our back door and continue hundreds of miles into the Dakotas. I gradually gave up the idea of hunting, the grasshoppers convincing me that there was no percentage in stealth. Even to doze was difficult, under such conditions, but I must have managed it. At least I was late coming to dinner, and so my introduction to the two missionaries took place at table. They were surprised, as most visitors are, to see me take the chair at Father Malt's right.

Father Malt, breaking off the conversation (if it could be called that), was his usual dear old self. "Fathers," he said, "meet Fritz."

I gave the newcomers the first good look that invariably tells me whether or not a person cares for cats. The mean old buck in charge of the team did not like me, I could see, and would bear watching. The other one obviously did like me, but he did not appear to be long enough from the seminary to matter. I felt that I had broken something less than even here.

"My assistant," said Father Malt, meaning me, and thus unconsciously dealing out our fat friend at the other end of the table. Poor Burner! There was a time when, thinking of him, as I did now, as the enemy, I could have convinced myself I meant something else. But he *is* the enemy, and I was right from the beginning, when it could only have been instinct that told me how much he hated me even while trying (in his fashion!) to be friendly. (I believe his prejudice to be acquired rather than congenital, and very likely, at this stage, confined to me, not to cats as a class —there *is* that in his favor. I intend to be fair about this if it kills me.)

My observations of humanity incline me to believe that one of us— Burner or I—must ultimately prevail over the other. For myself, I should not fear if this were a battle to be won on the solid ground of Father Malt's affections. But the old man grows older, the grave beckons to him ahead, and with Burner pushing him from behind, how long can he last? Which is to say: How long can *I* last? Unfortunately, it is naked power that counts most in any rectory, and as things stand now, I am safe only so long as Father Malt retains it here. Could I—this impossible thought is often with me now—could I effect a reconciliation and alliance with Father Burner? Impossible! Yes, doubtless. But the question better asked is: *How* impossible? (Lord knows I would not inflict this line of reason-

ALLEGORY

ing upon myself if I did not hold with the rumors that Father Burner will be the one to succeed to the pastorate.) For I do like it here. It is not at all in my nature to forgive and forget, certainly not as regards Father Burner, but it is in my nature to come to terms (much as nations do) when necessary, and in this solution there need not be a drop of good will. No dog can make that statement, or take the consequences, which I understand are most serious, in the world to come. Shifts and ententes. There is something fatal about the vocation of favorite, but it is the only one that suits me, and, all things considered—to dig I am not able, to beg I am ashamed—the rewards are adequate.

"We go through Chicago all the time," said the boss missionary, who seemed to be returning to a point he had reached when I entered: I knew Father Malt would be off that evening for a convention in Chicago. The missionaries, who would fill in for him and conduct a forty hours' devotion on the side, belonged to an order just getting started in the diocese and were anxious to make a good impression. For the present, at least, as a kind of special introduction offer, they could be had dirt-cheap. Thanks to them, pastors who'd never been able to get away had got a taste of Florida last winter.

"Sometimes we stay over in Chicago," bubbled the young missionary. He was like a rookie ballplayer who hasn't made many road trips.

"We've got a house there," said the first, whose name in religion, as they say, was—so help me—Philbert. Later, Father Burner would get around it by calling him by his surname. Father Malt was the sort who wouldn't see anything funny about "Philbert," but it would be too much to expect him to remember such a name.

"What kind of a house?" asked Father Malt. He held up his hearing aid and waited for clarification.

Father Philbert replied in a shout, "The Order owns *a house* there!"

Father Malt fingered his hearing aid.

Father Burner sought to interpret for Father Philbert. "I think, Father, he wants to know what it's made out of."

"Red brick—it's red brick," bellowed Father Philbert.

"*My* house is red brick," said Father Malt.

"I *noticed* that ," said Father Philbert.

Father Malt shoved the hearing aid at him.

"I know it," said Father Philbert, shouting again.

Father Malt nodded and fed me a morsel of fish. Even for a Friday, it wasn't much of a meal. I would not have been sorry to see this housekeeper go.

"All right, all right," said Father Burner to the figure lurking behind the door and waiting for him, always the last one, to finish. "She stands and looks in at you through the crack," he beefed. "Makes you feel like a condemned man." The housekeeper came into the room, and he addressed the young missionary (Burner was a great one for questioning the young): "Ever read any books by this fella Koestler, Father?"

"The Jesuit?" the young one asked.

"Hell, no, he's some kind of writer. I know the man you mean, though. Spells his name different. Wrote a book—apologetics."

"That's the one. Very—"

"Dull."

"Well . . ."

"This other fella's not bad. He's a writer who's ahead of his time—about fifteen minutes. Good on jails and concentration camps. You'd think he was born in one if you ever read his books." Father Burner regarded the young missionary with absolute indifference. "But you didn't."

"No. Is he a Catholic?" inquired the young one.

"He's an Austrian or something."

"Oh."

The housekeeper removed the plates and passed the dessert around. When she came to Father Burner, he asked her privately, "What is it?"

"Pudding," she said, not whispering, as he would have liked.

"*Bread* pudding?" Now he was threatening her.

"Yes, Father."

Father Burner shuddered and announced to everybody, "No dessert for me." When the housekeeper had retired into the kitchen, he said, "Sometimes I think he got her from a hospital and sometimes, Father, I think she came from one of *your* fine institutions"—this to the young missionary.

Father Philbert, however, was the one to see the joke, and he laughed.

"My God," said Father Burner, growing bolder. "I'll never forget the time I stayed at your house in Louisville. If I hadn't been there for just a day—for the Derby, in fact—I'd have gone to Rome about it. I think I've had better meals here."

At the other end of the table, Father Malt, who could not have heard a word, suddenly blinked and smiled; the missionaries looked to him for some comment, in vain.

"He doesn't hear me," said Father Burner. "Besides, I think he's listening to the news."

"I didn't realize it was a radio too," said the young missionary.

"Oh, hell, yes."

"I think he's pulling your leg," said Father Philbert.

"It's an idea," said Father Burner. Then in earnest to Father Philbert,

ALLEGORY

whom he'd really been working around to all the time—the young one was decidedly not his type—"You the one drivin that new Olds, Father?"

"It's not mine, Father," said Father Philbert with a meekness that would have been hard to take if he'd meant it. Father Burner understood him perfectly, however, and I thought they were two persons who would get to know each other a lot better.

"Nice job. They say it compares with the Cad in power. What do you call that color—oxford or clerical gray?"

"I really couldn't say, Father. It's my brother's. He's a layman in Minneapolis—St. Stephen's parish. He loaned it to me for this little trip."

Father Burner grinned. He could have been thinking, as I was, that Father Philbert protested too much. "Thought I saw you go by earlier," he said. "What's the matter—didn't you want to come in when you saw the place?"

Father Philbert, who was learning to ignore Father Malt, laughed discreetly. "Couldn't be sure this was it. That house on the *other* side of the church, now—"

Father Burner nodded. "Like that, huh? Belongs to a Mason."

Father Philbert sighed and said, "It would."

"Not at all," said Father Burner. "I like 'em better than K.C.s." If he could get the audience for it, Father Burner enjoyed being broad-minded. Gazing off in the direction of the Mason's big house, he said, "I've played golf with him."

The young missionary looked at Father Burner in horror. Father Philbert merely smiled. Father Burner, toying with a large crumb, propelled it in my direction.

"Did a bell ring?" asked Father Malt.

"His P.A. system," Father Burner explained. "Better tell him," he said to the young missionary. "You're closer. He can't bring me in on those batteries he uses."

"No bell," said the young missionary, lapsing into basic English and gestures.

Father Malt nodded, as though he hadn't really thought so.

"How do you like it?" said Father Burner.

Father Philbert hesitated, and then he said, "Here, you mean?"

"I wouldn't ask you that," said Father Burner, laughing. "Talkin' about that Olds. Like it? Like the Hydramatic?"

"No kiddin', Father. It's not mine," Father Philbert protested.

"All right, all right," said Father Burner, who obviously did not believe him. "Just so you don't bring up your vow of poverty." He looked at Father Philbert's uneaten bread pudding—"Had enough?"—

and rose from the table, blessing himself. The other two followed when Father Malt, who was feeding me cheese, waved them away. Father Burner came around to us, bumping my chair—intentionally, I know. He stood behind Father Malt and yelled into his ear, "Any calls for me this aft?" He'd been out somewhere, as usual. I often thought he expected too much to happen in his absence.

"There was something . . ." said Father Malt, straining his memory, which was poor.

"*Yes?*"

"Now I remember—they had the wrong number."

Father Burner, looking annoyed and downhearted, left the room.

"They said they'd call back," said Father Malt, sensing Father Burner's disappointment.

I left Father Malt at the table reading his Office under the orange light of the chandelier. I went to the living room, to my spot in the window from which I could observe Father Burner and the missionaries on the front porch, the young one in the swing with his breviary—the mosquitoes, I judged, were about to join him—and the other two just smoking and standing around, like pool players waiting for a table. I heard Father Philbert say, "Like to take a look at it, Father?"

"Say, that's an idea," said Father Burner.

I saw them go down the front walk to the gray Olds parked at the curb. With Father Burner at the wheel they drove away. In a minute they were back, the car moving uncertainly—this I noted with considerable pleasure until I realized that Father Burner was simply testing the brakes. Then they were gone, and after a bit, when they did not return, I supposed they were out killing poultry on the open road.

That evening, when the ushers dropped in at the rectory, there was not the same air about them as when they came for pinochle. Without fanfare, Mr. Bauman, their leader, who had never worked any but the center aisle, presented Father Malt with a travelling bag. It was nice of him, I thought, when he said, "It's from all of us," for it could not have come from all equally. Mr. Bauman, in hardware, and Mr. Keller, the druggist, were the only ones well off, and must have forked out plenty for such a fine piece of luggage, even after the discount.

Father Malt thanked all six ushers with little nods in which there was no hint of favoritism. "Ha," he kept saying. "You shouldn'a done it."

The ushers bobbed and ducked, dodging his flattery, and kept up a mumble to the effect that Father Malt deserved everything they'd ever done for him and more. Mr. Keller came forward to instruct Father Malt

ALLEGORY

in the use of various clasps and zippers. Inside the bag was another gift, a set of military brushes, which I could see they were afraid he would not discover for himself. But he unsnapped a brush, and, like the veteran crowd-pleaser he was, swiped once or twice at his head with it after spitting into the bristles. The ushers all laughed.

"Pretty snazzy," said the newest usher—the only young blood among them. Mr. Keller had made him a clerk at the store, had pushed through his appointment as alternate usher in the church, and was gradually weaning him away from his motorcycle. With Mr. Keller, the lad formed a block to Mr. Bauman's power, but he was perhaps worse than no ally at all. Most of the older men, though they pretended a willingness to help him meet the problems of an usher, were secretly pleased when he bungled at collection time and skipped a row or overlapped one.

Mr. Keller produced a box of ten-cent cigars, which, as a *personal* gift from him, came as a bitter surprise to the others. He was not big enough, either, to attribute it to them too. He had anticipated their resentment, however, and now produced a bottle of milk of magnesia. No one could deny the comic effect, for Father Malt had beeen known to recommend the blue bottle from the confessional.

"Ha!" said Father Malt, and everybody laughed.

"In case you get upset on the trip," said the druggist.

"You know it's the best thing," said Father Malt in all seriousness, and then even he remembered he'd said it too often before. He passed the cigars. The box went from hand to hand, but, except for the druggist's clerk, nobody would have one.

Father Malt, seeing this, wisely renewed his thanks for the bag, insisting upon his indebtedness until it was actually in keeping with the idea the ushers had of their own generosity. Certainly none of them had ever owned a bag like that. Father Malt went to the housekeeper with it and asker her to transfer his clothes from the old bag, already packed, to the new one. When he returned, the ushers were still standing around feeling good about the bag and not so good about the cigars. They'd discuss that later. Father Malt urged them to sit down. He seemed to want them near him as long as possible. They *were* his friends, but I could not blame Father Burner for avoiding them. He was absent now, as he usually managed to be when the ushers called. If he ever succeeded Father Malt, who let them have the run of the place, they would be the first to suffer— after me! As Father Malt was the heart, they were the substance of a parish that remained rural while becoming increasingly suburban. They dressed up occasionally and dropped into St. Paul and Minneapolis, "the Cities," as visiting firemen into Hell, though it would be difficult to imagine any other place as graceless and far-gone as our own hard little highway town—called Sherwood but about as sylvan as a tennis court.

They were regular fellows—not so priestly as their urban colleagues—loud, heavy of foot, wearers of long underwear in wintertime and iron-gray business suits the year round. Their idea of a good time (pilsner beer, cheap cigars smoked with the bands left on, and pinochle) coincided nicely with their understanding of "doing good" (a percentage of every pot went to the parish building fund). Their wives, also active, played cards in the church basement and sold vanilla extract and chances —mostly to each other, it appeared—with all revenue over cost going to what was known as "the missions." This evening I could be grateful that time was not going to permit the usual pinochle game. (In the midst of all their pounding—almost as hard on me as it was on the dining-room table—I often felt they should have played on a meat block.)

The ushers, settling down all over the living room, started to talk about Father Malt's trip to Chicago. The housekeeper brought in a round of beer.

"How long you be gone, Father—three days?" one of them asked.

Father Malt said that he'd be gone about three days.

"Three days! This is Friday. Tomorrow's Saturday. Sunday. Monday." Everything stopped while the youngest usher counted on his fingers. "Back on Tuesday?"

Father Malt nodded.

"Who's takin' over on Sunday?"

Mr. Keller answered for Father Malt. "He's got some missionary fathers in."

"Missionaries!"

The youngest usher then began to repeat himself on one of his two or three topics. "Hey, Father, don't forget to drop in the U.S.O. if it's still there. I was in Chi during the war," he said, but nobody would listen to him.

Mr. Bauman had cornered Father Malt and was trying to tell him where that place was—that place where he'd eaten his meals during the World's Fair; one of the waitresses was from Minnesota. I'd had enough of this—the next thing would be a diagram on the back of an envelope— and I'd heard Father Burner come in earlier. I went upstairs to check on him. For a minute or two I stood outside his room listening. He had Father Philbert with him, and, just as I'd expected, he was talking against Father Malt, leading up to the famous question with which Father Malt, years ago, had received the Sherwood appointment from the Archbishop: "Have dey got dere a goot meat shop?"

ALLEGORY

Father Philbert laughed, and I could hear him sip from his glass and place it on the floor beside his chair. I entered the room, staying close to the baseboard, in the shadows, curious to know what they were drinking. I maneuvered myself into position to sniff Father Philbert's glass. To my surprise, Scotch. Here was proof that Father Burner considered Father Philbert a friend. At that moment I could not think what it was he expected to get out of a lowly missionary. My mistake, not realizing then how correct and prophetic I'd been earlier in thinking of them as two of a kind. It seldom happened that Father Burner got out the real Scotch for company, or for himself *in* company. For most guests he had nothing—a safe policy, since a surprising number of temperance cranks passed through the rectory—and for unwelcome guests who would like a drink he kept a bottle of "Scotch-type" whiskey, which was a smooth, smoky blend of furniture polish that came in a fancy bottle, was offensive even when watered, and cheap, though rather hard to get since the end of the war. He had a charming way of plucking the rare bottle from a bureau drawer, as if this were indeed an occasion for him; even so, he would not touch the stuff, presenting himself as a chap of simple tastes, of no taste at all for the things of this world, who would prefer, if anything, the rude wine made from our own grapes—if we'd had any grapes. Quite an act, and one he thoroughly enjoyed, holding his glass of pure water and asking, "How's your drink, Father? Strong enough?"

The housekeeper, appearing at the door, said there'd been a change of plans and some of the ushers were driving Father Malt to the train.

"Has he gone yet?" asked Father Burner.

"Not yet, Father."

"Well, tell him goodby for me."

"Yes, Father."

When she had gone, he said, "I'd tell him myself, but I don't want to run into that bunch."

Father Philbert smiled. "What's he up to in Chicago?"

"They've got one of those pastors' and builders' conventions going on at the Stevens Hotel."

"Is he building?"

"No, but he's a pastor and he'll get a lot of free samples. He won't buy anything."

"Not much has been done around here, huh?" said Father Philbert.

He had fed Father Burner the question he wanted. "He built that fish pond in the back yard—for his minnows. That's the extent of the building program in his time. Of course he's only been here a while."

"How long?"

"Fourteen years," said Father Burner. *He* would be the greatest builder of them all—if he ever got the chance. He lit a cigarette and smiled. "What he's really going to Chicago for is to see a couple of ball games."

Father Philbert did not smile. "Who's playing there now?" he said.

A little irritated at this interest, Father Burner said, "I believe it's the Red Sox—or is it the Reds? Hell, how do I know?"

"Couldn't be the Reds," said Father Philbert. "The boy and I were in Cincinnati last week and it was the start of a long home stand for them."

"Very likely," said Father Burner.

While the missionary, a Cardinal fan, analyzed the pennant race in the National League, Father Burner sulked. "What's the best train out of Chicago for Washington?" he suddenly inquired.

Father Philbert told him what he could, but admitted that his information dated from some years back. "We don't make the run to Washington any more."

"That's right," said Father Burner. "Washington's in the American League."

Father Philbert laughed, turning aside the point that he travelled with the Cardinals. "I thought you didn't know about these things," he said.

"About these things it's impossible to stay ignorant," said Father Burner. "Here, and the last place, and the place before that, and in the seminary—a ball, a bat, and God. I'll be damned, Father, if I'll do as the Romans do."

"What price glory?" inquired Father Philbert, as if he smelt heresy.

"I know," said Father Burner. "And it'll probably cost me the red hat." A brave comment, perhaps, from a man not yet a country pastor, and it showed me where his thoughts were again. He did not disguise his humble ambition by speaking lightly of an impossible one. "Scratch a prelate and you'll find a second baseman," he fumed.

Father Philbert tried to change the subject. "Somebody told me Father Malt's the exorcist for the diocese."

"Used to be." Father Burner's eye flickered balefully.

"Overdid it, huh?" asked Father Philbert—as if he hadn't heard!

"Some." I expected Father Burner to say more. He could have told some pretty wild stories, the gist of them all that Father Malt, as an exorcist, was perhaps a little quick on the trigger. He had stuck pretty much to livestock, however, which was to his credit in the human view.

"Much scandal?"

"Some."

"Nothing serious, though?"

"No."

"Suppose it depends on what you call serious."

Father Burner did not reply. He had become oddly morose. Perhaps he felt that he was being catered to out of pity, or that Father Philbert, in giving him so many opportunities to talk against Father Malt, was tempting him.

"Who plays the accordion?" inquired Father Philbert, hearing it downstairs.

"He does."

"Go on!"

"Sure."

"How can he hear what he's playing?"

"What's the difference—if he plays an accordion?"

Father Philbert laughed. He removed the cellophane from a cigar, and then he saw me. And at that moment I made no attempt to hide. "There's that damn cat."

"His assistant!" said Father Burner with surprising bitterness. "Coadjutor with right of succession."

Father Philbert balled up the cellophane and tossed it at the wastebasket, missing.

"Get it," he said to me, fatuously.

I ignored him, walking slowly toward the door.

Father Burner made a quick movement with his feet, which were something to behold, but I knew he wouldn't get up, and took my sweet time.

Father Philbert inquired, "Will she catch mice?"

She! Since coming to live at the rectory, I've been celibate, it's true, but I daresay I'm as manly as the next one. And Father Burner, who might have done me the favor of putting him straight, said nothing.

"She looks pretty fat to be much of a mouser."

I just stared at the poor man then, as much as to say that I'd think one so interested in catching mice would have heard of a little thing called the mousetrap. After one last dirty look, I left them to themselves—to punish each other with their company.

I strolled down the hall, trying to remember when I'd last had a mouse. Going past the room occupied by the young missionary, I smiled upon his door, which was shut, confident that he was inside hard at his prayers.

The next morning, shortly after breakfast, which I took, as usual, in the kitchen, I headed for the cool orchard to which I often repaired on just such a day as this one promised to be. I had no appetite for the sparrows hopping from tree to tree above me, but there seemed no way to convince them of that. Each one, so great in his vanity, thinks himself eminently edible. Peace, peace, they cry, and there is no peace. Finally, tired of their noise, I got up from the matted grass and left, levelling my ears and flailing my tail, in a fake dudgeon that inspired the males to feats of stunt flying and terrorized the young females most delightfully.

I went then to another favorite spot of mine, that bosky strip of green between the church and the brick sidewalk. Here, however, the horseflies found me, and as if that were not enough, visions of stray dogs and children came between me and the kind of sleep I badly needed after an uncommonly restless night.

When afternoon came, I remembered that it was Saturday, and that I could have the rectory to myself. Father Burner and the missionaries would be busy with confessions. By this time the temperature had reached its peak, and though I felt sorry for the young missionary, I must admit the thought of the other two sweltering in the confessionals refreshed me. The rest of the afternoon I must have slept something approaching the sleep of the just.

I suppose it was the sound of dishes that roused me. I rushed into the dining room, not bothering to wash up, and took my customary place at the table. Only then did I consider the empty chair next to me—the utter void. This, I thought, is a foreshadowing of what I must someday face—this, and Father Burner munching away at the other end of the table. And there was the immediate problem: no one to serve me. The young missionary smiled at me, but how can you eat a smile? The other two, looking rather wilted—to their hot boxes I wished them swift return—talked in expiring tones of reserved sins and did not appear to notice me. Our first meal together without Father Malt did not pass without incident, however. It all came about when the young missionary extended a thin sliver of meat to me.

"Hey, don't do that!" said Father Philbert. "You'll never make a mouser out of her that way."

Father Burner, too, regarded the young missionary with disapproval.

"Just this one piece," said the young missionary. The meat was already in my mouth.

"Well, watch it in the future," said Father Philbert. It was the word "future" that worried me. Did it mean that he had arranged to cut off my sustenance in the kitchen too? Did it mean that until Father Malt returned I had to choose between mousing and fasting?

I continued to think along these melancholy lines until the repast, which had never begun for me, ended for them. Then I whisked into the kitchen, where I received the usual bowl of milk. But whether the housekeeper, accustomed as she was to having me eat my main course at table, assumed there had been no change in my life, or was now acting under instructions from these villains, I don't know. I was too sickened by

ALLEGORY

their meanness to have any appetite. When the pastor's away, the curates will play, I thought. On the whole I was feeling pretty glum.

It was our custom to have the main meal at noon on Sundays. I arrived early, before the others, hungrier than I'd been for as long as I could remember, and still I had little or no expectation of food at this table. I was there for one purpose—to assert myself—and possibly, where the young missionary was concerned, to incite sympathy for myself and contempt for my persecutors. By this time I knew that to be the name for them.

They entered the dining room, just the two of them.

"Where's the kid?" asked Father Burner.

"He's not feeling well," said Father Philbert.

I was not surprised. They'd arranged between the two of them to have him say the six- and eleven-o'clock Masses, which meant, of course, that he'd fasted in the interval. I had not thought of him as the hardy type, either.

"I'll have the housekeeper take him some beef broth," said Father Burner. Damned white of you, I was thinking, when he suddenly whirled and swept me off my chair. Then he picked it up and placed it against the wall. Then he went to the lower end of the table, removed his plate and silverware, and brought them to Father Malt's place. Talking and fuming to himself, he sat down in Father Malt's chair. I did not appear very brave, I fear, cowering under mine.

Father Philbert, who had been watching with interest, now greeted the new order with a cheer. "Attaboy, Ernest!"

Father Burner began to justify himself. "More light here," he said, and added, "Cats kill birds," and for some reason he was puffing.

"If they'd just kill mice," said Father Philbert, "they wouldn't be so bad." He had a one-track mind if I ever saw one.

"Wonder how many that black devil's caught in his time?" said Father Burner, airing a common prejudice against cats of my shade (though I do have a white collar). He looked over at me. "Sssssss," he said. But I held my ground.

"I'll take a dog any day," said the platitudinous Father Philbert.

"Me, too."

After a bit, during which time they played hard with the roast, Father Philbert said, "How about taking her for a ride in the country?"

"Hell," said Father Burner. "He'd just come back."

"Not if we did it right, she wouldn't."

"Look," said Father Burner. "Some friends of mine dropped a cat off the high bridge in St. Paul. They saw him go under in midchannel. I'm

DEATH OF A FAVORITE

talking about the Mississippi, understand. Thought they'd never lay eyes on that animal again. That's what they thought. He was back at the house before they were." Father Burner paused—he could see that he was not convincing Father Philbert—and then he tried again. "That's a fact, Father. They might've played a quick round of golf before they got back. Cat didn't even look damp, they said. He's still there. Case a lot like this. Except now they're afraid of *him*."

To Father Burner's displeasure, Father Philbert refused to be awed or even puzzled. He simply inquired: "But did they use a bag? Weights?"

"Millstones," snapped Father Burner. "Don't quibble."

Then they fell to discussing the burial customs of gangsters—poured concrete and the rest—and became so engrossed in the matter that they forgot all about me.

Over against the wall, I was quietly working up the courage to act against them. When I felt sufficiently lionhearted, I leaped up and occupied my chair. Expecting blows and vilification, I encountered only indifference. I saw then how far I'd come down in their estimation. Already the remembrance of things past—the disease of noble politicals in exile—was too strong in me, the hope of restoration unwarrantably faint.

At the end of the meal, returning to me, Father Philbert remarked, "I think I know a better way." Rising, he snatched the crucifix off the wall, passed it to a bewildered Father Burner, and, saying "Nice Kitty," grabbed me behind the ears. "Hold it up to her," said Father Philbert. Father Burner held the crucifix up to me. "See that?" said Father Philbert to my face. I miaowed. "Take that!" said Father Philbert, cuffing me. He pushed my face into the crucifix again. "See that?" he said again, but I knew what to expect next, and when he cuffed me, I went for his hand with my mouth, pinking him nicely on the wrist. Evidently Father Burner had begun to understand and appreciate the proceedings. Although I was in a good position to observe everything, I could not say as much for myself. "Association," said Father Burner with mysterious satisfaction, almost with zest. He poked the crucifix at me. "If he's just smart enough to react properly," he said. "Oh, she's plenty smart," said Father Philbert, sucking his wrist and giving himself, I hoped, hydrophobia. He scuffed off one of his sandals for a paddle. Father Burner, fingering the crucifix nervously, inquired, "Sure it's all right to go on with this thing?" "It's the intention that counts in these things," said Father Philbert. "Our motive is clear enough." And they went at me again.

After that first taste of the sandal in the dining room, I foolishly believed I would be safe as long as I stayed away from the table; there was something about my presence there, I thought, that brought out the

ALLEGORY

beast in them—which is to say very nearly all that was in them. But they caught me in the upstairs hall the same evening, one brute thundering down upon me, the other sealing off my only avenue of escape. And this beating was worse than the first—preceded as it was by a short delay that I mistook for a reprieve until Father Burner, who had gone downstairs muttering something about "leaving no margin for error," returned with the crucifix from the dining room, although we had them hanging all over the house. The young missionary, coming upon them while they were at me, turned away. "I wash my hands of it," he said. I thought he might have done more.

Out of mind, bruised of body, sick at heart, for two days and two nights I held on, I know not how or why—unless I lived in hope of vengeance. I wanted simple justice, a large order in itself, but I would never have settled for that alone. I wanted nothing less than my revenge.

I kept to the neighborhood, but avoided the rectory. I believed, of course, that their only strategy was to drive me away. I derived some little satisfaction from making myself scarce, for it was thus I deceived them into thinking their plan to banish me successful. But this was my single comfort during this hard time, and it was as nothing against their crimes.

I spent the night in the open fields. I reeled, dizzy with hunger, until I bagged an aged field mouse. It tasted bitter to me, this stale provender, and seemed, as I swallowed it, an ironic concession to the enemy. I vowed I'd starve before I ate another mouse. By way of retribution to myself, I stalked sparrows in the orchard—hating myself for it but persisting all the more when I thought of those bird-lovers, my persecutors, before whom I could stand and say in self-redemption, "You made me what I am now. You thrust the killer's part upon me." Fortunately, I did not flush a single sparrow. Since *my* motive was clear enough, however, I'd had the pleasure of sinning against them and their ideals, the pleasure without the feathers and mess.

On Tuesday, the third day, all caution, I took up my post in the lilac bush beside the garage. Not until Father Malt returned, I knew, would I be safe in daylight. He arrived along about dinnertime, and I must say the very sight of him aroused a sentiment in me akin to human affection. The youngest usher, who must have had the afternoon off to meet him at the station in St. Paul, carried the new bag before him into the rectory. It was for me an act symbolic of the counter-revoluton to come. I did not rush out from my hiding place, however. I had suffered too much to play the fool now. Instead I slipped into the kitchen by way of the flap in the screen door, which they had not thought to barricade. I waited under the stove for my moment, like an actor in the wings.

DEATH OF A FAVORITE

Presently I heard them tramping into the dining room and seating themselves, and Father Malt's voice saying. "I had a long talk with the Archbishop." (I could almost hear Father Burner praying, Did he say anything about *me*?) And then, "Where's Fritz?"

"He hasn't been around lately," said Father Burner cunningly. He would not tell the truth and he would not tell a lie.

"You know, there's something mighty funny about that cat," said Father Philbert. "We think she's possessed."

I was astonished, and would have liked a moment to think it over, but by now I was already entering the room.

"*Possessed!*" said Father Malt. "Aw, no!"

"Ah, yes," said Father Burner, going for the meat right away. "And good riddance."

And then I miaowed and they saw me.

"Quick!" said Father Philbert, who made a nice recovery after involuntarily reaching for me and his sandal at the same time. Father Burner ran to the wall for the crucifix, which had been, until now, a mysterious and possibly blasphemous feature of my beatings—the crucifix held up to me by the one not scourging at the moment, as if it were the will behind my punishment. They had schooled me well, for even now, at the sight of the crucifix, an undeniable fear was rising in me. Father Burner handed it to Father Malt.

"Now you'll see," said Father Philbert.

"We'll leave it up to you," said Father Burner.

I found now that I could not help myself. What followed was hidden from them—from human eyes. I gave myself over entirely to the fear they'd beaten into me, and in a moment, according to their plan, I was fleeing the crucifix as one truly possessed, out of the dining room and into the kitchen, and from there, blindly, along the house and through the shrubbery, ending in the street, where a powerful gray car ran over me—and where I gave up the old ghost for a new one.

Simultaneously, reborn, redeemed from my previous fear, identical with my former self, so far as they could see, and still in their midst, I padded up to Father Malt—he still gripping the crucifix—and jumped into his lap. I heard the young missionary arriving from an errand in Father Philbert's *brother's* car, late for dinner he thought, but just in time to see the stricken look I saw coming into the eyes of my persecutors. This look alone made up for everything I'd suffered at their hands. Purring now, I was rubbing up against the crucifix, myself effecting my utter revenge.

"What have we done?" cried Father Philbert. He was basically an emotional dolt and would have voted then for my canonization.

ALLEGORY

"I ran over a cat!" said the young missionary excitedly. "I'd swear it was this one. When I looked, there was nothing there!"

"Better go upstairs and rest," growled Father Burner. He sat down—it was good to see him in his proper spot at the low end of the table—as if to wait a long time, or so it seemed to me. I found myself wondering if I could possibly bring about his transfer to another parish—one where they had a devil for a pastor and several assistants, where he would be able to start at the bottom again.

But first things first, I always say, and all in good season, for now Father Malt himself was drawing my chair up to the table, restoring me to my rightful place.

Hook is primitive; he exists purely as a hawk, resolving his literal hunger, to fill his stomach, by eating; his hunger to kill by killing; his sexual hunger, when it comes, by releasing it. He is not personified; he is not conscious of his consciousness. He acts out his will as it surges and delights in the power born of that will: to eat, to kill, to lay claim to a female and to force himself upon her. His drives are as much a part of him as his wingedness and he knows the exaltation of flying. He never analyzes any of it; he is both joyfully and painfully aware of being alive but he is never aware of his awareness. Hook is a loner; he is the part of the human being that is always isolated, the part that strives to balance itself internally and to satisfy its solitary needs. The allegorical impact of "Hook" is proportional to how often and how much our will and our hunger move us. Hook is the hawk in us, the intrinsic loneliness that is our birthright: to be and to become a Self.

All three stories are concerned ultimately with the deaths of the animals therein. And their deaths are the result of their connection with mankind. Hook is the wildest, yet he too is fated to confront civilization as it extends deeper and deeper into the wilderness. There is finally only one power with which he grapples that he cannot subdue, and that is death. It comes, at last, clothed suspiciously like a Japanese farmer, accompanied by a dog, Man's best friend, the subservient canine. Ironic this meeting of the dog and the hawk, how they complement each other: the hawk the symbol of the raw, uncultivated range and the Airedale the symbol of the farming urge, the drive to cultivate the rawness of Hook's natural home.

As sad and hopeless as Hook's last battle is, it is courageous. "In this last conflict . . . there had been some minutes of the supreme fire of the hawk whose three hungers are perfectly fused in the one will, enough to burn off a year of shame." Hook's death was in a sense adventitious. He was already dead in terms of the power and virility he had known when he was young; assuredly he was weak and beaten and wingless to be forced to prey upon chickens. That he submitted to death in the form it took is the point, yes, for that is how Clark tells it to us. But the dog only killed him; he destroyed the invader of his master's henhouse. "The dog, smarting from his cuts, came to the master and was praised." No roaring, throbbing life force like the hawk's had ever been alive in the Airedale. Hook had reeked of dying for a year before the dog ever smelled him.

"A Mother's Tale," on the other hand, is of foreordained death. Cattle are raised by men to a specific end; they meet it in the slaughterhouse. Cows are a means of survival; we, as readers and as human *animals*, know, as soon as "A Mother's Tale" opens, where the cattle who are moving eastward and away from the rest, are going. But the calves don't know, and being *cow* animals, aren't yet aware of their destiny. It is determined by the material hungers of a society yet more collective than their own. Cattle, like men, seek to belong to the herd. It is that impulse to cluster that is common to them both.

The moving mass of cattle is the crowd. "They went at a walk, not very fast, but faster than they could imaginably enjoy. Those in front were compelled by those behind; those at the rear, with few exceptions, did their best to keep up; those who were locked within the herd could no more help moving than the particles inside a falling rock." This same motion is shared by crowds on buses or while emptying out of a theater onto the street.

"A Mother's Tale" is quite centrally concerned with the continuity in time of a collective heritage. The herd, though it mourns the death of the individual, resists dissolution upon that death. The end of the Self is not the end of the species. It is the herd who immortalizes The One Who Came Back. No tradition exists to assure us that Hook lived, no enduring memory of him, perhaps rightly; he was not conscious of himself that way. He passed on no legends to his offspring. The cattle in "A Mother's Tale" are terribly personified; yes, they are cattle, but Agee wants us to know they are mankind, too. He has infused his bovine creations with the spirit of humanity, endowed them with speech, the capacity for tale-telling and the development of a legendary tradition to ensure that the legend outlives them—they will it to their children.

Without the collective there can be neither written nor oral tradition, for there would be no group to receive what is verbally transmitted and no one to pass it on to the young. This is the mother's tale. " 'It was my great-grandmother who told me,' she said. 'She was told it by her great-

ALLEGORY

grandmother, who claimed she saw it with her own eyes, though of course I can't vouch for that. Because I wasn't even dreamed of then. . . .'"

Perhaps the deepest truth revealed in "A Mother's Tale" is the perpetuation of legend generation after generation, rendered possible only by those creatures who gather and form a collective. As a culture changes, so, too, does the legend. Its very repetition alters it; no two tale-tellers ever tell quite the same tale. With the practice of writing the process of change may be slowed somewhat, for the hand and the eye reproduce more precisely in conjunction than the ear and the tongue. But writing, too, is an act of interpretation and still the tale passes differently through every new mother, who heard it from her mother, and now in turn tells her child, who will some day be a mother. Legendry is a societal enterprise, a herd phenomenon. The allegorical strength of "A Mother's Tale" lies in its artful unfolding of a story within a story. The steer who returns, his very skin torn to shreds, his muscles raw and exposed to the wind, cries to the others, "Believe *me*. Oh, believe *me*." He echoes the plea inherent in legend; he begs for the trust of his listeners; he warns them. The ageless warning, the moral of the story, springs from the will of the species, apart from its independent members, to continue to survive. It is the reason that the legend, or the fable, or the tale, is ever told.

"Death of a Favorite" combines the simple, literal allegory of "Hook" with the allegorical technique of personification. Powers' cat retains throughout the story his integrity as a cat. He remains, in fact, proudly and aloofly feline and glad of it, for the men around him are mostly weak and despicable. He disdains their company, though he harbors a certain fondness for Father Malt, which fondness is based indubitably on the Father's kindness to him. This is the man who stands between Fritz and an unfortunate fate. "My observations of humanity incline me to believe that one of us—Burner or I—must ultimately prevail over the other. For myself, I should not fear if this were a battle to be won on the solid ground of Father Malt's affections. But the old man grows older, the grave beckons to him ahead, and with Burner pushing him from behind, how long can he last? Which is to say: How long can I last?"

Cats are highly domesticated yet they maintain an independence of mobility and a great degree of self-direction such as dogs have forfeited. The cat has made a compromise; he is supported by the efforts of his master, who feeds him, in return for which he might perform the function of ridding the premises of mice; a duty which Fritz, by the way, as the favorite, entirely neglects. Says he, "It is not at all in my nature to forgive and forget, certainly not as regards Father Burner, but it is my nature to come to terms (much as nations do) when necessary, and in this

DEATH OF A FAVORITE

solution there need not be a drop of good will. No dog can make that statement, or take the consequences, which I understand are most serious, in the world to come." Fritz is willing—in order to retain his position in the rectory—to negotiate.

Only "Death of a Favorite," of the three tales, is written in the first person. These are the thoughts of a cat, recorded by the cat himself we suppose, when he is not busy elsewhere. Powers is interested in persuading us of Fritz's feline nature; rather than the cat achieving manhood, the man achieves cathood. This is just the reverse of what Agee accomplishes in depicting his cow. Agee is more concerned that she behave humanly; she is a mother first and then she may be a cow. For his purposes, he makes use of one appropriate metaphorical device. We believe that Fritz, on the other hand, can observe humanity objectively because he is a cat.

Consider how you might appear to the feline who lives under your roof. Fritz has numerous opportunities to observe the priests at their meanest and most loathsome occupations. They neither realize nor care what he knows, for he is mute. It is just this, their ignorance of his keen perceptions, that is his triumph when Father Malt returns. Of this literary menagerie, it is the one animal who is close in, right in the house of man, who can outwit and escape him, though man may curse the cat and scare him to death. It is Fritz who outmaneuvers men; not the cattle, not the hawk who flies above men; Fritz, the pet, by virtue of suffering to abide with men, who knows and to a degree controls the humans around him. "Death of a Favorite" is humorous; we find nothing to laugh at in "Hook" or "A Mother's Tale." A cat's humor is wry. If he is not amused, we, at least, are.

The final twist to "Death of a Favorite" is a bit of superstition, a touch of magic: Fritz's self-sacrifice and subsequent rebirth. He throws himself beneath "Father Philbert's brother's car." A fitting use of a man's machine, a young priest at the wheel, to thwart the destiny in store for him. A cat, after all, has nine lives.

In the three tales, the same principle of fictional disguise—allegory—produces three entirely unique results.

VII | Dream as Crisis

To dream is to unwind the reels of our secret lives that lie below the level of consciousness. We are fascinated by dreams. They are the films shown in the dark theater of the mind, bringing to the surface wishing, fearing, and the lurking crises that trouble everyday existence. Dreams seem, in fact, to have a language of their own, strange upon awakening but quite acceptable during the term of the dream itself. The language of dream is often crisis. Its aspects can be the landscape of the real; the surreal (what the poet Marianne Moore has characterized as "imaginary gardens with real toads in them"—the more than real, objects clearly plausible but distorted in their relationships); the unreal; or the monstrous.

The title of Delmore Schwartz's story is of deep significance. It states clearly the early dread of assuming the responsibility for one's own identity, of leaving home and "becoming a person" on one's own, of going forth, in Blake's words, "to love without the help of any man on earth." It is not without significance either that Schwartz sets his story of a dream in a movie theater, where the storyteller and other witnesses can screen the history of his family events and share the growing terror of his coming birth. Life would be much simpler, wouldn't it, if it never began at all? In the easiest psychological definition, what we watch unfold in Schwartz' theater is an anxiety dream, put forth with such skill that we share the dream and the foreboding and leap up with the hero to protest.

In his story, Schwartz uses the dream as explicit scenario. Thus, as in film, dream sequences are used as shuttles beteweeen fantasy and reality, to undermine time as a linear or continuously simple experience, and to explain, underline, or advance the events of the plot. Yet well before movie-going slipped into common experience, the filmic quality of dream was expressed in Ambrose Bierce's "An Occurence at Owl Creek Bridge." This very quality tempted a French movie director, Robert Enrico, to record an event of the American Civil War with great fidelity to the story.

Dreaming, we are yet witnesses. "The Secret Room" takes place in the eye of the camera, and moves, as the camera often does, with the stealthy and *mysterious tread of dream. And like dream, its relationship to everyday experience is shattered because the dreamlike scenario begins without explanation or introductory exposition and ends without well-made solution. Like any dream, it has a vaguely disturbing resolution: the last word of the story. The realistic surface notwithstanding, more questions are provided than answered.*

(On the other hand, Fitzgerald's "The Curious Case of Benjamin Button" in Chapter II achieves a tone that is wide awake. Acerbic, reportorial, humorous, its style forces our attention to the problems of youth, age, and experience far from the cliché that "life is but a dream.")

The final story in this chapter is a fairy tale, a modern one, "The Seven Riders." Now, one belief is that fairy tales resulted from the tradition of telling dreams. A dictionary of some of the symbols of dreams can be bought from the local fortune teller. These dream books are interesting not so much because they translate dream into reality, but because they contain symbols which seeem universal to the dream experience. In another not unrelated way in the name of science, some psychologists have worked out an elaborate one-to-one symbology showing how an element of a fairy tale, say a frog, has Freudian overtones close to the interpretation of dreams.

Little do we find in fiction that will nicely conform to restrictive definitions. Stories are always trying to escape boundaries of neatly linear interpretation. What we can *say is that some stories are closer to dreaming than others, like "Bliss" (in Chapter IX), in which the shimmering imagery evokes the floating world of the heroine's life, or "The Ambitious Guest," where a fateful quality of experience unfolds.*

IN DREAMS BEGIN RESPONSIBILITIES

Delmore Schwartz

I

I think it is the year 1909. I feel as if I were in a moving-picture theater, the long arm of light crossing the darkness and spinning, my eyes fixed upon the screen. It is a silent picture, as if an old Biograph one, in which the actors are dressed in ridiculously old-fashioned clothes, and one flash succeeds another with sudden jumps, and the actors, too, seem

IN DREAMS BEGIN RESPONSIBILITIES

to jump about, walking too fast. The shots are full of rays and dots, as if it had been raining when the picture was photographed. The light is bad.

It is Sunday afternoon, June 12th, 1909, and my father is walking down the quiet streets of Brooklyn on his way to visit my mother. His clothes are newly pressed and his tie is too tight in his high collar. He jingles the coins in his pocket, thinking of the witty things he will say. I feel as if I had by now relaxed entirely in the soft darkness of the theater; the organist peals out the obvious approximate emotions on which the audience rocks unknowingly. I am anonymous. I have forgotten myself: it is always so when one goes to a movie, it is, as they say, a drug.

My father walks from street to street of trees, lawns, and houses, once in a while coming to an avenue on which a street-car skates and gnaws, progressing slowly. The motorman, who has a handle-bar mustache, helps a young lady wearing a hat like a feathered bowl onto the car. He leisurely makes change and rings his bell as the passengers mount the car. It is obviously Sunday, for everyone is wearing Sunday clothes and the street-car's noises emphasize the quiet of the holiday (Brooklyn is said to be the city of churches). The shops are closed and their shades drawn but for an occasional stationery store or drugstore with great green balls in the window.

My father has chosen to take this long walk because he likes to walk and think. He thinks about himself in the future and so arrives at the place he is to visit in a mild state of exaltation. He pays no attention to the houses he is passing, in which the Sunday dinner is being eaten, nor to the many trees which line each street, now coming to their full green and the time when they will enclose the whole street in leafy shadow. An occasional carriage passes, the horses' hooves falling like stones in the quiet afternoon, and once in a while an automobile, looking like an enormous upholstered sofa, puffs and passes.

My father thinks of my mother, of how lady-like she is, and of the pride which will be his when he introduces her to his family. They are not yet engaged and he is not yet sure that he loves my mother, so that, once in a while, he becomes panicky about the bond already established. But then he reassures himself by thinking of the big men he admires who are married: William Randolph Hearst and William Howard Taft, who has just become the President of the United States.

My father arrives at my mother's house. He has come too early and so is suddenly embarrassed. My aunt, my mother's younger sister, answers the loud bell with her napkin in her hand, for the family is still at dinner. As my father enters, my grandfather rises from the table and shakes

DREAM AS CRISIS

hands with him. My mother has run upstairs to tidy herself. My grandmother asks my father if he has had dinner and tells him that my mother will be down soon. My grandfather opens the conversation by remarking about the mild June weather. My father sits uncomfortably near the table, holding his hat in his hand. My grandmother tells my aunt to take my father's hat. My uncle, twelve years old, runs into the house, his hair tousled. He shouts a greeting to my father, who has often given him nickels, and then runs upstairs, as my grandmother shouts after him. It is evident that the respect in which my father is held in this house is tempered by a good deal of mirth. He is impressive, but also very awkward.

II

Finally my mother comes downstairs and my father, being at the moment engaged in conversation with my grandfather, is made uneasy by her entrance, for he does not know whether to greet my mother or to continue the conversation. He gets up from his chair clumsily and says "Hello" gruffly. My grandfather watches this, examining their congruence, such as it is, with a critical eye, and meanwhile rubbing his bearded cheek roughly, as he always does when he reasons. He is worried; he is afraid that my father will not make a good husband for his oldest daughter. At this point something happens to the film, just as my father says something funny to my mother: I am awakened to myself and my unhappiness just as my interest has become most intense. The audience begins to clap impatiently. Then the trouble is attended to, but the film has been returned to a portion just shown, and once more I see my grandfather rubbing his bearded cheek, pondering my father's character. It is difficult to get back into the picture once more and forget myself, but as my mother giggles at my father's words, the darkness drowns me.

My father and mother depart from the house, my father shaking hands with my grandfather once more, out of some unknown uneasiness. I stir uneasily also, slouched in the hard chair of the theater. Where is the older uncle, my mother's older brother? He is studying in his bedroom upstairs, studying for his final examinations at the College of the City of New York, having been dead of double pneumonia for the last twenty-one years. My mother and father walk down the same quiet streets once more. My mother is holding my father's arm and telling him of the novel she has been reading and my father utters judgments of the characters as the plot is made clear to him. This is a habit which he very much enjoys, for he feels the utmost superiority and confidence when he is approving or condemning the behavior of other people. At times he feels moved to utter a brief "Ugh," whenever the story becomes what he would call sugary. This tribute is the assertion of his manliness. My mother feels satisfied by the interest she has awakened; and she is showing my father how intelligent she is and how interesting.

They reach the avenue, and the street-car leisurely arrives. They are going to Coney Island this afternoon, although my mother really considers such pleasures inferior. She has made up her mind to indulge only in a walk on the boardwalk and a pleasant dinner, avoiding the riotous amusements as being beneath the dignity of so dignified a couple.

My father tells my mother how much money he has made in the week just past, exaggerating an amount which need not have been exaggerated. But my father has always felt that actualities somehow fall short, no matter how fine they are. Suddenly I begin to weep. The determined old lady who sits next to me in the theater is annoyed and looks at me with an angry face, and being intimidated, I stop. I drag out my handkerchief and dry my face, licking the drop which has fallen near my lips. Meanwhile I have missed something, for here are my father and mother alighting from the street-car at the last stop, Coney Island.

III

They walk toward the boardwalk and my mother commands my father to inhale the pungent air from the sea. They both breathe in deeply, both of them laughing as they do so. They have in common a great interest in health, although my father is strong and husky, and my mother is frail. They are both full of theories about what is good to eat and not good to eat, and sometimes have heated discussions about it, the whole matter ending in my father's announcement, made with a scornful bluster, that you have to die sooner or later anyway. On the boardwalk's flagpole, the American flag is pulsing in an intermittent wind from the sea.

My father and mother go to the rail of the boardwalk and look down on the beach where a good many bathers are casually walking about. A few are in the surf. A peanut whistle pierces the air with its pleasant and active whine, and my father goes to buy peanuts. My mother remains at the rail and stares at the ocean. The ocean seems merry to her; it pointedly sparkles and again and again the pony waves are released. She notices the children digging in the wet sand, and the bathing costumes of the girls who are her own age. My father returns with the peanuts. Overhead the sun's lightning strikes and strikes, but neither of them are at all aware of it. The boardwalk is full of people dressed in their Sunday clothes and casually strolling. The tide does not reach as far as the boardwalk, and the strollers would feel no danger if it did. My father and mother lean on the rail of the boardwalk and absently stare at the ocean. The ocean is becoming rough; the waves come in slowly, tugging strength from far back. The moment before they somersault, the moment when they arch

DREAM AS CRISIS

their backs so beautifully, showing white veins in the green and black, that moment is intolerable. They finally crack, dashing fiercely upon the sand, actually driving, full force downward, against it, bouncing upward and forward, and at last petering out into a small stream of bubbles which slides up the beach and then is recalled. The sun overhead does not disturb my father and my mother. They gaze idly at the ocean, scarcely interested in its harshness. But I stare at the terrible sun which breaks up sight, and the fatal merciless passionate ocean. I forget my parents. I stare fascinated, and finally, shocked by their indifference, I burst out weeping once more. The old lady next to me pats my shoulder and says: "There, there, young man, all of this is only a movie, only a movie," but I look up once more at the terrifying sun and the terrifying ocean, and being unable to control my tears I get up and go to the men's room, stumbling over the feet of the other people seated in my row.

IV

When I return, feeling as if I had just awakened in the morning sick for lack of sleep, several hours have apparently passed and my parents are riding on the merry-go-round. My father is on a black horse, my mother on a white one, and they seem to be making an eternal circuit for the single purpose of snatching the nickel rings which are attached to an arm of one of the posts. A hand organ is playing; it is inseparable from the ceaseless circling of the merry-go-round.

For a moment it seems that they will never get off the carousel, for it will never stop, and I feel as if I were looking down from the fiftieth story of a building. But at length they do get off; even the hand-organ has ceased for a moment. There is a sudden and sweet stillness, as if the achievement of so much motion. My mother has acquired only two rings, my father, however, ten of them, although it was my mother who really wanted them.

They walk on along the boardwalk as the afternoon descends by imperceptible degrees into the incredible violet of dusk. Everything fades into a relaxed glow, even the ceaseless murmuring from the beach. They look for a place to have dinner. My father suggests the best restaurant on the boardwalk and my mother demurs, according to her principles of economy and housewifeliness.

However they do go to the best place, asking for a table near the window so that they can look out upon the boardwalk and the mobile ocean. My father feels omnipotent as he places a quarter in the waiter's hand in asking for a table. The place is crowded and here too there is music, this time from a kind of string trio. My father orders with a fine confidence.

As their dinner goes on, my father tells of his plans for the future and

IN DREAMS BEGIN RESPONSIBILITIES

my mother shows with expressive face how interested she is, and how impressed. My father becomes exultant, lifted up by the waltz that is being played and his own future begins to intoxicate him. My father tells my mother that he is going to expand his business, for there is a great deal of money to be made. He wants to settle down. After all, he is twenty-nine, he has lived by himself since his thirteenth year, he is making more and more money, and he is envious of his friends when he visits them in the security of their homes, surrounded, it seems, by the calm domestic pleasures, and by delightful children, and then as the waltz reaches the moment when the dancers all swing madly, then, then with awful daring, then he asks my mother to marry him, although awkwardly enough and puzzled as to how he had arrived at the question, and she, to make the whole business worse, begins to cry, and my father looks nervously about, not knowing at all what to do now, and my mother says: "It's all I've wanted from the first moment I saw you," sobbing, and he finds all of this very difficult, scarcely to his taste, scarcely as he thought it would be, on his long walks over Brooklyn Bridge in the revery of a fine cigar, and it was then, at that point, that I stood up in the theater and shouted: "Don't do it! It's not too late to change your minds, both of you. Nothing good will come of it, only remorse, hatred, scandal, and two children whose characters are monstrous." The whole audience turned to look at me, annoyed, the usher came hurrying down the aisle flashing his searchlight, and the old lady next to me tugged me down into my seat, saying: "Be quiet. You'll be put out, and you paid thirty-five cents to come in." And so I shut my eyes because I could not bear to see what was happening. I sat there quietly.

V

But after a while I begin to take brief glimpses and at length I watch again with thirsty interest, like a child who tries to maintain his sulk when he is offered the bribe of candy. My parents are now having their picture taken in a photographer's booth along the boardwalk. The place is shadowed in the mauve light which is apparently necessary. The camera is set to the side on its tripod and looks like a Martian man. The photographer is instructing my parents in how to pose. My father has his arm over my mother's shoulder, and both of them smile emphatically. The photographer brings my mother a bouquet of flowers to hold in her hand, but she holds it at the wrong angle. Then the photographer covers himself with the black cloth which drapes the camera and all that one sees of him is one protruding arm and his hand with which he holds tightly to the rubber ball which he squeezes when the picture is taken. But he is not satisfied with their appearance. He feels that somehow there is something

DREAM AS CRISIS

wrong in their pose. Again and again he comes out from his hiding place with new directions. Each suggestion merely makes matters worse. My father is becoming impatient. They try a seated pose. The photographer explains that he has his pride, he wants to make beautiful pictures, he is not merely interested in all of this for the money. My father says: "Hurry up, will you? We haven't got all night." But the photographer only scurries about apologetically, issuing new directions. The photographer charms me, and I approve of him with all my heart, for I know exactly how he feels, and as he criticizes each revised pose according to some obscure idea of rightness, I become quite hopeful. But then my father says angrily: "Come on, you've had enough time, we're not going to wait any longer." And the photographer, sighing unhappily, goes back into the black covering, and holds out his hand, saying: "One, two, three, Now!", and the picture is taken, with my father's smile turned to a grimace and my mother's bright and false. It takes a few minutes for the picture to be developed and as my parents sit in the curious light they become depressed.

VI

They have passed a fortune-teller's booth and my mother wishes to go in, but my father does not. They begin to argue about it. My mother becomes stubborn, my father once more impatient. What my father would like to do now is walk off and leave my mother there, but he knows that that would never do. My mother refuses to budge. She is near tears, but she feels an uncontrollable desire to hear what the palm-reader will say. My father consents angrily and they both go into the booth which is, in a way, like the photographer's, since it is draped in black cloth and its light is colored and shadowed. The place is too warm, and my father keeps saying that this is all nonsense, pointing to the crystal ball on the table. The fortune-teller, a short, fat woman garbed in robes supposedly exotic, comes into the room and greets them, speaking with an accent, but suddenly my father feels that the whole thing is intolerable; he tugs at my mother's arm but my mother refuses to budge. And then, in terrible anger, my father lets go of my mother's arm and strides out, leaving my mother stunned. She makes a movement as if to go after him, but the fortune-teller holds her and begs her not to do so, and I in my seat in the darkness am shocked and horrified. I feel as if I were walking a tight-rope one hundred feet over a circus audience and suddenly the rope is showing signs of breaking, and I get up from my seat and begin to shout once more the first words I can think of to communicate my terrible fear, and once more the usher comes hurrying down the aisle flashing his searchlight, and the old lady pleads with me, and the shocked audience has turned to stare at me, and I keep shouting: "What are they doing? Don't they know what they are doing? Why doesn't my mother go after my father and beg him not to be angry? If she does not do that, what will she do? Doesn't my father know what he is doing?" But the usher has seized my arm, and is dragging me away, and as he does so, he says: "What are *you* doing? Don't you know you can't do things like this, you can't do whatever you want to do, even if other people aren't about? You will be sorry if you do not do what you should do. You can't carry on like this, it is not right, you will find that out soon enough, everything you do matters too much," and as he said that, dragging me through the lobby of the theater, into the cold light, I woke up into the bleak winter morning of my twenty-first birthday, the window-sill shining with its lip of snow, and the morning already begun.

AN OCCURRENCE AT OWL CREEK BRIDGE

Ambrose Bierce

A man stood upon a railroad bridge in northern Alabama, looking down into the swift water twenty feet below. The man's hands were behind his back, the wrists bound with a cord. A rope closely encircled his neck. It was attached to a stout cross-timber above his head and the slack fell to the level of his knees. Some loose boards laid upon the sleepers supporting the metals of the railway supplied a footing for him and his executioners—two private soldiers of the Federal army, directed by a sergeant who in civil life may have been a deputy sheriff. At a short remove upon the same temporary platform was an officer in the uniform of his rank, armed. He was a captain. A sentinel at each end of the bridge stood with his rifle in the position known as "support," that is to say, vertical in front of the left shoulder, the hammer resting on the forearm thrown straight across the chest—a formal and unnatural position, enforcing an erect carriage of the body It did not appear to be the duty of these two men to know what was occurring at the center of the bridge; they merely blockaded the two ends of the foot planking that traversed it.

Beyond one of the sentinels nobody was in sight; the railroad ran straight away into a forest for a hundred yards, then, curving, was lost to view. Doubtless there was an outpost farther along. The other bank of the stream was open ground—a gentle acclivity topped with a stockade of vertical tree trunks, loopholed for rifles, with a single embrasure through which protruded the muzzle of a brass cannon commanding the bridge. Midway of the slope between the bridge and fort were the spec-

DREAM AS CRISIS

tators—a single company of infantry in line, at "parade rest," the butts of the rifles on the ground, the barrels inclining slightly backward against the right shoulder, the hands crossed upon the stock. A lieutenant stood at the right of the line, the point of his sword upon the ground, his left hand resting upon his right. Excepting the group of four at the center of the bridge, not a man moved. The company faced the bridge, staring stonily, motionless. The sentinels, facing the banks of the stream, might have been statues to adorn the bridge. The captain stood with folded arms, silent, observing the work of his subordinates, but making no sign. Death is a dignitary who when he comes announced is to be received with formal manifestations of respect, even by those most familiar with him. In the code of military etiquette silence and fixity are forms of deference.

The man who was engaged in being hanged was apparently about thirty-five years of age. He was a civilian, if one might judge from his habit, which was that of a planter. His features were good—a straight nose, firm mouth, broad forehead, from which his long, dark hair was combed straight back, falling behind his ears to the collar of his well-fitting frock coat. He wore a mustache and pointed beard, but no whiskers; his eyes were large and dark gray, and had a kindly expression which one would hardly have expected in one whose neck was in the hemp. Evidently this was no vulgar assassin. The liberal military code makes provision for hanging many kinds of persons, and gentlemen are not excluded.

The preparations being complete, the two private soldiers stepped aside and each drew away the plank upon which he had been standing. The sergeant turned to the captain, saluted and placed himself immediately behind that officer, who in turn moved apart one pace. These movements left the condemned man and the sergeant standing on the two ends of the same plank, which spanned three of the crossties of the bridge. The end upon which the civilian stood almost, but not quite, reached a fourth. This plank has been held in place by the weight of the captain; it was now held by that of the sergeant. At a signal from the former the latter would step aside, the plank would tilt and the condemned man go down between two ties. The arrangement commended itself to his judgment as simple and effective. His face had not been covered nor his eyes bandaged. He looked a moment at his "unsteadfast footing," then let his gaze wander to the swirling water of the stream racing madly beneath his feet. A piece of dancing driftwood caught his attention and his eyes followed it down the current. How slowly it appeared to move! What a sluggish stream!

He closed his eyes in order to fix his last thoughts upon his wife and children. The water, touched to gold by the early sun, the brooding mists under the banks at some distance down the stream, the fort, the soldiers, the piece of drift—all had distracted him. And now he became conscious of a new disturbance. Striking through the thought of his dear ones was a sound which he could neither ignore nor understand, a sharp, distinct, metallic percussion like the stroke of a blacksmith's hammer upon the anvil; it had the same ringing quality. He wondered what it was, and whether immeasurably distant or near by—it seemed both. Its recurrence was regular, but as slow as the tolling of a death knell. He awaited each stroke with impatience and—he knew not why—apprehension. The intervals of silence grew progressively longer; the delays became maddening. With their greater infrequency the sounds increased in strength and sharpness. They hurt his ear like the thrust of a knife; he feared he would shriek. What he heard was the ticking of his watch.

He unclosed his eyes and saw again the water below him. "If I could free my hands," he thought, "I might throw off the noose and spring into the stream. By diving I could evade the bullets and, swimming vigorously, reach the bank, take to the woods, and get away home. My home, thank God, is as yet outside their lines; my wife and little ones are still beyond the invader's farthest advance."

As these thoughts, which have here to be set down in words, were flashed into the doomed man's brain rather than evolved from it the captain nodded to the sergeant. The sergeant stepped aside.

Peyton Farquhar was a well-to-do planter, of an old and highly respected Alabama family. Being a slave owner and like other slave owners a politician, he was naturally an original secessionist and ardently devoted to the Southern cause. Circumstances of an imperious nature, which it is unnecessary to relate here, had prevented him from taking service with the gallant army that had fought the disastrous campaigns ending with the fall of Corinth, and he chafed under the inglorious restraint, longing for the release of his energies, the larger life of the soldier, the opportunity for distinction. That opportunity, he felt, would come, as it comes to all in war time. Meanwhile he did what he could. No service was too humble for him to perform in aid of the South, no adventure too perilous for him to undertake if consistent with the character of a civilian who was at heart a soldier, and who in good faith and without too much qualification assented to at least a part of the frankly villainous dictum that all is fair in love and war.

One evening while Farquhar and his wife were sitting on a rustic bench near the entrance to his grounds, a gray-clad soldier rode up to the gate and asked for a drink of water. Mrs. Farquhar was only too happy to serve him with her own white hands. While she was fetching the

DREAM AS CRISIS

water her husband approached the dusty horseman and inquired eagerly for news from the front.

"The Yanks are repairing the railroads," said the man, "and are getting ready for another advance. They have reached the Owl Creek bridge, put it in order and built a stockade on the north bank. The commandant has issued an order, which is posted everywhere, declaring that any civilian caught interfering with the railroad, its bridges, tunnels or trains will be summarily hanged. I saw the order."

"How far is it to the Owl Creek bridge?" Farquhar asked.

"About thirty miles."

"Is there no force on this side the creek?"

"Only a picket post half a mile out, on the railroad, and a single sentinel at this end of the bridge."

"Suppose a man—a civilian and student of hanging—should elude the picket post and perhaps get the better of the sentinel," said Farquhar, smiling, "what could he accomplish?"

The soldier reflected. "I was there a month ago," he replied. "I observed that the flood of last winter had lodged a great quantity of driftwood against the wooden pier at this end of the bridge. It is now dry and would burn like tow."

The lady had now brought the water, which the soldier drank. He thanked her ceremoniously, bowed to her husband and rode away. An hour later, after nightfall, he re-passed the plantation, going northward in the direction from which he had come. He was a Federal scout.

As Peyton Farquhar fell straight downward through the bridge he lost consciousness and was as one already dead. From this state he was awakened—ages later, it seemed to him—by the pain of a sharp pressure up in his throat, followed by a sense of suffocation. Keen, poignant agonies seemed to shoot from his neck downward through every fiber of his body and limbs. These pains appeared to flash along well-defined lines of ramification and to beat with an inconceivably rapid periodicity. They seemed like streams of pulsating fire heating him to an intolerable temperature. As to his head, he was conscious of nothing but a feeling of fullness—of congestion. These sensations were unaccompanied by thought. The intellectual part of his nature was already effaced; he had power only to feel, and feeling was torment. He was conscious of motion. Encompassed in a luminous cloud, of which he was now merely the fiery heart, without material substance, he swung through unthinkable arcs of oscillation, like a vast pendulum. Then all at once, with terrible suddenness, the light about him shot upward with the noise of a loud plash; a frightful roaring was in his ears, and all was cold and dark. The power of thought was restored; he knew that the rope had broken and he had fallen into the stream. There was no additional strangulation; the noose about his neck was already suffocating him and kept the water from his lungs. To die of hanging at the bottom of a river—the idea seemed to him ludicrous. He opened his eyes in the darkness and saw above him a gleam of light, but how distant, how inaccessible! He was still sinking, for the light became fainter and fainter until it was a mere glimmer. Then it began to grow and brighten, and he knew that he was rising toward the surface—knew it with reluctance, for he was now very comfortable. "To be hanged and drowned," he thought, "that is not so bad; but I do not wish to be shot. No; I will not be shot; that is not fair."

He was not conscious of an effort, but a sharp pain in his wrist apprised him that he was trying to free his hands. He gave the struggle his attention, as an idler might observe the feat of a juggler, without interest in the outcome. What splendid effort! What magnificent, what superhuman strength! Ah, that was a fine endeavor! Bravo! The cord fell away; his arms parted and floated upward, the hands dimly seen on each side in the growing light. He watched them with a new interest as first one and then the other pounced upon the noose at his neck. They tore it away and thrust it fiercely aside, its undulations resembling those of a water snake. "Put it back, put it back!" He thought he shouted these words to his hands, for the undoing of the noose had been succeeded by the direst pang that he had yet experienced. His neck ached horribly; his brain was on fire; his heart, which had been fluttering faintly, gave a great leap, trying to force itself out at his mouth. His whole body was racked and wrenched with an insupportable anguish! But his disobedient hands gave no heed to the command. They beat the water vigorously with quick, downward strokes, forcing him to the surface. He felt his head emerge; his eyes were blinded by the sunlight; his chest expanded convulsively, and with a supreme and crowning agony his lungs engulfed a great draught of air, which instantly he expelled in a shriek!

He was now in full possession of his physical senses. They were, indeed, preternaturally keen and alert. Something in the awful disturbance of his organic system had so exalted and refined them that they made record of things never before perceived. He felt the ripples upon his face and heard their separate sounds as they struck. He looked at the forest on the bank of the stream, saw the individual trees, the leaves and the veining of each leaf—saw the very insects upon them: the locusts, the brilliant-bodied flies, the gray spiders stretching their webs from twig to twig. He noted the prismatic colors in all the dewdrops upon a million blades of grass. The humming of the gnats that danced above the eddies of the stream, the beating of the dragonflies' wings, the strokes of the water spiders' legs, like oars which had lifted their boat—all these made audible music. A fish slid along beneath his eyes and he heard the rush of its body parting the water.

He had come to the surface facing down the stream; in a moment the visible world seemed to wheel slowly round, himself the pivotal point, and he saw the bridge, the fort, the soldiers upon the bridge, the captain, the sergeant, the two privates, his executioners. They were in silhouette against the blue sky. They shouted and gesticulated, pointing at him. The captain had drawn his pistol, but did not fire; the others were unarmed. Their movements were grotesque and horrible, their forms gigantic.

Suddenly he heard a sharp report and something struck the water smartly within a few inches of his head, spattering his face with spray. He heard a second report, and saw one of the sentinels with his rifle at his shoulder, a light cloud of blue smoke rising from the muzzle. The man in the water saw the eye of the man on the bridge gazing into his own through the sights of the rifle. He observed that it was a gray eye and remembered having read that gray eyes were keenest, and that all famous marksmen had them. Nevertheless this one had missed.

A counter-swirl had caught Farquhar and turned him half round; he was again looking into the forest on the bank opposite the fort. The sound of a clear, high voice in a monotonous singsong now rang out behind him and came across the water with a distinctness that pierced and subdued all other sounds, even the beating of the ripples in his ears. Although no soldier, he had frequented camps enough to know the dread significance of that deliberate, drawling, aspirated chant; the lieutenant on shore was taking a part in the morning's work. How coldly and pitilessly—with what an even, calm intonation, presaging, and enforcing tranquillity in the men—with what accurately measured intervals fell those cruel words:

"Attention, company! . . . Shoulder arms! . . . Ready! . . . Aim! . . . Fire!"

Farquhar dived—dived as deeply as he could. The water roared in his ears like the voice of Niagara, yet he heard the dulled thunder of the volley and, rising again toward the surface, met shining bits of metal, singularly flattened, oscillating slowly downward. Some of them touched him on the face and hands, then fell away, continuing their descent. One lodged between his collar and neck; it was uncomfortably warm and he snatched it out.

As he rose to the surface, gasping for breath, he saw that he had been a long time under water; he was perceptibly farther down stream—nearer to safety. The soldiers had almost finished reloading; the metal ramroads flashed all at once in the sunshine as they were drawn from the barrels, turned in the air, and thrust into their sockets. The two sentinels fired again, independently and ineffectually.

The hunted man saw all this over his shoulder; he was now swimming vigorously with the current. His brain was as energetic as his arms and legs; he thought with the rapidity of lightning.

"The officer," he reasoned, "will not make that martinet's error a second time. It is as easy to dodge a volley as a single shot. He has probably already given the command to fire at will. God help me, I cannot dodge them all!"

An appalling plash within two yards of him was followed by a loud, rushing sound, *diminuendo*, which seemed to travel back through the air to the fort and died in an explosion which stirred the very river to its deeps! A rising sheet of water curved over him, fell down upon him, blinded him, strangled him! The cannon had taken a hand in the game. As he shook his head free from the commotion of the smitten water he heard the deflected shot humming through the air ahead, and in an instant it was cracking and smashing the branches in the forest beyond.

"They will not do that again," he thought; "the next time they will use a charge of grape. I must keep my eye upon the gun; the smoke will apprise me—the report arrives too late; it lags behind the missile. That is a good gun."

Suddenly he felt himself whirled round and round—spinning like a top. The water, the banks, the forests, the now distant bridge, fort and men—all were commingled and blurred. Objects were represented by their colors only; circular horizontal streaks of color—that was all he saw. He had been caught in a vortex and was being whirled on with a velocity of advance and gyration that made him giddy and sick. In a few moments he was flung upon the gravel at the foot of the left bank of the stream—the southern bank—and behind a projecting point which concealed him from his enemies. The sudden arrest of his motion, the abrasion of one of his hands on the gravel, restored him, and he wept with delight. He dug his fingers into the sand, threw it over himself in handfuls and audibly blessed it. It looked like diamonds, rubies, emeralds; he could think of nothing beautiful which it did not resemble. The trees upon the bank were giant garden plants; he noted a definite order in their arrangement, inhaled the fragrance of their blooms. A strange, roseate light shone through the spaces among their trunks and the wind made in their branches the music of Aeolian harps. He had no wish to perfect his escape—was content to remain in that enchanting spot until retaken.

A whiz and rattle of grapeshot among the branches high above his head roused him from his dream. The baffled cannoneer had fired him a random farewell. He sprang to his feet, rushed up the sloping bank, and plunged into the forest.

All that day he traveled, laying his course by the rounding sun. The forest seemed interminable; nowhere did he discover a break in it, not even a woodman's road. He had not known that he lived in so wild a region. There was something uncanny in the revelation.

By nightfall he was fatigued, footsore, famishing. The thought of his wife and children urged him on. At last he found a road which led him in what he knew to be the right direction. It was as wide and straight as a city street, yet it seemed untraveled. No fields bordered it, no dwelling anywhere. Not so much as the barking of a dog suggested human habitation. The black bodies of the trees formed a straight wall on both sides, terminating on the horizon in a point, like a diagram in a lesson in perspective. Overhead, as he looked up through this rift in the wood, shone great golden stars looking unfamiliar and grouped in strange constellations. He was sure they were arranged and in some order which had a secret and malign significance. The wood on either side was full of singular noises, among which—once, twice, and again—he distinctly heard whispers in an unknown tongue.

His neck was in pain and lifting his hand to it he found it horribly swollen. He knew that it had a circle of black where the rope had bruised it. His eyes felt congested; he could no longer close them. His tongue was swollen with thirst; he relieved its fever by thrusting it forward from between his teeth into the cold air. How softly the turf had carpeted the untraveled avenue—he could no longer feel the roadway beneath his feet!

Doubtless, despite his suffering, he had fallen asleep while walking, for now he sees another scene—perhaps he has merely recovered from a delirium. He stands at the gate of his own home. All is as he left it, and all bright and beautiful in the morning sunshine. He must have traveled the entire night. As he pushes open the gate and passes up the wide white walk, he sees a flutter of female garments; his wife, looking fresh and cool and sweet, steps down from the veranda to meet him. At the bottom of the steps she stands waiting, with a smile of ineffable joy, an attitude of matchless grace and dignity. Ah, how beautiful she is! He springs forward with extended arms. As he is about to clasp her he feels a stunning blow upon the back of the neck; a blinding white light blazes all about him with a sound like the shock of a cannon—then all is darkness and silence!

Peyton Farquhar was dead; his body, with a broken neck, swung gently from side to side beneath the timbers of the Owl Creek bridge.

AN OCCURRENCE AT OWL CREEK BRIDGE

The narration has the tone of a battle report, or a journalist's account in war. Bierce was a journalist and war correspondent. Thus the terse, straightforward prose contrasts with the momentous and horrifying deed. It is the understatement we have observed earlier in Hemingway.

Like other stories with which we have been dealing, "An Occurrence at Owl Creek Bridge" comments on the nature of enemies. "Evidently this was no vulgar assassin. The liberal military code makes provision for hanging many kinds of persons, and gentlemen are not excluded." A war story, it heightens the sense of dream induced by crisis. The dream-state is close to posthumous, a profound comment on the ancient cliché usually associated with drowning, that "his whole life swam before him."

It is no wonder that this tale found its way into the movies. The descriptions are intensely visual: the soldiers drawn up in military order for the hanging; different observations of the stream below the bridge from its sluggish force to its golden, dreamlike swirl in the moments after the tilting of the plank. A man dreaming a lifetime in a few seconds while we are privy to it all through our own eyes.

We move in the dream from the real to the surreal: "To die of hanging at the bottom of a river!" From the sensory with a description of sights and sounds—"He was now in full possession of his physical senses"—to the extrasensory, the surreal description of the "forests, the banks, the water . . . diamonds, rubies, emeralds. . . . The trees upon the bank were giant garden plants. . . . A strange roseate light shone through the spaces. . . ." We are in the land of Salvador Dali: "great golden stars looking unfamiliar and grouped in strange constellations. . . . he distinctly heard whispers in an unknown tongue." The landscape of dream. The waiting wife: slow the filmic action to show her arms outstretched in slow motion.

There is a passage part way through the story which interrupts the present and the dream. We are not sure whether it belongs to Farquhar's recollection or is the author's intrusion to tell us how the hanging came about and to introduce us to some of the planter's life. But because the passage ends with the words "He was a Federal scout" it is a brilliant stroke.

Alert as we are in these latter days to dream as psychological reality, we know the language of dream when we encounter it. Do responsibilities begin in dreams? Farquhar "was sure they were arranged in some order which had a secret and malign significance." Some years before Freud had entered the bloodstream of culture, Bierce had laid out the middle distance between trauma and its resolution.

DREAM AS CRISIS

THE SECRET ROOM

Alain Robbe-Grillet

To Gustave Moreau.

The first thing to be seen is a red stain, of a deep, dark, shiny red, with almost black shadows. It is in the form of an irregular rosette, sharply outlined, extending in several directions in wide outflows of unequal length, dividing and dwindling afterward into single sinuous streaks. The whole stands out against a smooth, pale surface, round in shape, at once dull and pearly, a hemisphere joined by gentle curves to an expanse of the same pale color—white darkened by the shadowy quality of the place: a dungeon, a sunken room, or a cathedral—glowing with a diffused brilliance in the semi-darkness.

Further back, the space is filled with the cylindrical trunks of columns, repeated with progressive vagueness in their retreat toward the beginning of a vast stone stairway, turning slightly as it rises, growing narrower, and narrower as it approaches the high vaults where it disappears.

The whole setting is empty, stairway and colonnades. Alone, in the foreground, the stretched-out body gleams feebly, marked with the red stain—a white body whose full, supple flesh can be sensed, fragile, no doubt, and vulnerable. Alongside the bloody hemisphere another identical round form, this one intact, is seen at almost the same angle of view; but the haloed point at its summit, of darker tint, is in this case quite recognizable, whereas the other one is entirely destroyed, or at least covered by the wound.

In the background, near the top of the stairway, a black silhouette is seen fleeing, a man wrapped in a long floating cape, ascending the last steps without turning around, his deed accomplished. A thin smoke rises in twisting scrolls from a sort of incense burner placed on a high stand of ironwork with a silvery glint. Nearby lies the milkwhite body, with wide streaks of blood running from the left breast, along the flank and on the hip.

It is a fully rounded woman's body, but not heavy, completely nude, lying on the back, the bust raised up somewhat by thick cushions thrown down on the floor, which is covered with oriental rugs. The waist is very narrow, the neck long and thin, curved to one side, the head thrown back into a darker area where even so, may be discerned the facial features, the partly opened mouth, the wide staring eyes, shining with a fixed brilliance, and the mass of long, black hair spread out in a complicated

THE SECRET ROOM

wavy disorder over a heavily folded cloth, of velvet perhaps, on which also rest the arm and shoulder.

It is a uniformly colored velvet of dark purple, or which seems so in this lighting. But purple, brown, blue also seem to dominate in the colors of the cushions—only a small portion of which is hidden beneath the velvet cloth, and which protrude noticeably, lower down, beneath the bust and waist—as well as in the oriental patterns of the rugs on the floor. Further on, these same colors are picked up again in the stone of the paving and the columns, the vaulted archways, the stairs, and the less discernible surfaces that disappear into the farthest reaches of the room.

The dimensions of this room are difficult to determine exactly; the body of the young sacrificial victim seems at first glance to occupy a substantial portion of it, but the vast size of the stairway leading down to it would imply rather that this is not the whole room, whose considerable space must in reality extend all around, right and left, as it does toward the far-away browns and blues among the columns standing in line, in every direction, perhaps toward other sofas, thick carpets, piles of cushions and fabrics, other tortured bodies, other incense burners.

It is also difficult to say where the light comes from. No clue, on the columns or on the floor, suggests the direction of the rays. Nor is any window or torch visible. The milkwhite body itself seems to light the scene, with its full breasts, the curve of its thighs, the rounded belly, the full buttocks, the stretched-out legs, widely spread, and the black tuft of the exposed sex, provocative, proffered, useless now.

The man has already moved several steps back. He is now on the first steps of the stairs, ready to go up. The bottom steps are wide and deep, like the steps leading up to some great building, a temple or theatre; they grow smaller as they ascend, and at the same time describe a wide helical curve, so gradually that the stairway has not yet made a half-turn by the time that it disappears near the top of the vaults, reduced then to a steep, narrow flight of steps without handrail, vaguely outlined, moreover, in the thickening darkness beyond.

But the man does not look in this direction, where his movement none the less carries him; his left foot on the second step and his right foot already touching the third, with his knee bent, he has turned around to look at the spectacle for one last time. The long, floating cape thrown hastily over his shoulders, clasped in one hand at his waist, has been whirled around by the rapid circular motion that has just caused his head and chest to turn in the opposite direction, and a corner of the cloth remains suspended in the air as if blown by a gust of wind; this corner, twisting around upon itself in the form of a loose S, reveals the red silk lining with its gold embroidery.

DREAM AS CRISIS

The man's features are impassive, but tense, as if in expectation—or perhaps fear—of some sudden event, or surveying with one last glance the total immobility of the scene. Though he is looking backward, his whole body is turned slightly forward, as if he were continuing up the stairs. His right arm—not the one holding the edge of the cape—is bent sharply toward the left, toward a point in space where the balustrade should be, if this stairway had one, an interrupted gesture, almost incomprehensible, unless it arose from an instinctive movement to grasp the absent support.

As to the direction of his glance, it is certainly aimed at the body of the victim lying on the cushions, its extended members stretched out in the form of a cross, its bust raised up, its head thrown back. But the face is perhaps hidden from the man's eyes by one of the columns, standing at the foot of the stairs. The young woman's right hand touches the floor just at the foot of this column. The fragile wrist is encircled by an iron bracelet. The arm is almost in darkness, only the hand receiving enough light to make the thin, outspread fingers clearly visible against the circular protrusion at the base of the stone column. A black metal chain running around the column passes through a ring affixed to the bracelet, binding the wrist tightly to the column.

At the top of the arm a rounded shoulder, raised up by the cushions, also stands out well lighted, as well as the neck, the throat, and the other shoulder, the armpit with its soft hair, the left arm likewise pulled back with its wrist bound in the same manner to the base of another column, in the extreme foreground; here the iron bracelet and the chain are fully displayed, represented with perfect clarity down to the slightest details.

The same is true, still in the foreground but at the other side, for a similar chain, but not quite as thick, wound directly around the ankle, running twice around the column and terminating in a heavy iron ring embedded in the floor. About a yard further back, or perhaps slightly further, the right foot is identically chained. But it is the left foot, and its chain, that are the most minutely depicted.

The foot is small, delicate, finely modeled. In several places the chain has broken the skin, causing noticeable if not extensive depressions in the flesh. The chain links are oval, thick, the size of an eye. The ring in the floor resembles those used to attach horses; it lies almost touching the stone pavement to which it is riveted by a massive iron peg. A few inches away is the edge of a rug; it is grossly wrinkled at this point, doubtless as a result of the convulsive, but necessarily very restricted, movements of the victim attempting to struggle.

The man is still standing about a yard away, half leaning over her. He looks at her face, seen upside down, her dark eyes made larger by their

294

surrounding eyeshadow, her mouth wide open as if screaming. The man's posture allows his face to be seen only in a vague profile, but one senses in it a violent exaltation, despite the rigid attitude, the silence, the immobility. His back is slightly arched. His left hand, the only one visible, holds up at some distance from the body a piece of cloth, some dark colored piece of clothing, which drags on the carpet, and which must be the long cape with its gold embroidered lining.

This immense silhoouette hides most of the bare flesh over which the red stain, spreading from the globe of the breast, runs in long rivulets that branch out, growing narrower, upon the pale background of the bust and the flank. One thread has reached the armpit and runs in an almost straight, thin line along the arm; others have run down toward the waist and traced out, along one side of the belly, the hip, the top of the thigh, a more random network already starting to congeal. Three or four tiny veins have reached the hollow between the legs, meeting in a sinuous line, touching the point of the V formed by the outspread legs, and disappearing into the black tuft.

Look, now the flesh is still intact: the black tuft and the white belly, the soft curve of the hips, the narrow waist, and, higher up, the pearly breasts rising and falling in time with the rapid breathing, whose rhythm grows more accelerated. The man, close to her, one knee on the floor, leans further over. The head, with its long, curly hair, and which is alone free to move somewhat, turns from side to side, struggling; finally the woman's mouth twists open, while the flesh is torn open, the blood spurts out over the tender skin, stretched tight, the carefully shadowed eyes grow abnormally larger, the mouth opens wider, the head twists violently, one last time, from right to left, then more gently, to fall back finally and become still, amid the mass of black hair spread out on the velvet.

At the very top of the stone stairway, the little door has opened, allowing a yellowish but sustained shaft of light to enter, against which stands out the dark silhouette of the man wrapped in his long cloak. He has but to climb a few more steps to reach the threshold.

Afterward, the whole setting is empty, the enormous room with its purple shadows and its stone columns proliferating in all directions, the monumental staircase with no handrail that twists upward, growing narrower and vaguer as it rises into the darkness, toward the top of the vaults where it disappears.

Near the body, whose wound has stiffened, whose brilliance is already growing dim, the thin smoke from the incense burner traces complicated scrolls in the still air: first a coil turned horizontally to the left, which then straightens out and rises slightly, then returns to the axis of its point

DREAM AS CRISIS

of origin, which it crosses as it moves to the right, then turns back in the first direction, only to wind back again, thus forming an irregular sinusoidal curve, more and more flattened out, rising, vertically, toward the top of the canvas.

What has been wrenched out of context, as compared with conventional short story narrative, is the method *of telling the story. There is still a plot: a beginning, a middle, an end, and a slice of action we can perceive. But we have become, as part of the process, not participants so much as watchers. We are the point of view. What we witness and watch is almost purely visual. We are the lens; the camera eye.*

A murder is committed. We do not know who is who, or why. The experience is filmic at a nearly technical level. We move as with a camera (the writer—director?—reminds us of the lighting), pan around the room, focus on the corpse. Blood oozes. This is a color film.

In watching and waiting we are fulfilled; strangely satisfied. The who and the why come not to bother us. The where, the secret room and its furnishings suffice. Why? The last word of the story is "canvas." Thus, the effect is genuinely like seeing a film of a painting that is finished, not being created. But that is a shock of apperception after the fact. We were fooled until we saw that word, "canvas." It is as if the author wishes us to be cut off from involvement, at two removes through paint and film.

Again, the story reads like directions for a film of Poe. But also like the directions for the film "Last Year in Marienbad," which Robbe-Grillet wrote, and which this story resembles in its luxurious environment and in its use of camera as narrator.

Of all the stories in this collection, this one can be reduced to the shortest paraphrase, like telling about a dream when you wake from it: I had the strangest experience. There was this body. . . . The strong visual aspects are close to the vivid ones of dreams, the action smooth-flowing but disconnected from reality. Freud is the producer-director. Unlike the hero of "In Dreams Begin Responsibilities" we do not care to jump up and stop the action. As with the action of "An Occurrence at Owl Creek Bridge," we relate deeply to the dreamlike state, strangely distanced from the affairs of the protagonists. Theirs is the reality of the dream. We gladly suspend our own realities to attend.

THE SEVEN RIDERS

Dino Buzzati

Since I left to explore my father's kingdom, I have travelled each day further from the town and news reaching me has become rarer and rarer. When I started out on this journey I was barely thirty years old and now more than eight years have passed—to be exact, eight years, six months and fifteeen days—of uninterrupted travelling. When I left I thought I should easily reach the boundaries of the kingdom within a few weeks, but all I have done is meet new people, and discover new villages and provinces; everywhere there are men speaking my language and claiming to be my vassals.

Sometimes I think my geographer's compass has gone mad and that, instead of going south as we think, we're only going round and round in a circle and never getting any further from the capital. This could explain why we never reach the frontiers of the kingdom.

More often, however, I feel obsessed by the idea that these frontiers don't exist, that the kingdom continues for ever and that, in spite of this endless travelling, I shall never reach its limits.

I was thirty when I began this journey—too old, perhaps. My friends, even those dearest to me, ridiculed the idea, for they considered I was wasting the best years of my life. In fact, only a few faithful ones agreed to accompany me.

Despite the lightheartedness with which I set out—a lightheartedness I no longer feel—I was determined to find a way of communicating during the journey with those dear to me and so I chose the seven best horsemen of my escort to be my messengers.

In my ignorance, I thought I was going a bit too far in choosing seven. But as time passed, I realized that far from being too many, this number was ridiculously small. Not one of them, however, has ever fallen ill, been captured by robbers, or ridden his horse into the ground. All seven of them have served me with a tenacity and devotion which I shall find it hard to repay. So that I might recognize them more easily, I gave them new names, in alphabetical order: Alexander, Batholomew, Caius, Dominic, Emile, Frederick and Gregory. I was not used to being away from home, so I sent the first, Alexander, back there on the evening of the second day of the journey, when we had covered almost eighty leagues. The following evening, so as to ensure a steady flow of news, I delegated the second messenger to leave, and then the third, then the fourth, and so on, until the eighth evening of the journey, when Gregory left. The first had not yet returned from the capital.

He rejoined us on the tenth day in a deserted valley where we were preparing to camp for the night. Alexander told me he had to travel less quickly than we had expected. I had thought that, since he was alone and mounted on an excellent charger, he would be able to cover the distance in half the time it took us. In fact, he'd only been able to cover one and a half times the distance we covered in a day—while we managed forty leagues he did sixty—but no more.

The same was true of the others. Bartholomew left for the city on the third evening of our journey and returned two weeks later. Caius set off on the fourth day and only arrived back on the twentieth. I quickly grasped that to estimate the return date of each messenger I had to multiply by five the number of days we had beeen travelling on the date of his departure.

Since we were advancing farther and farther from the capital, the messengers had to make longer and longer journeys. After fifty days, the interval beetween the return of one messenger and the next had become noticeably longer: whereas one arrived back at the camp every five days at the beginning, the interval now became twenty-five. In this way reports from my city became scarcer and scarcer; weeks passed without any news reaching me. When I had been travelling for six months—we had already crossed the Fasani mountains—the intervals between the arrival of each messenger had become a good four months. From this time onwards, they brought me only outdated news, handing me crumpled letters turning brown from the damp nights during which the messenger had to sleep on the prairies. We still carried on travelling. I tried in vain to persuade myself that the clouds which rolled above my head were still those of my childhood, that the sky over the distant town was in no way different from the blue dome hanging over me, that the air was the same, the puff of wind the same, the bird song the same. In reality the clouds, the sky, the air, the winds, the birds seemed new to me and I felt a complete stranger.

Let's go on! Let's go on! Tramps we met on the plains told me the frontiers weren't far. I encouraged my men to continue without respite, making the disillusioned words they were about to utter die on their lips. Four years had passed. What a weariness! The capital, my home, my father, all seemed curiously far away, in fact I hardly believed they existed any longer. A good twenty months of silence and loneliness separated the return of each messenger. They brought me curious missives, yellowed with age, in which I discovered forgotten names, unusual turns of phrases, opinions which I couldn't understand. And the following morning, after only one night's rest, while we continued on our way, the messenger would leave in the opposite direction, carrying a letter I had prepared long ago. Eight and a half years have passed. This evening I was eating supper alone in my tent when Dominic entered. He still managed to smile despite his overwhelming fatigue. And during these seven years he had done nothing but gallop across prairies, forests and deserts, changing his mount goodness knows how many times, to bring me this bundle of envelopes which I have no desire to open at this late hour. He has already retired to bed, for tomorrow morning at daybreak he will start out again.

He will be leaving for the last time. I have worked out in my notebook that if all goes well, if I continue my journey as I have until now, and he his, I will not see Dominic again until thirty-four years from now. I shall be seventy-two years old. But I am beginning to feel weary and death probably will have overtaken me by then. So I shall never see him again. In thirty-four years' time (even before, well before), Dominic will suddenly see the fires of my encampment, and will wonder how it's possible that I have taken so long to cover so few miles. He will enter my tent just as he did this evening, carrying letters yellowed by the years, full of absurd news of an obsolete age. But he will stop short in the doorway, seeing me motionless, stretched out dead on my couch, with two soldiers bearing torches on either side of me. But still, off you go, Dominic, and don't accuse me of cruelty. Carry my last greeting to the city where I was born. You are my only remaining link with a world which once was mine. The most recent letters tell me that many things have changed, that my father is dead, that the crown has passed to my eldest brother, that they consider me lost, that huge stone palaces are being built where in the past stood the oak trees under which I loved to go and play. But it is still, nevertheless, my old homeland. You, Dominic, are my last link with it. The fifth messenger, Emile, who will be returning in a year and eight months, God willing, won't be able to start out again. There won't be enough time for him to come back. After you, Dominic, silence! Unless I finally discover this expected frontier. But the further I travel, the more I am convinced the frontier doesn't exist. I suspect there is no frontier, at least not in the sense we commonly give to the word. There are no separating walls, no deep valleys, no mountains barring the route. I shall probably cross the boundaries of the kingdom without noticing it and in my ignorance will keep on going. For this reason, I intend that in future, when Emile and the others return, they will no longer set out again for my capital but will leave in the other direction, going on ahead so that I shall know in advance what is awaiting me. For some time now a strange new anxiety has come upon me in the evenings. It is no longer a question of longing for the joys I have left, as happened to me in the early days of the journey. It is rather that I am

DREAM AS CRISIS

impatient to discover the unknown lands towards which I am journeying. I am more and more aware—and until now I have never confided this to anyone—how, with each day that passes, as I advance towards the unlikely end of this journey, a strange light shines in the sky, a light I have never seen before, not even in my dreams. And how the shadows and the mountains and the rivers we traverse seem to take on a different nature: and the air is laden with omens of I know not what. Tomorrow evening fresh hope will carry me even farther towards those unexplored mountains still hidden by the shadows of the night. Once again I will roll up my tent while Dominic disappears over the horizon bearing my pointless message to the too-distant city.

VIII | Archetypes and Stereotypes: The Artificial Nigger and the Imaginary Jew

Fine works depend for their intelligibility upon the reader's participation with the author in certain cultural assumptions. In myth and Jungian psychology, archetypes represent figures larger than life in whose struggles we ennoble our own. Seeking heroes in literature has been a favorite pastime of our civilization—they seem to rescue us from the contemplation of our own lives. Shakespeare and his audience believed in royalty; even so he saw kings human.

The short story has peaked in an age when to some extent all people who read seriously share certain broad beliefs in common: we pull for the underdog, admiring comfort just the same. We are ambivalent. Granting our worship of and need for heroes, we suspect that we too can, in Frost's words, "rise from Nowhere up to Somewhere." In stories we can find explorations of our specialness at levels ignored by popular media. Good creators of fiction defy the easier assumptions about individuals even in the act of casting good fiction within a familiar setting. From them the synthesis is struck: we learn that we are in fact the heroes!

What we feared all along was that we are stereotypes, recognizable and faintly disturbing statistics of mass media and sociology. Every one of the main characters in this group of stories is undistinguished in fame, lacking the easy sensation of headlined stereotypes. But in creating the fiction, the writer was beyond sociology, beyond headlines. Each of these figures makes a perilous journey in life, flung headlong into the dangers of the commonplace. The two American writers, O'Connor and Berryman, in fact pit their characters against the problems of minorities, and the outcome has a complexity never reproduced in newspapers. Out of the stereotyped, the writer has created the archetypal. Berryman's narrator becomes the archetypal scapegoat; he is finally a Jew. J. F. Powers' priests (in a story in another part of this book) come very close to cliché. But the cat that starts out cute darkens into something that forces us out of the comfort of the parish house into the clutches of St. Augustine, and the reversal of some aspects of the Inquisition: the black priests thwarted and the good church ascendant.

Fashioned out of the popular elements of circus and sideshow, Kafka's "A Hunger Artist" (in Chapter III) reads like the unreal, wry, and bizarre case history of a fairy tale until we realize that we are involved with the archetypal artist, a creative force who performs his art because he cannot help it.

What saves James Joyce's protagonist in "Counterparts" from the stereotyped fate of just another drunken Irish clerk is the background we are provided of his frustrating life at home and at work. Farrington (who is given no first name) wants to live well, please the boss, but keep his dignity nevertheless. Yet he "blows the objective" and we understand why. His home life and his working life are counterparts of each other. Nor is there any real or lasting satisfaction in the company at the corner bar (there, the bartender is the curate; home, his wife is at the chapel). Farrington is surely more counter than part of his societies. A man of limited insight, Farrington resorts in the end to the only reaction he knows.

In the stratum below the level of the agony of a Farrington beats the accepting heart of Félicité. If Joyce makes a simple life complicated, Flaubert makes a simpler one immensely richer.

Both Joyce and Flaubert write of the life that seems extinct before death. But Farrington is battling with all his misdirected power that extinction of self, and Félicité in her grand solitude, and overflowing with love, becomes in always reaching outward a heroine because of her selfless service to others.

In the masterly portrayal of this lowly servant, we sense from Flaubert what it must be like to be Félicité, who lived all her life without any wide concourse with the world, and whose world was so, that when we hear, toward her end, that she became deaf and was "cut off from communication with everybody," we wonder whether she was ever in communication with anybody. The question applies, too, to Joyce's clerk and O'Connor's Grandpa Head, and in their lives upon these pages we share the consequent frustration of the one and the rage of the other, even while being repelled by their behavior.

In this way, we become Félicité, we become Farrington, just as the narrator of John Berryman's story becomes a Jew. Félicité is endowed by Flaubert with grace in her loneliness and in her ignorance. Mr. Head achieves grace on his own and after his excruciating journey.

We do love Félicité as we do not love Mr. Head and Mr. Farrington. Yet their creators afford us the luxury of compassion, so that, as with

A SIMPLE HEART

Shakespeare's kingly heroes, what we feel is pity, not envy. We are, if not purged, then self-indulged. Even in self-indulgence, though, we are made to think and to feel deeply. So we have here no stereotypes.

A SIMPLE HEART

Gustave Flaubert[*]

I

For half a century past the good folk of Pont-l'Évêque had envied Mme. Aubain her servant, Félicité.

For a wage of a hundred francs a year she cooked and did all the work of the house, sewing, washing, ironing; she knew how to harness a horse, how to fatten up poultry, and how to make butter; moreover, she remained loyal to her mistress, and her mistress was not an amiable person.

Mme. Aubain had married a handsome fellow, without means, who had died at the beginning of the year 1809, leaving her with two very young children and a quantity of debts. She then sold what landed property she owned, with the exception of two farms, named Toucques and Geffosses, the rents of which brought her in at most five thousand francs a year; and she gave up her Saint-Melaine house, and moved into another which was less expensive—one which had belonged to her ancestors, and which was situated at the back of the market place.

This house, roofed with slate, stood between a narrow alley and a lane which ended down by the riverside. Within there were differences of level that made one stumble. A narrow vestibule separated the kitchen from the sitting room in which Mme. Aubain, seated near the window in a wicker armchair, spent the entire day. Eight mahogany chairs stood in line against the wainscoting, which was painted white. A pyramid of small wooden and pasteboard boxes was heaped up on an old piano, beneath a barometer. The yellow marble chimneypiece, style Louis XV, was flanked by two shepherdesses in tapestry. The clock in the center represented a temple of Vesta. An atmosphere of mustiness pervaded the room, which was on a lower level than the adjoining garden.

On the first floor you came at once upon Madame's bedroom, very large, a pale flower design on its wallpaper, and for its chief decoration a portrait of "Monsieur" in dandified costume. It communicated with

[*] Translated by Frederick Whyte.

a smaller room in which were to be seen two children's beds, without mattresses. Next came the drawing room, always kept closed, and filled with furniture covered over with a dust sheet. Beyond, a corridor led to a study; books and waste papers occupied the shelves of a bookcase, the three sides of which embraced, as it were, a wide desk made of black wood. The opposite walls were almost covered with pen drawings, water-colors, and l'Audran engravings—souvenirs of better times and vanished luxury. On the second floor was Félicité's room, lit by a dormer window which looked out over the fields.

Félicité rose at daybreak so as to be able to get to mass, and worked on till the evening without interruption; then, dinner over, the plates and dishes cleared, and the door closed and bolted, she would smother the burning log in the ashes and would drop off to sleep before the hearth, her rosary in her fingers. There was no better hand at a bargain than Félicité—nobody equaled her in determination. As for her trimness, the polish of her saucepans was the despair of other servants. Very economical, she ate her food slowly and gathered together the breadcrumbs on the table with her fingers—her loaf was baked specially for her, weighed twelve pounds, and lasted her twenty days.

At all times and all seasons she wore a cotton handkerchief over her shoulders, pinned at the back, a bonnet hiding her hair, gray stockings, red petticoat, and, over her bodice, an apron like those of hospital nurses.

Her face was thin and her voice sharp. At twenty-five, people had taken her for forty. After she had reached fifty, she had ceased to show any signs of increasing age; and, with her silent ways, her erect carriage and deliberate movements, she gave the impression of a woman made of wood, going through her work like an automaton.

II

Yet, like any other, Félicité had had her love story.

Her father, a stonemason, had been killed by a fall from a scaffolding. Then her mother died, her sisters dispersed, and a farmer took her into his service, setting her while still a tiny child to look after the cows in the pastures. She shivered with cold in her thin rags, quenched her thirst in pools—lying full length on the ground to drink—was beaten frequently for nothing, and finally was turned away for a theft of thirty sous, which she had not committed. Then she got into another farm, where she tended the poultry yard, and where she gave so much satisfaction to her employers that the other servants became jealous of her.

One evening in August (she was now eighteen) she was taken to the merrymaking at Colleville. She was bewildered, stupefied almost, by the din of the fiddlers, by the dazzling lights hung from the trees, the medley of costumes, the wealth of lace and gold crosses, the immense concourse of people. She was holding timidly aloof when a young man, well-to-do in appearance, who had been smoking his pipe with his two elbows resting upon the pole of a cart, came up and asked her to dance. He treated her to some cider and to coffee, and brought her cakes and a silk handkerchief, and, supposing that she guessed what he had in mind, offered to see her home. As they were passing by a field of oats he threw her backwards roughly. She was frightened and began to scream. He took himself off.

Another evening, on the Beaumont road, as she was trying to hurry past a great wagon of hay which was progressing slowly in the same direction as herself, she recognized Theodore as she rubbed against the wheels.

He addressed her calmly, saying that she must forgive him everything, as it was "the fault of the drink."

She did not know what reply to make, and her impulse was to take flight.

He went on, however, at once to talk about the crops and about the notable folk of the commune. It seemed that his father had quitted Colleville and had taken the farm at Écots, so that they were now neighbors. "Oh!" said Félicité. He added that he was anxious to settle down. He was in no hurry, though, and could wait till he found a wife to his taste. She lowered her head. Then he asked her whether she had thought of marriage. She replied, smiling, that he ought not make fun of her. "I'm not doing so, I swear I'm not!" he rejoined, and he put his left arm round her waist; thus supported, she walked along. They slackened their pace. There was a gentle breeze, the stars were shining; in front of them the huge wagon oscillated from side to side, the four horses moving slowly, raising a cloud of dust. Presently, of their own accord, they took a turning to the right. He kissed her once again, and she made off into the darkness.

Next week Theodore got her to meet him.

They met in yard corners, behind walls, under isolated trees. She had not the innocence of young ladies of her age—the ways of the animals had been an education to her; but common sense and the instinct of self-respect safeguarded her virtue. Her resistance so stimulated Theodore's desires that to compass them (perhaps, indeed, ingenuously) he asked her to marry him. She was distrustful at first, but he gave her his word.

Soon, however, he communicated a disturbing piece of news. His parents had bought him a substitute the year previously, but now at any moment he was liable to conscription, and the idea of having to serve in the army frightened him. This cowardice, in Félicité's eyes, was evidence of his devotion to her, and she became increasingly devoted to him. She began to meet him at night, and while they were together Theodore tortured her with his fears and his entreaties.

At last he declared one evening that he would go himself to the Prefecture to make definite inquiries, and that he would come back with his news on the following Sunday between eleven o'clock and midnight.

When the time came Félicité hastened to meet him.

In his place she found one of his friends.

He told her that she would not see Theodore again. In order to escape the conscription he had married a very rich old woman, Mme. Lehoussais, of Toucques.

A fit of passionate grief ensued. Félicité threw herself down on the ground, uttering cries of misery and appeals to God. She lay there all alone in the field, weeping and moaning, until sunrise. Then she returned to the farm and announced her intention of leaving it; and at the end of the month, having received her wages, she tied up all her belongings in a handkerchief and made her way to Pont-l'Évêque.

In front of the inn, she accosted a dame wearing widow's weeds, who happened at that very time to be on the lookout for a cook. The young girl clearly did not know much, but she seemed so willing and so easily pleased that Mme. Aubain ended by saying:

"Good. I engage you."

Half an hour later Félicité was installed in her new situation.

At first she lived there in a state of nervousness caused by the style of the house and the memories of "Monsieur" by which it seemed to be pervaded. Paul and Virginie, aged respectively seven and barely four, seemed to her beings of a finer clay; she would let them ride upon her back; Mme. Aubain mortified her by telling her not to keep kissing them every minute. She was happy, however. Her sorrow melted away in these pleasant surroundings.

Every Thursday certain friends of Mme. Aubain's came to play a game of "Boston." Félicité had to get ready the cards and the foot-warmers. The guests arrived always at eight o'clock, and took their departure before the stroke of eleven.

Every Monday morning the curio-dealer who lived down the street spread out his wares on the ground in front. And on that day the whole town was filled with a babel of sounds, horses neighing, sheep bleating, pigs grunting—all these noises mingling with the sharp clattering of the carts in the streets. Towards midday, when the market was at its height, a tall old peasant with a hooked nose, his cap on the back of his head, would present himself at the hall door—this was Robelin, the tenant of the Geffosses farm. Shortly afterwards, Liébard, the Toucques farmer, would appear, short and fat and ruddy, wearing a gray coat and gaiters with spurs attached to them.

They both had fowls and cheeses to offer to Mme. Aubain. Félicité was always more than a match for them in guile, and they went off impressed by her astuteness.

At irregular intervals, Mme. Aubain received a visit from the Marquis de Gremanville, one of her uncles, a broken-down rake who lived now at Falaise on the last remnant of his estate. He always made his appearance at lunch time, accompanied by a hideous poodle whose paws left dirty tracks upon all the furniture. Despite his efforts to maintain the air of a gentleman of noble birth (he would, for instance, lift his hat every time he uttered the words, "my late father"), he had acquired the habit of filling himself glass after glass and giving forth questionable stories. Félicité would put him out of the house quite politely. "You have had enough, Monsier de Gremanville! You must come again another time!" she would say, and shut the door on him.

To M. Bourais, a retired lawyer, Félicité would open the door with pleasure. His white *cravate*, his bald head, his shirt frills, his ample brown frock coat, his way of curving his arm when he took a pinch of snuff—in fact, his whole personality, produced in her that slight feeling of excitement which we experience at the sight of men of mark.

As he looked after Madame's property, he would be shut up in Monsieur's "sanctum" with her for hours at a time; he was cautious always not to commit himself, had a boundless reverence for the magistracy, and was by way of being something of a Latin scholar.

With a view to imparting a little instruction to the children in an agreeable fashion, he presented them with a series of geographical prints which included representations of scenes in different parts of the world—cannibals with headdresses of feathers, an ape carrying off a young lady, Bedouin Arabs in the desert, the harpooning of a whale, and the like.

Paul explained these pictures to Félicité. This, in fact, was her sole literary education.

That of the children was undertaken by Guyot, a poor wretch employed at the *Mairie*, famous for his beautiful penmanship and for the way he sharpened his penknife on his boot.

In fine weather all the household would go off at an early hour to the Geffosses farm.

The farmyard is on a slope, with the house in the middle; in the distance is the sea, looking like a spot of gray.

Félicité would take some slices of cold meat out of her basket, and they would all sit down to their *déjeuner* in a room forming part of the dairy. It was all that was left of a pleasure house now disappeared. The wallpaper, falling into shreds, shook as the wind blew through the room. Mme. Aubain leaned forward, a victim to sad memories; the children did not dare to speak. "Why don't you go out and play?" she would say to them, and they would run off.

Paul climbed up into the loft, caught birds, played ducks and drakes with flat stones upon the pond, or tapped with a stick the rows of big barrels which sounded like so many drums.

Virginie fed the rabbits, or went to pick cornflowers, her legs moving so quickly that you caught glimpses of her little embroidered drawers.

One evening in autumn they were going back by the cornfields.

The moon in its first quarter lit up a portion of the sky, and a mist hung like a cloud over the winding course of the Toucques. Oxen, lying in the meadows, gazed tranquilly at the four passers-by. In the third field, some got up and formed round them in a circle.

"Don't be afraid," said Félicité, and making a soothing kind of noise with her mouth she stroked the back of the animal nearest to her, on which it turned right round and went off followed by the others. But the little party had scarcely traversed the adjoining meadow when they heard a fierce bellowing. It was a bull, invisible till then by reason of the mist. He advanced towards the two women. Mme. Aubain began to run. "No! No! don't go so fast!" cried Félicité; they hurried none the less and heard loud snorts closer and closer behind them. His hoofs had begun to beat the ground like strokes of a hammer—he was coming down upon them full gallop! Félicité turned round, and snatching up handfuls of earth threw them into the animal's eyes. He lowered his head, shook his horns, and stood trembling with fury, bellowing terribly. Mme. Aubain had by now reached the end of the field with her children, and was making desperate efforts to climb up the high bank. Félicité backed away slowly from the bull, and continued to throw bits of earth into his eyes. She kept calling out to the others, "Be quick! Be quick!"

Mme. Aubain got down into the ditch, pushing Virginie and Paul before her, but fell several times while struggling to climb up the other side, which she pluckily achieved.

The bull had forced Félicité back against some palings. Flakes of foam from his mouth splashed her face, and in another second he would have ripped her up. She had just time to slip between two bars, and the huge animal pulled up short, quite astonished.

This event was a subject of conversation at Pont-l'Évêque for many years. Félicité herself, however, took no pride in it, having no notion that she had achieved anything heroic.

Virginie monopolized her attention, for, as a result of the shock, the child had contracted a nervous affection, and M. Poupart, the doctor, had recommended sea baths for her at Trouville.

Trouville was not a fashionable watering place in those days. Mme. Aubain made inquiries about it, and consulted Bourais, making preparations as though for a long journey.

Her luggage was sent on ahead, on the eve of her departure, in a cart of Liébard's. Next day he himself brought round two horses, one provided with a lady's saddle covered with velvet, the other with a cloak rolled up to form a seat. Mme. Aubain got up on one of them, behind Liébard, while Félicité mounted the other with Virginie under her charge, and Paul rode a donkey lent by M. Lechaptois on the express understanding that great care was to be taken of it.

The road was so bad that two hours were taken to compass its eight kilometers. The horses sank in the mud down to their pasterns, and had to make violent movements with their haunches to extricate themselves; now they had to struggle with deep ruts, now clamber over obstacles. Now and again Liébard's mare would come to a standstill. He waited patiently until she decided to go ahead again, and he held forth upon the people whose estates bordered the road and indulged in moral reflections upon their history. Thus, in the center of Toucques, while passing under windows full of geraniums, he began with a shrug of his shoulders, "There's a Mme. Lehoussais, who instead of taking a young man . . ." Félicité did not catch the rest of the remark; the horses broke into a trot, the ass into a gallop; they now went down a narrow path single file, a gateway was opened to them, two boys made their appearance, and all dismounted in front of a dungheap on the very threshold.

Old "Mère" Liébard on seeing her mistress indulged in warm expressions of delight. She served a *déjeuner* consisting of a sirloin, tripe, black pudding, a fricassee of fowl, sparkling cider, a jam tart, and prunes in brandy—all to a running accompaniment of compliments to Madame herself, who seemed "in the best of health," to Mademoiselle, who looked "magnificent," to M. Paul "grown so big and strong," and inquiries after their deceased grandparents whom the Liébards had known, having been in the service of the family for several generations. The farm, like its occupiers, bore the appearance of age. The beams across the ceiling were worm-eaten, the walls blackened with smoke, the tiles gray with dust. An oak cupboard was covered with all kinds of utensils, jugs, plates, tin porringers, wolf traps, sheep clippers; a huge squirt amused the children. In the three adjoining yards there was not a tree but had mushrooms growing at its base, and tufts of mistletoe sprouting among its branches. The wind had blown down some of them. They had sprouted again, and all were weighed down by their quantity of apples. The thatched roofs of the outhouses, looking like brown velvet and of unequal thickness, withstood the most violent gusts of wind, but the carthouse lay in ruins. Mme. Aubain declared she would have it seen to, and gave orders for the horses to be reharnessed.

Another half-hour elapsed before they reached Trouville. The little caravan dismounted to pass the Écores, a cliff beneath which boats were moored, and three minutes later, at the end of the quay, they made their way into the courtyard of the Golden Lamb, kept by "Mère" David.

Virginie began from the very first to feel less weak—the result of the change of air and the action of the baths. She went into the water in her chemise, having no bathing dress, and her nurse dressed her in a customs-house shed which was placed at the disposal of the bathers.

In the afternoon they went with the donkey beyond the Roches Noires, Hennequeville way. The path rose, at first, through a countryside undulating like the greensward of a park, then came to an upland in which meadows alternated with plowed fields. To either side of the road holly bushes stood up from among the tangle of briars; while here and there a great lifeless tree made a zigzag pattern against the blue sky with its bare branches.

They nearly always had a rest when they reached a certain meadow, whence they could see Deauville to the left, Havre to the right, and the open sea in front of them. The sea flashed in the sunlight, its surface smooth as a mirror, and so calm that you could scarcely hear its murmuring; sparrows twittered out of sight; the immense vault of the heavens was over all. Mme. Aubain, sitting on the ground, busied herself with her sewing; Virginie, beside her, plaited reeds; Félicité weeded out sprigs of lavender; Paul found it dull and was restless to be off.

On other occasions they would cross over the Toucques by boat and go looking for shells. At low tide they would find sea urchins, anemones, and jellyfish; and the children would run to catch the flakes of foam carried by the breeze. The tranquil waves, breaking upon the sands, unrolled themselves along the entire length of the beach; the beach stretched out as far as you could see, but to landward it ended in the dunes which divided it from the Marais—a wide extent of meadowland, shaped like a hippodrome. When they returned that way they saw Trouville at the foot of the hillside. At each step they took the town seemed to grow bigger and to spread itself out, with all its multiform dwellings, in gay disorder.

On days when the weather was too hot they did not leave their sitting room. The dazzling radiance outside formed golden bars of light between the shutters of the Venetian blinds. Not a sound was to be heard in the village. Not a soul stirred in the street below. This pervading silence intensified their sense of restfulness. In the distance the hammers of caulkers beat upon keels and the smell of tar was wafted upwards on the heavy air.

Their principal amusement was found in the return of the ships to port. As soon as the vessels had passed the buoys they began to tack. They came in, topsails down, their foresails swelling like balloons; they glided along through the chopping waves until they were in the middle of the harbor, when the anchor was suddenly dropped. Finally, the vessel came alongside the quay. The sailors threw out their harvest of fish still palpitating and alive; a long line of carts stood in readiness, and a crowd of women wearing cotton bonnets rushed forward to fill their baskets and give their men a welcome.

One day one of these women went up to Félicité, who a few minutes later re-entered the family sitting room with her face beaming. She had found a sister; and Nastasie Barette, by marriage Leroux, presented herself, carrying a baby at her breast, while at her right hand was another young child, and at her left a small cabin boy, with his fists doubled on his hips and his sailor's cap cocked over one ear.

At the end of a quarter of an hour Mme. Aubain signified to her that it was time to go.

They were to be met continually outside the kitchen or on their walks. The husband did not show himself.

Félicité grew fond of them. She bought them a blanket, some shirts, and a stove; it was evident that they were taking advantage of her. This weakness exasperated Mme. Aubain, who moreover resented the familiar way in which the boy addressed Paul; and as Virginie had begun to cough and the weather was no longer good, she decided on a return to Pont-l'Évêque.

M. Bourais helped her to choose a college for Paul. That of Caen was considered to be the best, and thither he was sent. He went bravely through with his leavetaking, content to go and live in a house where he was to have companions.

Mme. Aubain resigned herself to the parting from her son, because it was absolutely necessary. Virginie missed him less and less. Félicité felt the loss of his noisy ways. A new occupation, however, served to distract her thoughts. After Christmas it became one of her duties to take the little girl to have her catechism lesson every day.

III

Having made a genuflection at the door of the church, Félicité advanced along the lofty nave between two rows of chairs, opened Mme. Aubain's pew, sat down, and allowed her gaze to travel all round her.

Boys to the right, girls to the left, occupied the choir stalls; the *curé* remained standing by the lectern; a stained glass window in the apse represented the Holy Ghost overshadowing the Blessed Virgin; another showed her on her knees before the Infant Jesus and behind the tabernacle there was a woodcarving of St. Michael destroying the dragon.

The priest began with an outline of sacred history. Félicité formed pictures in her mind of Paradise, the Deluge, the Tower of Babel, cities in flames, throngs of people being annihilated, idols being shattered, and these bewildering visions filled her with awe of the Almighty and terror of His wrath. The story of the Passion moved her to tears. Why had Jesus been crucified—He who had cherished little children, who had given food to the multitude, who had cured the blind, and who had chosen, out of love and kindness, to be born in the midst of the poor, in a stable? The seed times, the harvest times, the pressing of the grapes, these and all the other familiar things spoken of in the Gospel belonged to her life; the coming of the Savior sanctified them; and she began to love lambs more tenderly for love of The Lamb, doves, because of the Holy Ghost.

She found it difficult to imagine His Person, for He was not only a bird but also a flame, and at other times a breath. Perhaps it was His light that flew hither and thither at night by the borders of the marshes, His breath that moved the clouds, His voice that lent harmony to the bells? She remained lost in these moods of adoration, taking pleasure also in the freshness of the walls of the church and in its atmosphere of peace.

As for dogmas, she understood nothing of them, made no effort to understand them. The *curé* discoursed, the children repeated what they had learnt; presently she fell asleep, waking suddenly when they all got up to go and their sabots began to clatter on the flagstones.

It was in this fashion that she learnt her catechism, hearing it repeated out loud, her religious education having been neglected in her youth, and henceforward she imitated all Virginie's practices, fasting like her and going to confession. On the festival of Corpus Christi they erected a small altar together.

Virginie's first communion was a matter of great concern to her for many days in advance. She busied herself over the necessary shoes, the rosary beads, the prayer book and gloves. How her hands trembled as she helped Mme. Aubain to dress her!

Throughout the mass she endured an agony of nervousness. M. Bourais prevented her from seeing one side of the choir, but immediately in front of her the little troop of maidens, adorned with white crowns above their drooping veils, looked to her like a field of snow; and she recognized her little dear one from afar by her peculiarly slender neck and her devout bearing. The bell rang, the heads bent forward; there was a silence. Then the organ pealed out, and the choristers and the whole congregation sang the Agnus Dei; after which the boys moved out of their seats in single file, the girls following. Slowly, with hands joined, they progressed towards the brilliantly lit altar, knelt down upon the first step, received the Sacrament one by one, and returned to their places in the same order. When Virginie's turn came Félicité leant forward to watch her, and in imagination, as happens in cases of such true devotion, she felt as though she herself were this child—Virginie's face had become her own, Virginie's clothes she herself wore, Virginie's heart was beating in her bosom—when the moment came to open the mouth, with eyelids lowered, she all but fainted.

Next day, early in the morning, Félicité presented herself at the Sacristy and asked M. le Curé to give her communion. She received it devoutly, but not with the same rapture.

Mme. Aubain was anxious to make an accomplished person of her daughter, and as Guyot could teach her neither English nor music, she determined to send her as a boarder to the Ursuline Convent at Honfleur.

Virginie raised no objection. Félicité sighed, and it seemed to her that Mme. Aubain was unfeeling. Afterwards she reflected that perhaps her mistress was well advised. These things were beyond the scope of her own judgment.

At last an old convent van stopped one day in front of the house and there stepped out of it one of the nuns who was come to fetch "Mademoiselle." Félicité placed Virginie's luggage on the roof of the conveyance, imparted some instructions to the driver, and put in the box under the driver's seat six pots of jam, a dozen pears, and a bouquet of violets.

At the last moment Virginie burst into tears; she embraced her mother who kissed her on the forehead, bidding her to be brave. The steps were raised and the vehicle started.

Then Mme. Aubain broke down; in the evening all her friends, the Lormeau household, Mme. Lechaptois, "those" Rochefeuille women, M. de Houppeville, and Bourais looked in to console her.

The loss of her daughter was a great grief to her at first. But three times a week she had a letter from her, and on the other days she wrote to her, walked about in the garden, or read, and in this way succeeded in passing the time.

From force of habit Félicité continued to enter Virginie's bedroom every morning and looked all around it. It saddened her that she no longer had her hair to comb, her boots to lace, herself to tuck up in bed—that she no longer had her pretty little face to gaze upon or her hand to hold, out walking. Feeling the want of occupation, she tried her hand at making lace, but her fingers were too clumsy and she broke the threads; she seemed to herself no good at anything, she became unable to sleep—as she put it herself, she was simply worn out.

To distract her mind she asked permission to have her nephew Victor to visit her.

He arrived on Sunday after mass, his cheeks glowing, his chest bare, odorous of the country which he had crossed. Félicité had a meal ready for him at once. They sat down to it face to face, and Félicité, eating as little as possible herself from motives of economy, so stuffed him up that at last he fell asleep. When the bells began to peal for vespers she woke him, brushed his trousers, tied his bow, and went off to church with him, leaning on his arm with a kind of maternal pride.

His parents made him bring something home always from these visits; it might be a packet of brown sugar or of soap, or some brandy—sometimes it would be money. And he would leave Félicité his clothes to mend —a task she enjoyed especially because it meant that he had to come back to get them again.

In August his father took him off on a cruise along the coast.

It was holiday time. The arrival of the children consoled Félicité. But Paul had become capricious, and Virginie had grown too old to be addressed in the accustomed familiar way, and this produced a feeling of awkwardness, raised a barrier between them.

Victor sailed first to Morlaix, then to Dunkerque, then to Brighton, on his return from each trip he brought Félicité a present. On the first occasion it was a box contrived of shells; next time it was a coffee cup; the time after, a great figure of a man made of gingerbread. The boy was improving in appearance, he was growing into quite a fine fellow; a mustache began to make its appearance, and there was a frank look in his eyes. He wore a little leather hat on the back of his head like a pilot. It amused Félicité to listen to him telling his yarns full of sailor's lingo.

On Monday, July 14, 1819 (she never forgot the date), Victor announced to her that he had signed on for a long voyage, and that on the night of the following day, he would have to go away on the Honfleur packet boat to rejoin his ship, which was shortly to put in at Havre. It was possible that he might be away two years.

The prospect of so long a separation went to Félicité's heart; and, to say good-by to him again, on the Wednesday evening, after Madame had dined, she put on her galoshes and trudged twelve miles between Pont-l'Évêque and Honfleur.

On arriving at the Calvary, instead of turning to the left she went to the right, and getting lost among the shipbuilders' yards she had to retrace her steps; some people of whom she asked the way warned her that she must hurry up. She made her way round the harbor, which was full of

A SIMPLE HEART

ships, stumbling against ropes as she hastened along; then the ground sloped down to the water's edge, there was a confusion of light, and she thought she must have lost her sense, for she saw horses in the sky.

On the edge of the quay other horses were neighing, frightened at the sea. A crane was lifting them up and lowering them into a vessel, on the decks of which people were shoving their way between barrels of cider, hampers full of cheese, and sacks of grain; hens were to be heard clucking and the captain swearing; and a cabin boy was leaning over the cathead, regardless of all this. Félicité, who had not recognized him, called out "Victor." He raised his head; she rushed up, but they suddenly drew back the gangway.

The packet boat, towed at first by a number of women, cheering, moved out of port. Her timbers creaked, the heavy waves beat against her prow. Her sail had flapped round and nobody on board could now be seen. Soon nothing was visible upon the sea, silvered by the moon, but a black spot, which gradually grew less distinct, then sank and disappeared.

Félicité, passing close by the Calvary, wished to commend to God him whom she held nearest to her heart; and she stood there a long time praying, her face bathed in tears, her eyes turned towards the clouds. The town lay sleeping, the customs-house officials alone were moving about; there was the sound of water flowing unceasingly like a torrent through the holes in the lock-gates. Two o'clock struck.

The Convent would not be open until the morning. Mme. Aubain would be annoyed if she were delayed; and, in spite of her desire to see the other child, she went back. The girls at the inn were getting up when she reached Pont-l'Évêque.

For months and months to come that poor boy was to toss about on the waters of the deep. His cruises until then had given her no uneasiness. You might count on coming back safe from Brittany or from England; but America, the Colonies, the East Indies—these places were dubious regions, at the other end of the world.

Henceforth, all Félicité's thoughts were for her nephew. On sunny days she imagined him suffering from thirst; when it was stormy she dreaded the lightning for him. When she heard the wind shrieking down the chimney or blowing slates down from the roof, she saw him battered by this very tempest, on the top of a broken mast, drenched in foam. At another time—her imagination helped by those geographical pictures—she thought of him being eaten by savages, or in the grip of apes in a forest, or perishing on some desert shore. And she never spoke of these anxieties.

Mme. Aubain meanwhile experienced anxieties of another kind concerning her daughter. The good Sisters reported that she was an affectionate child, but delicate.

The least excitement upset her. They found it necessary to give up teaching her the piano.

Mme. Aubain expected the letters from the Convent to come to her with fixed regularity. One morning when there was no post, she became very impatient. She kept walking up and down the room from her armchair to the window. Really it was too extraordinary! Four whole days and no news!

To console her, Félicité remarked:

"It is six months, Madame, since I have heard any news."

"News from whom?"

"Why—from my nephew."

"Oh! Your nephew!" And Mme. Aubain, shrugging her shoulders, went on walking up and down, as much as to say, "You don't suppose I was thinking of him? He is nothing to me! A cabin boy, a little ragamuffin like that! The idea! It is my daughter I am talking about! Think a moment!"

Félicité, though hardened to rudeness by this time, took the affront to heart but presently forgot it.

It seemed to her natural enough to lose one's head over the little girl.

The two children were of equal importance in her eyes—they shared her heart, and their destinies were to be the same.

The chemist told her that Victor's ship had arrived at Havana. He had seen this item of news in a gazette.

On account of the cigars, Félicité imagined Havana to be a country in which people did nothing but smoke, and Victor went about among the Negroes in a cloud of tobacco. Would it be possible, "in case of need," to return from Havana by land? How far was it from Pont-l'Évêque? To find this out, she put the questions to M. Bourais.

He got out his atlas and entered upon explanations of longitudes and latitudes, and he smiled a very superior smile as he noted the dumbfounded expression on her face. He ended by pointing out to her a small black spot, barely perceptible, somewhere in the irregular outline of an oval section in the map. "Here it is," he said. She leaned over the map, but the network of colored lines merely tired her eyes and told her nothing; and on Bourais' asking her to say what it was that puzzled her, she begged him to point out to her the house in which Victor was staying. Bourais lifted up his arms, roaring with laughter—such simplicity delighted him. Félicité didn't understand why he was laughing—how should she, inasmuch as she very likely expected to see even her nephew's portrait in the map, within such narrow limits did her intelligence work.

It was fifteen days after this that Liébard entered the kitchen, at market time as usual, and handed her a letter from her brother-in-law. As neither of them could read it, she had recourse to her mistress.

A SIMPLE HEART

Mme. Aubain, who was counting the stitches of her knitting work, now put that aside, broke the seal of the letter, trembled, and said in a deep voice, a grave look in her eyes:

"This is to give you news of a calamity . . . your nephew——"

He was dead. That was all the letter told.

Félicité sank into a chair, and, leaning her head on the back of it, closed her eyes, which became suddenly red. Then bending forward, her eyes fixed, her hands drooping idly, she kept saying over and over again—

"Poor little fellow! Poor little fellow!"

Liébard, sighing, stood watching her. Mme. Aubain still trembled slightly.

She suggested to Félicité that she should go and visit her sister at Trouville.

Félicité signified by a gesture that she felt no need to do so.

There was a silence. Liébard thought it tactful for him to withdraw. Then Félicité exclaimed, "It means nothing to them."

Her head fell forward again; mechanically from time to time she lifted the long knitting needles upon the work table.

Some women passed into the yard with a cart from which odds and ends of linen kept falling out. Seeing them through the window, Félicité remembered her washing. Having soaked the things the day before, she had to wring them out today; she got up and left the room.

Her tub and her board were down by the Toucques. She threw a heap of underlinen down on the riverbank, rolled up her sleeves and took her bat in hand; the vigorous blows she dealt with it could be heard in the neighboring gardens. The meadows were empty, the wind ruffled the surface of the stream; lower down, tall grasses leaned over its sides, looking like the hair of corpses floating in water. Félicité restrained her feelings and was very brave until the evening; but in her own room she gave way to her sorrow and lay prostrate on her mattress, her face buried in the pillow, her hands clenched against her temples.

A good deal later she learned the particulars of Victor's death from the captain of the vessel. The boy had been bled to excess at the hospital for yellow fever. Four doctors had him in hand at the same time. He died immediately, and the principal doctor remarked:

"Good, one more!"

Victor's parents had always treated him brutally. Félicité preferred to see no more of them; and they for their part made no advance to her, either because they forgot all about her, or because of the callousness that comes from penury.

Virginie, meanwhile, was losing strength.

A weight on her chest, coughing, continued feverishness, and her flushed cheeks pointed to some deep-seated malady. M. Poupart had recommended a stay in Provence. Mme. Aubain decided upon this, and she would have fetched her daughter back again at once were it not for the climate of Pont-l'Évêque.

She made an arrangement with a man who let out carriages on hire, which enabled her to visit the Convent every Tuesday. There was in the garden a terrace from which a glimpse could be caught of the Seine. Virginie would walk up and down here over the vine leaves fallen on the ground, leaning on her mother's arm. Sometimes the sun, breaking through the clouds, forced her to lower her eyes, as she gazed upon the distant sails and along the entire horizon from the Château of Tancarville to the lighthouses at Havre. Afterwards they would have a rest in an arbor. Mme. Aubain had provided herself with a small cask of excellent Malaga; and, laughing at the idea of its possibly making her tipsy, Virginie would drink two thimblefuls, never more.

The girl's strength seemed to be coming back to her. The autumn passed smoothly. Félicité reassured Mme. Aubain. But one evening when she had been for a walk outside the town, she found M. Poupart's carriage outside the door on her return; and he himself was in the hall. Mme. Aubain was putting on her hat.

"Give me my foot-warmer, and my purse and gloves," she cried out. "Hurry up about it."

Virginie was suffering from inflammation of the lungs; perhaps it was already a hopeless case.

"Not yet," said the doctor; and he and Mme. Aubain stepped into the vehicle, beneath the whirling snowflakes. Night was approaching and the weather was very cold.

Félicité rushed off to the church to light a candle. Then she ran after the carriage, which she caught up with an hour later and jumped nimbly up behind, holding on to the hangings until suddenly the reflection came to her, "The yard was not closed. Supposing thieves found their way in!" And she got down.

First thing next day she presented herself at the doctor's. He had come back home, but had gone off again into the country. Then she stopped at the inn, thinking perhaps a letter might be brought thither by some stranger. Finally, towards dusk, she took the diligence for Lisieux.

The Convent was situated at the bottom of a steep lane. Half-way down it, she heard strange sounds—a death knell. "It must be for others," she thought; and she knocked vigorously at the Convent door.

After several minutes, she could hear the shuffling of shoes; the door was half opened and a nun appeared.

The good Sister, with a compassionate look, said that Virginie "had just passed away." At the same moment, the knell of Saint-Léonard was renewed.

Félicité made her way up to the second floor.

From the door she saw Virginie lying outstretched upon the bed, her arms clasped together, her mouth open, her head poised slightly backwards beneath a black cross leaning over her; between the motionless curtains, less white than her face, Mme. Aubain, clinging to the foot of the bed, gave out sobs of agony. The Mother Superior was standing to the right. Three candlesticks upon the chest of drawers made spots of red, and the fog spread a white mist over the windows. Some nuns led Mme. Aubain away.

For two nights Félicité did not leave the dead girl. She repeated the same prayers over and over again, throwing holy water over the sheets, and sitting down to gaze upon her. At the end of the first watch she noticed that the face had taken on a yellowish tint, the lips had become blue, the nose was thinner, the eyes were sinking in. She kissed them several times, and it would not have surprised her beyond measure had Virginie opened them again; for such souls the supernatural is quite simple. She dressed the body, wrapped it in the shroud, and laid it in the coffin, placed a wreath on her, and spread her hair. It was fair and extraordinarily long for her age. Félicité cut off a big lock of it and put half of it into her bosom, resolved never to part with it.

The corpse was taken back to Pont-l'Évêque, according to the wishes of Mme. Aubain, who followed the hearse in a closed carriage.

After the mass, it took the funeral *cortège* three-quarters of an hour to reach the cemetery. Paul walked at its head, sobbing. M. Bourais followed, and then the principal inhabitants of the village, the women wearing black cloaks, Félicité among them. Her thoughts went back to her nephew, and not having been able to render him these tokens of regard, she felt her sadness doubled—as if her nephew were also being taken to the grave.

Mme. Aubain's despair was boundless.

At first she revolted against God, accusing Him of injustice in robbing her of her child when she had never done any harm, and her conscience was so pure. . . . But no! She ought to have taken Virginie to the south! . . . Perhaps other doctors would have saved her life! She accused herself, wished to follow her child, and cried out distressfully in her dreams. One in particular obsessed her. Her husband, wearing the garb of a sailor, had returned from a long voyage and was saying to her, weeping the while, that he had been commanded to take Virginie away. Then he and she endeavored together to find a hiding place somewhere.

Once, she re-entered the house from the garden, quite overcome. A moment ago (she could point out the exact spot), father and child had appeared to her side by side. They were doing nothing; they were only looking at her.

For several months she remained in her room, listless. Félicité would lecture her gently—she must rouse herself for the sake of her son, and besides—in remembrance of "her."

"Of her," replied Mme. Aubain, as though coming back to consciousness. "Oh, of course! . . . You do not forget." She had been scrupulously forbidden any allusion to the cemetery.

Félicité went to it every day.

At four o'clock precisely she would walk past the houses, go up the hill, open the gate, and make her way to Virginie's grave. There was a little column of rose-colored marble, with a tablet at its base, and a chain all round enclosing a miniature garden plot. The borders were almost hidden by flowers. Félicité watered them and renewed the sand, going down on her knees the better to dress the ground. Mme. Aubain, when she was able to visit the grave, derived some relief and a kind of consolation from it.

After this, years passed by, all very much alike, and without other incidents than the return of the great festivals—Easter, the Assumption, All Saints. Domestic events constituted dates to serve as landmarks in years to come. Thus, in 1825, two glaziers whitewashed the hall; in 1827, a portion of the roof, falling down into the courtyard, nearly killed a man. In the summer of 1828 it fell to Madame to offer the Blessed Bread; Bourais, about this time, absented himself mysteriously; and gradually old acquaintances passed out of sight; Guyot, Liébard, Mme. Lechaptois, Robelin, the uncle Gremanville, paralyzed now for a considerable time past.

One night the mail-cart driver announced in Pont-l'Évêque the Revolution of July. A new subprefect was nominated some days later: the Baron de Larsonnière, who had been previously a consul in America, and who brought with him, in addition to his wife, his sister-in-law and her three daughters, almost grown up. They were all to be seen on their lawn, wearing loosely made blouses; they were the owners of a Negro and a parrot. Mme Aubain received a visit from them and duly returned it. Félicité used always to run to her mistress to let her know whenever she saw any of them approaching, no matter how far off they might be. But the only things that could now arouse Mme. Aubain were her son's letters.

He could not follow any profession, spending all his time in drinking houses. She paid his debts, but he contracted new ones; and Mme.

Aubain's sighs, as she sat knitting by the window, reached the ears of Félicité, turning her spinning wheel in the kitchen.

They used to walk together under the fruit wall; they talked always of Virginie, speculating as to whether such and such a thing would have pleased her, what she would have said on this occasion or on that.

All her little belongings were gathered together in a cupboard in the double-bedded room. Mme. Aubain abstained as much as possible from inspecting them. One summer's day she resigned herself to doing so, and moths flew out of the cupboard.

Her dresses lay folded under a shelf on which were three dolls, some hoops, a set of doll's-house furniture, and the basin she used. Mme. Aubain and Félicité also took out the petticoats, stockings, and handkerchiefs, and spread them out upon the two beds before folding them up again. The sun shining on these poor little treasures revealed spots and stains and the creases made by the movements of the body that had worn them. Outside, the atmosphere was warm and the sky blue; a thrush was warbling; the world seemed steeped in peace. Presently they came upon a small plush hat, with deep pile, chestnut colored; but it was all moth-eaten. Félicité took possession of it for herself. The eyes of the two women met and filled with tears. Then the mistress opened wide her arms and the servant threw herself into them; and they held each other fast, finding vent for their common grief in the kiss that annulled all difference of rank.

It was the first time in their lives that they had embraced, for Mme. Aubain was not demonstrative by nature. Félicité felt grateful to her as for some actual benefit, and henceforth tended her with as much devotion as a dumb animal, and with a religious veneration.

The benevolence of her heart developed.

When she heard in the street the drums of a regiment marching past, she would take up her position in front of the door with a jug of cider and invite the soldiers to drink. She helped to nurse those on the sick list. She took the Poles under her special protection, and one of them declared he wanted her to marry him. But she had a tiff with him; for, returning one morning from the angelus, she found him in her kitchen in her kitchen in which he had settled down comfortably to the consumption of a salad.

After the Poles came Père Comiche, an old man who was reputed to have been guilty of enormities in '93. He lived down by the riverside in what was left of a disguised pigsty. The street urchins spied at him through chinks in the wall, and chucked stones which fell down on the squalid bed upon which he lay, shaken continually by a cough, his hair worn long, his eyelids inflamed, and on one of his arms a tumor bigger than his head. She provided him with linen and made efforts to cleanse his hovel; she wanted, indeed, to establish him in the bakehouse, if only it could be managed without disturbance or annoyance to Madame. When the cancerous growth burst she doctored the sore every day, sometimes bringing him some cake which she would place in the sun in a box lined with straw. The poor old man, dribbling and trembling, thanked her in his faint voice, and, fearing always lest he should lose her, stretched out his arms as he watched her retreating figure. He died, and she had a mass said for the repose of his soul.

It was on that day that a piece of great good fortune befell her. Just as dinner was served, the Negro belonging to Mme. de Larsonnière made his appearance, carrying the parrot in its cage, with its perch, chain, and padlock. A note from the *baronne* informed Mme. Aubain that, her husband having been promoted to a prefecture, they were going away that evening, and begged her to accept the bird as a souvenir and a mark of her regard.

It had long excited Félicité's imagination, for it came from America, and the word recalled Victor—so much so that she had sometimes questioned the Negro on the subject. Once she had gone so far as to say, "How pleased Madame would be if she had it!"

The Negro had repeated the remark to his mistress, who, being unable to take it away with her, was glad to dispose of it in this manner.

IV

Its name was Loulou. Its body was green, the tips of its wings pink, its forehead blue, its throat golden.

But it had a tiresome habit of biting its perch, and it tore out its feathers, splashed about the water in its drinking trough, and made such a mess that Mme. Aubain found it a nuisance and handed it over altogether to Félicité.

She set about educating it; soon it learnt to say, "Charmant garçon." . . . "Serviteur, monsieur." . . . "Je vous salue, Marie." It was placed by the door, and people used to be surprised that it would not answer to the name of Jacquot, for all parrots are called Jacquot. It used to be likened sometimes to a turkey, sometimes even to a log of wood. These remarks stabbed Félicité to the heart. Certainly it was very perverse of Loulou to stop talking the moment anyone looked at it.

Yet it liked to have company, for on Sunday when "those" Rochefeuille women, Monsieur de Houppeville, and certain new members of Madame's social circle—the apothecary Onfroy, Monsieur Varin, and Captain Mathieu—were playing cards, it would beat against the window panes

A SIMPLE HEART

with its wings and conduct itself so violently that it was impossible to hear oneself speak.

No doubt old Bourais' countenance struck the bird as very droll. The moment it saw him it always began to laugh—to laugh with all the vigor at its command. Its clattering voice resounded through the courtyard; an echo repeated it, and the neighbors coming to their windows laughed too. M. Bourais, to avoid being seen by the parrot, used to slink along the wall, covering his face with his hat, and, getting down to the river, would enter the house from the garden; and the looks he would direct towards the bird were lacking in affection.

Loulou had been given a slap by the butcher's boy one morning, having taken the liberty of inserting its head into his basket; and ever since it had tried to pinch him through his shirt-sleeves. Fabu threatened to wring its neck for it, though in reality he was not cruel, despite his tattooed arms and heavy whiskers. Indeed, he had a liking for the parrot, and even insisted in his jovial way on teaching it how to curse. Félicité, horrified, removed it to the kitchen. It was now relieved of its chain and was allowed to wander about the house.

When coming downstairs it would first lean its beak upon each step, then raise its right claw, its left following. Félicité used to be afraid that these gymnastic exercises would make it dizzy. It became ill and could no more talk nor eat. There was a thickness under its tongue, such as poultry sometimes suffer from. She cured it by removing this growth with her fingernails. M. Paul one day was so imprudent as to puff the smoke of his cigar into the bird's nostrils. On another occasion Mme. Lormeau worried it with the end of her umbrella and it snatched at the ferrule. Finally, it got lost!

She had put it out on the grass to give it some fresh air and had gone away for a minute. When she returned there was no parrot to be seen. At first she looked about for it in the bushes, by the riverside, and on the roofs, paying no attention to her mistress, who was crying out to her, "Mind what you are doing. Have you taken leave of your senses?" Then she explored all the gardens of Pont-l'Évêque; and she inquired of everyone she met, "Do you happen by any chance to have seen my parrot?" To those who did not know the parrot she gave a description of its appearance. Suddenly she thought she descried something green flying behind the windmills at the bottom of the hill, but when she got near there was no sign of it. A peddler maintained that he had come across it shortly before at Saint-Melaine, in Mère Simon's shop. She ran thither. They knew nothing about it there. At last she returned home quite worn out, her shoes in rags, despair in her heart; and, sitting on the garden bench side by side with Madame, she had begun a recital of all her adventures, when suddenly a light weight fell upon her shoulder—it was Loulou! What in the world had it been up to? Perhaps it had gone for a turn in the neighborhood.

It took her a long time to recover from the effects of her overexertion—in fact, she never really recovered.

As a result of a cold, she had an attack of quinsy, followed soon afterwards by an affection of the ears. Three years later she was deaf and had got into the way of talking very loud even in church. Although her sins might have been made known in every corner of the diocese without shame to her or evil effect upon the world at large, the *curé* deemed it well to hear her confession henceforth only in the sacristy.

She suffered from buzzing in her ears. Often her mistress would cry out, "Mon Dieu! how stupid you are," and she would answer merely, "Yes, Madame," and go looking about for something close at hand.

The narrow field of her ideas became still further limited, and the pealing of bells and the lowing of cattle no longer existed for her. Living creatures of every description moved and acted with the noiselessness of phantoms. The only sound that penetrated to her ears was the voice of the parrot.

As though to amuse her, it would mimic the ticktock of the turnspit, the sharp cry of the fish vendor, the sound of the carpenter's saw from across the road, and, when the bell rang, Mme. Aubain's voice calling out "Félicité, the door! the door!"

They would talk together, the bird going incessantly through its three stock phrases, and Félicité replying in words which were no less inconsequent, yet in which her heart poured itself out. In her isolation Loulou was almost a son to her, or a lover. He walked up and down her fingers, nibbled at her lips, hung on to her kerchief, and when she leaned forward, shaking her head in the way nurses do, the great wings of her cap and the wings of the bird flapped in unison.

When the clouds gathered and the thunder rolled, Loulou would give forth cries, remembering perhaps the inundations of its native forests. The streaming down of the rain made it wild with excitement; it would dash about violently, flying up to the ceiling, knocking everything about, and escaping out of the window, would dabble about in the garden; but it would soon make its way in again to the fireplace, and, hopping about to dry its feathers, would display now its tail, now its beak.

One morning in the terrible winter of 1837, when Félicité had put the bird in front of the fire on account of the cold, she found it dead in the center of its cage, its head down, its claws grasping the iron bars. Doubtless it had died of a cold, but Félicité attributed its death to poisoning by eating parsley, and despite the lack of any kind of proof her suspicions fell upon Fabu.

She wept so much that her mistress said to her, "Well, well, have it stuffed."

She asked the advice of the chemist who had always been friendly to the parrot.

He wrote to Havre. A certain Fellacher volunteered to undertake the job. As parcels sometimes went astray when sent by diligence, Félicité preferred to take it to Honfleur herself.

Leafless apple trees lined both sides of the road. The water in the ditches was frozen. Dogs barked on the edges of farmyards. Félicité, her hands hidden under her cloak, trudged along briskly in the middle of the road, wearing her little black *sabots* and carrying her basket.

She crossed the forest, passed by the Haut-Chêne, and reached Saint-Gatien.

Behind her, in a cloud of dust, gathering momentum as it came, a mail cart at full gallop rushed down the incline like a waterspout. Catching sight of the woman, who turned neither to the right nor left, the driver jumped up from his seat and the postilion began to shout out warning, but the four horses clattered along ever faster. The two leaders grazed her; with a sudden jerk of the reins he contrived to swerve to one side of the road, but, furiously, he raised his arm and, as he passed, lashed Félicité with his great whip round stomach and neck so violently that she fell on her back.

Her first action when she regained consciousness was to open the basket. Loulou was all right, thank goodness! She felt a burning pain on her right cheek; putting her hands to it, she found them red. The blood was running.

She sat down on a heap of stones and stopped the bleeding of her face with a handkerchief; then she ate a crust of bread which she had had the forethought to put in her basket, and took consolation for her own wound in contemplating the bird.

When she had got to the summit of Ecquemanville, she saw the lights of Honfleur sparkling in the night like stars; beyond, the sea spread out indistinctly. Then a feeling of weakness overcame her, and her childhood's misery, the disillusionment of her first love, her nephew's departure, Virginie's death, came back all at once like a flood tide, rising to her neck and suffocating her.

Then the urge came upon her to speak to the captain of the vessel herself, and, without saying what it was she was consigning to his cure, she gave him his instructions.

Fellacher kept the parrot a long time. He kept promising it for the following week; at the end of six months he announced its dispatch in a box, and then for a period there was no further news. It looked as though Loulou would never return to her. "They have stolen him from me," she thought.

But at last it arrived—and looking a magnificent sight, perched on the branch of a tree which was fixed on to a mahogany pedestal. One claw was in the air, the head was cocked on one side. Loulou was biting a nut to which the bird-stuffer, carried away by his love for the grandiose, had given a gilt coating!

Félicité put it away safely in her own room.

This spot, to which she admitted very few visitors, had the aspect at once of a chapel and a bazaar; it contained so many religious objects as well as other miscellaneous treasures.

A large cupboard was so placed as to make it difficult to open the door. Opposite the window which overlooked the garden there was a round one from which you could see the courtyard; on a table, standing near the folding bed, stood a jug of water, two combs, and a piece of blue soap on a notched plate. On the walls were hung rosaries, medals, several statues of the Blessed Virgin, and a holy-water font made of cocoanut wood; on the chest of drawers, covered with a cloth like an altar, stood the box made of shells which Victor had given her, together with a watering pot, a toy balloon, some copybooks, the series of geographical charts, and a pair of boots; Virginie's little plush hat was tied by its ribbons to the nail from which hung the looking glass. Félicité carried this form of respect so far as even to keep an old frock coat of Monsieur's. She took to this rooom of hers, in fact, all the old belongings for which Mme. Aubain had no use. This accounted for a case of artificial flowers on one side of the chest of drawers, and a portrait of the Comte d'Artois at the side of the window.

By means of a small bracket Loulou was set up on a portion of the chimney which projected into the room. Every morning, on waking, she caught sight of it in the clear light of the dawn, and without pain, full of peace, she recalled days that had gone and insignificant events in all their slightest details.

Cut off from communication with everybody, she continued to live on like a somnambulist, in a kind of trance. The Corpus Christi processions revived her. She applied to her neighbors for the loan of torches and colored mats in order to decorate the altar that was being erected in the street.

In church she would sit gazing at the Holy Ghost, and discovered in

A SIMPLE HEART

him some resemblance to the parrot. This resemblance came out in a more marked degree in an Épinal picture representing the Baptism of Our Lord. With the purple wings and emerald body, this really presented a portrait of Loulou.

She bought this picture, and hung it up in the place by the window where she had previously put the Comte d'Artois, so that she could see the parrot and it together in the same glance. They became associated together in her mind, the parrot becoming sanctified by this connection with the Holy Ghost, who thus became more real in her eyes and easier to understand. God the Father, to announce Himself, could not have chosen a dove, for these birds have no voice, but rather one of Loulou's ancestors. And Félicité prayed before the sacred picture but would turn slightly from time to time in the direction of the bird.

She wanted to enroll herself in the confraternity of the *Demoiselles de la Vièrge*, but Mme. Aubain dissuaded her from doing so.

Presently an important event took place—Paul's marriage.

After having been first a clerk in a notary's office, and then in business, in the Customs and Revenue services, and after making an effort to get into the Rivers and Forests Department, as last in his thirty-sixth year he had discovered, as though by a heavenly inspiration, his natural calling, his *métier*: that of a registrar. He displayed such remarkable qualifications for this position that an inspector had offered him his daughter in marriage, promising at the same time to use his influence in his favor.

Paul, now sobered, brought her to visit his mother.

She sniffed at the ways of Pont-l'Évêque, played the princess, and hurt Félicité's feelings. Mme Aubain felt relieved when she took her departure.

The following week news came of the death of M. Bourais, in Lower Brittany, in an inn. A rumor that he had committed suicide was confirmed, and doubts were raised as to his honesty. Mme. Aubain examined her books and was not long in learning the litany of his disdeeds: misappropriations, fictitious sales of timber, forged receipts, and the like. To add to this, he was the father of an illegitimate child, and had had "illicit relations with a creature from Dozule."

These iniquities afflicted her very much. In the month of March, 1853, she began to feel a pain in her chest; her tongue became clouded, and the application of leeches afforded her no relief. On the ninth evening she died, aged seventy-two precisely.

She had been believed to be less old on account of her brown hair, plaits of which framed her pallid face, marked by smallpox. Few friends regretted her, for her proud manners had kept people at a distance.

Félicité, however, mourned her in a way that masters are seldom mourned. It seemed to upset all her calculations that Madame should die before she did; it seemed out of keeping with the order of things, unallowable and uncanny.

Ten days later (it took ten days to rush up from Besançon) Paul and his wife appeared upon the scene. The latter turned out every drawer in the house, chose some furniture and sold the rest. The pair then returned home.

Mme. Aubain's armchair, her round table, her foot-warmer, the eight sitting-room chairs, disappeared. The wall space once occupied by the pictures was now a series of yellow squares. The children's beds with their mattresses had also been carried off, and the cupboard in which Virginie's belongings had been cherished was now empty. Félicité went upstairs, beside herself with misery.

Next day there was a notice posted up on the front door; the apothecary shouted in her ear that the house was for sale.

She tottered and had to sit down.

What chiefly troubled her was the idea of having to give up her own room—it suited poor Loulou so well. Gazing with anguish at the bird, she prayed fervently to the Holy Ghost. She contracted the idolatrous habit of kneeling in front of the parrot to say her prayers. Sometimes the sun coming through the window struck its glass eye, making it emit a great luminous ray, which threw her into an ecstasy.

She had an income of three hundred and eighty francs a year, bequeathed her by her mistress. The garden provided her with vegetables; as for clothes, she had enough to last her until the end of her days, while she saved lighting by going to bed at dusk.

She rarely went out, not liking to pass the second-hand shop in which some of the old furniture of the house was now displayed for sale. She had dragged one leg since her shock; and as she was losing her strength, Mère Simon, whose grocery business had come to grief, came now every morning to cut up wood and draw water for her.

Her eyes became weak. She gave up opening the window shutters. Many years passed. And the house remained unlet and unsold.

For fear lest they should get rid of her, Félicité refrained from asking for repairs. The laths of the roof began to rot; for an entire winter the bolster on her bed was damp. After the following Easter she spat blood.

Then Mère Simon had recourse to a doctor. Félicité wanted to know what was the matter with her. But, too deaf to hear, she could only catch one word—"Pneumonia." It was familiar to her, and she said softly, "Ah! like Madame!" finding it natural to follow her mistress.

The time for the temporary altars now approached.

The first of them was erected always at the foot of the hill, the second in front of the post office, the third about half-way down the street. There

A SIMPLE HEART

was some contention as to the exact position of this one, and the parishioners had at last decided to place it in Mme. Aubain's courtyard.

Félicité's sufferings increased, and she worried over her inability to do anything for the altar. If only she could have put something on it! Then the parrot occurred to her. The neighbors objected; it was not suitable, they maintained. But the *curé* granted her permission, and this made her so happy that she begged him to accept Loulou, her only valuable, when she should die.

From the Tuesday until Saturday, the eve of Corpus Christi, she coughed more and more frequently. In the evening her face shriveled up, her lips clove to her gums, and she began to vomit; next day at early dawn, feeling herself to be very low, she had the priest call.

Three good women stood round her while she received extreme unction. Then she declared she wanted to speak to Fabu.

He arrived in his Sunday clothes, ill at ease in the dismal atmosphere.

"Forgive me," she said to him, trying to hold out her arms; "I believed it was you who killed him!"

What in the world was she talking about? The idea of her suspecting a man like him of murder! Fabu grew indignant, and began to get excited. "She is off her head! Anybody can see that!"

From time to time Félicité talked with shadows. The neighbors left her. Mère Simon ate her breakfast.

A little later she took Loulou and held him out towards Félicité.

"Come! Bid him good-by!"

Though it was not a corpse, the worms had begun to eat it; one of its wings was broken, and the stuffing had begun to escape from its stomach. But, quite blind now, she kissed it on the forehead, and pressed it against her cheek. Then Mère Simon took it away again to place it upon the altar.

V

The scent of summer came from the meadows; there was a buzzing of flies; the sunshine made the surface of the river sparkle, and warmed the slates upon the roof. Mère Simon had returned to the room, and was slumbering peacefully.

The striking of a bell woke her. People were coming away from vespers. Félicité's delirium left her, and, her thoughts intent on the procession, she saw it as though she were making part of it.

All the children from the schools, together with the choristers and the firemen, walked along the pavements, whilst in the middle of the road came first the Swiss with his halberd, the beadle with a great cross, the schoolmaster looking after his boys, the sister watching anxiously the little girls under her charge; three of the smallest of these, with curly hair like angels, threw rose petals into the air as they advanced; the deacon, his arms outstretched, beat time for the music; and two incense-bearers bowed at every step in front of the Blessed Sacrament, carried by M. le Curé, wearing his beautiful chasuble, beneath a daïs of red velvet, held up by four churchwardens. A mass of people followed, between the white cloths covering the walls of the houses. They arrived at the foot of the hill.

A cold sweat moistened Félicité's temples. Mère Simon wiped them with a piece of linen, saying to herself that some day her own time would come.

The murmur of the crowd grew in volume, for a moment waxed very loud, then faded away.

A fusillade shook the windows. It was the postilions firing a salute in front of the monstrance. Félicité, rolling her eyes, inquired in as low a tone as she could:

"Is he all rgiht?"

She was worrying about the parrot.

Her death agony commenced. A rattle, more and more violent, shook her sides. Bubbles of foam rose to the corners of her mouth, and her whole body was in a tremble.

Now, the blare of the wind instruments made itself heard, the clear voices of children, the deep voices of men. There were intervals of silence, and the trampling of feet, muffled by the flowers strewn along the ground, sounded like the pattering of sheep upon the grass.

The priests appeared in the courtyard. Mère Simon climbed up on a chair so that she might look out of the circular window, and thus got a view of the altar.

Green garlands hung over the altar, which was decorated with a frill of English lace. In the center there was a small casket containing relics, two orange trees at either end, and all along it silver candlesticks and porcelain vases, from which rose sunflowers, lilies, peonies, foxgloves, and tufts of hydrangea. This mass of brilliant coloring sloped downwards, extending from above the altar down to the carpet which had been spread over the ground. A variety of rare objects caught the eye. A vermilion sugar basin had a wreath of violets; pendants of Alençon stone shone on tufts of moss; two Chinese screens depicted landscapes. Loulou, hidden beneath roses, displayed only his blue forehead, which looked like a slab of lapis lazuli.

The churchwardens, the choristers, and the children stood in a line along the three sides of the courtyard. The priest ascended slowly the steps of the altar and put down his great, shining, golden sun upon

A SIMPLE HEART

the lacework cloth. All knelt down. There was a deep silence. And the incense burners, swinging to and fro, grated upon their chains.

A cloud of blue smoke rose to Félicité's bedroom. She distended her nostrils, breathing it in with a mystical sensuousness; then closed her eyes. Her lips smiled. The movements of her heart became gradually more faint, more gentle, as a fountain runs out, as an echo fades away; and when she gave up her last breath, she believed she saw in the opening heavens a tremendous parrot hovering above her head.

Felicity. Félicité. The name is one of the few details we have of the life of the woman—girl, peasant, creature—for she lived a long time, and Flaubert in a story we may read within an hour, cannot after all, supply every detail. She was seventy years old or so when she died, we have spent only an hour with her, and yet we seem to have known her all her life.

As sidereal time is measured, I first met Félicité twenty years ago and she was vivid to me then. Meeting her again, I wondered whether she would have changed; for I had changed. But no, there she was, trudging the country road, struck by the "mail cart at full gallop" at that point at which I knew something was about to happen, but I could not remember from the last time exactly what. Have we not seen, even in modern times, old poor folk trudging the roads between towns? Did they seem to us anonymous, lacking life, too obscure for our consideration, almost so little real that we make no attempt to construct in our minds a past life or a present for such a person. "Yet, like any other, Félicité had her love story"—and her whole life, too.

If her heart was simple, so was her day (she rose always at dawn), her life, her love. Her face "thin and her voice sharp," she ceased to show any signs of increasing age. Indeed. That is to say, she was timeless, seen from the window of a vehicle by Flaubert, Tolstoy, Faulkner, in France, Russia, America. She was betrayed at love. She was scarcely literate. Without children of her own, her employer's children became hers, and she seems to have cared for them, and grieved after them, more deeply than their natural mother.

Félicité achieves local fame when she saves her little family from an agitated bull, but she had "no notion that she had achieved anything heroic." Flaubert's purpose in writing this story is unknown, but we may not be far wrong if we say he chose to celebrate the common man, to contemplate a life less dramatic than a hero's; to affect our hearts by visions which may have moved his, of the peasant, ugly, poor, misshapen, and afflicted.

So the question Flaubert must have confronted, and passed on to us to deal with, is: What does it feel like to be Félicité? *Not that she was simply poor, or that she was simply humble, but that she was alone. In always serving others she is grander and more sensitive than her mistress, Mme. Aubain, who was envied by the "good folk" of the town for having such a fine servant. But the good folk envied Mme. Aubain only the good servant. They missed the sensitive humanity of Félicité, who was in that way sure, even "superior" to these householders who may order her about, or patronize her. Bereft of lovers, Félicité loves. Loves the children who are her charges, loves wandering Polish soldiers, loves a disgusting, stinking, dying man of the village, nursing him in his stench to his dying hour, and loves at last a final object, a parrot Loulou, loves Loulou even after Loulou is dead and stuffed, and prays to Loulou, perhaps in a last gesture indicating she believed (if she thought about it at all) that all other gods had failed her.*

She outlives her household. The pictures on the wall disappear, becoming only "a series of yellow squares." Years pass without event for her, without details for us. She dies.

Of course. A simple life. A simple death. But she was more real, more vivid, more alive, because more loving, than many of her contemporaries, and it may have been these qualities, by whatever name Flaubert called them, which fascinated his consciousness. Or her humility, her faith, her love, her loyalty, her long suffering, her self-denial, her grief, her tenderness, her passing, her vision of Heaven, all abstractions which suggest but do not show. It is not so simple a task, after all, to write of a simple life, or to discover or to celebrate the nobility of simplicity. A mighty heart and talent may be required to tell of a simple heart.

THE IMAGINARY JEW

John Berryman

The second summer of the European War I spent in New York. I lived in a room just below street-level on Lexington above 34th, wrote a good deal, tried not to think about Europe, and listened to music on a small gramophone, the only thing of my own, except books, in the room. Haydn's London Symphony, his last, I heard probably fifty times in two months. One night when excited I dropped the pickup, creating a series

THE IMAGINARY JEW

of knocks at the beginning of the last movement where the oboe joins the strings which still, when I hear them, bring up for me my low dark long damp room and I feel the dew of heat and smell the rented upholstery. I was trying, as one says, to come back a little, uncertain and low after an exhausting year. Why I decided to do this in New York—the enemy in summer equally of soul and body, as I had known for years—I can't remember; perhaps I didn't, but was held on merely from week to week by the motive which presently appeared in the form of a young woman met the Christmas before and now the occupation of every evening not passed in solitary and restless gloom. My friends were away; I saw few other people. Now and then I went to the zoo in lower Central Park and watched with interest the extraordinary behavior of a female badger. For a certain time she quickly paced the round of her cage. Then she would approach the sidewall from an angle in a determined, hardly perceptible, unhurried trot; suddenly when an inch away, point her nose up it, follow her nose up over her back, turning a deft and easy somersault, from which she emerged on her feet moving swiftly and unconcernedly away, as if the action had been no affair of hers, indeed she had scarcely been present. There was another badger in the cage who never did this, and nothing else about her was remarkable; but this competent disinterested somersault she enacted once every five or ten minutes as long as I watched her,—quitting the wall, by the way, always at an angle in fixed relation to the angle at which she arrived at it. It is no longer possible to experience the pleasure I knew each time she lifted her nose and I understood again that she would not fail me, or feel the mystery of her absolute disclaimer,—she has been taken away or died.

The story I have to tell is no further a part of that special summer than a nightmare takes its character, for memory, from the phase of the moon one noticed on going to bed. It could have happened in another year and in another place. No doubt it did, has done, will do. Still, so weak is the talent of the mind for pure relation—immaculate apprehension of p alone—that everything helps us, as when we come to an unknown city: architecture, history, trade-practices, folklore. Even more anxious our approach to a city—like my small story—which we have known and forgotten. Yet how little we can learn! Some of the history is the lonely summer. Part of the folklore, I suppose, is what I now unwillingly rehearse, the character which experience has given to my sense of the Jewish people.

Born in a part of the South where no Jews had come, or none had stayed, and educated thereafter in States where they are numerous, I somehow arrived at a metropolitan university without any clear idea of what in modern life a Jew was,—without even a clear consciousness of

ARCHETYPES AND STEREOTYPES

having seen one. I am unable now to explain this simplicity or blindness. I had not escaped, of course, a sense that humans somewhat different from ourselves, called "Jews," existed as in the middle distance and were best kept there, but this sense was of the vaguest. From what it was derived I do not know; I do not recall feeling the least curiosity about it, or about Jews; I had, simply, from the atmosphere of an advanced heterogeneous democratic society, ingathered a gently negative attitude towards Jews. This I took with me, untested, to college, where it received neither confirmation nor stimulus for two months. I rowed and danced and cut classes and was political; by mid-November I knew most of the five hundred men in my year. Then the man who rowed Number Three, in the eight of which I was bow, took me aside in the shower one afternoon and warned me not to be so chatty with Rosenblum.

I wondered why not. Rosenblum was stroke, a large handsome amiable fellow, for whose ability in the shell I felt great respect and no doubt envy. Because the fellows in the House wouldn't like it, my friend said. "What have they against him?" "It's only because he's Jewish," explained my friend, a second-generation Middle European.

I hooted at him, making the current noises of disbelief, and went back under the shower. It did not occur to me that he could be right. But next day when I was talking with Herz, the coxswain, whom I knew very well, I remembered the libel with some annoyance, and told Herz about it as a curiosity. Herz looked at me oddly, lowering his head, and said after a pause, "Why, Al *is* Jewish, didn't you know that?" I was amazed. I said it was absurd, he couldn't be! "Why not?" said Herz, who must have been as astonished as I was. "Don't you know I'm Jewish?"

I did not know, of course, and ignorance has seldom cost me such humiliation. Herz did not guy me; he went off. But greater than my shame at not knowing something known, apparently, without effort to everyone else, were my emotions for what I then quickly discovered. Asking careful questions during the next week, I learnt that about a third of the men I spent time with in college were Jewish; that they knew it, and the others knew it; that some of the others disliked them for it, and they knew this also; that certain Houses existed *only* for Jews, who were excluded from the rest; and that what in short I took to be an idiotic state was deeply established, familiar, and acceptable to everyone. This discovery was the beginning of my instruction in social life proper— construing socal life as that from which political life issues like a somatic dream.

My attitude toward my friends did not alter on this revelation. I merely discarded the notion that Jews were a proper object for any special attitude; my old sense vanished. This was in 1933. Later, as word of the German persecution filtered into this country, some sentimentality undoubtedly corrupted my no-attitude. I denied the presence of obvious defects in particular Jews, feeling that to admit them would be to side with the sadists and murderers. Accident allotting me close friends who were Jewish, their disadvantages enraged me. Gradually, and against my sense of impartial justice, I became the anomaly which only a partial society can produce, and for which it has no name to the lexicons. In one area, not exclusively, "nigger-lover" is flung in a proximate way: but for a special sympathy and liking for Jews—which became my fate, so that I trembled when I heard one abused in talk—we have no term. In this condition I still was during the summer of which I speak. One further circumstance may be mentioned, as a product, I believe, of this curious training. I am spectacularly unable to identify Jews as Jews—by name, cast of feature, accent, or environment—and this has been true, not only of couse before the college incident, but during my whole life since. Even names to anyone else patently Hebraic rarely suggest to me anything. And when once I learn that So-and-so is Jewish, I am likely to forget it. Now Jewishness—the religion or the race—may be a fact as striking and informative as someone's past heroism or his Christianity or his understanding of the subtlest human relations, and I feel sure that something operates to prevent my utilizing the plain signs by which such characters—in a Jewish man or woman—may be identified, and prevent my retaining the identification once it is made.

So to the city my summer and a night in August. I used to stop on Fourteenth Street for iced coffee, walking from the Village home (or to my room rather) after leaving my friend, and one night when I came out I wandered across to the island of trees and grass and concrete walks raised in the center of Union Square. Here men—a few women, old—sit in the evenings of summer, looking at papers or staring off or talking, and knots of them stay on, arguing, very late; these the unemployed or unemployable, the sleepless, the malcontent. There are no formal orators, as at Columbus Circle in the nineteen-thirties and at Hyde Park Corner. Each group is dominated by several articulate and strong-lunged persons who battle each other with prejudices and desires, swaying with intensity, and take on from time to time the interrupters: a forum at the bottom of the pot,—Jefferson's fear, Whitman's hope, the dream of the younger Lenin. It was now about one o'clock, almost hot, and many men were still out. I stared for a little at the equestrian statue, obscure in the night on top of its pedestal, thinking that the misty Rider would sweep again away all these men at his feet, whenever he liked—what symbol for power yet in a mechanical age rivals the mounted man?—and moved to the nearest group; or I plunged to it.

The dictator to the group was old, with dark cracked skin, fixed eyes in an excited face, leaning forward madly on his bench towards the half-dozen men in semicircle before him. "It's bread! it's bread!" he was saying. "It's bitter-sweet. All the bitter and all the sweetness. Of an overture. What else do you want? When you ask for steak and potatoes, do you want pastry with it? It's bread! It's bread! Help yourself! Help yourself!"

The listeners stood expressionless, except one who was smilling with contempt and interrupted now.

"Never a happy minute, never a happy minute!" the old man cried. "It's good to be dead! Some men should kill themselves."

"Don't you want to live?" said the smiling man.

"Of course I want to live. Everyone wants to live! If death comes, suddenly it's better. It's better!"

With pain I turned away. The next group were talking diffusely and angrily about the Mayor, and I passed to a third, where a frantic olive-skinned young man with a fringe of silky beard was exclaiming:

"No restaurant in New York had the Last Supper! No. When people sit down to eat they should think of that!"

"Listen," said a white-shirted student on the rail, glancing around for approbation, "listen, if I open a restaurant and put *The Last Supper* up over the door, how much money do you think I'd lose? Ten thousand dollars?"

The fourth cluster was larger and appeared more coherent. A savage argument was in progress between a man of fifty with an oily red face, hatted, very determined in manner, and a muscular fellow half his age with heavy eyebrows, coatless, plainly Irish. Fifteen or twenty men were packed around them, and others on a bench near the rail against which the Irishman was lounging were attending also. I listened for a few minutes. The question was whether the President was trying to get us into the War,—or rather, whether this was legitimate, since the Irishman claimed that Roosevelt was a goddamned warmonger whom all the real people in the country hated, and the older man claimed that we should have gone into the f—ing war when France fell a year before, as everybody in the country knew except a few immigrant rats. Redface talked ten times as much as the Irishman, but he was not able to establish any advantage that I could see. He ranted, and then Irish either repeated shortly and fiercely what he had said last, or shifted his ground. The audience were silent—favoring whom I don't know, but evidently much interested. One or two men pushed out of the group, others arrived behind me, and I was eddied forward towards the disputants. The young Irishman broke suddenly into a tirade by the man with the hat:

"You're full of s. Roosevelt even tried to get us in with the communists in the Spanish war. If he could have done it we'd have been burning churches down like the rest of the Reds."

"No, that's not right," I heard my own voice, and pushed forward, feeling blood in my face, beginning to tremble. "No, Roosevelt as a matter of fact helped Franco by non-intervention, at the same time that Italians and German planes were fighting against the Government and arms couldn't get in from France."

"What's that? What are you, a Jew?" He turned to me contemptuously, and was back at the older man before I could speak. "The only reason we weren't over there four years ago is because you can only screw us so much. Then we quit. No New Deal bastard could make us go help the goddamned communists."

"That ain't the question, it's if we want to fight *now* or *later*. Them Nazis ain't gonna sit!" shouted the redfaced man. "They got Egypt practically, and then it's India if it ain't England first, It ain't a question of the communists, the communists are on Hitler's side. I tellya we can wait and wait and chew and spit and the first thing you know they'll be in England, and then who's gonna help us when they start after us? Maybe Brazil? Get wise to the world! Spain don't matter now one way or the other, they ain't gonna help and they can't hurt. It's Germany and Italy and Japan, and if it ain't too late now it's gonna be. Get wise to yourself. We shoulda gone in—"

"What with?" said the Irishman with disdain. "Pop pop. Wooden machine-guns?'

"We were as ready a year ago as we are now. Defense don't mean nothing, you gotta have to fight!"

"No, we're much better off now," I said, "than we were a year ago. When England went in, to keep its word to Poland, what good was it to Poland? The Germany Army—"

"Shut up, you Jew," said the Irishman.

"I'm not a Jew," I said to him. "What makes—"

"Listen, Pop," he said to the man in the hat, "it's O.K. to shoot your mouth off, but what the hell have you got to do with it? You aren't gonna do any fighting."

"Listen," I said.

"You sit on your big ass and talk about who's gonna fight who. Nobody's gonna fight anybody. If we feel hot, we ought to clean up some of the sons of bitches here before we go sticking our nuts anywhere to help

England. We ought to clean up the sons of bitches in Wall Street and Washington before we take any ocean trips. You want to know something? You know why Germany's winning everything in this war? Because there ain't no Jews back home. There ain't no more Jews, first shouting war like this one here"—nodding at me—"and then skinning off to the synagogue with the profits. Wake up, Pop! You must have been around in the last war, you ought to know better."

I was too nervous to be angry or resentful. But I began to have a sense of oppression in breathing. I took the Irishman by the arm.

"Listen, I told you I'm not a Jew."

"I don't give a damn what you are." He turned his half-dark eyes to me, wrenching his arm loose. "You talk like a Jew."

"What does that mean?" Some part of me wanted to laugh. "How does a Jew talk?"

"They talk like you, buddy."

"That's a fine argument! But if I'm not a Jew, my talk only—"

"You probably are a Jew. You look like a Jew."

"I *look* like a Jew? Listen"—I swung around with despair to a man standing next to me—"do I look like a Jew? It doesn't matter whether I do or not—a Jew is as good as anybody and better than this son of a bitch." I was not exactly excited. I was trying to adapt my language as my need for the crowd, and sudden respect for its judgment, possessed me. "But in fact I'm not Jewish and I don't look Jewish. Do I?"

The man looked at me quickly and said, half to me and half to the Irishman, "Hell, I don't know. Sure he does."

A wave of disappointment and outrage swept me almost to tears. I felt like a man betrayed by his brother. The lamps seemed brighter and vaguer, the night large. Glancing round I saw sitting on a bench near me a tall, heavy, serious-looking man of thirty, well dressed, whom I had noticed earlier, and appealed to him, "Tell me, do I look Jewish?"

But he only stared up and waved his head vaguely. I saw with horror that something was wrong with him.

"You look like a Jew. You talk like a Jew, You *are* a Jew," I heard the Irishman say.

I heard murmuring among the men, but I could see nothing very clearly. It seemed very hot. I faced the Irishman again helplessly, holding my voice from rising.

"I'm *not* a Jew," I told him. "I might be, but I'm not. You have no bloody reason to think so, and you can't make me a Jew by simply repeating like an idiot that I am."

"Don't deny it, son," said the redfaced man, "stand up to him."

"God damn it"—suddenly I was furious, whirling like a fool (was I

afraid of the Irishman? had he conquered me?) on the redfaced man—
"I'm *not* denying it! Or rather I am, but only because I'm not a Jew!
I despise renegades, I hate Jews who turn on their people, if I were a Jew
I would say so, I would be proud to be: what is the vicious opinion of a
man like this to me if I were a Jew? But I'm not. Why the hell should
I admit I am if I'm not?"

"Jesus, the Jew is excited," said the Irishman.

"I have a right to be excited, you son of a bitch. Suppose I call you a
Jew. Yes, you're a Jew. Does that mean anything?"

"Not a damn thing." He spat over the rail past a man's head.

"Prove that you're not. I say you are."

"Now listen, you Jew. I'm a Catholic."

"So am I, or I was born one, I'm not one now. I was born a Catholic."
I was a little calmer but goaded, obsessed with the need to straighten
this out. I felt that everything for everyone there depended on my proving
him wrong. If *once* this evil for which we have not even a name could
be exposed to the rest of the men as empty—if I could *prove* I was not a
Jew—it would fall to the ground, neither would anyone else be a Jew
to be accused. Then it could be trampled on. Fascist America was at stake.
I listened, intensely anxious for our fate.

"Yeah?" said the Irisman. "Say the Apostles' Creed."

Memory went swirling back. I could hear the little bell die as I hushed
it and set it on the left. Father Boniface looked at me tall from the top
of the steps and smiled greeting me in the darkness before dawn as I
came to serve, the men pressed around me under the lamps, and I could
remember nothing but *visibilum omnium* . . . et invisibilium?

"I don't remember it."

The Irishman laughed with his certainty.

The papers in my pocket; I thought them over hurriedly. In my
wallet. What would they prove? Details of ritual, Church history: anyone
could learn them. My piece of Irish blood. Shame, shame: shame for my
ruthless people. I will not be his blood. I wish I were a Jew, I would
change my blood, to be able to say *Yes* and defy him.

"I'm not a Jew." I felt a fool. "You only say so. You haven't any
evidence in the world."

He leaned forward from the rail, close to me. "Are you cut?"

Shock, fear ran through me before I could make any meaning out of
his words. Then they ran faster, and I felt confused.

From that point, nothing is clear for me. I stayed a long time—it
seemed impossible to leave, showing him victor to them—thinking of
possible allies and new plans of proof, but without hope. I was tired to
the marrow. The arguments rushed on, and I spoke often now but

seldom was heeded except by an old fat woman, very short and dirty, who listened intently to everyone. Heavier and heavier appeared to me to press upon us in the fading night our general guilt.

In the days following, as my resentment died, I saw that I had not been a victim altogether unjustly. My persecutors were right: I was a Jew. The imaginary Jew I was was as real as the imaginary Jew hunted down, on other nights and days, in a real Jew. Every murderer strikes the mirror, the lash of the torturer falls on the mirror and cuts the real image, and the real and the imaginary blood flow down together.

THE ARTIFICIAL NIGGER

Flannery O'Connor

Mr. Head awakened to discover that the room was full of moonlight. He sat up and stared at the floor boards—the color of silver—and then at the ticking on his pillow, which might have been brocade, and after a second, he saw half of the moon five feet away in his shaving mirror. It rolled forward and cast a dignifying light on everything. The straight chair against the wall looked stiff and attentive as if it were waiting an order, and Mr. Head's trousers, hanging to the back of it, had an almost noble air, like the garment some great man had just flung to his servant; but the face on the moon was a grave one. It gazed across the room and out the window where it floated over the horse stall and appeared to contemplate itself with the look of a young man who sees his old age before him.

Mr. Head could have said to it that age was a choice blessing and that only with years does a man enter into that calm understanding of life that makes him a suitable guide for the young. This, at least, had been his own experience.

He sat up and grasped the iron posts at the foot of his bed and raised himself until he could see the face on the alarm clock which sat on an overturned bucket beside the chair. The hour was two in the morning. The alarm on the clock did not work, but he was not dependent on any mechanical means to awaken him. Sixty years had not dulled his responses; his physical reactions, like his moral ones, were guided by his will and strong character, and these could be seen plainly in his features. He had a long tubelike face with a long, rounded open jaw and a long depressed nose. His eyes were alert but quiet, and in the miraculous moonlight they

THE ARTIFICIAL NIGGER

had a look of composure and of ancient wisdom as if they belonged to one of the great guides of men. He might have been Virgil summoned in the middle of the night to go to Dante; or better, Raphael, awakened by a blast of God's light to fly to the side of Tobias. The only dark spot in the room was Nelson's pallet, underneath the shadow of the window.

Nelson was hunched over on his side, his knees under his chin and his heels under his bottom. His new suit and hat were in the boxes that they had been sent in, and these were on the floor at the foot of the pallet where he could get his hands on them as soon as he woke up. The slop jar, out of the shadow and made snow-white in the moonlight, appeared to stand guard over him like a small personal angel. Mr. Head lay back down, feeling entirely confident that he could carry out the moral mission of the coming day. He meant to be up before Nelson and to have the breakfast cooking by the time he awakened. The boy was always irked when Mr. Head was the first up. They would have to leave the house at four to get to the railroad junction by five-thirty. The train was to stop for them at five-forty-five.

This would be the boy's first trip to the city, though he claimed it would be his second because he had been born there. Mr. Head had tried to point out to him that when he was born he didn't have the intelligence to determine his whereabouts, but this had made no impression on the child at all, and he continued to insist that this was to be his second trip. It would be Mr. Head's third trip. Nelson had said, "I will've already been there twicet and I ain't but ten."

Mr. Head had contradicted him.

"If you ain't been there in fifteen years, how you know you'll be able to find your way about?" Nelson had asked. "How you know it hasn't changed some?"

"Have you ever," Mr. Head had asked, "seen me lost?"

Nelson certainly had not, but he was a child who was never satisfied until he had given an impudent answer and he replied, "It's nowhere around here to get lost at."

"The day is going to come," Mr. Head prophesied, "when you'll find you ain't as smart as you think you are." He had been thinking about this trip for several months, but it was for the most part in moral terms that he conceived it. It was to be a lesson that the boy would never forget. He was to find out from it that he had no cause for pride merely because he had been born in a city. He was to find out that the city is not a great place. Mr. Head meant him to see everything there is to see in a city so that he would be content to stay at home for the rest of his life. He fell asleep thinking how the boy would at last find out that he was not as smart as he thought he was.

He was awakened at three-thirty by the smell of fatback frying and he leapt off his cot. The pallet was empty, and the clothes boxes had been thrown open. He put on his trousers and ran into the other room. The boy had a cornpone on cooking and had fried the meat. He was sitting in the half-dark at the table, drinking cold coffee out of a can. He had on his new suit and his new grey hat pulled low over his eyes. It was too big for him, but they had ordered it a size large because they expected his head to grow. He didn't say anything, but his entire figure suggested satisfaction at having arisen before Mr. Head.

Mr. Head went to the stove and brought the meat to the table in the skillet. "It's no hurry," he said. "You'll get there soon enough and it's no guarantee you'll like it when you do, neither," and he sat down across from the boy whose hat teetered back slowly to reveal a fiercely expressionless face, very much the same shape as the old man's. They were grandfather and grandson but they looked enough alike to be brothers, and brothers not too far apart in age, for Mr. Head had a youthful expression by daylight, while the boy's look was ancient, as if he knew everything already and would be pleased to forget it.

Mr. Head had once had a wife and daughter, and when the wife died, the daughter ran away and returned after an interval with Nelson. Then one morning, without getting out of bed, she died and left Mr. Head with sole care of the year-old child. He had made the mistake of telling Nelson that he had been born in Atlanta. If he hadn't told him that, Nelson couldn't have insisted that this was going to be his second trip.

"You may not like it a bit," Mr. Head continued, "it'll be full of niggers."

The boy made a face as if he could handle a nigger.

"All right," Mr. Head said. "You ain't ever seen a nigger."

"You wasn't up very early," Nelson said.

"You ain't ever seen a nigger," Mr. Head repeated. "There hasn't been a nigger in this county since we run that one out twelve years ago and that was before you were born." He looked at the boy as if daring him to say he had even seen a Negro.

"How you know I never saw a nigger when I lived there before?" Nelson asked. "I probably saw a lot of niggers."

"If you seen one, you didn't know what he was," Mr. Head said, completely exasperated. "A six-month-old child don't know a nigger from anybody else."

"I reckon I'll know a nigger if I see one," the boy said and got up and straightened his slick, sharply creased grey hat and went outside to the privy.

THE ARTIFICIAL NIGGER

They reached the junction some time before the train was due to arrive and stood about two feet from the first set of tracks. Mr. Head carried a paper sack with some biscuits and a can of sardines in it for their lunch. A coarse-looking orange sun coming up behind the east range of mountains was making the sky a dull red behind them, but in front of them it was still grey, and they faced a grey transparent moon, hardly stronger than a thumbprint and completely without light. A small tin switch box and a black fuel tank were all there was to mark the place as a junction; the tracks were double and did not converge again until they were hidden behind the bends at either end of the clearing. Trains passing appeared to emerge from a tunnel of trees and, hit for a second by the cold sky, vanish terrified into the woods again. Mr. Head had had to make special arrangements with the ticket agent to have this train stop and he was secretly afraid it would not, in which case he knew Nelson would say, "I never thought no train was going to stop for you." Under the useless morning moon the tracks looked white and fragile. Both the old man and the child stared ahead as if awaiting an apparition.

Then suddenly, before Mr. Head could make up his mind to turn back, there was a deep warning bleat, and the train appeared, gliding very slowly, almost silently around the bend of trees about two hundred yards down the track, with one yellow front light burning. Mr. Head was still not certain it would stop and he felt it would make an even bigger idiot of him if it went by slowly. Both he and Nelson, however, were prepared to ignore the train if it passed them.

The engine charged by, filling their noses with the smell of hot metal, and then the second coach came to a stop exactly where they were standing. A conductor with the face of an ancient bloated bulldog was on the step as if he expected them, though he did not look as if it mattered one way or the other to him if they got on or not. "To the right," he said.

Their entry took only a fraction of a second, and the train was already speeding on as they entered the quiet car. Most of the travelers were still sleeping, some with their heads hanging off the chair arms, some stretched across two seats, and some sprawled out with their feet in the aisle. Mr. Head saw two unoccupied seats and pushed Nelson toward them. "Get in there by the winder," he said in his normal voice which was very loud at this hour of the morning. "Nobody cares if you sit there because it's nobody in it. Sit right there."

"I heard you," the boy muttered. "It's no use in you yelling," and he sat down and turned his head to the glass. There he saw a pale ghost-like face scowling at him beneath the brim of a pale ghost-like hat. His grandfather, looking quickly too, saw a different ghost, pale but grinning, under a black hat.

ARCHETYPES AND STEREOTYPES

Mr. Head sat down and settled himself and took out his ticket and started reading aloud everything that was printed on it. People began to stir. Several woke up and stared at him. "Take off your hat," he said to Nelson and took off his own and put it on his knee. He had a small amount of white hair that had turned tobacco-colored over the years, and this lay flat across the back of his head. The front of his head was bald and creased. Nelson took off his hat and put it on his knee, and they waited for the conductor to come ask for their tickets.

The man across the aisle from them was spread out over two seats, one foot propped on the window and the other jutting into the aisle. He had on a light blue suit and a yellow shirt unbuttoned at the neck. His eyes had just opened, and Mr. Head was ready to introduce himself when the conductor came up from behind and growled, "Tickets."

When the conductor had gone, Mr. Head gave Nelson the return half of his ticket and said, "Now put that in your pocket and don't lose it or you'll have to stay in the city."

"Maybe I will," Nelson said as if this were a reasonable suggestion.

Mr. Head ignored him. "First time this boy has ever been on a train," he explained to the man across the aisle, who was sitting up now on the edge of his seat with both feet on the floor.

Nelson jerked his hat on again and turned angrily to the window.

"He's never seen anything before," Mr. Head continued. "Ignorant as the day he was born, but I mean for him to get his fill once and for all."

The boy leaned forward, across his grandfather and toward the stranger. "I was born in the city," he said. "I was born there. This is my second trip." He said it in a high positive voice, but the man across the aisle didn't look as if he understood. There were heavy purple circles under his eyes.

Mr. Head reached across the aisle and tapped him on the arm. "The thing to do with a boy," he said sagely, "is to show him all it is to show. Don't hold nothing back."

"Yeah," the man said. He gazed down at his swollen feet and lifted the left one about ten inches from the floor. After a minute he put it down and lifted the other. All through the car people began to get up and move about and yawn and stretch. Separate voices could be heard here and there and then a general hum. Suddenly Mr. Head's serene expression changed. His mouth almost closed, and a light, fierce and cautious both, came into his eyes. He was looking down the length of the car. Without turning he caught Nelson by the arm and pulled him forward. "Look," he said.

A huge coffee-colored man was coming slowly forward. He had on a light suit and a yellow satin tie with a ruby pin in it. One of his hands rested on his stomach which rode majestically under his buttoned coat,

THE ARTIFICIAL NIGGER

and in the other he held the head of a black walking stick that he picked up and set down with a deliberate outward motion each time he took a step. He was proceeding very slowly, his large brown eyes gazing over the heads of the passengers. He had a small white mustache and white crinkly hair. Behind him there were two young women, both coffee-colored, one in a yellow dress and one in a green. Their progress was kept at the rate of his, and they chatted in low throaty voices as they followed him.

Mr. Head's grip was tightening insistently on Nelson's arm. As the procession passed them, the light from a sapphire ring on the brown hand that picked up the cane reflected in Mr. Head's eye, but he did not look up, nor did the tremendous man look at him. The group proceeded up the rest of the aisle and out of the car. Mr. Head's grip on Nelson's arm loosened. "What was that?" he asked.

"A man," the boy said and gave him an indignant look as if he were tired of having his intelligence insulted.

"What kind of a man?" Mr. Head persisted, his voice expressionless.

"A fat man," Nelson said. He was beginning to feel that he had better be cautious.

"You don't know what kind?" Mr. Head said in a final tone.

"An old man," the boy said and had a sudden foreboding that he was not going to enjoy the day.

"That was a nigger," Mr. Head said and sat back.

Nelson jumped up on the seat and stood looking backward to the end of the car, but the Negro had gone.

"I'd thought you'd know a nigger since you seen so many when you was in the city on your first visit," Mr. Head continued. "That's his first nigger," he said to the man across the aisle.

The boy slid down into the seat. "You said they were black," he said in an angry voice. "You never said they were tan. How do you expect me to know anything when you don't tell me right?"

"You're just ignorant is all," Mr. Head said and he got up and moved over in the vacant seat by the man across the aisle.

Nelson turned backward again and looked where the Negro had disappeared. He felt that the Negro had deliberately walked down the aisle in order to make a fool of him and he hated him with a fierce, raw, fresh hate; and also, he understood now why his grandfather disliked them. He looked toward the window, and the face there seemed to suggest that he might be inadequate to the day's exactions. He wondered if he would even recognize the city when they came to it.

After he had told several stories, Mr. Head realized that the man he was talking to was asleep and he got up and suggested to Nelson that they walk over the train and see the parts of it. He particularly wanted the boy to see the toilet, so they went first to the men's room and examined the plumbing. Mr. Head demonstrated the ice-water cooler as if he had invented it and showed Nelson the bowl with a single spigot where the travelers brushed their teeth. They went through several cars and came to the diner.

This was the most elegant car in the train. It was painted a rich egg-yellow and had a wine-colored carpet on the floor. There were wide windows over the tables, and great spaces of the rolling view were caught in miniature in the sides of the coffeepots and in the glasses. Three very black Negroes in white suits and aprons were running up and down the aisle, swinging trays and bowing and bending over the travelers eating breakfast. One of them rushed up to Mr. Head and said, holding up two fingers, "Space for two!" but Mr. Head replied in a loud voice, "We eaten before we left!"

The waiter wore large brown spectacles that increased the size of his eye whites. "Stan' aside then, please," he said with an airy wave of the arm as if he were brushing aside flies.

Neither Nelson nor Mr. Head moved a fraction of an inch. "Look," Mr. Head said.

The near corner of the diner, containing two tables, was set off from the rest by a saffron-colored curtain. One table was set but empty, but at the other, facing them, his back to the drape, sat the tremendous Negro. He was speaking in a soft voice to the two women while he buttered a muffin. He had a heavy sad face, and his neck bulged over his white collar on either side. "They rope them off," Mr. Head explained. Then he said, "Let's go see the kitchen," and they walked the length of the diner, but the black waiter was coming fast behind them.

"Passengers are not allowed in the kitchen!" he said in a haughty voice. "Passengers are *not* allowed in the kitchen!"

Mr. Head stopped where he was and turned. "And there's good reason for that," he shouted into the Negro's chest, "because the cockroaches would run the passengers out!"

All the travelers laughed, and Mr. Head and Nelson walked out, grinning. Mr. Head was known at home for his quick wit, and Nelson felt a sudden keen pride in him. He realized the old man would be his only support in the strange place they were approaching. He would be entirely alone in the world if he were ever lost from his grandfather. A terrible excitement shook him, and he wanted to take hold of Mr. Head's coat and hold on.

As they went back to their seats they could see through the passing windows that the countryside was becoming speckled with small houses and shacks and that a highway ran alongside the train. Cars sped by on it,

THE ARTIFICIAL NIGGER

very small and fast. Nelson felt that there was less breath in the air than there had been thirty minutes ago. The man across the aisle had left, and there was no one near for Mr. Head to hold a conversation with, so he looked out the window, through his own reflection, and read aloud the names of the buildings they were passing. "The Dixie Chemical Corp!" he announced. "Southern Maid Flour! Dixie Doors! Southern Belle Cotton Products! Patty's Peanut Butter! Southern Mammy Cane Syrup!"

"Hush up!" Nelson hissed.

All over the car people were beginning to get up and take their luggage off the overhead racks. Women were putting on their coats and hats. The conductor stuck his head in the car and snarled, "Firstoppppmry," and Nelson lunged out of his sitting position, trembling. Mr. Head pushed him down by the shoulder.

"Keep your seat," he said in dignified tones. "The first stop is on the edge of town. The second stop is at the main railroad station." He had come by this knowledge on his first trip when he had got off at the first stop and had had to pay a man fifteen cents to take him into the heart of town. Nelson sat back down, very pale. For the first time in his life he understood that his grandfather was indispensable to him.

The train stopped and left off a few passengers and glided on as if it had never ceased moving. Outside, behind rows of brown rickety houses, a line of blue buildings stood up, and beyond them a pale rose-grey sky faded away to nothing. The train moved into the railroad yard. Looking down, Nelson saw lines and lines of silver tracks multiplying and crisscrossing. Then before he could start counting them, the face in the window started out at him, grey but distinct, and he looked the other way. The train was in the station. Both he and Mr. Head jumped up and ran to the door. Neither noticed that they had left the paper sack with the lunch in it on the seat.

They walked stiffly through the small station and came out of a heavy door into the squall of traffic. Crowds were hurrying to work. Nelson didn't know where to look. Mr. Head leaned against the side of the building and glared in front of him.

Finally Nelson said, "Well, how do you see what all it is to see?"

Mr. Head didn't answer. Then as if the sight of people passing had given him the clue, he said, "You walk," and started off down the street. Nelson followed, steadying his hat. So many sights and sounds were flooding in on him that for the first block he hardly knew what he was seeing. At the second corner, Mr. Head turned and looked behind him at the station they had left, a putty-colored terminal with a concrete dome on top. He thought that if he could keep the dome always in sight, he would be able to get back in the afternoon to catch the train again.

ARCHETYPES AND STEREOTYPES

As they walked along, Nelson began to distinguish details and take note of the store windows, jammed with every kind of equipment—hardware, dry goods, chicken feed, liquor. They passed one that Mr. Head called his particular attention to where you walked in and sat on a chair with your feet upon two rests and let a Negro polish your shoes. They walked slowly and stopped and stood at the entrances so they could see what went on in every place, but they did not go into any of them. Mr. Head was determined not to go into any city store, because on his first trip here he had got lost in a large one and had found his way out only after many people had insulted him.

They came in the middle of the next block to a store that had a weighing machine in front of it and they both in turn stepped up on it and put in a penny and received a ticket. Mr. Head's ticket said, "You weigh 120 pounds. You are upright and brave and all your friends admire you." He put the ticket in his pocket, surprised that the machine should have got his character correct but his weight wrong, for he had weighed on a grain scale not long before and knew he weighed 110. Nelson's ticket said, "You weigh 98 pounds. You have a great destiny ahead of you but beware of dark women." Nelson did not know any women and he weighed only 68 pounds, but Mr. Head pointed out that the machine had probably printed the number upside down, meaning the 9 for a 6.

They walked on, and at the end of five blocks the dome of the terminal sank out of sight, and Mr. Head turned to the left. Nelson could have stood in front of every store window for an hour if there had not been another more interesting one next to it. Suddenly he said, "I was born here!" Mr. Head turned and looked at him with horror. There was a sweaty brightness about his face. "This is where I come from!" he said.

Mr. Head was appalled. He saw the moment had come for drastic action. "Lemme show you one thing you ain't seen yet," he said and took him to the corner where there was a sewer entrance. "Squat down," he said, "and stick your head there," and he held the back of the boy's coat while he got down and put his head in the sewer. He drew it back quickly, hearing a gurgling in the depths under the sidewalk. Then Mr. Head explained the sewer system, how the entire city was underlined with it, how it contained all the drainage and was full of rats and how a man could slide into it and be sucked along down endless pitch-black tunnels. At any minute any man in the city might be sucked into the sewer and never heard from again. He described it so well that Nelson was for some seconds shaken. He connected the sewer passages with the entrance to hell and understood for the first time how the world was put together in its lower parts. He drew away from the curb.

Then he said, "Yes, but you can stay away from the holes," and his face

THE ARTIFICIAL NIGGER

took on that stubborn look that was so exasperating to his grandfather. "This is where I come from!" he said.

Mr. Head was dismayed but he only muttered, "You'll get your fill," and they walked on. At the end of two more blocks he turned to the left, feeling that he was circling the dome; and he was correct, for in a half hour they passed in front of the railroad station again. At first Nelson did not notice that he was seeing the same stores twice, but when they passed the one where you put your feet on the rests while the Negro polished your shoes, he perceived that they were walking in a circle.

"We done been here!" he shouted. "I don't believe you know where you're at!"

"The direction just slipped my mind for a minute," Mr. Head said, and they turned down a different street. He still did not intend to let the dome get too far away, and after two blocks in their new direction he turned to the left. This street contained two- and three-story wooden buildings. Anyone passing on the sidewalk could see into the rooms, but Mr. Head, glancing through one window, saw a woman lying on an iron bed, looking out, with a sheet pulled over her. Her knowing expression shook him. A fierce-looking boy on a bicycle came driving down out of nowhere, and he had to jump to the side to keep from being hit. "It nothing to them if they knock you down," he said. "You better keep closer to me."

They walked on for some time on streets like this before he remembered to turn again. The houses they were passing now were all unpainted, and the wood in them looked rotten; the street between was narrower. Nelson saw a colored man. Then another. Then another. "Niggers live in these houses," he observed.

"Well, come on and we'll go somewheres else," Mr. Head said. "We didn't come to look at niggers," and they turned down another street but they continued to see Negroes everywhere. Nelson's skin began to prickle, and they stepped along at a faster pace in order to leave the neighborhood as soon as possible. There were colored men in their undershirts standing in the doors, and colored women rocking on the sagging porches. Colored children played in the gutters and stopped what they were doing to look at them. Before long they began to pass rows of stores with colored customers in them but they didn't pause at the entrances of these. Black eyes in black faces were watching from every direction. "Yes," Mr. Head said, "this is where you were born—right here with all these niggers."

Nelson scowled. "I think you done got us lost," he said.

Mr. Head swung around sharply and looked for the dome. It was nowhere in sight. "I ain't got us lost either," he said. "You're just tired of walking."

"I ain't tired, I'm hungry," Nelson said. "Give me a biscuit."

They discovered then that they had lost the lunch.

"You were the one holding the sack," Nelson said. "I would have kep aholt of it."

"If you want to direct this trip, I'll go by myself and leave you right here," Mr. Head said and was pleased to see the boy turn white. However, he realized they were lost and drifting farther every minute from the station. He was hungry himself and beginning to be thirsty, and since they had been in the colored neighborhood, they had both begun to sweat. Nelson had on his shoes and he was unaccustomed to them. The concrete sidewalks were very hard. They both wanted to find a place to sit down, but this was impossible and they kept on walking, the boy muttering under his breath, "First you lost the sack and then you lost the way," and Mr. Head growling from time to time, "Anybody wants to be from this nigger heaven can be from it!"

By now the sun was well forward in the sky. The odor of dinner cooking drifted out to them. The Negroes were all at their doors to see them pass. "Whyn't you ast one of these niggers the way?" Nelson said. "You got us lost."

"This is where you were born," Mr. Head said. "You can ast one yourself if you want to."

Nelson was afraid of the colored men and he didn't want to be laughed at by the colored children. Up ahead he saw a large colored woman leaning in a doorway that opened onto the sidewalk. Her hair stood straight out from her head for about four inches all around, and she was resting on bare brown feet that turned pink at the sides. She had on a pink dress that showed her exact shape. As they came abreast of her, she lazily lifted one hand to her head, and her fingers disappeared into her hair.

Nelson stopped. He felt his breath drawn up by the woman's dark eyes. "How do you get back to town?" he said in a voice that did not sound like his own.

After a minute she said, "You in town now," in a rich low tone that made Nelson feel as if a cool spray had been turned on him.

"How do you get back to the train?" he said in the same reedlike voice.

"You can catch you a car," she said.

He understood she was making fun of him but he was too paralyzed even to scowl. He stood drinking in every detail of her. His eyes traveled up from her great knees to her forehead and then in a triangular path from the glistening sweat on her neck down and across her tremendous bosom and over her barm arm back to where her fingers lay hidden in her hair. He suddenly wanted her to reach down and pick him up and draw him against her and then he wanted to feel her breath on his face. He wanted to look down and down into her eyes while she held him tighter and

THE ARTIFICIAL NIGGER

tighter. He had never had such a feeling before. He felt as if he were reeling down through a pitch-black tunnel.

"You can go a block down yonder and catch you a car take you to the railroad station, Sugarpie," she said.

Nelson would have collapsed at her feet if Mr. Head had not pulled him roughly away. "You act like you don't have any sense!" the old man growled.

They hurried down the street, and Nelson did not look back at the woman. He pushed his hat sharply forward over his face which was already burning with shame. The sneering ghost he had seen in the train window and all the foreboding feelings he had on the way returned to him and he remembered that his ticket from the scale had said to beware of dark women and that his grandfather's had said he was upright and brave. He took the old man's hand, a sign of dependence he seldom showed.

They headed down the street toward the car tracks where a yellow rattling trolley was coming. Mr. Head had never boarded a streetcar and he let that one pass. Nelson was silent. From time to time his mouth trembled slightly, but his grandfather, occupied with his own problems, paid him no attention. They stood on the corner and neither looked at the Negroes who were passing, going about their business just as if they had been white, except that most of them stopped and eyed Mr. Head and Nelson. It occurred to Mr. Head that since the streetcar ran on tracks, they could simply follow the tracks. He gave Nelson a slight push and explained that they would follow the tracks on into the railroad station, walking, and they set off.

Presently to their great relief they began to see white people again, and Nelson sat down on the sidewalk against the wall of a building. "I got to rest myself some," he said. "You lost the sack and the direction. You can just wait on me to rest myself."

"There's the tracks in front of us," Mr. Head said. "All we got to do is keep them in sight and you could have remembered the sack as good as me. This is where you were born. This is your old home town. This is your second trip. You ought to know how to do," and he squatted down and continued in this vein, but the boy was easing his burning feet out of his shoes.

"And standing there grinning like a chim-pan-zee while a nigger woman gives you directions. Great Gawd!" Mr. Head said.

"I never said I was nothing but born here," the boy said in a shaky voice. "I never said I would or wouldn't like it. I never said I wanted to come. I only said I was born here and I never had nothing to do with that. I want to go home. I never wanted to come in the first place. It was all your big idea. How you know you ain't following the tracks in the wrong direction?"

This last had occurred to Mr. Head, too. "All these people are white," he said.

"We ain't passed here before," Nelson said. This was a neighborhood of brick buildings that might have been lived in or might not. A few empty automobiles were parked along the curb and there was an occasional passer-by. The heat of the pavement came up through Nelson's thin suit. His eyelids began to droop, and after a few minutes his head tilted forward. His shoulders twitched once or twice and then he fell over on his side and lay sprawled in an exhausted fit of sleep.

Mr. Head watched him silently. He was very tired himself but they could not both sleep at the same time and he could not have slept anyway because he did not know where he was. In a few minutes Nelson would wake up, refreshed by his sleep and very cocky, and would begin complaining that he had lost the sack and the way. You'd have a mighty sorry time if I wasn't here, Mr. Head thought; and then another idea occurred to him. He looked at the sprawled figure for several minutes; presently he stood up. He justified what he was going to do on the grounds that it is sometimes necessary to teach a child a lesson he won't forget, particularly when the child is always reasserting his position with some new impudence. He walked without a sound to the corner about twenty feet away and sat down on a covered garbage can in the alley where he could look out and watch Nelson wake up alone.

The boy was dozing fitfully, half conscious of vague noises and black forms moving up from some dark part of him into the light. His face worked in his sleep, and he had pulled his knees up under his chin. The sun shed a dull dry light on the narrow street; everything looked like exactly what it was. After a while Mr. Head, hunched like an old monkey on the garbage-can lid, decided that if Nelson didn't wake up soon, he would make a loud noise by bamming his foot against the can. He looked at his watch and discovered that it was two o'clock. Their train left at six, and the possibility of missing it was too awful for him to think of. He kicked his foot backwards on the can, and a hollow boom reverberated in the alley.

Nelson shot up onto his feet with a shout. He looked where his grandfather should have been and stared. He seemed to whirl several times and then, picking up his feet and throwing his head back, he dashed down the street like a wild maddened pony. Mr. Head jumped off the can and galloped after, but the child was almost out of sight. He saw a streak of grey disappearing diagonally a block ahead. He ran as fast as he could looking both ways down every intersection, but without sight of him

THE ARTIFICIAL NIGGER

again. Then as he passed the third intersection, completely winded, he saw about a half a block down the street a scene that stopped him altogether. He crouched behind a trash box to watch and get his bearings.

Nelson was sitting with both legs spread out, and by his side lay an elderly woman, screaming. Groceries were scattered about the sidewalk. A crowd of women had already gathered to see justice done, and Mr. Head distinctly heard the old woman on the pavement shout, "You've broken my ankle and your daddy'll pay for it! Every nickel! Police! Police!" Several of the women were plucking at Nelson's shoulder, but the boy seemed too dazed to get up.

Something forced Mr. Head from behind the trash box and forward, but only at a creeping pace. He had never in his life been accosted by a policeman. The women were milling around Nelson as if they might suddenly all dive on him at once and tear him to pieces, and the old woman continued to scream that her ankle was broken and to call for an officer. Mr. Head came on so slowly that he could have been taking a backward step after each forward one, but when he was about ten feet away, Nelson saw him and sprang. The child caught him around the hips and clung panting against him.

The women all turned on Mr. Head. The injured one sat up and shouted, "You, sir! You'll pay every penny of my doctor's bill that your boy has caused. He's a juve-nile delinquent! Where is an officer? Somebody take this man's name and address!"

Mr. Head was trying to detach Nelson's fingers from the flesh in the back of his legs. The old man's head had lowered itself into his collar like a turtle's; his eyes were glazed with fear and caution.

"Your boy has broken my ankle!" the old woman shouted. "Police!"

Mr. Head sensed the approach of the policeman from behind. He stared straight ahead at the women who were massed in their fury like a solid wall to block his escape. "This is not my boy," he said. "I never seen him before."

He felt Nelson's fingers fall out of his flesh.

The women dropped back, staring at him with horror, as if they were so repulsed by a man who would deny his own image and likeness that they could not bear to lay hands on him. Mr. Head walked on, through a space they silently cleared, and left Nelson behind. Ahead of him he saw nothing but a hollow tunnel that had once been the street.

The boy remained standing where he was, his neck craned forward and his hands hanging by his sides. His hat was jammed on his head so that there were no longer any creases on it. The injured woman got up and shook her fist at him, and the others gave him pitying looks, but he didn't notice any of them. There was no policeman in sight.

In a minute he began to move mechanically, making no effort to catch up with his grandfather but merely following at about twenty paces. They walked on for five blocks in this way. Mr. Head's shoulders were sagging, and his neck hung forward at such an angle that it was not visible from behind. He was afraid to turn his head. Finally he cut a short hopeful glance over his shoulder. Twenty feet behind him, he saw two small eyes piercing into his back like pitchfork prongs.

The boy was not of a forgiving nature, but this was the first time he had ever had anything to forgive. Mr. Head had never disgraced himself before. After two more blocks, he turned and called over his shoulder in a high, desperately gay voice, "Let's us go get us a Co' Cola somewheres!"

Nelson, with a dignity he had never shown before, turned and stood with his back to his grandfather.

Mr. Head began to feel the depth of his denial. His face as they walked on became all hollows and bare ridges. He saw nothing they were passing but he perceived that they had lost the car tracks. There was no dome to be seen anywhere, and the afternoon was advancing. He knew that if dark overtook them in the city, they would be beaten and robbed. The speed of God's justice was only what he expected for himself, but he could not stand to think that his sins would be visited upon Nelson, and that even now he was leading the boy to his doom.

They continued to walk on block after block through an endless section of small brick houses until Mr. Head almost fell over a water spigot sticking up about six inches off the edge of a grass plot. He had not had a drink of water since early morning but he felt he did not deserve it now. Then he thought that Nelson would be thirsty and they would both drink and be brought together. He squatted down and put his mouth to the nozzle and turned a cold stream of water into his throat. Then he called out in the high desperate voice, "Come on and getcher some water!"

This time the child stared through him for nearly sixty seconds. Mr. Head got up and walked on as if he had drunk poison. Nelson, though he had not had water since some he had drunk out of a paper cup on the train, passed by the spigot, disdaining to drink where his grandfather had. When Mr. Head realized this, he lost all hope. His face in the waning afternoon light looked ravaged and abandoned. He could feel the boy's steady hate, traveling at an even pace behind him and he knew that (if by some miracle they escaped being murdered in the city) it would continue just that way for the rest of his life. He knew that now he was wandering into a black strange place where nothing was like it had ever been before, a long old age without respect and an end that would be welcome because it would be the end.

As for Nelson, his mind had frozen around his grandfather's treach-

THE ARTIFICIAL NIGGER

ery as if he were trying to preserve it intact to present at the final judgment. He walked without looking to one side or the other, but every now and then his mouth would twitch and this was when he felt, from some remote place inside himself, a black mysterious form reach up as if it would melt his frozen vision in one hot grasp.

The sun dropped down behind a row of houses and, hardly noticing, they passed into an elegant suburban section where mansions were set back from the road by lawns with birdbaths on them. Here everything was entirely deserted. For blocks they didn't pass even a dog. The big white houses were like partially submerged icebergs in the distance. There were no sidewalks, only drives, and these wound around and around in endless ridiculous circles. Nelson made no move to come nearer to Mr. Head. The old man felt that if he saw a sewer entrance he would drop down into it and let himself be carried away; and he could imagine the boy standing by, watching with only a slight interest, while he disappeared.

A loud bark jarred him to attention, and he looked up to see a fat man approaching with two bulldogs. He waved both arms like someone shipwrecked on a desert island, "I'm lost" he called. "I'm lost and can't find my way and me and this boy have got to catch this train and I can't find the station. Oh Gawd, I'm lost! Oh hep me Gawd, I'm lost!"

The man, who was bald-headed and had on golf knickers, asked him what train he was trying to catch, and Mr. Head began to get out his tickets, trembling so violently he could hardly hold them. Nelson had come up to within fifteen feet and stood watching.

"Well," the fat man said, giving him back the tickets, "you won't have time to get back to town to make this train but you can catch it at the suburb stop. That's three blocks from here," and he began explaining how to get there.

Mr. Head stared as if he were slowly returning from the dead, and when the man had finished and gone off with the dogs jumping at his heels, he turned to Nelson and said breathlessly, "We're going to get home!"

The child was standing about ten feet away, his face bloodless under the grey hat. His eyes were triumphantly cold. There was no light in them, no feeling, no interest. He was merely there, a small figure, waiting. Home was nothing to him.

Mr. Head turned slowly. He felt he knew now what time would be like without seasons and what heat would be like without light and what man would be like without salvation. He didn't care if he never made the train and if it had not been for what suddenly caught his attention, like a cry out of the gathering dusk, he might have forgotten there was a station to go to.

He had not walked five hundred yards down the road when he saw, within reach of him, the plaster figure of a Negro sitting bent over on a low yellow brick fence that curved around a wide lawn. The Negro was about Nelson's size and he was pitched forward at an unsteady angle because the putty that held him to the wall had cracked. One of his eyes was entirely white, and he held a piece of brown watermelon.

Mr. Head stood looking at him silently until Nelson stopped at a little distance. Then as the two of them stood there, Mr. Head breathed, "An artificial nigger!"

It was not possible to tell if the artificial Negro were meant to be young or old; he looked too miserable to be either. He was meant to look happy, because his mouth was stretched up at the corners, but the chipped eye and the angle he was cocked at gave him a wild look of misery instead.

"An artificial nigger!" Nelson repeated in Mr. Head's exact tone.

The two of them stood there with their necks forward at almost the same angle and their shoulders curved in almost exactly the same way and their hands trembling identically in their pockets. Mr. Head looked like an ancient child and Nelson like a miniature old man. They stood gazing at the artificial Negro as if they were faced with some great mystery, some monument to another's victory that brought them together in their common defeat. They could both feel it dissolving their differences like an action of mercy. Mr. Head had never known before what mercy felt like because he had been too good to deserve any, but he felt he knew now. He looked at Nelson and understood that he must say something to the child to show that he was still wise, and in the look the boy returned he saw a hungry need for that assurance. Nelson's eyes seemed to implore him to explain once and for all the mystery of existence.

Mr. Head opened his lips to make a lofty statement and heard himself say, "They ain't got enough real ones here. They got to have an artificial one."

After a second, the boy nodded with a strange shivering about his mouth, and said, "Let's go home before we get ourselves lost again."

Their train glided into the suburb stop just as they reached the station and they boarded it together, and ten minutes before it was due to arrive at the junction, they went to the door and stood ready to jump off if it did not stop; but it did, just as the moon, restored to its full splendor, sprang from a cloud and flooded the clearing with light. As they stepped off, the sage grass was shivering gently in shades of silver, and the clinkers under their feet glittered with a fresh black light. The treetops, fencing the junction like the protecting walls of a garden, were darker than the sky which was hung with gigantic white clouds illuminated like lanterns.

Mr. Head stood very still and felt the action of mercy touch him again, but this time he knew that there were no words in the world that could name it. He understood that it grew out of agony, which is not denied to any man and which is given in strange ways to children. He understood it was all a man could carry into death to give his Maker, and he suddenly burned with shame that he had so little of it to take with him. He stood appalled, judging himself with the thoroughness of God, while the action of mercy covered his pride like a flame and consumed it. He had never thought himself a great sinner before but he saw now that his true depravity had been hidden from him lest it cause him despair. He realized that he was forgiven for sins from the beginning of time, when he had conceived in his own heart the sin of Adam, until the present, when he had denied poor Nelson. He saw that no sin was too monstrous for him to claim as his own, and since God loved in proportion as He forgave, he felt ready at that instant to enter Paradise.

Nelson, composing his expression under the shadow of his hat brim, watched him with a mixture of fatigue and suspicion, and as the train glided past them and disappeared like a frightened serpent into the woods, he muttered, "I'm glad I've went once, but I'll never go back again!"

COUNTERPARTS

James Joyce

The bell rang furiously and, when Miss Parker went to the tube, a furious voice called out in a piercing North of Ireland accent:

"Send Farrington here!"

Miss Parker returned to her machine, saying to a man who was writing at a desk:

"Mr. Alleyne wants you upstairs."

The man muttered "*Blast* him!" under his breath and pushed back his chair to stand up. When he stood up he was tall and of great bulk. He had a hanging face, dark wine-coloured, with fair eyebrows and moustache: his eyes bulged forward slightly and the whites of them were dirty. He lifted up the counter and, passing by the clients, went out of the office with a heavy step.

He went heavily upstairs until he came to the second landing, where a door bore a brass plate with the inscription *Mr. Alleyne*. Here he halted, puffing with labour and vexation, and knocked. The shrill voice cried:

"Come in!"

The man entered Mr. Alleyne's room. Simultaneously Mr. Alleyne, a little man wearing gold-rimmed glasses on a clean-shaven face, shot his head up over a pile of documents. The head itself was so pink and hairless it seemed like a large egg reposing on the papers. Mr. Alleyne did not lose a moment:

"Farrington? What is the meaning of this? Why have I always to complain of you? May I ask you why you haven't made a copy of that contract between Bodley and Kirwan? I told you it must be ready by four o'clock."

"But Mr. Shelley said, sir——"

"*Mr. Shelley said, sir.* . . . Kindly attend to what I say and not to what *Mr. Shelley says, sir.* You have always some excuse or another for shirking work. Let me tell you that if the contract is not copied before this evening I'll lay the matter before Mr. Crosbie. . . . Do you hear me now?"

"Yes, sir."

"Do you hear me now? . . . Ay and another little matter! I might as well be talking to the wall as talking to you. Understand once for all that you get a half an hour for your lunch and not an hour and a half. How many courses do you want, I'd like to know. . . . Do you mind me now?"

"Yes, sir."

Mr. Alleyne bent his head again upon his pile of papers. The man stared fixedly at the polished skull which directed the affairs of Crosbie & Alleyne, gauging its fragility. A spasm of rage gripped his throat for a few moments and then passed, leaving after it a sharp sensation of thirst. The man recognised the sensation and felt that he must have a good night's drinking. The middle of the month was passed and, if he could get the copy done in time, Mr. Alleyne might give him an order on the cashier. He stood still, gazing fixedly at the head upon the pile of papers. Suddenly Mr. Alleyne began to upset all the papers, searching for something. Then, as if he had been unaware of the man's presence till that moment, he shot up his head again, saying:

"Eh? Are you going to stand there all day? Upon my word, Farrington, you take things easy!"

"I was wating to see . . ."

"Very good, you needn't wait to see. Go downstairs and do your work."

The man walked heavily towards the door and, as he went out of the room, he heard Mr. Alleyne cry after him that if the contract was not copied by evening Mr. Crosbie would hear of the matter.

He returned to his desk in the lower office and counted the sheets which remained to be copied. He took up his pen and dipped it in the ink but he continued to stare stupidly at the last words he had written: *In no case shall the said Bernard Bodley be* . . . The evening was falling and in a few minutes they would be lighting the gas: then he could write. He felt that he must slake the thirst in his throat. He stood up from his

COUNTERPARTS

desk and, lifting the counter as before, passed out of the office. As he was passing out the chief clerk looked at him inquiringly.

"It's all right, Mr. Shelley," said the man, pointing with his finger to indicate the objective of his journey.

The chief clerk glanced at the hat-rack, but, seeing the row complete, offered no remark. As soon as he was on the landing the man pulled a shepherd's plaid cap out of his pocket, put it on his head and ran quickly down the rickety stairs. From the street door he walked on furtively on the inner side of the path towards the corner and all at once dived into a doorway. He was now safe in the dark snug of O'Neill's shop, and filling up the little window that looked into the bar with his inflamed face, the colour of dark wine or dark meat, he called out:

"Here, Pat, give us a g.p., like a good fellow."

The curate brought him a glass of plain porter. The man drank it at a gulp and asked for a caraway seed. He put his penny on the counter and, leaving the curate to grope for it in the gloom, retreated out of the snug as furtively as he had entered it.

Darkness, accompanied by a thick fog, was gaining upon the dusk of February and the lamps in Eustace Street had been lit. The man went up by the houses until he reached the door of the office, wondering whether he could finish his copy in time. On the stairs a moist pungent odour of perfumes saluted his nose: evidently Miss Delacour had come while he was out in O'Neill's. He crammed his cap back again into his pocket and re-entered the office, assuming an air of absentmindedness.

"Mr. Alleyne has been calling for you," said the chief clerk severely. "Where were you?"

The man glanced at the two clients who were standing at the counter as if to intimate that their presence prevented him from answering. As the clients were both male the chief clerk allowed himself a laugh.

"I know that game," he said. "Five times in one day is a little bit . . . Well, you better look sharp and get a copy of our correspondence in the Delacour case for Mr. Alleyne."

This address in the presence of the public, his run upstairs and the porter he had gulped down so hastily confused the man and, as he sat down at his desk to get what was required, he realised how hopeless was the task of finishing his copy of the contract before half past five. The dark damp night was coming and he longed to spend it in the bars, drinking with his friends amid the glare of gas and the clatter of glasses. He got out the Delacour correspondence and passed out of the office. He hoped Mr. Alleyne would not discover that the last two letters were missing.

The moist pungent perfume lay all the way up to Mr. Alleyne's room.

ARCHETYPES AND STEREOTYPES

Miss Delacour was a middle-aged woman of Jewish appearance. Mr. Alleyne was said to be sweet on her or on her money. She came to the office often and stayed a long time when she came. She was sitting beside his desk now in an aroma of perfumes, smoothing the handle of her umbrella and nodding the great black feather in her hat. Mr. Alleyne had swivelled his chair round to face her and thrown his right foot jauntily upon his left knee. The man put the correspondence on the desk and bowed respectfully but neither Mr. Alleyne nor Miss Delacour took any notice of his bow. Mr. Alleyne tapped a finger on the correspondence and then flicked it towards him as if to say: *"That's all right: you can go."*

The man returned to the lower office and sat down again at his desk. He stared intently at the incomplete phrase: *In no case shall the said Bernard Bodley be* . . . and thought how strange it was that the last three words began with the same letter. The chief clerk began to hurry Miss Parker, saying she would never have the letters typed in time for post. The man listened to the clicking of the machine for a few minutes and then set to work to finish his copy. But his head was not clear and his mind wandered away to the glare and rattle of the public-house. It was a night for hot punches. He struggled on with his copy, but when the clock struck five he had still fourteen pages to write. Blast it! He couldn't finish it in time. He longed to execrate aloud, to bring his fist down on something violently. He was so enraged that he wrote *Bernard Bernard* instead of *Bernard Bodley* and had to begin again on a clean sheet.

He felt strong enough to clear out the whole office single-handed. His body ached to do something, to rush out and revel in violence. All the indignities of his life enraged him. . . . Could he ask the cashier privately for an advance? No, the cashier was no good, no damn good: he wouldn't give an advance. . . . He knew where he would meet the boys: Leonard and O'Halloran and Nosey Flynn. The barometer of his emotional nature was set for a spell of riot.

His imagination had so abstracted him that his name was called twice before he answered. Mr. Alleyne and Miss Delacour were standing outside the counter and all the clerks had turned round in anticipation of something. The man got up from his desk. Mr. Alleyne began a tirade of abuse, saying that two letters were missing. The man answered that he knew nothing about them, that he had made a faithful copy. The tirade continued: it was so bitter and violent that the man could hardly restrain his fist from descending upon the head of the manikin before him:

"I know nothing about any other two letters," he said stupidly.

"*You—know—nothing.* Of course you know nothing," said Mr. Alleyne. "Tell me," he added, glancing first for approval to the lady beside him, "do you take me for a fool? Do you think me an utter fool?"

COUNTERPARTS

The man glanced from the lady's face to the little egg-shaped head and back again; and, almost before he was aware of it, his tongue had found a felicitous moment:

"I don't think, sir," he said, "that that's a fair question to put to me."

There was a pause in the very breathing of the clerks. Everyone was astounded (the author of the witticism no less than his neighbours) and Miss Delacour, who was a stout amiable person, began to smile broadly. Mr. Alleyne flushed to the hue of a wild rose and his mouth twitched with a dwarf's passion. He shook his fist in the man's face till it seemed to vibrate like the knob of some electric machine:

"You impertinent ruffian! You impertinent ruffian! I'll make short work of you! Wait till you see! You'll apologise to me for your impertinence or you'll quit the office instanter! You'll quit this, I'm telling you, or you'll apologise to me!"

He stood in a doorway opposite the office watching to see if the cashier would come out alone. All the clerks passed out and finally the cashier came out with the chief clerk. It was no use trying to say a word to him when he was with the chief clerk. The man felt that his position was bad enough. He had been obliged to offer an abject apology to Mr. Alleyne for his impertinence but he knew what a hornet's nest the office would be for him. He could remember the way in which Mr. Alleyne had hounded little Peake out of the office in order to make room for his own nephew. He felt savage and thirsty and revengeful, annoyed with himself and with everyone else. Mr. Alleyne would never give him an hour's rest; his life would be a hell to him. He had made a proper fool of himself this time. Could he not keep his tongue in his cheek? But they had never pulled together from the first, he and Mr. Alleyne, ever since the day Mr. Alleyne had overheard him mimicking his North of Ireland accent to amuse Higgins and Miss Parker: that had been the beginning of it. He might have tried Higgins for the money, but sure Higgins never had anything for himself. A man with two establishments to keep up, of course he couldn't.

. . .

He felt his great body again aching for the comfort of the public-house. The fog had begun to chill him and he wondered could he touch Pat in O'Neill's. He could not touch him for more than a bob—and a bob was no use. Yet he must get money somewhere or other: he had spent his last penny for the g.p. and soon it would be too late for getting money anywhere. Suddenly, as he was fingering his watch-chain, he thought of Terry Kelly's pawn-office in Fleet Street. That was the dart! Why didn't he think of it sooner?

He went through the narrow alley of Temple Bar quickly, muttering to himself that they could all go to hell because he was going to have a good night of it. The clerk in Terry Kelly's said *A crown!* but the consignor held out for six shillings; and in the end the six shillings was allowed him literally. He came out of the pawn-office joyfully, making a little cylinder of the coins between his thumb and fingers. In Westmoreland Street the footpaths were crowded with young men and women returning from business and ragged urchins ran here and there yelling out the names of the evening editions. The man passed through the crowd, looking on the spectacle generally with proud satisfaction and staring masterfully at the office-girls. His head was full of the noises of tram-gongs and swishing trolleys and his nose already sniffed the curling fumes of punch. As he walked on he preconsidered the terms in which he would narrate the incident to the boys:

"So, I just looked back at him—coolly, you know, and looked at her. Then I looked back at him again—taking my time, you know. 'I don't think that that's a fair question to put to me,' says I."

Nosey Flynn was sitting up in his usual corner of Davy Byrne's and, when he heard the story, he stood Farrington a half-one, saying it was as smart a thing as ever he heard. Farrington stood a drink in his turn. After a while O'Halloran and Paddy Leonard came in and the story was repeated to them. O'Halloran stood tailors of malt, hot, all round and told the story of the retort he had made to the chief clerk when he was in Callan's of Fownes's Street; but, as the retort was after the manner of the liberal shepherds in the eclogues, he had to admit that it was not as clever as Farrington's retort. At this Farrington told the boys to polish off that and have another.

Just as they were naming their poisons who should come in but Higgins! Of course he had to join in with the others. The men asked him to give his version of it, and he did so with great vivacity for the sight of five small hot whiskies was very exhilarating. Everyone roared laughing when he showed the way in which Mr. Alleyne shook his fist in Farrington's face. Then he imitated Farrington, saying, *"And here was my nabs, as cool as you please,"* while Farrington looked at the company out of his heavy dirty eyes, smiling and at times drawing forth stray drops of liquor from his moustache with the aid of his lower lip.

When that round was over there was a pause. O'Halloran had money but neither of the other two seemed to have any; so the whole party left the shop somewhat regretfully. At the corner of Duke Street Higgins and Nosey Flynn bevelled off to the left while the other three turned back towards the city. Rain was drizzling down on the cold streets and, when they reached the Ballast Office, Farrington suggested the Scotch House. The bar was full of men and loud with the noise of tongues and glasses.

COUNTERPARTS

The three men pushed past the whining matchsellers at the door and formed a little party at the corner of the counter. They began to exchange stories. Leonard introduced them to a young fellow named Weathers who was performing at the Tivoli as an acrobat and knockabout *artiste*. Farrington stood a drink all round. Weathers said he would take a small Irish and Apollinaris. Farrington, who had definite notions of what was what, asked the boys would they have an Apollinaris too; but the boys told Tim to make theirs hot. The talk became theatrical. O'Halloran stood a round and then Farrington stood another round, Weathers protesting that the hospitality was too Irish. He promised to get them in behind the scenes and introduce them to some nice girls. O'Halloran said that he and Leonard would go, but that Farrington wouldn't go because he was a married man; and Farrington's heavy dirty eyes leered at the company in token that he understood he was being chaffed. Weathers made them all have just one little tincture at his expense and promised to meet them later on at Mulligan's in Poolbeg Street.

When the Scotch House closed they went round to Mulligan's. They went into the parlour at the back and O'Halloran ordered small hot specials all round. They were all beginning to feel mellow. Farrington was just standing another round when Weathers came back. Much to Farrington's relief he drank a glass of bitter this time. Funds were getting low but they had enough to keep them going. Presently two young women with big hats and a young man in a check suit came in and sat at a table close by. Weathers saluted them and told the company that they were out of the Tivoli. Farrington's eyes wandered at every moment in the direction of one of the young women. There was something striking in her appearance. An immense scarf of peacock-blue muslin was wound round her hat and knotted in a great bow under her chin; and she wore bright yellow gloves, reaching to the elbow. Farrington gazed admiringly at the plump arm which she moved very often and with much grace; and when, after a little time, she answered his gaze he admired still more her large dark brown eyes. The oblique staring expression in them fascinated him. She glanced at him once or twice and, when the party was leaving the room, she brushed against his chair and said *"O, pardon!"* in a London accent. He watched her leave the room in the hope that she would look back at him, but he was disappointed. He cursed his want of money and cursed all the rounds he had stood, particularly all the whiskies and Apollinaris which he had stood to Weathers. If there was one thing that he hated it was a sponge. He was so angry that he lost count of the conversation of his friends.

When Paddy Leonard called him he found that they were talking about feats of strength. Weathers was showing his biceps muscle to the company and boasting so much that the other two had called on Farrington to uphold the national honour. Farrington pulled up his sleeve accordingly and showed his biceps muscle to the company. The two arms were examined and compared and finally it was agreed to have a trial of strength. The table was cleared and the two men rested their elbows on it, clasping hands. When Paddy Leonard said *"Go!"* each was to try to bring down the other's hand on to the table. Farrington looked very serious and determined.

The trial began. After about thirty seconds Weathers brought his opponent's hand slowly down on to the table. Farrington's dark wine-coloured face flushed darker still with anger and humiliation at having been defeated by such a stripling.

"You're not to put the weight of your body behind it. Play fair," he said.

"Who's not playing fair?" said the other.

"Come on again. The two best out of three."

The trial began again. The veins stood out on Farrington's forehead, and the pallor of Weathers' complexion changed to peony. Their hands and arms trembled under the stress. After a long struggle Weathers again brought his opponent's hand slowly on to the table. There was a murmur of applause from the spectators. The curate, who was standing beside the table, nodded his red head towards the victor and said with stupid familiarity:

"Ah! that's the knack!"

"What the hell do you know about it?" said Farrington fiercely, turning on the man. "What do you put in your gab for?"

"Sh, sh!" said O'Halloran, observing the violent expression of Farrington's face. "Pony up, boys. We'll have just one little smahan more and then we'll be off."

A very sullen-faced man stood at the corner of O'Connell Bridge waiting for the little Sandymount tram to take him home. He was full of smouldering anger and revengefulness. He felt humiliated and discontented; he did not even feel drunk; and he had only twopence in his pocket. He cursed everything. He had done for himself in the office, pawned his watch, spent all his money; and he had not even got drunk. He began to feel thirsty again and he longed to be back again in the hot reeking public-house. He had lost his reputation as a strong man, having been defeated twice by a mere boy. His heart swelled with fury and, when he thought of the woman in the big hat who had brushed against him and said *Pardon!* his fury nearly choked him.

His tram let him down at Shelbourne Road and he steered his great body along in the shadow of the wall of the barracks. He loathed returning to his home. When he went in by the side-door he found the kitchen empty and the kitchen fire nearly out. He bawled upstairs:

"Ada! Ada!"

His wife was a little sharp-faced woman who bullied her husband when he was sober and was bullied by him when he was drunk. They had five children. A little boy came running down the stairs.

"Who is that?" said the man, peering through the darkness.

"Me, pa."

"Who are you? Charlie?"

"No, pa. Tom."

"Where's your mother?"

"She's out at the chapel."

"That's right. . . . Did she think of leaving any dinner for me?"

"Yes, pa. I——"

"Light the lamp. What do you mean by having the place in darkness? Are the other children in bed?"

The man sat down heavily on one of the chairs while the little boy lit the lamp. He began to mimic his son's flat accent, saying half to himself: *"At the chapel. At the chapel, if you please!"* When the lamp was lit he banged his fist on the table and shouted:

"What's for my dinner?"

"I'm going . . . to cook it, pa," said the little boy.

The man jumped up furiously and pointed to the fire.

"On that fire! You let the fire out! By God, I'll teach you to do that again!"

He took a step to the door and seized the walking-stick which was standing behind it.

"I'll teach you to let the fire out!" he said, rolling up his sleeve in order to give his arm free play.

The little boy cried *"O, pa!"* and ran whimpering round the table, but the man followed him and caught him by the coat. The little boy looked about him wildly but, seeing no way of escape, fell upon his knees.

"Now, you'll let the fire out the next time!" said the man, striking at him vigorously with the stick. "Take that, you little whelp!"

The boy uttered a squeal of pain as the stick cut his thigh. He clasped his hands together in the air and his voice shook with fright.

"O, pa!" he cried. "Don't beat me, pa! And I'll . . . I'll say a *Hail Mary* for you. . . . I'll say a *Hail Mary* for you, pa, if you don't beat me. . . . I'll say a *Hail Mary*. . . ."

IX | Irony–Epiphany

Irony is what most of our lives are about. In the fictional treatment of irony, myth spirals down from invulnerable heroes and grandly inescapable fate, forcing the reality that besets us all. The wiser we grow, the less we see ourselves as larger than life. That is an irony upon which many writers inform us.

Symmetry, the perfect resolution of enormous problems, is the very stuff of myth, predictable, reliable. On the other hand, real life displays asymmetry—that is our order, our geometry. A function of the art of fiction is the struggle for synthesis between the symmetry of myth and the asymmetry of real life. And the tone of that synthesis is irony.

A great deal of literature is rich in the kind of irony in which we are involved very distinctly in the sadness or disappointment of hope or expectation. We understand the fateful implications of irony as the characters do not, as in Mansfield's "Bliss."

We are involved with characters of fiction in their moment of awareness, an insight into life, or perhaps even an overwhelming change in it. Such a moment Joyce called "epiphany." We share this discovery, can in fact see it coming sometimes before the character does, in a series of ironic events such as befall Lally in A. E. Coppard's story, "Fifty Pounds," and old Mr. Watford in Paule Marshall's "Barbados." What differs in these two stories is the tone of the irony. Lally's epiphany is accompanied by her rueful resignation to it; the old man's flashes upon him like lightning, accompanied by shattering physical pain and remorse.

In another way, Hawthorne's ambitious guest has intimations that he may not achieve his wished-for destiny. He cannot foretell, as the clues of the story might lead us to suspect, that the immediate future, with terrible quick force, will deprive him of possibility. That, of course, is the final irony.

IRONY—EPIPHANY

BLISS

Katherine Mansfield

Although Bertha Young was thirty she still had moments like this when she wanted to run instead of walk, to take dancing steps on and off the pavement, to bowl a hoop, to throw something up in the air and catch it again, or to stand still and laugh at—nothing—at nothing, simply.

What can you do if you are thirty and, turning the corner of your own street, you are overcome, suddenly, by a feeling of bliss—absolute bliss!—as though you'd suddenly swallowed a bright piece of that late afternoon sun and it burned in your bosom, sending out a little shower of sparks into every particle, into every finger and toe? . . .

Oh, is there no way you can express it without being "drunk and disorderly"? How idiotic civilization is! Why be given a body if you have to keep it shut up in a case like a rare, rare fiddle?

"No, that about the fiddle is not quite what I mean," she thought, running up the steps and feeling in her bag for the key—she'd forgotten it, as usual—and rattling the letter-box. "It's not what I mean, because—Thank you, Mary"—she went into the hall. "Is nurse back?"

"Yes, M'm."

"And has the fruit come?"

"Yes, M'm. Everything's come."

"Bring the fruit up to the dining-room, will you? I'll arrange it before I go upstairs."

It was dusky in the dining-room and quite chilly. But all the same Bertha threw off her coat; she could not bear the tight clasp of it another moment, and the cold air fell on her arms.

But in her bosom there was still that bright glowing place—that shower of little sparks coming from it. It was almost unbearable. She hardly dared to breathe for fear of fanning it higher, and yet she breathed deeply, deeply. She hardly dared to look into the cold mirror—but she did look, and it gave her back a woman, radiant, with smiling, trembling lips, with big, dark eyes and an air of listening, waiting for something . . . divine to happen . . . that she knew must happen . . . infallibly.

Mary brought in the fruit on a tray and with it a glass bowl, and a blue dish, very lovely, with a strange sheen on it as though it had been dipped in milk.

"Shall I turn on the light, M'm?"

"No, thank you. I can see quite well."

There were tangerines and apples stained with strawberry pink. Some yellow pears, smooth as silk, some white grapes covered with a silver bloom and a big cluster of purple ones. These last she had bought to tone in with the new dining-room carpet. Yes, that did sound rather far-fetched and absurd, but it was really why she had bought them. She had thought in the shop: "I must have some purple ones to bring the carpet up to the table." And it had seemed quite sense at the time.

When she had finished with them and had made two pyramids of these bright round shapes, she stood away from the table to get the effect—and it really was most curious. For the dark table seemed to melt into the dusky light and the glass dish and the blue bowl to float in the air. This, of course in her present mood, was so incredibly beautiful. . . . She began to laugh.

"No, no. I'm getting hysterical." And she seized her bag and coat and ran upstairs to the nursery.

Nurse sat at a low table giving Little B her supper after her bath. The baby had on a white flannel gown and a blue woollen jacket, and her dark, fine hair was brushed up into a funny little peak. She looked up when she saw her mother and began to jump.

"Now, my lovey, eat it up like a good girl," said Nurse, setting her lips in a way that Bertha knew, and that meant she had come into the nursery at another wrong moment.

"Has she been good, Nanny?"

"She's been a little sweet all the afternoon," whispered Nanny. "We went to the park and I sat down on a chair and took her out of the pram and a big dog came along and put its head on my knee and she clutched its ear, tugged it. Oh, you should have seen her."

Bertha wanted to ask if it wasn't rather dangerous to let her clutch at a strange dog's ear. But she did not dare to. She stood watching them, her hands by her side, like the poor little girl in front of the rich little girl with the doll.

The baby looked up at her again, stared, and then smiled so charmingly that Bertha couldn't help crying:

"Oh, Nanny, do let me finish giving her her supper while you put the bath things away."

"Well, M'm, she oughtn't to be changed hands while she's eating," said Nanny, still whispering. "It unsettles her; it's very likely to upset her."

How absurd it was. Why have a baby if it has to be kept—not in a case like a rare, rare fiddle—but in another woman's arms?

"Oh, I must!" said she.

Very offended, Nanny handed her over.

"Now, don't excite her after her supper. You know you do, M'm. And I have such a time with her after!"

IRONY—EPIPHANY

Thank heaven! Nanny went out of the room with the bath towels.

"Now I've got you to myself, my little precious," said Bertha, as the baby leaned against her.

She ate delightfully, holding up her lips for the spoon and then waving her hands. Sometimes she wouldn't let the spoon go; and sometimes, just as Bertha had filled it, she waved it away to the four winds.

When the soup was finished Bertha turned round to the fire.

"You're nice—you're very nice!" said she, kissing her warm baby. "I'm fond of you. I like you."

And, indeed, she loved Little B so much—her neck as she bent forward, her exquisite toes as they shone transparent in the firelight—that all her feeling of bliss came back again, and again she didn't know how to express it—what to do with it.

"You're wanted on the telephone," said Nanny, coming back in triumph and seizing *her* Little B.

Down she flew. It was Harry.

"Oh, is that you, Ber? Look here. I'll be late. I'll take a taxi and come along as quickly as I can, but get dinner put back ten minutes—will you? All right?"

"Yes, perfectly. Oh, Harry!"

"Yes?"

What had she to say? She'd nothing to say. She only wanted to get in touch with him for a moment. She couldn't absurdly cry: "Hasn't it been a divine day!"

"What is it?" rapped out the little voice.

"Nothing. *Entendu*," said Bertha, and hung up the receiver, thinking how more than idiotic civilization was.

They had people coming to dinner. The Norman Knights—a very sound couple—he was about to start a theatre, and she was awfully keen on interior decoration, a young man, Eddie Warren, who had just published a little book of poems and whom everybody was asking to dine, and a "find" of Bertha's called Pearl Fulton. What Miss Fulton did, Bertha didn't know. They had met at the club and Bertha had fallen in love with her, as she always did fall in love with beautiful women who had something strange about them.

The provoking thing was that, though they had been about together and met a number of times and really talked, Bertha couldn't yet make her out. Up to a certain point Miss Fulton was rarely, wonderfully frank, but the certain point was there, and beyond that she would not go.

Was there anything beyond it? Harry said "No." Voted her dullish, and "cold like all blond women, with a touch, perhaps, of anæmia of the brain." But Bertha wouldn't agree with him; not yet, at any rate.

"No, the way she has of sitting with her head a little on one side, and smiling, has something behind it, Harry, and I must find out what that something is."

"Most likely it's a good stomach," answered Harry.

He made a point of catching Bertha's heels with replies of that kind . . . "liver frozen, my dear girl," or "pure flatulence," or "kidney disease," . . . and so on. For some strange reason Bertha liked this, and almost admired it in him very much.

She went into the drawing-room and lighted the fire; then, picking up the cushions, one by one, that Mary had disposed so carefully, she threw them back on to the chairs and the couches. That made all the difference; the room came alive at once. As she was about to throw the last one she surprised herself by suddenly hugging it to her, passionately, passionately. But it did not put out the fire in her bosom. Oh, on the contrary!

The windows of the drawing-room opened on to a balcony overlooking the garden. At the far end, against the wall, there was a tall, slender pear tree in fullest, richest bloom; it stood perfect, as though becalmed against the jade-green sky. Bertha couldn't help feeling, even from this distance, that it had not a single bud or a faded petal. Down below, in the garden beds, the red and yellow tulips, heavy with flowers, seemed to lean upon the dusk. A grey cat, dragging its belly, crept across the lawn, and a black one, its shadow, trailed after. The sight of them, so intent and so quick, gave Bertha a curious shiver.

"What creepy things cats are!" she stammered, and she turned away from the window and began walking up and down. . . .

How strong the jonquils smelled in the warm room. Too strong? Oh, no. And yet, as though overcome, she flung down on a couch and pressed her hands to her eyes.

"I'm too happy—too happy!" she murmured.

And she seemed to see on her eyelids the lovely pear tree with its wide open blossoms as a symbol of her own life.

Really—really—she had everything. She was young. Harry and she were as much in love as ever, and they got on together splendidly and were really good pals. She had an adorable baby. They didn't have to worry about money. They had this absolutely satisfactory house and garden. And friends—modern, thrilling friends, writers and painters and poets or people keen on social questions—just the kind of friends they wanted. And then there were books, and there was music, and she had found a wonderful little dressmaker, and they were going abroad in the summer, and their new cook made the most superb omelettes. . . .

IRONY—EPIPHANY

"I'm absurd. Absurd!" She sat up; but she felt quite dizzy, quite drunk. It must have been the spring.

Yes, it was the spring. Now she was so tired she could not drag herself upstairs to dress.

A white dress, a string of jade beads, green shoes and stockings. It wasn't intentional. She had thought of this scheme hours before she stood at the drawing-room window.

Her petals rustled softly into the hall, and she kissed Mrs. Norman Knight, who was taking off the most amusing orange coat with a procession of black monkeys round the hem and up the fronts.

". . . Why! Why! Why is the middle-class so stodgy—so utterly without a sense of humour! My dear, it's only by a fluke that I am here at all—Norman being the protective fluke. For my darling monkeys so upset the train that it rose to a man and simply ate me with its eyes. Didn't laugh—wasn't amused—that I should have loved. No, just stared—and bored me through and through."

"But the cream of it was," said Norman, pressing a large tortoiseshell-rimmed monocle into his eye, "you don't mind me telling this, Face, do you?" (In their home and among their friends they called each other Face and Mug.) "The cream of it was when she, being full fed, turned to the woman beside her and said: 'Haven't you ever seen a monkey before?'"

"Oh, yes!" Mrs. Norman Knight joined in the laughter. "Wasn't that too absolutely creamy?"

And a funnier thing still was that now her coat was off she did look like a very intelligent monkey—who had even made that yellow silk dress out of scraped banana skins. And her amber ear-rings; they were like little dangling nuts.

"This is a sad, sad fall!" said Mug, pausing in front of Little B's perambulator. "When the perambuator comes into the hall—" and he waved the rest of the quotation away.

The bell rang. It was lean, pale Eddie Warren (as usual) in a state of acute distress.

"It *is* the right house, *isn't* it?" he pleaded.

"Oh, I think so—I hope so," said Bertha brightly.

"I have had such a *dreadful* experience with a taxi-man; he was *most* sinister. I couldn't get him to *stop*. The *more* I knocked and called the *faster* he went. And *in* the moonlight this *bizarre* figure with the *flattened* head *crouching* over the *lit-tle* wheel. . . ."

He shuddered, taking off an immense white silk scarf. Bertha noticed that his socks were white, too—most charming.

"But how dreadful!" she cried.

"Yes, it really was," said Eddie, following her into the drawing-room. "I saw myself *driving* through Eternity in a *timeless* taxi."

He knew the Norman Knights. In fact, he was going to write a play for N. K. when the theatre scheme came off.

"Well, Warren, how's the play?" said Norman Knight, dropping his monocle and giving his eye a moment in which to rise to the surface before it was screwed down again.

And Mrs. Norman Knight: "Oh, Mr. Warren, what happy socks!"

"I *am* so glad you like them," said he, staring at his feet. "They seem to have got so *much* whiter since the moon rose." And he turned his lean sorrowful young face to Bertha. "There *is* a moon, you know."

She wanted to cry: "I am sure there is—often—often!"

He really was a most attractive person. But so was Face, crouched before the fire in her banana skins, and so was Mug, smoking a cigarette and saying as he flicked the ash: "Why doth the bridegroom tarry?"

"There he is, now."

Bang went the front door open and shut. Harry shouted: "Hullo, you people. Down in five minutes." And they heard him swarm up the stairs. Bertha couldn't help smiling; she knew how he loved doing things at high pressure. What, after all, did an extra five minutes matter? But he would pretend to himself that they mattered beyond measure. And then he would make a great point of coming into the drawing-room, extravagantly cool and collected.

Harry had such a zest for life. Oh, how she appreciated it in him. And his passion for fighting—for seeking in everything that came up against him another test of his power and of his courage—that, too, she understood. Even when it made him just occasionally, to other people, who didn't know him well, a little ridiculous perhaps. . . . For there were moments when he rushed into battle where no battle was. . . . She talked and laughed and positively forgot until he had come in (just as she had imagined) that Pearl Fulton had not turned up.

"I wonder if Miss Fulton has forgotten?"

"I expect so," said Harry. "Is she on the 'phone?"

"Ah! There's a taxi, now." And Bertha smiled with that little air of proprietorship that she always assumed while her women finds were new and mysterious. "She lives in taxis."

"She'll run to fat if she does," said Harry coolly, ringing the bell for dinner. "Frightful danger for blond women."

"Harry—don't," warned Bertha, laughing up at him.

Came another tiny moment, while they waited, laughing and talking, just a trifle too much at their ease, a trifle too unaware. And then Miss Fulton, all in silver, with a silver fillet binding her pale blond hair, came in smiling, her head a little on one side.

"Am I late?"

"No, not at all," said Bertha. "Come along." And she took her arm and they moved into the dining-room.

What was there in the touch of that cool arm that could fan—fan—start blazing—blazing—the fire of bliss that Bertha did not know what to do with?

Miss Fulton did not look at her; but then she seldom did look at people directly. Her heavy eyelids lay upon her eyes and the strange half smile came and went upon her lips as though she lived by listening rather than seeing. But Bertha knew, suddenly, as if the longest, most intimate look had passed between them—as if they had said to each other: "You, too?"—that Pearl Fulton, stirring the beautiful red soup in the grey plate, was feeling just what she was feeling.

And the others? Face and Mug, Eddie and Harry, their spoons rising and falling—dabbing their lips with their napkins, crumbling bread, fiddling with the forks and glasses and talking.

"I met her at the Alpha show—the weirdest little person. She'd not only cut off her hair, but she seemed to have taken a dreadfully good snip off her legs and arms and her neck and her poor little nose as well."

"Isn't she very *liée* with Michael Oat?"

"The man who wrote *Love in False Teeth?*"

"He wants to write a play for me. One act. One man. Decides to commit suicide. Gives all the reasons why he should and why he shouldn't. And just as he has made up his mind either to do it or not to do it—curtain. Not half a bad idea."

"What's he going to call it—'Stomach Trouble'?"

"I *think* I've come across the *same* idea in a li-ttle French review, *quite* unknown in England."

No, they didn't share it. They were dears—dears—and she loved having them there, at her table, and giving them delicious food and wine. In fact, she longed to tell them how delightful they were, and what a decorative group they made, how they seemed to set one another off and how they reminded her of a play by Tchekof!

Harry was enjoying his dinner. It was part of his—well, not his nature, exactly, and certainly not his pose—his—something or other—to talk about food and to glory in his "shameless passion for the white flesh of the lobster" and "the green of pistachio ices—green and cold like the eyelids of Egyptian dancers."

When he looked up at her and said: "Bertha, this is a very admirable *soufflée!*" she almost could have wept with child-like pleasure.

Oh, why did she feel so tender towards the whole world tonight? Everything was good—was right. All that happened seemed to fill again her brimming cup of bliss.

And still, in the back of her mind, there was the pear tree. It would be silver, now, in the light of poor dear Eddie's moon, silver as Miss Fulton, who sat there turning a tangerine in her slender fingers that were so pale a light seemed to come from them.

What she simply couldn't make out—what was miraculous—was how she should have guessed Miss Fulton's mood so exactly and so instantly. For she never doubted for a moment that she was right, and yet what had she to go on? Less than nothing.

"I believe this does happen very, very rarely between women. Never between men," thought Bertha. "But while I am making the coffee in the drawing-room perhaps she will 'give a sign.'"

What she meant by that she did not know, and what would happen after that she could not imagine.

While she thought like this she saw herself talking and laughing. She had to talk because of her desire to laugh.

"I must laugh or die."

But when she noticed Face's funny little habit of tucking something down the front of her bodice—as if she kept a tiny, secret hoard of nuts there, too—Bertha had to dig her nails into her hands—so as not to laugh too much.

It was over at last. And: "Come and see my new coffee machine," said Bertha.

"We only have a new coffee machine once a fortnight," said Harry. Face took her arm this time; Miss Fulton bent her head and followed after.

The fire had died down in the drawing-room to a red, flickering "nest of baby phoenixes," said Face.

"Don't turn up the light for a moment. It is so lovely." And down she crouched by the fire again. She was always cold . . . "without her little red flannel jacket, of course," thought Bertha.

At that moment Miss Fulton "gave the sign."

"Have you a garden?" said the cool, sleepy voice.

This was so exquisite on her part that all Bertha could do was to obey. She crossed the room, pulled the curtains apart, and opened those long windows.

"There!" she breathed.

And the two women stood side by side looking at the slender, flowering tree. Although it was so still it seemed, like the flame of a candle, to stretch up, to point, to quiver in the bright air, to grow taller and taller as they gazed—almost to touch the rim of the round, silver moon.

How long did they stand there? Both, as it were, caught in that circle of unearthly light, understanding each other perfectly, creatures of another world, and wondering what they were to do in this one with all this blissful treasure that burned in their bosoms and dropped, in silver flowers, from their hair and hands?

For ever—for a moment? And did Miss Fulton murmur: "Yes. Just *that*." Or did Bertha dream it?

Then the light was snapped on and Face made the coffee and Harry said: "My dear Mrs. Knight, don't ask me about my baby. I never see her. I shan't feel the slightest interest in her until she has a lover," and Mug took his eye out of the conservatory for a moment and then put it under glass again and Eddie Warren drank his coffee and set down the cup with a face of anguish as though he had drunk and seen the spider.

"What I want to do is to give the young men a show. I believe London is simply teeming with first-chop, unwritten plays. What I want to say to 'em is: 'Here's the theatre. Fire ahead.' "

"You know, my dear, I am going to decorate a room for the Jacob Nathans. Oh, I am so tempted to do a fried-fish scheme, with the backs of the chairs shaped like frying pans and lovely chip potatoes embroidered all over the curtains."

"The trouble with our young writing men is that they are still too romantic. You can't put out to sea without being seasick and wanting a basin. Well, why won't they have the courage of those basins?"

"A *dreadful* poem about a *girl* who was *violated* by a beggar *without* a a nose in a lit-tle wood. ..."

Miss Fulton sank into the lowest, deepest chair and Harry handed round the cigarettes.

From the way he stood in front of her shaking the silver box and saying abruptly: "Egyptian? Turkish, Virginian? They're all mixed up," Bertha realized that she not only bored him; he really disliked her. And she decided from the way Miss Fulton said: "No, thank you, I won't smoke," that she felt it, too, and was hurt.

"Oh, Harry, don't dislike her. You are quite wrong about her. She's wonderful, wonderful. And, besides, how can you feel so differently about someone who means so much to me. I shall try to tell you when we are in bed to-night what has been happening. What she and I have shared."

At those last words something strange and almost terrifying darted into Bertha's mind. And this something blind and smiling whispered to her:

"Soon these people will go. The house will be quiet. The lights will be out. And you and he will be alone together in the dark room—the warm bed. . . ."

She jumped up from her chair and ran over to the piano.

"What a pity someone does not play!" she cried. "What a pity somebody does not play."

For the first time in her life Bertha Young desired her husband.

Oh, she'd loved him—she'd been in love with him, of course, in every other way, but just not in that way. And, equally, of course, she's understood that he was different. They'd discussed it so often. It had worried her dreadfully at first to find that she was so cold, but after a time it had not seemed to matter. They were so frank with each other—such good pals. That was the best of being modern.

But now—ardently! ardently! The word ached in her ardent body! Was this what that feeling of bliss had been leading up to? But then then—

"My dear," said Mrs. Norman Knight, "you know our shame. We are the victims of time and train. We live in Hampstead. It's been so nice."

"I'll come with you into the hall," said Bertha. "I loved having you. But you must not miss the last train. That's so awful, isn't it?"

"Have a whisky, Knight, before you go?" called Harry.

"No, thanks, old chap."

Bertha squeezed his hand for that as she shook it.

"Good night, good-bye," she cried from the top step, feeling that this self of hers was taking leave of them for ever.

When she got back into the drawing-room the others were on the move.

". . . Then you can come part of the way in my taxi."

"I shall be *so* thankful *not* to have to face *another* drive *alone* after my *dreadful* experience."

"You can get a taxi at the rank just at the end of the street. You won't have to walk more than a few yards."

"That's a comfort. I'll go and put on my coat."

Miss Fulton moved towards the hall and Bertha was following when Harry almost pushed past.

"Let me help you."

Bertha knew that he was repenting his rudeness—she let him go. What a boy he was in some ways—so impulsive—so—simple.

And Eddie and she were left by the fire.

"I *wonder* if you have seen Bilk's *new* poem called *Table d'Hôte*," said Eddie softly. "It's *so* wonderful. In the last Anthology. Have you got a copy? I'd *so* like to *show* it to you. It begins with an *incredibly* beautiful line: 'Why Must it Always be Tomato Soup?' "

"Yes," said Bertha. And she moved noiselessly to a table opposite the drawing-room door and Eddie glided noiselessly after her. She picked up the little book and gave it to him; they had not made a sound.

While he looked it up she turned her head towards the hall. And she saw ... Harry with Miss Fulton's coat in his arms and Miss Fulton with her back turned to him and her head bent. He tossed the coat away, put his hands on her shoulders and turned her violently to him. His lips said: "I adore you," and Miss Fulton laid her moonbeam fingers on his cheeks and smiled her sleepy smile. Harry's nostrils quivered; his lips curled back in a hideous grin while he whispered: "To-morrow," and with her eyelids Miss Fulton said: "Yes."

"Here it is," said Eddie. " 'Why Must it Always be Tomato Soup?' It's so *deeply* true, don't you feel? Tomato soup is so *dreadfully* eternal."

"If you prefer," said Harry's voice, very loud, from the hall, "I can phone you a cab to come to the door."

"Oh, no. It's not necessary," said Miss Fulton, and she came up to Bertha and gave her the slender fingers to hold.

"Good-bye. Thank you so much."

"Good-bye," said Bertha.

Miss Fulton held her hand a moment longer.

"Your lovely pear tree!" she murmured.

And then she was gone, with Eddie following, like the black cat following the grey cat.

"I'll shut up shop," said Harry, extravagantly cool and collected.

"Your lovely pear tree—pear tree—pear tree!"

Bertha simply ran over to the long windows.

"Oh, what is going to happen now?" she cried.

But the pear tree was as lovely as ever and as full of flower and as still.

FIFTY POUNDS

A. E. Coppard

After tea Phillip Repton and Eulalia Burnes discussed their gloomy circumstances. Repton was the precarious sort of London journalist, a dark deliberating man, lean and drooping, full of genteel unprosperity, who wrote articles about Single Tax, Diet and Reason, The Futility of this that and the other, or The Significance of the other that and this; all done with a bleak care and signed P. Stick Repton. Eulalia was brown-haired and hardy, undeliberating and intuitive; she had been milliner,

FIFTY POUNDS

clerk, domestic help, and something in a canteen; and P. Stick Repton had, as one commonly says, picked her up at a time when she was drifting about London without a penny in her purse, without even a purse, and he had not yet put her down.

"I can't understand! It's sickening, monstrous!" Lally was fumbling with a match before the penny gas fire, for when it was evening, in September, it always got chilly on a floor so high up. Their flat was a fourth-floor one and there was—oh, fifteen thousand stairs! Out of the window and beyond the chimney you could see the long glare from lights in High Holborn and hear the hums and hoots of buses. And that was a comfort.

"Lower! Turn it lower!" yelled Phillip. The gas had ignited with an astounding thump; the kneeling Lally had thrown up her hands and dropped the matchbox saying "Damn" in the same tone as one might say good morning to a milkman.

"You shouldn't do it, you know," grumbled Repton. "You'll blow us to the deuce." And that was just like Lally, that was Lally all over, always: the gas, the nobs of sugar in his tea, the way she . . . and the, the . . . oh dear, dear! In their early life together, begun so abruptly and illicitly six months before, her simple hidden beauties had delighted him by their surprises; they had peered and shone brighter, had waned and recurred; she was less the one star in his universe than a faint galaxy.

This room of theirs was a dingy room, very small but very high. A lanky gas tube swooped from the middle of the ceiling towards the middle of the tablecloth as if burning to discover whether that was pink or saffron or fawn—and it *was* hard to tell—but on perceiving that the cloth, whatever its tint, was disturbingly spangled with dozens of cup-stains and several large envelopes, the gas tube in the violence of its disappointment contorted itself abruptly, assumed a lateral bend, and put out its tongue of flame at an oleograph of Mona Lisa which hung above the fireplace.

Those envelopes were the torment to Lally; they were the sickening monstrous manifestations which she could not understand. There were always some of them lying there, or about the room, bulging with manuscripts that no editors—they *couldn't* have perused them—wanted; and so it had come to the desperate point when, as Lally was saying, something had to be done about things. Repton had done all *he* could; he wrote unceasingly, all day, all night, but all his projects insolvently withered, and morning, noon, and evening brought his manuscripts back as unwanted as snow in summer. He was depressed and baffled and weary. And there was simply nothing else he could do, nothing in the world.

IRONY—EPIPHANY

Apart from his own wonderful gift he was useless, Lally knew, and he was being steadily and stupidly murdered by those editors. It was weeks since they had eaten a proper meal. Whenever they obtained any real nice food now, they sat down to it silently, intently, and destructively. As far as Lally could tell, there seemed to be no prospect of any such meals again in life or time, and the worst of it all was Phillip's pride—he was actually too proud to ask anyone for assistance! Not that he would be too proud to accept help if it were offered to him: oh no, if it came he would rejoice at it! But still, he had that nervous shrinking pride that coiled upon itself, and he would not ask; he was like a wounded animal that hid its woe far away from the rest of the world. Only Lally knew his need, but why could not other people see it—those villainous editors! His own wants were so modest and he had a generous mind.

"Phil," Lally said, seating herself at the table. Repton was lolling in a wicker armchair beside the gas fire. "I'm not going on waiting and waiting any longer, I must go and get a job. Yes, I must. We get poorer and poorer. We can't go on like it any longer, there's no use, and I can't bear it."

"No, no, I can't have that, my dear . . ."

"But I will!" she cried. "Oh, why are you so proud?"

"Proud! Proud!" He stared into the gas fire, his tired arms hanging limp over the arms of the chair. "You don't understand. There are things the flesh has to endure, and things the spirit too must endure. . . ." Lally loved to hear him talk like that; and it was just as well, for Repton was much given to such discoursing. Deep in her mind was the conviction that he had simple access to profound, almost unimaginable wisdom. "It isn't pride, it is just that there is a certain order in life, in my life, that it would not do for. I could not bear it, I could never rest; I can't explain that, but just believe it, Lally." His head was empty but unbowed; he spoke quickly and finished almost angrily. "If only I had money! It's not for myself. I can stand all this, any amount of it. I've done so before, and I shall do so again and again I've no doubt. But I have to think of you."

That was fiercely annoying. Lally got up and went and stood over him.

"Why are you so stupid? I can think for myself and fend for myself. I'm not married to you. You have your pride, but I can't starve for it. And I've a pride, too. I'm a burden to you. If you won't let me work now while we're together, then I must leave you and work for myself."

"Leave! Leave me now? When things are so bad?" His white face gleamed his perturbation up at her. "Oh well, go, go." But then, mournfully moved, he took her hands and fondled them. "Don't be a fool, Lally; it's only a passing depression, this. I've known worse before, and it never lasts long, something turns up, always does. There's good and bad in it all, but there's more goodness than anything else. You see."

"I don't want to wait for ever, even for goodness. I don't believe in it. I never see it, never feel it, it is no use to me. I could go and steal, or walk the streets, or do any dirty thing—easily. What's the good of goodness if it isn't any use?"

"But, but," Repton stammered, "what's the use of bad, if it isn't any better?"

"I mean—" began Lally.

"You don't mean anything, my dear girl."

"I mean, when you haven't any choice it's no use talking moral, or having pride; it's stupid. Oh, my darling"—she slid down to him and lay against his breast—"it's not you, you are everything to me; that's why it angers me so, this treatment of you, all hard blows and no comfort. It will never be any different. I feel it will never be different now, and it terrifies me."

"Pooh!" Repton kissed her and comforted her: she was his beloved. "When things are wrong with us our fancies take their tone from our misfortunes, badness, evil. I sometimes have a queer stray feeling that one day I shall be hanged. Yes, I don't know what for, what *could* I be hanged for? And, do you know, at other times I've had a kind of intuition that one day I shall be—what do you think?—Prime Minister of the country! Yes, well, you can't reason against such things. I know what I should do, I've my plans, I've even made a list of the men for my Cabinet. Yes, well, there you are."

But Lally had made up her mind to leave him; she would leave him for a while and earn her own living. When things took a turn for the better she would join him again. She told him this. She had friends who were going to get her some work.

"But what are you going to do, Lally? I—"

"I'm going away to Glasgow," said she.

"Glasgow?" he had heard things about Glasgow! "Good heavens!"

"I've some friends there," the girl went on steadily. She had got up and was sitting on the arm of his chair. "I wrote to them last week. They can get me a job almost anywhere, and I can stay with them. They want me to go—they've sent the money for my fare. I think I shall have to go."

"You don't love me, then!" said the man.

Lally kissed him.

"But *do* you? Tell me!"

"Yes, my dear," said Lally, "of course."

An uneasiness possessed him; he released her moodily. Where was their wild passion flown to? She was staring at him intently, then she tenderly said: "My love, don't you be melancholy, don't take it to heart so. I'd cross the world to find you a pin."

"No, no, you mustn't do that," he exclaimed idiotically. At her indulgent smile he grimly laughed too, and then sank back in his chair. The girl stood up and went about the room doing vague nothings, until he spoke again.

"So you are tired of me?"

Lally went to him steadily and knelt down by his chair. "If I was tired of you, Phil, I'd kill myself."

Moodily he ignored her. "I suppose it had to end like this. But I've loved you desperately." Lally was now weeping on his shoulder and he began to twirl a lock of her rich brown hair absently with his fingers as if it were a seal on a watch-chain. "I'd been thinking that we might as well get married, as soon as things had turned round."

"I'll come back, Phil"—she clasped him so tenderly—"as soon as you want me."

"But you are not really going?"

"Yes," said Lally.

"You're not to go!"

"I wouldn't go if—if anything—if you had any luck. But as we are now I must go away, to give you a chance. You see that, darling Phil?"

"You're not to go; I object. I just love you, Lally, that's all, and of course I want to keep you here."

"Then what are we to do?"

"I—don't—know. Things drop out of the sky, but we must be together. You're not to go."

Lally sighed: he was stupid. And Repton began to turn over in his mind the dismal knowledge that she had taken this step in secret, she had not told him while she was trying to get to Glasgow. Now here she was with the fare, and as good as gone! Yes, it was all over.

"When do you propose to go?"

"Not for a few days, nearly a fortnight."

"Good God," he moaned. Yes, it was all over, then. He had never dreamed that this would be the end, that she would be the first to break away. He had always envisaged a tender scene in which he could tell her, with dignity and gentle humour that—Well, he never had quite hit upon the words he would use, but that was the kind of setting. And now here she was with her fare to Glasgow, her heart towards Glasgow, and she as good as gone to Glasgow! No dignity, no gentle humour—in fact he was enraged sullen but enraged, he boiled furtively. But he said with mournful calm:

"I've so many misfortunes, I suppose I can bear this too."

Gloomy and tragic he was.

"Dear, darling Phil, it's for your own sake I'm going."

Repton sniffed derisively. "We are always mistaken in the reasons for our commonest actions; Nature derides us all. You are sick of me; I can't blame you."

Eulalia was so moved that she could only weep again. Nevertheless she wrote to her friends in Glasgow promising to be with them by a stated date.

Towards the evening of the following day, at a time when she was alone, a letter arrived addressed to herself. It was from a firm of solicitors in Cornhill inviting her to call upon them. A flame leaped up in Lally's heart: it might mean the offer of some work that would keep her in London after all! If only it were so she would accept it on the spot, and Phillip would have to be made to see the reasonability of it. But at the office in Cornhill a more astonishing outcome awaited her. There she showed her letter to a little office boy with scarcely any fingernails and very little nose, and he took it to an elderly man who had a superabundance of both. Smiling affably, the long-nosed man led her upstairs into the sombre den of a gentleman who had some white hair and a lumpy yellow complexion. Having put to her a number of questions relating to her family history, and appearing to be satisfied and not at all surprised by her answers, this gentleman revealed to Lally the overpowering tidings that she was entitled to a legacy of eighty pounds by the will of a forgotten and recently deceased aunt. Subject to certain formalities, proofs of identity and so forth, he promised Lally the possession of the money within about a week.

Lally's descent to the street, her emergence into the clamouring atmosphere, her walk along to Holborn, were accomplished in a state of blessedness and trance, a trance in which life became a thousand times aerially enlarged, movement was a delight, and thought a rapture. She would give all the money to Phillip, and if he very much wanted it she would even marry him now. Perhaps, though, she would save ten pounds of it for herself. The other seventy would keep them for . . . it was impossible to say how long it would keep them. They could have a little holiday somewhere in the country together, he was so worn and weary. Perhaps she had better not tell Phillip anything at all about it until her lovely money was really in her hand. Nothing in life, at least nothing about money, was ever certain; something horrible might happen at the crucial moment and the money be snatched from her very fingers. Oh, she would go mad then! So for some days she kept her wonderful secret.

IRONY—EPIPHANY

Their imminent separation had given Repton a tender sadness that was very moving. "Eulalia," he would say, for he had suddenly adopted the formal version of her name; "Eulalia, we've had a great time together, a wonderful time, there will never be anything like it again." She often shed tears, but she kept the grand secret still locked in her heart. Indeed, it occurred to her very forcibly that even now his stupid pride might cause him to reject her money altogether. Silly, silly Phillip! Of course, it would have been different if they had married; he would naturally have taken it then, and really it would have *been* his. She would have to think out some dodge to overcome his scruples. Scruples were *such* a nuisance, but then it was very noble of him: there were not many men who wouldn't take money from a girl they were living with.

Well, a week later she was summoned again to the office in Cornhill and received from the white-haired gentleman a cheque for eighty pounds drawn on the Bank of England to the order of Eulalia Burnes. Miss Burnes desired to cash the cheque straightway, so the large-nosed elderly clerk was deputed to accompany her to the Bank of England close by and assist in procuring the money.

"A very nice errand!" exclaimed that gentleman as they crossed to Threadneedle Street past the Royal Exchange. Miss Burnes smiled her acknowledgment, and he began to tell her of other windfalls that had been disbursed in his time—but vast sums, very great persons—until she began to infer that Blackbean, Carp & Ransome were universal dispensers of largesse.

"Yes, but," said the clerk, hawking a good deal from an affliction of catarrh, "I never got any myself, and never will. If I did, do you know what I would do with it?" But at the moment they entered the portals of the bank, and in the excitement of the business Miss Burnes forgot to ask the clerk how he would use a legacy; and thus she possibly lost a most valuable slice of knowledge. With one fifty-pound note and six five-pound notes clasped in her handbag she bade good-bye to the long-nosed clerk, who shook her fervently by the hand and assured her that Blackbean, Carp & Ransome would be delighted at all times to undertake any commissions on her behalf. Then she fled along the pavement, blithe as a bird, until she was breathless with her flight. Presently she came opposite the window of a typewriter agency. Tripping airily into its office, she laid a scrap of paper before a lovely Hebe who was typing there.

"I want this typed, if you please," said Lally.

The beautiful typist read the words of the scrap of paper and stared at the heiress.

"I don't want any address to appear," said Lally. "Just a plain sheet, please."

A few moments later she received a neatly typed page molded in an envelope, and after paying the charge she hurried off to a district messenger office. Here she addressed the envelope in a disguised hand to P. Stick Repton, Esq., at the address in Holborn. She read the typed letter through again:

Dear Sir,
In common with many others I entertain the greatest admiration for your literary abilities, and I therefore beg you to accept this tangible expression of that admiration from a constant reader of your articles, who for purely private reasons, desires to remain anonymous.
Your very sincere
Wellwisher

Placing the fifty-pound note upon the letter Lally carefully folded them together and put them both into the envelope. The attendant then gave it to a uniformed lad, who sauntered off whistling very casually, somewhat to Lally's alarm—he looked so small and careless to be entrusted with fifty pounds. Then Lally went out, changed one of her five-pound notes, and had a lunch—half a crown, but it was worth it. Oh, how enchanting and exciting London was! In two days more she would have been gone; now she would have to write off at once to her Glasgow friends and tell them she had changed her mind, that she was now settled in London. Oh, how enchanting and delightful! And tonight he would take her out to dine in some fine restaurant, and they would do a theatre. She did not really want to marry Phil, they had got on so well without it, but if he wanted that too she did not mind—much. They would go away into the country for a whole week. What money would do! Marvellous! And looking round the restaurant she felt sure that no other woman there, no matter how well-dressed, had as much as thirty pounds in her handbag.

Returning home in the afternoon she became conscious of her own betraying radiance; very demure and subdued and usual she would have to be, or he might guess the cause of it. Though she danced up the long flight of stairs, she entered their room quietly, but the sight of Repton staring out of the window, forlorn as a drowsy horse, overcame her and she rushed to embrace him, crying: "Darling!"

"Hullo, hullo!" he smiled.

"I'm so fond of you, Phil dear."

"But—but you're deserting me!"

"Oh, no," she cried archly; "I'm not—not deserting you."

"All right." Repton shrugged his shoulders, but he seemed happier.

IRONY — EPIPHANY

He did not mention the fifty pounds then; perhaps it had not come yet—or perhaps he was thinking to surprise her.

"Let's go for a walk, it's a screaming lovely day," said Lally.

"Oh, I dunno," he yawned and stretched. "Nearly tea-time, isn't it?"

"Well, we—" Lally was about to suggest having tea out somewhere, but she bethought herself in time. "I suppose it is. Yes, it is."

So they stayed in for tea. No sooner was tea over than Repton remarked that he had an engagement somewhere. Off he went, leaving Lally disturbed and anxious. Why had he not mentioned the fifty pounds? Surely it had not gone to the wrong address? This suspicion once formed, Lally soon became certain, tragically sure, that she had misaddressed the envelope herself. A conviction that she had put No. 17 instead of No. 71 was almost overpowering, and she fancied that she hadn't even put London on the envelope—but Glasgow. That was impossible, though, but—oh, the horror!—somebody else was enjoying their fifty pounds. The girl's fears were not allayed by the running visit she paid to the messengers' office that evening, for the rash imp who had been entrusted with her letter had gone home and therefore could not be interrogated until the morrow. By now she was sure that he had blundered; he had been so casual with an important letter like that! Lally never did, and never would again, trust any little boys who wore their hats so much on one side, were so glossy with hair-oil, and went about whistling just to madden you. She burned to ask where the boy lived but in spite of her desperate desire she could not do so. She dared not, it would expose her to—to something or other she could only feel, not name; you had to keep cool, to let nothing, not even curiosity, master you.

Hurrying home again, though hurrying was not her custom and there was no occasion for it, she wrote the letter to her Glasgow friends. Then it crossed her mind that it would be wiser not to post the letter that night; better wait until the morning, after she had discovered what the horrible little messenger had done with her letter. Bed was a poor refuge from her thoughts, but she accepted it, and when Phil came home she was not sleeping. While he undressed he told her of the lecture he had been to, something about Agrarian Depopulation it was, but even after he had stretched himself beside her, he did not speak about the fifty pounds. Nothing, not even curiosity, should master her, and she calmed herself, and in time fitfully slept.

At breakfast next morning he asked her what she was going to do that day.

"Oh," replied Lally offhandedly, "I've a lot of things to see to, you know; I must go out. I'm sorry the porridge is so awful this morning, Phil but—"

FIFTY POUNDS

"Awful?" he broke in. "But it's nicer than usual! Where are you going? I thought—our last day, you know—we might go out somewhere together."

"Dear Phil!" Lovingly she stretched out a hand to be caressed across the table. "But I've several things to do. I'll come back early, eh?" She got up and hurried round to embrace him.

"All right," he said. "Don't be long."

Off went Lally to the messenger office, at first as happy as a bird, but on approaching the building the old tremors assailed her. Inside the room was the cocky little boy who bade her "Good morning" with laconic assurance. Lally at once questioned him, and when he triumphantly produced a delivery book she grew limp with her suppressed fear, one fear above all others. For a moment she did not want to look at it: truth hung by a hair, and as long as it so hung she might swear it was a lie. But there it was, written right across the page, an entry of a letter delivered, signed for in the well-known hand, P. Stick Repton. There was no more doubt, only a sharp indignant agony as though she had been stabbed with a dagger of ice.

"Oh yes, thank you," said Lally calmly. "Did you hand it to him yourself?"

"Yes'm," replied the boy, and he described Phillip.

"Did he open the letter?"

"Yes'm."

"There was no answer?"

"No'm."

"All right." Fumbling in her bag, she added: "I think I've got a sixpence for you."

Out in the street again she tremblingly chuckled to herself. "So that is what he is like, after all. Cruel and mean! He was going to let her go and keep the money in secret to himself!" How despicable! Cruel and mean, cruel and mean! She hummed it to herself. "Cruel and mean, cruel and mean!" It eased her tortured bosom. "Cruel and mean!" And he was waiting at home for her, waiting with a smile for their last day together. It would *have* to be their last day. She tore up the letter to her Glasgow friends, for now she *must* go to them. So cruel and mean! Let him wait! A bus stopped beside her, and she stepped on to it, climbing to the top and sitting there while the air chilled her burning features. The bus made a long journey to Plaistow. She knew nothing of Plaistow, she wanted to know nothing of Plaistow, but she did not care where the bus took her; she only wanted to keep moving and moving away, as far away as possible from Holborn and from him, and not once let those hovering tears down fall.

IRONY—EPIPHANY

From Plaistow she turned and walked back as far as the Mile End Road. Thereabouts wherever she went she met clergymen, dozens of them. There must be a conference, about charity or something, Lally thought. With a vague desire to confide her trouble to someone, she observed them; it would relieve the strain. But there was none she could tell her sorrow to, and failing that, when she came to a neat restaurant she entered it and consumed a fish. Just beyond her, three sleek parsons were lunching, sleek and pink; bald, affable, consoling men, all very much alike.

"I saw Carter yesterday," she heard one say. Lally liked listening to the conversation of strangers, and she often wondered what clergymen talked about among themselves.

"What, Carter! Indeed. Nice fellow, Carter. How was he?"

"Carter loves preaching, you know!" cried the third.

"Oh yes, he loves preaching!"

"Ha, ha, ha, yes."

"Ha, ha, ha, oom."

"Awf'ly good preacher, though."

"Yes, awf'ly good."

"And he's awf'ly good at comic songs, too."

"Yes?"

"Yes!"

Three glasses of water, a crumbling of bread, a silence suggestive of prayer.

"How long has he been married?"

"Twelve years," returned the cleric who had met Carter.

"Oh, twelve years!"

"I've only been married twelve years myself," said the oldest of them.

"Indeed!"

"Yes, I tarried very long."

"Ha, ha, ha, yes."

"Ha, ha, ha, oom."

"Er—have you any family?"

"No."

Very delicate and dainty in handling their food they were; very delicate and dainty.

"My rectory is a magnificent old house," continued the recently married one. "Built originally 1700. Burnt down. Rebuilt 1784."

"Indeed!"

"Humph!"

"Seventeen bedrooms and two delightful tennis courts."

"Oh, well done!" the others cried, and then they fell with genteel gusto upon a pale blancmange.

From the restaurant the girl sauntered about for a while, and then there was a cinema wherein, seated warm and comfortable in the twitching darkness, she partially stilled her misery. Some nervous fancy kept her roaming in that district for most of the evening. She knew that if she left it she would go home, and she did not want to go home. The naphtha lamps of the booths at Mile End were bright and distracting and the hum of the evening business was good despite the smell. A man was weaving sweetstuffs from a pliant roll of warm toffee that he wrestled with as the athlete wrestles with the python. There were stalls with things of iron, with fruit or fish, pots and pans, leather, string, nails. Watches for use—or for ornament—what d'ye lack? A sailor told naughty stories while selling bunches of green grapes out of barrels of cork dust which he swore he had stolen from the Queen of Honolulu. People clamoured for them both. You could buy back numbers of the comic papers at four a penny, rolls of linoleum for very little more—and use either for the other's purpose.

"At thrippence per foot, mesdames," cried the sweating cheap jack, lashing himself into ecstatic furies, "that's a piece of fabric weft and woven with triple-strength Andalusian jute, double-hot-pressed with rubber from the island of Pagama, and stencilled by an artist as poisoned his grandfather's cook. That's a piece of fabric, mesdames, as the king of heaven himself wouldn't mind to put down in his parlour—if he had the chance. Do I ask thrippence a foot for that piece of fabric? Mesdames, I was never a daring chap."

Lally watched it all, she looked and listened; then looked and did not see, listening and did not hear. Her misery was not the mere disappointment of love, not that kind of misery alone; it was the crushing of an ideal in which love had had its home, a treachery cruel and mean. The sky of night, so smooth, so bestarred, looked wrinkled through her screen of unshed tears; her sorrow was a wild cloud that troubled the moon with darkness.

In miserable desultory wanderings she had spent her day, their last day, and now, returning to Holborn in the late evening, she suddenly began to hurry, for a new possibility had come to lighten her dejection. Perhaps, after all, so whimsical he was, he was keeping his "revelation" until the last day, or even the last hour, when (nothing being known to her, as he imagined) all hopes being gone and they had come to the last kiss, he would take her in his arms and laughingly kill all grief, waving the succour of a flimsy bank-note like a flag of triumph. Perhaps even, in fact surely, that was why he wanted to take her out today! Oh, what a blind, wicked, stupid girl she was, and in a perfect frenzy of bubbling faith she panted homewards for his revealing sign.

From the pavement below she could see that their room was lit. Weakly she climbed the stairs and opened the door. Phil was standing up, staring so strangely at her. Helplessly and half-guilty she began to smile. Without a word said he came quickly to her and crushed her in his arms, her burning silent man, loving and exciting her. Lying against his breast in that constraining embrace, their passionate disaster was gone, her doubts were flown; all perception of the feud was torn from her and deeply drowned in a gulf of bliss. She was aware only of the consoling delight of their reunion, of his amorous kisses, of his tongue tingling the soft down on her upper lip that she disliked and he admired. All the soft wanton endearments that she so loved to hear him speak were singing in her ears, and then he suddenly swung and lifted her up, snapped out the gaslight, and carried her off to bed.

Life that is born of love feeds on love; if the wherewithal be hidden, how shall we stay our hunger? The galaxy may grow dim, or the stars drop in a wandering void; you can neither keep them in your hands nor crumble them in your mind.

What was it Phil had once called her? Numskull! After all it was his own fifty pounds, she had given it to him freely, it was his to do as he liked with. A gift was a gift, it was poor spirit to send money to anyone with the covetous expectation that it would return to you. She would surely go tomorrow.

The next morning he awoke her early and kissed her.

"What time does your train go?" said he.

"Train!" Lally scrambled from his arms and out of bed.

A fine day, a glowing day. Oh, bright, sharp air! Quickly she dressed and went into the other room to prepare their breakfast. Soon he followed, and they ate silently together, although whenever they were near each other he caressed her tenderly. Afterwards she went into the bedroom and packed her bag; there was nothing more to be done, he was beyond hope. No woman waits to be sacrificed, least of all those who sacrifice themselves with courage and a quiet mind. When she was ready to go she took her portmanteau into the sitting room; he, too, made to put on his hat and coat.

"No," murmured Lally, "you're not to come with me."

"Pooh, my dear!" he protested; "nonsense!"

"I won't have you come," cried Lally with an asperity that impressed him.

"But you can't carry that bag to the station by yourself!"

"I shall take a taxi." She buttoned her gloves.

"My dear!" His humorous deprecation annoyed her.

"Oh, bosh!" Putting her gloved hands around his neck she kissed him coolly. "Good-bye. Write to me often. Let me know how you thrive, won't you, Phil? And"—a little wavering—"love me always." She stared queerly at the two dimples in his cheeks; each dimple was a nest of hair that could never be shaved.

"Lally, darling, beloved girl! I never loved you more than now, this moment. You are more precious than ever to me!"

At that, she knew her moment of sardonic revelation had come—but she dared not use it, she let it go. She could not so deeply humiliate him by revealing her knowledge of his perfidy. A compassionate divinity smiles at our puny sins. She knew his perfidy, but to triumph in it would defeat her own pride. Let him keep his gracious, mournful airs to the last, false though they were. It was better to part so, better from such a figure than from an abject scarecrow, even though both were the same inside. And something capriciously reminded her, for a flying moment, of elephants she had seen swaying with the grand movement of tidal water—and groping for monkey nuts.

Lally tripped down the stairs alone. At the end of the street she turned for a last glance. There he was, high up in the window, waving good-byes. And she waved back at him.

BARBADOS

Paule Marshall

Dawn, like the night which had preceded it, came from the sea. In a white mist tumbling like spume over the fishing boats leaving the island and the hunched, ghost shapes of the fishermen. In a white, wet wind breathing over the villages scattered amid the tall canes. The cabbage palms roused, their high headdresses solemnly saluting the wind, and along the white beach which ringed the island the casuarina trees began their moaning—a sound of women lamenting their dead within a cave.

The wind, smarting of the sea, threaded a wet skein through Mr. Watford's five hundred dwarf coconut trees and around his house at the edge of the grove. The house, Colonial American in design, seemed created by the mist—as if out of the dawn's formlessness had come, magically, the solid stone walls, the blind, broad windows and the portico of fat columns which embraced the main story. When the mist cleared, the

IRONY—EPIPHANY

house remained—pure, proud, a pristine white—disdaining the crude wooden houses in the village outside its high gate.

It was not the dawn settling around his house which awakened Mr. Watford, but the call of his Barbary doves from their hutch in the yard. And it was more the feel of that sound than the sound itself. His hands had retained, from the many times a day he held the doves, the feel of their throats swelling with that murmurous, mournful note. He lay abed now, his hands—as cracked and callused as a cane cutter's—filled with the sound, and against the white sheet which flowed out to the white walls he appeared profoundly alone, yet secure in loneliness, contained. His face was fleshless and severe, his black skin sucked deep into the hollow of his jaw, while under a high brow, which was like a bastion raised against the world, his eyes were indrawn and pure. It was as if during all his seventy years, Mr. Watford had permitted nothing to sight which could have affected him.

He stood up, and his body, muscular but stripped of flesh, appeared to be absolved from time, still young. Yet each clenched gesture of his arms, of his lean shank as he dressed in a faded shirt and work pants, each vigilant, snapping motion of his head betrayed tension. Ruthlessly he spurred his body to perform like a younger man's. Savagely he denied the accumulated fatigue of the years. Only sometimes when he paused in his grove of coconut trees during the day, his eyes tearing and the breath torn from his lungs, did it seem that if he could find a place hidden from the world and himself he would give way to exhaustion and weep from weariness.

Dressed, he strode through the house, his step tense, his rough hand touching the furniture from Grand Rapids which crowded each room. For some reason, Mr. Watford had never completed the house. Everywhere the walls were raw and unpainted, the furniture unarranged. In the drawing room with its coffered ceiling, he stood before his favorite piece, an old mantel clock which eked out the time. Reluctantly it whirred five and Mr. Watford nodded. His day had begun.

It was no different from all the days which made up the five years since his return to Barbados. Downstairs in the unfinished kitchen, he prepared his morning tea—tea with canned milk and fried bakes—and ate standing at the stove while lizards skittered over the unplastered walls. Then, belching and snuffling the way a child would, he put on a pith helmet, secured his pants legs with bicycle clasps and stepped into the yard. There he fed the doves, holding them so that their sound poured into his hands and laughing gently—but the laugh gave way to an irritable grunt as he saw the mongoose tracks under the hutch. He set the trap again.

392

BARBADOS

The first heat had swept the island like a huge tidal wave when Mr. Watford, with that tense, headlong stride, entered the grove. He had planted the dwarf coconut trees because of their quick yield and because, with their stunted trunks, they always appeared young. Now as he worked rearranging the complex of pipes which irrigated the land, stripping off the dead leaves, the trees were like cool, moving presences; the stiletto fronds wove a protective dome above him and slowly, as the day soared toward noon, his mind filled with the slivers of sunlight through the trees and the feel of earth in his hands, as it might have been filled with thoughts.

Except for a meal at noon, he remained in the grove until dusk surged up from the sea; then returning to the house, he bathed and dressed in a medical doctor's white uniform, turned on the lights in the parlor and opened the tall doors to the portico. Then the old women of the village on their way to church, the last hawkers caroling, "Fish, flying fish, a penny, my lady," the roistering saga-boys lugging their heavy steel drums to the crossroad where they would rehearse under the street lamp—all passing could glimpse Mr. Watford, stiff in his white uniform and with his head bent heavily over a Boston newspaper. The papers reached him weeks late but he read them anyway, giving a little savage chuckle at the thought that beyond his world that other world went its senseless way. As he read, the night sounds of the village welled into a joyous chorale against the sea's muffled cadence and the hollow, haunting music of the steel band. Soon the moths, lured in by the light, fought to die on the lamp, the beetles crashed drunkenly against the walls and the night—like a woman offering herself to him—became fragrant with the night-blooming cactus.

Even in America Mr. Watford had spent his evenings this way. Coming home from the hospital, where he worked in the boiler room, he would dress in his white uniform and read in the basement of the large rooming house he owned. He had lived closeted like this, detached, because America—despite the money and property he had slowly accumulated—had meant nothing to him. Each morning, walking to the hospital along the rutted Boston streets, through the smoky dawn light, he had known—although it had never been a thought—that his allegiance, his place, lay elsewhere. Neither had the few acquaintances he had made mattered. Nor the woman he had occasionally kept as a younger man. After the first months their bodies would grow coarse to his hand and he would begin edging away. . . . So that he had felt no regret when, the year before his retirement, he resigned his job, liquidated his properties and, his fifty-year exile over, returned home.

The clock doled out eight and Mr. Watford folded the newspaper and brushed the burnt moths from the lamp base. His lips still shaped the last words he had read as he moved through the rooms, fastening the windows against the night air, which he had dreaded even as a boy. Something palpable but unseen was always, he believed, crouched in the night's dim recess, waiting to snare him. . . . Once in bed in his sealed room, Mr. Watford fell asleep quickly.

The next day was no different except that Mr. Goodman, the local shopkeeper, sent the boy for coconuts to sell at the racetrack and then came that evening to pay for them and to herald—although Mr. Watford did not know this—the coming of the girl.

That morning, taking his tea, Mr. Watford heard the careful tap of the mule's hoofs and looking out saw the wagon jolting through the dawn and the boy, still lax with sleep, swaying on the seat. He was perhaps eighteen and the muscles packed tightly beneath his lustrous black skin gave him a brooding strength. He came and stood outside the back door, his hands and lowered head performing the small, subtle rites of deference.

Mr. Watford's pleasure was full, for the gestures were those given only to a white man in his time. Yet the boy always nettled him. He sensed a natural arrogance like a pinpoint of light within his dark stare. The boy's stance exhumed a memory buried under the years. He remembered, staring at him, the time when he had worked as a yard boy for a white family, and had had to assume the same respectful pose while their flat, raw, Barbadian voices assailed him with orders. He remembered the muscles in his neck straining as he nodded deeply and a taste like alum on his tongue as he repeated the "Yes, please," as in a litany. But because of their whiteness and wealth, he had never dared hate them. Instead his rancor, like a boomerang, had rebounded, glancing past him to strike all the dark ones like himself, even his mother with her spindled arms and her stomach sagging with a child who was, invariably, dead at birth. He had been the only one of ten to live, the only one to escape. But he had never lost the sense of being pursued by the same dread presence which had claimed them. He had never lost the fear that if he lived too fully he would tire and death would quickly close the gap. His only defense had been a cautious life and work. He had been almost broken by work at the age of twenty when his parents died, leaving him enough money for the passage to America. Gladly had he fled the island. But nothing had mattered after his flight.

The boy's foot stirred the dust. He murmured, "Please, sir, Mr. Watford, Mr. Goodman at the shop send me to pick the coconut."

Mr. Watford's head snapped up. A caustic word flared, but died as he noticed a political button pinned to the boy's patched shirt with "Vote for the Barbados People's Party" printed boldly on it, and below that the motto of the party: "The Old Shall Pass." At this ludicrous touch (for what could this boy, with his splayed and shigoed feet and blunted mind, understand about politics?) he became suddenly nervous, angry. The button and its motto seemed, somehow, directed at him. He said roughly, "Well, come then. You can't pick any coconuts standing there looking foolish!"—and he led the way to the grove.

The coconuts, he knew, would sell well at the booths in the center of the track, where the poor were penned in like cattle. As the heat thickened and the betting grew desperate, they would clamor: "Man, how you selling the water coconuts?" and hacking off the tops they would pour rum in the water within the hollow centers, then tilt the coconuts to their heads so that the rum-sweetened water skimmed their tongues and trickled bright down their dark chins. Mr. Watford had stood among them at the track as a young man, as poor as they were, but proud. And he had always found something unutterably graceful and free in their gestures, something which had roused contradictory feelings in him: admiration, but just as strong, impatience at their easy ways, and shame. . . .

That night, as he sat in his white uniform reading, he heard Mr. Goodman's heavy step and went out and stood at the head of the stairs in a formal, proprietary pose. Mr. Goodman's face floated up into the light— the loose folds of flesh, the skin slick with sweat as if oiled, the eyes scribbled with veins and mottled, bold—as if each blemish there was a sin he proudly displayed or a scar which proved he had met life head-on. His body, unlike Mr. Watford's, was corpulent and, with the trousers caught up around his full crotch, openly concupiscent. He owned the one shop in the village which gave credit and a booth which sold coconuts at the race track, kept a wife and two outside women, drank a rum with each customer at his bar, regularly caned his fourteen children, who still followed him everywhere (even now they were waiting for him in the darkness beyond Mr. Watford's gate) and bet heavily at the races, and when he lost gave a loud hacking laugh which squeezed his body like a pain and left him gasping.

The laugh clutched him now as he flung his pendulous flesh into a chair and wheezed, "Watford, how? Man, I near lose house, shop, shirt and all at races today. I tell you, they got some horses from Trinidad in this meet that's making ours look like they running backwards. Be Jese, I wouldn't bet on a Bajan horse tomorrow if Christ heself was to give me the top. Those bitches might look good but they's nothing 'pon a track."

Mr. Watford, his back straight as the pillar he leaned against, his eyes unstained, his gaunt face planed by contempt, gave Mr. Goodman his cold, measured smile, thinking that the man would be dead soon, bloated with rice and rum—and somehow this made his own life more certain.

IRONY—EPIPHANY

Sputtering with his amiable laughter, Mr. Goodman paid for the coconuts, but instead of leaving then as he usually did, he lingered, his eyes probing for a glimpse inside the house. Mr. Watford waited, his head snapping warily; then, impatient, he started toward the door and Mr. Goodman said, "I tell you, your coconut trees bearing fast enough even for dwarfs. You's lucky, man."

Ordinarily Mr. Watford would have waved both the man and his remark aside, but repelled more than usual tonight by Mr. Goodman's gross form and immodest laugh, he said—glad of the cold edge his slight American accent gave the words—"What luck got to do with it? I does care the trees properly and they bear, that's all. Luck! People, especially this bunch around here, is always looking to luck when the only answer is a little brains and plenty of hard work. . . ." Suddenly remembering the boy that morning and the political button, he added in loud disgust, "Look that half-foolish boy you does send here to pick the coconuts. Instead of him learning a trade and going to England where he might find work he's walking about with a political button. He and all in politics now! But that's the way with these down here. They'll do some of everything but work. They don't want work!" He gestured violently, almost dancing in anger. "They too busy spreeing."

The chair creaked as Mr. Goodman sketched a painful and gentle denial. "No, man," he said, "you wrong. Things is different to before. I mean to say, the young people nowadays is different to how we was. They not just sitting back and taking things no more. They not so frighten for the white people as we was. No, man. Now take that said same boy, for an example. I don't say he don't like a spree, but he's serious, you see him there. He's a member of this new Barbados People's Party. He wants to see his own color running the government. He wants to be able to make a living right here in Barbados instead of going to any cold England. And he's right!" Mr. Goodman paused at a vehement pitch, then shrugged heavily. "What the young people must do, nuh? They got to look to something . . ."

"Look to work!" And Mr. Watford thrust out a hand so that the horned knuckles caught the light.

"Yes, that's true—and it's up to we that got little something to give them work," Mr. Goodman said, and a sadness filtered among the dissipations in his eyes. "I mean to say we that got little something got to help out. In a manner of speaking, we's responsible . . ."

"Responsible!" The word circled Mr. Watford's head like a gnat and he wanted to reach up and haul it down, to squash it underfoot.

Mr. Goodman spread his hands; his breathing rumbled with a sigh. "Yes, in a manner of speaking. That's why, Watford man, you got to provide little work for some poor person down in here. Hire a servant at least! 'Cause I gon tell you something . . ." And he hitched forward his chair, his voice dropped to a wheeze. "People talking. Here you come back rich from big America and build a swell house and plant 'nough coconut trees and you still cleaning and cooking and thing like some woman. Man, it don't look good!" His face screwed in emphasis and he sat back. "Now, there's this girl, the daughter of a friend that just dead, and she need work bad enough. But I wouldn't like to see she working for these white people 'cause you know those men will take advantage of she. And she'd make a good servant, man. Quiet and quick so, and nothing a-tall to feed and she can sleep anywhere about the place. And she don't have no boys always around her either. . . ." Still talking, Mr. Goodman eased from his chair and reached the stairs with surprising agility. "You need a servant," he whispered, leaning close to Mr. Watford as he passed. "It don't look good, man, people talking. I gon send she."

Mr. Watford was overcome by nausea. Not only from Mr. Goodman's smell—a stench of salt fish, rum and sweat—but from an outrage which was like a sediment in his stomach. For a long time he stood there almost kecking from disgust, until his clock struck eight, reminding him of the sanctuary within—and suddenly his cold laugh dismissed Mr. Goodman and his proposal. Hurrying in, he locked the doors and windows against the night air and, still laughing, he slept.

The next day, coming from the grove to prepare his noon meal, he saw her. She was standing in his driveway, her bare feet like strong dark roots amid the jagged stones, her face tilted toward the sun—and she might have been standing there always waiting for him. She seemed of the sun, of the earth. The folktale of creation might have been true with her: that along a riverbank a god had scooped up the earth—rich and black and warmed by the sun—and molded her poised head with its tufted braids and then with a whimsical touch crowned it with a sober brown felt hat which should have been worn by some stout English matron in a London suburb, had sculptured the passionless face and drawn a screen of gossamer across her eyes to hide the void behind. Beneath her bodice her small breasts were smooth at the crest. Below her waist, her hips branched wide, the place prepared for its load of life. But it was the bold and sensual strength of her legs which completely unstrung Mr. Watford. He wanted to grab a hoe and drive her off.

"What it 'tis you want?" he called sharply.

"Mr. Goodman send me."

"Send you for what?" His voice was shrill in the glare.

She moved. Holding a caved-in valise and a pair of white sandals, her head weaving slightly as though she bore a pail of water there or a tray

IRONY—EPIPHANY

of mangoes, she glided over the stones as if they were smooth ground. Her bland expression did not change, but her eyes, meeting his, held a vague trust. Pausing a few feet away, she curtsied deeply. "I's the new servant."

Only Mr. Watford's cold laugh saved him from anger. As always it raised him to a height where everything below appeared senseless and insignificant—especially his people, whom the girl embodied. From this height, he could even be charitable. And thinking suddenly of how she had waited in the brutal sun since morning without taking shelter under the nearby tamarind tree, he said, not unkindly, "Well, girl, go back and tell Mr. Goodman for me that I don't need no servant."

"I can't go back."

"How you mean can't?" His head gave its angry snap.

"I'll get lashes," she said simply. "My mother say I must work the day and then if you don't wish me, I can come back. But I's not to leave till night falling, if not I get lashes."

He was shaken by her dispassion. So much so that his head dropped from its disdaining angle and his hands twitched with helplessness. Despite anything he might say or do, her fear of the whipping would keep her there until nightfall, the valise and shoes in hand. He felt his day with its order and quiet rhythms threatened by her intrusion—and suddenly waving her off as if she were an evil visitation, he hurried into the kitchen to prepare his meal.

But he paused, confused, in front of the stove, knowing that he could not cook and leave her hungry at the door, nor could he cook and serve her as though he were the servant.

"Yes, please."

They said nothing more. She entered the room with a firm step and an air almost of familiarity, placed her valise and shoes in a corner and went directly to the larder. For a time Mr. Watford stood by, his muscles flexing with anger and his eyes bounding ahead of her every move, until feeling foolish and frighteningly useless, he went out to feed his doves.

The meal was quickly done and as he ate he heard the dry slap of her feet behind him—a pleasant sound—and then silence. When he glanced back she was squatting in the doorway, the sunlight aslant the absurd hat and her face bent to a bowl she held in one palm. She ate slowly, thoughtfully, as if fixing the taste of each spoonful in her mind.

It was then that he decided to let her work the day and at nightfall to pay her a dollar and dismiss her. His decision held when he returned later from the grove and found tea awaiting him, and then through the supper she prepared. Afterward, dressed in his white uniform, he patiently waited out the day's end on the portico, his face setting into a grim mold.

Then just as dusk etched the first dark line between the sea and sky, he took out a dollar and went downstairs.

She was not in the kitchen, but the table was set for his morning tea. Muttering at her persistence, he charged down the corridor, which ran the length of the basement, flinging open the doors to the damp, empty rooms on either side, and sending the lizards and the shadows long entrenched there scuttling to safety.

He found her in the small slanted room under the stoop, asleep on an old cot he kept there, her suitcase turned down beside the bed, and the shoes, dress and the ridiculous hat piled on top. A loose nightshift muted the outline of her body and hid her legs, so that she appeared suddenly defenseless, innocent, with a child's trust in her curled hand and in her deep breathing. Standing in the doorway, with his own breathing snarled and his eyes averted, Mr. Watford felt like an intruder. She had claimed the room. Quivering with frustration, he slowly turned away, vowing that in the morning he would shove the dollar at her and lead her like a cow out of his house....

Dawn brought rain and a hot wind which set the leaves rattling and swiping at the air like distraught arms. Dressing in the dawn darkness, Mr. Watford again armed himself with the dollar, and with his shoulders at an uncompromising set, plunged downstairs. He descended into the warm smell of bakes and this smell, along with the thought that she had been up before him, made his hand knot with exasperation on the banister. The knot tightened as he saw her, dust swirling at her feet as she swept the corridor, her face bent solemn to the task. Shutting her out with a lifted hand, he shouted, "Don't bother sweeping. Here's a dollar. G'long back."

The broom paused and although she did not raise her head, he sensed her groping through the shadowy maze of her mind toward his voice. Behind the dollar which he waved in her face, her eyes slowly cleared. And, surprisingly, they held no fear. Only anticipation and a tenuous trust. It was as if she expected him to say something kind.

"G'long back!" His angry cry was a plea.

Like a small, starved flame, her trust and expectancy died and she said, almost with reproof, "The rain falling."

To confirm this, the wind set the rain stinging across the windows and he could say nothing, even though the words sputtered at his lips. It was useless. There was nothing inside her to comprehend that she was not wanted. His shoulders sagged under the weight of her ignorance, and with a futile gesture he swung away, the dollar hanging from his hand like a small sword gone limp.

She became as fixed and familiar a part of the house as the stones—and as silent. He paid her five dollars a week, gave her Mondays off and in the evenings, after a time, even allowed her to sit in the alcove off the parlor, while he read with his back to her, taking no more notice of her than he did the moths on the lamp.

But once, after many silent evenings together, he detected a sound apart from the night murmurs of the sea and village and the metallic tuning of the steel band, a low, almost inhuman cry of loneliness which chilled him. Frightened, he turned to find her leaning hesitantly toward him, her eyes dark with urgency, and her face tight with bewilderment and a growing anger. He started, not understanding, and her arm lifted to stay him. Eagerly she bent closer. But as she uttered the low cry again, as her fingers described her wish to talk, he jerked around, afraid that she would be foolish enough to speak and that once she did they would be brought close. He would be forced then to acknowledge something about her which he refused to grant; above all, he would be called upon to share a little of himself. Quickly he returned to his newspaper, rustling it to settle the air, and after a time he felt her slowly, bitterly, return to her silence. . . .

Like sand poured in a careful measure from the hand, the weeks flowed down to August and on the first Monday, August Bank holiday, Mr. Watford awoke to the sound of the excursion buses leaving the village for the annual outing, their backfire pelleting the dawn calm and the ancient motors protesting the overcrowding. Lying there, listening, he saw with disturbing clarity his mother dressed for an excursion—the white headtie wound above her dark face and her head poised like a dancer's under the heavy outing basket of food. That set of her head had haunted his years, reappearing in the girl as she walked toward him the first day. Aching with the memory, yet annoyed with himself for remembering, he went downstairs.

The girl had already left for the excursion, and although it was her day off, he felt vaguely betrayed by her eagerness to leave him. Somehow it suggested ingratitude. It was as if his doves were suddenly to refuse him their song or his trees their fruit, despite the care he gave them. Some vital past which shaped the simple mosaic of his life seemed suddenly missing. An alien silence curled like coal gas throughout the house. To escape it he remained in the grove all day and, upon his return to the house, dressed with more care than usual, putting on a fresh, starched uniform, and solemnly brushing his hair until it lay in a smooth bush above his brow. Leaning close to the mirror, but avoiding his eyes, he cleaned the white rheum at their corners, and afterward pried loose the dirt under his nails.

Unable to read his papers, he went out on the portico to escape the unnatural silence in the house, and stood with his hands clenched on the balustrade and his taut body straining forward. After a long wait he heard the buses return and voices in gay shreds upon the wind. Slowly his hands relaxed, as did his shoulders under the white uniform; for the first time that day his breathing was regular. She would soon come.

But she did not come and dusk bloomed into night, with a fragrant heat and a full moon which made the leaves glint as though touched with frost. The steel band at the crossroads began the lilting songs of sadness and seduction, and suddenly—like shades roused by the night and the music—images of the girl flitted before Mr. Watford's eyes. He saw her lost amid the carousings in the village, despoiled; he imagined someone like Mr. Goodman clasping her lewdly or tumbling her in the canebrake. His hand rose, trembling, to rid the air of her; he tried to summon his cold laugh. But, somehow, he could not dismiss her as he had always done with everyone else. Instead, he wanted to punish and protect her, to find and lead her back to the house.

As he leaned there, trying not to give way to the desire to go and find her, his fist striking the balustrade to deny his longing, he saw them. The girl first, with the moonlight like a silver patina on her skin, then the boy whom Mr. Goodman sent for the coconuts, whose easy strength and the political button—"The Old Order Shall Pass"—had always mocked and challenged Mr. Watford. They were joined in a tender battle: the boy in a sport shirt riotous with color was reaching for the girl as he leaped and spun, weightless, to the music, while she fended him off with a gesture which was lovely in its promise of surrender. Her protests were little scattered bursts: "But, man, why don't you stop, nuh . . . ? But, you know, you getting on like a real-real idiot. . . ."

Each time she chided him he leaped higher and landed closer, until finally he eluded her arm and caught her by the waist. Boldly he pressed a leg between her tightly closed legs until they opened under his pressure. Their bodies cleaved into one whirling form and while he sang she laughed like a wanton, with her hat cocked over her ear. Dancing, the stones moiling underfoot, they claimed the night. More than the night. The steel band played for them alone. The trees were their frivolous companions, swaying as they swayed. The moon rode the sky because of them.

Mr. Watford, hidden by a dense shadow, felt the tendons which strung him together suddenly go limp; above all, an obscure belief which, like rare china, he had stored on a high shelf in his mind began to tilt. He sensed the familiar specter which hovered in the night reaching out to embrace him, just as the two in the yard were embracing. Utterly unstrung, incapable of either speech or action, he stumbled into the house, only to meet there an accusing silence from the clock, which had missed

IRONY—EPIPHANY

its eight o'clock winding, and his newspapers lying like ruined leaves over the floor.

He lay in bed in the white uniform, waiting for sleep to rescue him, his hands seeking the comforting sound of his doves. But sleep eluded him and instead of the doves, their throats tremulous with sound, his scarred hands filled with the shape of a woman he had once kept: her skin, which had been almost bruising in its softness; the buttocks and breasts spread under his hands to inspire both cruelty and tenderness. His hands closed to softly crush those forms, and the searing thrust of passion, which he had not felt for years, stabbed his dry groin. He imagined the two outside, their passion at a pitch by now, lying together behind the tamarind tree, or perhaps—and he sat up sharply—they had been bold enough to bring their lust into the house. Did he not smell their taint on the air? Restored suddenly, he rushed downstairs. As he reached the corridor, a thread of light beckoned him from her room and he dashed furiously toward it, rehearsing the angry words which would jar their bodies apart. He neared the door, glimpsed her through the small opening, and his step faltered; the words collapsed.

She was seated alone on the cot, tenderly holding the absurd felt hat in her lap, one leg tucked under her while the other trailed down. A white sandal, its strap broken, dangled from the foot and gently knocked the floor as she absently swung her leg. Her dress was twisted around her body—and pinned to the bodice, so that it gathered the cloth between her small breasts, was the political button the boy always wore. She was dreamily fingering it, her mouth shaped by a gentle, ironic smile and her eyes strangely acute and critical. What had transpired on the cot had not only, it seemed, twisted the dress around her, tumbled her hat and broken her sandal, but had also defined her and brought the blurred forms of life into focus for her. There was a woman's force in her aspect now, a tragic knowing and acceptance in her bent head, a hint about her of Cassandra watching the future wheel before her eyes.

Before those eyes which looked to another world, Mr. Watford's anger and strength failed him and he held to the wall for support. Unreasonably, he felt that he should assume some hushed and reverent pose, to bow as she had the day she had come. If he had known their names, he would have pleaded forgiveness for the sins he had committed against her and the others all his life, against himself. If he could have borne the thought, he would have confessed that it had been love, terrible in its demand, which he had always fled. And that love had been the reason for his return. If he had been honest, he would have whispered—his head bent and a hand shading his eyes—that unlike Mr. Goodman (whom he suddenly envied for his full life) and the boy with his political button (to whom he had lost the girl), he had not been willing to bear the weight of his own responsibility.... But all Mr. Watford could admit, clinging there to the wall, was, simply, that he wanted to live—and that the girl held life within her as surely as she held the hat in her hands. If he could prove himself better than the boy, he could win it. Only then, he dimly knew, would he shake off the pursuer which had given him no rest since birth. Hopefully, he staggered forward, his step cautious and contrite, his hands, quivering along the wall.

She did not see or hear him as he pushed the door wider. And for some time he stood there, his shoulders hunched in humility, his skin stripped away to reveal each flaw, his whole self offered in one outstretched hand. Still unaware of him, she swung her leg, and the dangling shoe struck a derisive note. Then, just as he had turned away that evening in the parlor when she had uttered her low call, she turned away now, refusing him.

Mr. Watford's body went slack and then stiffened ominously. He knew that he would have to wrest from her the strength needed to sustain him. Slamming the door, he cried, his voice cracked and strangled, "What you and him was doing in here? Tell me! I'll not have you bringing nastiness round here. Tell me!"

She did not start. Perhaps she had been aware of him all along and had expected his outburst. Or perhaps his demented eye and the desperation rising from him like a musk filled her with pity instead of fear. Whatever, her benign smile held and her eyes remained abstracted until his hand reached out to fling her back on the cot. Then, frowning, she stood up, wobbling a little on the broken shoe and holding the political button as if it was a new power which would steady and protect her. With a cruel flick of her arm she struck aside his hand and, in a voice as cruel, halted him. "But you best move and don't come holding on to me, you nasty, pissy old man. That's all you is, despite yuh big house and fancy furnitures and yuh newspapers from America. You ain't people, Mr. Watford, you ain't people!" And with a look and a lift of her head which made her condemnation final, she placed the hat atop her braids, and turning aside picked up the valise which had always lain, packed, beside the cot—as if even on the first day she had known that this night would come and had been prepared against it.

Mr. Watford did not see her leave, for a pain squeezed his heart dry and the driven blood was a bright, blinding cataract over his eyes. But his inner eye was suddenly clear. For the first time it gazed mutely upon the waste and pretense which had spanned his years. Flung there against the door by the girl's small blow, his body slowly crumpled under the weariness he had long denied. He sensed that dark but unsubstantial figure which roamed the nights searching for him wind him in its chill embrace. He struggled against it, his hands clutching the air with the spastic eloquence a drowning man. He moaned—and the anguished sound reached beyond the room to fill the house. It escaped to the yard and his doves swelled their throats moaning with him.

X | The Shape of Fiction

The history of the wife of Martin Guerre is one of those tales in which the truth is so remarkable that it can hardly be believed. I do not know whether the original documents pertaining to the case are still available at Toulouse. Phillips, whose works were, during the early years of the nineteenth century, the standard English authority on the rules of evidence, transcribed the case in one of his discussions of circumstantial evidence, giving the details very fully, and the facts, however strange, bequeathed us by so eminent a jurist can hardly be discredited. The rules of evidence vary from century to century and country to country, and the morality which compels many of the actions of men and women varies also, but the capacities of the human soul for suffering and for joy remain very much the same.*

THE WIFE OF MARTIN GUERRE

Janet Lewis

I. ARTIGUES

One morning in January, 1539, a wedding was celebrated in the village of Artigues. That night the two children who had been espoused to one another lay in bed in the house of the groom's father. They were Bertrande de Rols, aged eleven years, and Martin Guerre, who was no older, both offspring of rich peasant families as ancient, as feudal and as proud as any of the great seignorial houses of Gascony. The room was cold. Outside the snow lay thinly over the stony ground, or, gathered into long shallow drifts at the corners of houses, left the earth bare. But higher, it extended upward in great sheets and dunes, mantling the ridges and choking the wooded valley, toward the peak of La Bacanère and the long

---

* This foreword was written by Janet Lewis, the author of "The Wife of Martin Guerre," when her story was first published in 1941.

405

ridge of Le Burat, and to the south, beyond the long valley of Luchon, the granite Maladetta stood sheathed in ice and snow. The passes to Spain were buried under whiteness. The Pyrenees had become for the winter season an impassable wall. Those Spaniards who were in French territory after the first heavy snowfall in September, remained there, and those Frenchmen, smugglers or soldiers or simple travelers who found themselves on the wrong side of the Port de Venasque were doomed to remain there until spring. Sheep in fold, cattle in the grange, faggots heaped high against the wall of the farm, the mountain villages were closed in enforced idleness and isolation. It was a season of leisure in which weddings might well be celebrated.

Bertrande had not spoken to Martin in all her life until that morning, although she had often seen him; indeed she had not known until the evening before that a marriage had been arranged. That morning she had knelt with Martin before his father and then had walked with him across the snow, dressed bravely in a new red cape and attended by many friends and relatives and by the sound of violins, to the church of Artigues where the marriage ceremony had been completed. She had found it quite as serious an affair as first communion.

Afterwards, still to the music of the violins, which sounded thin and sharp in the cold air, she had returned to the house of her husband where a huge fire of oak logs garnished with vine-trimmings roared in the big fireplace, and where the kitchen, the principal room of the house, was set with improvised tables, long boards laid over trestles. The stone floor had been freshly strewn with broken boughs of evergreen. The sides and bottoms of the copper pans flashed redly with the reflection of the flames, and the air was rich with the good smell of roasting meat and of freshly poured wine. Underfoot the snow from the sabots melted and sank beneath the trodden evergreens. A smell of humanity and of steaming wool mingled with the odors of the food, and the room was incredibly noisy with conversation.

It was a gay, an important event. Everyone was intensely jubilant, but the small bride received very little attention. After the first embraces and compliments, she sat beside her mother at the long table and ate the food which her mother served her from the big platters. Now and again she felt her mother's arm steal warmly about her shoulders, and felt herself pressed briefly against her mother's breast, proudly and reassuringly, but as the feast proceeded her mother's attention became more engrossed with the conversation of the curé, who sat opposite, and of the groom's father, who sat upon her other side, and Bertrande, immune from observation in the midst of all this commotion which was ostensibly in her honor, looked about the room at her ease, and fed pieces of hard bread dipped in grease

THE WIFE OF MARTIN GUERRE

to the woolly Pyrenean sheep dog with the long curly tail who nosed his head into her lap from his place beneath the table. By and by, when the dishes of soup and roast had given way to the boiled chestnuts, cheese, honey and dried fruits, she slipped from her place and began quietly to explore the room.

Behind the table where she had been sitting the beds were ranged, end to end, the curtains of yellow serge drawn close, each one an apartment in itself. The child brushed between these curtains and the stout backs of the merrymakers, moving slowly toward the nearer corner of the room, where she stood, her back against a tall cupboard, and surveyed the scene. Across from her the blackened fireplace occupied at least a third of the wall, and the brightness of the leaping flames left the corners on either side in confused semi-darkness. In the middle of the wall to the right, however, she spied a door, and toward that she gradually made her way. It proved to be the entrance to a long cold corridor, from which doors opened into storerooms, rooms for the shepherds, and lighted only by a small window of which the wooden shutters were closed. Another person had taken refuge from the festivities in this corridor, and was intent upon undoing the bolts of the shutters. The half of the shutter folded back, a flood of sharp snowy sunlight fell into the corridor, and in its brightness she recognized Martin. She made a step forward, uncertainly, and Martin, hearing it, turned and advanced upon her, his hands outstretched and a fearsome expression on his long, young face. He had disliked being married, and, in order to express his dislike of the affair, and also to express the power of his newly acquired sovereignty, he cuffed Bertrande soundly upon the ears, scratched her face and pulled her hair, all without a word. Her cries brought a rescuer, her mother's sister, who rebuked the bridegroom and led the bride back into the kitchen, where she remained beside her mother until the hour when she was led by her mother and her mother-in-law into the Chamber, the room on the opposite side of the kitchen, where stood the master's bed, now dedicated to the formalities of the wedding.

Bertrande was disrobed and attired in night garments and a bonnet-de-nuit. Martin was brought in and similarly attired, and the two children were put to bed together in the presence of all the company. In deference to the extreme youth of the bridal couple, however, the serge curtains were not pulled, and a torch, fastened to the wall, was left blazing.

The company remained in the room for a time, laughing at jokes of a time-honored nature, while the two children lay very still and did not look at each other. By and by the merrymakers drifted into the kitchen, and last of all the father of Martin Guerre paused in the doorway to wish his children a formal goodnight. Bertrande saw his features, exaggerated

THE SHAPE OF FICTION

in the flare of the torch, bent in an expression of great seriousness, and the realization that henceforth her life lay beneath his jurisdiction came suddenly and overwhelmingly to the little girl. The door closed behind him. The unglazed window was also closed, but between the leaves of the shutter a draft came which shook the flame of the torch. Otherwise the air was still and dead. The floor was bare, and the room was unfurnished save for a row of carved chests against the wall and the great bed in which she lay. She was tired and frightened. She did not know what Martin might not take it into his head to do to her. Presently she felt him stir.

"I am tired of all this business," he said, turning on his side and burrowing his head into his pillow. Soon his breathing became regular, and, without daring to move her body, Bertrande relaxed. She was safe. Her husband was asleep.

From her high pillow she watched the torch, as the flame wavered, and little particles of blazing lint detached themselves and fell, smoking, to the stone floor. One was long in falling; it clung, a blazing thread, making the flame of the torch irregular and smoky. Then it too dropped. The warmth of the flock bed began to enclose the small thin body in something like security, a feeling almost as good as that of being home again. The light of the torch seemed to go out. The child began to doze.

An hour or so later the door opened and a large figure entered, substantially clothed in ample folds of brown wool and coifed in white linen, and bearing a tray; and crossed with leisured tread to the bedside. Whether it was merely the sense of being observed, or whether the stone floor had resounded or the silver rattled a little on the tray, Bertrande awoke and, opening her eyes, looked up into the square, benevolent face and the pleasant brown eyes of a woman whom she recognized dimly as a part of the house of Guerre. But it was not the face of her mother-in-law, no, it was the face of the servant who had stood at the doorway as the bridal party had returned from the church.

"You are awake. That is well," said the woman, smiling. "I warrant, if the boy were eight years older he would not be sound asleep at such an hour."

She rested the tray on the bed, and, reaching across the body of Bertrande, shook Martin by the shoulder.

"Surely, it is not already morning," said Bertrande.

"No, my dear, it is réveillon. I have brought you your little midnight feast."

"Oh," said Bertrande, "they forgot to tell me about it."

She sat up, looking a little dazed and worried. Without instruction she might not know what to do, she might do the wrong thing. Martin, roused, also sat up, and together they surveyed the tray.

"It is not a bad idea at all," said Martin, his voice foggy with sleep, and, strangely enough, perfectly good-natured.

"Eat," said the woman, beaming upon them. "You have had all the rest of the affair—you may as well enjoy now your little feast, just the two of you. I prepared it myself."

Thus urged, the children rubbed their eyes and fell to, while the woman stood by, her hands on her well-draped hips.

"It is all kinds of an affair, this getting married," she said as she watched the children. "Don't overlook the custard—it is my specialty. And by and by you will appreciate all that your parents have done for you. And meanwhile what peace there is and what friendship in the village of Artigues! You are a pretty little girl, Madame, a little thin, perhaps, but with the years the limbs grow rounder. A little more flesh and you will be altogether charming. And you have a fine, bright color in your cheeks. Look at her, Martin. She is even prettier now than she was at the church, when she was so pale with emotion."

Bertrande ate gravely, licking the yellow custard from the large silver spoon. This was more attention than she had received all day, and, moreover, it was the sort of attention that she could understand. The woman continued in a rich, comfortable voice:

"Take Martin now. He will not be a pretty man, but he will be very distinguished, like his father. There is a kind of ugliness which is very fine in a man. For the rest, I doubt not but that he will be capable of all that is required of a man."

She smiled upon them with no intention of hurrying them, and continued:

"Also, Martin, look at your wife—she has the lucky eyes, the two-colored eyes, brown and green, and the lucky people bring luck to those they love."

They finished everything upon the tray, even dividing amicably the last bit of pastry between them, and the servant departed with a final word of commendation. Madame Martin Guerre, born Bertrande de Rols, comforted by the inward presence of pastry and custard and by the wholesome unconcern of her husband, fell into a deep untroubled slumber. In the morning she returned to the house of her parents, there to await an age when she should be more fitted to assume her married responsibilities.

So began for the wife of Martin Guerre the estate which was to bring her so much joy and also such strange and unpredictable suffering.

For the present, life went on as usual. She had not gained in personal importance or in liberty by becoming the wife of Martin Guerre; indeed she had not expected to do so. Advantages there were, certainly, from the marriage, but for the present they were all for the two families of Guerre and de Rols; later, Martin and Bertrande would profit from the increased dual prosperity. The solemn ceremony in the church, the recollection of awakening at night to be served royally with delicacies shining on the family plate of les Guerre, receded, overshadowed by the multiplicity of the daily tasks that were her education.

The union of the house of de Rols and that of Guerre had long been considered. It had appeared to three generations as almost inevitable, so many were the advantages for both families to be expected from such an alliance. Three generations ago the matter had been practically settled, until a remark by the great-grandfather of Bertrande de Rols upset the plans of the great-grandfather of Martin Guerre.

"I have a nice little granddaughter whom I'm keeping for you," said the ancestor of Martin to old de Rols, affably, at the close of a conversation which had covered the extent of the mutual benefits which might result from a union between the two families.

"If you wish to keep her well," said the great-grandfather of Bertrande, humorously, "if you wish to keep her very well, my friend, you have only to salt her."

The great-grandfather of Martin regarded de Rols for a moment without speaking, but he was no longer affable.

"You wish to imply then, that she will be easy to keep. You imply that the suitors will not be many. You imply that I may salt her and cover her with oil, like the carcase of a chicken, and she will keep, eh, she will keep indefinitely!"

"My friend, I imply nothing of the sort," said the other old man, patiently. "I only like to have my little joke."

"Your joke," replied Martin's great-grandfather, "your joke is an insult." And he spat in the face of Bertrande de Rols' ancestor.

The negotiations for the marriage were discontinued, and not only that, but great-grandfather Guerre and all his mesnie, that is to say, his sons and daughters and their families, his uncles and aunts and their families, and all the servants whose families had been accustomed to serve these families of the house of Guerre, conceived and maintained an intense hatred of the mesnie of the house of de Rols, which was continued until the birth of Bertrande. Then, since the house of Guerre had rejoiced in the birth of a son but a short time previous, it occurred to the descendants of the jesting and offended great-grandfathers that the best and only way to end a feud of such long standing was to affiance the infants in their cradles. This was accordingly done, and peace was restored.

One should not judge too harshly the pride of the grandfather who was insulted by so mild a jest. As head of his family, the *cap d'hostal,* he carried great responsibilities; the safety and prosperity of all his household depended largely upon the strict obedience and reverence which he could demand from his children, his wife and his servants. From great responsibility arose great pride. No one questioned his right to be offended and no one hesitated to follow his example in hating the offender—offenders, one should say, because the deed of one man became immediately the deed of his family. It is perhaps surprising, however, that the feudal structure should have been maintained so strictly and upon so large a scale by these peasants of Artigues, for these peasants were closer to the *seigneur campagnard* whom the close of the sixteenth century saw coming into prominence than they were to the average peasant of the lowlands, whose families were sprung from the emancipated serfs of the middle ages. The crags and valleys of the Pyrenees were the cause of their prosperity and of their pride.

The hot mineral baths in the valley of Luchon, it is true, were on one of the direct routes from Spain into France, and it is said that the soldiers of Caesar stopped there to soak their battle-weary limbs in the muddy sulphur pools, but the court of Navarre neglected Luchon. The Marguerite of Princesses took her entourage to Cauterets, nearer Pau. Neither was Artigues upon the direct way through the valley of Luchon to the valley of the Garonne. It stood nearer to a small tributary to the Neste in a higher fold of the mountains. It was on the way to no other village. No one visited Artigues who had not business there. And so from generation to generation, while the lowland villages were plundered and burned and their fields laid waste by the religious wars which swept southern France through the thirteenth century and down to the middle of the sixteenth, Artigues enjoyed its isolation and its lack of fame, and actual gold accumulated in the coffers of its more prosperous families. The feudal feeling maintained its value also, as strong as in the earlier centuries, although Francis the First had been for twenty-one years upon the throne of France and although Languedoc had belonged to the French crown almost three hundred years.

When she was fourteen years of age, perhaps a little earlier than might have been the case had it not been for the death of her own mother, Bertrande de Rols went to live finally with the house of Guerre. One deceptively warm autumn forenoon, attended by the servant who had brought the réveillon to the young bridal couple, she crossed the courtyard, barefoot, dressed quite simply in her usual workaday clothes, and found herself on the threshold of the big kitchen. Her mother-in-law kissed her on both cheeks, and led her to the hearth. The wooden coffers which contained her personal effects and the linen and silver of her dowry were carried in and set against the wall, her mother-in-law indicated to her the large bed with the curtains of yellow serge which was to be hers and Martin's, and, without too great haste, she was set to grinding meal in a big stone mortar. Martin and his father were in the fields. Her own father had ridden off to oversee the vintaging. None of the field-workers returned until nightfall. But meanwhile she had time to become familiar with the kitchen, with Martin's four sisters and the servants, with the dogs and cats and with the feathered inhabitants of the basse-cour. She had not visited the house since the day of her wedding, but the scene was much as she had remembered it. The big table on trestles had been removed; there remained only a square table near the hearth, for the family, and a long one beside it for the workers. The floor was strewn only with dried grass, and the walls were not garnished with evergreen; but festoons of garlic and onions, the long stems braided together, hung from the rafters, together with bunches of dried elder blossoms and linden flowers. Bunches of dried rosemary, mountain thyme, and parsley were there also; and, in the hood of the chimney, meats and sausages were freshly hung to benefit from the resinous smoke.

Not again for a long time did Bertrande enjoy as much of her mother-in-law's attention as she did that afternoon, but the leisured kindness and interest which Madame Guerre bestowed upon her son's young wife threw a long warm shadow which extended forward for many days. She showed Bertrande the farm in detail, the stables, the granary, low stone buildings roofed with tile, like the house, set to the right and left of the courtyard before the house; showed her the room used for the dairy, the storerooms with their pots of honey and baskets of fruit, baskets of chestnuts, stone crocks of goose and chicken preserved in oil, eggs buried in bran, cheeses of goat's milk and of cow's milk, wine, oil. In the Chamber she showed her wool and flax for the distaff, the loom on which the clothing for the household would be woven. She showed her the garden, now being set in order for the early frost, the straw-thatched beehives, the sheepfold of mud and wattles, and last of all, returning to the Chamber in which the marriage bed had been dressed, Madame Guerre opened certain chests filled with bran and showed the young girl the coats of mail of the ancestors, thus preserved from rust. She did all this, as Bertrande well knew, that the young wife might understand the household which she would one day be called upon to direct. At no season of the year could she have summarized more happily all that the labors of the spring and summer were working to achieve.

The dusk came early with a chill that presaged winter. It was fully dark before the men began to assemble from the fields and pastures. The tables were set, and fresh bundles of vine trimmings were flung on the fire. The cattle were driven home and stabled, as was necessary every night

THE WIFE OF MARTIN GUERRE

in the year because of the depredations of bears. The sheep came next, their voices filling the courtyard with a high prolonged babble. The shepherd and the cowherd, entering the kitchen, brought the smell of the beasts into the room. The swineherd came next, and the men who were, turn and turn about, waggoners, vine dressers, or harvesters of grain. Last of all came the head of the family, Martin's father, squired by his son. His wife met him on the threshold with a cup of warmed wine, which he drank before he entered the house. He removed his cape and gave it to one of his daughters. He seated himself at the head of the table. The eldest daughter brought him a bowl of water and a napkin. He washed and wiped his hands, and then, searching the room with his eyes, found Martin's wife and signaled her to approach.

"Sit here, my daughter," he said, indicating a place beside him. "Tonight you shall be waited on. Tomorrow you shall have your own share of the labors of the house."

He did not smile, but the deed and the voice were kind. Bertrande, gazing cautiously into his face as his attention was directed elsewhere, now to the conversation of the shepherd, now toward the blazing hearth, remembered the severe paternal countenance as she had seen it by torchlight from the high pillow of the marriage bed, and she thought that the torchlight had changed it. Here, in the more even flow of the fire, the face of her new father held nothing terrifying. Seamed, coarsened by exposure to rough weather, the darkened skin caught the gold reflections squarely, without compromise or evasion, admitting all the engravures of time. The beard was short, rough and grizzled, parted to show a cleft in the long chin. The mouth, not smiling, but just, had a heavy lower lip which could admit of anger. The nose was short and flattened, the cheek bones were high, the forehead was high and wide, the eyes, now gray, now black, as the light changed, were calmly interested, calm in the assurance of authority. He sat at ease in the stiff-backed rush-bottomed chair, his dark jerkin laced to the throat, his right hand resting on the edge of the table, vigilantly surveying his household, like some Homeric king, some ruler of an island commonwealth who could both plow and fight, and the hand which rested on the table was scarred as from some defensive struggle in years long gone by. Without bearing any outward symbol of his power, he was in his own person both authority and security. He ruled, as the contemporary records say, using the verb which belongs to royalty, and the young girl seated beside him, in feeling this, felt also the great peace which his authority created for his household. It was the first of many evenings in which his presence should testify for her that the beasts were safe, that the grain was safe, that neither the wolves, whose voices could be heard on winter nights, nor marauding bands of mercenaries such as the current hearsay from the larger valleys sometimes reported, could do anything to harm the hearth beside which this man was seated. Because of him the farm was safe, and therefore Artigues, and therefore Languedoc, and therefore France, and therefore the whole world was safe as it should be.

Martin was sufficiently kind to her, in spite of her apprehensions. He treated her with rather more affection than he did his sisters, bullying her occasionally, as he never bullied them, leaving her for the most part to her own affairs. At night they slept together in their own bed, shoulders turned away from each other, the tired young heads buried deep in the feather-stuffed pillows. Bertrande continued, day by day, her long apprenticeship for the position which she was destined to fill, that of mistress of the farm.

A year went by, during which Bertrande was aware of no other sentiment for her husband than a mild gratitude for his leaving her alone. Then, in the early autumn, Martin went bear-hunting. A cordon had been organized in the parish, according to custom, in order to check to some extent the increasing boldness of those animals which not only destroyed the young barley in the spring but also attacked cattle and sheep. It was generally maintained that there were two species of bear in the Pyrenees, those which were vegetarians strictly and those which were carnivorous. The latter were a far greater menace than the wolves, which were not seen in summer and which were dangerous only in the winter months when stock was likely to be safe in stable or fold. Martin had heard of the cordon, and, without saying anything to anyone, had risen early and gone off to join the hunters. He was not seen all that day. When evening came, the workers returned to the farm, shepherd, swineherd, carter, vintager, but no Martin. Monsieur Guerre inquired for his son, but no one had any information to offer. According to custom, the farm workers and the household servants sat down with their master while Madame Guerre and Bertrande waited upon them. The usual talk of the day's work went on, the meal was finished, the tables were cleared away, and the hour for prayers drew near, before the door burst open and Martin entered, staggering under a load of bearmeat done up in the yet bloody hide of the bear. He was exultant. But when he saw his father's expectant eyes, his exuberance died away, and, depositing his booty before his father, he made his excuses for being absent from the farm labor, and recounted, more briefly than he had intended, the adventures of his day. His father watched him quietly. When the boy had finished, his father said,

"That is all you have to say?"

"Yes, my father."

"Very well. Kneel."

Martin dropped on his knees, and his father, leaning forward, struck him with the knuckles of his right hand full upon the left side of his jaw. Martin said nothing. Madame Guerre caught her breath but made no outcry. In a moment Martin stood up and went to spit blood into the fire.

"Prayers, my children," said the father.

The household, upon its knees, with bowed heads, attended to the prayers which the father repeated, and then, dispersing, went off to bed. Several hours later that evening when the house was quiet and only a small gleam of firelight shone through the folds of serge which enclosed their bed, Bertrande said to Martin:

"Are you awake?"

"Certainly. My jaw aches. He has broken me two teeth."

"It was not just," she whispered with indignation.

"Certainly it was just. I didn't ask him if I might go. I was afraid that he might refuse me. But it was well done, was it not, to kill a bear?"

"Oh, yes," she replied fervently, "Martin, you are brave."

He said nothing to that, agreeing in his heart, but as he fell asleep, later, his arm rested on her shoulder. She had sided with him against the paternal authority, however just that authority might be. They were two, a camp within a camp. As for Bertrande, to her own surprise she began to understand that Martin belonged to her and that her affection for him was even greater than her respect and admiration for his father.

In the morning Madame Guerre, examining the damage done to her son's teeth, wept, but did not protest against her husband's severity.

"You understand, my son, it is necessary," she said. "If you have no obedience for your father, your son will have none for you, and then what will become of the family? Ruin. Despair."

"Yes, my mother, I understand," said Martin.

No one but Bertrande had hinted that the punishment was arbitrary and severe, and nothing further was said by anyone about the matter.

But gradually Bertrande's affection for her husband became a deep and joyous passion, growing slowly and naturally as her body grew. All about her, life flourished and increased itself, in field, in fold, in the rose-flushed bramble stems of spring before the green leaf unfurled, and in the vine leaves of autumn that lay like fire along the corded branches. She felt this passion within herself like the wine they drank in the early days of spring, light, tart, heady, and having a special fragrance, and her delight illuminated her love like the May sunshine pouring downward into the cupped wine. Early in her twentieth year she gave birth to a son, and her happiness seemed crowned and sanctified beyond anything she had ever dreamed. They called the boy Sanxi. His grandfather, receiving him in his arms a few minutes after his birth, rubbed his lips with garlic and touched them with a few sour drops of the wine of the country, welcoming him as

THE SHAPE OF FICTION

a true Gascon. The boy thrived, and his mother thrived with him, as if they lent each other well-being.

Being the mother of an heir, Bertrande now received from her parents-in-law a new esteem which was manifest in little favors. This filled her with pride and contributed in no small measure to the grace with which she carried her dark head. More than ever she understood her position in the household, part of a structure that reached backward in time towards ancestors of whose renown one was proud and forward to a future in which Sanxi was a young man, in which Sanxi's children were to grow tall and maintain, as she and Martin now helped to maintain, the prosperity and honor of the family.

Martin had been placed in full charge of certain labors of the farm and more especially in charge of certain fields. He was responsible to his father for all he did, but the method and the details were in his own hands. It was a part of his progress toward the assumption of the full authority of the farm, which could not come to him until after his father's death, but for which he must be early prepared.

His situation was moreover curious in this respect; for the extent of his father's lifetime Martin would remain legally a minor. He might grow old, Sanxi might marry and have sons, but as long as the elder Guerre survived, so long was he absolute head of the house, and such liberty as Martin might enjoy was to be enjoyed only under his father's rule. This was so well understood together with the necessity for the law, that it never occurred to Martin to suppose it might be otherwise. It was known throughout Languedoc that a father owned the privilege of freeing his son, if he chose, from the parental authority, but this could only be done through a deliberate and formal ceremony; and although there were fathers who sometimes so liberated their sons, if anyone had asked Martin Guerre what he thought of such a procedure, he would almost certainly have replied that he thought ill. All such authority as belonged to the *cap d'hostal* Martin Guerre wished to retain, however much he might personally suffer for the time being under such authority. After the lapse of years he expected himself to be *cap d'hostal*, and when that responsibility should rest upon him he would have need of all the accumulated authority of antiquity, even as his father had need of it now.

Martin resembled his father greatly, both physically and in disposition. B̶ ̶t̶rande, who sometimes observed his smothered resentment, or impa-
 at his inferior position, understood both the impatience and the
  which kept it in control, the acceptance of things as they were,
   ietly to herself:
    y he will make a protector for this family as like his own
     en well may be, and for that thanks to God."

Outwardly, Martin had the swarthy skin, the high forehead, the gray eyes, the flat, short nose, the lips, the high cleft chin of his father, and something of his father's build. Too early labor at the plow had rounded his shoulders. Nevertheless he was a skillful swordsman and boxer, agile, tall, and well-developed for his years. "Not a pretty man," as the servant had said, "but a very distinguished man." His ugliness was ancestral, and that in itself was good.

People so reasonable, so devoted, so strongly loving and hard working should have been exempt, one feels, from the vagaries of a malicious fate. Nevertheless, the very virtues of their way of life gave rise to a small incident, and from that incident developed the whole train of misfortune which singled out Bertrande de Rols from the peace and obscurity of her tradition.

It was a day in autumn. The vintage was done and the winter wheat was being put in the ground. Since the men were not expected to return to the farm at noon, Bertrande had taken Martin's lunch to him, and while he ate, she sat beside him on the sun-warmed, roughened earth at the edge of the field. She was bare-footed and bare-headed, the bodice of her gown open a little at the throat because of the noonday heat. The flesh at the edge of the gown was creamy, and the color deepened upward into a warm tan, growing richer and brighter on the rounded cheeks; and at the edge of the hair, in the shadow of the thick dark locks, the creamy color showed again, now moist from the sheltered heat. She watched her husband with tender, happy eyes. Before them, the cultivated ground slanted downward to a hazel copse. They could hear above them the murmur of the stream, reduced from its full summer flow, where it ran under the chestnut trees, before it circled the field, running below them through the copse and on into the narrowing valley. Across the valley and on the higher slopes, the beech and oak woods were tinged with gold and russet, and higher still a blue haze seemed to be gathering, like threads of smoke. Leaf, earth, and wine in the still sunlight gave forth the odors of their substances; the air was full of autumn fragrance. Martin, when he had finished his lunch, wrapped the fragments of bread and cheese and put them in his wallet. He returned the earthen wine jug to the hands of his wife and said:

"I am going away for a little while."

Bertrande made an exclamation of surprise.

"You may well be astonished," replied Martin. "This is the way of it. This morning I took from my father's granary enough seed wheat to plant the half of this field."

"You did not ask him for it?" cried Bertrande in alarm.

"Certainly, no. He would have denied it to me because it is his notion that I should put aside whatever grain I need from my own harvesting. But this year I have more land under cultivation than I had hoped to have. Should I let it go to waste? He has finished his planting; the wheat remains unused. So I took it, and I have planted it. Was it not well done?"

"It was well done," she answered, "but I'm afraid for you."

"I am afraid for myself," he said with a smile. "Without a doubt, he would flay me. Therefore I am going away. When he has had time to reflect, he will see that it was well done, and he will forgive me. Then I can return. You remember the bear?"

He rubbed his hand reminiscently along his jaw while Bertrande also smiled a little.

"You will have to be gone at least a week," she said. "Perhaps longer. If I could send you word . . ."

"Eight days should be enough," said Martin. "It is done for the good of the house—he will see that. And it is better that you should not know where I am in case he asks you. I shall go to Toulouse, then further, so that you can answer honestly, 'I do not know where he is.' Embrace my little son for me, and do not be disturbed."

She kissed him on both cheeks, feeling the warmth of the sun upon his flesh, caressing with her hand the short smooth beard, and then, in a brief premonition of disaster, held to his arm and would not let him go.

"Do not distress yourself," he repeated tenderly. "I shall be safe. I shall enjoy myself, moreover. And I shall see you in a week."

So he went off. Once he turned to wave with a free, elated gesture, and then the shadows of the trees engulfed his figure. Bertrande returned to the farm, swinging the empty jug from a forefinger and thinking of the path which led down the valley beside the torrent falling and tumbling toward the Neste. Once she stepped aside to let pass a herd of swine being driven up into the oak forest to feed on acorns. She greeted the swineherd absently, thinking of Martin's journey, and how he would pass village after village, ford the cold streams, follow the narrow passes beside the Neste and eventually emerge into the greater valley of the Garonne, see the level fields, the walled cities, broad roads traversed by bands of merchants and armed men. The woods were still after the passage of the beasts—no insects and few birds. She wished that she might have gone with Martin. At the farm she found Sanxi, and was glad that she had not gone.

The afternoon passed as usual, but at suppertime, when Monsieur Guerre asked her where Martin was, and she answered, as had been arranged between them, "I do not know," she trembled beneath the cold gray gaze, penetrating and clear as a beam of light reflected from a wall of ice.

When it was learned that certain baskets of grain had been removed from the granary, the anger of Monsieur Guerre was terrible, as she had known it would be, and she was thankful that Martin's shoulders were beyond the reach of his father's heavy whip. At the end of a week the anger of Monsieur Guerre had not abated. Apprehensively Bertrande listened at the approach of every passer-by, started and turned cold each time the door to the house creaked on its broad hinges, and hoped that Martin might be fortunately delayed. Again and again she wished that some arrangement had been made between them by which she might meet and warn him. As week followed week, alarm at his prolonged absence began to mingle with the fear of his premature return. At the end of a month she was almost certain that some evil must have befallen him, and in great fear and agitation presented herself before the father of the family and confessed all that she knew of Martin's design.

Monsieur Guerre listened to her in silence, without moving a finger. Then he answered coldly:

"Madame, that my son should have become a thief is the greatest shame I have ever been asked to bear. Since he is my son, my only son, and since the welfare of the house depends upon the succession of an heir, I consider it my duty to forgive him. When he returns and confesses his crime, and has borne his punishment, I shall withdraw my anger. Until that time, no matter how distant it may be, rest assured, Madame, my anger shall exist. You may return to your work, Madame."

It was terrible to her to be addressed in this manner by a man whom she so greatly respected. "For their children," wrote the learned Etienne Pasquier a few years later, "fathers and mothers are the true images of God upon earth," and this was not an opinion which Pasquier imposed upon his time, but one in which he had been schooled. Bertrande admitted the inflexible justice of Martin's father, and regretted bitterly that she had fallen in with Martin's plans for avoiding punishment. How much better if he had stayed and submitted! He would now be forgiven and all would be well. She now prayed that he return at once. But the winter deepened about the village of Artigues, the ways were blocked with snow, and as even the mountain torrent became locked under ice she abandoned all hope of seeing him that winter.

It was lonely without him. The days, shortened by the double shadow of winter and of the steep mountain-sides, held little gaiety for the wife of Martin Guerre, and the nights were unutterably long. When spring came, the snow melted and all the valley was murmurous with the sound

THE SHAPE OF FICTION

of rushing water. Still Martin delayed his return, and she said to herself:

"It is too early to hope for him. All the streams are flooded, the fords are impassable. Men and horses have beeen drowned trying to cross La Neste in flood."

She said this, but still her heart unreasonably demanded that he return and that quickly. With the first fine weather, the young wheat sprouting, the vines beginning to put forth tufts of silvery, crumpled leaves, with the half-wooded, half-cultivated valley ringing, now far, now near, with birdsong, her own youth and beauty quickened; and together with her consciousness of her youth, her beauty, her desire deepened for her husband. Somehow, with the winter, had died the fear that Martin might have been hurt or killed. She was at that time too young to believe in the reality of death. The reviving season held only her love and her impatience.

But spring went by, and Martin did not return. Through the deepening summer she looked for him in vain and only when the first heavy snow again closed the mountain passes did she admit to herself that her husband had left her. She knew that he had found the experience of liberty sweet, that to be master of his own actions was more precious to him than the society of his wife, the enjoyment of his son, or his share in the prosperity of the house. She believed that Martin was waiting until the time when he might return as head of the house, that he could not brook the idea of returning, not only to punishment, but to the continued rigors of his father's authority. She said nothing of this to anyone, but the thought was not an easy one to live with.

He had deserted her in the full beauty of her youth, in the height of her great passion, he had shamed her and wounded her, and when he returned, if he should return after the death of his father, his authority would be as great as his father's then was, and to murmur against his treatment of her would then be improper in the highest degree.

Martin's absence weighed upon the whole family. Although his father never mentioned his name, it was evident to those who knew him well that he had aged since Martin's departure. The second year after the disappearance of her son, Madame Guerre died. She was not an old woman, and it may have been possible, as her daughters believed, that the illness from which she suffered during the last year of her life was greatly aggravated by the prolonged absence of her son. Bertrande assumed her duties and mourned her, for whatever their differences, always unexpressed by Bertrande, on other matters, the deserted wife had felt that her mother-in-law retained no anger against Martin. With Monsieur Guerre it was quite another matter. However perfect his courtesy to her, Bertrande felt always in his presence the just, inflexible displeasure that he maintained toward her husband, and she was reminded, also, that she had shared in Martin's plan. To his original offense, as time went by, Martin was also adding the greater offense of neglecting his inheritance.

The displeasure of Monsieur Guerre had become as necessary and inevitable a part of his character as his spine was of his body. When he entered a room that displeasure entered with him. The household, meanwhile, had changed and was no longer gay. Martin's elder sisters had married and lived elsewhere. The youngest, having married a cadet, or younger son, still lived at home and her husband had come to live with her. He was a quiet soul, deferring easily to Bertrande and to Monsieur Guerre. His presence did not greatly enliven the scene. Sanxi, who was excessively healthy, did not know how to be unhappy, and whether he played or rested, the place where he happened to be was for his mother the only joyous spot on the farm. For the rest, the household waited. Work went on, but the feeling of expectation was always in the air.

The fourth year after Martin's departure his father, though an expert horseman, was thrown from his horse, and, his head striking against a rock as he fell, he was killed instantly. Bertrande, who had seen him ride away from the house, firm and erect in the saddle, could hardly believe the servants who came with the news an hour later. Still, there was something fitting in the manner of his death, which was abrupt, violent and absolute. The peremptory summons and the prompt obedience were like everything else in his way of living. It would have been difficult to conceive of him as grown old, yielding, little by little, perforce, his authority, hesitating and dwindling, and yet, if Martin had not returned, holding on to a life thoroughly exhausted in order not to leave the house without a master.

The shock of his death threw the family into confusion. Something like a panic seemed to overpower the servants and to reduce the four sisters of Martin to helpless children. And yet at the end of the day, Bertrande, finding for the first time a moment to herself, was surprised to consider how completely his death had been accepted, how long he seemed to have been dead who was not yet buried, whose death, early that morning, has been almost as remote as the day of judgment.

Pierre Guerre, the brother of Monsieur Guerre, had arrived in the afternoon and had announced his position as head of the family. He was a lesser man than his brother, shorter and broader of frame, with something of the family countenance but without the quality of great distinction that somehow had belonged to the old master. No less honest, but more simple, easier to approach, a good farmer, a solid soldier, Uncle Pierre had entered the kitchen and crossed with sober dignity to his brother's chair by the hearth. He had assigned tasks, taken the legal matters into consideration, sent for the priest and made public the news of the death. The panic had subsided, the servants had gone about their business as usual, the older sisters had returned to their homes, and Bertrande had said to herself:

"Now it will be safe for Martin to return."

She did not expect him to appear magically. She made her own estimate of the time that it might take the news, traveling uncertainly about the countryside, to reach him and how long it would take him to make the journey home. And hope flourished and wore greener branches than in many a long day. But as the year which she had allowed passed on and drew to a close, her hope again declined, and there were times when despair took its place entirely. She no longer had the fine sense of immortality which she had felt before the death of Martin's parents. Death had now become an actuality rather than a possibility. Death was something that not only could happen but that did happen.

A new fear assailed her. When she thought of Martin as perhaps dead, his remembered features suddenly dissolved, and the more she strove to recollect his appearance, the vaguer grew her memory. When she was not trying to remember him, his face would sometimes reappear, suddenly distinct in color and outline. Then she would start and tremble inwardly and try to hold the vision. But the harder she tried, the dimmer grew the face. The same thing had happened to her, she now remembered, after her mother's death. The beloved image had faded. An impression of warmth, of security, the tones of the voice, the pressure of the hand had remained, but she could not see her mother's face. She had spoken of this to Madame Guerre, who had replied:

"There are people like that. They do not remember with their eyes, but with their ears, maybe. With me, it is the eye, and I could tell you at any moment in which chest I have laid away anything that you might want. I do not remember where it is, I see it. I cast my eye, as it were, over all my arrangements, and I see where I have laid the article which you desire."

Once indeed Bertrande thought that Martin had returned. She was walking on the path to the lower fields and was near the place where she had said farewell to her husband almost five years before. A man coming toward her under the shadow of the trees moved with Martin's gait and was so like him in build that Bertrande stopped, her hand on her breast and her heart leaping suddenly in such wild delight that she could hardly breathe. But the figure, approaching, lost its likeness to the man she loved. She saw presently that he was a stranger and that his features did not resemble those of Martin Guerre in the least. He did not even come near enough to pass her, but some few yards away turned off into the woods in the direction of Sode. Their eyes had met, like those of strangers who met in a narrow path, and he had saluted her, but without recognition.

After he had gone, she stood there, ready to weep in her sick disappointment. The day was cool, a day toward the end of winter, and she wore a heavy black wool cape with a hood, and on her feet were the pointed wooden sabots of her mountains, but she seemed to be standing barefoot on the moss, and bareheaded. Martin's hands were upon hers; she could see the familiar scars, the torn fingernail; and Martin's head was bent and touching hers. She could not see his face for his cheek was against her forehead. From the pressure of his hands upon hers such peace and joy flowed into her body that all the woods seemed warm, bathed in autumnal sunlight. The moment faded and she stood alone again in the thin winter air. She realized then that she had not seen his face, and wondered if that might be of good or bad omen. But the touch of his hand had been very living, and she renewed her hope.

If she heard of there being strangers in town, as there so often were, smugglers from Spain, or deserters from one army for another passing from kingdom to kingdom by way of the Port de la Venasque who delayed their wanderings to visit awhile in the rich mountain villages, she sent for them and entertained them overnight, giving them food, wine and a warm place to sleep. Of these she inquired for news of Martin. Had they, while serving with the Duke of Savoy or under the old Constable Montmorency or with the young Duke of Guise, heard of any man named Martin Guerre? Or bivouacked with him? Or perhaps fought by his side? None of these wanderers had met with such a man. They gave her, in return for her hospitality, other news, of how, before the death of the old king, Guienne, Angoumois and Saintonge had risen in insurrection because of the salt tax, of how at Angoulême the king's tax collectors had been beaten to death and sent "to salt the fish of the Charente," their flesh being flung into the river. She heard of the cruel revenge which Montmorency took under the new king, Henry, the second of that name, at Bordeaux, burning alive those who had killed the tax collectors, and oppressing and humiliating the whole city most grievously. She learned of the siege of Metz and of Henry's continuance of the quarrels of his father with the Emperor from men who had fought with Guise under the walls of that city. The Emperor had said, "I see now that Fortune is a woman; she prefers a young king to an old emperor," and, fatigued and ill, "his face all pale and his eyes sunk in his head, his beard as white as the snow," had made his resolve to abdicate and withdraw to Yuste, there on the other side of the Pyrenees in the Spanish monastery of the Cordeliers. Her imagination traveled far afield, thinking that wherever there was fighting, there Martin was likely to be; but of Martin himself

THE SHAPE OF FICTION

she learned nothing. She charged these wanderers, upon their leave-taking, with a message to her husband, if they should chance to meet him:

"The old Master is dead. Come home."

She even made a journey once to Rieux, where her mother's sister then lived, thinking that to that town, which was a bishopric, almost as many travelers must come as to Toulouse. The town lay in a green meadow in a curve of the Arize, near to the spot at which that turbulent stream hurls itself into the Garonne. Behind it stood the wall of the Pyrenees. The delicate, bold spire of the cathedral, rising above the tiled roofs of the houses, seemed less tall than it was because of the height of the mountains. At the inn and at the cathedral doors Bertrande made her inquiries, and besought her aunt to question travelers whenever she might have the opportunity. She also begged that the death of Martin's father be announced from the cathedral. But a nostalgia came upon her there—she had never before left the parish of Artigues. She missed Sanxi, and everything seemed strange. Even the room in which she slept in her aunt's house seemed turned around, and the sun rose in the west and shone through western windows all the morning. Or so it seemed to Bertrande. After a few days she made her excuses to her aunt, and went home to Artigues.

And time went by. Meanwhile Sanxi, who in his earliest infancy had given some slight promise of growing to look like his father, daily grew more and more to resemble the sisters of Martin Guerre, who had their mother's features and proportions rather than those of their father. This was at first a grief to Bertrande, although in considering Sanxi with his fresh young face and thick smooth chestnut hair, he seemed to her so altogether remarkable and charming that she could not wish him otherwise in any detail. She began to listen instead for the tones of his father's voice in the boy's light treble. So, nourishing her devotion with hope and with imagination, she took charge of Martin's household, tended his child, and waited.

The house flourished, Sanxi grew, and Bertrande increased in beauty. Her sorrow and her new sense of responsibility ennobled her physical charm. She acquired unconsciously a manner of gracious command. Eight years after the departure of her husband she no longer had the first tender radiance which had so pleased the young man, but a greater and more mature beauty had taken its place.

Eight years after the departure of Marin Guerre, Bertrande his wife was seated in the Chamber instructing her son in the catechism. The first warm days of summer were come, and neither mother nor son was paying as great attention as might have been paid to the lesson in hand. The room, large, dusky, cool, shut them effectively from the affairs of

THE WIFE OF MARTIN GUERRE

the kitchen and the courtyard. The wooden shutters were opened wide, but the window was high. It let in the sunshine but did not permit a view of the yard. The peace of the summer day without, the quiet half hour alone with Sanxi, the release from the continual round of practical duties had relaxed Bertrande. She looked at Sanxi's cool young cheek beside her knee and thought, "At last I begin to be at peace."

And her thought, sweeping backward quickly over all the moments of anguish, of desire, of hatred, even, hours of fierce resentment against Martin for making her suffer, for holding her from any other life than a prolonged fruitless waiting for his return, hours of terror when she had contemplated his death in some engagement of the Spanish wars, hours to be remembered with horror in which she had desired his death that she might be free of the agony of incertitude—all these reviewed in a moment with a sharp inward knowledge of herself, her thought returned like a tired dove to this moment of peace in which love was only love for Sanxi, as innocent and cool and gentle as the curve of his cheek. She regarded him thoughtfully and tenderly, and Sanxi, lifting his eyes to hers, smiled with a secret amusement.

"Repeat the answer, my son," said Bertrande.

Sanxi did so, his delight deepening.

"But you have given me that reply for two questions, Sanxi. You do not attend."

"No, mother, for three questions, the same answer," said Sanxi, suddenly hilarious.

"You must not make fun of sacred things," she said to him as gravely as she could, but neither of them was deceived, and as they smiled at each other, a hubbub arose in the courtyard which made Sanxi run to the window. Standing on his tiptoes, he still could not see much but the adjoining buildings. The tumult increased, with shrill cries, definitely joyous. Bertrande de Rols turned toward the door, leaning slightly forward in her chair. The noise, advancing through the kitchen, was approaching the Chamber, and suddenly the door swung open to admit Martin's Uncle Pierre, his four sisters and a bearded man dressed in leather and steel, who paused on the threshold as the others crowded forward. Behind him all the household servants and one or two men from the fields showed their excited ruddy faces. The old housekeeper, pushing past him, almost beside herself with joy, curtsied as low as she could, and cried:

"It is he, Madame!"

"It is Martin, my child," said Uncle Pierre.

"Bertrande," cried the sisters in chorus, "here is our brother Martin!"

Their voices filled the room, echoing from the low beams and the stone walls; they were all talking at once, and, as Bertrande rose to her feet, keeping one hand on the back of the chair to steady herself against a sudden, quickly passing dizziness, the bearded figure advanced gravely, surrounded by the agitated forms of the sisters, the uncle, the servants, who were now all swarming in behind the original group.

It was dark at the far end of the room. Bertrande stood in the sunlight and met, as in a dream, the long-anticipated moment, her breath stilled and her heart beating wildly. The figure in leather and steel advanced with even tread, a stockier figure than that of the man who had gone away eight years before, broader in the shoulder, developed, mature. The beard was strange, being rough and thick, but above it the eyes were like those of Martin, the forehead, the whole cast of the countenance, like and unlike to Bertrande's startled recognition, and as he advanced from the shadow he seemed to Bertrande a stranger, the stranger of the wooded pathway, then her loved husband, then a man who might have been Martin's ancestor but not young Martin Guerre.

When he had advanced to within a few feet of her, he stopped, and she read in his eyes a surprise and an admiration so intense that her limbs seemed all at once bathed in a soft fire. She was frightened.

"Madame," said the stranger who was her husband, "you are very beautiful."

"Cap de Diou!" exclaimed the uncle. "Are you surprised that your wife is beautiful?"

"Beautiful, yes, I knew, but beauty such as this I did not remember."

"Yes, Martin, yes," cried the sisters. "She has changed, you are right. It is another beauty."

"But why do you stand there? Embrace her, my nephew."

And then Bertrande felt on her cheek the imprint of the bearded lips, and on her shoulders the weight of the strong hands, felt with a shock the actual masculinity of the embrace, so strange for one who had been long accustomed only to the light touch of Sanxi's mouth. The embrace released her from her trance, reminding her of the last kiss which she had given Martin at the edge of the wheat field, and all the emotion tightly held in check for so many years was in her voice as she cried:

"Ah, why have you been away so long! Cruel! Cruel! I have almost forgotten your face! Even your voice, Martin, is strange in my ears."

"Bertrande," said Pierre Guerre with gravity, "this is no proper welcome for your husband, to overwhelm him with reproaches. You forget youself, my child, indeed you do. My nephew, you must pardon her. It is the excess of emotion. We cannot tell you how we rejoice at your return. It was the greatest sorrow to your father that you were gone so long. But that is over. I praise God that you are safely with us, no

THE WIFE OF MARTIN GUERRE

longer a boy, but a man grown. In times like these a house has need of a master and a child of a protector."

"I praise God also," said Bertrande softly, "and I ask your pardon, my husband."

"No, Uncle," came the reply. "She does well to reproach the man who left you all so long unprotected. It is I who should ask pardon of her. But you must believe me: until I passed through Rieux I did not know that my father was dead." And, bending above her hand, he promised Bertrande that he would never again leave her and that he would do all in his power to atone for the neglect which he had shown her. Bertrande was deeply touched and not a little surprised. Uncle Pierre remarked:

"It is well done, my nephew. I can see that the wars have done more for you than strengthen bone and muscle. You have spoken like a true father and like the head of a house."

Behind him the four sisters of Martin were agitated by murmurs of approval, and there were cries of approval and admiration from the servants, who, crowding forward, all wished to salute their long-absent master.

He greeted them all, inquiring for certain ones who had died during his absence, questioned them about their families, and their health, praised them for their loyalty and good service, and appeared so genuinely pleased to see them all that their enthusiasm redoubled.

Bertrande, watching him, said to herself:

"He is noble, he is generous, he is like his father again, but become gracious."

But suddenly the master, putting aside gently the servants who stood between him and Bertrande, cried:

"But where is Sanxi? Where is my son, that I may embrace him?"

At this Sanxi, who had been hiding behind his mother, burrowed his head into her skirts, drawing the ample folds about his shoulders.

"Come, Sanxi," said his mother, taking him by the shoulders. "Here is your father, your good father of whom we have talked so many times. Salute him."

"Ah, my little monsieur," exclaimed a great voice, "it is good to see you," and Sanxi, clinging like a kitten to his mother's skirts, so that she had to disengage his fingers one by one, felt himself hoisted into the air and then folded close to a hard shoulder, smelt the reek of leather and horse-sweat, and then felt the wiry beard rubbed joyously against his face.

"Mama!" he cried. "Mama!"

"It is the strangeness," he heard his mother's voice saying apologetically. "Do not hold it against him. Consider, how sudden and how strange —for him, as for me."

THE SHAPE OF FICTION

"Tonnèrre!" cried the great voice. "He is hard to hold. But never mind. We shall be friends, in time."

The boy felt himself set on his feet firmly, and then his parents turned away from him. Some people pushed in between him and his mother, and as the crowd moved toward the door, everyone laughing and talking, it carried her along, clinging to the arm of the stranger. The swineherd and the boy who cared for the horses were the last to leave the room. They lagged behind, buffeting each other out of sheer good will, and the swineherd, turning, saw young Sanxi still standing in front of his mother's chair.

"What a fine day for you," he called. "It isn't everyday that a boy gets a father."

An hour later Sanxi had recovered himself sufficiently to dare sit beside his father on the long bench before the fireplace. On the other side of his father was the priest; in front of him, on a stool, was Uncle Pierre. His mother kept coming and going from the table to the fireplace, pausing sometimes with her hand on the shoulder of Uncle Pierre to gaze happily and incredulously at his father.

Uncle Pierre had to tell again how he had met Sanxi's father, "away by the church, far from the road to the farm. I knew him at once, and that from the back of his head. I cried, 'Hollah, Martin, my nephew, where are you going, away so far from your own house? You have returned,' I said. 'Pray do not leave us before you have seen your own roof.' And what answer did he make, this excellent man? 'I am going,' said he, 'to the church to give thanks to God for my safe return and to pray for the soul of my father of whose death I learned only yesterday.'"

The priest nodded with grave approval; the uncle wiped an actual tear from his eye.

"So then I cried, 'Good boy, embrace me, Martin, embrace your old Uncle Pierre,' and we went and knelt in the church. I am glad that I have lived to see this day."

Then Sanxi's father had to hear from the priest and from Uncle Pierre all the story of how Sanxi's grandfather had fallen from his horse and been killed instantly, and of how his grandmother had died very quietly in her bed with all her family and her servants round about, weeping, all save her son Martin, and through all these recitals Sanxi was puzzled to see how his mother alternately wept and smiled. His father did not cry. He was very serious, very serious and strong, and Sanxi, sitting beside him, observed minutely all the straps and buckles of his armor and how the metal of his gorget had chafed the leather of his jerkin, and began to admire him, silently.

For the rest of the day he attached himself to his father's person, like a small dog who does not mind whether he is noticed or not, provided he is permitted to be present. He heard his father's brief account of his wanderings. He listened to the servants as they poured out to his father their stories of everything that had taken place since his departure, eight years ago. He even listened unnoticed while Uncle Pierre went over the business of the house with his father. And in the evening there were violins and flutes, roast meat as if it were a fête day, and neighbors riding in from miles around to welcome his father home. Sanxi had not known that his own household could be so gay. The very walls of the kitchen were animated and seemed to tremble in the ruddy glow from the chimney. The copper vessels winked and blazed. The glazed pottery on the dresser also gave back the quivering light, and his father's armor, as he flung himself in his chair, or rose to meet a newcomer, was momentarily like the sky of an autumn sunset.

But the seasons are tyrannical for the farmer. In the morning the flutes and violins were put away, and before dawn the men were about the usual work of the farm. The master to the fields, the mistress to the dairy —everything was just as usual until evening, and then, after supper before the hour for prayers, there was much talk by the fireplace of foreign lands, sieges and marches, the slaying of heretics, and finally, instead of saying, "Prayers, my friends," there was the master of the house, like Sanxi's grandfather, announcing,

"My children, it is time for prayer."

The estate prospered surprisingly after the return of the master. The vigor of the man was contagious, and he had a way of noticing the work that a servant was doing and saying a word of approval that the old master had never had. For Bertrande, as for Sanxi, it was a new life, almost a new world. Gladly she surrendered the responsibilities of the farm to her husband's care, and surrendered herself to his love. From having been a widow for eight years, she was suddenly again a wife. The loneliness of the house was dissipated. Even when there were not old friends come from a distance to greet Martin Guerre, even when the priest was not established in the corner of the hearth to hear accounts of the world below the mountains, there was good conversation in the house, and sometimes music, and Sanxi flourished and grew manly in the companionship of a hero. His newly-found father was no less to him.

At the end of a few months Bertrande found herself with child. She rejoiced thereat, and she also trembled, for at times a curious fear assailed her, a fear so terrible and unnatural that she hardly dared acknowledge it in her most secret heart. What if Martin, the roughly bearded stranger, were not the true Martin, the one whom she had kissed farewell that noonday by the side of the freshly planted field? Her sin, if such indeed were a fact, would be most black, for had she not experienced an instinctive warning? On the night of his return, overcome by desire and astonishment, she had trembled in his embrace and murmured again and again:

"Martin, it is so strange, I cannot believe it to be true."

To which the bearded traveler had replied:

"Poor little one, you have been too long alone."

In the morning her fear had vanished, Martin's family and friends, the servants, the very animals of the place, it seemed, affirming his identity, and putting her heart at peace.

So she had been happy, and had rejoiced in the presence of this new Martin even more than in that of the old, and it was not until she began to feel the weight of the child in her body that the fear returned. Even so, it did not stay. It was like the shadow of a dark wing sweeping suddenly across the room, and then departing swiftly as it had come, leaving all things standing as usual under the cold, normal light of day. But one day, seeing Martin returning from a ride with Sanxi, and seeing the easy comradeship between the two, she said aloud:

"It is not possible that this man should be Martin Guerre. For Martin Guerre, the son of the old master, proud and abrupt, like the old master, could never in this world speak so gaily to his own son. Ah! unhappy woman that I am, so to distrust the Good God who has sent me this happiness! I shall be punished. But this is also punishment in itself."

No one heard her speak, and, weeping bitterly, she withdrew to her own room where she remained until a servant came to find her at the hour of the evening meal. Nevertheless, in spite of her contribution, she could not refrain, the moment that they were left alone that evening, from accusing her husband of being other than the man he represented, and of asking for proof of his identity.

She had expected passionate proof or passionate denial. The man before her regarded her gravely, even tenderly, and said:

"Proof? But why proof? You have seen me. You have felt the touch of my lips. Behold my hands. Are they not scarred even as you remember them? Do you remember the time my father struck me and broke my teeth? They are still broken. You have spoken with me; we have spoken together of things past. Is not my speech the same? Why should I be other than myself? What has happened to give you this strange notion?"

Bertrande replied in a barely audible voice:

"If you had been Martin Guerre you would perhaps have struck me just now."

He answered with gentle surprise:

"But because I struck you on the day we were married, is that a reason I should strike you now? Listen to me, my dearest. Am I who speak to you now more different from the young man who left you, than that young man was different from the child you married?"

"When you left me," said Bertrande, "you resembled your father in flesh and spirit. Now you resemble him only in the flesh."

"My child," said her husband, ever more gravely, "my father was arrogant and severe. Just, also, and loving, but his severity sent from home his only son. For eight years I have traveled among many sorts and conditions of men. I have been many times in danger of death. If I return to you with a greater wisdom than that which I knew when I departed, would you have me dismiss it, in order again to resemble my father? God knows, my child, and the priest will so instruct you, that a man of evil ways may by an act of will so alter his actions and his habits that he becomes a man of good. Are you satisfied?"

"And then," said Bertrande, in a still smaller voice, marshaling her last argument, "Martin Guerre at twenty had not the gift of the tongue. His father, also, was a silent man."

At this her husband, hitherto so grave, burst into a laugh which made the Chamber echo, and still laughing, with his broad hand he wiped the tears from her wet face.

"My darling, how funny you are," he said. "Weep no more. Every Gascon has the gift of the tongue. Some employ it, some do not. Since I am become no longer arrogant and severe, I choose to employ my gift." Then, more gently, he continued. "Madame, you are demented. It happens sometimes to women who are with child. Pay no attention to it. It will pass, and when your time is over, you will look back to this with astonishment."

"Perhaps that is it," said Bertrande in acquiescence. "For God knows I do not wish you to be otherwise than my true husband. When I went to visit my aunt in Rieux, being in a strange town, I became confused as to the directions, and not until I left that house did it seem to me, when I was within doors, that the east was not the west. So it must be with me now. For when I look at you it seems to me that I see the flesh and bone of Martin Guerre, but in them I see dwelling the spirit of another man."

"When I was in Brittany," said her husband, "I heard a strange story of a man who was also a wolf, and there may also have been times when the soul of one man inhabited the body of another. But it is also notorious that men who have been great sinners have become saints. What would become of us all if we had no power to turn from evil toward good?"

And so he led her on to talk of other matters, of foreign lands and battles in Flanders until she was again calm. She put her fear away, or rather, she regarded it as a delusion, and she gave herself over to the happy anticipation of her second child. In her affection for her husband was now mingled a profound gratitude, for he had delivered her, at least for the present, from the terror of sin. When, upon a certain day she asked him if he remembered such and such a little incident, and he responded, smiling, "No, and do you remember when I told you that your eyes are speckled like the back of a mountain trout?" she only smiled in return, full of confidence and ease.

"You did not say such things when you were twenty," she replied.

It was the time of year when the grapes were being harvested, and the odor of ripe muscats was in the air. When the wine was made and the leaves on the vine stocks had turned scarlet, Bertrande rode out among valleys that dipped in fire toward Luchon between the irregular advances of the woods, saw the conical haystacks burning with dull gold beside the stone walls of farm buildings, felt, as she rode in the sunshine, the cold invigorating sweep of wind from the higher mountains, lifted her eyes and saw how the white clouds piled high above the rich green of the pine woods and how the sky was intensely blue beyond, blue as a dream of the Mediterranean or of the Gulf of Gascony. And returning, toward evening to her own house, as the blue haze of evening began to intercept and transmute the shapes of things, she smelled the wood smoke from her own hearth fire and thought it as sweet as the incense which was burned in the church at Artigues. Or she saw at the far end of a field, a man wearing a scarlet jerkin working in a group of men uniformly clothed in brown, a small dot of scarlet moving about on long brown legs against the golden surface of the earth, and these things, intensely perceived as never before since she could remember, filled her with a piercing joy. The cold metallic gleam of halberds moving forward under a steely sky against the background of the russet woods, as a band of soldiers passed her by; the very feel and pattern of the frost upon the threshold early in the morning as the season advanced; the motion and songs of birds, until their numbers diminished; and then the iron sound of the churchbell ringing in somber majesty across the cold valleys—all these she noticed and enjoyed as never before. And even, when winter had closed around them, one night from a far-off hillside, the crying of wolves had filled her with a pleasure enhanced with dread, for the doors were safely closed and all the animals safe within walls, and a good fire roared in the great fireplace, spreading shifting constellations of gold against the black throat of the chimney, so that the dread was a luxury, and her enjoyment of the strange distant voices all the greater. And all this vividness of feeling, this new awareness of the life around her, was because of her love for this new Martin Guerre, and because of the delight and health of her life-giving body. Yet even this love was intensified, like her pleasure in the cry of the wolves, by the persistent illusion, or suspicion, that this man was not Martin.

The illusion, if such it was, did not pass away at the termination of her pregnancy, as he had prophesied it would do, but she had grown used to it. It lent a strange savor to her passion for him. Her happiness, and the happiness of her children, especially that of the newly born, the son of the new Martin, shone the more brightly, was the more greatly to be treasured because of the shadow of sin and danger which accompanied it. She wrapped the little body in swaddling bands, sheltering the little bald head from the chill spring air with her softest woolen cloth, and walked out into the fields along paths still wet from melting snow, where the earliest spring blossoms had already pricked the dead leaves. The winter wheat showed its point of new sharp green, and the air alternately misted, showered, and shone in confusing variability.

In June the wheat was harvested and the brook of the valley was turned loose by irrigating ditches upon the stubble fields, which had already begun to parch and burn in the midsummer heat. The steep fields, being so flooded, were like a series of cascades and terraces, running and shining; yet the water also sank deep into the rich earth and before long the fields were bright, some with flowers and grass, some with the new crop of buckwheat. And still the happiness of Bertrande continued, accompanied always by the shadow of her suspicion, and she could no longer say:

"It will pass when I am delivered of the child."

Through the summer, little by little the shadow increased in the mind of Bertrande. In vain did she contend with it. In a thousand ways her suspicion was strengthened, in ways so small that she was ashamed to mention them. She thought of speaking of the matter in confession, but checked herself, saying:

"The priest will think me mad." She did not say, "Or worse, he will find a way to prove that which I only suspect."

But this was in her mind, and day after day she turned aside, she doubled her tracks, like a pursued creature, trying to avoid the realization which she knew was waiting for her. But as time went on she found herself more and more surely faced with the obligation of admitting herself to be hopelessly insane or of confessing that she was consciously accepting as her husband a man whom she believed to be an impostor. If the choice had lain within her power she would undoubtedly have chosen to be mad. For days and weeks she turned aside, as in a fever, from what she felt to be the truth, declaring to her distracted soul that she was defending the safety of her children, of her household, from Uncle Pierre down to the smallest shepherd, and then at last, one morning as she was seated alone, spinning, the truth presented itself finally, coldly, inescapably.

"I am no more mad than is this man. I am imposed upon, deceived, betrayed into adultery, but not mad."

The spindle dropped to the floor, the distaff fell across her knees, and though she sat like a woman turned into stone and felt her heart freezing slowly in her bosom, the air which entered her nostrils seemed to her more pure than any she had breathed in years, and the fever seemed to have left her body. She began then quietly to array before her in this clear passionless light the facts of her situation as she must now consider it, no longer distorted through fear or shame or through the desire of the flesh. She knew that she would never again be able to pretend that this man was the man whom she had married. Although she had loved him passionately and joyously, and perhaps loved him still, and although he was the father of her son, she must rid herself of him. But could she rid herself? If she asked him to go, would he go? If she were to accuse him publicly of his crime, could she prove it? And if she could not prove it, in bringing such an accusation would she not be wronging the entire family from Sanxi and herself to the least of the cousins and cousins-in-law? And what of her youngest son, the son of the impostor? Had he no claim upon her, that she should of her own free will dishonor his birth? Terror assailed her lest she be trapped inescapably, and in her profound agitation and fear she rose and paced back and forth in the long, silent room until she was fatigued and trembling. She crossed to the window, and, leaning on the high sill, looked down into the courtyard.

Dusk was gathering, an autumn dusk. The paving stones were black with damp, but by morning they would be lacy white. While she stood there, looking down, her husband rode into the yard. A boy ran to meet him, and led his horse away after he had dismounted. The smith, whose fire glowed dimly in the cold gray light, left his work for a moment to salute his master, and returned to his work, smiling and rubbing his blackened hands together; and the old housekeeper, she who had brought the réveillon to the child bride and groom, so many years ago, appeared on the doorstep, holding a cup of warm wine. The master paused on the threshold to drink the wine and thank the old woman, and Bertrande could see quite plainly the look of adoration with which she received the empty cup.

The next day, an occasion presented itself as Martin's younger sister was praising his conduct his to wife, Bertrande ventured:

"Yes, he is very kind, very gentle. One would almost say, is this the same man who so resembled in action and in feature your father?"

"One would almost say so," assented the sister amiably.

"But I do say so," returned Bertrande. "Often I ask myself, can this man be an impostor? And the true Martin Guerre, has he been slain in the wars?"

"Mother of Heaven," replied the sister, shocked, "how can you say such a thing, even think so? It is enough to tempt the saints to anger. Oh, Bertrande, you have not said such a thing to anyone else, have you?"

"Oh, no," she answered lightly.

"Then for the love of Our Lady, never speak of it again to me or to anyone. It is unkind. Martin could consider it an insult. He might be very angry if he heard it."

"Very well,'" said Bertrande. "I was jesting," and she smiled, but her heart was sick.

At confession, kneeling in the stale, cold semi-darkness, her hands muffled in her black wool capuchon, her head bowed, she said, as she had long meditated but never dared:

"Father, I have believed my husband, who is now master of my house, not to be Martin Guerre whom I married. Believing this, I have continued to live with him. I have sinned greatly."

"My child," replied the voice of the priest, without indicating the least surprise, "for what reason have you suspected this man not to be the true Martin Guerre?"

"Ah, he also has suspected him," said Bertrande to herself, and her heart gave a great leap of joy, like that of an imprisoned animal who sees the way to escape.

She replied to the priest as she had replied to her husband, giving instances of his behavior which seemed to her unnatural.

"What shall I do," she besought him finally, "what shall I do to be forgiven?"

"Softly, my child," said the calm voice of the priest. "It is then for his kindness to you that you accuse him?"

"Not for his kindness, but for the manner of his kindness."

"No matter," said the priest. "It is because of a great change in his spirit. He spoke to me of this long since, being concerned for you, and it seems to me that he has been toward you both wise and gentle. Go now in peace, my daughter. Be disturbed no more."

Bertrande continued to kneel, only drawing her cloak closer about her shoulders. The cold air seemed to draw slowly through the meshes of the wool and rise from the cold stones on which she knelt. At last she replied incredulously:

"You then believe him to be no impostor?"

"Surely not," said the easy voice of the priest, warm, definite and uncomprehending. "Surely not. Men change with the years, you must remember. Pray for understanding, my daughter, and go in peace.'"

Slowly she got to her feet and slowly made her way through the obscurity to the doorway, pushed aside the unwieldy leather curtain, stepped outside into the freely moving air and the more spacious dusk, and descended the familiar steps.

Familiar figures passed her, greeting her as they went on into the church. She answered them as in a dream, and as in a dream took the path to her farm. She felt like one who has been condemned to solitude, whether of exile or of prison. All the circumstances of her life, the instruction of the church, her affection for her children and her kindred rose up about her in a wall implacable as stone, invisible as air, condemning her to silence and to the perpetuation of a sin which her soul had learned to abhor. She could not by any effort of the imagination return to the happy and deluded state of mind in which she had passed the first years since the return of her husband. The realization that she was again with child added to her woe, and the weight, such as she had carried before in her body joyously, now seemed the burden of her sin made actual and dragged her down at every step.

The path, turning to follow the contours of the mountainside, brought her after a time to the crest of a slope above her farm. There it lay, house, grange and stable, set about with its own orchards, its chimney smoking gently, infinitely more familiar, more her own after all these years than the house in which she had been born; yet as she looked down toward it from the hillside she thought that it was no longer hers. An enemy had taken possession of it and had treacherously drawn to his party all those who most owed her loyalty and trust. Her eyes filled with tears, and when she drew her hands away from her face, a commotion had arisen in the courtyard below. People were running about with torches, gathering into a group from which excited cries, staccato and sonorous, rose toward the hillside, and presently three figures on horseback detached themselves from the group and rode away, the hoofs ringing on the stones. She remembered then that Martin had promised to make one of a cordon for a bear hunt from the parish of Sode, and knew that these must be his neighbors come for him.

When she reached her doorway, the housekeeper greeted her.

"The Master is gone to Sode. Ah, they are fortunate to have him! He is famous as a hunter of bear." She laughed, helping Bertrande to remove her cape, and did not see that her mistress's face had been stained with tears.

The next evening as they sat together, her husband said to Bertrande:

"Why do you look at me so strangely with your lovely two-colored eyes, your lucky eyes?"

"I was wondering when you would leave me to return again to the wars."

"I have told you never, never until you cease to love me."

"I have ceased to love you. Will you go?"

Something in the quality of her voice restrained the man from jesting.

"I do not believe you," he said, courteously.

"You must believe me," she cried with passion. "I beg of you to go. You have been here too long already," and a fire kindled in the eyes which the Gascons call lucky, the eyes of hazel and green, which made her husband lean forward and look long and searchingly into her face.

At last he said:

"You are still cherishing that madness of which you spoke, long since. Can you suppose that while you believe this thing of me, I will ever leave you? That would serve only to deepen your madness and increase your suffering. Do you not understand?"

"You are intricate," she cried. "You have the subtlety of the Evil One himself."

The man straightened, and rose from his chair. When he spoke, the quality of his voice had changed completely.

"I am sorry, Madame. There are others to be considered besides yourself. School yourself, Madame, to the inevitable."

He lifted her hand to his lips, and without another word turned and left her.

"Ah," exclaimed Bertrande bitterly, "that was the true manner of Martin Guerre. He has profited well from my complaints, this impostor."

Then began for the woman a long game of waiting and scrutinizing. Some day, she told herself, he will be off his guard, some day, if I do not warn him too often, I shall catch him in his deception, and free myself of him. "Ah, Martin, Martin," she cried in her loneliness, "where are you and why do you not return?" And as she observed the man whom she now called the impostor, considered the tranquillity of his demeanor and the ease with which he accomplished all his designs, confidently winning all people to him, the terrifying thought occurred to her that his great sense of security might lie in some certain knowledge, unshared by herself or by anyone else at Artigues. Perhaps the real Martin was indeed dead. Perhaps this man had seen his body on some distant battlefield, besmeared with blood and mutilated, the face turned downward to the bloody grass.

Perhaps, and at this last thought her soul recoiled in horror, perhaps he had himself slain Martin Guerre that he might come to Artigues in perfect safety and inherit his lands.

She watched him as he sat by the fire, fatigued from the day's work, yet playing gently with the children, holding the youngest child upon his knee, and discoursing meanwhile to Sanxi, and he did not appear a monster. The priest came still, through the winter evenings, as before Bertrande had made her momentous confession, and, hearing the talk between the curé and the master of the house, Bertrande could not but admit that this man was wise, subtle, and, if not learned, infinitely skilled in argument. The priest valued him, the children loved him, and these virtues of his which entrenched him with those who should have supported her, but made her the more bitter against him. Passionate as had once been her love for this stranger, so passionate became her hatred of him, and her fear; yet in order that his power over her might not become greater, she dissembled her hatred and veiled her fear; for this reason and also because the innocent and observant eyes of Sanxi were upon her. Now all the years of loneliness before the return of Martin Guerre, or rather, before the coming of the impostor, stood her in good stead. She enclosed in her heart a single fierce determination, and outwardly her life went on as usual.

Still, she sickened. When her pallor was mentioned to her, she explained it by her physical condition. She grew more thin in cheek and shoulder as her belly grew more round. The bones of her face, the delicate arch of the nose, the high cheek bones, the wide and well-shaped skull, defined themselves under the white skin, and beneath the high arching brows her lucky eyes shone with an extraordinary luminosity.

Her husband was extremely attentive to her health, ordering all things that he could imagine to increase her comfort, excusing her from work whenever it was possible, and if there was a battle between them, apparently only Bertrande herself was aware of it. Sometimes she wondered, so unfailing were his courtesies, whether he was indeed aware of the fact that they were enemies. However, in the beginning of the spring and toward the termination of her pregnancy, an incident occurred which defined their positions beyond any doubt.

Martin's younger sister and her husband, Uncle Pierre Guerre, the curé and Martin Guerre himself, whom Bertrande called the impostor, were returning from mass at Artigues to Martin's farm. As they approached the inn, the landlord, leaning from an upper story window—for the ground floor was given over to the accommodation of the horses of his guests, according to custom—called to Martin Guerre:

"Hollah, Master Guerre, here is a friend of yours from Rochefort, an old comrade in arms who asks the way to your house."

He drew in his head, turning around to speak to a person in the room behind him, and as Martin's party came up to the door of the inn, there issued from that door a thick-set figure wearing a coat of link armor over a red woolen jerkin, who carried a cross-bow slung over one shoulder and a short sword fastened to his belt. His face was scarred from more than battle wounds, and one eye was clouded by some kind of infection that was gradually masking the lens.

"I was at Luchon," he said, coming close to them, without hesitation, "soaking my old carcass and my scabby hide in that unspeakable mud. It smells of bad eggs, pah, but it is warm, and that feels good. There I learned of your being home again, and I came to stretch my legs before your fire. Eh, Martin, we shall have much to say of Picardy, eh, and other matters less heroic." He laughed, thrusting his thumbs through his belt, but the man whom he addressed neither laughed nor smiled but regarded him with a somewhat puzzled countenance.

"Eh, Martin?" repeated the soldier, and, indicating by a nod of his head Martin's younger sister, "Is this your wife?"

"My friend of Rochefort," said Martin slowly, "I cannot for the life of me remember when or where we met. I am not so certain that we ever met at all."

The soldier cocked his head to one side, and then, with the gesture of a man who feels the leg of a spavined horse, bent quickly, and grasping Martin below the left knee, gave the leg a sharp squeeze and then a slap. Straightening himself abruptly, he announced:

"Certainly, you do not remember me! You are not even sure you know me, eh? Impostor! You are Monsieur Martin Guerre, my friend? You return from the mass, you are neat and proper, you have a great distaste for the smelly old soldier! You are nothing but a fraud. The true Martin Guerre—I knew him very well. There was a man. He could see beyond the dirt on the face of a friend. He lost a leg before St. Quentin in the year fifty-seven."

There was a dead silence, during which Martin Guerre lifted his left eyebrow the while he contracted the right, a trick, as his sister remembered, which had been characteristic of his father.

Then Uncle Pierre said:

"Brute! You have the manners of a pig. Take yourself away before you force me to roll you in the dirt."

"I do not go away so easily," said the soldier from Rochefort.

The man whom he had accused still regarded him calmly, and slowly remarked:

"Doubtless he wishes me to bribe him to leave. I have heard that there was employed under the Duke of Savoy a man who resembled me greatly in feature. Perhaps it was he who lost a leg."

"Ventre de Dieu," exclaimed the soldier with increased impatience and scorn. "I knew him well, the true Martin Guerre. He was a Gascon and he lost his left leg at the battle of St. Laurent before St. Quentin. It is all one to me if this man is a rogue. He is your relative, not mine. If he had been Martin Guerre, he would have known me."

And with many oaths he turned back to the inn, of which all the windows now stood wide open as those within tried to see and hear what went on; he was still cursing under his breath and in more languages than one as he disappeared within the shadow of the doorway, but he made no further effort to have his story believed.

"He is malicious," said Pierre Guerre with indignation, as the small party proceeded on the way to the farm.

"He was disappointed," said Martin. "He thought to find a welcome with good lodging and food for a week. I do not grudge him the food, but I cannot have him sitting about every evening telling stories of gallant adventures—which I did not commit—before my wife, who is so sick.'"

The curé said nothing, but Martin's sister and uncle discussed the matter of having the soldier apprehended.

"Let it pass," said Martin. "It was a mistake; there is truly a man who resembles me. I have heard of him more than once. And the fellow was disappointed. Had he been less foul with disease I would have brought him home with us anyway, to hear the news from Spain." To the priest he added, "I could wish that this had not happened."

The priest nodded, said nothing, but the sister continued indignant and voluble, and when they reached the farm, and found Bertrande waiting for them in the kitchen, she burst at once into an account of the adventure.

"Imagine it," exclaimed Uncle Pierre as the young woman paused for breath. "Only imagine it! He leaned over, this pig of a man, and pinched Martin below the knee as if he had been a horse for sale at the market. I wonder that he did not offer to look at his teeth."

"He called Martin a rogue," repeated the sister, ever more indignant.

"Worse than that," said the brother-in-law. "He called Martin an impostor."

Bertrande, looking from one hot, excited face to another, turned at last her brilliant eyes full upon her husband's quiet countenance, in a look of triumph and scorn.

"At last," she cried suddenly in a strange hoarse voice, "at last, dear God, Thou wilt save me!"

She pressed her hands to her temples, then turned, and ran from the room.

"Go with her," said Martin, his face immediately full of concern.

"Go with her quickly, my sister. Do you not see? She is ill." To the priest he said, "You understand to what a pass it has come? I would give half my farm if this soldier from Rochefort had never come to Luchon. This will unsettle her reason."

The sister, who had followed Bertrande, found her kneeling beside the bed, clutching the coverlet in agony. To all questions and reproaches she answered only:

"I am dying, I am dying. I beg of you, send for my nurse."

She was delivered that night in great suffering of a daughter who died before she had lived an hour. Bertrande herself was very ill, and in the fever which followed the birth of the child, asked only to see the soldier from Rochefort. To humor her, for he thought her hours were numbered, the curé sent for the soldier, but the man was not to be found. He had not lingered at Artigues. He had been seen at St. Gaudens some days later. After that all trace of him was lost. However, the curé caused to be written down and properly witnessed the soldier's accusation, and these papers he brought to the invalid. Immediately after she had received them, the condition of Madame Guerre began to improve, a fact which could not fail to impress not only the curé but her entire family.

"She is mad," they said to each other, "but if we humor her and are patient, God willing, she may recover."

The improvement continued. She gained strength slowly but steadily and was soon able to walk about a little in her room, but she refused steadily to leave the Chamber. She refused to see her husband, to admit him to her room, or in any way to have anything to do with him. Everyone on the farm could see how heavily this weighed upon the master. He was as patient as ever with his people, and as kind, but there was little merriment.

"Madame is not herself since her illness," the housekeeper said to the priest, "and it is breaking the Master's heart."

The priest sought out Martin Guerre, and found him at work in the fields. Together they sat down in the shade of the beech trees, and the priest said:

"Who would have thought that kindness could have worked so much sorrow!"

Martin shook his head.

"There would have been no sorrow, Father, if I had not tried to run away from my father's anger. The trouble begins there. But what shall I do to help her? Once she asked me to leave her."

The priest surveyed his friend intently. If this man were not indeed his friend and the son of his friend, surely his eyes would betray him.

"And you refused to leave?" the priest said.

"At that time I refused," said the man before him, evenly, his sad eyes meeting those of the priest without hesitation. "I thought that to leave her then would but confirm her in this madness, and that I should be deserting her to years of pain—as if I were to fasten upon her the guilt of a sin—" he hesitated—"a sin of which she must not be accused."

His voice was vehement, and he stopped speaking abruptly, overcome with emotion. To the priest, who knew the voice, who knew the race, there could be no doubt whatever but that the grief, the concern and the humility were real. He passed a hand over his forehead and looked away toward the empty wheat field.

"My son," he answered at last, "I do not know what to advise you. What you have said is true. If you run away—if you disappear again—it will look like an admission of guilt. Unless, of course, you go with my consent and knowledge, leaving word of where you may be found, and denying the accusation of the fellow from Rochefort. It is conceivable that your absence might improve the condition of your wife. Your presence but adds continual fuel to the fire. The spirit is ill, and it has need of rest to heal itself, of rest as well as prayer. But you cannot leave the farm indefinitely. Your people have need of you. The parish, also—I have need of you. Is there no journey you could make about some business of the farm?"

Martin shook his head.

"The business of the farm is all in the parish of Artigues."

"You left a sum of money with your uncle when you were a boy. I think that it has never been spent. Take it, and journey to Toulouse and there purchase a gift for Our Lady. Be home again before the snow. Say farewell to your wife before you go."

"She will not speak to me," said the man with a wry smile. "But I shall say farewell to you before I go. I must help them with the wheat harvest before I leave. Meanwhile"—he hesitated—"let us say nothing of the matter until it is accomplished. There will be less talk."

The priest nodded, and blessed him. Martin Guerre returned to his work.

A few days later Bertrande herself sent for Pierre Guerre. The honest man found her seated in the highbacked chair near the curtained bed, but as he approached her, she rose.

"I have sent for you, my uncle," she said in a low voice, "because you are still the head of our family, and I must beseech your help."

The room was cool, and to the diminished vitality of the invalid it seemed even cold. She stood wrapped in her black wool capuchon, the hood thrown back on her shoulders. Her illness had aged her, but there showed in her face such poise and clarity of spirit that the uncle was unaccountably moved.

"Sit down, my child," he said gently. "You will tire yourself."

She shook her head.

"I ask you to believe me, believe me at last, when I say to you now, 'I am not mad.' All my household believe me to be mad. I have only yourself to whom to look for help."

"I believe you, my child," he answered quietly. "Sit down. Look, I will sit down beside you on the coffer."

"I have no proof," said she, "unless the story of the soldier from Rochefort can be considered proof."

"It is a strange story," replied the uncle. "I was angered that day, but since then, the picture seems to move, like people changing places in a dance. If there is another man who resembles Martin, this must be the man. You are Martin's wife, and you would be the first to know. Moreover, he has behaved strangely of late."

"In what manner?" said Bertrande.

"He came to me demanding a sum of money which he left with me before he ran away. I replied that the money had made part of the sum for the purchase of the lower fields. It was a matter of which his father had approved. The purchase was made after his father's death, according to his father's plan."

"I remember," said Bertrande. "What then?"

"He was angered," said Pierre shortly.

"I understand," said Bertrande slowly. "He wishes money in hand in order to leave us. Now that he fears detection, now that he has pillaged us, now that he has almost killed me, he will go away." She began to weep and hid her face in her hands.

A deliberate, abiding wrath grew in the old uncle as he watched her bent head and listened to her sobs. "Madame," he said, striking with his clenched hand upon his knee, "give me your permission to accuse this man of his crime. He shall not leave us unpunished."

Bertrande could hardly speak for her tears. But:

"Accuse him, punish him, do as you like with him, only rid me of his presence," she implored.

Less than a week later armed men from Rieux arrived at the farm and arrested the master of the house. They brought him in irons from the field to the kitchen for a final identification by Bertrande. His own men followed after, angry and sullen. Standing beside the master's chair, before the hearth, Bertrande identified him as the man who had claimed, but falsely, to be her husband.

"I accuse him," she said clearly, "of being an impostor and not the true Martin Guerre."

It was the first time since the birth of the child that she had left her room. Uncle Pierre stood beside her. It was evident that the man from Rieux had been expected.

Sanxi, seeing his father in chains, burst into a passion of weeping, flung himself, first upon his father, and then, kicking and scratching, upon the two guardsmen.

"Madame," said his father quietly, above the turmoil thus raised, "is it indeed you who do this to me?"

Bertrande bowed her head, and turned her back upon him.

The man sighed, and nodded, as if to himself. Then, turning to the housekeeper, he asked that the youngest child be brought. The old woman, all in tears, held up the little one to his father to be kissed. The people of the farm crowded about, and the priest, entering in haste, cried to the men-at-arms:

"This is folly—you do not know what you are doing!" He stretched out his hands and would have prevented their departure.

"Let be," said the prisoner, still quietly. "It is not the fault of the men. They must do as they have been commanded." And then, addressing his people, he said: "Good-by, my children. God willing, I shall return to you safely."

"It is a mistake," said the priest again to the guardsmen. "You do not understand that the woman is mad."

But the guard moved forward, with the prisoner between them, through the wide doorway into the courtyard of the farm. The housekeeper, Sanxi and the other servants followed closely behind them. There was some delay in the courtyard as a horse was brought for the prisoner. Bertrande, who had continued to stand with her back to the room, her eyes upon the hearth, turned now and looked about her. She was entirely alone. In the courtyard the servants shouted their last farewells. She heard Sanxi's voice.

"Good-by, my father, my dear father!"

II. RIEUX

The accusation had been made at Rieux, since Artigues was too small a place to boast a court, and thither Bertrande went with her uncle, Pierre, and the servants who were to be called as witnesses. She stayed in the house of her mother's sister, occupying the same room which she had been given on her earlier visit, and in which the sun had always seemed to shine through western windows in the morning. But this time the sun shone from the east, as it should do, and Bertrande marveled that she had ever felt confused about the direction. In the same fashion she marveled that she should have permitted herself to be deceived concerning the identity of the man who had called himself her husband. Her present belief was inescapable and plain, and yet she found herself alone in it, alone, that is, save for the support of honest Pierre. She left in Artigues a house in which the very servants looked at her askance. Of Martin's four sisters, two had not hesitated to declare that they thought her malicious. They said openly, so that the report returned to her:

"For years during Martin's absence she was sole mistress of the farm. Now she cannot bear to be put back into her proper place. She has a greed of authority, and of money. She was severe to us before we married, severe and miserly. This is all a plan to destroy Martin and possess the farm."

The other sisters, particularly the youngest, defended her. She had done no more in the management of the estate and of the family than their mother would have required her to do, and her strange fancy that Martin was not her husband had arisen from the grief of the long separation. They were sure that she was insane. The charity and the coldness were alike difficult for Bertrande; and at Rieux, even her aunt supported the claim of the impostor.

"My poor child," she said to Bertrande, "your years of suffering have told on your brain in a strange way. Why, I have known the boy all his life! Of course I shall testify in his favor, if I am asked, and when the courts have decided that he is really your husband, perhaps you will have some peace, although it's all a great pother to go through with in order to convince a wife of what she ought to know without help."

At the first session of the court the crime was formally charged to the prisoner of misrepresentation and theft. Bertrande then demanded through Pierre Guerre, and in fact only because of the uncle's insistence, that the prisoner be made to do penance publicly, that he pay a fine to the king, and that he pay to herself the sum of ten thousand livres. She was then asked to state her reasons for the accusation.

"My lords," she began, "there is the testimony of the soldier from Rochefort."

She was interrupted.

"We ask you for your testimony only," they reminded her.

She bent her head, and after a moment, told them just what she had told the priest. Upon being questioned further, she added:

"I also found it curious, upon remarking the prisoner at sword practice with my son, that Martin Guerre should fence so awkwardly; he was known to be distinguished in the art."

The prisoner smiled, and shrugged his shoulder slightly. A brief smile also flitted across the face of one of the judges, and Bertrande, seeing it, exclaimed:

"You may smile, my lord, and my testimony may seem innocent to you and of small importance, but I swear by God and all His holy angels that this man is not my husband. Of that I am certain, though I should die for it."

"Well, we shall inquire, Madame, we shall inquire," said the justice, and called for the accused to be examined.

The prisoner stepped forward with an easy manner, as if he stood before his own hearth. He explained that during his absence he had served the King of Spain, that he had traveled extensively both through Spain and France, and that he had not known until he came to Rieux, some three years earlier, that his parents were dead; that upon learning that he was head of the house, he had made all haste to return to his wife and child, and had endeavored in every way to make up for his past neglect. He furnished the names and addresses of people who could verify the story of his wanderings. He told of his return to Artigues, of how Pierre Guerre, his uncle, had been the first person in the village to recognize and welcome him, and averred that Pierre had been to him in all things friendly until he, Martin, had found reason to question Pierre about the disposition of a certain sum of money which he had left in the care of his uncle. Since that time, he said, his uncle had sought to destroy him. He even hinted in conclusion that an attempt had been made upon his life.

The judges then asked him a great number of questions regarding the history of his family, the date of his own wedding, the date of birth of Sanxi, to all of which he answered without hesitation.

"Madame," said the judges to Bertrande, "you have heard these answers. Are they correct?"

"They are all correct, my lords," said Bertrande, "but still the man is not my husband."

The judges conferred together and presently announced that the case would be dismissed for a short time while an examination should be made into the characters of the accusers. Bertrande, her face burning with shame at this implication, turned to Martin's uncle.

"This is because we have asked for money," she said bitterly. "All that I ask, all that I hope is to be rid of his presence."

Uncle Pierre shrugged his shoulders.

"You must not be unreasonable," he told her. "After all, there will be the expense of the trial."

However, the investigation determined that the characters of Bertrande and Pierre were above reproach, and the case was ordered to proceed. In the interval, word of the dispute had gone round the countryside, and a great number of persons had either presented themselves voluntarily or had been called by the court as witnesses. On the morning when the case reopened, the chambers of the judges were crowded with interested persons, of whom no fewer than one hundred and fifty were present in the quality of witnesses.

The examination of relatives began, followed by that of the farm servants, then of neighbors from Artigues. Without a dissenting voice they all declared that the man in fetters was no other than Martin Guerre himself. The priest, being called, declared that the man was Martin and gave an eloquent account of Bertrande's illness and her madness, as he had discussed it with her husband and herself.

The day was wearing to a close, and Bertrande, sadly, said to Pierre Guerre:

"Do not all these people begin to convince you that you may be mistaken?"

"I am not one to change my mind every five minutes," said honest Pierre. "I have thought him a rogue, and a rogue he remains."

The priest departed and a new witness was called.

"Your name?" said the judge.

"Jean Espagnol."

"And whence do you come?"

"From Tonges, my lord."

"Your occupation?"

"Soldier of fortune."

"Do you know the prisoner?"

"That I do, my lord."

"And by what name do you know him?"

"Arnaud du Tilh, my lord. Sometimes we call him Pansette."

A murmur ran over the room. People stretched themselves, and Bertrande shot a glance at the accused man, whose face, however, showed no guilt, no surprise and only a very natural interest in the proceeding.

"And how long have you known the prisoner?"

"Oh, from the cradle, my lord."

"Have you had any conversation with him of late?"

"My lord, he told me less than half a year ago that he was playing the part of one Martin Guerre, that he had met this said Guerre in the wars, and that this Guerre made over to him, for certain considerations, the whole of his estate and the permission to impersonate himself."

"Ah, it is a lie," cried the voice of Bertrande, passionately.

"Well said, Madame," added the prisoner.

"Silence," demanded the judge.

The witness spread his hands palm outwards with the expression of a

THE SHAPE OF FICTION

man who has done his best for the cause of truth and justice, and, being dismissed, took his place again in the crowd.

From then on the case began to appear most dubious for the prisoner, for although it was rather a tall story that Martin Guerre would have made over all his possessions to a wandering rogue for whatever considerations, there were many witnesses examined who declared that the prisoner was in fact a Gascon by the name of Arnaud du Tilh. There were also among the witnesses called, some who were acquainted with both Martin Guerre and the rogue du Tilh. Of these, some said that the prisoner was Martin, some that he was Arnaud, and some declared themselves unable to decide between the two. The examination of witnesses ran on at such length that it was necessary to reconvene the court on the following day. Finally, when the last witness had given his testimony, the judges sent for Sanxi, and tried to find in his face some resemblance to the man who claimed to be his father. But since the boy so obviously resembled his father's sisters, who were said to resemble their mother, rather than their father, the countenance of Sanxi was of little aid to the judges.

The judges withdrew and debated the case at length. Bertrande, sitting clasping and unclasping her hands, overheard two of the spectators who were commenting freely on the case. Said one:

"They have proved nothing against the man, and the woman demands a great sum of money."

"If she denies him to be her husband," said the other, "why did she not deny it immediately? She lived with him for three years without complaining. Why does she quarrel with him now?"

"She has lost her pains, without a doubt," said the first.

"My God, my God," said Bertrande, bowing her head and clasping and unclasping her long hands in a passion of despair, "deliver me from sin."

The judges returned and prepared to speak:

"Whereas, out of one hundred and fifty witnesses called by this court of Rieux, forty have testified that the prisoner is Martin Guerre, sixty have refused to testify to his identity, and fifty have testified that he is none other than Arnaud du Tilh, and whereas the wife of Martin Guerre, whose opinion should bear more weight with us than that of any other living person, has testified that the prisoner is not her husband, we do affirm that the prisoner is in fact Arnaud du Tilh, commonly known as Pansette. And we do condemn the said Arnaud du Tilh to do public penance before the church of Artigues, and before the house of Martin Guerre, and to suffer death by decapitation before the house of Martin Guerre."

A gasp as of astonishment and pity swept the room, and Bertrande de Rols, rising from her seat, cried out in a clear, terrified voice:

"Not death! Not death! No, no, I have not demanded his death!"

She stood, grown very pale, confronting the judges with surprise and horror in her features; and then, putting out her hand gropingly, she half-turned toward Pierre Guerre, and fell unconscious into his arms.

The prisoner had started also at Bertrande's cry. In spite of the sentence just passed upon him, his eyes were clear, and his face bright, one would have said, with joy.

III. TOULOUSE

It is difficult to relate all that Bertrande de Rols suffered in the days which followed directly upon this decision. She returned to Artigues, to a house in which all peace and contentment had been destroyed. Nor was there anyone in Artigues, except Martin's uncle, who did not by word or gesture blame her for this destruction. Sanxi regarded her with frightened, incredulous eyes, or slipped from a room as she entered, like a small animal who has been beaten continuously and without having offended. Nor was the matter ended. If the sentence had been carried through without delay, Bertrande felt, she might have borne the horror with some courage and reached, afterwards, a certain peace of finality, and time might have justified her action; but the case had been appealed at once by Martin's sisters to the parliament of Toulouse, and the summer dragged forward through a long, heart-breaking uncertainty.

The wheat was harvested, but without exultation, and threshed, but without merriment. As in other years the water of the mountain stream was turned upon the stubble fields and ran in shining cascades across the parched and broken earth, but Bertrande de Rols did not walk out to see it, nor did it matter to her that the flowers sprang up after the passage of the water as if a carpet had suddenly been spread, a carpet of a thousand flowers and a thousand pleasant odors. During the last days of August word was brought to Artigues that the parliament of Toulouse had found the evidence inconclusive and had called the witnesses for a second trial.

The curé visited Bertrande.

"My daughter," he said, as persuasive and kindly as if she had not now for almost a year steadily refused his advice, "it is no more than my duty to entreat you to consider once more that which you have undertaken."

"Reverend Father," said Bertrande abruptly, "have you never once thought but that I might be right? Consider the soldier from Rochefort. Is it not possible that this man may indeed be Arnaud du Tilh? Is it not more than likely?"

"All things are possible with God," said the priest, "but I cannot think it likely that the man of whom we speak should be one and the same with a most notorious rogue." His voice softened and his eyes became very sad. "The man of whom we speak was one whom I had grown to value greatly. His ways, his thoughts, were kindly. There was no soul in my parish of Artigues who did not benefit in some way from his presence here."

"You valued him," said Bertrande quietly, "more than you valued Martin Guerre who ran away?"

"Indeed, more," said the priest. "What was that boy? A raw, impatient youth, a thoughtless boy, selfish in the extreme. He had in him, it is true, the qualities of a great man. I like to think that he has grown into that man. His selfishness has become generosity, his impatience has become energy well-directed. It did not happen suddenly. He was eight years in a hard school." He paused, and in a curious voice asked her, "It does not pain you to hear me praise him?"

"No," she answered slowly, as if she questioned herself. "It is no more than just to remember that he has been kind to us—kind to all, save me, and kind even to me after a strange fashion."

"Then if it does not pain you to hear him praised," said the priest, pursuing his slight advantage, "if it pleases you a little to hear good of him, then you cannot have ceased entirely to love him, and does not this love convince you that he is truly Martin Guerre?"

"No," said Bertrande fiercely and quickly. "No, Father. Can you not see, it is in this love that he has wronged me most, that he has damned my soul? I have sinned, through him, and you will not understand it even long enough to give me absolution! No, Father, I cannot believe him to be other than the rogue, Arnaud du Tilh."

Her cheeks had flushed, as if with a fever, and to the priest her eyes held a strange luminosity. He lifted his hand and then, helplessly, dropped it upon his knee. He said:

"There is a doubt, nevertheless. While there remains a doubt you run the risk of unwillingly, unwittingly, assisting at the destruction of your own husband. I counsel you to withdraw the charges before it is too late. Those who love you, and him, have given you an opportunity of retreating from this whole affair.

"Is it for you to assume vengeance? You believe that you have sinned. You are in danger of sinning far more greatly. If there is evil in the matter, God will unravel it in His own good time. No, do not answer now. I advise you to withdraw the accusation. If you cannot do this, if your heart will not permit you to do this, then I shall pray for you that you may be prevented against your will from so harming, not only yourself, but all who love you."

He left her sorely shaken, as he had meant to do, not in her opinion of the man's guilt, but in her belief in the wisdom of her action. The event had gone beyond her plan. "I did not demand his death," she reminded herself; "but now I must demand it."

After the priest came Martin's youngest sister. She knelt in front of Bertrande and, covering Bertrande's two hands with her own, looked up into the face of her sister-in-law, and said most pleadingly:

"Bertrande, my dearest sister, we were always good friends. Do not be angry with me now. When you come before the judges of Toulouse, say to them, 'I withdraw the charges made against my husband. I do not know how it happened—I think that I was mad.' Our uncle will not press the charges, if you do not. Martin will forgive you. We shall all be happy again. Dear God," and she suddenly began to weep, "we cannot have him killed before his own house."

She bowed her head on her hands, and Bertrande felt upon her own cold fingers the warm tears.

"Little sister," she answered in despair, "how can I deny the truth?"

"It is only the truth for you, not for us," returned the weeping girl. "For the truth, that none of us believe, you would destroy us all. We shall never be happy again. The farm will never prosper again."

"Your uncle believes as I do," said Bertrande.

"Ah, but he is old. He wants nothing to be changed that was not just as it was when our father died. He would not change a cobble stone. And Martin changes everything, and is changed himself, so that we all love him more."

"Well, then," said Bertrande, "if the man be Martin, as you would have me say, why does not Arnaud du Tilh come forward and declare himself? Why should he let an innocent man suffer in his name?"

"He has enough to answer for with the law," replied the girl with some impatience. "It is to his advantage to be considered dead. The law will cease to seek for him. And why should a rogue put his neck into a halter for the sake of another?"

Bertrande sighed and laid her hand gently on the girl's shoulder.

"I am so sorry," she said, "so sorry." But she promised nothing.

September came, reddening the vines, making the mornings and evenings cool. Bertrande, returning from church the evening before her departure, whither she had gone in preparation for the journey to Toulouse, crossed the courtyard toward her house, wearily. She saw the housekeeper sitting near the doorway killing doves, and sat down beside the old woman.

"You have made your prayers, Madame," said the old woman.

"Yes."

"I wish that you had made them for a better cause."

"How can you know what prayers I made?"

"I cannot know, Madame. I only know that since you have had this strange idea of yours, nothing goes well for us. And all was well before. So well."

She sighed, leaning forward, holding the dove head down between her hands, the smooth wings folded close to the smooth soft body, while the dark blood dripped slowly from a cut in the throat into an earthen dish. The dish, already filled with blood, darker than that which was falling into it, spilled over slightly, and a barred gray cat, creeping cautiously near, elongated, its belly close to the ground, put out a rasping pale tongue and licked the blood. The housekeeper, after a little, pushed it away with the side of her boot. A pile of soft gray-feathered bodies already lay beside her on the bench. The living dove turned its head this way and that, struggled a little, clasping a pale cold claw over the hand that held it, and relaxed, although still turning its head. The blood seemed to be clotting too soon, the wound was shrunken, and the old woman enlarged it with the point of the knife which she had in her lap. The dove made no cry. Bertrande watched with pity and comprehension the dying bird, feeling the blood drop by drop leave the weakening body, feeling her own strength drop slowly away like the blood of the dove.

"What would you have me do?" she asked at length. "The truth is only the truth. I cannot change it, if I would."

The old woman turned her head without lifting her shoulders, still leaning forward heavily above her square, heavy lap. Her face was much more lined than in the days when Bertrande had first known her. There were creases above and below her lips, parallel with the line of the lips, as well as creases at the corners of the mouth. Her forehead was scored with lines that arched one above the other regularly, following the arches of the eyebrows. There were fine radiating lines about her eyes. The skin was brown and healthy, with ruddy patches on the cheek bones, but nevertheless the face was worn.

"I, Madame?" she said.

Bertrande looked into the tired affectionate brown eyes and nodded.

"Ah," said the housekeeper, turning once more to the dove which now lay still in her hands, "Madame, I would have you still be deceived. We were all happy then." She laid the dead dove with the others, and stooped to pick up the dish of blood.

All the way to Toulouse the echoes of these three conversations rang through the mind of Bertrande de Rols, making a slow, confused accompaniment to the clop-clop of the horses' hooves. The housekeeper rode behind her, Uncle Pierre before. They descended the valley of the Neste, the road running close to the stream, until the valley closed about them narrowly, leaving barely room for the passage of the torrent and the path above it. The woods were yellowing, but were still rich in leafy shadow. They came from the deep gorge to the wider valley of the Garonne, the stream coming in swiftly from the right, from the valley of Aran, saw St. Bertrand de Comminges with its narrow buttresses rising from its stony pedestal far below them in the green cup of the hills, crossed the Garonne and came into the more spacious country where the heavy-laden vines were trained from maple tree to maple tree in natural festoons. They passed St. Gaudens and St. Martory; they approached Muret. It was the journey which Bertrande had taken in imagination with Martin that autumn when he had first left her, and it was all rich and lovely, the wild mountain scenery giving way gradually to more thickly clustered farms, thorn hedges around the autumn gardens, and fruit trees set about the houses, medlars, plums and cherries, and always the fresh running of the water beyond the road; but now she traveled in great bitterness of heart, hearing through the noise of the hooves and the splashing of the Garonne, only the reproaches and prayers of those dependent upon her.

It had come to be a fixed idea with her that Martin was dead. It was incredible to her that any man could stand so calmly to face the extravagant charges brought against him as Arnaud du Tilh had done, if he had not certain knowledge that the man was dead whose place he usurped. Justly or unjustly she believed also that du Tilh had had something to do with Martin's death. Being so bereaved, and so unjustly blamed, herself, she would have welcomed almost any plan that would have given her back the sympathy and understanding of those she loved. And they had entreated her to withdraw the charges against du Tilh. Well, and if she did? Was it too late? Might she not restore to them the happier days?

"I, Madame? I could wish you still to be deceived."

The words recurred to her again and again. Might she not purchase for her people with this one secret weight of shame against her soul the peace and happiness which she desired for them and for herself their forgiveness and gratitude?

Again, if the court of Toulouse should reverse the decision of the court of Rieux, what then? Might she not feel released from this necessity of pursuit and revenge? The judges of Toulouse were very learnèd men and very near to the king in authority. The king, in turn, was appointed of God. Might she not consider it in some sense an indication from heaven, if the court should command her to receive this man as her husband, and might she not thereby find peace?

She had not seen the man whom she accused since the day in court when she had cried out against the sentence of death. His face had grown a little shadowy, the whole quality of his person a little unreal. Riding in the late afternoon under the shadow of trees, and out from that shadow into the light of a meadow, then again into the shadow of other, farther trees, she let herself slip for a time into a dream of surrender, and drooping over the saddle-bow, giving herself easily to the slow motion of the horse, she thought only of the restored tranquillity in the big kitchen, the contented faces bent above the evening meal—little of the man seated in the chair by the hearth, and, for the time being, nothing of herself in that new and impossible relationship. Meanwhile Pierre Guerre rode before her, and when she lifted her eyes from the roadway, or from the contemplation of the roadside grass, she saw his broad and honest back going steadily on.

She remembered then that he was not only her one supporter in the task which she had undertaken, but that he was also the one remaining defender of the old authority of her husband's house. He was that authority, simple and direct, without need of subterfuge or of superfluous charm, which before the coming of the stranger had kept them all in a secure and wholesome peace. He was for her that day a tradition more potent than the church. In her country the church had sometimes been denied, but even the Albigenses, hunted from town to town, from town to mountain cavern, and mercilessly destroyed for that denial, had never denied the tradition of which Pierre Guerre was the symbol. When she lay down that night in a strange bed in a strange valley, it was with a fatigue which overwhelmed body and soul, so that she felt she would have been fortunate never to waken.

On the third day of their journey they had come to the lowlands, and the September heat was excessive. There were no more cool ravines with belated shadows, where the water dripped from rocks, and where ferns grew. Now the fields lay parched and dusty. A white dust rose constantly from the road under the horses' hooves, and the leaves of the plane trees were dulled by dust. Earlier in the day they traversed the waste lands, filled with rocks and patches of wild lavender. At noon the heat was so great that they stopped to rest for nearly three hours under a grove of plane trees. Here there was shade for them and for their beasts, but the cicadas, boring into the bark of the trees for cooling drinks in the hot weather, beat their cymbals so loud in their great content, at the heat, at the sweet liquid which they sucked all day, that the whole grove rang, harshly reverberant. The air seemed to tremble to the sound, and for Bertrande they were a torment made audible. She was glad to resume the way, although the noise of the cicadas accompanied them still, now near, now far, as they passed other groves.

The Garonne ran, broader now, no longer splashing and sparkling, but sullenly, a yellow flood weighted with earth from the mountain-sides where the goats browsed. They crossed it toward evening over a wooden bridge into the city of Toulouse. Farther downstream, the first four arches of the Pont Neuf, the new stone bridge which was to be so well and so cleverly constructed that it would withstand even the most violent of the spring floods, projected its incompleted ramp less than half way across the yellow tide. Before them on the quay, the western sunlight shone full upon the whitened brick façade of Notre Dame de la Dalbade, and behind them the Pyrenees, of which a long spur had accompanied them almost to the city, retreated range upon snowy range, now turning slowly rose-color, far away, even into Spain. Behind La Dalbade lay Toulouse, a huddle of buildings of a dusty, rose-colored brick, intricate, noisy and odorous. The mountain peasants crossed the quay, passed the white façade of the church, and plunged into the network of echoing streets.

They found an inn and ordered supper, after engaging lodging for the night. The ordinary was full of guests, mostly merchants from the neighboring small towns, with a sprinkling of city men. Bertrande found a place in a corner, and, leaning back against the stained plastered wall, took refuge from herself and her companions in the public confusion of the room. Gradually, through the fog of personal misery which enveloped her, she observed that the talk was not general and easy, as one might have expected it to be, but that a group of men was giving great attention to a small number of travelers, and that there was a great deal of head-shaking, and of sober looks. When the hostess brought her supper, she detained her long enough to ask of what the men were talking.

"Of Amboise Madame. You have heard nothing of Amboise?"

Bertrande shook her head.

"You are Catholic, Madame?"

Bertrande nodded.

"And so am I, Madame, but Amboise was the work of the Guises. God be praised, we have no such Catholics in Toulouse. It seems there was a conspiracy of a sort, not greatly proved—there was more talk than evidence. And for that—every kind of death: hangings, decapitations, drownings, without number every day, and so for a whole month. I am a Catholic like yourself, Madame, but in Toulouse for every Catholic there is at least one Protestant. And they are good people, Madame. I promise you, I would as soon cut off my own head as that of my neighbor, and that for his being merely a Protestant!"

"But judging from those faces," said Pierre Guerre, indicating the talkers on the other side of the room, "one would think it a rebellion sooner than a conversation."

"A rebellion, yes," said the hostess. "I would not think it impossible. Toulouse has not always been bound to the French crown."

She went off, and the somber discussion continued, never more animated, never less intense, like a storm cloud that hangs patiently at the edge of an horizon, waiting for a wind to blow it into action.

"I do not know what is the matter with the world," said Pierre Guerre. "It seems to be breaking up in little pieces. In the days of Francis we were strongly French."

The room in which they slept, the entire party of mountaineers, for the inn was crowded, was hot and close. In the morning the streets were still warm and in the unmoving air the odors and stenches of the previous days remained, like a kind of disembodied refuse. There was none of the early morning crispness of the mountains, nor the amplitude of the purified air in which odors of the farm, of the beasts and of cooking, stood like symbols of the force and vigor, the healthiness of life. Bertrande awoke unrefreshed and felt in the air, as in her mind, the sultriness which paralleled the sullen temper of the men in the eating-room the evening before.

After the cup of wine, which seemed sour, and a piece of bread, which seemed bitter, she followed Pierre Guerre bare-headed through the streets to the council chambers of the Parliament in the Château Narbonnais.

The streets were crowded. People were speaking, not the mountain patois, but Languedocien, and with a curiously clanging, hard resonance, which made, in the narrower passages, everything seem to be spoken twice, re-echoed in metallic vigor from the dusty walls. And all the way Bertrande asked of herself, What am I doing here, in this unhappy town, in this prolonged stench, this heat, this desolating strangeness? I am pursuing a man to his death, a man who has been many times kind to me, who is the father of my smallest child. I am destroying the happiness of my family. And why? For the sake of a truth, to free myself from a deceit which was consuming me and killing me. She remembered herself speaking to Martin's sister.

"What would you have, my sister? The truth is only the truth. I cannot change it."

The sister had replied:

"It is true only for you."

"And might I be wrong?" she asked herself again as she mounted the stone steps and stood waiting before the great, closed door. She felt, in approaching this tribunal of Toulouse, a finality she had not felt at Rieux. It would not be possible for her to appeal this decision. It waited for her, behind those doors, in the quality of a doom. Suddenly her confidence deserted her, and terror engulfed her. She saw herself as borne forward helplessly on a great tide of misunderstanding and mischance to commit even a greater sin than that of which she had been afraid. The words of the priest returned to her. It had been holy counsel; she had refused it.

She broke into a heavy sweat which turned cold on her skin and made her shudder even in the meridional heat. She was dizzied. The door before her grew insubstantial, invisible, as if she had walked into an icy cloud on the summit of La Bancanère. Blindly, she reached out her hand for Uncle Pierre, and, the doors being opened, she entered the courtroom leaning on his arm.

The judges of Toulouse wished to confront the two accusers with the accused, but singly, feeling that much might be revealed to the acute observer in the countenances of the accusers which had not been recorded in the account of the case forwarded to them by the judges of Rieux. Accordingly, once inside the courtroom, Bertrande was constrained to leave the support of Uncle Pierre, and, attended by a guard, advanced before the very seat of the judges. A hum of voices which had filled the room ceased suddenly as she appeared. In the abrupt silence she heard the admonition and then the question of the judge and, lifting her eyes, saw before her at the distance of only a few feet, the man for whom she had felt for one extraordinary year a great and joyous passion. He was regarding her with a look at once patient, tender and ironic. In her distress she saw no other face, and could not bear the contemplation of that tender gaze. She looked down, dropping her head forward, while the blood beat upward into her face and then receded. Who was this Arnaud du Tilh? What manner of man was he that he did not return her hatred with hatred, and why had he not made good his escape from this most dangerous justice on the day when she had first suspected him? Her face turned very white, while a return of the giddiness which had seized her just before she entered the court made it almost impossible for her to continue standing. She replied to the question of the judges in a half-audible voice, and was then escorted to a small doorway through which she gained the courtyard, the sunlight, and a degree of solitude. She was instructed to return to the inn and to remain there until sent for. She went to her room and lay down.

Inside of an hour Pierre Guerre, who had been similarly instructed, joined her there. He was morose, annoyed at being detained at the inn, feeling himself a prisoner and having no occupation, large or small, with which to while away the time. He felt that he had behaved badly at the trial, and it was true that, although his conviction was as sound as ever, his manner had been hesitating, and embarrassed. He had felt himself stared at and smiled at as a peasant, a mountaineer. He had overheard, as the guard led him through the crowded room, an amused comment on his dress, the wit of which he had not understood, but the intent of which he had understood only too well. Annoyed at the crowd, humble before the judges, suddenly for the first time in his life acutely self-conscious, he had lost, for the space of five minutes, the simple dignity which had lent, at Rieux, such great weight to his testimony. Added to this discomfort was the spectacle of the impostor who had lost during his period of imprisonment some of his healthy brown color but none of his air of being arrogantly in the right.

"We are lost," said old Pierre to himself as he returned to the inn. "If it depended on me, we are lost indeed."

He dared not mention his discomfort to his niece, but it was the principal reason for the morose silence with which he rejoined her and set himself to wait out the day.

Bertrande lay upon the bed and regarded the stained canopy. Or she turned her head idly and surveyed the wall, or the figure of old Pierre seated on a straight bench under the window. She felt a great illness. A weight seemed to lie upon her breast which made breathing difficult, and the air which entered her lungs, after she had made so great an effort to expand them, contained no freshness, no reviving quality. Her mind had gone numb through prolonged self-examination. Exhausted and trapped by all these walls, by all these circumstances, she lay still and remembered that the one thing she desired was to be free of Arnaud du Tilh.

Meanwhile the court was proceeding with the examination of witnesses. One hundred and fifty witnesses had been called from the hearing at Rieux, and thirty new ones. Jean Espagnol testified as he had done at the former trial, and introduced a friend, Pelegrin de Liberos by name.

Pelegrin de Liberos, being sworn, testified that he was an old friend of Arnaud du Tilh, and that Arnaud had recently not only admitted his identity to him, but had given him a handkerchief to be delivered to Arnaud's brother, Jean du Tilh.

Gradually a body of information was built up, minute details contributed now by one witness, now by another. The shoemaker of Artigues testified that the foot of Martin Guerre exceeded slightly that of the accused. Certain witnesses to the number of five who had formerly testified with assurance that the accused was indeed Martin Guerre, now declared that they could not be sure whether he was or whether he was not. Of the thirty new witnesses, twelve declared themselves unable to make any decision regarding the identity of the accused. He might be either Martin Guerre or Arnaud du Tilh, for all they could observe. On the other hand, seven of the new witnesses were quite sure that he was du Tilh, and ten were equally convinced that he was Martin Guerre. It was established that Martin Guerre had appeared to be taller and more slender than Arnaud du Tilh, and that he had been somewhat round-shouldered. However there was also the argument that since the accused was eleven years older than was Martin Guerre when last seen, the natural increase in weight and age might make him seem shorter than had appeared Martin Guerre, the boy of twenty.

Still, as the day went on, it was decided beyond a doubt that Martin Guerre had two teeth broken in the lower left jaw, as had also the accused; that Martin Guerre had a scar on the right eyebrow and the trace of an ulcer on one cheek, as had also the accused; that Martin Guerre had a drop of extravasated blood in the left eye, as had also the prisoner; that Martin Guerre had the nail of the left forefinger missing, and three warts on the left hand, two of which were on the little finger, as had also the man in fetters. So that the evidence tended well toward the defense, when there appeared before the judges an old man in the clothes of a mountaineer but with a somewhat more distinguished bearing than the costume might have seemed to warrant. He was sworn and his name was asked.

"I am called Carbon Bareau."

"And do you recognize the prisoner?"

"Gentlemen, this man in irons is the child of my own sister."

The old man then began to weep, and it was some time before he had recovered composure sufficient to continue.

"I have loved this boy," he said at last, "for he has a way with him, a way of stealing the heart, but I have feared for him ever since he grew old enough to talk. He has had no respect for the laws, gentlemen. It breaks my heart to say that he has even declared there is no God. He has revered his parents not at all. With no faith, no respect for family, nor for the law of the kingdom, what could one hope for, gentlemen? He has a good heart, that is all. But what is a good heart when he can so disgrace an honorable family?"

The two brothers of Arnaud du Tilh were then called and testified that the prisoner "resembled" their brother. Further than that they would not commit themselves.

After this came a long succession of witnesses for the defense, forty-five people all of blameless reputation and well-qualified to know what they were talking about. Martin's four sisters testified that the accused was their brother, as did also two brothers-in-law. Many people who had been guests at the wedding of Bertrande and Martin testified that the accused was certainly Martin Guerre. The curé of Artigues testified in favor of his friend.

Last witness of all came the old housekeeper who had brought to the bridal couple the little midnight repast, or réveillon. She had a story to tell after she had identified the prisoner as her young master. She stood before the judges with her hands clasped firmly at her belt, her brown eyes, good, honest, kind, fixed steadily upon the revered faces, and cleared

THE SHAPE OF FICTION

her throat. Shortly after the return of Monsier, she testified, she had heard Madame remark to Monsier that she had kept certain chests unopened since his departure, so long ago. Upon hearing this, Monsieur had described certain white culottes wrapped in a piece of taffeta and requested that they be fetched him. Whereupon Madame had given to the housekeeper the key to the chest and requested her to fetch the *pantalons*, and the housekeeper had done so, finding them wrapped exactly as Monsieur had described. She made her recital bravely, greatly impressed herself at the gravity with which the judges heard it, and then, trembling with triumph and embarrassment, crept back to her place.

It was now late in the afternoon. The day's heat seemed to have accumulated in the crowded room along with the testimony of the witnesses, and the place was stifling. The light which entered through the high windows struck almost levelly upon the wall opposite, above the heads of the judges. The scribe laid down his pen, and the judges leaned forward to confer with each other. The examination was over, and it remained only to interpret the information. Those who had most to lose or gain by the decision had been dismissed to an inner room, but the courtroom was still packed.

It was neither reasonable nor just, the court argued first of all, to permit the bad reputation of the rogue Arnaud du Tilh to affect the fate of the prisoner if he was indeed Martin Guerre. Secondly, the judges argued, if it were so easy for the wife of Martin Guerre to mistake Arnaud for her husband, even if only for a short time, it would have been just as easy for the soldier from Rochefort to mistake Arnaud for Martin; there was no way of proving that the man who lost a leg at the battle of St. Laurent before St. Quentin was Martin Guerre rather than Arnaud du Tilh. Thirdly, they argued, it was beyond human ingenuity for any man to impersonate so well, to know so many intimate details of the life of another man, and to exhibit so close a physical resemblance to another man as the accused. Last of all, the court considered that the confusion of Bertrande at the sight of the accused, together with the report of her outcry in the court of Rieux when the sentence of death had been pronounced against the prisoner, testified badly for her case. Therefore the judges decided, and doubtless to their own relief, for they had been sadly puzzled, that the prisoner must be in truth none other than Martin Guerre, as he himself affirmed. The populace seemed pleased with the decision, and the clerk of the court prepared to put the verdict down in writing.

As this individual drew up his inkpot and sharpened his pen, and as the judges of Toulouse relaxed in their chairs and mopped their foreheads, conversing among themselves, and not, shrewdly, overlooking the smiles which overspread the courtroom, a commotion was heard at the outer door in which could be distinguished a great deal of stamping and of beating on the stone floor with the butt of a halberd, and a vigorous exposition of an undeterminable nature in an unmistakably Gascon voice. The court sent to inquire; the messenger returned with news of some importance, for, as the audience twisted about and necks were craned in curiosity, a way was cleared through the crowd so that a Gascon soldier in travel-stained garments was permitted to walk directly up to the seats of the justices.

The halberds of the attendants sounded on the floor as the men halted, one on each side of the soldier; but there also sounded, during the entrance of the group, what resembled the butt of a third halberd, but which was, remarkably enough, a wooden leg worn by the Gascon soldier.

The judges surveyed the newcomer. He was sunburned, and bearded, but through the beard the shape of the high, cleft chin was easily discernible. His left eyebrow was scarred; and there was a trace of an old ulcer on one cheek. He returned the scrutiny of the judges of Toulouse with eyes which were arrogant, gray and cold.

"Body of God," said one of the justices, sinking back in his seat in something not unlike despair, "this is either Martin Guerre or the devil," and he gave an order to the attendants to put the newcomer under arrest.

After brief deliberation among the judges, the order was also given to remove the accused man to an adjoining chamber and to close the doors against further entrance. This done, the weary justices proceeded to examine the soldier with the wooden leg.

"I am without any doubt Martin Guerre," said the soldier. "I lost my leg before St. Quentin in the year fifty-seven. I am the father of Sanxi Guerre, and of no other children."

To all the questions which had previously been put to the accused man, the soldier was able to reply with reasonable accuracy. Once or twice his answers were at variance with those of Bertrande to the same question, now and again he hesitated before answering, but in the main he showed a knowledge of the affairs of Martin Guerre which might well have justified his claim to be that man. He also manifested an unusual knowledge of the career of Arnaud du Tilh. This was interesting, for the accused man had known nothing at all of the affairs of du Tilh; he had heard rumors of his existence—that was all. But the newcomer seemed no better informed concerning the affairs of Martin Guerre than the accused had seemed. At the end of an hour the judges were no nearer a decision than they had been early that morning.

There remained a final test, however. The prisoner was summoned and made to stand face to face with the one-legged soldier. Then, one by one, the relatives of the two men were called, and asked to make their choice.

THE SHAPE OF FICTION

Carbon Bareau, the first of the relatives of du Tilh to be called, stared for a moment with great surprise at the soldier, then, turning without any hesitation at all, laid his hand on the shoulder of the prisoner and said:

"Gentlemen, this is my nephew."

The brothers of Arnaud, confronted by the two men so extraordinarily similar, hesitated, and then, turning from the prisoner as from the soldier, besought the court to excuse them from bearing witness. The court, with a humanity rare in that century, dismissed them. They had in their request testified more than they realized.

When the youngest sister of Martin Guerre was admitted, she lifted her hands to her forehead in a gesture full of amazement and distress, and then, without hesitation, flung herself upon the breast of the soldier with the wooden leg and burst into tears. One by one the other relatives of Martin Guerre, being admitted, stared with surprise from the soldier to the prisoner and back again, and confessed with many apologies and protestations of sorrow at their mistake that the soldier with one leg was undeniably Martin Guerre, who had been so long away.

It was remarkable that while Martin Guerre received this succession of tearful recognitions with a consistent, stern reserve, Arnaud du Tilh the prisoner, although growing perceptibly graver, lost none of his calm air of assurance and none of his dignity.

Meanwhile the judges, seeing which way the case had turned, sent to their hotel for Pierre Guerre and Bertrande de Rols. The day had been long. For these two lonely defenders of a cause it had seemed longer than a century. When the messenger came for them, they left the confinement of the inn and followed him through the still-confining streets with the intense fatalism of the defeated. The messenger had been instructed to tell them nothing, but rumor had preceded the messenger with the advice that the case had been decided against them. Pierre Guerre was admitted alone, and Bertrande, left in an ante-chamber with a guard, was clearly and sharply aware for the first time in that exhausting day of one thing, and that was that she could not return to Artigues as the wife of Arnaud du Tilh.

After a time the door to the courtroom opened, and she was admitted. She made her way through the crowd toward the space before the judges. Without looking up to see it, she yet felt the intense curiosity of all these unfamiliar faces bent upon her like a physical force. In the silence of the room the insatiable interest of the crowd beat upon her like a sultry wave. She reached the open space, and stopped. There she lifted her eyes at last and saw, standing beside Arnaud du Tilh the man whom she had loved and mourned as dead. She uttered a great cry and turned very pale. The pupils of her parti-colored eyes, the lucky eyes, expanded until the iris was almost lost. Then, reaching out her hands to Martin Guerre, she sank slowly to her knees before him. He did not make any motion toward her, so that, after a little time, she clasped her hands together and drew them toward her breast, and, recovering herself somewhat, said in a low voice:

"My dear lord and husband, at last you are returned. Pity me and forgive me, for my sin was occasioned only by my great desire for your presence, and surely, from the hour wherein I knew I was deceived, I have labored with all the strength of my soul to rid myself of the destroyer of my honor and my peace."

The tears began to run quietly down her face.

Martin Guerre did not reply immediately, and in the pause which followed, one of the justices, leaning forward, said to Bertrande:

"Madame, we have all been very happily delivered from a great error. Pray accept the profound apologies of this court which did not earlier sufficiently credit your story and your grief."

But Martin Guerre, when the justice had finished speaking, said to his wife with perfect coldness:

"Dry your tears, Madame. They cannot, and they ought not, move my pity. The example of my sisters and my uncle can be no excuse for you, Madame, who knew me better than any living soul. The error into which you plunged could only have been caused by willful blindness. You, and you only, Madame, are answerable for the dishonor which has befallen me."

Bertrande did not protest. Rising to her feet, she gazed steadily into the face of her husband and seemed there to see the countenance of the old Monsieur, the patriarch whose authority had been absolute over her youth and over that of the boy who had been her young husband. She recoiled from him a step or two in unconscious self-defense, and the movement brought her near to the author of her misfortunes, the actual Arnaud du Tilh.

In the silence which filled the courtroom at Martin's unexpected severity, a familiar voice close to her elbow pronounced gently:

"Madame, you wondered at the change which time and experience had worked in Martin Guerre, who from such sternness as this became the most indulgent of husbands. Can you not marvel now that the rogue, Arnaud du Tilh, for your beauty and grace, became for three long years an honest man?"

"Sirrah," answered Bertrande, "I marvel that you should speak to me, whose devotion has deprived me even of the pity of my husband. I once seemed to love you, it is true. I cannot now hate you sufficiently."

"I had thought to ask you to intercede for mercy for me," said Arnaud du Tilh.

THE SHAPE OF FICTION

"You had no mercy upon me, either upon body or upon soul," replied Bertrande.

"Then, Madame," said du Tilh, and there was at last neither arrogance nor levity in his voice, "I can but die by way of atonement."

Bertrande had turned to look at him as he spoke. She turned now from him towards her husband, and then, without speaking, moved slowly toward the door. The court did not detain her, and the crowd, in some awe, drew aside enough to let her pass without interruption. Bertrande did not see the crowd. Leaving the love which she had rejected because it was forbidden, and the love which had rejected her, she walked through a great emptiness to the door, and so on into the streets of Toulouse, knowing that the return of Martin Guerre would in no measure compensate for the death of Arnaud, but knowing herself at last free, in her bitter, solitary justice, of both passions and of both men.

Arnaud du Tilh, being confined in the prison at Artigues in the days which followed immediately upon the hearing at Toulouse, made a confession in which he stated that he had been tempted to the imposture by the frequency with which he had been mistaken for Martin Guerre. All that he knew of Martin's life and habits he had gleaned from Martin's friends, from his servants and from members of his family. He added that he had not originally intended to take Martin's place in his household, but had intended to stay only long enough to pick up a little silver or gold.

The court decreed that he had been convicted of the several crimes of imposture, falsehood, substitution of name and person, adultery, rape, sacrilege, plagiat, which is the detention of a person who properly belongs to another, and of larceny; and the court condemned him to do penance before the church of Artigues on his knees, in his shirt, with head and feet bare, a halter around his neck and a burning taper in his hand, asking pardon of God and of the king, of Martin Guerre and of Bertrande de Rols, his wife; the court then condemned him to be handed over to the common executioner, who should conduct him by the most public ways to the house of Martin Guerre, in front of which, upon a scaffold previously prepared, he should be hanged and his body burned. All his effects were forfeit to the crown. And this decree bears the date of September the twelfth, in the year 1560, in the city of Toulouse.

Of Martin Guerre nothing more is recorded, whether he returned to the wars or remained in Artigues, nor is there further record of Bertrande de Rols, his wife. But when hate and love have together exhausted the soul, the body seldom endures for long.

To enter the landscape of "The Wife of Martin Guerre" is like abandoning yourself in a most nonlinear fashion to the center of a Provencal

THE WIFE OF MARTIN GUERRE

Renaissance painting—it is to enter another dimension of time in another country, and hence abandon some of our modernity or sophistication. As we enter the painting we leave behind our skepticism and our questions; we must accept the values of light and shade in their own terms.

In order to understand a little better this experience we might harken back to another setting that puzzles and even annoys us—that of Hawthorne's The Scarlet Letter, where the puritanical persecution of Hester Prynne for having loved freely is almost beyond our ability to grasp it, while in the interior of that story almost no one questions the righteousness of the community's stand. Yet to us it amounts to tyranny.

That is the interesting and vital tension of both circumstances. We know what we know, but that hardly shatters the psychological reality of "The Wife of Martin Guerre." We have moved in historic time from a very special sort of religious morality, spatially confined in ways now seeming "narrow," to the multiple options made possible by the influence of Freud. Does that make our decisions any easier, or any wiser?

If we are speaking, in one sense, of entrapment, let us compare this story to Mansfield's "Bliss," another tale of another marriage. Fifty years after the fact of its publication we are still trying to determine woman's role in this most intimate and difficult relationship. The heroine, in no sense as heroic as Bertrande, has married the wrong man, utterly deceived in him and in her own powers. Behind the Sire de Malétroit's door, in another story, we witness a delicate and charming romance, also predicated on mistaken identity. But what will happen when the happy pair goes out the door? Will the young man carry with him a nagging sense of his wife's guilt, or his wife a sense of what she has lost? We do not know, or even care. That is what is meant by romance.

The moral and spatial confinement of "The Wife"—the shape of the enclosure within which the action occurs—is linked also to the economic foundations of the society it portrays. The marriage of Martin Guerre and Bertrande de Rols is a result of negotiations between their families in the interest of fortifying their material holdings. "It had appeared to three generations as almost inevitable, so many were the advantages for both families to be expected from such an alliance."

Out of this pressing need to maintain the land grew the tradition of a strong, male figure at the head of the family. We have all seen the motion picture, "The Godfather." Without absolute rule the farm might collapse into chaos; democracy is a slow and inefficient system in contrast to tyranny. "Without bearing any outward symbol of his power, [Martin's father] was in his own person both authority and security. He ruled, as the contemporary records say, using the verb which belongs to royalty, and the young girl seated beside him, in feeling this, felt also the great peace which his authority created for his household." The responsibility for decision must rest upon someone.

But limits invite violation, and it is of course the very autocracy of his father which drives Martin away. How modern this tale is, springing from annals 400 years old! Martin fears both his father and his father's justice, and he discovers, once he has left his father's house, that he cannot return to it. He is a rebel, and he is rare, but it is Bertrande, after all, who gives her life to perpetuate the ancient pattern of the elite French peasantry which Martin has attempted to destroy. She *is the wife of Martin Guerre and she will remain the wife of Martin Guerre* though the act sicken her body and exhaust her soul.

Her fate was shaped by forces greater than the fire of her spirit: the demands of the soil, the tenets of her Church. She served two gods. " 'For their children,' wrote the learned Etienne Pasquier a few years later, 'fathers and mothers are the true images of God upon earth,' and this was not an opinion which Pasquier imposed upon his time, but one in which he had been schooled."

How determined a woman Bertrande was to sustain her existence, wondering first whether she was insane, and knowing finally that the man she had loved was not her husband—throwing him off, ridding herself of him and of the sin he had thrust upon her! "I am pursuing a man to his death, a man who has been many times kind to me, who is the father of my smallest child. I am destroying the happiness of my family. And why? For the sake of a truth, to free myself from a deceit which was consuming me and killing me."

One of the great experiences of this story is in its explosion of sensory detail. We see the countryside in its various seasons, infinite with color. Even the chiaroscuro of the winter landscapes tempers the description of the indoor blaze of the fires, the rooms festooned with foods and evergreens. The flow of change throughout is reflected in the cyclic passage of the seasons. The story opens on a winter's day with snow outside the window, and ends in the "excessive" heat of a later September: when Martin Guerre appears at last after long absence "he was sunburned." The sensory experience has persisted throughout the story—we feel of things, we smell them, we hear the sounds of talk, work, music.

But in the foreground of this gorgeous design we witness the steady tread of tradition and its morality, absolutely materialistic, rooted in the family, and surviving by its transmission from generation to generation. Religion and justice are as severe as these circumstances can make them, a compassionate priest and an appealing rogue notwithstanding; and all is cyclical—war, politics, planting and harvesting, and the births and deaths of kings and rich farmers. We must then understand Bertrande's decision in the light of these things. Really, she has no wide choice. Her religion, her family, her first son's accession to the head of family, her attunement to her culture, all contrive to bring about the bitter unremitting end.

Humanly, she loved Martin with the growth and familiarity of her developing life. Her joy in the imposter was greater. Her torment in bringing forth intuition to fact (was it "willful blindness"?) spares neither her body nor her soul. In the end she is steel. She opts for the stronger force, the cycles of the life she knows, and its truths. And it is the death of her.

Of the works of this collection "The Wife of Martin Guerre" is longest, and yet its strength is in its succinctness—no sentence is irrelevant, no character appears who is not somehow entwined with the bizarre fate of Bertrande de Rols. The story is woven like cloth: each thread, each strand, whether cultural, economic, or psychological, inescapably colors the whole. The tale is a tribute to the particularly Western philosophy that no effect exists without a cause, and no cause exists without producing an effect.

Is "The Wife of Martin Guerre" a novel? A novella? Is it a long short story or a short novel? Do such things matter? This collection opened with an item of the shortest fiction—"The Use of Force"—whose brief action occurs during a few minutes in a modest house in New Jersey in the twentieth century. The collection concludes with an item of fiction whose actions covers a period of twenty-one years in France in the sixteenth century. In each story the central character is a woman of pride and secrecy, one in conflict with a claimant-husband.

Fiction is fiction. Length *may distinguish one example of fiction from another, but it remains the* shape *of the test, not its length, which defines the nature of our experience. In recent years we have heard a certain amount of careless talk about "the nonfiction novel," as if fiction could somehow be both true and invented. No such thing exists, and we do well to remain clear in this respect, as in others: stories, however long or short, are fiction; novels are fiction. If we can read fiction with pleasure we can read either stories or novels, however long, however short, nor are we under any obligation to describe strict boundaries between adjoining categories. (Young writers sometimes confuse themselves by imagining a progression in their writing from short stories to novels, as if one is a preparation for the other.)*

Traditionally, so long as men and women have told stories, whether on paper, at fireside, or into an electronic tube, fiction has had a beginning, a middle, and an end: a shape. Fiction introduces problem and crisis, characters in conflict—the doctor must see the little girl's throat—"it is a social necessity"; and Bertrande must name her true husband, for that, too, is a social necessity.

All fiction demands the reader's surrender, the willing suspension of disbelief, and once the reader has surrendered to a tale neither its length nor the labels applied by custom ought to affect the reader's relationship to his reading. Not a story's length but its shape affects us. Fiction differs in size from story to story, novel to novel, now shorter, now longer, but it never differs in the single demand we make upon it—that it engage us, that its conflicts interest us, excite us, that it be credible, that it speak to our condition. Good fiction succeeding in this way bears a closer resemblance to other good fiction of whatever length than it bears to "bad" fiction.

Fiction need be only long enough or short enough to tell itself. "Too long" or "too short" is not a measurable quality but a felt quality. The writer has his story to tell, and a writer of experience knows above all the importance of his or her remaining open to chance, to opportunity, and to accident. Many works of fiction begun one way ended quite another—stories turned to novels, novels turned to plays, plays turned to stories; stories were abandoned; work begun as nonfiction turned to fiction.

As the writer works he measures values. Dr. Williams wished to convey the idea of a single moment. Janet Lewis, in "The Wife of Martin Guerre," chose a much broader sweep. Dr. Williams saw his event through the eyes of the doctor. Janet Lewis, seeing her event through the eyes of Bertrande, might have chosen to see it another way (through Martin's eyes, let us say; or Arnaud's); or she might have chosen to see it from several alternating viewpoints. Knowing her own skills, she chose to see those twenty-one years mainly through Bertrande's sensibilities, and thus was length ordained, not preconceived; and ordained, too, by style, by diction, by the sound for which the writer might have strived; by the balance required between, on one hand, attention to detail, and, on the other hand, attention to the illusion of the passage of time.

> But gradually Betrande's affection for her husband became a deep and joyous passion, growing slowly and naturally as her body grew. All about her, life flourished and increased itself, in field, in fold, in the rose-flushed bramble stems of spring before the green leaf unfurled, and in the vine leaves of autumn that lay like fire along the corded branches. She felt this passion within herself like the wine they drank in the early days of spring, light, tart, heady, and having a special fragrance, and her delight illuminated her love like the May sunshine pouring downward into the cupped wine. Early in her twentieth year she gave birth to a son. . . .

The writer wrote to fulfill the needs of her story, not to meet the specifications of arbitrary length. When she was done she might have said to herself, "So that's how long it came to!"

HANDBOOK FOR TEACHERS AND STUDENTS

Contents

I. REALISM	473
The Use of Force *William Carlos Williams*	473
The Procurator of Judaea *Anatole France*	475
II. HIGH STYLE VERSUS JUST PLAIN GOOD	
The Sire de Malétroit's Door *Robert Louis Stevenson*	477
The Short Happy Life of Francis Macomber *Ernest Hemingway*	478
The Curious Case of Benjamin Button *F. Scott Fitzgerald*	479
But For This . . . *Lajos Zilahy*	481
III. HUMOR	481
A Hunger Artist *Franz Kafka*	482
Dying *Richard Stern*	483
The Gonzaga Manuscripts *Saul Bellow*	485
The Iron Fist of Oligarchy *Mark Harris*	485
IV. THE READER	486
The Ambitious Guest *Nathaniel Hawthorne*	486
The Real Right Thing *Henry James*	487
Life-Story *John Barth*	488
V. MYTH AND SYMBOL	489
Persephone *Meridel Le Sueur*	489
Red Leaves *William Faulkner*	490
VI. ALLEGORY	493
Hook *Walter Van Tilburg Clark*	494
A Mother's Tale *James Agee*	495
Death of a Favorite *J. F. Powers*	496

VII. DREAM AS CRISIS   497

In Dreams Begin Responsibilities   *Delmore Schwartz*   497
The Seven Riders   *Dino Buzzati*   498

VIII. ARCHETYPES AND STEREOTYPES   501

The Imaginary Jew   *John Berryman*   501
The Artificial Nigger   *Flannery O'Connor*   502
Counterparts   *James Joyce*   504

IX. IRONY—EPIPHANY   506

Bliss   *Katherine Mansfield*   506
Fifty Pounds   *A. E. Coppard*   508
Barbados   *Paule Marshall*   509

X. THE SHAPE OF FICTION   513

The Wife of Martin Guerre   *Janet Lewis*   513

I. REALISM

THE USE OF FORCE
William Carlos Williams

Accept, if you will, a sweeping statement: the story, "The Use of Force," is the shape of all fiction. It has theme, plot, conflict. It has a beginning, a middle, and an end. It is fiction in miniature. What is fiction? Surprisingly, many students are unclear on that point. What is true? Is a story true? Distinguish between a story which is fiction and a newspaper "story."

In a sense, the events of "The Use of Force" actually occurred to its author, Dr. Williams, a physician in New Jersey. Does that make "The Use of Force" something other than fiction? Write up the action of "The Use of Force" as it would appear in a local newspaper. Notice how different the newspaper "story" is from the story as fiction.

What is the plot of "The Use of Force"? Let the word "plot," like all other more or less technical literary words, circulate without definition. After a while one finds that classroom use has defined the word for practical purposes. If you have other purposes for the definition of that word or any other word, you may wish to consult dictionaries or glossaries. Most of the words we know, however, we learned outside the dictionary, and we may acquire literary vocabulary, too, by observation as opposed to conscious inquiry.

What does each of the two main characters of "The Use of Force" hope to achieve? Does the goal of each conflict with the goal of the other?

What does the story symbolize? Think of the word "symbolize" in a commonsense way. What classes of people do the characters symbolize, "stand for"? Of what other action is the action symbolic: for example, does the action suggest that at a philosophical level the story is about war? About rape?

Isn't a story always first of all "about" what it appears to be about? In this case, it is about a doctor and a patient and the patient's parents. What discovery does the doctor make about himself during the course of the action? If a discovery is to be made, we expect that the doctor will make it, not the child, not the parents. Why?

One reason may be that the doctor is, after all, the narrator. Does this mean that he is also the author? What is the difference between narrator and author? Can they sometimes be the same person? Distinguish between the doctor who wrote the story and the doctor who narrates it.

The doctor reflects: "The damned little brat must be protected against her own idiocy, one says to one's self at such times. Others must be protected against her. It is a social necessity. And all these things are true. But a blind fury, a feeling of adult shame, bred of a longing for muscular release are the operatives. One goes on to the end." Discuss with students the nature of the doctor's conflict with himself. Instantly he overpowers the girl with an "unreasoning" assault. Consider the ways in which we and our students are in conflict with ourselves, as the doctor is.

This story reveals its meaning rhythmically, viscerally. The doctor's insight into his inner conflict occurs at the moment of his "blind fury . . . shame . . . longing for muscular release." A good way to hear the rhythm of this story, or of others, is to hear it read aloud. A story heard in the voice of someone who understands it well will usually offer meanings in ways we fail to hear with our inner ear only.

Why did the author of "The Use of Force" choose to punctuate his story in a minimal way? Obviously his punctuation is not "correct." Why no quotation marks? Does his indifference to punctuation impede our clearing reading of the story? Is it now safe for the rest of us to abandon punctuation?

What "facts" do we have about the social or economic class of Mathilda's family? Notice how many factual details are unobtrusively provided—the family name, its habit of cleanliness, its housekeeping practices, the size of its house, its grammar, and its deferences to a member of the professional class.

A skillful writer conveys the idea of a relationship with a touch of detail. "As often, in such cases, they weren't telling me more than they had to, it was up to me to tell them; that's why they were spending three dollars on me."

Literature is "about" life, and no one is an "expert" on life. A story's meaning may not even be clear to the author. A good author is often surprised at the number of interpretations placed upon his story, but he is also open to a variety of interpretations. Nobody owns the truth.

Remember that one reader's realism is not another's. Thus, judgments of the stories grouped as "realism" will vary from person to person, depending upon each person's own real experiences.

Write about a story memorable to you from a period five years ago. Reexamine a story, a fable, a fairy tale, a moving picture, a play, which you once found important, but which you now find beneath your interests. How can this decline in influence be explained in terms of altered reality? Whose reality has altered? Was it Mark Twain who said, "It's amazing how much my father has learned in twenty years."?

Time alters realities. People change. Can we agree that judgments of stories are to a large degree subjective? And yet, some stories are clearly "better" than others. Can we agree, then, to a seeming contradiction?

Above all, is it necessary to decide if one story is better than another? Can we avoid contests in these matters, and read each work of literature for the value it offers?

THE PROCURATOR OF JUDAEA

Anatole France

What is the weakness, if any, of "The Procurator of Judaea"? Is the surprise ending—the O. Henry ending—a weakness? If so, is the story more than redeemed by the characterizations and the daring imagination which raises it far above the level of a frail story topped by a "twist"? Does this story depend heavily upon our knowing enough of the myth or legend upon which it is based to appreciate the bold manner of Anatole France's breaking from that familiar tale?

A story, to be real, must provide more than a series of words and sentences leading to a climax or surprise. It must be real *within*. Does "The Procurator" offer a picture of Roman life sufficiently persuasive to satisfy our desire for realism? But are we interested in Rome for Rome's sake? Are we interested in more than Rome?

Can we see that this story is truly about our time and our place, based upon Anatole France's interpretation of the story of Jesus' life, trial, and death? Is "The Procurator of Judaea" really a story of our own time, although it was written many years ago about events occurring in the time of Jesus?

One may enjoy discussing modern instances resembling the events of "The Procurator of Judaea." Would the story make a good motion picture? Some of us perhaps recall the motion picture "Jesus Christ Superstar," in which the story of Jesus is seen in modern terms. Does casting an old story in modern dress necessarily make it relevant?

What *does* make a story relevant? Does the meaning of relevance vary from person to person, like interpretations of reality? We tend to elicit similarities between events of our own lives and events of stories we read. One ought not look upon such discussions as digressions: they may be, in fact, routes back to the heart of the literature in question.

And if they are not, we can try again tomorrow.

Reread stories. Sometimes a second reading makes all the difference; in a second marriage, one learns immensely from the first. A story cannot occur in an entirely linear manner. When it does it creates doubts about itself (see our discussion of "But For This . . ."). Many things the author wishes the reader to know or to remember cannot be presented to the reader at the precisely convenient moment. The author confronts at least two kinds of chronology: one is linear time; the other is dramatic time. Therefore, important information may reside at a distance from its "logical" location. What is the logic of linear time? What is the logic of dramatic time?

Have you had this experience: After reading a story you discover that you have "forgotten" some data located early in the story. But upon rereading you find that this data is really remembered, and adds to the dramatic effect? Can we, should we learn to depend upon subliminal effects in reading?

A test of a story may be its capacity to bear rereading. Often a second reading will be in many ways more exciting than a first reading. Can you explain why this phenomenon occurs? Are there stories you have read many times with continuing pleasure? Why does a young child sometimes read (or hear) a book dozens of times without growing tired of it?

II. HIGH STYLE VERSUS JUST PLAIN GOOD

We have included four stories in this section. Which of them do you think are written in "high style"? What influences a person in making this decision?

Two of the stories are about whole lives. Which two? The other two are about parts of lives, the beginnings and the endings of things. The beginnings are endings, too: the beginning of Denis' marriage becomes the end of his single life; the beginning of Macomber's short happy life is the end of him.

THE SIRE DE MALÉTROIT'S DOOR
Robert Louis Stevenson

The Sire de Malétroit is extremely anxious that his niece be married, for she has disgraced his name through a harmless but indiscreet flirtation with a young captain. Does he believe that Denis de Beaulieu is really that man? He thinks Denis "A likely stripling—not ill born...." Is there any reason the Sire should care whether he has trapped the wrong gentleman?

At first, Denis thinks he is dealing with a madman, a lunatic. Why is it so chilling to him to realize that the old man is sane?

Remember that the year is 1429. The Sire says, "I had little more acquaintance with my own late lady ere I married her; which proves that these impromptu marriages may often produce an excellent understanding in the long run." Speculate on the circumstances of the marriage of the Sire himself.

What are his motives in the arrangement of Blanche's marriage? He states his feelings quite clearly in the story. Is the Sire a just man?

Why is the old gentleman constantly chirping? "[He] meanwhile surveyed Denis from head to foot with a smile, and from time to time emitted little noises like a bird or a mouse, which seemed to indicate a high degree of satisfaction."

Alain Malétroit was once a young man of one and twenty. What, do you suppose, would *he* have done in Denis' situation? Would he have let himself be hanged from an old man's window before he married a pretty, plump girl? Remember the circumstances of his marriage; perhaps it was "arranged."

What are you feelings toward the Sire de Malétroit and how do your feelings change as you read the story? Indeed he is clever. By the standards of *his* time, is he also cruel? He tells Blanche, "If your father had been alive, he would have spat on you and turned you out of doors. His was the hand of iron. You may bless your God you have only to deal with the hand of velvet, mademoiselle."

Explain what you think happened between Blanche and Denis in the two hours before dawn. Do you think they "fell in love" so quickly? What did Stevenson think about love at first sight? We know, don't we, what the Sire thought.

What irony is there in the name Blanche? In French, it is the feminine form of *blanc,* meaning white. What is Blanche wearing when she emerges from the chapel?

The end of the story leaves us curious about what happened to Denis and Blanche once they were married. Talk about what their married life might have been like; how well they got along, where they lived. Were their children comely? The story holds quite an appeal for young people of a marriageable age. It is a sort of involuntary romance. Ultimately, what difference does it make how you meet the person you marry?

THE SHORT HAPPY LIFE OF FRANCIS MACOMBER
Ernest Hemingway

Discuss the ways in which "Macomber" "qualifies" as story and "But For This . . ." does not. For example, Hemingway's characters are explored in depth. They are real people with distinct personalities. How is Wilson's Englishness offset by the Macombers' Americanness?

What does Hemingway mean by "the short happy life of Francis Macomber"? In the beginning we might think it an ironic title. Though Macomber is young, only thirty-five, his short life certainly hasn't been happy. When *did* his life become happy?

About two-thirds of the way through the story, Macomber begins to change. "He expected the feeling he had had about the lion to come back but it did not. For the first time in his life he really felt wholly without fear. Instead of fear he had a feeling of definite elation." Then again: "Macomber felt a wild unreasonable happiness that he had never known before." And again: " 'Do you have that feeling of happiness about what's going to happen?' Macomber asked, still exploring his new wealth." Why does Hemingway use the word "wealth"? Where are other indications that Macomber is changing? Part of Hemingway's craft is his artful preparation of the reader for what is to come. How do these lines give us clues about the end of the story? What is Hemingway telling us?

What does Memsahib mean? In what language?

Hemingway frequently writes rather detailed physical descriptions of his characters and of the landscape. Where, in his description of Macomber, does he set the mood for Macomber's later "coming of age"?

Hemingway tells us that Francis and Margot "had a sound basis of union." What *is* the basis of their union? How does this explain Margot's fear and anxiety as she senses the changes in her husband at the conclusion of the story? " 'You've gotten awfully brave, awfully suddenly,' his wife said contemptuously, but her contempt was not secure. She was very afraid of something."

Wilson is a highly sensitive man. He will not leave the wounded lion in the bush because he knows the animal is suffering. "Macomber did not know how the lion had felt before he started his rush, nor during it when the unbelievable smash of the .505 with a muzzle velocity of two tons had hit him in the mouth.... Wilson knew something about it and only expressed it by saying 'Damned fine lion.' " Where else are we let into Wilson's private thoughts? How does he know immediately that Macomber was awake when his wife returned to their tent in the early hours of the morning?

What do you suppose Wilson means when he refers to Macomber as a "four-letter man" and later "If a four-letter man marries a five-letter woman, he was thinking, what number of letters would their children be?" What does Wilson think of American women?

We wonder at the end of another story in this book, "Barbados," whether Mr. Watford dies. We know that Macomber dies, but we wonder if he is murdered. Reread the last page or so of this story; rereading can often reveal what we have missed in the excitement of the first reading. Wilson suggests leaving a gun in the car with Margot. " 'We'll leave the Mannlicher in the car with the Memsahib.' " Here again is a hint of what's to come.

What does Wilson think about Macomber's death? What does he mean when he says to Margot, " 'He *would* have left you too.' " Then a few sentences farther on: " 'Why didn't you just poison him? That's what they do in England.' "

Do we know anything about Margot's marksmanship? What, if anything, do we assume? If Margot shot to kill her husband, what were her motives? If not, why did she shoot at all? The conclusion of this story holds almost unlimited possibilities for exploration and interpretation since Hemingway never provides us with an *answer*. There is perhaps no answer. We can only make what we will of the situation with the information we are given in the text.

THE CURIOUS CASE OF BENJAMIN BUTTON
F. Scott Fitzgerald

Fitzgerald has actually given us a humorous story; at least, certain lines in it are humorous. Consider, for example, "To his relief, she complained to his parents, and he was removed from the school. The Roger Buttons told their friends that they felt he was too young." Or: "Of the life of Benjamin Button between his twelfth and twenty-first year I intend to say little. Suffice to record that they were years of normal ungrowth." In what other stories in the book do we find humor alongside serious intent?

Can you find any serious intent in "The Curious Case of Benjamin Button"? Perhaps Fitzgerald is trying to say something about the social structure of the South or the nature of scandal. Benjamin's birth is scandalous: to his parents, to Doctor Keene, who washes his hands of it, to the nurses in the hospital—in fact, to all of Baltimore. How would you feel if your newborn son were seventy years old; would you worry about what people thought? Remember that the Buttons were "related to the This Family and the That Family, which, as every Southerner knew, entitled them to membership in that enormous peerage which largely populated the Confederacy."

Do you know who Methuselah is? Look in the Bible. Why does Fitzgerald say "—for it was by this name they called him instead of by the appropriate but invidious Methuselah—"? Why appropriate? Why invidious? Here is another instance of humor in the story.

Read the following quotations chosen from the story and arranged as they appear. We have here a rather structured piece of writing, for Benjamin's age coincides, as he moves backward through life, very neatly at points, with the ages of his male kin, from his grandfather to his grandson. You could take a piece of chalk and draw a picture of the process on a blackboard.

> *When his grandfather's initial antagonism wore off, Benjamin and that gentleman took enormous pleasure in one another's company.*
>
> *Roger Button was now fifty, and he and his son were more and more companionable—in fact, since Benjamin had ceased to dye his hair (which was still grayish) they appeared about the same age, and could have passed for brothers.*
>
> *He and his son [Benjamin's son Roscoe] were, in fact, often mistaken for each other.*
>
> *Five years later Roscoe's little boy had grown old enough to play childish games with the little Benjamin under the supervision of the same nurse.*

What do you imagine finally happens to Benjamin? "When the sun went his eyes were sleepy—there were no dreams, no dreams to haunt him.... And then he remembered nothing." What *would* happen to someone growing inevitably younger and younger? Would he soon just cease to exist; would Nana come one morning to find nothing at all in his crib?

There are two cribs and two canes in this story. Find them. They appear first at the opening and then at the closing of Benjamin's cockeyed life. What do they mean for Benjamin? What do they mean to us?

BUT FOR THIS . . .
Lajos Zilahy

The editors have included "But For This . . ." in a collection of short stories. But is it actually a story? Perhaps "chronology" would be a better word; Zilahy examines none of his characters in depth. In fact, the most important thing about each of them is that he or she dies.

"But For This . . ." is a series of brief sentences describing the events that lead ultimately to the total annihilation of the memory of a man. What does the title imply? Why is it also the last phrase of the "chronology"? We might ask "But for what?"

What feeling does "But For This . . ." inspire in you? Many human beings live and die and leave no trace of their existence behind them. John Kovacs "left no wife, no child behind. . . ." What could be one of the reasons that people have children? In another story in this book, "A Mother's Tale," James Agee offers a partial answer to this question. John Kovacs took his name and his legend to the grave.

III. HUMOR

Often students are afraid of acting in the "wrong" way in the eyes of their teachers. Like well-made characters in good stories, students have their motivations: for better or for worse, grades matter. Teachers, in their turn, don't wish to be seen doing "wrong," either. For both students and teacher the tradition of the American school clings to seriousness.

Since literature is one of those "serious" things, we're all afraid to look "wrong" by smiling in its presence. This well might bring a frown to the face of an author, who may have smiled or laughed outright in the moment of composition!

Is literature always solemn? Always "serious"? Do "serious" matters necessarily preclude laughter? If we smile as we read is the story or book we are reading therefore by definition *not* literature, *not* serious, *not* worthy of our classroom? Write in a paragraph what you think literature is. Was it written only by grave men?

What are some reasons why laughter is mistrusted? Compare literature to politics in this respect, bearing in mind that a candidate who mingles light-heartedness with seriousness is widely mistrusted.

The four stories categorized as "humor" in this volume appear to be critical of aspects of modern society. In what ways are they critical? What are they critical *of*? Humor is often more than merely laughter. Humor may be thought of as a certain *spirit*, a certain *approach*, a direction from which to explore or expose enormously serious social questions. For example, *The Adventures of Huckleberry Finn* is a humorous book, yet its subject is a white boy's conscience in the days of black slavery. Jonathan Swift's essay, "A Modest Proposal," is certainly humor—once we are sure of the point—although the question it addresses itself to is immensely serious: poverty in Ireland.

Can you name some stories in this volume which could not, by any stretch of the imagination, be thought of as humor? But can you also discover, even in the least humorous stories of this volume, some few moments which evoke smiles? Discuss humor as perhaps a matter of balance, proportion, emphasis, taste.

One of the most grievous social errors we can commit is to laugh at another person's misfortune. Is it possible that this is the reason we hesitate to smile, to laugh, to enjoy fully a certain work of literature—we hesitate to laugh at another's misfortune. But laughter cannot liberate us until we are prepared to receive it. Thus we depend somewhat upon others to show us the way.

Discuss the importance of the difference between that which is "serious" and that which is "tragic." Consider the statement: "Jokes about me are not funny." Discuss this paradoxical statement: "Humor must be serious enough to hurt."

To hurt whom? Humor may be potentially painful to the reader, who escapes pain by laughing at the absurd victim as he exists in the story. The victim is therefore apart from oneself, apart from the reader; he is objectified in the story. On the other hand, of course, when humor too deeply hurts, the reader cannot laugh under any circumstances.

What is the essence of the humor of these stories? Try to cite, as you read, or to recall afterward, the moment at which you grasped the idea that a given story *was* humor. Or was the idea missed altogether? (If so, no need to be discouraged: the taste for humor can be developed.) Does a student, upon rereading a story, see humor where he hadn't seen it before? Literature increasingly unfolds upon rereading.

A HUNGER ARTIST

Franz Kafka

Do you think actually believe that "professional fasting" is a recent public spectacle? Do we do a "double-take" when we read the first sentence of "A Hunger Artist"?

Did you have some advance notion of a story by Franz Kafka. Had you heard about things being "Kafkaesque"? Do you approach Kafka's story with the idea that the author is a highly intellectual and therefore somewhat grim and humorless commentator on the state of the world? Were you for that reason unprepared to laugh with "A Hunger Artist"? Did you glide by that first sentence without even a secret smile?

Is it bad to be momentarily baffled by a story? Should readers demand instant clarity? Is discussion with friends and classmates a valid means of clarifying a story which may have been at first perplexing? Can students clarify things for teachers? Should teachers be prepared to revise their own views in the light of student interpretations of literary works?

In "A Hunger Artist" we learn that the artist was "honored by the world, yet in spite of that troubled in spirit...." Why is he so difficult to please? Why can't he accept his honors on the world's terms?

A fruitful discussion may begin with Kafka's statement that "We live in a different world now." As the story proceeds, however, we may become increasingly sensible that the world of Kafka's "hunger artist" is very much like our own. Is the modern artist, for example, in competition with TV?

Explain the statement, "Humor arises from contradiction and paradox." The artist, rejecting materialism and the competitive life, nevertheless finds himself forced to come to terms with those characteristics of society. Consider the stories grouped as "Humor" in that light—as the paradox of each author's being, like Kafka's hunger artist, "all the more troubled because no one would take his trouble seriously."

DYING

Richard Stern

Why does the offer of F. Dorfman Dreben to Professor Bly arouse the professor's resistance rather than his cooperation? Since cooperation could be so easily given, why doesn't Professor Bly *give* it? Kafka's hunger artist says he has not eaten "because I couldn't find the food I liked." Could Professor Bly, in some figurative sense, be saying the same thing to Mr. Dreben? Compare Mr. Dreben to the hunger artist's night watchers, engrossed in their card game, who believe that the artist keeps food in a "private hoard."

How is the poetry which Mr. Dreben wants similar to the panther who replaces the hunger artist? Consider this passage: "Even the most insensitive felt it refreshing to see this wild creature leaping around the cage that had so long been dreary. The panther was all right. The food he liked was brought him without hesitation by the attendants; he seemed not even to miss his freedom...." Would Professor Bly be impairing or securing his own freedom by dashing off a bit of poetry for Mr. Dreben for 200 dollars?

In "Dying," with whom do our sympathies lie? Our appreciation of the humor of the story depends a great deal upon whether we share Professor Bly's dilemma. Are we pleased or displeased at the outcome of "Dying"? Are we angry at Professor Bly for his failure to win the money? And isn't our attitude crucial to our appreciating the humor of the story? With which of the two main characters of "Dying" does the author find *his* identity?

Can Professor Bly and Mr. Dreben ever achieve a meeting of their minds? Often they appear to be talking at cross-purposes. Mr. Dreben frequently misses the point of Professor Bly's statements. Is the reverse true?

Discuss Richard Stern's comment that his story, "Dying," is a "more or less serious comedy or farce."

Discuss the gulf between the mind of Mr. Dreben and the mind of Professor Bly as it is symbolized in the following seemingly simple wordplay:

> He said, "You'd invited other—there were other poets writing verses for you?"
> "Two others, Professor. Bladwin Kerner, editor of the Township School year-book, a fine young poet, and then a dear friend of my sister's, Mrs. Reiser."
> "Which won?"
> "I have only one."

Professor Bly said to Mr. Dreben, "After all, I didn't even know your mother. Not even her name." Mr. Dreben replies by telling Bly his mother's name. Again the gulf! Is it funny? Is it also, in its way, sad? Isn't it both? May a moment express two apparently opposite moods? In humor, nobody is mortally hurt. Yet, in "Dying," someone lies dying; and the professor is studying death in plants. Does this dilute humor? Does it heighten humor? In his essay on the story Professor Stern has written, "Death is a theme to which few writers are not alive." Have you observed his statement to be true?

HANDBOOK FOR TEACHERS AND STUDENTS

THE GONZAGA MANUSCRIPTS
Saul Bellow

At what point in "The Gonzaga Manuscripts" do you begin to be aware that the mood of the story is humor? Would all readers reach this moment of awareness at the same point?

Does our mood begin to find itself when we encounter the lines of Gonzaga's poetry? What are we to make of those verses? Does the direction of our mood now depend somewhat upon our literary judgment itself? If the reader is unable to judge the quality of Gonzaga's poetry the reader is uncertain how to feel, whether to laugh. Can we begin to understand the real merit of those verses as we come to understand Clarence's character?

How do we begin to know Clarence from the following passage? "Clarence disliked black-marketing, but the legal rate of exchange was ridiculous; he was prepared to pay a lot of money for those manuscripts and at eighteen to one he might spend a small fortune." Isn't there some hypocrisy there? Does Clarence *really* dislike black-marketing?

The humor or laughter of "The Gonzaga Manuscripts" may overtake the reader gradually. Short bursts of detail frequently call our attention to the widespread absurdity of things. What is the meaning of the old general's "bothering" his soup? How is our comic sense served by the author's bold comment on a lady's hair—"Tresses of dark-reddish hair fought strongly for position on her head"?

At tea Clarence is feeling uncomfortable. "Instead of a saucer, he felt as though he were holding on to the rim of Saturn." Can you explain that sentence?

THE IRON FIST OF OLIGARCHY
Mark Harris

At several points in "The Iron Fist of Oligarchy" Sy Appleman's idealism is contrasted with the pragmatism or even cynicism of his father and other elders. Do most students necessarily find identity with Sy, who is of their age? Describe, perhaps in writing, situations in your own lives when your idealism has clashed with the more conservative or cautious outlooks of your elders.

Is Sy in some respect like Professor Bly, suffering the artist's pride, unable to perform at command? Is Sy also to some extent like the hunger artist, competing with circuses? In each case, these three principal characters of these stories confront antagonists. What is the common denominator of their antagonists? If Sy, Bly, and the hunger artist represent art, what do their antagonists represent?

Does the slight obtuseness of the narrator of "The Iron Fist of Oligarchy" heighten or lessen the humor of the story? How does the narrator reveal his own true character when he says, "In the slaughterhouse they talked about man's relationship to animals, of the ethics of killing them, and of the wonders and dangers of man's technological environment, thoughts which you and I had when we were younger"? Does the character of the narrator enlighten readers on the character of Sy's father? How? Has Sy's father abandoned idealism?

Has television changed since the days of "Kanine Kapers"? Sy contends that that television program foretells the decline of Western civilization. Is he dramatizing things? What do you make of his more specific complaint that "Kanine Kapers" lacked teamwork, that he never met the actors, that the actors never met the writers, and so forth? What is Sy trying to say? Is his father the man to try to say it to?

On the diving board Sy Appleman recites from *Winnie the Pooh*. Is his choice of that book significant? What is the significance of his instantaneous response to his father's voice?

IV. THE READER

THE AMBITIOUS GUEST
Nathaniel Hawthorne

Three of the four stories of this group announce their unashamed devotion to matters related to literature—especially the act of composition. In "The Ambitious Guest," however, the subject seems to be the quest for fame. How do you think "The Ambitious Guest" might be related to Hawthorne's daydreams at the time he wrote the story? How old was he when he wrote it?

In "The Ambitious Guest" the "stranger" is nameless, and his way is solitary. Do you think he might be a writer? What characteristics does he have that might make you think so? He appears resigned to living an "undistinguished life" in exchange for immortality. But do you suppose the attraction of the seventeen-year-old daughter of the family might have brought him toward the present? How is romanticism about "immortality" like the romanticism of romance? Compare the young stranger's statement of his ambition to the humbler last request of the "aged grandmother."

Has Hawthorne written elsewhere about sexual attraction? Good extra reading might be *The Scarlet Letter*. In what sector of the country does "The Ambitious Guest" occur? Could it have occurred elsewhere? Compare this story to "But For This . . .".

The scene of the family by the fireplace is vivid. How is this vividness brought about? Would this story make a good short film—for example, a TV "Hitchcock"?

If it is true that the stories of this group arise from preoccupations of their authors, it is also true, of course, that many stories appear to bear no *direct* relationship to their authors' lives. Can you identify stories in this volume which do not appear to feature their authors in a visible way? Would "Red Leaves" be one story of that type? "A Simple Heart"? And yet, isn't an author always in some manner "in" his story?

THE REAL RIGHT THING

Henry James

Where is Henry James in "The Real Right Thing"? Is it possible that he has cast himself, consciously or otherwise, in *two* roles? George Withermore thinks of Ashton Doyne as "the master"—a phrase often used with reference to James himself. What does Withermore mean by his use of the word? Is Withermore's reverence perhaps one reason for his being unable to work in Doyne's house?

Withermore, working on the Life of Doyne, "was learning many things that he had not suspected, drawing many curtains, forcing many doors, reading many riddles, going, in general, as they said, behind almost everything." Let us pretend for a moment that ghosts cannot possibly exist. How, then, do you explain the actions of the "mystical assistant" who often seems to be sharing the work with Withermore?

If you were making a moving picture of this story how would you manage the mystery of the "mystical assistant"? Is it really Mrs. Doyne? Is it Withermore's imagination?

Why, on page 165, is the word "Life" spelled in that fashion?

LIFE-STORY

John Barth

In John Barth's "Life-Story" the author seems to be turning his distress to playfulness. Do you suppose that much writing is inspired by authors' distress?

In a sense, "Life-Story" sets forth the problem of the modern writer, who yearns to be "linear" in the old-fashioned sense, but cannot be. Why is "old-fashioned" storytelling difficult for the modern writer? Consider, for example, plots involving boy-meets-girl, trial marriage, or the scandal of a young man's being discovered in a young lady's dormitory room. How do changing social attitudes alter plot possibilities?

Notice, in this connection, Barth's passionate paragraph beginning on page 178: "Neither had his wife and adolescent daughters, who for that matter preferred life to literature and read fiction when at all for entertainment. Their kind of story (his too, finally) would begin if not once upon a time at least with arresting circumstance, bold character, trenchant action...." Does life in our time overwhelm the possibilities for literature? But what are some of the ways in which literature can serve, for which no substitute has yet presented itself?

Barth, in "Life-Story," contends that his (or his character's) "fiction inevitably made public his private life." Does that seem to inhibit Barth in the present story?

Here's a chance for a little detective work. In "Life-Story" Barth speaks in an odd phraseology at one point: "V. S. Pritchett, English critic and author, will put the matter succinctly in a soon-to-be-written essay on Flaubert...." What is the meaning of that odd phraseology? Is it reminiscent of a passage in "In Dreams Begin Responsibilities," in which we hear that "the older uncle" is "in his bedroom upstairs, studying for his final examinations at the College of the City of New York, having been dead of double-pneumonia for the last twenty-one years"?

On page 177 Barth speaks of the "ground-situation" of the story the writer would like to be able to write. What does he mean by that interesting new word? Is he speaking of something like plot?

V. MYTH AND SYMBOL

PERSEPHONE

Meridel Le Sueur

Demeter (her Roman name was Ceres) was the venerable Greek goddess of fertility, and Persephone, her daughter by Zeus. The myth has undergone changes in the tellings and the two goddesses are represented variously in different cultures, but the story line itself persists. One day as she was gathering flowers, the maiden Persephone was kidnapped by Hades, king of the underworld, and taken by him there to rule as his consort. Disconsolate, Demeter ranged the world in search of her beloved daughter, in her deprivation and distraction searing the earth and producing famine. Zeus finally intervened and Persephone was allowed to return to her mother, but only on a limited basis. For Persephone had eaten the seed of a pomegranate, the sacred fruit of hell, and thus she must return to her husband beneath the earth for part of each year. The mythological expression or explanation for spring fertility and its disappearance in the fall is clear. Quest, which Northrop Frye terms the central myth of literature, gives this myth its contour, or form.

Thus, Demeter's search for Persephone represents the light looking for the dark; the bountiful seeking the spare. The situation is resolved in compromise: the flowering-forth balanced with loss, the joy with sorrow.

In the Le Sueur story, the setting has been changed to a Kansas farming community. Demeter has become in the story the farm wife Freda (a spelling variation of the Norse goddess of fertility). She oozes fertility; fairly smells of it. She is fruitful in planting and in harvesting. Her mare (Demeter is the goddess of mares) easily establishes at any given moment her owner's whereabouts in the community. Freda is identified with that mare. Freda's daughter, of mysterious origin (Zeus's numerous begettings are always disguised mysteries), is born in the spring "as the first white violets bloomed." (Persephone has one mythic identity as the goddess of flowers.) She is a strange child, wind-swift, haunted, and with a growing reputation for wantonness. It is not unexpected when she is spirited away by an outsider, a stockman. We have, then, in this narrative the intense decline of the mother; Freda's wanderings, and the corresponding death of the earth:

That year the spring never came. The flowers died beneath the ground and the fields burned in the sun.

With the daughter's strange reappearance, the rains begin to fall. At the end of the story, the narrator is accompanying the sick and failing daughter on a train, in terror, through the autumn's dark and cavernous landscapes to the "dead, glowing ... mineral worlds of her strange lord."

The story abounds in the symbols, the representations, of the details of the myth itself: seed; the black bulls of Hades; the country people *dreaming* over their farm work "half-unconsciously touched by the mystery of their tasks"; the partaking in the ritual birth and death of the soil. Elegies of other myths echo as well. One is the rape of Freda's daughter, like the rape of Europa, as the bulls stand in the wind.

But we have also and finally the narrative itself. And we see, too, the Kansas prairie, the young girls with bright ribbons in their hair, the summer, the animals, and the sere winter. One of these girls is the narrator, who has a vision of her everyday life that is larger than humdrum. *She* sees the working out of the cycle of growth, birth, and dying in mythic terms, and she peoples her world with the prototypes of the gods, her own neighbors. She ends her narration with questions: who are these people—the dream, the myth, or the reality? The last words of the story are "And I did not know."

Yet what we know from the story is that in the precise sense of "real" identities we also do not know; in the larger sense, in the sense of the race's collective unconscious, we know what we know. And that is the human heritage.

RED LEAVES

William Faulkner

This story concerns survival, and three societies with respect to that.

The first society is that of the (Chickasaw) Indian, the *red* leaves of the title, in final flaring glory before the fall. Even their first-mentioned leader is nicknamed "Doom," perhaps because he was the first to fall in love with the white man's ways and artifacts, slavery and finery and the like. The white man's is the second society of the story, but represented only by the corruption of his things and his ways.

Each of Doom's descendants—there are two in the story—becomes increasingly physically passive and withdrawn, desiccated. The true power of the Indian, to meditate, not to act, has become vitiated as it is entangled with white-black mores. The worst commitment is to slavery. To them, it is a great bother. We know, from our perspective, that it too ended—

violently! The author must surely wish us to keep that in mind. The Indian is not committed to the work ethic, which is white and has communicated to the black ("they like to sweat"), and is associated with vigor.

Quite apart from the ritualistic aspects of the chase after the runaway slave, the black man, representing the third society, wishes to resist death, not go to it willingly as the Indian wants him to—"they would even rather work in the sun than to enter the earth."

The black man, who will survive, "endure," is also infected by white mores, but he is on the move up, however slowly. He is not passive, and his group will not dissolve. His blood, in the story, has been mixed with the Indian, as it has been and will continue to be with the white, and that is the design. To embrace the blood is to invite the doom of "pure" culture; the Indian's will not survive. Whatever process is being served, metaphysics or sociology, miscegenation will merely hasten it.

The construct of this story is in the nature of a grand poem, with certain lines and phrases reiterated, giving us the rhythm of a chant. The writing, most carefully crafted, leaves us no surprises. When we reread we discover that all the clues have been planted early to be reaped later. The recurring themes, the use of language transliterated ("Issetibbeha became dead . . . tomorrow is today . . . it is today"), simple and echoic, give the feeling too of primitivism. There are two kinds of primitivism in this "poem," black and red, and we are led carefully to the characteristics of each.

There are several references to "the clan," the Indian totem divisions of family and tribe, distinguished, Freud tells us, to avoid incest. There are references to Siam, to Sumatra, and "Malay god." Cannibalism is practiced by the Indians. The black practices of primitivism are mentioned in ceremonies, in the phases of the moon, in the drums of the jungle, hidden away. There are differentiations. The buryable black man has no name, for us or the Indians. He is a body servant, "a Guinea man" of forty. Such is to be his identity for 150 years or more. Like many of the clothes of the Indians, his acquisitions are borrowed—"dungaree pants bought by Indians from white men" and an amulet from his owner, Issetibbeha. Both primitives, the one now advanced in living scale over the other, enter into the ritual of chase and live burial.

From the first page, "I know what we will not find," the plot and the ritual aspects of the chase are signaled. We learn that when Doom died something similar occurred. On the first page as well, there is Basket wearing clamped through one ear, an enameled snuff box. This affectation, like the stiff Sunday clothes at the funeral later, the rotting steamboat, the useless gilt bed, and above all, the red shoes which have become the lineal mark of leadership, all reiterate the theme of the Indian's succumbing to the puerile and dangerous white possessions.

The shoes, indeed, operate as a one-to-one symbol. Acquired in aristocratic circumstances, they have been handed down. Moketubbe plays with them when he is small, and later sneaks the wearing of them, a fact not lost upon his father. They have to be forced on to Moketubbe when he is carried forth on the litter into the chase. We do not usually associate feet with respiration; nevertheless these shoes almost suffocate Moketubbe. They combine with his obesity and thus immobility to inform us that the end of everything has begun.

Are we troubled with the stereotyped description of the Negroes? There are recurring "rolling eyeballs" and the stink. The story is full of smells, those of death, and of fear. They are coefficients of primitivism. Faulkner's work is very strong, not anesthetized by deodorants of mind and body. The important thing is his description of the black group as being like a "single octopus . . . the roots of a huge tree uncovered, the *earth broken* momentarily upon the writhen, thick fetid tangle of its lightless and *outraged* life." The blacks have been wrenched from their natural life in Africa, abused, their simplicity misused, their existence a form of being buried alive. It will not always be so: " 'They are thinking something,' the second [Indian] said. 'I do not want to be here.' "

And lo! they were, finally, not.

Nobody really knows how ancient myths got started, but we can guess. Looking at present-day sports heroes or entertainment figures, we can see that they become endowed with virtues—or vices—larger than life. Secretly, enviously, we may attribute to such people wish fulfillments of our own. They can do our exciting living for us, vicariously cavorting, sinning, reaping the glory, reaping the consequences. They become, so endowed, like gods.

Stories promulgate myth.

On the other hand, in dealing with the fiction of James Joyce's *Ulysses* or Meridel Le Sueur's "Persephone," we can see that something of the opposite was true. Stories of the gods were thought about in human proportions, and adapted to human scale. Thus, the wily Ulysses becomes a Jewish advertising solicitor living in Dublin. The writer may very well ask of a myth, as of anything else, "How did this come to be?" And then set about using familiar materials, perhaps from life, to reconstruct and reinterpret myth.

Can you see how Le Sueur implies that an incident in a rural community can become a basis for interpreting a mystery, a myth? The story becomes a two-way proposition, then: How do the facts of the story become larger than life in the telling? How has the myth itself been used to work out the facts in this Kansas prairie town?

The French word for story is *l'histoire*, very close to the word we have for history in English. Which of these stories applies myth to personal history? Which would you say applies history, and demonstrates how it becomes myth?

What two modern meanings apply when we say a story is a myth? How, then, does Faulkner illustrate the "myth" of the noble savage, the Indian?

Would we have less understanding of these two stories if we did not have background in or knowledge of (1) the myth of Persephone or (2) the history of the fate of the red man in America? Do these two make any difference in our appreciation of the stories?

Who tells the story of "Persephone"? What is the narrator's relationship to the community?

A symbol is said to be a dramatic shorthand for shared experience. What is the difference between myth and symbol? How does the one employ the other? How are they related? Is it valid to say that Persephone has become a symbol of lost innocence?

What are the ritual aspects of these two stories? What do we recognize in them as setting forth patterns of deeply significant human behavior? What are the two kinds of Quest, or search, in these stories, for instance? In the Le Sueur story, there are definite occasions that seem to be rituals, like planting and harvesting. Why then is it necessary to explain drought in terms of mystery?

Within primitive groups, the tribes or clans often adopted totems for protection and good luck. A totem is an emblem or symbol believed to be an ancestor. The snake is a frequent totem animal. What, then, is symbolized when the snake slashes at the slave in "Red Leaves"?

VI. ALLEGORY

If you were going to write a story about yourself but instead of appearing as a person, appear as an animal, what animal would you choose? How would your choice be influenced by the experience in your life about which you were writing?

Of the three animals represented in these stories, with which do you most identify? Which animal, do you suppose, is most commonly owned by human beings? Maybe you don't identify with any of them; you would rather be a deer or an elephant or a camel.

A reader brings to these stories a knowledge of the nature of the beasts that he encounters. We already know something of each animal before we read, either through photographs or through direct experience; we have a sense of how the animal kingdom lives. Could Walter Van Tilburg Clark have written the same story about a sparrow or a pigeon?

We find allegory in fables and in fairy tables. Children love stories about bears who talk and the wolf who pretends he is Red Riding Hood's grandmother. Why are handsome princes confined to frog bodies by wicked witches? How does a frog look to you? To a child? Does a frog look the same to everyone? Is he the opposite of a handsome prince? The fables and fairy tales of our childhood are part of our education. Through them we learn something about the behavior of creatures, even what they look like, what color they are. We take some of this knowledge with us to our adult reading, when we meet again the same animals but in more sophisticated literature.

HOOK

Walter Van Tilburg Clark

Why did Clark write this story in five parts? Discuss what happens to Hook in each "chapter" that changes his life. Each of the five parts covers a different amount of time; how does the time in years or months differ from the duration of certain processes of living and dying that Hook experiences? Where does Clark tell us how long Hook lives?

How do the last months of Hook's life resemble the first? "But gradually he learned to believe that he could not fly, that his life must now be that of the discharged nestling again." You may recall the sphinx's riddle that Oedipus was finally able to answer. "What walks on four legs in the morning, two legs in the afternoon, and three legs in the evening?" In terms of allegory, how can we relate Hook's life to man's and therefore to this riddle?

Why does Clark make so much of Hook's attacks on the gulls? What do the gulls represent to Hook? To us? To begin with he drives them from their kill and eats what they have left. Then he commences to attack and kill the gulls themselves. Reread the paragraphs of the story that deal with the mass attack of the gulls upon Hook. What betrays Hook's weakness to the gulls, giving them the courage to attack him? Where else in the story do we find references to the gulls?

Toy with the idea of "personification," defining it in a practical and useful way. Is Hook a personified character? Do we find any evidence in the story that Hook does any thinking as we know it? If not, how does he make his decisions? What are his "three hungers" and his "one will"?

Because Hook is a creature of the wild outdoors, his life is influenced greatly by such things as the weather. Clark tells us about the rains and the drouths and their effects on Hook and on the other animals of the range, upon some of whom Hook feeds. Go through the story and analyze the changing of the seasons. How could you in this way determine how long Hook lives without Clark's reference to his lifetime in years?

In the end, Hook steals into the henhouse and preys upon the flightless chickens. This is reminiscent of his behavior toward the gulls. His last battles are fought first with a cock and then with a dog. Why do you feel satisfaction when he kills the rooster, if indeed you do feel it? Clark says "The great eye flashed more furiously than it ever had in victorious battle." Explain why. How is Hook's last battle his most courageous one, the most worthy of the nature of a hawk?

A MOTHER'S TALE

James Agee

A case could be made for "A Mother's Tale" as religious allegory. What does religion, especially Judeo-Christian, tell us about life on earth? It has told us that all our suffering has "been sent us as a kind of harsh trying or proving of our worthiness; and that it was entirely fitting and proper that we could earn our way through to such rewards as these, only through suffering, and through being patient under pain which was beyond our understanding; and that now at the last, to those who had borne all things well, all things were made known: for the mystery of suffering stood revealed in joy."

The cattle made up a mythlogy to explain their long journey. Were they now in Heaven? Can you find other sections of "A Mother's Tale" that seem to relate to religion? For example, why does Agee capitalize the words "He," "Him," "Hammer" and "One Who Came Back"? If there is a Christ in the story, who is it?

The journey of the steer in his righteous fury is rather incredible. How *did* he know where he was going, whether he was headed in the right direction? Discuss his uncanny sense of "home."

Many times prophet or seers are *not* believed by their people. "Others suspected that he had been sent among us with his story for some mischievous and cruel purpose, and the fact that they could not imagine what this purpose might be, made them, naturally, all the more suspicious . . . whether anyone in his right mind would go to such trouble for others."

Why did the men who "came quietly" among the ancestors shoot the One Who Came Back? What does the mother believe? Does she believe the old legend as she tells it to the calves?

Explore the suggestion that Agee makes that there was something the mother could not bring herself to ask her son. Why couldn't she ask him?

Why does Agee end the story with "What's a train?" Perhaps the calf has missed the whole point of the fable; out of the mother's recital, his young mind grasps only the merest word. Yet, this word is practically the pivot point of the whole story. Discuss the mingled innocence and insight of the calf expressed in his final question.

DEATH OF A FAVORITE

J. F. Powers

Are you surprised to discover that the narrator is a cat? How long does it take for the reader to find that out? Meanwhile, we are trying to imagine what kind of person mouses for sport, not diet, in midwestern fields.

What opinion does Fritz hold of himself? Consider that he tells us "There is something fatal about the vocation of favorite, but it is the only one that suits me. . . ." And later he laments: "Already the remembrance of things past—the disease of noble politicals in exile—was too strong in me, the hope of restoration unwarrantably faint." Fritz likens himself to aristocracy.

Some of us have seen the movie "The Exorcist." What does it mean to be possessed? " 'Association,' said Father Burner with mysterious satisfaction, almost zest." Explain what he means. How successful are the two priests in their endeavor to bewitch the cat?

Find the part in this story where Fritz tells us what color he is and how he is marked. What other characters in the story wear black with white collars? During the conversation between Father Burner and Father Philbert, at which Fritz is present, Fritz remarks that he has been celibate since coming to live at the rectory. What characters in the story take vows of celibacy?

There is a saying, "When the cat's away, the mice will play." The cat makes a similar remark about the priests. Find the quotation. Who is the "cat" and who are the "mice"?

What is the source of Father Burner's hostility toward Fritz? The story opens with Father Malt introducing Fritz to the visiting missionaries as "My assistant." What do we learn when we read: " 'His assistant!' said Father Burner with surprising bitterness. 'Co-adjutor with right of succession' "? Father Burner unwittingly reenforces Fritz's idea of himself as some kind of aristocrat, with the rights of succession and restoration. Why might Burner resent the presence of such a favorite in the rectory? What position does Burner himself hold there?

What motive could Father Philbert have in allying himself with Burner's anger toward Fritz and therefore toward Father Malt? What is Father Malt's position in the parish?

As a small matter of literary sleuthing, can you find indirect evidence in the story that it is Father Malt who named the cat "Fritz"? A clue lies in a "famous question" that Father Malt once asked, and that Burner passes on to his friend Philbert.

What is significant about Father Burner saying "Scratch a prelate and you'll find a second baseman"? The priests do seem to have concern outside their divine mission. Why does Father Philbert insist that the "clerical gray" car is not his but his *brother's*? What is a prelate? A curate?

Discuss the anecdote Father Burner tells at the noon meal on Sunday about another cat. Why does he conclude: "Case a lot like this. Except now they're afraid of him"?

Fritz says, "I wanted nothing less than my revenge." Does he get it? How is it a limitation of his species that he couldn't control his reaction to the crucifix upon Father Malt's return? We all remember Pavlov's dogs. Fritz has to destroy himself to eradicate his fear. What does Fritz mean when he says that Father Philbert "was basically an emotional dolt and would have voted then for my canonization"? What is canonization?

How does this phrase ". . . for now Father Malt himself was drawing my chair up to the table, restoring me to my rightful place" indicate to us that Fritz has retained his identity and his original sentiments about his proper elevation in life? The exiled ruler has been reinstated on his throne.

VII. DREAM AS CRISIS

IN DREAMS BEGIN RESPONSIBILITIES

Delmore Schwartz

The story flows quickly into its three channels: the dream (announced in the title beforehand), the film ("I feel as if I were in a moving-picture theater"), the motion backward in time. Dream isn't necessarily confined in time this way. It goes forward, goes senselessly, or can invoke any kind of time sense, really. Even so, this story is told in the present tense though the events point backward.

"In Dreams" is a fine place to begin a consideration of the influence of dream upon fiction because it so clearly and realistically announces its own theme: fantasy tamed by actuality.

If we wish to impose deeper enlightenment from psychology upon Schwartz's story, we can find in the mother and the father archetypal components of anima and animus, the female and the male principles that Carl Jung sees as dominating dream and symbol. They are expressions of both hope and fear.

This story is also scenario. Alone of the stories in this section, it is in the first person. So that if Jung can still be applied, seeing *oneself* in one's dream refers to the conscious embattled against itself; the other parties to the dream represent the unconscious. At the same time, the point of view gives the story an immediacy, while the vehicle of dreaming-on-film gives a distance, in both of which we can participate.

"Why was I born?" has ever been a concern of the young. The dream announces the responsibility for the self.

THE SEVEN RIDERS

Dino Buzzati

The imagery is that of dream, riding without ever reaching a frontier, forward motion arriving nowhere in time and space. The narrator has set out to explore his *father's* kingdom, but who really sent him on the journey? As in dream, the origin of the impulse is lost in the quest.

Despite the continual arithmetic of computed time and distance which gives the story a notebook validity, we are really in the realm of fairy tale. This is a prince. His horses are called chargers. The situation is right out of descriptions of dreams by Carl Jung. Jung sees the fairy tale as archetypal expression of the symbolic landscape of dream. That is, man universally has certain kinds of dreams; they surface in his tales and are given a verbal expression to which we all respond, not only because of the fantasy, but because we have been *there*, in the unconscious. To Jung, a mountain pass, for instance, is a well-known symbol for a "situation of transition" that leads from an old attitude of mind to a new one. The conflicting opposites of past and future are expressed in boundaries. "I shall probably cross the boundaries of the kingdom without noticing it and in my ignorance will keep on going." The prince tells one of his riders, "After you, Dominic, silence," a clear reference to the past. For the future, the others will set out *ahead* to bring news of the waiting terrain. After all this *time*, the prince looks ahead, not back, to "a strange light" shining in the sky, the longed-for unknown.

The prince's other riders would represent to Jung an "old state of passivity." For when the dreamer's ego decides on activity, Jung says, "the other figures [in the dream] stand for his more or less unknown, unconscious qualities."* The symbols of fairy tale are the symbols of self.

※※※

It is the editors' belief that the stories represented in this section achieve, by various means, that human state called dream. Furthermore, each of these stories reflects the dream-state as displaying crisis, close to nightmare. Burrowing into the unconscious, the writers have produced experiences that we better understand if we see them as dream, and as dream-surrogates, surreal and filmic. These stories are, like dreams, intensely visual; that is their chief sensory impact. A good centering for their discussion is to ask, "What do you *see* of these stories when you close your eyes, open your mind, and invite their pictures?"

Then:

What *are* the conditions called dreaming? What do we describe in trying to recreate the texture of dreams? Try describing the conditions of lassitude, of trance, of hypnosis.

Do you *know* you are dreaming when you are in the middle of a dream?

What is surrealism? Seeking out the work of Salvador Dali, can you see why his paintings are said to look like the landscape of dream? Which of these stories would you paint like a Dali?

Logic is the tissue of reality. Dreams display the opposite of logic: the progression of time is unpredictable, for one thing. Which of these stories skew time? How?

Three of the stories are written in the present tense. How does the immediacy of the present tense serve to produce a dreamlike state in each case? In the stories using past tense, obviously other methods achieved a sense of dream. Which? Look for elements of time, motion, earth, water, sky.

Often, we are one of two kinds of spectators in dreams. In one kind, we are crucially involved in the events of the dream. We make things happen; things happen to us. In the other, we merely watch, sometimes because we are helpless, sometimes because we are purposely aloof, not

---

* Carl Jung, *Man and His Symbols* (London: Aldus Books Ltd., 1964), p. 279.

HANDBOOK FOR TEACHERS AND STUDENTS

choosing to "mix in." How do the narrator and the main character of each of these stories represent involvement or mere watching? Does the author involve you as participant or viewer?

How does the movie-house simulate a sense of dream?

Film is a play of light and shadow projected on a screen. It is photographed make-believe. Isn't it? Why do we get a sense of crisis when the film breaks in the story, "In Dreams Begin Responsibilities"?

If an important aspect of dream is crisis, what is the significance of the awakening of the young man in "In Dreams Begin Responsibilities" to his twenty-first birthday?

Definite kinds of language and imagery in these stories evoke dream qualities. Look for, "In Dreams Begin Responsibilities," ". . . an automobile, looking like an enormous upholstered sofa. . . ." "I feel as if I were looking down from the fiftieth story of a building." Again, "I feel as if I were walking a tight-rope one hundred feet over a circus audience. . . ." There are many such references in this story and the others. Notice how such phrases and statements indeed recreate the sense of dreaming.

Dreaming offers its own urgency as the present, mingling aspects of the past and the future. What is the startling effect in "In Dreams Begin Responsibilities" of this: "He is studying in his bedroom upstairs, studying for his final examinations . . . having been dead of double pneumonia for the last twenty-one years"?

In this story, the characters of the mother and the father are sharply differentiated. With which does the son identify? Why do both the narrator and the mother identify with the photographer?

Death is at the center of several of these stories. The story, "An Occurrence at Owl Creek Bridge," announces the impending death of its protagonist at the outset. What, then, happens to sustain our attention between the announcement and the resolution? What is an obituary? What does it tell of a life?

Most dreams are said to be of very short duration: twenty-seven seconds has been mentioned. From the time Peyton Farquhar "closed his eyes," his neck "in the hemp," till the author's stark last sentence, are we aware of the condensation of time? What is a "kaleidoscope effect"?

Notice the style of Robbe-Grillet's "The Secret Room." What is staccato? How does the depersonalization of the narrator here serve to create the sense of a camera lens? Are you shocked by the appearance of the body? Why does the story end with the word "canvas"? Has *this word* some other function? What are the possibilities of irony in making a film of a painting?

Two of these stories are translations. Do they seem to you to demonstrate cultural differences from each other? From the other stories?

One interpretataion of "The Seven Riders" is that it symbolizes how childhood recedes from the adult in ever-increasing distances of experience and memory. How do the events of the story seem to bear out this interpretation? What other meanings might the story hold for you? What does the narrator mean when he says, "After you, Dominic, silence!"? And "I suspect there is no frontier . . ."?

All these stories, closely related in theme, take a different tack of narration. Two are told in the first person. Which? In which of these stories would you say the writer wants us as reader to be the least intensely involved, the watcher? In which, the most, the participant?

VIII. ARCHETYPES AND STEREOTYPES

THE IMAGINARY JEW

John Berryman

The opening of the story gives us the design of the narrator's life in what turned out to be a crucial summer. We are invited in to glimpse him as he lived. His preoccupation with the acrobatic badger serves as a memory of his months in New York, but it is placed carefully as a comment upon mindless reflexing. Yet we are presented a stern disclaimer: his story needed no part of these details of his private life, or of that time or that place. It is a tale of probability—notice the math symbol p. He talks about "pure relation—immaculate apprehension . . ." and history as opposed to folklore. Let us step carefully below the glassy surface of fact, now. His history is in part his lonely summer. Part of the folklore is "the character which experience has given to my sense of the Jewish people." The word "experience" is most important, and it has several meanings.

In one sense it deals with the metaphysical, nonlinear "experience." That is, the narrator is forced to live the experience of folklore so that the history of it becomes individually true. He who cannot imaginatively know p must experience it.

He begins his history with tabula rasa, a clean slate. He has no history of Jews, no imagination of them; can't physically identify them or make their names significant. A Southerner of Irish Catholic background he can, however, quickly identify the Irishman later among the orators at Union Square. How curiously, almost comically, naive is the personal accidental experience of ethnology.

But this is no comedy, for of Jews he says he "trembled when I heard one abused in talk." He is making ready for his identity, for suffering, for being bloodied, for expiating for "his" sins through experience to understanding.

His experience is a journey among madmen. He finds himself in Union Square, a bughouse square, as such places are called. Matters take a biblical turn. The Last Supper is mentioned. He is "thinking that the misty Rider would sweep again away all these men at his feet, whenever he liked," an apocalyptic thought. There are four horsemen of the apocalypse, one of whom is war, and war is again threatening Europe and the world. The story was published in 1945, a year when the extent of the destruction of World War II was well known. In the midst of a mob, hatred and insanity swirling around him, our hero finds himself helplessly, idiotically repeating that he is not a Jew. It is at once a biblical denial, like Thomas' in the New Testament, and a resentment of the stereotype.

In tranquillity, at the ending, the probability—the *p*—has been translated by experience into history, his history too. Imagination defined by reality leads to an understanding of John Donne's sermon, a Christian sermon, "it tolls for thee," and the stereotyped Jew has become an archetype of the ideal.

THE ARTIFICIAL NIGGER

Flannery O'Connor

There is a surprise ending to this story, particularly its next-to-last paragraph. We resent being taken aback so, because O'Connor is a superb storyteller who ought to show, not just tell. That next-to-last paragraph is like a little essay, almost parochial in its religious implications, forcing us to cast back for clues, to reread and to wonder why such an Archie Bunker as Mr. Head has achieved grace in momentous ephiphany and is shriven to enter into the Roman Catholic heaven.

Yes, we cast back for clues and wonder what this marvelously described journey of an old man and a boy *means*. For a reduction of the story is simple enough, and the incongruities of race prejudice, explicit upon Mr. Head's tongue, are balanced in one moment by the boy's response to a large black woman. The child accosts her for directions back to the train, and longs to be enveloped in her arms.

The story really does begin at its beginning, in full moonlight, just before morning, like the "Inferno" of Dante's *Divine Comedy*. Mr. Head is, in fact, compared to Virgil going to summon Dante for his journey through hell. "Or better," to the archangel Raphael, like the Greek Titan

Prometheus in his power and compassion for Man; Raphael summoned by God to Tobias in his journey to slay an important demon. In view of the invocation of the Bible and of Dante's suprareligious poem, the significance of the dark people in this story seems puzzling.

First off, Nelson, the boy, does not even recognize the coffee-colored man on the train as a "nigger." "You never said they were tan." Nelson suspects right away on the train what his grandfather later discovers, that their journey is to turn out a small season in hell, and that is dark enough.

For they get lost. They enter the city in a dream that turns to dread. There are sewers that swallow people up; even a penny weighing machine warns against dark women. Mr. Head's cry turns everything to nightmare, "I'm lost! . . . I'm lost and can't find my way to the station. Oh, Gawd, I'm lost! Oh hep me Gawd, I'm lost!"

Just when Mr. Head knows his greatest desolation, time without seasons, heat without light, he spies the artificial nigger. It draws the two like a plaster saint. Their quarrel is resolved. In a moment of crisis, when Nelson had knocked over an old woman, the grandfather denied his grandchild. It is a denial in terror, like the denial of Berryman's imaginary Jew. It is Mr. Head's blackest moment. But he has *found* the boy again. The two stand gaping at the statue, Mr. Head looking like "an ancient child" and Nelson like a "miniature old man."

> *They stood gazing at the artificial Negro as if they were faced with some great mystery, some monument to another's victory that brought them together in their common defeat.*

In the next moment Mr. Head feels mercy, which he is to feel touch him again just before the end of the story. To him, the experience is unnameable ("there were no words in the world that could name it. He understood it grew out of agony."). The train, the city, the blacks, seem to represent the means, the locale, and the destination of the unnameable.

The black people have turned out to be threatening, however, only in Mr. Head's head. They seem benign enough to us, going about their business. It is the whites, in fact, who are involved in the troublesome incident with Nelson.

The difficulties of the man and the boy are really with each other, they are the ancient ones of mind and heart. They are their own worst enemies. In forgiveness (the boy's) and mercy (the old man's) they have overcome their own darkness. The environment they sought is only a tacit image of their blackest fears. The evil was in themselves, caused by themselves, their own actions, their own uninformed behavior. Of that image of black Mr. Head had said, "... they ain't got enough real ones here. They got to have an artificial one."

The "monument to another's victory," Dante's great experience in his "comedy" is that of the journey from dominance of the mind to pure and holy emotion. Mr. Head all too glibly "says." In order truly to feel, his journey is difficult and deep.

In both the foregoing stories, one written by a Southern Catholic (O'Connor), the other about a Southern Catholic (Berryman's), there is a metaphysical sense that "the pure relation—immaculate apprehension" must move through folklore to history. To know probability, it must be felt. Grace is achieved through experience. That is what O'Connor is trying to tell us in the troublesome next to last paragraph.

COUNTERPARTS

James Joyce

In his fiction and in his statements about his own life, James Joyce said he hated Dublin. Physically, he left that city, yet he entitled his first collected work of fiction, *Dubliners.* "Counterparts" is a story from that collection. Violent emotion leads to its own perception. In Joyce's case, it looks very much like hatred recollected-in-tranquillity. A most autobiographical writer, he used members of his own family from which to fashion Farrington and even Farrington's son. And, something of a drinker himself, who better knew the frustrations and disappointments that lead to the corner bar?

"Counterparts" is a savage story, heart-rending in its ending. Did you ever have a day in which "everything" went wrong? This is a day in the life of Farrington in which that life went wrong. The commitment to end his job and waste what was left of his substance is final. Farrington is unloved and unloving. He senses his plight, but acts out of malaise rather than of deepest feeling. His incapacity is a lack of understanding. We leave him sore tried, but unredeemed.

What are the counterparts of this story's title? Conventionally viewed, religion, marriage, and fatherhood should sustain and support working-class life. They are the solid institutions of society, but how does Joyce view them? Where in the story do you find evidence for these views?

Do you know any "Pat and Mike" jokes? They are so-called Irish jokes. What are the assumptions of these jokes about Irishmen? What *is* a stereotype? What, if anything, makes Farrington, an Irishman, distinctive in this way? Does Joyce deal with the stereotype?

❧❧❧

Of the characters in this series of stories—Félicité, Nelson, Mr. Head, Mr. Farrington, and the narrator in the "Imaginary Jew"—who has the best insights into the events that befall them?

Most of these characters lead marginal lives. What does that mean? What keeps our interest up, then?

Both "A Simple Heart" and "Counterparts" give us a complete sense of a certain kind of life. How does Flaubert use time to convey this sense? How does Joyce? What can you say about the differences of technique in these two stories as to, say, time and place? *Are* time and place significant to each story? Is there a special flavor involved in the different times and the different locales? What?

In both the Joyce and the J. F. Powers stories, the Church is central to the plot. Notice how the same institution can be background information or in the forefront of developments. The stories in this entire category are affected by the Roman Catholic Church. What is the difference between theology and church-going suggested in these stories? Does it matter to you that the Church is a common factor? Does it make a difference in your approach anew to the stories, or their outcome? What is the effect of this knowledge upon your relationship to each story?

Consult Carl Jung; consult the dictionary: what is the definition of an archetype? In what ways and in what characters in this section can you see the definition carried out? A good litmus test for an archetype might be: ah yes, that is how it is! Or, that is how it must *be*. Another test is that a stereotype is shallow, the archetype deep. For help here, pursue the difference between a cartoon and a painting judged to be of deep significance. Try Michelangelo's "The Creation" from the Sistine Chapel.

In what ways are the titles, "The Imaginery Jew" and "The Artificial Nigger" ironic? Consider that Jews and blacks are perennially considered "threats" to certain societies. How are the two stories affected by such threats? In the stories, what are the *realities* of the threats? What is the relationship between the statue of "The Artificial Nigger" and the identity forced upon the narrator of "The Imaginary Jew"? Notice how Berryman uses the phrase "nigger-lover" in his story. How does he compare this phrase with "special sympathy" for Jews?

The protagonists of both these stories are journey-takers. Set forth the realistic journeys and relate them to the deeper journeys that the authors wish us to understand have been undertaken, the "real" versus the "metaphysical" journeys, that is. Don't fail to note the authenticity of both kinds of journeys.

Félicité's is also a journey. How could it be handled so that it resembled Benjamin Button's in the Fitzgerald story?

Is there a student in the class who is working with the mathematical symbol p, the probability factor? Encourage its application to the literary experience.

If you were to develop a scale of self-realization, who of the characters in these stories would place highest upon it? Lowest? On a scale of acceptance of the hard knocks of life, who accepted the most? The least?

What is a parable? What is the New Testament meaning of "And a little child shall lead them?" Children are often used in stories to represent figures of innocence. What is Nelson's role in this way in "The Artificial Nigger"? How is Félicité like a child? What is the role of the child, Farrington's son, who ends the story "Counterparts"? Is Freda's daughter in "Persephone" an archetypal figure? Is Freda herself?

IX. IRONY—EPIPHANY

BLISS

Katherine Mansfield

Like the musical composition it greatly resembles, this piece illustrates one difference between a short story and a long work of fiction. It is a symphonic or tone poem, not a symphony only because it is a short composition. The downbeat is an ode to joy, the bliss of the title and of the second paragraph. We are floating, we are dancing down the street with Bertha Young, in love with life and possibility. We are reminded of Emily Dickinson's "inebriate of dew am I." Fit as Bertha feels, it is not as a "rare, rare fiddle" shut up in a case: life is to play and be played. Yet rather quickly thereafter with the introduction of the "cold mirror" and Bertha's ironic (as it will turn out) notion that she can "see quite well" there are introduced the first somber notes or measures.

If we have music, then, in the sense of the construction of this story, it is in the mood of "dark comedy." This is instanced in Bertha's encounter with her baby and the nurse. Bertha feels happy and charmed, in her airy and yet physical way, about being a mother but the baby doesn't quite belong to her. Here we have again the little motif of the "rare, rare fiddle" and discover why valuable instruments are kept in a case; the baby in another woman's arms.

Enter Harry the husband, by way of the telephone. We are made to notice that he will be late. Why will he be late? Because they are connected only by telephone ("idiotic civilization"), it is impossible to *communicate* with him.

Next we get a preview, really a key to their characters, of the guests who will be coming to dinner; there is some mystery to Miss Fulton, and Harry seems a disinterested conspirator in uncovering the mystery. Much is made by the writer, but with great skill, of his disinterest.

Then the theme of the pear tree is introduced in its perfect, shimmering beauty. Bertha feels the pear tree as a symbol of her life. We have not heard the last of the pear tree, and we know, alas, if we dwell on it, how transitory are spring blossoms. There are the notations of small, but to her, perfect, things of Bertha's life; the music of joy recurs. She dresses most carefully in the colors of and around the pear tree. When the first guests arrive, Bertha's "petals rustled softly into the hall." She is the pear tree!

We have the late arrival of Miss Pearl, and the delineation of the Youngs' guests in all their superficiality. Bertha loves it all. Loves them. They are living in a play by Chekhov. But living in a play is no more real than the feeble plans for plays that Norman Knight has. (Norman Knight—is his name an ironic reference to England's portentous date, 1066?) Harry's appetite for the pleasures of the physical *are* real. So is his lack of enthusiasm for the baby. Bertha and Pearl (another ironic name?) seem to share a moment of affinity involving the pear tree. All these observations and emotions are building to something for Bertha. They are unseen, unrealized yearnings and responses, and they culminate in physical desire for her husband, a new experience.

But the climax of the evening will be an unexpected one. Pearl is discovered by Bertha in Harry's arms. There is habitual intimacy between them. In leaving, Pearl Fulton mentions "your pear tree" to Bertha. Then she is gone with their friend Eddie, the two like the cats under the pear tree that, earlier in the evening, had cost Bertha a shiver. There is a horrible note of irony, "Your lovely pear tree—pear tree—pear tree." The gossamer, the symbolic pear tree has been ripped to shreds. Cacophony sounds.

Bertha asks what is going to happen now. Well, tomato soup, a veritable emblem of domesticity and civilization, is "*dreadfully* eternal." Pear trees are far less robust.

The coda is dark, in the bass clef. Only innocence has been changed. The comedy is over.

FIFTY POUNDS

A. E. Coppard

Coppard's art may not look like art, but look again. "Fifty Pounds" is an artful story, well made, its author employing his art in a way which is probably basic to artistic motivation, as an expression of indignation, outrage, protest against the imperfection of the world. But the impulse is softened by comedy.

In "Fifty Pounds" the object of indignation is hypocrisy, principally the hypocrisy of P. Stick Repton, a writer upon many subjects. (Coppard himself wrote much, undoubtedly very swiftly, almost too easily, mechanically, or repetitiously. When he was good he was very, very good.)

At one point we eavesdrop with Lally upon hypocrisy. She sits in a restaurant near "three sleek parsons." "There must be a conference about charity or something," Lally thought, when she saw "dozens" of clergymen in the neighborhood. But no, when she sat among them in the restaurant they revealed to her that their charity began with themselves—that they cared for their own comfort first, even as P. Stick Repton did "who wrote articles about Single Tax, Diet and Reason," and so forth. Poor Lally, she "loved to hear him talk like that." She believed in the possibilities of purity, of devotion, of love, religious ideals. She has not yet become a hypocrite, and we hope she never will. She has learned a great lesson, however, at a cost of fifty pounds.

It isn't only that Lally will grow, as we hope, from innocence to urbanity without falling into hypocrisy. We need not patronize her. Lally is already there. She has already, by her Nature, by her wisdom, by precocity, achieved that liberation about which our Mr. Repton so often writes and lectures. Lally is capable of loving well outside of marriage. "She did not really want to marry Phil, they had got on so well without it . . . ." What has she to learn from him? Nothing, really, for she has grown beyond the teacher. The loss is finally Phil's—a point he'd not understand or accept, lacking as he does Lally's unself-conscious subtlety, her *instinctive* liberalism. Instinct to her, dogma to him.

This story appears at first to be "easy reading," and in one sense it is. It moves fluidly, without Jamesian or Faulknerian complication. However, we deprive ourselves by haste, for the plot is most carefully laid, hints and clues effectively planted.

We must act it out for ourselves, perhaps as if we are directors of a stage or screen production, to savor the tension of certain scenes. Notice, for example, "Repton staring out of the window, forlorn as a drowsy horse," in the moment of Lally's first sight of him after sending the money. Why forlorn? He has, in fact, already received the fifty pounds from Wellwisher. It should be for him a moment of exaltation, the finest of all rewards for a "precarious sort of London journalist." We may suspect, as Lally does, that the money has gone astray. Thus Phil's forlornness. Looking back, however, with the truth in our possession, we become aware of the depths of his hypocrisy. The irony is richest then, all doubt dissolved.

Simply told, simply made—an art seeming artless! "Fifty Pounds" is a dramatized description of a great part of the known world, especially those quarters where men enunciate liberated ideals in the very moment of their betrayal of their sincerest lovers.

BARBADOS

Paule Marshall

The technique of epiphany, so-named by James Joyce, is meant to illuminate the essence of a character's life or personality. The process itself is all too human, but in fiction, the process is often speeded up, accelerated for the dramatic force of revelation upon the character or upon the reader, often upon the reader alone. It is a technique usually reserved for the ending of a story.

Joyce is represented in this volume in another section, because his story illustrates a masterstroke of story writing, lifting the commonplace into the emotionally uncommon. "Counterparts" represents, however, one kind of epiphany. Farrington will never "know his ail," but his son reaches out to save his father in the defense of his own innocence, and we are moved even if Farrington is not.

The question of innocence and guilt, of the juxtaposition of white and black—"there it is in black and white; believe it" we are often told—is worked out in Paule Marshall's "Barbados" with enormous attention to structure and to the detail of structure.

The story opens in whiteness. There are half a dozen references to "white" in the first three paragraphs alone. "White" will reappear throughout. The story ends at night, with the use in the last paragraph of the word "dark."

The writing style is leisurely with long, languorous sentences—the scene, after all, is the Caribbean—interspersed with rare, short statements, bursts of fact, "I's the new servant." The writer's flowing diction is balanced with the lilt of Island English, crisp, truncated, ignoring the niceties of rules.

The first word of this story is "Dawn." The day begins. It is heralded too by creamy-white Barbary doves, whose sound will also end the story. We feel dawn to be a promise, a proper start for waking, for rising. Perhaps we are guided, therefore, to feel that something is at its beginning for Mr. Watford. His passing through the house will lead somewhere, to something. So it must. A story must lead us somewhere.

So it will, for this story is of a classical pattern, fulfilling a promise of completion, of a beginning and an end. "It was no different from all the days which made up the five years since his return to Barbados." But will it be?

"For some reason, Mr. Watford had never completed the house." This the author observes as we accompany Mr. Watford through its rooms. His day only just beginning, he "strode" through his house. He is seventy years old, and one might think him entitled to be at leisure. Nevertheless, he "strode." There is something about himself that Mr. Watford denies. He denies being seventy, perhaps. But more than that, he may be one of those people Thoreau hoped not to be—one who, when his time came to die, discovered he had not lived. Like his house, Mr. Watford's life will never be complete.

We soon sense his deliberate loneness. He lives alone, works alone, according to strict routine, beginning with his rising, his striding through his house, his day of hard work which is a denial of his age and of his right to rest, his return to the house, his bathing, his dressing in a "stiff . . . white . . . medical doctor's uniform," his reading the Boston newspaper.

Yet in America he had felt totally detached from his surroundings. Women he spent time with finally bored him. He paid no allegiance to America, ". . . his place lay elsewhere." But upon his return to Barbados, he isolated himself from the community, in a Colonial American house, his Grand Rapids furniture reflecting the popular taste of mid-America, he lived in grand isolation and dealt only with Mr. Goodman to sell his coconuts. In America he knew his place to be in Barbados. In Barbados he devoured newspapers from Boston, weeks old, and with a "little savage chuckle at the thought that beyond his world that other world went its senseless way."

Watford, a man who was somewhere else wherever he was, and always solitary, will somehow be repaid by the "senseless" world for his "savage chuckle." He can't really avoid the world, which comes, on the second day of our acquaintance with him, in the form of a visit somewhat out of the ordinary: the arrival of Mr. Goodman's "boy," which will lead, as the author tells us, to the coming of the girl as well.

These events will take Mr. Watford our of his routine and into a moment during which he is captured at last by something the "senseless" world offers, after all. And then his denial will haunt him to the end.

Mr. Goodman's "boy" wears a political pin. "The Old Shall Pass," it proclaims. And continues, "Vote for the Barbados People's Party." The message is political, but Mr. Watford rejects it politically and personally ("You ain't people . . ." we will hear later). For what is old, after all—and who are people, when one is sealed behind 500 coconut trees in a fine white house?

Mr. Goodman who sent the boy will also send the girl. When she came to be his maid, the girl reminded Mr. Watford of his mother, a reminder he will curse himself for later. He alone has survived of the ten children his mother bore; he alone has escaped death.

The girl has come expecting to be a devoted servant, like Félicité, spending years in the service of a good house. She expects as well to violate Mr. Watford's solitude, to be treated, in her innocence and willingness to serve, like a human being. She would have preferred the abuse of white men who would "take advantage of she," as Mr. Goodman had warned her, to the distance, silence, and indifference of Mr. Watford. He could not raise his eyes from his evening reading to acknowledge her existence.

And when, resenting her pleasure more than her existence, he charged to her room, expecting to find her there in embrace with Mr. Goodman's boy, finding her, instead, alone, Mr. Watford's shame is complete, especially because his "inner eye was suddenly clear." Whom did he see with his inner eye? It was himself. *She* had not violated his house. Not at all. It was he who had violated—something; he, who had lived this long, almost to his time to die, to hear from the mouth of a servant girl fifty years younger, "You ain't people, Mr. Watford, you ain't people!"

He had achieved. He had achieved. What? She condemns his house, his furniture, his papers from America. She herself has achieved—something, for she has achieved if nothing more quite yet, an evening's intensity with the storekeeper's boy.

He has seen only guilt in the innocence of her natural act. For in her womanhood, the girl is full of caring, full of life. "Below her waist, her hips branched wide, the place prepared for its load of life." So that when she strikes her small blow, it is the "woman's force in her aspect" that flings Mr. Watford against the door.

It is not she who is alone, unhuman, inhuman, not people, not a person; condemned, life cast away. This is the charge against *him*. His conscience, acknowledging, pleads guilty.

Goodman, whose person disgusts him, speaks to Mr. Watford of responsibility, really the "weight of his own responsibility" to extend love. Mr. Goodman relates to people. The boy has won the girl by giving her his political button. All took the responsibility of relating to others. Not Mr. Watford. He has feared death and thus shirked his responsibility to life, by detachment and withdrawal.

He has always believed in a "presence," something crouched in the night to ensnare him. Fearing death, the presence of death, he has failed to live life. In the moment of self-revelation, in the fullest light of the moon, there is no longer an opportunity to compensate himself for the loss.

The story ends as it began, with Mr. Watford alone.

◈◈◈

Of the characters discussed in this section of the book—Mr. Watford, Lally, Bertha—whose lives will undergo change as a result of the events in their stories? Whose will not? Why?

We are all acquainted with fairy tales. In what ways is Bertha living a life of "make-believe"? Consider the ironic title, "Bliss."

One of the themes running-through this group of stories is that "things are seldom what they seem." What illusions are some of the characters here protecting? How does the reality of their situations occur in the stories? Think, again, of Lally, Bertha, Mr. Watford.

Katherine Mansfield wrote about the heroine of "Bliss" in 1920. What decisions do you think Bertha of that story would make now, confronted with the same circumstances?

Often writers set up a counterpoint between characters to develop their stories. For instance, how are P. Stick Repton and Eulalia (Lally) contrasted in the first paragraph of "Fifty Pounds"? Their characters are set there.

Consider making a motion picture of "Fifty Pounds." It is a highly "visual" story. Which of these visual scenes would you choose to dramatize? How would you use in your film the scene when Lally, beginning to suspect the worst about Repton, "hummed" as she walked, "Cruel and mean, cruel and mean"? How would you depict for film the scene where the two part? How would you show what each is thinking—he in deceit, possibly looking forward to his "fun"; she, knowing that they will not meet again?

Imagine that you are Lally. After all, fifty pounds is a *lot* of money. How would you go about retrieving the money? Or would you?

"Barbados" is a story by a woman "about" a man. In "The Artificial Nigger," Flannery O'Connor, a woman, writes about a man and a boy. Flaubert's "A Simple Heart" is "about" a woman. How might an author

HANDBOOK FOR TEACHERS AND STUDENTS

"transfer" emotions to the other sex? In "Barbados" could Paule Marshall be writing of someone she knows rather than about herself? What are we saying here about the act of imagination?

Where is Barbados? Does the question of its geography matter?

What *does* matter? Does it matter that Mr. Watford is black? If the writer had eliminated all references to race in her story, would the story remain essentially the story we have read?

Does Mr. Watford die in the end?

There are many ironies in "Barbados." Consider the irony of the artifacts: what is the significance of the Grand Rapids furniture? The "Colonial American" house? The Boston newspapers? Consider the irony of role. Mr. Watford is the "master." The Girl is the servant. What about the mastery of self?

How do these stories illuminate the questions of "role" for us? Is there a continuity of women, young or old, always serving in several stories? What other roles stand out for you in this book of stories?

Some writers confound our expectation of role by deepening their characters with dignity, or grace, or irony; salvaging or twisting the turn of events. Which stories stand out for you in this way?

X. THE SHAPE OF FICTION

THE WIFE OF MARTIN GUERRE

Janet Lewis

How do the first three sentences of the story transport us in time and place?

As heroines, what do Félicité of "A Simple Heart" and Bertrande share in common? How do they differ—in strength, loyalty, and subservience, for example? Both are French. Do we perceive more information about the country of France in one story or the other?

In this story, as in "The Sire de Malétroit's Door," we have to accept another code, another set of values, different from our own, in order to receive the story on its own terms. How does "The Wife of Martin Guerre" confront us with our own standards of such abstractions as marriage, morality, law and order, love, "the head of the house"? What human capacities endure? Think about joy, passion, suffering, as emotions with which we can identify even though we quarrel with code.

During her husband's eight years of absence, for instance, Bertrande is essentially in charge of the household. What light does her stewardship cast upon the significance of the title? Constantly caught between pressure from her family, authority, and her own convictions, Bertrande generally errs in the direction of law and order. In what portions of the story is she called upon for such choices, and how do her decisions reflect, again, the title of the story?

When "she was fourteen years of age" Bertrande made the transition from her childhood to her new life at the Guerres'. Analyze the style of these passages signifying Bertrande's new life. Notice with what simplicity the sentence, " 'Sit here, my daughter, tonight you shall be waited on' . . ." effects the transition from one life to the other.

Great changes occur in the three main characters of the story. Discuss the interrelatedness of these changes and, in turn, their relationship to the code of authority that rules the life of the Guerres.

First, Martin: He is the rebel who sloughs off his responsibility, possibly with the intention never to return to his family, until his name is defiled and he reappears at the end. Where do we discover his sense of frustration? Look first at the incident in which he boxes the ears of his child bride. How does it indicate his resentment toward a lifetime commitment? What can you say of the incident regarding the hunting of the bear? Why did his father strike him? For what was he really being punished? Worrying his father? How does Martin use the climactic incident with the grain? In what terms would you describe his departure? Does he leave with trepidation? With anxiety? Or how? In what ways does he finally come to resemble his father?

Second, Arnaud: What does he confess was his original intention in taking Martin's place? What accounted for his decision to remain as Martin? As readers, do we share Bertrande's sense of him, or that of the family group? We know this "Martin" has changed after eight years. Are we suspicious of the changes?

Third, Bertrande: Why does the author say that her husband's long absence prepared her to hold to her conviction that "Martin" is not Martin? Under what circumstances does she waiver in her conviction? Why? How does the sentence, "Once indeed Bertrande thought that Martin had returned" forecast a set of mind? How is Bertrande's belief in her code relevant to her statement to Arnaud, "You had no mercy upon me, either upon body or upon soul"? The judgment of the court and the judgment of God: with which of these was Bertrande really concerned? She is asked by a judge why she waited three years to denounce her husband the impostor. How would *you* answer that?

What occupied each of the Martins in the eight years when Bertrande, alone, was raising her child and supervising the household?

Bertrande's suspicions of Martin-the-pretender grow as the new child grows within her. How does the soldier from Rochefort affect Bertrande? The family? Your own suspicions?

To what extent do you share the housekeeper's inclination in her advice to Bertrande to let well enough alone?

A contemporary commentator upon the real trial of Arnaud asked why Martin Guerre did not "deserve a punishment as severe as that of Arnaud . . . for having been by his absence the cause of this wrong-doing?" How do you feel in that matter? What difference would it have made, do you believe, in Bertrande's reactions?

The author has based her story upon a real incident. What are some ways in which the style, the descriptions, the sense of work and life, the atmosphere of the courtroom, make this story seem authentic? What facets of the story do you believe the writer had to recreate or invent?

The following notices of copyright in materials included in this book are a continuation of the copyright page (p. iv) and are incorporated therein for the purposes of Copyright law.

"A Mother's Tale," by James Agee from *The Collected Short Prose of James Agee.* Copyright © 1968, 1969 by The James Agee Trust. Reprinted by permission of the publisher Houghton Mifflin Company.

"Life-Story," copyright © 1968 by John Barth from *Lost in the Funhouse.* Reprinted by permission of Doubleday & Company, Inc.

"The Gonzaga Manuscripts." From *Mosby's Memoirs* by Saul Bellow. Copyright 1954 by Saul Bellow. Reprinted by permission of The Viking Press, Inc.

"The Imaginary Jew." Reprinted with the permission of Farrar, Straus & Giroux, Inc. from *Recovery* by John Berryman. Copyright 1945 by John Berryman, copyright renewed 1973 by Kate Berryman.

"The Seven Riders" by Dino Buzzati. Reprinted by permission of Arnoldo Mondadori Editore.

"Fifty Pounds." From *The Collected Tales of A. E. Coppard.* Copyright 1948 by A. E. Coppard. Reprinted by permission of Alfred A. Knopf, Inc.

"Red Leaves." Copyright 1930 and renewed 1958 by The Curtis Publishing Company from *Collected Stories of William Faulkner*, by permission of Random House, Inc.

"The Curious Case of Benjamin Button" (Copyright 1922 F. P. Collier & Son Co.) is reprinted by permission of Charles Scribner's Sons from *Tales of the Jazz Age* by F. Scott Fitzgerald.

"The Iron Fist of Oligarchy" by Mark Harris. Copyright © 1959 by the Virginia Quarterly. Reprinted by permission of the author.

"The Short Happy Life of Francis Macomber" (copyright 1936 Ernest Hemingway) is reprinted by permission of Charles Scribner's Sons from *The Short Stories of Ernest Hemingway.*

"Counterparts." From *Dubliners* by James Joyce. Copyright © 1967 by the Estate of James Joyce. All rights reserved. Reprinted by permission of The Viking Press, Inc.

"A Hunger Artist." Reprinted by permission of Schocken Books Inc. from *The Penal Colony* by Franz Kafka. Copyright © 1948 by Schocken Books Inc.

"Persephone" by Meridel Le Sueur. Reprinted by permission of the author.

The Wife of Martin Guerre © 1941, 1967 by Janet Lewis. Reprinted with permission of The Swallow Press, Chicago, Ill.

"Bliss" by Katherine Mansfield. Copyright 1920 by Alfred A. Knopf, Inc. and renewed 1948 by John Middleton Murry. Reprinted from *The Short Stories of Katherine Mansfield,* by permission of the publisher.

"Barbados." Copyright © 1961 by Paule Marshall.

"The Artificial Nigger." Copyright © 1955 by Flannery O'Connor. Reprinted from her volume *A Good Man Is Hard to Find and Other Stories* by permission of Harcourt Brace Jovanovich, Inc.

"Death of a Favorite," copyright © 1950 by The New Yorker Magazine, Inc. from *The Presence of Grace* by J. F. Powers. Reprinted by permission of Doubleday & Company, Inc.

"The Secret Room" by Alain Robbe-Grillet from *Snapshots*. Reprinted by permission of Grove Press, Inc. Copyright © 1968 by Grove Press, Inc.

"In Dreams Begin Responsibilities." Delmore Schwartz, *The World Is a Wedding*. Copyright © 1948 by Delmore Schwartz. Reprinted by permission of New Directions Publishing Corporation.

"Dying" from *Teeth, Dying and Other Matters* by Richard G. Stern. Copyright © 1964 by Richard G. Stern. By permission of Harper & Row, Publishers, Inc.

"Hook." Reprinted by permission of International Creative Management. Copyright © 1940, 1968 by Walter Van Tilburg Clark.

"The Use of Force." William Carlos Williams, *The Farmers' Daughters*. Copyright 1938 by William Carlos Williams. Reprinted by permission of New Directions Publishing Corporation.

"But For This . . ." by Lajos Zilahy. Reprinted by permission of Mrs. Piroska Zilahy.